HENRI seized her hand and pulled her towards him, roughly and strongly. "You're a fool, Celeste."

SHE struggled with him briefly. But he took her face in his hands and kissed her brutally on the lips. He took her in his arms, and kissed her over and over, until she was blinded and stunned, and could not resist.

SHE pressed her hands against his chest. "Let me go," she said, through her clenched teeth. But her knees were weak beneath her. If he had released her, she would have fallen. Her lips burned as if stung by flame.

"NO," he said softly, kissing her again. "I'll never let you go again. You never wanted me to go. You're a shameless woman, aren't you, darling? I've watched you these last weeks. I knew I had only to reach for you, and you'd come. You knew that too. I've reached; you've come. It's as simple as all that, isn't it?"

Also by Taylor Caldwell:

DYNASTY OF DEATH
THE EAGLES GATHER
THE EARTH IS THE LORD'S
THE STRONG CITY
THE ARM AND THE DARKNESS*
THE TURNBULLS
THE WIDE HOUSE
THIS SIDE OF INNOCENCE
THERE WAS A TIME
MELISSA
LET LOVE COME LAST
THE BALANCE WHEEL
MAGGIE—HER MARRIAGE*
THE DEVIL'S ADVOCATE
YOUR SINS OR MINE
NEVER VICTORIOUS, NEVER DEFEATED
TENDER VICTORY
THE SOUND OF THUNDER
DEAR AND GLORIOUS PHYSICIAN
THE LISTENER
A PROLOGUE TO LOVE
GRANDMOTHER AND THE PRIESTS*
THE LATE CLARA BEAME*
WICKED ANGEL*
THE ROMANCE OF ATLANTIS*
A PILLAR OF IRON*
NO ONE HEARS BUT HIM*
DIALOGUES WITH THE DEVIL*
TESTIMONY OF TWO MEN*
GREAT LION OF GOD*
ON GROWING UP TOUGH*
CAPTAIN AND THE KINGS*
TO LOOK AND PASS*
GLORY AND THE LIGHTNING*
CEREMONY OF THE INNOCENT*
BRIGHT FLOWS THE RIVER*
ANSWER AS A MAN*

*Published by Fawcett Books

TAYLOR CALDWELL

The
Final Hour

All Rights Reserved under International and Pan-American Copyright Conventions including the right to reproduce this book or portions thereof in any form. Published in the United States by Ballantine Books, a division of Random House, Inc., New York, and simultaneously in Canada by Random House of Canada Limited, Toronto.

ISBN: 0-449-20038-8

This edition published by arrangement with Charles Scribner's Sons.

Printed in Canada

First Fawcett Crest Edition: May 1976
First Ballantine Books Edition: May 1982
Seventh Printing: February 1983

FAWCETT CREST • NEW YORK

To

Burt and Phoebe Wetherbee

with love

ACKNOWLEDGMENT

The author here makes grateful acknowledgment to Marcus Reback, for his constant encouragement, sympathy and assistance.

CONTENTS

CONTENTS

"To every people there comes one terrible and inevitable final hour, when it must choose between those things by which men live, or those by which they die."

—BARON OPPERHEIM

Book One

OUR OWN DRUMS

"   ——*Look, sir, my wounds!*
I got them in my country's service, when
Some certain of you brethren roared and ran
From the noise of our own drums."

Shakespeare (*Coriolanus*)

CHAPTER 1

"A charming place," said Count Wolfgang von Bernstrom, as he looked about him. "Each time I see it, it appears more delightful to me. I am very fortunate, my dear Ramsdall, in leasing it from you for the rest of the summer."

"And I," said George, Lord Ramsdall, somewhat drily, "am fortunate in leasing it to you. There is a plague on Cannes this season." He paused, and glanced obliquely at the German.

Von Bernstrom shrugged stiffly, his hard military shoulders moving as if made of wood and not flesh and bone. He adjusted his monocle and surveyed the terrace with unaffected pleasure before replying: "So many rumors, my dear Ramsdall. So much hysteria. I, for one, believe nothing, know nothing, see nothing, hear nothing. A very comfortable state of mind. I recommend it with enthusiasm. Why anticipate an unpleasantness that most probably will never arrive? Such a dispersal of energy! One needs to conserve energy these turbulent days. One must be aware, yet not too aware." He smiled, and his pale dry face wrinkled with a kind of mirth which was really mirthless. His eyes, too, were pale and dry, with a curious sort of brilliance in their whites, as if they were made of polished marble. His light thin hair was cropped in the Junker fashion; he had a sharp spade-like chin, a colorless slash of a mouth which opened frequently in a smile that was oddly charming, despite its lack of human warmth. That smile revealed excellent and flashing teeth. His cheeks were sunken, as if sucked in, and between them his thin hooked nose was aggressive, yet possessing a translucence as though formed solely of cartilage and skin. He gave the impression of fleshlessness, because he was unusually tall and thin; there might have been only aristocratic bones under his lovingly tailored English tweeds. The pared cleanliness of the Teuton appeared exaggerated in him. An aura of soap, cold water, shaving lotion and aseptic cologne wafted from him to Lord Ramsdall on the warm salt wind.

It was said of Lord Ramsdall that he amazingly resembled Winston Churchill, whom he hated with hysterical passion. Short, stocky, with a rosy cherubic face and prominent blue eyes and a button of a pink nose, he appeared all amiable shrewdness. He had a big round head covered with tendrils of faded blond hair, through which his skull shone rosily, like a baby's scalp, quite unlike Mr. Churchill's. He was fond of being called "Johnnie Bull," and tried unremittingly to carry out this characterization by a bluff and hearty manner, a rich and rotund laugh, a robust manner of speaking, and an open and engaging smile. If he was ever aware that his only and beloved daughter, Ursula, was called the "Bitch of Cannes and points East," or that she was at the present time the mistress of Count von Bernstrom, he gave no evidence of it. If he was loathed and hated in England because of his oppression of the workers in his great steelmill (subsidiary of Robsons-Strong), and if he was strongly suspect among those he spoke of contemptuously as "Reds," and, too, if his newspaper, the *London Opinion*, was accused of pandering to the pacifistic policies of the doddering Chamberlain (to the danger of the British Empire), these matters were of no apparent importance to the happy and generous peer. On this beautiful morning of May 9, 1939, all seemed well with George, Lord Ramsdall, and he appeared to have nothing more on his mind than a warm affection for von Bernstrom and a simple delight that his white elephant of a villa (which he had happily been able to lease to the young American couple for the past five years, at a most satisfying sum) was about to pass into the hands of his dear friend, with a substantial lease.

The villa, situated close to the sea between Juan-les-Pins and Cannes, shone white and gleaming in the brilliant May sunshine, every french window sparkling. It stood on brown rock, but on three sides of it were narrow green lawns, immaculately fresh and clipped, and beautifully landscaped with shrubs and beds of flowers. It faced the blue and incandescent ocean, and the air about it was sweet and pure with salt and the fragrance of the gardens. Everything was so still, so warm, so peaceful, that Lord Ramsdall momentarily regretted that he must leave Cannes almost immediately for dusty gritty London, where so much was to be done, and done without delay. Thinking this, he glanced again at von Bernstrom, and his full lids almost closed over the bulge of his eyes.

The German appeared much younger to the casual eye than he truly was, for he was in his fifties. But there was a lean agelessness about him, like the agelessness of a predatory

14

hawk. He had been the Kaiser's youngest general in the late war, but he refused to be called by his former title. "I am done with things military," he would say in a tight tone, with a stiff lift of his bony hand. He would avert his narrow head when saying this, and would present his profile, that harsh profile, as if something impossibly nauseating had been mentioned. Nor did he ever speak of the Third Reich, or Hitler, and if these were spoken of in his presence, he would relapse into grim silence, pent and angular, and would soon make an excuse to leave the company. Never did he at any time give the impression of loathing or abominating the present regime of his country, except for these slight manifestations. But the latter were quite enough, for the naive. As for the initiate, von Bernstrom's attitudes and expressions occasioned them grim if secret mirth. He visited Germany very seldom. He had lived in France for nearly ten years, an apparently gloomy and reticent exile, an aristocrat who could not even mention the vulgar upstarts, vagabonds and criminals who now infested his country. Consequently, to romantic ladies in particular, he was a fascinating figure, and they quite forgave him his dun fat little wife. In truth, they usually forgot her. His affair with Ursula Ramsdall had their approval, their admiration and affection. If the lady had formerly expressed the most vitriolic passion for the Nazis, it was discerned that since her amorous entanglement with von Bernstrom she had apparently had a change of heart.

Also, there were persistent rumors that his estates in Prussia had been confiscated by the omnipotent Hitler in revenge for a lack of enthusiasm for the Austrian paper-hanger, and that his visits to Germany, infrequent though they were, were filled with danger for him. However, for one rumored to be practically without resources of a financial nature, he lived well, even lavishly. Ramsdall had once remarked vaguely that "probably the chap has a recent account in the Bank of England, and in France and America." At any rate, there was no affair of any importance occurring without von Bernstrom's presence, and the Casino saw him frequently, losing or winning vast sums with great indifference.

If anyone with a suspicious nature questioned the background of this fine aristocrat, it was pointed out severely that he had lived for some time at the villa of Baron Israel Opperheim on the Riviera, and that the two were the most affectionate of friends.

Von Bernstrom moved about the terrace, softly, on the balls of his feet, regarding everything with reserved pleasure.

He peered briefly through an open window at the drawing-room, whose blue dusk was invitingly cool and fresh. He saw the dim mirror of the floors, the crystal chandelier, the shape of a grand piano, the white marble fireplace. There were flowers on the dark glass of every table top, and their sweet fragrance seemed to fill the quiet air like incense. He allowed the bleached harshness of his expression to soften with anticipation. Lord Ramsdall watched him. There was a cunning lift to his heavy red lips.

"Ah," breathed the count, "charming! Charming! It is strange how delightful a prospect seems when it is about to become one's own." His voice, light and only elusively accented, was very agreeable. "What taste, my dear Ramsdall! But you were always known for your taste, were you not?"

Ramsdall inclined his head. "Very sporting of you to say that, Wolfgang. But there has been a woman's touch here, too, you know. A young lady of taste, herself, considering that she is an American."

They heard a soft footfall. The count immediately retreated to a position on the flagged terrace near his friend, and they both affected to be engrossed in happy contemplation of the blue sea.

A young lady, who had entered the drawing-room, now stood in one of the windows, gazing at them from the threshold a moment before she stepped down upon the terrace. The count and Ramsdall turned, with a look of pleasant surprise and pleasure. They bowed.

"I trust we are not too early, dear Mrs. Bouchard," said Ramsdall. "But, as Wolfgang is to be my next tenant, he decided he wished to arrive a little beforehand. To gloat, probably."

The lady smiled faintly. She extended her hand, and the count took it and raised it to his lips. He studied her with real delight and covetousness.

"I gain a pleasure, to lose one, dear Madame," he murmured. "We shall be disconsolate when you are gone."

As Mrs. Bouchard and her husband were accustomed to entertain only rarely, and cared little for those who swarmed ravenously along the Coast, this was an extravagant statement of the count's. But the young lady showed no surprise.

"How very kind of you, Count," she said, in a sweet but disinterested voice. The count was annoyed, but, as always, piqued. These American women! The most beautiful in the world, with such bosoms, such waists, such legs. But cold as death. He, himself, preferred the French, who knew much about love, and a great deal about wickedness. He adored wicked women. American women were never wicked, even those foolish and intoxicated expatriates who swarmed noisily (in exquisite toilettes) around the tables at the Casino. They lacked maturity, poise, grace, and their imitations of vice were the imitations of children. When they went too far, they were gross and disgusting. It was the Puritan in them, he suspected. A debased Puritan was the most revolting of creatures, for he had no taste, no reticence.

Mrs. Bouchard, however, was not in the least wicked, he meditated. But cold as a stone, as rigid as death. A beautiful statue of frozen flesh. Extraordinary, too, for so young a woman, in her early thirties. Most delicately designed for love and intrigue, his reflections continued. Yet, she had lived in this villa, within sight and sound of all the subtle and dainty viciousness of the notorious Coast, and had remained, like Cæsar's wife—uncorrupted, aloof and indifferent. Was it innocence, or distaste? The count believed it was neither. It was simply a lack of capacity for joy, for living, for delight. No doubt she was stupid, almost as stupid as his own German women. This reflection soothed his vanity, and so he regarded her with more amiability, and even superior pity. How most appalling to have lived here in the very presence of gaiety and pleasure and intoxication for over five years, and never to have experienced one moment of excitement and intrigue! But that, most certainly, was because of her invalid husband, and her devotion to him.

The count's large and transparent nose twitched with aversion. How pitiable, this lovely young creature's martyrdom to one who was apparently less than half a man! He, Wolfgang von Bernstrom, would have been only too delighted to have been allowed to relieve the tedium of her onerous life, if she had permitted it. He, and so many others. But she had allowed no man to approach her. What devotion! What stupidity!

He drew out a white chair for her on the terrace, and she sat down. The gentlemen seated themselves, also, and smiled tenderly upon her.

She directed an indifferent look upon the German. "I'm afraid this is going to be a very dull luncheon," she said, without the slightest regret. "I have invited only you, Count, and you, Lord Ramsdall, and Baron Opperheim. You are all such friends, and you have been kind to my husband, So, there will be only six of us, you three, my mother, and my husband—no one else. Peter hasn't been very well lately, and so I didn't wish to disturb him. You understand?"

"My dear, dear Mrs. Bouchard!" exclaimed Ramsdall, with an expression of fond understanding and regret upon his ruddy face. "Of course, we understand. It was very kind of you, indeed, to invite us. We're grateful, I assure you."

"We are leaving tomorrow," continued the young lady. "We are to stop in Paris for a few days, and then we go directly home."

For a moment she wore a betraying expression, sad and wistful, and very tired. She does not wish to return, thought the count. She is not entirely stupid, then. It had been his experience that very rich American ladies were invariably stupid and insensitive. But this delightful little creature, with such incredible wealth, had moments, too, of human regret, human insecurity and sorrow. Ah, had he but discovered this sooner! He might have corrupted her into joy.

He looked at her intently, without betraying his scrutiny. She was small and exquisitely made, with a beautiful figure, if slightly too slender for his taste. And most excessively chic, he acknowledged. She almost always wore a thin black dress, very plain, but of impeccable style, relieved only by a small necklace of rosy pearls. What lovely slender legs, lovingly curved at the calf, tapering to the most fragile of ankles and the tiniest of little arched feet! She sat gracefully in her chair, remote, and unconscious of herself, and most probably of her visitors, too. The count delighted his eye with the frailness of her waist, the perfect line of her small breasts under the filmy black stuff. His gaze rose to the whiteness of her throat, where the pearls moved with her quiet breath. After a moment, he looked at her face. How perfectly adorable, how exquisite in its perfection!

For her face, small and pointed, seemed carved of new ivory, so firm and clear were all its contours, its lines, and its curves. He could find no flaw, no hastiness, no crudeness or lack of expertness in that carving. However, there was a sort of rigidity about her features, a delicate sternness, which, to him, was somewhat repellent, inhuman. Too, she had a worn look, not so much patient as repressed and determined. That look lingered about her small red mouth with its deep corners, around the thin flaring nostrils of her nose, and hovered in a kind of stony fixity about her deeply set and beautiful dark blue eyes, over which the clear black lines of her brows were like the satin curves of a bird's wings. Her black hair, very lustrous and vital and full of deep shining waves, was brushed upwards to rest like an old-fashioned coronet upon the top of her head. Her little ears, with their pearl earrings, were white and as translucent as alabaster, and fully revealed. She had a luminous pallor, very vivid, and there was not the slightest stain of color upon her cheeks, whose smoothness and clarity aroused the hatred and envy of every woman who looked upon her.

The count remembered that she was of French descent. Yes, in those cheekbones, in the line of her shoulders, in the smallness of her hands and feet, in the grace of her carriage and posture, there was a distinctly French suggestion. But the spirit was not French! She had English blood also. That might account for her remoteness, her indifference, her iciness of manner, her withdrawn hauteur. However, he recalled that on one or two rare occasions, he had seen a flash about her, a restrained vehemence, a hint of hidden and wistful warmth, a generosity of temperament immediately hidden. He felt a tender pity for her again. How most deplorable, to have been victimized into service to an abominable invalid, a husband who apparently had not been a husband. Not amazing, then, that the life had gone from her.

He thought of her husband, and the bleached skin of his face, wrinkled like parchment.

In the meantime, the young lady and Lord Ramsdall had been conversing with amiable disinterest about nothing at all. "The servants, of course, will remain on for the count," she said. She hesitated. "Except the chef, Pierre, and his wife, Elise. They told me they preferred to return to Paris, if they can't find positions here."

The count came to himself at this catastrophe. He scowled. "But Madame! That is impossible. Intolerable. How am I to maintain a ménage here without them? You have been the envy of all our friends, for possessing such treasures. It is unendurable, not to be countenanced." He turned with a scowl to his friend. "My dear Ramsdall, I understood that the servants were attached to the villa."

Before Ramsdall could reply, the young lady looked directly at the count. Now for the first time there was a sudden breath of agitation about her, as if she was angered or indignant. Her dark blue eyes flashed. But she said quietly: "They are not attached. Pierre and Elise came with me from Paris. It was understood perfectly that if they did not wish to remain, after we left, they were to return to their home."

But the count hardly heard her. He made a rude gesture with his hand, which dismissed her as a stupid child, an intruder, one who does not need to be considered. All his native arrogance, his intolerance, were implicit in the cold violence of his manner. He looked only at Ramsdall.

"I insist these creatures remain. How am I to continue without them? I will not countenance their leaving."

Mrs. Bouchard sat upright in her chair. Her cheeks were suddenly stained with scarlet. "This is not Germany, my dear Count," she said, and her voice rose, clear and hard. "Pierre and Elise are free citizens of France. You 'insist' on their remaining. That is very incredible." And she laughed angrily, and with contempt.

He turned to her, and she saw the intolerant hatred in his eyes, the will to dominance, the fury of a man unaccustomed to resistance, the cowardly rage of a race that will not be refused what it desires. Peter is right, she thought. They are impossible. They are dangerous. They are deadly.

She continued, before he could speak: "When Pierre told me they would return to Paris, I tried to replace them for you. Tomorrow, a Belgian couple will come to you for an interview. I understand they are very reliable and expert."

Ramsdall tried to mollify his friend. He leaned towards him eagerly, and said: "Yes, yes. Mrs. Bouchard told me about this. She has been very kind, Wolfgang, in trying to replace these two. It was really generous of her. There was no obligation on her part. I understand the Belgians are really excellent——"

The count clenched his fist and struck the arm of his chair with it. It made a dull but curiously violent sound. "I am not interested in Madame's 'kindness,'" he said, brutally. "I had planned on Pierre and his wife."

Mrs. Bouchard, with a small choked exclamation, grasped the arms of her chair as if to rise with indignant haste. She said, speaking quickly and sharply, with a slight breathlessness:

"It may interest you to know, Count, that Pierre's son, Bernard, was killed in Spain. Captured, then tortured, then murdered by a German officer."

Her eyes were blue fire; she was very white. Her breast rose on an arch of passionate if repressed feeling. She looked at the count, and her face expressed her deep emotion.

He was taken aback by her look, relapsed into a fulminating silence. Then he said, unpleasantly, with a nasty smile: "Ah, Communists, our dear Pierre and Elise! Very interesting. Exceedingly interesting."

She made a small gesture of disgust. "Nonsense. You know it is nonsense. If one hates the fascists, must one be a Communist? My husband hates them. I hate them. That is why we are leaving." She paused, as if conscious of vulgar impetuousness, of indiscretion and ill-bred impulsiveness. Then her passion overcame her repressiveness, and she continued, more quickly than ever: "Will you call me a Communist, Count? Because I hate and despise this corrupt and useless society at Cannes, these parasites, these worthless creatures who connive with every foreign fascist who comes here to seduce the whining privileged from every country in Europe? Am I a Communist because I detest the kept women of French, Spanish, German and English politicians that swarm about this coast? The contemptible creatures who would sell the freedom and honor of their countries for soft beds and safety and the security of bank accounts? If this makes me a Communist, then I am proud to be one!"

They regarded her with amazement. The little cold creature, the exquisite and inhuman little statue, had come to wild and indignant life, filled with ardor and passion. The count almost forgot her words, so intrigued, so excited was he. He saw how her breast trembled, how her hands clenched the arms of her chair so that the fragile knuckles were white, how her eyes glowed with a molten blueness. And she turned those eyes first upon Ramsdall, and then upon von Bernstrom, with disgust and loathing, significant and aware.

"My dear Mrs. Bouchard," said Ramsdall, hastily. "The count was unfortunate in his choice of words. He doesn't believe what he said, himself. I am sure you know that he is virtually an exile from Germany, because he can't endure that—that abominable upstart of an Austrian." He coughed, and out of the corner of his eye he glanced at the German. Von Bernstrom saw that glance; it was furious, warning. He bit his lip. "I am sure," continued Ramsdall, "that Wolfgang is entirely in agreement with you. He spoke out of temper." The noble peer smiled ingratiatingly at the lady, who had paled excessively, and was very still and silent in her chair. "Naturally, he was annoyed at the bad news of losing the best chef in Cannes. Who wouldn't be? We must allow for his disappointment, my dear Mrs. Bouchard. As you know, he intended to give his first dinner party next week in honor of a most distinguished, I might even say, royal, couple, and this disturbs all his plans. A royal couple, in virtual exile," he added, with a meaning and significant smile at her.

She lifted her little hand in a scornful gesture. It was an eloquent gesture, and Ramsdall's full and folded cheeks turned crimson with inner fury. She said, lightly, and softly: "Yes, I know that couple. I would not allow them in this house while I was a tenant. They are very good friends of yours, are they not, Count von Bernstrom?"

He answered, with muffled dignity: "Indeed, Madame. I am proud to acknowledge it."

"I know," she said, very gently. Now her eyes were vivid again, full of things too portentous for speech, but completely understanding. And then she sighed, and sank back in her chair, as if exhausted. She was very pale; even her lips had turned white. She appeared ill. After a moment she resumed, and now her voice was drained: "The Belgians will satisfy you. However, there is no obligation on your part to accept them."

The count had recovered from his rage, at least, on the surface. He said placatingly, and with smooth haste: "Madame, I am very sorry. I spoke without thinking. I am very grateful. You have been more than kind. I cannot think of anyone else who would have had my welfare in mind to this extent."

She said, not looking at him: "I am sure this—royal couple —will find the cooking to their satisfaction."

The count overwhelmed her with extravagant protestations of his gratitude. In the meantime, he was mentally adding another item concerning her and her ridiculous husband to a certain dossier which was kept among secret documents in Berlin. He smiled, remembering those items, all concerning the antics of one Peter Bouchard, member of a family with whom the count was very familiar—very familiar indeed. His smile became more amiable and confident, as he expressed, over and over again, his contrition, his gratitude. He saw she was not listening. He was greatly annoyed. He was not accustomed to having women so oblivious of his fascination. She seemed to be involved in thoughts that greatly disturbed, angered, and sickened her.

He said: "Though I will not pretend that I am not delighted to be the next tenant in this villa, I should resign it gladly if you, and your husband, dear Madame, would only remain. However, I can assume that Mr. Bouchard has now so far recovered his health that he feels he can return to his own country? That is exceedingly happy news."

She came up from her thoughts and gazed at him with that pure directness which had in it the quality of a child's regard. "My husband feels much stronger, he says. Of course, he has not recovered, can never completely recover, from the injury to his lungs from poison gas during the war. But now he wishes to return home." She paused. "He feels we must return home. Before the war."

" 'Before the war'!" said Ramsdall, with an incredulous smile. "My dear child, there'll be no war."

"I have it on the most confidential authority," affirmed the count.

" 'Confidential authority'?" murmured Mrs. Bouchard. "Whose? Hitler's?" Her tone was sadly satirical.

The count allowed an expression of distaste to appear on his face. He averted his head with an abrupt movement, as he always did at the mention of that "loathsome" name. "Madame," he said, stiffly, "I must protest. No, my information comes from those who have balanced and very wise minds."

"Nevertheless, there will be war," said Mrs. Bouchard. She smiled strangely at the count. He saw that smile. His pale brows drew together suspiciously.

"Your distinguished husband truly believes this?" he asked. "How very depressing for him. It must pain him very much. We all know how he detests and abominates war. His book, *The Terrible Swift Sword*, the exposé of the armaments industry, the international plotters against the peace of the world, was very popular in Germany. It is still exceedingly popular. My friends in Germany so assure me."

She was unaccountably, to him, agitated. "Count von Bernstrom, I must ask you not to mention that book to my husband today! It upsets him. His whole meaning was distorted. No one understood. It was not only the armaments industry which he intended to expose. That was a minor matter to him. He wished only to draw attention to the sickness of the world, the hatred, the cruelty, the viciousness, of every man in every country. He wished to show that wars are not caused by a single group of men, but by the disease in every man—everywhere. The armaments industry merely pandered to that insane disease. Catered to it. Without the disease, Peter thinks, there would be no armaments industry. Wars are caused by the hatreds and corruptions in the minds of all men. They are the breakdown of the moral responsibility every man owes to his neighbor. Peter wished to show," she continued, her agitation making her incoherent, "that wars are the expression of the violence already in existence in men's hearts. He quoted someone to the effect that war is merely an extension of politics, their most primitive and direct extension, and conclusion. If he hated, and still hates, the armaments industry, it is because that industry is in itself an expression of greed on the part of those men who would profit by the wickedness of all the world."

The count affected to be bewildered by her rushing words, and uncomprehending. He lifted his hands artlessly, and smiled at her with deprecation. "I am afraid I do not follow, dear Madame. It is very confusing. Has not someone said that war is the most natural expression of man? Doubtless, he was wrong, and was attempting to simplify a most complex situation. Nevertheless, there is some reason in his remark."

She was not deceived by his artlessness. "Peter says that the intention of Christianity is to sublimate man's primitive instincts to an awareness of his moral responsibilities. Now, he believes, Christianity has failed. Not because it was wrong, but because it is ignored and perverted. In its most concentrated perversion—clerical fascism in Spain, Italy and France—it has become a horror, a death and a menace to the existence of civilization and democracy."

Ramsdall listened to her acutely, with a hidden and ominous smile.

"I am sure," he said, soothingly, "that those intelligent enough will appreciate Mr. Bouchard's intention. I know I had no difficulty. No difficulty at all. Does Mr. Bouchard intend to carry on his work further, upon his return to America?"

She was abruptly still. Then, after a moment, she said, clearly: "Yes." And she looked at them with the blue shining of her eyes. "He will try to tell America what he has learned here, what he has seen, what he knows. Before it is too late."

The count and Ramsdall exchanged a swift look.

"But Mr. Bouchard has hardly ever stepped from the villa," said Ramsdall, tentatively, leaning forward a little so that his chest extended itself over his paunch.

"He has listened," she answered, firmly.

Ramsdall's mind ran rapidly over the few years during which he had known the Bouchards. He tried to remember every man and woman who had visited them. He felt something sinister in the pattern of those who had been invited. He recalled that at the times he had been present there had been strange people here, also, whom he had detested, of whom he had had reason to be suspicious. He was alarmed. He smiled tolerantly, but said nothing.

An elderly lady, slight and bent, soft of movement, and gentle of expression, stepped onto the terrace. She had a worn and wrinkled face, kind and sad, and large brown eyes full of wisdom. Her hair was smooth and white. She wore black, also, but a hanging and spiritless black. The men rose and bowed. Mrs. Bouchard kissed the lady's cheek with deep affection. "How are you, Mama?" she said, in a sweet tone. "Not too tired, I hope, after all that packing?"

She smiled tenderly at her daughter. "No, dear. I am quite well." She turned and regarded the gentlemen with an expression suddenly very tired and remote, and full of shrinking. She sat down in a chair the count pulled forward for her.

"We are going to miss you very much, Mrs. Bouchard," said Ramsdall, gallantly.

"That is very kind of you, indeed," she murmured. She looked at him steadfastly, with those full brown eyes of hers, so simple, so intelligent, so ingenuous. For some reason he felt a heat rising about his thick throat.

She turned to her daughter. "It is almost twelve, dear. I haven't seen Peter this morning. He is well?"

"Yes, Mama," replied young Mrs. Bouchard. "He has been up since eight. Baron Opperheim is with him now. They have been together since ten."

The count moved slightly. "I beg your pardon, Madame. You said: 'Opperheim'?"

"Yes, Count. They are great friends, you know, and have been, for five years. The baron comes here very often."

The count's parched countenance remained smooth and only politely interested. "Of course. It was stupid of me to forget." He smiled with pleasure. "The baron and I have much to say to each other. I have not seen him for a month. When I called for him this morning, I was told he had already left his hotel."

"He has been in Paris," said young Mrs. Bouchard, indifferently.

Old Mrs. Bouchard said nothing. She looked slowly from the count to Lord Ramsdall. Only she saw the swiftness of their exchanged glances. She shivered.

She could not bear to look at these two any longer. Her gaze wandered over the terrace, barred and dappled with sunlight. She looked beyond, to the blue brilliance of the sea. She heard its soft and whispering sound, saw the light of the wings of the doves that circled the gulf. Far out, a white sail divided the water from the pure incandescence of the noonday sky. There was a faint rustling of leaves in the air, the warm scent of grass and salt and flowers. How peaceful it was, how gentle and serene. Her body felt very cold, and ancient.

She turned her mournful brown gaze to her daughter. She saw the worn fixity about the beautiful blue eyes and the deep corners of the lips of Celeste Bouchard. And her heart was torn with a grief too deep for words, for thought, or even for tears.

CHAPTER II

The wind came in on waves of radiant light through the open windows. Here, one could see the immense and glittering azure of the ocean, the wet brown rocks on which the villa perched, the scythe-like sweep of the gulls against the pure and passionate sky of France. The peace and shimmering brilliance of the noonday pervaded the serene air like a benediction. From these windows, there was no sign of the feverish and decadent life of Cannes, nothing but the wash of waves, the cries of the gulls, the soft rustling of the wind.

There was silence in the room. The pale and lofty walls and ceiling sparkled with shadowy brightness. There was a dancing reflection upon the cool dim floors, the edges of simple but perfect dark furniture, the bowls and vases of flowers scattered about on the tables and on the fireplace. In a far corner was a canopied bed, turned down, as if waiting. But near the windows, looking out upon the summer radiance and serenity, sat two men, in utter quietness.

But it was not the quietness of peace, tranquility or calm meditation. Things had been said, in a hushed voice, and behind them they had left an aura of bitter violence, of despair, of hopelessness and impotent sorrow. The younger man lay on a chaise-longue, a light shawl over his emaciated knees. His head rested on a plump pillow, and his face was turned to the windows. And that face was white and still, as quiet as the death which never seemed far from him. He was a man in his early forties, his coloring fair and pale, his light hair smooth and faded. His face, so ominously gaunt, appeared formed of the most frail but strangely strong angles, jutting or sunken, the bones sharply visible under the thin flesh. It was a gentle face, severe, sad, reflective, and full of intense intellect and mournfulness. His attitude revealed profound exhaustion, but also a spirit which would not allow his dying flesh to rest, so imbued was it with passion and indomitable courage and endless grief. His hands, emaciated, but fine and narrow, lay on the shawl, and though he had said nothing for a long time, the fingers flexed, trembled, convulsively clenched under the impetus of his tumultuous thoughts. The eyes that looked out upon the sea were strongly blue and pellucid, full of valor and fearlessness, and, now, burning with frantic misery.

The man who sat near him was much older. He was a very little man, brown, dry, shrivelled, with a tiny gray goatee and a bald head. His expression, whimsical and bitter, but kind and resigned, reflected itself in his large brown eyes as they fixed themselves upon the younger man. There was a quietness about him, a thoughtfulness, a sense of great wise age, which contrasted themselves remarkably with the agonized prostration implicit in the attitude of the other. He thought: They never accept, these Gentiles. They clamor, grow tempestuous, and out of their despair they abandon everything. That is because they live in the circle of the today, the bubble of Now. Beyond them, they cannot see the past or the future. Who can endure without a sense of yesterday and tomorrow? Despair is the prerogative of the child, but the stupidity of the man. I am desolate, yes. Ruined, true. I see no hope for myself. But I do not despair. Of what importance am I? The tomorrow is not for me. And life outwits tomorrows, inevitably, world without end. Why cannot my dear friend understand that? He is engrossed with today. He sees in it the shapes of all the tomorrows. But today, though it is exceedingly dreadful, and throws its bloody shadow on the future, carries in it a hope also for that future. Man dies, but mankind persists. But these Gentiles believe that each individual man's agonies are the world's agonies; his death, the world's death. They are bounded by their narrow flesh. We, at least, have the larger vision of humanity, its diversity, its bounding recovery from anguish, the distant light from other suns shining upon its face. I perish, but my brother shall live.

The young man stirred slightly on his pillows. He said, in a faint voice, in German: "It is not to be endured, Israel. Not to be endured!" And now his voice rose in a thin cry. He lifted his worn hands and clasped them together with a suppressed convulsion. "What can I do? What can anyone do?"

Baron Opperheim regarded his friend with deep compassion. He rubbed the side of his Phoenician nose, and coughed gently. He murmured something. The young man turned his face towards him. The baron spoke louder. "I was quoting a passage from Goethe's *Egmont*. You remember the cry of Ferdinand?: 'Must I stand by, and look passively on; unable to save thee, or to give thee aid! What voice avails for lamentation! What heart but must break under the pressure of such anguish?' "

The young man was silent. But his eyes fixed themselves with deathly and weary intensity upon the other. His hands clasped themselves together.

The baron inclined his head, and smiled his wry and whimsical smile. But his look was still compassionate, as he said softly: "And Ferdinand continues to his dear friend, Egmont: 'Thou canst be calm, thou canst renounce, led on by necessity, thou canst advance to the direful struggle, with the courage of a hero. What can I do? What ought I to do? Thou dost conquer thyself and us; thou art the victor; I survive both myself and thee. I have lost my light at the banquet, my banner on the field. The future lies before me, dark, desolate, perplexed.' "

He was silent a moment, then smiled tenderly. He leaned towards his friend, and repeated with soft insistence: " 'Thou canst advance to the direful struggle, with the courage of a hero.' "

The young man suddenly turned his face away so that his friend might not see what there was to be seen in his eyes.

"Goethe," continued the baron, reflectively, "was a great man. Until he forgot the world for himself. When he saw all men, he had a tremendous stature. When he remembered only himself, he was a pygmy. When he lamented over the torments of every man, his voice was as wide as the wind. When he began to lament for himself, bewail his impotence in a fretful voice, cry out in a woman's shrilling at his own sufferings, then his voice was crushed against his own teeth. It was not the later Goethe who said, in *Egmont* again: 'It was my blood, and the blood of many brave hearts. No! It shall not be shed in vain! Forward! Brave people!—And as the sea breaks through and destroys the barriers that would oppose its fury, so do ye overwhelm the bulwark of tyranny, and with your impetuous flood sweep it away from the land which it usurps.—I die for freedom, for whose cause I have lived and fought, and for whom I now offer myself up a sorrowing sacrifice.' "

He sighed. "Yes, Goethe was a great man, when he believed in the power of a single soul. He was a lost and little man, when he no longer believed that."

The younger man opened his pale lips as if to speak, then closed them again. Lines of chronic suffering were cleft deep beside them.

"You must go on. You must speak. You must warn, dear Peter. Nothing must close your mouth, so long as you live. The ruin is here. But it is not incurable. It will not utterly destroy the world, so long as there lives a single man with a great soul. You have a great soul. If only a few men listen to you, they are enough to save mankind. Do you remember the story of Sodom? It was necessary only to produce a few righteous men to save the city from God's just wrath." He smiled. "Surely you are not alone? Surely there are ten righteous men in the world like you to save the city!" He laughed gently. "Perhaps God will compromise. Perhaps He will agree to spare the city if only ten, if only five, if only one, righteous soul can be found."

Peter Bouchard lifted his clasped hands from his lap, and breathed with difficulty. There was a rasping sound in his breath, which came from his spirit as well as his lungs.

"It is strange," continued the baron. "I, like everyone else, never believed in God during the years of peace and security. But now I believe." He turned his head towards the windows, and Peter saw his Hebraic profile, serene, meditative, sorrowful, full of sadness, but very calm. "I believe," he repeated.

"Because you can do nothing else. You, like all of us, are impotent," said Peter, with a bitterness from the bottom of his heart.

The baron turned his head back to him, quickly. His eyes were alive, sparkling. "No! I am not impotent! I believe in God."

Peter pressed his hands over his face, over his eyes. His thoughts were full of deathlike despair. For it seemed to him that the world of men was a world of hatred, in which it was impossible to live, to draw a single free and happy breath. He felt the doom hanging over the world like a sword. Its shadow had already fallen on every city, on every hamlet, on every sea and river and stream. The thread by which it was held trembled in a wind of rising fury. The doom was just. Let the sword fall! The world deserved it. Courage, tenderness, honor, peace, compassion and justice and mercy: these were lies. There was no love—never, never was there love. Honor? Oh, above all things there was no honor! There was only hatred. Always, the word came back to him with an iron clangor, the doomful echo of man's perfidy and enormity.

He thought: I can't live in such a world, in the world which is coming.

The baron's words: "I believe," seemed to him the very essence of sad absurdity. He could only come back to the things which the baron had told him.

He said: "You are certain, Israel? Hitler will attack Poland? There will be war? I have always said there would be war, but I hardly believed it. You have made me believe it."

The baron nodded. "Yes, my dear Peter, there will be war. When Hitler will strike at Poland I am not certain. Next month? August, September, October? I do not know. But it will be soon. We must accept it."

"And France? England?"

"England will enter. This time she dare not ignore the challenge. I have faith in England. Under the corruption, the treachery, the pusillanimity of her leaders, under the hatred of her leaders, there is the English people. Always, under the greed of the powerful, there remains the people. Everywhere. Not only in England. Everywhere." He looked through the windows again. "Even in France."

"You can say that, after all we have seen, and known?"

"Yes, my dear Peter. Even after all that. When the captains and the kings depart with the banners and the trappings of their infamy, the people are left on the battlefield. It is they, at the last, who win, who understand, who build again, and bury the dead." He added, very softly: "And it is they who listen to the voice of the ten, the five, righteous men of Sodom."

Peter was silent. The baron regarded him with profound compassion. There was death in this younger man. It was there, in the gray shadows of his gaunt face. It was there, like a spectral light, on his forehead. But the voice still lived. The voice could still speak, and in the rising madness and tumult some would hear, and remember.

"When you return to America, speak, write, never rest. Tell your country what you know. You will be hated and derided by those who are plotting against other people. You will be called many foul names. What is all that to you. Somewhere, a few men will hear you. They will not forget. They will remember when the storm is at its most terrible."

He continued: "I went not only to Paris, where the decadent and the vicious live, and plot. I went over the whole countryside. I talked to the people. They are bewildered, and terrified. They are lost. They will be betrayed. One cannot escape acknowledging that. They know it, in their patient hearts. That is why they are so bewildered. But there will come a day when they will not be bewildered or frightened any longer. When they will understand who they are who have betrayed them. That will be a terrible day. But it will also be the day of strength and courage and valor. For the people are the children of those who destroyed the rights of kings, the power of the oppressors, the grasp of a murderous and corrupted clergy. They will remember. They will beat again with the pulses of their fathers."

Peter did not speak. But he looked at the other with a sudden awakening in his exhausted eyes. His hand lifted, and remained in the air in a gesture of intense listening.

"And America," said the baron. "The people, too, will remember. You must help them to remember. The coming war will not be between leaders, generals, kings, monsters and oppressors. It will be a war between philosophies. The philosophy of courage and life and freedom, and the philosophy of cowardice, death and slavery."

There was a light footfall, and Celeste entered the room. The baron rose and bowed quickly. She smiled at him, and the delicate sternness of her lips and expression softened. She bent over Peter and felt his forehead. He turned his lips to her soft palm and kissed it. She patted his cheek and looked down at him with infinite tenderness and anxiety.

"You are tiring yourself, dear," she said. "Do you feel up to going down to luncheon?" She paused. "Count von Bernstrom and Lord Ramsdall are already here."

Peter looked at the baron, who returned his glance swiftly.

"Yes, darling," said Peter. "I am feeling quite well." He paused. He looked at the baron again. "I am feeling quite well," he repeated. "In fact, I have never felt better."

CHAPTER III

It was a delightful if simple luncheon, there on the shaded terrace within sight and sound of the sea. The count was again incensed that he was to lose those paragons, Pierre and

Elise, those miracle-makers who had transformed a dull bird into a pheasant cooked by angels in heaven. The prawns, the salad, the crusty sweet bread, the coffee, the tiny petits-fours, only added to his rage as they lingered in rapturous memory on his tongue. He felt much abused. In consequence, his ire rose against the Bouchards, whom he obstinately credited with his deprivation.

He lusted after Celeste Bouchard, but now with sadism. He sneered inwardly at her husband. An example of pure decadence, most certainly. What could one expect from such inbreeding? The count was very familiar with the ramifications of the Bouchard family, that mighty munitions company which dominated all other armaments concerns in the world, and whose thin winding fingers grasped so many allied industries. This Peter Bouchard: the count ruminated. He was third cousin to his wife, born Celeste Bouchard. The count admitted that inbreeding frequently emphasized fine traits, eliminated grossnesses. One had only to consider horse-breeding. But it inevitably led to decadence, also, a refinement so extended that it became tenuous and implicit with decay. The father of Celeste had been Jules Bouchard, that brilliant and unscrupulous rascal who had become legendary. His cousin had been Honoré Bouchard, a man of intelligence and integrity. It was evident he had bequeathed these qualities to his youngest son, Peter. The count sneered again. Intelligence and integrity! The attributes of fools. Pure decadence.

The count glanced fleetingly at the older Mrs. Bouchard, the widow of Jules. Not a true Bouchard, but like so many aristocrats she, too, had that faint aura of physical and spiritual deterioration, he commented to himself. He, too, he reflected, was an aristocrat. But German aristocracy, because of its comparative youth, still retained the virility and ruthlessness of the barbarian. The French and the English were old; done. He smiled to himself.

Adelaide, mother of Celeste, mysteriously felt the thoughts of the German. She turned her weary brown eyes to him, reluctantly. He saw her look, inclined his head courteously and with a question. She turned away in silence.

Lord Ramsdall had been making himself very agreeable to his hostess and her husband. He repeated, bluffly, that Cannes was not going to be the same after their departure.

"I can't believe that," said Peter, who had only listlessly sampled the luncheon. He looked up, and his light blue eyes, square of corner and exhausted, were direct. "It's very kind of you, of course, Ramsdall, to say so, but Celeste and I haven't exactly been the life of the Coast." He glanced at his wife, and for a moment his expression became sad and regretful. "We've kept pretty much to ourselves, I'm afraid. So, no one will miss us."

As if she felt his sadness, his apology, his regret, Celeste reached under the lace edge of the cloth and pressed his hand warmly and tenderly. She looked at Ramsdall. "Candidly, we haven't had much in common with the tourists or the permanent residents. We haven't cared for the things which attracted them. We came here for a rest, for quiet, for the climate."

Baron Opperheim had been very silent during the luncheon. But his expressive old face, so wise and brown, the glance of his keen and sunken eye, so compassionate, so rueful and gently embittered, had seemed to add much to the desultory conversation around the table. Now he slowly glanced at each face, and his silent comments seemed actual and audible remarks. He came at last to the elder Mrs. Bouchard, and smiled at her. His bearded lips made that smile sweet and intimate.

"Will you regret leaving us, Madame?" he asked.

Her worn abstraction lightened as she turned to him. Apparently there was something in him which aroused some deep emotion in her. "There are a few," she said, in her tired and gentle voice. "You, most especially, Baron."

He bowed his head in acknowledgment of her kindness. "I wish I were going with you, dear friend," he said.

Peter turned to him with weary alertness. "Yes. I wanted to ask you again, Israel. Why can't you go? It will be an easy matter to get you a passport. I—I was able to do that for your daughter and her husband, and their children."

"Good, good of you! Do you think I forget? But for me— no." He paused, touched his beard. Von Bernstrom listened attentively, and with an expression of affection on his parchment features.

"Israel is no alarmist," he said. "He does not believe, like you, Mr. Bouchard, that there will be war."

The baron turned to him with bland but penetrating simplicity. His eyes regarded his friend with fixed concentration. "On the contrary, Wolfgang, I do believe there will be war. Are you going to deny that you know this, also?"

"Nonsense! Nonsense!" cried Ramsdall, sturdily, holding his glass of wine in his pudgy hand. "Why should there be war? Granting all that we know of Hitler—that he is a paranoiac madman, that he has delusions of grandeur, that he is a monster—we must also grant that he is no fool. He knows that he cannot win. He will try for bloodless victories, such as——"

"Munich," said Peter, and a pale convulsion passed over his face.

Ramsdall coughed. He said, gravely: "You know I never agreed with you, Peter, about Munich. 'Peace in our time.' What a noble phrase! And I don't doubt its validity." He leaned back in his chair and smiled at the younger man. "I admit that I never understood that about you, Peter. I should have thought you, above all others, would have been delighted over Munich. You've always hated war with commendable and civilized passion. Yet, you weren't delighted. No matter. You've explained that——"

"I've said, over and over, that Munich brought war closer to the world than any other one act during the past five years," Peter remarked, with feverish impatience. "Had we admitted Russia to the discussions, had Chamberlain and Daladier refused to go to Berchtesgaden without a representative of Stalin, had such a representative been there, there would not have been a 'Munich' in the present meaning of the word. When we repudiated Russia, we signed our agreement to war. Now, the blood of the world will be on our heads."

Ramsdall smiled indulgently. "I must disagree with you, Peter. Had a Russian representative been there, there would have been war indeed. The Bolsheviks are lusting for war. They'd like to see us all destroy ourselves, so that they can take over. Any student of modern history knows that. Stalin would have egged us on to fight Hitler, and then would have sat back, grinning, watching us cut our own throats. But, we were too clever for him."

"Much too clever," remarked Peter, with somber emphasis. "We'll fight Hitler alone, now."

"*Drang nach Osten,*" murmured the baron.

"Perfectly true, dear Israel!" exclaimed the count. "*Drang nach Osten!* If Hitler fights, which most certainly he will not, he will attack Russia. Not England; not France; not America."

The baron smiled wryly. He crumbled a bit of bread in his brown fingers and slowly glanced about the table again.

Peter sighed, as if the conversation wearied him. He looked at the baron. "But we were talking about you, Israel. Why can't you go with us? We'll be in Paris for a while. You can secure a passport; we'll even wait for you."

The baron shook his head. "For me—no. It is very simple, but no one understands. What has happened in Europe—it is the fault of all of us. Its doom will be upon all of us. Am I a coward?" He shrugged. "It appears to me that for me to leave will be the most exquisite cowardice. Could I have helped prevent this most horrible and imminent débâcle? Could any of us have done so? I am not making myself clear," he added apologetically. "We are all guilty, Englishman, Frenchman, German." He tapped his brown forehead, and then his chest, significantly. "It is in here, and here, that the guilt lies, that the disease first had its blossoming. Not in Hitler; not in Franco; not in Mussolini. Only in here, and here. In the soul. In the heart. In the mind. In every man. To run, and leave the doom to fall upon one's fellow sinners is cowardice."

"What could you have done?" cried Peter, impatiently. "You, a Jew? You, the first victim?"

But the baron looked at Ramsdall, at his friend von Bernstrom, with that bland and fatal directness of his. He replied to Peter, but looked only at those two.

"What could I have done? I could have thought with my soul. I could have turned to God. I could have believed. I—we—did not. There is strange power in God," he added, in a soft and almost inaudible tone, and his face became old and profound with pain.

Ramsdall's full red lips pursed themselves with amusement. But there was a baleful gleam in his eye, full of inimical contempt. "Jews always return to God when the power of their money fails," he said.

Peter, his wife, his mother-in-law, looked at him with shock and outrage. The count grimaced.

But the baron inclined his head almost with humility. "You are correct," he murmured, gently. "So we differ from you. You never return. To the last, you believe in money, in power. Even at the gallows, you believe in it. You never comprehend."

Ramsdall coughed. "I hope I didn't offend you, Opperheim. I didn't intend that, I assure you. In a way, I was complimenting your people. You return much sooner than we do. But, frankly, don't you consider that real cowardice?"

The baron smiled, and did not answer. His hands continued their crumbling of the bread, and now the movements of his fingers seemed fateful as they slowly dropped crumb after crumb so that they lay in a little mound like ashes upon the table.

There was a silence about the table. The brilliant wind lifted the edges of the lace cloth, glittered on the silver.

There was the perfume of roses strong in the air. The sea rushed in with a deep breath, and despite the light and the sun there was an ominous quality in its cosmic breathing.

The baron looked at the heap of crumbs on the cloth, and impelled by his absorption, the others gazed at it also. No one could have explained what so compelled their attention. But the crumpled and abandoned mound seemed of enormous and terrible significance to them. They felt a pressure in the atmosphere, a constriction in their chests, even Ramsdall, even von Bernstrom.

"I had an old nurse, when I was a child," said the baron, in a soft voice. "I wasted bread; I was a very wilful child. I piled up crumbs—like this. It was a favorite occupation of mine. She said to me, once: 'When you waste bread, holy bread, in this fashion, your soul will never rest after it leaves your body. It will go roaming about the world, until every last crumb is gathered up, out of the earth, out of the bellies of birds and animals, out of the water. You will look long and far. For you have done a great sin.'"

He lifted his head, and for the last time he looked slowly at each face.

"'Long and far.' The world will soon be full of souls, searching. We have done a great sin."

The count lit a cigarette, with his graceful if wooden gesture. He blew a plume of blue smoke into the bright air, and watched it curl. His thoughts were virulent, and full of contempt. But he kept his harsh face impassive and aloof. When he returned his attention to the others, after a long moment or two, the baron was watching him, his nut-brown eyes intent, significant, filled with melancholy and deep thoughtfulness. For some strange reason, the count was immediately imbued with impotent rage and hatred.

Ramsdall stirred his fat bulk uneasily on the chair. "Well, in speaking for myself, I am glad to say that I am returning to England. There are currents here, in France. I confess I don't like them. I don't like the implication of doom here lately. The air in England is more wholesome, even if it rains almost constantly." He laughed with affection.

He turned to Peter. "You will be glad to hear that I intend to continue my policy of peace, in my newspaper. I have always supported Chamberlain, of whom you don't approve, my dear lad. Nevertheless, I believe the old codger is right. We've nothing to gain by war, even if there was the remotest chance of such a catastrophe, which there is not. Your articles in my paper, Peter, were much approved by thoughtful people. May we hope for others like them?"

"No," said Peter, quietly.

Ramsdall raised his eyebrows at this impoliteness. He assumed a whimsical expression, and sighed, leaning over to deposit the ash of his excellent cigar in the silver tray.

The count said: "If I thought there was to be war, my dear Mr. Bouchard, I should leave France immediately. I have my friends in Germany who keep me informed. You observe that I am quite comfortable in France. I do not leave. I remain. Does that mean nothing of significance to you?"

"Yes," said Peter.

The eyes of the two men met, and held.

In the ringing silence, which followed Peter's reply, Celeste rose, and the gentlemen with her, all except Peter, who was kept in his chair by the light pressure of his wife's hand on his shoulder.

"You must please excuse Mama and me," said Celeste, in her sweet low voice. "We have still some packing to do."

She extended her hand to Lord Ramsdall, who took it warmly. Her face wore its worn look of delicate sternness, but her eyes were direct between their curved black lashes. "It is good-bye, then, Lord Ramsdall."

"No, rather au revoir, dear Mrs. Bouchard," he said, gallantly. "I expect to be in America in October. I trust I shall see you then?"

She smiled briefly, then turned to the count, who raised her hand to his lips. Now her sternness became fixed and hard.

Her mother, Adelaide, received the gentlemen's regretful remarks in polite silence. The ladies left the terrace. Their departure was soon followed by that of Lord Ramsdall and Count von Bernstrom. The baron remained.

He and Peter sat for a long time on the sunlit terrace, not speaking, but looking out over the gulf where the sea sighed restlessly.

"It will be an unhappy day for France, if or when von Bernstrom becomes the *gauleiter*," said the baron, wearily.

Peter moved in his chair, and clasped his hands together.

"You are sure, Israel? That is the plan? It is incredible!"

The baron shrugged. " 'I have my friends in Germany who keep me informed,' " he quoted, with his sad and quizzical smile.

"But France! The Maginot Line!"

"I have told you so often, dear Peter, that a thousand Maginot Lines cannot resist the wickedness in men's hearts."

"Israel, I must ask you again: Why don't you inform Daladier, Bonnet, Reynaud, all of them? The authorities? That this scoundrel is a spy, a dangerous plotter?"

Again the baron shrugged, and spread out his hands. "I have told you: they already know. They are helpless, or are in the plot. What is one to do?"

Peter groaned under his breath. "I tell you, I can't believe it! You must be mistaken! This is fantastic. It is a nightmare."

"It is a Walpurgis Night," agreed the baron. "The world is entering on the long night." He added: "The dance of madmen. The carnival of the clowns. The merriment of the murderers. Listen: you can hear the wailing of the insane flutes, the beat of the terrible drums. The stage is set. The world is the audience. The world has paid the actors, and called them on the stage. It has paid its price to see them, in greed and hatred and treachery. It will leave the theatre knee-deep in blood. Its own blood."

He continued, in so low a tone that Peter hardly heard him: "Not Hitler. Not Mussolini. No. These are not the guilty. It is all the world. Not only Germany. No. England, France, America. This is the play they have demanded. These are the actors they have evoked. And may God have mercy on our souls."

His old enormous sickness seized Peter again, a sickness of the soul, an anguish and impotence of the mind.

"There was Manchuria," said the baron. "And God said to the world: 'Now? You will oppose the evil ones now?' But the greedy ones replied: 'No. We shall make money by this conquest.' God is patient. There was Ethiopia: 'Now?' said God. But no, it was not now. There was the same answer of the greedy, and the stupid whimpered and cried: 'Am I my brother's keeper?' And then there was Spain. 'O!' cried God. 'Surely now? Look at the blood of the innocent, the righteous, the just, the lovers of freedom, the poor and honest men!' But the wicked sneered, the greedy reached forth their hands, the treacherous turned away. And the stupid, as always, shivered and hid their faces. Then came Czecho-Slovakia, Austria. Out of their depths, out of Germany, came the appeal of good men, innocent men, helpless men. 'World,' said God, sternly, 'it is now? Surely it is now?' But there was only silence, or laughter, or cries of hatred."

He paused. Now his voice was solemn, low, very cold. "There will come another day. Very soon. And God's voice will fill the universe like a cosmic and awful thunder, saying: 'Men, ye shall surely die, for ye have ignored the cries of your tortured brother. The punishment is upon you. This is the final hour. To every people there comes one terrible and inevitable final hour, when it must choose between those things by which men live, or those by which they die. The hour is upon you. It is Now. Shall it be now, O faithless and adulterous generation?' "

Peter listened with passionate attention. He said: "Will it be 'now,' Israel?"

The baron lifted his head and looked at the sky. He clasped his hands as if in urgent prayer, humble and profound.

"I believe," he whispered, "surely I believe: it will be Now."

CHAPTER IV

Celeste and her mother occupied seats of honor at the table of the captain of the *Ile de France*. The captain was a sour Breton, who disliked the sea, and particularly disliked wealthy passengers. He came of a long line of fishermen, who regarded the sea as a vast brute whose existence could be tolerated only because it separated the coast of France from England, and contained fish. He had no romantic illusions about the great waters; he had seen too many men, including his own father, die in them. Safety and food; these the sea provided. Thus it had a reason for being. But he could not believe that one of its reasons was to furnish luxurious transportation between continents for the idle and the rich and the vicious. One used the sea as a bulwark, as a necessity. To use it for recreation, to ride on the top of its watery chasms and profound horrors was to him something frightful. He brooded on this constantly. He would stand on the bridge at night and regard the seething blackness with hatred, unmoved by the shattered silver path of the moon, or the phosphorescence that sparkled in the wake of the ship. In his hatred was fear. But the fools sleeping, drinking, dancing, fornicating and lying and eating below knew nothing of fear, except the dread that the coming years might not be so well for them.

The captain would clench his fists, and smile grimly. The coming years! He had once been first officer on a French warship. He flexed his arm. He was not old! He could still fight. With his inner ear, he heard the echoing hollow boom of guns riding the waves like the bellowing of giants. Ah, how he would fight! The sea had another use besides safety and food. It could bear the prows of iron ships into the guts of the enemy. He saw banners against the sky. The Boche! How he hated the Boche! Almost as much as he hated the sea. The Boche seemed to him more of a horror than the waters, for the Boche had a mind and did his evil deliberately. The captain, his heart beating more strongly than it had beaten in years, felt temporarily superior to the sea. He leaned over the bridge and spat into it. "You are very foul," he addressed it. "You do not sink the ships of the Boche immediately when he embarks on you. If you did that, I could endure you. I could forgive you."

He wondered how long it would be before the Boche would rise to his feet again, ankle-deep in blood, and set out on his ancient path to war. He, the captain, had in his safe a certain sealed envelope, which was not to be opened except in the event of sudden war. What did that envelope contain? What orders? The dark lined face of the captain tightened. Would he be ordered to remain in a neutral port with his ship? That would be bad. Now he felt ill. Or, would he be ordered to surrender that ship with all hands on board to the Boche? He thought this, incredulously. He recalled that during the last war he had never thought such a thing. To think it would have been dishonor, deserving of death. But in these malignant days all things were possible. It was no dishonor, to think them. That seemed very terrible to the captain. He contemplated the hidden enemies of France, lurking like foul slugs under stones, like poisonous vipers hidden in little caves, under ferns, in wet sunless places. Always they lived, these enemies, but in the past they had not dared come forth lest a strong heel crush them. Now, they waited. The strong heels were no more, or were tied. There were the clergy, the haters of liberalism, enlightenment and freedom, always waiting, with their interdictions, their narrow venomous faces, their crosses, their chants, their chains, their cruelty, and their hatred. There were the pusillanimous statesmen, the plotters, the servers of raucous and venal women, the cowards, the whimperers, the creatures without fortitude or honor, the diseased, the liars and the traitors, the rich fools who remembered nothing and hated always.

What had France become! He thought of his countrymen, whom he brought for idle pleasure to America, and then returned them to France a little later. There was not even a robust zest in their dirty women. They were rotten with disease; they had no gay light in their vicious eyes. He thought of the fat and swarthy industrialists, the politicians, the perfume purveyors, the diplomats, the dressmakers, the male milliners, the writers of obscene and elegant literature, the Jesuitical and attenuated gentlemen, impotent and milky. Were they France? No, said his heart, with sudden passion. There were still the Breton fisherfolk, the peasant in his field, the little artisan, the man in the factory and the mines. He knew them, did the captain. France was dead and stinking at the top. But the trunk was sound. Then he felt ill again. A tree always died first at the top. Who, in this extremity, would cut away the dead wood with a ruthless hand, so that new branches could grow? Who would save the tree before decay engulfed even its roots? There was a prelate of the Church on board, with a thin and sinister face. He, too, sat at the captain's table. The captain belched, and put his hand to his belly. No, he did not need bismuth. He only needed to drown the prelate. Then he could digest adequately again.

On this journey he had an unusually large percentage of Americans on board. Ah, the rats had heard the quaking of the timbers of Europe! They had smelt the distant fire. They had heard the rumble of iron feet. They had sniffed the effluvia of poison gas. So, they were returning to their vast fat homeland, where they could hide behind their banks and the barricades of their bonds. They thought they were safe. They were too stupid to know that no man was safe anywhere in the world, this time. The trumpets of doom were sounding below every wall in the world. The mortar was already sifting from between the stones and filling the air with choking dust. The great stones were already groaning as they shifted uneasily one upon another. The gates were rocking and squealing. Could these fools, these rich vagabonds, these useless imbeciles, these rotten posturers, hear and feel all this? He doubted it. No, they remembered nothing, they learned nothing, they thought nothing. They thought of nothing but their flesh, their bellies, their lusts, men and women alike.

Perhaps the coming ruin would be a good thing. Perhaps it would destroy these ravenous feeders, as collapsing walls destroyed the termites that devoured them. The gilt and plaster walls of cathedrals would fall, burying the fetidness within them; the thrones of kings, the lie-impregnated roofs of government: these too were trembling in the coming earthquake. And when the smoke drifted away from broken cities, would it be found that the fire had cleansed them of liars, exploiters, murderers, plotters and fools?

The captain really hated Americans. So famously did they believe that they were apart from the common world, that they lived on some esoteric plane that could be in communication with the plane of other men, but could not be invaded by them! When they said: "I am an American," they smiled smugly as if they had declared that they were inhabitants of Mars or the moon, and had nothing in common with Europe or Asia, that they breathed another air, were pressed upon by another atmosphere, had their being in another kind of flesh and another universe, whirling placidly above the world like an impregnable nebula. Who had told them this? What liars, what plotters, what traitors, in their own government, among their own people, had imparted this lie to them to their own coming death? There was only one world; there was only one race of men. If the Americans did not learn this soon, they must surely die. He thought of the prattling silly American women on board the ship, the vicious jewelled women with their high sharp laughter, their equally brainless and complacent men, and he muttered an imprecation.

Then he paused. He remembered the two American ladies at his table, the Mesdames Bouchard. But these ladies were very strange; they were not like their fellow Americans. They were quiet, well-bred, soft-voiced, almost always silent and restrained. The younger lady reminded him of his own daughter, who had been reared in a convent. Madame Bouchard had the same softness and delicacy and shyness, and the same aristocratic pride. Ah, and what a face, so stern and fragile, so clear of contour, so beautiful! There was her mother, also, a great lady. He felt kinder and easier in his mind. He had not met many such American ladies, but perhaps they were not the only ones.

Then, too, there was poor Monsieur Bouchard, with the face of death, the firm clear voice, the penetrating light-blue eyes, the integrity and honor. Not a typical American. The captain shuddered as he thought of the typical male American, who was either obese or athletic, a gambler or a lover of horses and women, noisy, dogmatic, ignorant, egotistic, arrogant, believing that all things were for sale— (But, were they not? reflected the captain with acid irony.) Monsieur Bouchard was not one with his fellow Americans. It was sad that he had come only twice to table during the past four days of the voyage. He was ill. But he had no nurse, no court physician, though his family was one of the richest in the world. Nor had he engaged the most expensive suite. (That was now occupied by an American female whose sole claim to fame was her notorious adulteries, from which she had extracted truly impressive sums. And all this during her career as soubrette, swimmer, naked dancer with fans, and mouther in the cinema! Truly a fantastic country, this America!) No, the suite occupied by the Bouchards was modest: three bedrooms, a common little sitting-room, and one bath. It was rumored that young Mrs. Bouchard was her husband's nurse, and that she served him with endless devotion. That was probably the reason for the fixed and worn look about her eyes and mouth, the certain grimness in the bluish shadow about her delicate nostrils. The captain sighed. These were not the usual expatriates. He understood Monsieur Bouchard had lived in France for reasons of health. If so, he had not improved. Death was breathing his icy breath upon his neck. But one could understand that such a gentleman was returning to America not out of fear. It was something else.

Young Mrs. Bouchard had not attended a single dance or party during the voyage. It was not to be expected that she would attend the last dance, which was to be held tonight. Tomorrow, they would reach New York.

So young a woman, so beautiful, and there was no light in her, no life, no young gaiety or joy. Only that dainty grimness of one dedicated to duty. How very *pathétique!*

Celeste tapped gently on Peter's bedroom door, and at his invitation to enter, she put her face archly into the room, and then went in, smiling brightly. Peter was in bed, his medicine on the lighted bed-table at his right hand. He was sitting high on his pillows, for he could no longer lie flat. Sometimes, during the night, the long and lonely night, Celeste could hear his coughing until she could no longer bear it, but must put her hands over her ears and sob soundlessly.

The soft light of the lamp emphasized all the hollows and pallor of his attenuated carved face, the quiet mouth with its hint of intellectual fanaticism, the shadows about his eyes, the strong resolution of his forehead. He returned his wife's smile with weary passion and love. He extended his hand to her.

43

"Hello, angel. Come to say good-night to your miserable husband?"

To smother a momentary revolt against his faint self-pity, she bent and kissed him gently and humorously. "Hello, wretch," she said, fondly. Her soft voice caught a little. She shook up his pillows, glanced at her jewelled watch, poured out a dose of the sedative he always took. It usually acted in about fifteen minutes. He took it obediently, looking at her with yearning tenderness. Then he lifted her hand, kissed its palm. He sighed. She sat down on the corner of the bed. Now her face was beautiful in its compassion, its courage, and its love.

"Our last night out," she said. "Tomorrow, we'll be in New York. Then what?"

He was silent. He lifted his hand and touched his lips with it, coughing automatically. Then he said: "We're homeless vagabonds. What a life I've led you! Plans?"

She bent and lifted one small box after another on his bed-table, examining the contents. "Peter! You didn't take your vitamins at dinner! If I don't watch you constantly, you neglect yourself. Just like a child. Well, it's too late tonight. Tomorrow, you take a double dose."

She turned to him and smiled again. "Yes, plans. I don't know. We have a choice of half a dozen homes or more, of our loving relatives. Who would you prefer? Until we can find a place of our own, or build? Of course, it would take a year to build, and we can circulate among the family, staying until each kicks us out."

She laughed merrily. He only smiled absently, looking away from her.

Then he began to speak with hesitation: "Look here, this might be awkward. Today, I got a radiogram from Henri, inviting us to stay with him and Annette at Robin's Nest."

She was rigid with surprise and shock. But she did not speak, only watched him intently.

He spoke in a louder tone, as if justifying himself, or trying to break down what he believed would be her inevitable resistance:

"Francis, Jean, Hugo, my precious brothers. I had a kind of liking for Francis at one time. Now, I don't know. They've all invited us. The whole damn family. Very generous and affectionate of them. We can knock around from one to the other indefinitely, until we decide what to do. Somehow, I don't admire the prospect. Besides, they make me ill. Have I ever told you how I despise all of them?"

He laughed shortly, which brought on a fit of coughing. Celeste gave him a glass of water. He did not see that her hand was trembling a little. He drank; the cough subsided. He lay back on his pillows, breathing exhaustedly, drops of sweat out over his forehead and upper lip. His light-blue eyes were bloodshot. She looked at him, and her cool heart was torn as by iron fingers. His face was no paler than her own.

In the sudden silence they could hear the wash and suck of the sea outside the port-holes, the laughter and footsteps of men and women on the deck, the distant sound of dance music.

He said, suddenly, looking at her with suffering: "My darling, what a life you'd had with me! What have I given you? You were so young when we were married, hardly more than a child. You were so happy, before you knew me. What have I brought you? Attendance on a contemptible invalid, vagabondage, homelessness, sleepless nights, constant nursing. You've never had a home. You've never had a husband," he added, in a lower tone, very quiet, but heavy with pain, and even shame. "How can I forgive myself? How can I hope you'll ever forgive me? I despise myself."

The aching wound in her heart increased, expanded, until all her flesh was engulfed in its pangs. She laid her face beside his on the pillows. She could feel its heat, could hear the rasp of his uneasy breathing. She kissed his cheek, his lips, and tears smarted like molten metal in her eyes.

"Peter, how can you say that? I love you so. I've always loved you so terribly. I never really cared about anyone else but you. You've brought me such happiness. I've hated myself because I could do so little for you. I've been so frightened. You don't know what a coward I am. I never believed in anything—really. But since I've been married to you—I've prayed. Really prayed." She laughed, chokingly. "You've made me quite religious, darling."

He moved his head and pressed his cheek against her with feverish strength, and he sighed over and over, the mournful sound seeming to come from the very tortured depths of him. He smoothed the tumbled black hair on the pillow beside him with infinite tenderness and pain.

"Whatever we've had has been so precious," she whispered, smiling radiantly into his eyes, her tears on her cheeks. "So very, very precious. I wouldn't exchange that for anything in the world. That's why I've prayed."

He continued to smooth her hair with his emaciated fingers. He thought: It will be better for her when I am dead. I must hurry. I must do what I've set out to do. When that's done, I'll let go. It'll be easy to let go. But, I must hurry, before she suffers too much. Before it's too late for her to pick up her life, that I've almost ruined, and go on, alone. She's still young. She still has time to be happy.

The thought gave him a sudden joy, sudden ease. A faint color came back into his livid face. He patted her cheek lightly.

"Well, the prayers must have had some effect. I've been much better this last year. You know that. Before the last twelve months I was practically bedridden for two years. Now, I'm almost normal. I can get up for four—six—hours a day. I'll be leaving the ship under my own steam. You must tell me about your new religion. Perhaps I could use a little of it, myself!"

She sat up, wiping her tears away, laughing a little. "O Peter, remember how I dragged you to Lourdes? Wasn't it ridiculous? Wasn't it absurd? Making you drink that abominable water, kneeling among those gibbering people, looking at that silly grotto? I was so earnest! I knelt with you. I've wondered so often why you indulged me, by going."

He said, smiling only slightly, holding her hand again: "But it did you some good, my angel. Didn't it, now? You looked quite refreshed after it, quite hopeful."

She shook her head, her smile making her white teeth sparkle in the soft light. "Well, there were all those crutches, and people whooping and crying out they were cured. Really hopeless cases. And all you had was a few damaged spots in your lungs. I considered you quite a bargain for the mystical powers. Just a few spots. It was quite a job to cure the cripples, I thought, and the blind and the deaf. During the super-natural handouts, your spots would only be a slight flicker of the ghostly wrist, a mere bagatelle of generosity. And, speaking of hopefulness, you didn't cough for two months after that, so there!"

They laughed together, in the fullness of love and remembrance.

"Psychology," said Peter, at last. "You know, fully half of human ailments come from the mind. We know that, at last, just as the jungle witch-doctors and the medicine men and the alleged saints have always known it. Modern medicine is just bumbling along in a dishevelled and panting state in the rear of the ancient wizards and pagan faith-healers. Perhaps some day it will catch up. Kissing the stony hem of a statue of Hera or Juno, or the image of Isis, or the relics of Christian martyrs and saints, are all the same profound mumbo-jumbo. The altar of Diana—the grotto of Lourdes. One and the same. Supernaturalism? Only the supernaturalism, the un-understandableness, of the human soul and mind. And, perhaps, the mystery of God, which is probably the same thing. Yes, I was helped at Lourdes. You can't be in the presence of faith, even superstitious and ignorant faith, without being affected."

"I felt, I had cheapened you, and myself," she said. "It seemed so mediæval. Gruesome, sickening, morbid, superstitious."

"Nevertheless, I was helped. We can't get over that. I've often wondered if there aren't localities in the world which are strongly impregnated with what we call 'supernaturalism.' Which probably isn't supernaturalism at all, but the remnant of unknown and mysterious charges of power, cosmic power. Like deposits of coal, or oil. They might have crystallized, like diamonds, when the world was cooling from its molten state. What are those deposits of unseen power? We know that the universe consists of tremendous atomic charges of neutrons and electrons, that what we know as 'matter' is only those charges, constantly in flux, in incredible motion. The Hindoos never believed in 'matter' at all, and countless mystics never believed in it either. They believed that 'matter' and God are synonymous. When I take the time to think, I believe it, also."

He continued, reflectively: "I really almost believe in those cosmic deposits of mysterious power in certain localities of the world. Just as I sometimes believe that while there are benevolent deposits of unseen power of what we choose to call 'good,' there are also deposits of what we call 'evil.' And this evil explodes into the world periodically like an active volcano, affecting all men. It is exploding now. You can feel it. Reason, like a candle, can only illuminate a little of the caverns. But beyond its feeble light we hear strange cosmic echoes, catch shadows of mystery."

He turned to her, laughing gently. "Well, we are getting philosophical. Let us return to the surface and get back to things as they seem."

He hesitated. "Well, there's Henri's cable. I've given the matter thought. You and Annette were very close. Would you like to be with her for a while?"

Her face became closed. He could not know her agitation. She thought: He's forgotten. That is very sensible, of course. How foolish we were, once!

She said: "I received a cable from Annette, inviting us.

You'll laugh at me, but I thought you'd refuse. I remembered that you and Henri were very antagonistic once. Even though he and Annette came nicely to our wedding, and you both shook hands very cordially afterwards."

Peter was amused. He looked almost well now, as he laughed.

"That was a long time ago. We're getting along in years now."

He paused, and was no longer amused. He regarded her with steadfast earnestness. "I'll tell you the truth, my darling. You know what I've set out to do. As soon as possible, I must get to work. Another book. Perhaps several. You know my plans. That is why we are returning to Windsor. I must study the Bouchards. I've studied them from France, from England, from Germany, from Italy, from Russia. I know what they've been doing. I know whose hands move the State Department, the American and foreign diplomats. And I know whose is the strongest hand. Henri's."

"But, darling," she said, "our family isn't that omnipotent. I know it's pretty powerful. But it is only one organization. It can't manipulate the whole world so easily."

"You forget its ramifications. You forget that it is entangled with all the men of power, in politics, in industry, in government. It is symbolic of all the men of power, the men of evil. In writing, one must confine the general to the particular. You can't embrace the whole of mankind in a single book. You can use only a few characters, a few incidents. One symphony doesn't contain all music. But it hints at all of it. It contains elements of all written and heard harmony.

"Henri is the most powerful of the Bouchards. He is the 'key man' of the 'key men' of power. That's why I want to study him at close hand."

She looked down at the sparkling ring on her left hand. She shook her head, smiling somewhat. "Isn't that a little treacherous? We accept his hospitality, and you put him under a microscope!" She laughed.

He took her seriously. "You think it would be dishonorable? If you do, we won't accept his invitation. I wouldn't violate even the slightest compunction in you, my darling."

She laughed again. "O my pet! How humorless you are! I was only joking. You have your work to do. You know how devoted I am to your work. Almost as much as you are. I'd do anything to help you. We'll go, then. I'll radiogram Annette immediately. She and Henri have come especially to New York to meet us, and I think that is very kind of them. They are staying at the Ritz-Plaza, she says."

She bent and kissed him. The sedative had begun its work. His eyelids were heavy. There was a look of uneasy peace on his exhausted face. He watched her leave the room for her own room. His eyes followed her with passionate yearning to the last.

CHAPTER V

Adelaide was sitting alone by her reading table in her bedroom when her daughter tapped softly on the door. Celeste entered, smiling faintly.

"Mama? Am I disturbing you?" She held the cable sent to Peter in her hand.

"No, darling," answered Adelaide, putting aside her book. She regarded her daughter with sad fondness. The girl was so pale, so contained, so poised. Adelaide's heart ached. She had lived in close intimacy with Celeste and Peter during these past five years, but she knew less about her daughter now than she had done fourteen years ago when Celeste had married Peter. There was never any indication of what she was thinking on that lovely ivory face, no flicker of her deepest thoughts in those dark blue eyes. Adelaide's sorrow was more than she could endure. Had she been wrong when she had maneuvered this marriage, believing it best for Celeste? Surely the marriage had brought nothing but pain and anxiety to the child, nothing but fear and sleepless nights. Had it brought a profound love? In the beginning, Adelaide had believed this. Now, she was not too sure. If there had only been a child! But she knew, with the subtle omniscience of a mother, that for the last ten years, at least, there had been no possibility of a child. She thought of the tender devotion, unremitting and patient service, Celeste had given her husband. Surely that must be love! But one could not tell, with Celeste. There was a grim Puritanism about the girl, a passion for silent duty, for hard self-immolation.

Adelaide had often wanted to cry out to her beloved daughter, in anguish and tears: "Tell me, darling! Are you happy? Do you love poor Peter? Are you without regret? You must tell me, if I am to have just a little peace!"

But she had never been able to say this. She was an old woman now, very old. She would die soon. She was so very tired. But never, even if she lived forever, could she bring herself to ask these questions. If she heard the answer, she might expire in one convulsion of remorseful agony. Or, she might be at peace. She dared not risk the first terrible possibility.

At times she comforted herself with the remembrance that it was Celeste who had made the final decision to marry Peter, who had broken her engagement to the ruthless and coldly violent Henri Bouchard, her cousin. There was no weakness in Celeste. Under that exquisite poise and gentleness was a character like stone, something hard and uncompromising and determined. Nothing could have forced Celeste into a repugnant marriage. Yes, she had loved Peter. Of that, Adelaide was now sure. Did she still love him? Was she, Adelaide, never to know?

Perhaps Celeste had always known that these questions tormented her mother. Perhaps that was the reason for her firm aloofness, her steadfast look that dared Adelaide to intrude impertinently, her quiet removal when the conversation showed any signs of becoming intimate. "Thus far shall you go, and no farther," had been the silent law of Celeste Bouchard. Adelaide had not been hurt by this hardness. She had only been frightened that perhaps Celeste did not dare allow any intimacy, for the sake of her own soul, her own fortitude, her own safety. She had done this thing; she had married Peter. All this was irrevocable. She had chosen her path, and she walked bravely and quietly upon it, not looking back, not turning aside, not even sighing.

Sometimes, Adelaide, with terror, wondered if Celeste had loved Henri Bouchard. Oh, she dared not think of this! During the engagement, she, Adelaide, had been able to think of nothing but that Henri, with his cold viciousness, his arrogance, his relentless strength, would destroy the girl. He would violate the virtue in Celeste. Now, Adelaide was not so sure. Sometimes her terror overwhelmed her. She remembered her own part in the breaking of the engagement. Was it now her punishment to watch the uncomplaining and patient suffering of her daughter? Was she to be given no chance to set her own mind at rest, to offer consolation, sympathy and affection? To pray for forgiveness?

The hopeless question was again in her mind as Celeste seated herself near her mother. She was smiling her usual faint and quiet smile. She wore a thin black lace frock, through which her white flesh glowed like sun-warmed marble. Her bright black hair was exquisitely coiffed, though she had no personal maid. Her red mouth would have been perfect in her pale and luminous face had it not been for that deep and delicate hardness at the corners, the hardness of long patience. She fluttered the paper, and laughed a little.

"You know, we are to stay at Crissons, for the summer, Mama?" she said.

"Yes, dear," replied Adelaide, with yearning love in her tremulous voice.

Celeste laughed a little, and stared into space. Her dark blue eyes were reflective, and somewhat satirical.

"It has just occurred to me that we really have no home at all! Crissons is Christopher's estate, even though he lives in Florida now, and rarely goes to Crissons. Let me see: it has been three years since he has been there. It's sweet of him to offer me Crissons."

"You are his sister," said Adelaide, shrinking as always at the mention of the name of her youngest son. "Why shouldn't you use Crissons? After all, I contributed to the furnishings, though heaven knows I thought them atrocious."

Celeste smiled. "Yes, the house is rather astringent. I never liked it, either inside or out. Edith hated it. I think she was glad she and Christopher went to Florida when they were married. We've never visited them in Florida. We might, this summer. Christopher has invited us. The climate might help Peter." She paused. As she spoke her husband's name, the faint dim shadow, as always, touched her features, making their calmness waver and break up for a moment. She continued, in a slightly firmer tone: "Yes, it might be good for Peter. But you know the antagonism between him and Christopher. I haven't asked him yet. Perhaps it would be better to say nothing at all about it."

"If you don't care for Crissons, we could go to Windsor, and stay at Endur," said Adelaide, hopefully, remembering her old home.

Celeste shrugged. "Somehow, I don't think Endur appeals to me. I never liked that house, either. Besides, hasn't Armand's new superintendent rented it? Yes, I remember Armand writing me about that."

She laughed again, without merriment. "We really haven't

a home! The first two years Peter and I were married we spent in New York." She lifted the fingers of her left hand and counted the years off with the index finger of her right hand. "Then, we spent four years in England, at Torquay. We came back to New York for a year. That was when poor old Etienne died. We occupied his apartment. What a fantastic place it was! Then, thinking the mountains might help Peter, we went to Switzerland for two years, or a little more. Then Paris for a few months. Then Germany, Italy. Finally Cannes, for five years. What horrible expatriates we are!"

She smiled thoughtfully, then with wryness.

"Why not remain in New York a little, then you and Peter could look about and see where you would prefer to live," suggested Adelaide, her knotted hands twisting together with their chronic gesture of old pain.

Celeste, not replying, lifted the paper on her knee and studied it thoughtfully. The slightest frown appeared between her eyes. She was silent for a short space.

Then she said: "I love Windsor. I feel I have roots there. Perhaps it is because it is practically infested with Bouchards. All of us. We own it, mentally, physically, spiritually. And, financially. I feel important in Windsor. Not useless, as I do now. Peter hasn't said he hated it. I think he is perfectly indifferent. I also think he could come to love the little city as I do."

She was silent again. She studied the paper intently. There were only a few lines on it. Adelaide recognized it as a cable. Then she had the feeling that Celeste was playing for time, that for once she was hesitant, she who was always so assured and resolute.

"Is that a cable, dear?" asked Adelaide, tentatively.

Celeste, still looking at the paper, nodded. She lifted her head and stared, rather than looked at her mother, almost challengingly.

"We could stay with Armand, or Emile, or Jean, or any of the rest of our numerous relatives for a while, until we made up our minds. They've all invited us. Francis, after all, is Peter's brother, and they've had something in common. Of course, Georges has invited us to stay with him and Marion on their farm in Dutchess County. I shouldn't like that, even though he and Peter are great friends. I really detest Marion. I wonder if she is as 'clear-eyed' as ever. Remember? Papa always spoke of her going about the whole damned place with 'clear eyes.' Dear me," she added, after a moment, "we've been away so long that I haven't been able to keep up with the family. Surely we have some younger relatives!"

With sudden unreasoning terror, Adelaide thought: She is thinking of something. For once, she is afraid to speak it. She is hesitating!

She made herself speak calmly and indifferently: "Well, you'll soon learn all about your relatives again when we return. What have you decided to do, dear?"

Celeste again stared at her mother, and now Adelaide detected a hint of hard ruthlessness in the young woman's beautiful eyes.

"There was really only one of my multitudinous relatives with whom I ever had anything in common. Annette," she added, speaking of her niece, daughter of her eldest brother, Armand. "Yes, Annette. We loved each other. We are almost the same age. I always loved Annette."

Now the terror was close upon Adelaide. Annette, wife of Henri Bouchard! Poor weak little Annette, who had almost died when Celeste had become engaged to Henri! Since the marriage between Annette and Henri, Celeste had seen those two only three times in fourteen years, and then only for a short while. It was true that Annette and Celeste had corresponded vigorously, always, with affection, long letters passing between them. But letters are not personal contact.

Adelaide drew a deep breath. She met Celeste's eyes, and her withered lips dried.

"Are you trying to tell me that you are really considering staying with Henri and Annette at Robin's Nest, Celeste? You and Peter? Remembering—everything?"

Celeste still stared. Her face was smooth and still. One black eyebrow rose in a whimsical curve.

"O Mama. That is so tiresome. Because I was once a silly girl, and engaged to Henri, means nothing at all. That was so long ago. We've all forgotten it. 'Remembering—everything,' you say. So melodramatic. What is there to remember, except a short mistake? Henri, I am sure, has forgotten a long time ago. If you recall, he wasn't inconsolable. He married Annette almost immediately."

Adelaide compelled herself to speak in as indifferent a tone as her daughter's. But her voice was somewhat faint. "But why Annette, darling? After all, there is Emile, your own brother, and his wife, Agnes. Emile is my son. I should much prefer to be with my son, rather than with my granddaughter, Annette, and her husband."

Celeste gazed at her with a frankness which was, however, opaque and unreadable.

"Well, that brings us to a situation, Mama. We can't all three of us descend in a body on our relatives, can we? So, I suggest that you go to Emile, or to Armand, and Peter and I will consider going to Annette and Henri, until we can settle ourselves."

Adelaide regarded her daughter speechlessly. Her seamed and saddened face took on a sunken look. She thought: I have exiled myself with you and your husband, my child. I have roamed all the terrible world with you. I have dragged my old bones in your wake, wanting only to be with you, to serve you and help you, because you, alone, of all my children, have I loved. Because you, of all my children, had integrity of character, honesty, virtue. So I believed. Is it possible I have deceived myself all these years? And, are you repaying me for my service by this cold and cruel dismissal? What is behind it? Why are you doing this thing to me, to yourself?

And she knew that, once separated from Celeste, she would never be allowed to be with her again. Did Celeste understand this? She searched her daughter's face with painful earnestness, with passionate imploring. If Celeste understood that she would be forever separated from her mother— had she intended this? And if so, why?

Could it be she was afraid?

The smooth pale face opposite her, with the firm blooming mouth and the eyes almost violet in their color and as polished as an amethyst in their brilliant hardness, told her nothing. But Adelaide was sick with her fear, her real terror.

With a last supreme and desperate effort, she cried, leaning towards Celeste, extending her hands: "My darling, let us be frank, for once, in all these fourteen years! Do you wish to rid yourself of me? Tell me, honestly? Have I failed you in some way?"

Celeste's features expressed nothing but impatient surprise. "Mama! How can you say that? You are so imaginative. Wouldn't I be the nastiest of creatures if I forgot what you've done for me, and for Peter? What in the world would I have done without you?"

Adelaide paused. She wrung her hands together. She looked down at them, so discolored and mottled, so veined, so large and gaunt of knuckle. She heard a soft movement. Celeste was kneeling beside her and putting her warm white arms about her shoulders, laughing a little, shaking her mother fondly.

"O Mama, how can you be so silly! Look at me. Don't you know how much I love you, dearest?"

Adelaide looked down at her daughter's smiling face, and at the deep eyes, so tender now. But she thought: Never has she been so unreadable as now.

A horrible impotence came over her, and a new fear, even though she kissed her daughter's cheek, and took one of the little hands and pressed it. We are speaking through a glass, she thought. We are not making real sense.

"Of course, I know you love me, my dear. You were always my favorite child. I've done what I could. Do you think these years have been easy for me? I'm an old woman, very old. I'm in my seventies. I won't live much longer. You see," she added, incoherently, "I am so afraid. I've always thought you were very vulnerable, darling. The honest and the virtuous are always vulnerable. I've been so afraid for you."

She took Celeste's face in her hands, feeling its warm and velvety texture against her trembling palms. She held that face in trembling despair. She saw how a thin white sheath seemed to slide subtly over it, hiding all thoughts, all expression.

"Now, Mama, that is foolish," said Celeste, lightly. She gently removed her mother's hands, pressed them, rose, and resumed her seat. "You know, I'm a pretty strong party, myself. I don't think I was ever very much afraid of anyone." She laughed a little. "Except Christopher, once or twice. But that was my imagination. I've outgrown that.

"You know, we're making much ado about nothing. Here I am, suggesting we accept Annette's invitation, Peter and I, and that you go to Emile, or to Armand, your own sons, for a little while, until we can all get settled. Frankly, I don't intend to leave Windsor again. I was born there. Dozens of us Bouchards were born there. I want to feel rooted again. Peter can't travel very much any longer. I'm not deceiving myself. Probably we won't be with Annette at Robin's Nest for more than a week or so. It's better than a hotel, I'm sure."

Adelaide's sense of hopelessness, of confusion, grew. "But why Henri and Annette?" she urged again. "Have you thought how Peter would regard this? You know how he dislikes Henri. He always did."

Celeste laughed again, her light laugh that was brittle and indifferent. "Mama, dear. That was a long time ago. If you remember, he and Henri have written to each other several times since we've been abroad. Very amiable letters, too. Do you think either of them has had the time to remember a silly romantic feud? After all, Henri is about forty now, and Peter is even older. Mama, you, like so many—older—people, live acutely in the past. We've forgotten everything. Everything, about our youth, and our adolescence. It was all so foolish. Have you forgotten that Peter has had Henri manage his affairs for him while we've been away, and that he didn't ask that of his own brothers, Francis, Hugo, and Jean? Yet, here you come, with Victorian trappings, talking like the parents of Romeo and Juliet! Now, isn't that very silly?"

She added, with rising impatience: "This is all so absurd. I'm going to radio Annette and Henri that we accept their invitation."

She stood up, smoothing the folds of her black lace dress.

Adelaide thought: Am I indeed stupid? Am I making something of nothing? Do I, like all the old, think of nothing but the past? My darling is still young. She has forgotten the past.

Nevertheless her fear remained. She thought, with sharp pain: The child is afraid. But, of what?

CHAPTER VI

"Ah, there she is, the darling!" cried Annette Bouchard, standing on tiptoe to peer over bobbing heads at the deck of the great liner. She fluttered her wisp of a lace handkerchief, blew kisses. "Celeste! Celeste!" she called. "Look, Henri, there's Peter beside her, waving. Why, he seems quite well, bless him. Celeste!" she cried again, almost dancing with delight, then composing herself. But her delight remained, a radiance upon her poor little face, brighter than the brilliant sun.

"She can't hear you, pet," said Henri, indulgently. "Yes, she sees you. But don't scream so."

He turned to Rosemarie Bouchard who stood beside him, and smiled slightly. Rosemarie returned that smile with a quirk of her vividly painted lips, and a wink of contempt. She reached behind Annette's small and agitated back, caught his hand, pressed in the little finger sharply to the palm. He made a grimace of affected pain. She pursed her mouth in an exaggerated kiss.

According to the ramifications of the Bouchard clan, Henri and Rosemarie were distant cousins. Henri's father had been François Bouchard, brother of Jules Bouchard, both cousins to Honoré, grandfather of Rosemarie. Thus, Rosemarie was also a vague cousin of Celeste's, as Jules, Celeste's father, had been cousin to her own grandfather. (Her father, Francis, was second-cousin to the late Jules.) Rosemarie's grandmother, the late Ann Richmond Bouchard, had been quite a genealogist, and had kept charts of family relationships. But no one bothered now. It was too complex. It was the family name, rather than involved relationships, that kept the clan welded together. Old family portraits lined the walls of every Bouchard household, but it was too complicated to trace out the lines of descent and intermarriage, and resulting progeny. The name, and mutual hatred, were better for unity than recollections of blood. Even those ladies who married into the clan, though perfectly friendly and amiable and affectionate creatures to begin with, invariably soon absorbed the pride and the hatred and out-Boucharded the Bouchards. The former Estelle Carew, mother of Rosemarie, had been a wholesome nice woman in the beginning, hating no one. Now she merely disliked the Bouchards, so she was apparently a woman without true character.

Phyllis Bouchard, sister of Rosemarie, had married the son of the Morse National Bank of New York. That is how he was designated by the Bouchards, though his father had had the individual name of Richard Morse. Phyllis now had four young daughters. Though the Bouchard family had long been Episcopal, Phyllis (married to an official Presbyterian) had suddenly reverted to the ancient Catholicism of the Bouchard clan, and her children went about with jewelled crosses, medals and scapulars, made their first communions, and attended convent schools. All this, much to the risibility of the Bouchards, who considered Phyllis an affected fool, full of romanticism. They remembered her as "the little tart" of Christopher's naming, and this abrupt conversion of Phyllis's endlessly entertained them. From a wild and ribald girl, who in earlier days might have been called "no better than she should be," she had become a prim dark matron, sedulously pious, and, necessarily, fanatically vicious in her new religion. If one mentioned the Roman Church with the slightest indifference, or ridicule, or with the faintest contempt, she became quite hysterical, her voice trembling, her dark thin face flushing, her black eyes sparkling with what Henri called "the auto-da-fé light." She was constantly feuding with her relatives, trying to convince them of "the truth," praying for them with virulent hatred, making novenas for their conversion, and paying out tremendous sums of her own and her husband's cash for masses for the souls of her grandparents, and other relatives, now pining in Purgatory awaiting release via the Bouchard money. Though the Bouchards affectionately hated every other member of the family, Phyllis hated them all with becoming cruelty and madness. They baited her, teased her, when in good humor. She bored them to complete ennui, almost constantly.

Rosemarie was attractively ugly, very chic, very French. She had been to school in France. Now, she spoke with a French accent, a pure affectation, very amusing to the Bouchards. Her voice was hoarse, fashionably husky, though in moments of stress she forgot, and allowed it to become naturally shrill. (Her mother had once distressedly, and in Irish forthright fashion, warned her during a family gathering that she would ruin her vocal cords by compression, for which her daughter had never forgiven her. When her voice was most husky, it was customary for the family to murmur something about "compression," a word calculated to make the young lady quite violent.)

She had a tall lank figure, but with elegance and litheness. She wore her exquisite and simple clothing with an air, so that the eye of the beholder was fascinated. Part of this fascination was due to her personal magnetism, for she was witty, daintily obscene, full of original repartee, and humor. Too, she was exceptionally intelligent and disingenuous. She was too clever to be cynical, that attribute of the eternal adolescent, but she had no trust in her for her fellow man or woman, which did not prevent her from having many adoring friends. Humanity constantly amused her; she despised, rather than hated it, and found it unremittingly entertaining. She rarely admired anyone, felt no affection for a single soul, though she was capable of a fiery and ferocious passion, as Henri Bouchard had discovered at least five years ago. Disloyal, treacherous, brilliant, malicious, even venomous at times, unsentimental and hard-hearted and greedy, and, like all the Bouchards, intrinsically selfish, she had infinite variety and was never dull.

She made much of her ugliness, until it became fascination.

Her lank hair, so like an Indian's, was always severely dressed, brushed back in blue-black and polished smoothness behind her excellent ears, and wound in a coil at the nape of her neck. It reached to her knees; she had let it grow very long. Her great-great grandmother, Antoinette, wife of the founder of the Bouchards, Armand, had been an Italian, and this accounted, perhaps, for her pale olive complexion, her malevolent black eyes, rather small, but very vivacious, and her long Moorish nose with the jerking nostrils. She had a wide thin mouth, which she painted to a vivid slash, and mobile and very thick black eyebrows under a low brow. She was in constant activity, even when apparently the most serene. Her expression, sly, twinkling, wary, amused and disillusioned, gave her plain but attractive face a look of alert life, and lively malice. She had been one of Henri Bouchard's numerous mistresses for at least four years. She was now twenty-seven, and had found no one she cared to marry, except Henri, who seemed firmly wedded to Annette.

She knew Henri did not love his wife. She, perhaps alone of the Bouchards, knew that he still loved Celeste, and in consequence she hated Celeste with wild passion. She had been in New York to shop, and had been invited by the innocent Annette to accompany her and Henri to the docks, to meet the returning expatriates. She had not been able to resist the invitation, wishing to see Henri's reaction at the sight of Celeste. So far as she had been able to discern, his manner had been quite calm and indifferent.

Annette's excitement grew momentarily. She could hardly keep still. She twittered and fluttered like an agitated bird. She was about thirty now, but she had never lost her childlikeness, her immaturity of body. Undersized, and underdeveloped, always with a shy and diffident soft manner, she walked so gently and with such a deprecating stoop to her small thin shoulders, that she gave an effect of deformity. But she was not in the least deformed, her body being all flatness and fragility. She could never wear sophisticated clothing, which would have looked absurd on her delicate angles and only vaguely formed breast. In consequence, she was compelled to wear childish styles, pretty, ribbonned, bouffant, which made her appear even more immature than she was. One guessed that even in old age she would be childish of figure. When she laughed, it was with apology and deprecation, and she would look at others with birdlike shyness and gentle fear, for she was a tender soul, all sweetness and chastity and kindness. She had a tiny triangular face, very white, worn with pain (she had been tubercular in her youth). The little mouth, the porcelain nose, the lines of chin and brow and cheek were negligible, but she had the most extraordinary large light-blue eyes, filled with light, and angelic in their purity. They had the inner radiance of those who are pure in heart, without guile or cruelty. Her father called her "Angel," as did her husband on those rare occasions when she touched him unbearably, and aroused his almost moribund compassion. Her ashen hair, full of bright ripples, had been cut, and framed her little face in tendrils like an infant's.

None of the Bouchards could hate this little soft creature, who believed no evil of them. They pitied her, some even loved her. Rosemarie merely despised her in an indolently affectionate fashion. She was her father's darling, he who loved no one but her. She was even beloved of her malignant brother, Antoine, who was spoken of laughingly as the reincarnation of the lethal and elegant Jules, his grandfather.

Beside the dark and fashionable Rosemarie, in her thin black linen suit, Annette was more childish than ever in her ruffled white dress and large white lace hat. Her head hardly came above her husband's shoulder, and he was no giant in stature.

If Antoine, brother of Annette, was the reincarnation of Jules, Henri Bouchard was the reincarnation of Ernest Barbour, his great-grandfather, the real founder, the real spirit, of the great armaments firm now called Bouchard & Sons. Stocky, broad, powerful of shoulders, calm and impressive of movement, he gave one the sense of inexorable strength. He had an unusually large head for a man of his height, and this, combined with his vital crest of light hair (one could not tell if it was gray, merely pale of color, or faded) gave him a look of agelessness. He might have been in his early thirties, or fifty. In fact, he was about forty now. His face, also large, was broad, almost squarish, with thick folds about the heavy almost brutal lips. He had Ernest Barbour's short broad nose, with the flaring coarse nostrils, and his square hard chin, with the deep dimple. It was his eyes, however, which were the dominant feature. Pale, staring, implacable, with bright black pinpoints of pupils, they fascinated the beholder, filled him with instinctive fear. When he smiled, it was a mere convulsion of his lips. His eyes never smiled. He had a compact and vital body, for all its stockiness, and there was a squareness about it, also. His clothing was invariably excellent, all angles, all neatness. His old friend, Jay Regan, the financial master of the world, declared that Henri looked incongruous in modern dress. He needed the long buff coat, the light pantaloons, the stock and the ruffles of his great-grandfather to be appropriately attired. His voice was quiet, firm, indomitable.

He was the power of the Bouchards. His father-in-law, the fat, pursy, irresolute Armand, had retired. Henri was now president of Bouchard & Sons, master of its subsidiaries, plotter of its destiny, and through it, plotter of America, and, with others, plotter of the world.

He stood beside his wife and Rosemarie, and idly watched the travellers leave the liner. Annette was all gentle impatience to seek out her beloved Celeste, and Peter. But Henri restrained her. "Wait, love. There's the Customs, you know. Do you want to meet them under the 'B's'? Or shall we wait a little?"

"Under the 'B's', please," she implored, looking at him with all the love of her pure heart standing in her pellucid eyes. She touched his arm timidly. He pressed his own hand over her gloved fingers. Rosemarie grimaced.

"Why all the hurry?" she asked, in her husky voice. "It's only a matter of a few minutes." She added, indolently: "Are you really going back tomorrow morning? Why all the rush?"

"There's Peter," said Annette, with that breathless and apprehensive apology she always used to the exigent, the greedy and the selfish, as if she must appease their cruelty. "He's been so ill, you know."

Ill, thought Henri. It is fourteen years. I had given him five, at the most. Fourteen years! I won't wait any longer.

They found Celeste, Peter and Adelaide, among their trunks, boxes and other luggage. Adelaide looked very old and dim. Celeste, in her brown and gold toilette, was calm and efficient, serene and assured, assisting the Customs officers, whom she had already charmed. Under the broad brim of her brown hat her face was cool and luminous, like white stone flecked with sunlight. Peter sat on a suitcase, emaciated and weak, his lips set grimly to restrain his fainting exhaustion of body. His eyes were sunken, shadowed with pain. He coughed hoarsely, held a handkerchief to his lips as he watched his wife.

It was Peter, rather than Celeste, that Henri saw first, and what he saw made him smile internally, with brutal satisfaction.

Annette, in a flutter of white lace, ran, crying, to her young aunt, her thin little arms extended, tears on her lashes, smiling radiantly. "Celeste! O my darling! It's been so long!" She flung her arms about Celeste, standing on tiptoe to reach her lips, hugging her with passion.

Celeste, laughing lovingly, returned the kisses and embraces. She held off Annette a moment, to study, with secret earnestness, the small triangular face under the white lace hat. What she saw made her heart sink.

"Granny, dear," said Annette, turning to Adelaide, and kissing her. "You don't know how good it is to see you again." She kissed Peter's damp cheek, with warm compassion. He had struggled to his feet, and he looked down at his distant cousin with a smile as gentle as her own.

"It seems we're forgotten," said Rosemarie, with amusement. But her sparkling black eyes, as she regarded Celeste, were pointed with hatred and ferocity. She had hoped that the long nursing of Peter, the long absence, might have destroyed that beauty which was so dangerous to her own peace of mind.

Celeste, laughing, a faint color now in her cheeks, apologized, extended her gloved hands to Rosemarie, and gave her a cool kiss. "Handsome as ever, I see," she smiled. "Not married yet, Rosy?"

Henri came forward, and Celeste turned to him. She looked at him steadfastly as he approached. The smooth white sheath slipped over her features, and her smile was the smile of a statue. She gave him her hand. He held it strongly, and looked down into her eyes with gravity. Her heart began to beat with the strangest sensation, and she felt a heat in her flesh, a long thrill like a shiver passing up her arm from the hand he held. Her nostrils distended a little, as if she found it difficult to breathe.

"Welcome home," he said, quietly. "It's been a long time. You haven't changed in the least, Celeste."

How blue her eyes were in the shadow of the hat! Like violets, like lobelia, like amethysts. Yes, there was a jewel-like brilliance and hardness in them, a colored light without expression. She was a woman now, he thought. More beautiful than ever. She belongs to me; she has always belonged to me. She is afraid. She has always been afraid of me. Why? I think I know. She is really afraid of herself. Poor fool.

He smiled slightly, pressed her hand, released it, turned to Adelaide. "How are you, Aunt Adelaide?" His heavy lips, for all their smile, were sullen. He had not forgotten, then, that she had been his enemy, that she had helped defeat him, that, in all the world, she alone had ever defeated him.

But he was very courteous, and inclined his head, almost with a stiff bow, a remnant of his European training.

She regarded him with fear. She remembered Ernest Barbour so well. This might have been the terrible man she remembered, inexorable, full of power, as dangerous as an army, as relentless as death. How could she have forgotten that resemblance of this man to his dead great-grandfather? Even the voice, silent now for nearly half a century, was the same. Her fear mounted.

"It was so good of you all to meet us," she said, in a quavering tone. Her brown eyes were alive with her unreasoning terror. She glanced swiftly at Celeste, the glance of a mother whose child is threatened.

She was not conscious of Rosemarie's careful kiss, nor the fact that a streak of paint remained on her withered cheek from that salute. All her thoughts and sensations were centered on Celeste, who had turned away composedly to answer a question put to her by a Customs officer.

In the meantime, Peter and Henri were shaking hands. Henri's voice had become hearty, full of friendliness. "Well! You are looking much better than you did the last time you were home!"

Peter was smiling. There was a glisten of dampness on his livid face. He regarded Henri with a penetrating look, his light-blue eyes, with their square corners of the heroic martyr, more intense than ever.

"Thanks," he said, trying to make his tone as strong as Henri's, and, as a result, having to suppress a cough. "Good of you to meet us, to invite us. I hope we aren't imposing on you, Henri."

"Not at all. We're delighted to have you. You ought to know that." Nothing could have been heartier than Henri's manner and smile. But the pale basilisk eyes did not warm in the least. Peter felt his personality, with coldness and dread. The man of power. The most terrible man of power. The old hatred, the old fear, the old loathing, overcame him. Afraid that Henri might sense his thoughts, he forced himself to be overly cordial.

"Very good, just the same. I'm afraid you'll find us tiresome. But it'll be just for a little while."

His thin hand was stinging from Henri's grasp when he turned to Rosemarie, who had been watching the two men with a cynical and hating smile. She kissed him heartily. He was her uncle, brother to her father, Francis Bouchard, and related to her also through other ramifications of the clan.

"Well, Pete, home again. Contemplating any new wanderings?"

People like Rosemarie invariably caused him to shrink. They were so compact, so ruthless, so polished of contour and so inhuman. His voice stammered as he tried to reply to her airily.

"We've engaged a suite for the night for you at the Ritz," said Henri. "Better to rest before starting for home."

Celeste was having some difficulty with the Customs. Henri immediately went to her assistance. In an incredibly short space of time he had adjusted matters. Celeste watched him, a little apart, saw the almost grovelling respect of the officers. She smiled, somewhat somberly. Everyone watched him. He impelled eyes, and was completely unaware of them, as if he disdained the very existence of others.

Henri's limousine was waiting. The heat of New York was intense this last day of May. Yellow dust swirled with chaff against the windows of the car. The light on the great towers was too intense, the noise aching. Celeste sat back on the cushions and closed her eyes. But she could feel Henri's look upon her face, the pressure of his arm against hers. His manner had been indifferent, his attitude casual. He was talking now to Peter, asking him amiable questions. But she felt his thoughts engrossed with her, like exigent and resistless hands upon her very body, and her body responded with heat and terror. Weakness flowed over her; her heart beat so loudly in her ears that she could not hear the conversation that went on about her. It came to her, muffled and disjointed. Her knees were like water; her fingers trembled in her gloves.

We should never have accepted, she thought, her spirit struggling with the invisible but terrible hands that gripped her, subdued her, just as her body would have struggled with fleshly hands. She panted with a desire to escape, and when she was conscious of the desire, the will left her, voluptuously. Chill tendrils ran over her face and neck and breasts. She hated him; feared him; could not resist him. She felt the moving of his shoulder against hers, as he breathed, and knew, without glancing at him, when he looked at her out of the corner of his eye.

We'll have to make some excuse, she thought. Tomorrow, we'll make some excuse. Emile is still in Windsor. We can change our minds. Yes, that is it. I can't endure him. Once, I could. Once, I even thought I loved him. Now, I hate him. How dare he think of me, how dare he look at me! Tomorrow we've got to make other plans. I don't remember, now, why I accepted. Other plans——

She made no other plans. The next evening she and Peter occupied a fine apartment in Robin's Nest, in Roseville, suburb of Windsor, Pennsylvania.

CHAPTER VII

Celeste had vaguely hoped that the breathless and ominously shining peace that had lain over Europe this summer of 1939 would be absent from America, from her old home in Windsor. But it was not absent. It had invaded America, too, like a sea of glittering chromium, which might part momentarily to reveal the points of blinding bayonets. The Depression, "that man in the White House," labor, unemployment, the "New Deal," were still important in discussion, in newspapers, in books, and on the radio. But the main topic was Hitler, the Polish Corridor, the prospect of war.

There was a silent seething in America, a restlessness, a looking to the east with hatred or fear or hope. Across those blue seas, so calm and sweet this summer, so filled with gay traffic, there came sinister murmurs, the breath of cold winds, the sounds of invisible armies. And with them came the cries of those in torment, the shadow of a multitude of lifted arms appealing for help, the long foggy shapes of duplicity and treachery, greed and murder, terror and doom, casting their reflections on the chromium ocean like spectral portents of destiny.

Celeste forced herself to believe in peace, against what she really knew, against the tired voice of Peter. She refused to discuss anything with him. "Let us just rest a little, darling," she pleaded. "Just a little."

She knew now that she had been homesick for very long. Even her multitudinous relatives, the Bouchards, whom she had once so feared and disliked, seemed lovable to her. She accepted their surface cordiality and affection. Her two brothers, Armand and Emile, still at Windsor, and their families, were always in and out of Robin's Nest. Her other relatives, Francis, Hugo, and Jean, and their wives and children, were frequent visitors, and even Nicholas, that "dirty man." André Bouchard, his wife and children, came also. Only Christopher, her beloved brother, and his wife Edith, sister of Henri, had not yet arrived from Florida, but were expected daily.

Celeste felt the warmness of family. It was entirely in her mind, as Adelaide might drearily have told her. But Adelaide was with her son, Emile, and his family. She had always had a faint liking for Agnes, Emile's wife, who, besides being cynical, cruel, dissipated and greedy, was also honest. For some reason Agnes did not "feel up to" visiting Robin's Nest very often, though Emile often dropped in on his way home from the office. Therefore Adelaide saw her daughter and Peter not more than once a week, or even less. She felt something resistless in the atmosphere, and however she tried to reason it away, it remained. She knew she had only to demand a car, that she had only to call a cab, and she could go to Robin's Nest alone. But that strange wall erected against her, which she felt, which she could not credit even in her strongest imagination, prevented her from doing this. However, she telephoned Celeste at least once a day, to listen achingly to the tone of Celeste's voice rather than to her affectionate words.

There were many other relatives, too, of other than the Bouchard name, and many friends, who called upon Celeste. She was quite touched. She had not forgotten that they had not cared for her before, more especially since her marriage to Peter. She was hardly ever at home. Peter, recuperating from the voyage from France, rarely accompanied her to the numerous houses where she was entertained. She had at first refused, because Peter was unable to go, but seeing that she had suddenly and inexplicably manifested a desire for gaiety, for the presence of her people, he had urgently implored her not to think of him for a time, but to enjoy herself. "You deserve it, dear," he had said, gently, kissing her hand. "I'm quite comfortable. I only need a rest. In a week or two, I'll be able to go with you anywhere."

He noticed that she was often out to dinner. He and Henri and Annette dined alone almost every night. Henri made no comment. Annette beamed with pleasure. "I've never seen anyone so popular," she would say. "It is so good for the darling, too."

Henri, at this, would incline his head, and smile a little to

66

himself. He had a fairly good idea why he so infrequently encountered Celeste in his own house. He could wait a little longer. He understood this flight. Had Celeste not fled so often, so persistently, he might not have been so satisfied. Her absence told him much, to his savage satisfaction.

Peter's strength was not returning. This, then, prevented him and Celeste from settling down to discuss their future plans. He was in no condition to be disturbed, to be moved, to be agitated, his doctors had informed his wife. They profoundly agreed with Henri, who had had a private discussion with them. He had warned them not to give Peter the slightest hint of this discussion.

A competent trio of nurses had appeared at Robin's Nest. Celeste had protested; Peter had protested. "You wish to recover your health as quickly as possible, do you not?" Henri had asked impatiently, while Annette lovingly pleaded. "Besides," Henri had said privately to his guest, "if you refuse, Celeste will be imprisoned here. Don't you think she deserves a little freedom, after all these years?"

So, miserable though he was, and strangely apprehensive, Peter agreed to the nurses, bore down Celeste's protests. He felt rewarded by the new youth and happiness and gaiety which became evident in Celeste's face. She had acquired her girlhood vivacity again. Sometimes, this vivacity appeared feverish to her husband. Certainly, though she laughed so often, and had acquired quite a wit, she seemed tired in repose. She was more loving than ever; sometimes she clung to Peter with a kind of despair. During these times, she slept in his room on the nurse's cot, and obstinately refused to be ousted.

When Peter became restless, demanded paper and certain books, seemed about to engage Henri in serious discussion, all this was dexterously evaded by the courteous host. Later, the physician would call upon the irritable invalid, with urgings that he "rest" a little longer, that he relax, be calm, that his health was improving and it would be folly to destroy the gains already made. Peter, for Celeste's sake, would subside. But his sleeplessness increased.

He felt surrounded by enemies, though everyone was extremely solicitous. Sometimes, in vague but feverish words, he suggested this to Celeste. But Celeste, who had been in consultation with the physician, would plead with him to be patient. Peter would become silent. But he would regard his wife with passionate eyes in which the confused light of a prisoner would glimmer.

He was experiencing the sluggish impotence of one in chains. He was encompassed with care and friendliness, and the affection of Annette, who was very fond of him. He heard nothing of significance in the kind voices of his relatives. He remembered the deviousness, craft and greed of his brothers, their murderous exigency. But now he saw only bland smooth faces, heard only expressions of solicitude, and easy laughter. Where were the undercurrents he remembered, the hatred, the plottings, the sensation of terrible things occurring in silence and in secrecy? They were not present in the least. Utter amiability and calm prevailed. Everyone appeared on the best of terms, engrossed with nothing but smilingly contemptuous opinions of the President, golf, summer plans, and family affections. They joked, laughed, brought small gifts for the invalid, and many invitations. The Depression did not appear to affect them. "We're marking time," said Francis, Peter's brother, he of the frigid blondness, now graying.

"Marking time?" Peter would say, somberly. "For what?"

But no one would answer him except with light laughter, a pressure on the shoulder, a change of subject.

However, very slowly, as the days passed, he began to feel undercurrents again, more powerful, more frightful, more significant and sinister, than he had ever remembered. They threw him into a frenzy. He was a blind man groping through awful caverns filled with muffled echoes, with the brushing-by of appalling enemies, with the breath of unseen terrors. He could not speak of them even to Celeste, who was engrossed only with his health now. He never saw Adelaide more than once a week, she who had been his confidante even more than had been his wife. When he did see her, she was always with others.

He was alone. He was paralyzed with the inertia of those who are alone. He stretched out his hands in the dark, to the suspected shapes, the whispering voices, and encountered nothing. But his dread and fear grew as the days glided like a silver dream into June, into July. He heard the urgent call from a distance, and could not rise. He prayed. In his prayers was the terror of the threatened, the terror of one who knew but had no power, no words, to express his knowledge.

We must leave here, he thought. I've done no good coming here. He suggested to Celeste leaving Robin's Nest, but frightened by the private words of the physicians, she resisted, with murmured soothing words and loving touches.

It came to him slowly, with overpowering and almost superstitious fear, that he was being watched. That even while his many relatives talked to him idly and comfortably of the most unimportant things, he was watched by them. He told himself that he was acquiring the suspiciousness and querulous introspection of an invalid. But it was no use. He saw the sudden gleam of an eye here and there, immediately averted. Why were they watching him; if they were? It was absurd. He was a fool. He was no power among the Bouchards. It is true his anti-war, anti-munitions, book, *The Terrible Swift Sword,* had been enormously popular in America. He had thought it had had much influence. (His relative, Georges Bouchard the publisher, had amicably assured him, however, that a writer's influence was romantically and grossly overestimated, especially in America, where so few were mentally literate.) But the book was no longer mentioned, even casually, in the papers, or in literary magazines. He thought this inevitable. The book had been published so long ago. He did not know that his family had had much to do with the suppression in periodicals and newspapers of any mention of the book. Nor did he know that his family had prevented its sale to the moving picture industry, and that a large sum had exchanged discreet hands.

Why, then, should he have the sensation of being unremittingly watched? And all this while no one would discuss anything of importance with him. He was asked, affectionately, about the celebrities he had met in France, Germany, Italy, and England. But the instant he spoke, with rising passion, of what he had seen there, and understood, the subject was languidly changed, faces became disinterested, and bored. He thought at first that it was because his relatives discerned that he was becoming upset, and this annoyed him, for only when he spoke of these things did he come alive. But later, he began to wonder.

He read the *Windsor Courier,* the newspaper owned by his people. Everything in it was restrained and conservative. It deprecated the imminence of war. It laughed tolerantly at any Governmental suggestion of dire future events. He found it intolerable. He subscribed to various liberal periodicals, but they came to him desultorily, and had a habit of disappearing.

By the end of July, he was in a ferment. His terror was a living thing.

Sometimes he would almost forcibly seize on Henri, the power of the Bouchards, and demand to be told what was taking place in the company, in its subsidiaries. Henri would raise his eyebrows over those pale and implacable eyes, and say, humorously: "We're just getting by. Marking time. What can interest you in our affairs? Frankly, I don't know what we'll do, if we don't get rid of that man in the White House next year. Business is at a standstill."

It is not true, Peter would think, in dread and despair. I know. I know what you are doing. But he could do nothing but look at Henri with impotent fear, with gathering hatred, and overwhelming confusion.

He tried to engage his relatives in discussions of politics. But beyond the fact that they were enthusiastically vitriolic at the mention of Mr. Roosevelt's name, they said nothing of significance, except to hint at a Republican victory in the coming Presidential election next year. "We have our man picked," Jean was indiscreet enough to acknowledge, but when Peter asked to be enlightened, Jean drifted away followed by the dark glances of other relatives.

So, he discovered nothing. He ought not to have come to Robin's Nest, to be smothered in this sinister solicitude. He was imprisoned. He was kept incommunicado.

In the meantime, the shining air of peace was constantly agitated by winds full of portent and horror. It might have been his imagination, so far as the Bouchards were concerned. Moreover, instead of improving, he grew worse. He was being subtly poisoned by an inertia inflicted upon him by others. He would lie awake at night, thinking of this, thinking that he was going mad. His reason repudiated his terror. But his instinct warned him ominously.

Engrossed with himself, smothering at Robin's Nest, he did not see the fever gathering in Celeste's pale face, which was losing its luminous quality. He did not see her desperate eyes, the increasing worn repression about her mouth.

There was another thing: for all the discussions of summer plans, Peter saw that none of the Bouchards was absent from Windsor for more than a few days. They, too, waited, as he waited. He felt their eyes, fixed and dangerous, turned eastward, across the sea. The world waited.

CHAPTER VIII

On July 26, 1939, Christopher Bouchard ("the Chromium Robot") and his wife Edith, sister to Henri, came to Robin's Nest from Florida, Christopher ostensibly to see his beloved only sister, Celeste. He had been her guardian, substituting for Jules, the father he had hated so monstrously. He had almost destroyed the girl. She had never known this. At the end, before the final implacability, he had been weak. He could not complete the destruction. Celeste's faith in him had saved herself, and strangely, also her brother.

Christopher was within sight of fifty now, but he had the agelessness of those of his temperament and his coloring. He was much like his father, except for that coloring, which was fair, pallid, steel-tinted, with that glimmering hint of polished chromium which had given him his nickname. Bloodless, with a small sleek skull with thin gray-brown hair, earlobes so delicate and small that they were almost transparent, slight and slender rather than excessively tall, toneless and unemphatic of voice, he at first gave no hint of the deadliness of his personality, his sadistic cruelty, his inner selfish terror, his murderous exigency. His hands were delicate also, with blue veins and pale nails. He moved softly, like the "silver snake" his brother, Armand, had declared he resembled. His features were refined and attenuated, expressing nothing, and there was a silvery paleness in his "Egyptian" eyes. When he smiled, it was an immobile smile. He trusted no one. He hated everyone. There was a quality of hatred even in his love for his wife and his sister. And only his wife and his mother and his sister loved him. For his mother, Adelaide, he had only the most indifferent malice and contempt. Usually, he forgot her existence, and once, when reminded that she was still alive, he exclaimed, to Edith: "What! Isn't she dead yet? Good God, she's almost eighty, then!"

He never forgot that it was Adelaide who had helped

thwart his scheming to marry his sister to Henri, and so advance his own fortunes, his own plottings against his brother Armand, their father's heir. He was now president of Duval-Bonnet, airplane manufacturers, in Florida.

Edith Bouchard, sister of Henri, great granddaughter of the terrible Ernest Barbour, wife of Christopher, was a plain but aristocratic woman now in her early forties. She had the dark coloring of the "Latin" Bouchards, as opposed to the blondness of the "Saxon" Bouchards. Small, and erect of head, she held herself with a kind of cold arrogance. Her body was somewhat hard, and very slender, with broad thin shoulders, and she was about as tall as her brother, appearing taller because of her straight, quickly moving figure. In some features, she resembled the chic Rosemarie, for her face was very narrow, hard and high of cheekbone, the nose too long and thin and prominent, the chin square and uncompromising. She used little artifice, and her naturally sallow tint of complexion was covered only by a film of dark face-powder, unrelieved by rouge or lipstick. Her eyes were nut-brown, but had no hint of the warmth of such a color; they were direct and forthright, and completely honest, for all her native cleverness and disillusion. But, she had éclat, breeding, taste, and a certain elegance which the more flamboyant Rosemarie did not possess. Even her hair, black and straight and lusterless though it was, and dressed in a fashion similar to Roemarie's, added to her appearance of smartness.

She had no children, had never desired them, for, while she had a deep and hidden kindness and integrity, she was without sentiment, and completely selfish. There was also another reason, which she hardly admitted even to herself. She was afraid of giving birth to another Bouchard.

Completely undeluded about her husband, she nevertheless loved him with the only passion of her life. She and her brother, Henri, had been close and affectionate, but she had never felt for him this complete dedication of heart and soul. However, had it come to a real contest between her brother and her husband, as she knew it must some day, she would have surveyed the situation dispassionately, her opinion and support going unswervingly to the one she deemed less evil. Christopher knew this. He often chaffed her about her "Puritanism," but he respected her for it.

For Celeste, she had a casual fondness, a wry amusement, a pity, and sometimes, a regret. She loathed poor little Annette, as she loathed all that was sickly and impotent. Peter was the one exception, and she felt for him only compassion

72

and an indifferent sense of indignation for his sufferings.

Often she reflected that fourteen years had passed since the marriage of Celeste to Peter, and each year was like another fort in the vulnerable area that surrounded Peter. But now Celeste and her husband were under the very roof of the inexorably patient Henri, and her first reaction to the news had been disgust and apprehension. She knew Henri very well indeed. Surely, even those innocents, Peter and Celeste, ought to know him a little by now. Surely, they might have remembered, with vagueness, that he never forgot, never forgave, and never gave up what he had desired. He had desired Celeste. The blue-eyed lamb had taken "shelter" in the very ambush of the wolf.

Christopher and Edith had arrived unexpectedly, on a Sunday morning, by airplane. It was still very early. Henri met them at the door, in the wake of the servants, who bustled about the cab, extracting baggage. Edith kissed him warmly, subjected his face to a furtive but very keen searching, even while she knew it was no use. Henri never revealed anything he desired to keep hidden. He shook hands heartily with Christopher. He stood there on the terrace, strong, somewhat stocky, in loose morning dress, for the day was very hot, and his sister felt again the impact of his formidable power. Even while he shook hands with Christopher, his left hand retained the cool brown fingers of his sister, and he pressed them with real affection.

"They're all in bed, except me," he said. He walked up towards Robin's Nest between his sister and Christopher. "But they've been called. They'll be down almost at once. How was the trip?"

"Excellent. Duval-Bonnet plane, of course," replied Christopher, with his metallic grin, which warped his dry fine skin into a web of wrinkles. There was about him, reflected Henri, as he often had reflected, the quality of a parched and brittle death's-head, sardonic and evil.

The two men went into the mansion, but Edith lingered alone in the morning, looking about her with a strange dark wistfulness on her plain face, a softness that was unusual. She had always loved Robin's Nest, the house built by her grandparents in the suburb of Roseville. She had not been here for two years. Now her cold heart ached with nostalgia.

This was the great Georgian house of gray stone, built for the tragic Gertrude Barbour by her husband, Paul. Through those grilled windows, Gertrude must often have glanced down the winding road that led through the park-like estate.

For whom had she always been watching, until her early death? For Phillippe, the cousin whom she was to have married, and who had been sent away by her father? The parkway lay all about her granddaughter Edith, serene, golden in the summer sun, shadowed with the purple shade of the moving trees, so tall and majestic with the early rosy light on their upper branches. There was a stern and formal beauty about the grounds. But in the rear, Edith knew there were immense rose gardens, grottoes, little winding paths, fountains, and bending willows full of wind and mysterious whispers.

By American standards, the house was "old," and impossibly archaic. The tremendous square rooms were without "style" as the lady Bouchards often declared. But Edith remembered their cool and gracious quality, their quiet duskiness in the heat of the day, their immense fireplaces in every room, their dignity and classic grace, their lofty ceilings and darkly polished floors. She remembered the air of formality, even during the most intimate parties, the restraint of panelled wood and damask walls. From the heroic proportions of the reception hall, a graceful and strongly delicate spiral staircase curved upwards. Sometimes, on dim and lonely nights when she had lived there, Edith, lying in her bed, had imagined she had heard the rustling of taffeta on the stairs, the echo of a sad young sigh coming from a heart that was slowly breaking.

She stood alone on the pathway to the house, listening to the flow of warm wind in the trees, breathing the scent of warm damp morning and the illusive fragrance of the rose gardens and the living earth. The sunlight shone on the dark severe face under the smart hat, and she felt its early heat on her gloved hands. The breeze stirred her thin black suit, fluttered the plain white collar. Birds, lulled by her immobility, ran over the plush of the green grass almost at her narrow feet. She heard their sweet twitterings in the trees, saw the flash of sunlight on their wings as they darted into shadows. The fresh and shining silence of the morning flowed over everything like water. Sometimes the ivy on the gray stones of the mansion turned white in the wind.

The long sweep of the driveway, the greenness, the flowing trees, suddenly were a bright dazzle before her stern eyes. She and Henri had been born here. This was her home. She felt her flesh one with the house, the very living substance of her part of the earth. The house was almost a hundred years old, but only two people had been born here, herself and her brother. It was a house built for large families of happy children, who would play in those running mauve shadows under the trees, who would fill the lofty rooms with laughter and bright frocks and rosy faces. The music room should resound with small fingers at the immense grand piano. There was a harp there now, reflected Edith, Annette's harp. No doubt the twilight would tinkle with silvery notes evoked by fragile fingers. She felt a sense of outrage.

Perhaps, if Christopher and I lived here, instead of Henri and Annette, I might have had children, she thought. The house would compel it. But, there might be a curse upon it, she reflected, with wry humor. Even her mother, Alice, had not been born here, but in Ernest Barbour's house. Birth fled from these majestic precincts.

Her sense of courage grew. How could Henri have been so obtuse as not to realize that the frail Annette would never bear him children? All at once, Edith, in spite of her fundamental hardness, felt the profundity of earth. It seemed, for the first time in her existence, that life was more important than power and wealth. She was startled. She was a true Bouchard, indifferent, disingenuous, and even cunning, for all her honesty and forthrightness. Never had she thought these things before—that children, that home, that serenity and love might be more valuable than the things by which the Bouchards lived. They had had a sense of dynasty—yes. And so had produced children to carry on that dynasty. But children as flesh, as life, as health and sweetness and strength of heart and soul—this had never occurred to them. Power and revenge had moved Henri. He had not cared that they had also made his virility impotent in the sterile Annette. Did he never long for children, if even for the sake of dynasty? He was her brother; surely at times he must have felt this stirring that now created such sad havoc in her own flesh. She was filled with burning compassion for him.

Henri had married Annette as his last forceful blow to regain the power that had been ruthlessly stolen from the great-grandchildren of Ernest Barbour by his nephew, Jules Bouchard. Now, to Edith, all this remorseless regaining of power seemed foolish and tragic, and very childish.

I'm absurd, she thought.

And then, under the shadow of the smart black sailor hat with its white ribbon, her nut-brown eyes widened. Her heart quickened uneasily. Henri, married to the sterile and ailing Annette; Celeste, married to the dying Peter. Henri—and Celeste. She had a mysterious and frightened premonition that destiny, as well as Henri, could be seen as a vague but gigantic shadow behind the presence of Celeste in this house.

Henri, too, must have felt the impelling force of this house—
No! she thought, I am absurd.

But her uneasiness quickened to fear. She bent her head
and hurried into the cool dim immensity of the reception hall.
Her one stern thought was: Look here, it's hands off. Earlier
in the morning, she had not thought that. She had had an
entirely different idea. Now, the enchantment and the power
of the house were upon her, and the strong air warned her.

Celeste had always impressed Edith with her childlikeness
and singleness of mind and thought. An eternal child, she
had once thought. But now she discerned that Celeste was a
woman. There might still be a childlike quality in the direct
dark-blue eyes that met hers quietly. There might be a
simplicity in her dignified manner. But she was a woman
now. She might not be as disingenuous as all the other
Bouchards, but she was without illusion. This, too, Henri
must know.

Edith and Celeste had never been friends. Edith had felt
only an amused superiority towards the silent child that her
brother had so desired. She had not believed Celeste worthy of
such a man. She, too, had had a large part in the thwarting
of Henri, convinced that he would find no happiness in the
pure innocence of Celeste. Had she been mistaken? She
asked herself this question somberly, as Adelaide had asked
it so often of herself.

The five of them, Celeste, Henri, Annette, Christopher and
Edith, had breakfasted in the sunny morning-room, whose
french windows opened out upon the rose gardens. Peter
did not as yet come downstairs for breakfast.

Annette was lovingly delighted at the presence of her
guests. Her flat little body, so fragile and thin, was clad in
a white lace morning gown. The tendrils of her bright fair
hair curled about her small triangular face, emphasizing its
pallor. But her extraordinarily beautiful light-blue eyes, so
large and tender, were filled with radiance. Beside her sat
Henri. He listened to her gay prattle with a smile, and sometimes looked at her with casual fondness. She was no longer
very young, but she appeared still immature. When she
glanced at her husband her eyes lit up with a dazzling and
pathetic light, and there would be a flutter of faint rose in
her little face.

How can Henri endure that sickly little thing? thought
Edith, as she had always thought it, but now with new and
awakened disgust, sorrowful and outraged. But he betrayed
nothing but mixed kindness and solicitude for his wife. He

rarely glanced at Celeste, sitting across from him in her dark-blue frock which matched her eyes.

It had been many years since Edith had seen her sister-in-law, who was also related to her by blood. It was the same Celeste, but with an unfamiliar sternness in her repose, a worn look about her nostrils and lips. There was patience there, repressed and firm, and a sureness. She smiled rarely. But she was more beautiful than ever, in her maturity. Christopher could hardly look away from his beloved sister. When she met his look, he smiled, and there was a strange searching tenderness in his smile, for all its immobile and metallic quality.

He had inquired politely of Peter, and had listened to Celeste intently when she replied. "He is much better," she said. "He only coughs a little at night. Soon, we'll look about for a place of our own."

Henri, at this, lifted his head, and directed a pale glance at Celeste. But the heavy lips with the brutal folds about them did not move. A moment later he lifted his eyes to Christopher, bland blank eyes which expressed nothing at all. However, all Christopher's lean muscles tightened with a kind of alert surprise, and calculation.

Impossible, he thought. That's over and done with. Then he thought: But nothing is ever over and done with, with such men. Nevertheless, he felt a black and dangerous amusement. He turned his own glittering stare upon his sister, and the chromium wheels of his mind began a soundless but rapid whirling. She had undone him, by her marriage to Peter, against his plans. He, like Henri, never forgot, never wholly forgave. But, as he studied her, that inner treachery of his which could never withstand the love he had for her filled him with gloomy anxiety. The little love, the little utter fool! She had ruined her life, ruined Henri's life, ruined his own. She had caused that tight deep look about her eyes and mouth, the patient look of vicarious suffering. He felt the marble core of her, and wondered, for the hundredth time, how he had never known of it when she had been a child and under his care. His anxiety lifted a little. She had been a match for all of them, because she had been defenseless. She was a better match now, because she understood so many things, and was a woman at last.

His scrutiny of her intensified. Henri was speaking idly to her of nothing at all. She was returning his regard indifferently. There was no sign of any emotion on her grave pale face. Her little white hand rested near her coffee cup in a supine attitude. It did not tremble in the least.

Christopher's mind increased its speed. Henri was in control of the Bouchards, through his marriage to Annette, because of his own power of character. Annette. Christopher glanced at his sister-in-law, who was also his niece. As brittle and delicate as a figurine. But one could not always count on the early demise of such little creatures. They had tenacity, and clung to life until they dropped from it as a fluttering leaf drops from a tree in autumn. However, such as she died when their hearts broke. He remembered she had almost died when Celeste had been engaged to Henri. Now, if she should die——

If she should die. Christopher's mind fastened on the thought as greedy hands fasten on ripe fruit, the juice spilling through the fingers in the clenched grip. If Peter should die. A look of utter malevolence shone in his inhuman eyes for an instant. Then, there would be only Henri and Celeste. A swift warmth, almost like a fever, touched his face.

He felt someone looking at him, and glanced up to see that it was Henri. And Henri was smiling, his eyelids narrowed.

But Henri said in the most casual of tones: "Would you like to go up to see Peter, Chris?"

"I'll wait a while," said Edith, who hated invalids. "We girls have a lot to talk about."

The two men rose and left the breakfast table. They entered the long corridor that led to the reception hall. Christopher walked behind Henri, and could not look away from the back of that large Napoleonic head, the set of those broad shoulders. Henri moved quickly and firmly. Reaching the foot of the staircase, he turned and regarded his brother-in-law with that bland blank expression.

Nothing had been said, nothing hinted. But, as the two men stared at each other in the purplish dusk, the impalpable air was full of portent. Christopher saw the pale gleaming of Henri's eyes, his faint smile. He saw the broad strong hand on the stair-rail. Henri had planted one of his feet on the first step. He stood there, did not move, and only gazed at his brother-in-law, and waited.

Christopher began to smile.

He said, very softly: "So, he's here. How is he?"

"Dying," said Henri, with impassive calm.

Again, there was silence.

"As insane as ever?"

Henri shrugged. He glanced down at his hand, lifted it absently, and bit the nail of his index finger. Christopher, with a shock, remembered from his own boyhood that immemorial gesture of Ernest Barbour.

"I have an idea," said Henri, at last, examining the nail he had bitten, "that he knows a great deal. Too much. He's bursting with it. But, he doesn't know enough—from this side. He is hell-bent on finding out. He will, too. He has the obsession that we nasty Bouchards are plotting war." He smiled.

Christopher smiled also. "It might interest him to know we have other thoughts, this time. But that might be worse than his present ideas. Much worse. In fact, with the stupid obsession he now has he can be of invaluable assistance." He coughed gently.

"My thought, exactly," agreed Henri, with friendly warmth. They regarded each other with amusement.

"He could be delicately encouraged—" continued Christopher.

"Exactly," repeated Henri.

"Must be dexterously handled——"

"With finesse. It can be managed. We'll have a gathering of the clan. He never was very bright," Henri added.

"He's big with book again?"

"About to hatch, I'd say. He couldn't have returned at a happier time, in my opinion. But, we've got to work fast. He'll hardly last more than a few months. I've seen the X-rays."

There was a ringing silence, there in the hallway, while the two men stared impassively at each other.

Then Christopher touched his lips with his skeletal fingers. "And little Celeste? It'll be bad for her."

Henri's fixed regard did not leave his brother-in-law. "Perhaps," he murmured. "Who can tell?"

Christopher, who hated Henri more than did any of the other Bouchards, because of the public humiliation and ignominy Henri had once inflicted on him, reached out and pressed the other's arm with affection.

"We'll be on hand, to help her bear it," he said, in a jocular tone.

But Henri said nothing. He went up the stairway. Christopher followed, watching him with narrowed eyes.

Henri tapped on a door in the upper hall, and he and Christopher entered Peter's apartments.

CHAPTER IX

Peter was sitting in a deep chair near one sunny window, which was opened to admit the shining wind. On a table near his right elbow was heaped a mass of orderly papers and books and magazines. Somehow, he had been able to obtain a few sheets of paper, and had apparently been making rapid notes upon them for some time. A housemaid was busily dusting his bedroom beyond.

Christopher, smiling, glanced acutely at his brother-in-law, and missed no detail of that exhausted and pallid face, with the sunken cheeks and white lips, the suffering eyes. What he saw made his spirits rise excessively.

"Well!" he exclaimed, "so here we are!"

He approached Peter, his hand extended. Peter looked at him in silence, even while he mechanically took that hand. He felt a thrill of the old loathing and disgust at the touch of that dry cool flesh and the light pressure of the bony fingers. "The Robot" had not improved with marriage. He was easier in manner, yes, had even more of the inhuman sang-froid which had always distinguished him. But the lethal quality of him was still there, waiting, like poison in a vial.

"You haven't changed, Christopher," he said.

Christopher laughed lightly. "Oh, come now. We're none of us any younger, you know that. But thank you, anyway, Pete."

Henri smiled irrepressibly. Peter was not known for his tact; he had no deviousness. Henri discerned that he might even elucidate his real meaning, which might have its amusing aspects. But Peter, by an effort, did not elucidate. He withdrew his feverish hand from Christopher's, and was silent again.

"We're all delighted you are home," said Christopher, sitting down near the other. "It's been a long time."

"Too long," remarked Peter.

"I think so, too. How are you? You seem perfectly well to me." Nothing could have been more affectionate than Christopher's smile, his air of solicitude.

"I am much better," murmured Peter. He hesitated. "In fact, I am going to insist that everyone stop treating me as an invalid."

"Quite right," said Henri, moving to the window and glancing idly through it. "There's been enough of this pampering. But, you know women. Hens cackling over chicks. Celeste's been coddling you enough, Pete. How do you think you would stand a dinner party, with the whole damned family?"

"I'd like it," said Peter, in a low tone. Henri's profile was toward him, brutal, blunt, carved harshly as if by a powerful knife. "I've wanted that."

He could not look away from Henri. The man seemed to fascinate him. In the meantime, Christopher was fondly studying the heap of papers and books on the table. "Another book, Pete? I hope a more charitable one this time."

Peter laid his shrunken hand protectingly over the contents of the table nearest to him. He regarded Christopher with eyes that were suddenly blue fire.

"I have my plans," he said, very quietly. He drew a deep breath. The two other men heard the rasping in his chest, the wheezing. "I've been gathering material." He lifted a thin book, and Christopher saw the German lettering on it: *Deutsche Wehr*. Peter held it in his hands and stared down at it.

"A German military publication, June 13, 1935," said Christopher. "It must be interesting. If only as a psychological study of the German mentality. I've always hated the Germans. A vicious and perverted people. Quite mad. But, I suppose you don't agree with me, Pete? You never did believe in the virulence of people."

But Peter said calmly: "On the contrary. I do agree with you. This time. I didn't, at first. A Swedish nobleman once told me that they had a proverb in his country: 'As mad as a German.' Yes, they are an insane people. It isn't Hitler. It's Germany, itself. Every German, man, woman or child. Any German, anywhere. There's a mass insanity there. But that doesn't mean we should cater to that insanity, you know. Every man of intelligence understands that insane people should be isolated. But there are men, everywhere in the world, who intend to turn the dementia of Germany to their own uses. They think that afterwards they can put chains on Germany. But you can't easily put madmen back in the madhouse after you've used them."

"'You can't indict a whole people,'" murmured Henri. "Didn't you say that yourself, in your own book?"

"I'm not indicting the Germans," replied Peter. A febrile color rushed to his cheeks. "In a way, I pity them. They are intrinsically mad. You don't murder madmen. You pity them, incarcerate them where they won't harm society. You try to cure them by suggestion, or drugs, or treatment—if you can."

He paused. The flush left his cheek. It became livid. He half raised himself in his chair, and despite his own inner warnings, he could not control himself. "I tell you, I've seen so much in Europe! No one will listen to me—I went everywhere. I saw so terribly much. That's why I came back—to tell what I've seen! Perhaps a few will listen."

"My God," interrupted Henri, wearily, turning from the window and looking down at Peter. "We've had a measles-rash of books about Europe. Prophets have been going wildly up and down America, shrieking warnings. Jeremiahs have been howling on every doorstep. The people are sick of it, I'm afraid. You don't intend to add yourself to the prophets and the Jeremiahs, do you, Pete? It's no use. We've got legions of them already. They bore us to death."

Peter was trembling violently. They could see that. Henri and Christopher exchanged a malignant look of amusement. Christopher thought: He's been suppressed. He's not been allowed to speak. Henri has seen to that. Now, he lets him talk. He wants me to hear. He, Christopher, felt the old rising of excitement, a satisfaction that his deadly brother-in-law was conspiring with him again.

Peter cried out in a thin and choking voice: "'Bore you to death!' My God, can't you see?" He stopped. His hands clenched on the German military publication. His eyes were blue flame, and his mouth was grim. "Yes," he said, in a lower tone. "You see, all right. I know that. There's nothing I can tell you. You know it all. That's what I was afraid of."

Henri shrugged, smiled. "My God. You believe that, don't you? You will continue to flatter us with omnipotence and omnipresence and prescience. You are our best advertiser, our best boaster, Pete. Never mind. Calm yourself. Maybe Germany isn't as mad as we all think. It will blow over. You'll see."

Peter's shaking hands opened the book. "Let me read this to you," he said, in such a strained and agitated voice that it was hardly audible: "'Totalitarian victory means the utter destruction of the vanquished nation and its complete and final disappearance from the historical arena. In reality, totalitarian warfare is nothing but a gigantic struggle of elimination whose upshot will be terrible and irrevocable in its finality.' " He closed the book, looked slowly from one to the other with his moved eyes. "I suppose you've read that before?"

Henri laughed, with indulgent disgust. "I've heard it somewhere, yes. Who listens to the bombast of Germans? They're all bullies and cowards and shouters. We ought to have enforced the Versailles Treaty. We didn't. That was our sentimentality——"

"Your expediency!" cried Peter, aroused now from the sluggish inertia of the many past weeks. Christopher was silent, smiling slightly. Henri was "egging" the fool on, for his own purposes. So Christopher listened intently, understanding that in this apparently incoherent and silly conversation there was a plan and a pattern which Henri intended him to discern.

"Our expediency?" said Henri, becoming colder and heavier as Peter's passionate agitation grew. He was studying the sick man with implacable interest. "Don't be a fool, Pete. Yes, I remember what you said in your book: 'Evil men will seek to destroy the Versailles Treaty, call a moratorium on reparations from Germany, help her secretly to arm and loose her madness on the world again—for profits.' "

He paused. He smiled with pleasant savagery. He extended one of his broad index fingers at Peter, and continued: "Now, let me tell you something, Pete. You, and your kind, destroyed the Versailles Treaty. You and your kind influenced Hoover in his dangerous moratorium. You, in consequence, are the cause of Germany's rearming and the present danger implicit in her for the world. You and your pacifist writers; you and your anti-munitions writers. You and your muckrakers. What have we now, here in America? A sluggish and obstinate people determined on no more European entanglements, a people eyeing all munitions and armaments makers with suspicion and hatred. A rash of anti-war and pacifist societies of squawking women and ink-blooded eunuchs. Look at our military situation now. What real planes have we? What tanks? What army, what navy? What vital defense?"

He paused. He dropped his pointing finger. His smile remained. The pale eyes were gleaming with amused malevolence. "Yes, Peter, you've helped us disarm America. We

Bouchards can't make a move now without the stupid masses bellowing that we're 'plotting wars.' Our public relations men tell us there is absolutely no use in our lobbying, or appealing or working. Roosevelt himself, urging rearmament, is being called a 'war-monger.' If it had been left to us Bouchards, with others like us, America might not be eyeing Europe with such terror now, England might not have had a Munich, France might not be in such a foul condition of degeneracy and decadence. Say we're after profits; we admit that. We're in business. The business of rearming America."

He paused again. Peter had fallen back in his chair. He was staring at Henri unblinkingly. His eyes were blue and steadfast holes in his exhausted face. Henri inclined his head, and looked down at the sick man with that murderously cold smile of his.

Then Peter said, very quietly: "You simplify things. You imply I am a fool. You see, you don't know what I know." He drew a sharp and audible breath.

Henri raised his eyebrows. "So, we don't know what you know? I assure you, we know a great deal, my friend. Wait. I've not finished. Look at America again. See us, a fat unarmed nation, clamorous with silly voices shrieking against rearmament. You've raised that storm of voices, Pete. You, and others like you, with your heedless and hysterical books. Now, we're impotent. And, now you rush back home to America to cry out the 'truth'! If there is a war—which there won't be, of course—and America is plunged into it, defenseless, and is conquered by Germany, you will have the satisfaction of knowing you have helped bring it about. Do you know what pacifist societies you have helped create here? You'll have an opportunity to find out, soon. It ought to give you quite a sense of power. That's what you were after, weren't you?"

Peter was silent. He was gazing at Henri with a kind of still horror, as if something in that large pale countenance fascinated him. He appeared not to have heard what the other had said.

"Yes," said Christopher, gently. "It's all quite true, Pete. You've helped. You've helped bring about the very situation which you now have galloped home to warn us about. Very, very inconsistent." •

Peter regarded them in that frozen and immobile silence which had come upon him. There was a kind of horrified incredulity in his look. His hands clenched on the arms of his chair. These terrible men! These smooth and evil liars! He felt his heart swelling and rising in his chest so that he thought he might choke to death, there before them, to their satisfaction and amusement. Do not speak, a still voice in him urged. Do not let them know all that you know. They are trying to discover——

But his passion would not let him keep completely silent.

He lifted his hand and directed it towards Henri, standing with such strong ease near him. He used it partly to point, partly to keep that formidable man away.

"Answer one question for me, Henri Bouchard," he said, in a tone almost a whisper. "Tell me what you were doing in Italy last December, in Germany in January, in Spain in March."

For the first time, Henri involuntarily stirred. Christopher looked up, alertly, his fleshless body drawing together in his chair. He and Henri exchanged one of their swift looks.

"Yes!" cried Peter, raising himself a little. "Yes! Tell me, 'Mr. Britton'! That is what they called you, wasn't it? You thought no one knew. Only a few knew. I was one of them."

A heavy and dangerous silence filled the sunny room. Peter sat upright in his chair, shaking violently. Henri looked down at him, and that broad colorless face was tight and grim. But he was not disconcerted.

He said at last: "I don't suppose it occurred to your heated mind that I might have been there on a secret mission to help keep the peace, did it? To survey the situation incognito?"

Peter, for all his knowledge of the Bouchards, was freshly aghast, freshly made frantic by a feeling of new impotence and despair. They had been trying to reduce him to foolishness, to ridiculousness. Above all, they had dared to lie so impudently to him, as if he were a fool, a moron, a contemptible and squirming little sparrow in a nest of hawks. For a moment his own vanity was outraged and infuriated. This was immediately superseded by a real and enormous terror.

Be quiet, the still voice in him warned him sternly. You are playing into their hands. Be quiet, in the name of God.

But he could not be quiet, and this terrified him even more.

"When you were in Italy, Henri, was it possible that you visited the Associazone fra Industriali Metallurgici Mecannici ed Affini? The Fiat automobile works? Lega Industriale of Turin? Societa Ansaldo, the shipbuilders? The steel works of Venezia Giulia? Banca Commerciale of Milan, Banca Italiana di Sconto? And, when you were in Spain, is it possible you had a quiet talk with the Duke of Alba, one of the murderous possessors of Spain and Fascism? Did you see Juan March, that incredibly wealthy criminal, that assassin of the Spanish poor and helpless? Did you see Cardinal de Llano, that panderer to Franco, that destroyer of new Spanish liberty and enlightenment? And, while in Spain, did you visit the officers of Rio Tinto, the greatest mining venture in the world today?"

Henri said nothing. He only watched Peter with alert and immobile interest. He lifted his index finger to his teeth, and abstractedly bit a hangnail. Christopher had covered his lips with his pale fingers.

Peter was bolt upright in his chair. Again he stretched out his hand and cried: "And when you were in Germany, was it possible that you did not see Hitler, Goering, Thyssen, the I.G. Farbenindustrie, the president of the Reichsbank? And when Mr. Claude Bowers, the American Ambassador to Spain, called upon you, did he not tell you, in the presence of the British Ambassador to Spain, that with the victory of Franco over the Spanish people Britain would find Hitler at Gibraltar, and thus would lose control of the Mediterranean? And were you not amused by the British Ambassador's reply that 'private interests in England are stronger than national interests'?"

Christ! thought Christopher. Who told the swine this? Where was the leak?

But Henri was very calm. He said, indifferently: "All this is possible. You seem to forget that we have interests all over the world, that American stockholders in our companies and subsidiaries have to be protected. It was my duty to investigate, in the interest of America, in the interest of ourselves, and our stockholders. So, why all this shining-eyed agitation?"

Peter pressed his hands together, and literally wrung them. You are a fool, said his inner voice, sternly. What have you accomplished? These men are more powerful than you. They are reducing you to ridiculous impotence.

Henri said, in a suddenly loud and cruel voice: "My only interest is in protecting America. Let me tell you this, my friend, and you may believe it or not: I am not interested in war. I shall do all I can—we shall all do all we can—to keep America out of any war which might occur in Europe."

That voice rang through the room, inexorable and powerful. Peter listened to it. Suddenly, a sense of fainting overwhelmed him. The room swung about him in great slow circles filled with bands of light.

In the midst of the chaos which surrounded him, he thought with incredulous and desperate horror: It is true. He has told me the truth at last. They do not want war, for America. An hour ago, I believed they were plotting to engulf us in such a war. Now, I believe, I know, they do not want it—for America. They will do all they can to keep us out of any conflict. They will never rest.

Why?

A faint glimmering of the appalling truth began to appear before him. He dared not look at it. He thought: If I could only die! I cannot live, and know. He felt his heart beating with great agony in his smothering chest.

Henri's voice filled his ears, very close, like a great and choking wind: "So, if you've had the idea that you would 'expose' us, as you 'exposed' us before, you're wasting your time. If you've thought that we were 'hatching wars' again— (my God, what stupidity!)—you can set your mind at rest. If you've thought to show that we have been intriguing or manipulating to get America into any damned mess cooked up in Europe, I can tell you quite frankly that you're a fool. America won't get in. We'll see to that. That ought to soothe you considerably."

It is true, thought Peter. Why? O God, why?

The great and crushing voice continued: "I'll tell you a secret, Pete. The instant war occurs in Europe, we'll have peace societies in America, which our money has helped organize. Big societies, which will stamp down any attempts to foment good feeling for Britain, for France, for Spain. We shall be neutral as we've never been neutral before. You'll find us openly supporting any Neutrality Act which Congress finds it necessary to pass. You see, you've helped stir up a lot of nasty muck against us. In the interest of self-preservation, no one will be more anti-war than ourselves."

Then Peter, outraged, appalled, heard his feeble voice saying: "America must prepare——"

He heard a great shout of laughter about him. It seemed to come from whirling space. He could not connect it with Henri's open mouth, in which the big teeth were glistening. Nor, to his confused senses did it seem to come from Christopher.

"My God!" Henri was crying. "Is it possible that it is *you* who are saying this; you, the pacifist, the anti-munitions muck-raker, the brotherly-lover?"

And then Peter knew that there was a most terrible power in this room, more terrible than had ever lived among the Bouchards before, or in the world. He gripped the arms of his chair to keep from fainting. He felt the impact of cosmic winds on his flesh, on his face. He felt the vast movement of unseen and frightful things.

Why? one strong voice cried out in him. Why is all this?

He dared not try to answer. He could only sit there and look at Henri. He did not know that his expression was quite deathlike.

As in a dream of horror, in which everything moved slowly and sleepily, he saw the door opening. Celeste was entering. Christopher sprang up to draw a chair for her. She was smiling, somewhat anxiously. She looked only at Peter. She came directly to him. What she saw made all expression leave her face. She swung upon her brother and Henri.

"What have you been doing to him?" she cried. "He is so very ill again. His pulse is—is—" Her fingers were clasped about her husband's wrist, and her eyes were filled with passionate anger. Her lips, very pale now, shook.

Henri frowned. He took a step towards her. "For God's sake, Celeste, don't be a fool. We've done nothing. Your husband has been up to his old accusations again—that we're 'fomenting war.' We've just convinced him otherwise. What is wrong with that? It ought to give him some peace of mind."

She regarded Henri in agitated silence, and the look in her dark-blue eyes made him frown again, a dull color rose harshly in his cheeks. But he returned her gaze formidably, and with considerable contempt.

Then she turned to her brother, and in a trembling voice she exclaimed: "Christopher, you always upset Peter so. What have you done now?"

Christopher looked at her quizzically. "Now, my darling, that is absurd. We've thought, for the sake of Peter's health, and peace-of-mind, that he ought to be disillusioned. Apparently the truth is too much for him."

Peter's breathing filled the room with faint rasping sounds. He was struggling for self-control. He took Celeste's hand, and his own was cold and damp with sweat. Yet he could speak so very calmly, looking up at her with a smile:

"Yes, dear, that's quite right. They've just told me the truth. And, as Chris says: 'it is apparently too much for me.' " He pressed her hand, and she gazed down at him, bewildered, enormously shaken.

"Don't worry, darling. I'm quite well. I've—come to life. All these weeks, just sitting here, I really feel impossibly strong. I've got a lot of work to do, and you must help me." He lifted her hand and pressed his lips to the small and tremulous palm.

Henri's eyebrows, pale and thick, drew together as he watched this little scene, and now his eyes were pin-pricks of malignancy. Christopher, watching him acutely, saw how his fists clenched, and how his upper lip drew back from his teeth.

Celeste said, quietly, seeing only her husband: "We'll leave here, Peter dear, at once. We'll go away. Anywhere. Tomorrow?"

Christopher rose, smiling to himself. "It seems we aren't wanted here, Henri, my lad. So, let us leave this devoted couple together."

They left the room. They carefully closed the door, seeing, for a last scene, Celeste kneeling beside Peter, her head on his shoulder, her arms about him. He was smoothing her bright black hair tenderly and slowly. She was weeping.

The two men moved away. Henri was very calm. Christopher touched his arm. "Well?" he said.

Henri turned to his brother-in-law. He said, very softly: "He knew too much. Now, he knows much too much."

"So?" said Christopher, gently.

Henri shrugged, and smiled. "Homicide,—or is it fratricide? —isn't approved of by the police. Not even for the Bouchards. Come; what do you suggest?"

Christopher raised his eyebrows. "It is apparent he can't stand the truth. Now, huge doses of it might——"

"And," reflected Henri, "he can always be kept impotent. No one would dare publish whatever the imbecile might say. There are still libel laws, you know. Not even our dear relative, Georges, would dare. By the way, his publishing business hasn't been doing so well lately. There are other matters of his, too, which might not stand the light of day. I've a feeling one of us ought to visit dear Georges."

Christopher whistled soundlessly. "Georges? What've you got on old Georges?"

Henri smiled again. "I've overlooked no contingencies. Georges, who doesn't like us much, might easily be induced to publish any insanity. So, I've done a little investigating. Never mind. I may never need to use it. By the way, didn't he recently publish a little pamphlet about 'doing business with Hitler'? Called, I believe: 'The Madman and the Industrialist'? All about the impossibility of carrying on normal commercial relationships with the paper-hanger? It had quite a sale, I believe. Even though it was too technical for the average American-cow mind. It was read almost exclusively by our more Christian, but smaller, competitors. Not important. No harm done. But Pete's insanity might be important. Never mind. I can nip all that before it gets dangerous."

In the room they had left, Peter was saying to Celeste: "They don't want war! They will try to keep us out. Why? Celeste, can you tell me why? My God, why?" He continued chokingly: "They secretly helped Germany rearm. They furnished the money, through American, French and British banks. But they don't want us in the war. Why? Why?"

CHAPTER X

Henri went in to see his wife, Annette.

She was dressing for dinner, having just bathed and rested. Her frail health necessitated prolonged periods of rest and sleep. During the first year of her married life, instinctively understanding that sickliness and weakness of body were repugnant to her husband, she had attempted to dispense with these periods, and had pathetically assumed a sprightliness and activity which had later prostrated her and had confined her to her bed for nearly three months. Thereafter, there was no question of afternoon engagements. She retired almost invariably at ten at night, not rising until almost nine the next morning. It was not that she was an invalid, but a congenital infirmity and fragility of physique compelled her to live a quiet and semi-convalescent life.

Her great agony of mind was that her physician had warned her that any attempt to have children would probably result in her death, and that in any event she might not live long after the birth of a child. At the best, she could expect invalidism. She had been willing to chance these desperate contingencies, but Henri would not allow it. He had been very "noble" about the situation, she had tearfully confided to Celeste. No one could have been more considerate, more understanding, more gentle. He would not allow her even to talk about the matter to him. "No, my dear," he had said, "we can't discuss it. Your life is more valuable to me than the possibility of any children. I can't afford to lose you, you know."

He had smiled a little when he had said this, not in a jocular fashion, but somewhat grimly. Annette had not understood this smile in the least. Her heart had ached with passionate gratitude, and with joy. The subsequent years of her marriage had been illuminated with happiness. She had loved Henri with overwhelming rapture before she had married him. She had discerned that he had had for her no such passion and absorption, but only an indifferent affection, if even that. Why had he married her under these circumstances she did not quite know. It had been enough for her that he had. There had been a few times when she had caught his glance fixed upon her, and it had terrified her, during their engagement. Her naïveté, her innocence, her unfamiliarity with human emotions and reactions, had protected her from seeing the full meaning of his glance, implicit with disgust, repulsion, and contemptuous pity. Only the vague leaping of her heart, rather than her reason, caused her terror. And then, seeing her face, her fear, her dread, he would become suddenly solicitous, considerate and even tender. He betrayed an almost extravagant concern for her, which, rather than arousing her suspicions, allayed them.

It never occurred to her that he had married her because she was the only and beloved daughter of Armand Bouchard, the president of Bouchard & Sons. Was he not the powerful holder of Bouchard bonds? What more might he desire? She did not know Henri Bouchard. There was to be a time when she would know, but it was not yet. She, until that hour, was not to understand his sleepless hatred because Jules Bouchard, her grandfather, had so manipulated Henri's mother's affairs that her son, great-grandson of Ernest Barbour, had been rendered impotent. Henri had dissipated that impotence. He was now the power of the Bouchards, and the president of the mother company since the retirement of the diabetic Armand. But the hatred remained. It was part of his personality. It was not in him to forget an offense, an injury. Sometimes, he looked at her in the strangest and most formidable fashion, remembering that she was the granddaughter of the subtle and Machiavellian Jules.

Annette had made objective the power he held behind the scenes. She had been too frail and gentle a thing to know or understand what he had done immediately prior to her marriage to him. She had heard the faint echoes of the thunderbolt, the dim shaking of the earth under all the Bouchards. But her marriage had made her unaware of anything else. She knew that the Bouchards had a kind of terribleness about them, but she believed it was because she was so weak and frail, and they were so strong. She hated no one; she did not even dislike the most repellent of the Bouchards. She longed only for affection, for kindness, for gentle hands and voices and eyes. Now that she was Henri's wife, she had them in good measure. Her gratitude was touching, even to the hardest heart. She rejoiced that her family now accepted her as a complete human being, that many listened to her respectfully, and that they were solicitous of her. She asked no questions. She was too sweet, too humble, too timid.

It was these qualities that protected her from the cold furies and remorseless brutality of Henri Bouchard. When he had first seen his cousin in 1925 (his father and her grandfather had been brothers) he had known immediately that here was a poor little creature instinctively overwhelmed by a subconscious knowledge of the character of her family. He had known they despised her, whenever she infrequently came to their attention. Only her father's former position as dominant executive of the Bouchard affairs had prevented her from open or covert abuse. Her very gentle youth, her timidity, her frailness of body, her air of deformity (which really did not exist) reminded them of an old legendary figure of the family: Jacques Bouchard, son of the co-founder of the Dynasty, old Armand, her grandfather's grandfather. The legend had persisted in the family, a furtive tale which still could arouse sniggers among the meaner-minded. It was said that Jacques had been "in love" with Martin Barbour, brother of the terrible Ernest, and had killed himself when Martin had married Amy Drumhill, cousin to Ernest's wife, May Sessions. Emile, Annette's brother, had an old and faded miniature of Jacques, and indeed, the poor deformed cripple was strangely like little Annette. There were the same large blue eyes, light and radiant, the same delicate features, the same small triangular face, so pale and drawn, the same mass of light and buoyant hair. Even the expression, gentle and tragic and appealing, was startlingly similar.

Henri's first emotion upon seeing Annette had been an indifferent compassion. Later, he was slightly interested by her intelligence, sweetness and innocence. But he never recovered from a sense of strong repugnance for her. Sometimes he hated her, as if she had wronged him by her mere existence, though she had saved him years of work in gaining control of Bouchard & Sons. His reason was annoyed at this emotional reaction against a gentle creature who had done him no harm, and who loved him with such passionate shy consecration. His annoyance at himself caused those intervals of coldness towards her which so puzzled and frightened her, and filled her with a sense of guilt. The intervals came rarely. She was now only his hostess, his tender little friend whenever he would permit it, his idolatress. And there are few men who can resist idolatry. He had only to be kind and courteous to satisfy her, to transform her into radiant joy.

The family was completely aware of why he had married Annette, and they admired him for it, even while they snickered in private at the spectacle of the implacable Henri mated to that fluttering little bird. They knew of his many liaisons, but out of fear of him did not acquaint Annette with the luscious facts. And especially not since the advent of Rosemarie in his amorous life. They also had Francis Bouchard, her father, with whom to reckon in the event of an open scandal. Did Francis know? They believed he did. They shrewdly conjectured that Francis even countenanced the affair, in the hope of Annette's early death and Henri's marriage to Rosemarie.

A wall of affectionate silence, then, surrounded Annette. Occasionally, however, she saw the dim shapes of reality passing behind the glass, heard the faint harsh echoes of cruel voices, but strain as she would, with fear, she discerned nothing definite enough to shatter the glass and leave her bereft and shuddering. Perhaps this was because she dared not look too closely. She forced herself to be satisfied with things as they appeared on the surface. Always, she had been too introspective, too sensitive, too fearful, she would reproach herself. Even in Paradise she would look for the serpent, watch the eternal sun for signs of storm, believe that the whispering winds of heaven contained the sly voices of enemies. Thus she told herself.

For Annette was no fool. Years of quiet and secluded living had turned her mind to books and music, to long thoughts and meditative silences. This had given her a clarity of perception, very dangerous for the helpless. Her consciousness had been like a mass of trembling antennae waving in every subtle wind that emanated from other personalities. She had been able to feel the thoughts of others, their reactions not only to herself, but to circumstance, to environment, to voices, to the very sun and weather. She had sensed their backgrounds, and their response to their backgrounds. This had frequently given her such a strange sense of disorientation and confusion that she had often felt her own personality disintegrating in the general mass of reactions all about her, and she could not tell whether she was thinking thus and so, or whether others were thinking in this manner.

Now she knew that if she was to retain her identity, if she was to live at all, endure at all, she must protect herself from this exhausted surrender to impressions of others, and helpless identification with their personalities. She must grow a skin; better, she must enclose herself in concrete. If, as she sometimes thought, that concrete had in it the quality of a sarcophagus, at least she would be comparatively safe from a perceptiveness that threatened her very existence, physical as well as mental.

For, like her relative, Peter, she knew that she would surely die if she understood too much about the world of men. Her life now was an unending struggle not to see more than was necessary for her survival, not to read the true meaning under casual and guarded words, to accept the statements of others with simple faith, to believe that their gestures meant only what they were intended to convey, that their faces expressed what they apparently desired them to express.

So, she had a kind of happy if static peace in her tortured heart. If she caught herself listening to the dim and ominous echo behind friendly and casual voices, if she found herself searching for the arched lip and cruel eye beyond affectionate smiles, she sternly covered her spiritual ears with her hands and closed her clear and desperate eyes. Who could know the truth about mankind, and live? she would whisper to herself.

When Henri would enter her apartments during the early months, or even years, of their marriage, her gaze would instinctively and fearfully fasten upon him, her heart would rise with quick and perceptive dread, her blood would cool so that she shivered as if expecting a mortal shock. She had overcome that now. She accepted him as he desired to be accepted by her. If he smiled affectionately, as he did this evening, she accepted that affection. But she still could not control the instinctive lurching of a heart that demanded the truth, even if it died for it.

Her maid placed a lace négligé over her thin bare shoulders, and discreetly left the room. Annette smiled joyously at her husband, extended her little narrow hand to him. He took it; it trembled a little, as always. Her great light eyes fixed themselves upon him with a helpless pleading to which he had become accustomed, and which never failed, despite himself, to give him a qualm of compassion. So he bent and kissed her white forehead, then touched her hair with a briefly tender hand.

"Am I interfering with something important, darling?" he asked.

She sighed, and smiled. The imminent danger was passed. It always passed. But she always waited for it, in bottomless terror. She sat down in a puffed satin chair, as if weak. He sat near her.

"No, dearest. Nothing else is important, when you come," she said. Her hands fluttered, as if she desperately desired to take hold of him and feel his strength.

"Well then, how would you like to give a large family party for Celeste and Peter?" he asked, regarding her with indulgent fondness. His pale expressionless eyes had even a slight smile in them.

"Oh, lovely!" she exclaimed, in her fluting voice. She clapped her hands together, softly. Now she was all joy, and delight. Then the small face clouded. "But Peter. Is he well enough? Would he want it?"

"I think he is well enough, pet. Frankly, I think we've pampered him too much. That is just like you, Annette; you are always so brooding and solicitous, like a damned little wren."

She laughed happily at this, and adored him. "Oh, Henri, that's unfair. Didn't you warn me, yourself, that poor Peter mustn't be disturbed, that he needed careful nursing? Didn't you suggest the nurses, yourself? That was so kind of you, so very, very good. But it was you, you know, who insisted on all this.

"If you really think Peter could stand a party, then I'll be so happy to give him and darling Celeste one. When do you think?"

But he was silent a moment, eyeing her with penetration. She was immediately uneasy. He said: "You are very fond of Celeste, aren't you, sweet?"

She was immediately radiant. "Oh, yes, I am," she said, very swiftly. "We were always such good friends. You can't know. Celeste was my only friend. We are almost the same age, even if she is my aunt. We were together, whenever

Uncle Christopher would allow it. I think I was the only friend the poor darling ever had, too. Uncle Christopher kept her like a little nun. I would do anything for Celeste," she added, with the swiftness of pain and love. "I know she is so unhappy now, over Peter."

He did not move a muscle, yet she had the queer sensation that he had moved closer to her, as if not to miss a single expression, or a solitary intonation of her voice.

"Why do you think she is so unhappy, Annette?"

She felt the pressing power of his personality, his intentness. This confused her, so that she could only falter: "Well, isn't it obvious, dear? Peter has been so ill, is still so ill. There doesn't seem much hope for his complete recovery. And Celeste is so devoted to him, loves him so. It is awfully touching; sometimes I can't bear it." Her voice faded; there were tears in her eyes.

Henri shrugged. "She married him, didn't she? Knowing that he was a sick man? What could she expect?"

She spoke eagerly, as if pleading for his compassion for Celeste and Peter: "Yes, she knew it. Or, as much as she could. She was so young. She believed that he would recover. After all, the doctors were optimistic. The damage to his lungs was quite bad, but not irreparable, they said. But he didn't recover. He got worse." She hesitated, pleading again with her illumined eyes for his pity. "Celeste once hinted to me, not long ago, that it was something else that was making Peter so ill. She said—she thought it was because he couldn't stand the things he had learned about—about—" Her voice fell into distressed silence, and now those eyes were filled with a personal terror, as if she heard the echo in herself of things she dared not hear.

Henri raised his eyebrows in a broad expression of amusement. He laughed. "Now, let's not get metaphysical. I don't follow you when you talk such nonsense, little mouse. It's my opinion, and the doctors uphold it, that Peter's too introspective, too absorbed in himself and in what he believes. The supreme egoist. Now, I'm not intending to be unkind, so don't look at me like that. I'm telling you my considered opinion, after long study of our sensitive invalid.

"So, that's why I'm suggesting a party. It might help him. Take him out of himself. Besides, Celeste needs it, too. It's my observation that she's pretty miserable. I've sometimes wondered if she didn't regret marrying Peter."

"O no!" cried Annette, in a tone unusually loud and desperate. "You're wrong, Henri! She loves him so. I know that."

"How can you know that?" he asked, obviously bored, and standing up. "After all, she's had her bellyful of dancing attendance. She hasn't had a normal life. I wouldn't blame her if she was sick of it."

She looked up at him, her eye-sockets widening and stretching, until her whole small face seemed filled with anguished blueness.

"Henri, you don't understand. Celeste is so—so stern. She wouldn't allow herself to think such things, even if they were there. I—I know Celeste. I know that she'd rather have had her life with Peter, wretched and anxious though it has been at times, than a more serene and normal life with anyone else. Please believe me. I know."

"Celeste has told you this?" She felt again that he had moved too close to her. There was a nameless sense of smothering in her thin throat. She lifted her hands as if to hold him off, and he thought: He did that, too, this morning. They're alike, these pathetic wretches.

"No, no, she didn't tell me!" she cried. "I just know." Now she dropped her hands and pressed them on the cushion beside her, as if to spring to her feet and flee.

He saw her distress, but he was remorseless. He studied her intently. He thought: She is frightened. She is afraid to look too sharply at the truth. She knows the truth.

He relaxed, and smiled. He took her face in his hands. It felt chill and damp to his touch. He bent down and kissed her again. She was vibrating, like a tuning fork which had been struck too violently. But under his strong touch, under his smile, under the eyes deliberately affectionate, she subsided, feeling only a profound weakness.

"Now, we're getting too excited over nothing at all," he said, soothingly. "Why do you upset yourself, you little fool?" He pressed her cheeks again, then straightened up. He took out the gold cigarette case she had given him on his last birthday, and nonchalantly lighted a cigarette. She watched all his motions, deliberate, heavy, calm, and could not look away from him. He puffed a moment, frowning thoughtfully at the curling smoke.

"I have a feeling you are perhaps right," he acknowledged. "Only this morning Celeste said something, before Peter, of leaving us very shortly."

She uttered a light cry of protest. The weakness was still strongly upon her, but she forgot its cause in this new development. "Oh, I couldn't bear that! I've hoped Celeste and Peter might stay with us indefinitely. I couldn't bear losing her now, Henri."

He smiled with hidden satisfaction. "Well, we can't chain them, you know. However, you might mention your feelings to Celeste very soon. Tell her you need her, or something. She's very good at being needed."

There was something in his tone, something cruel or sardonic, which made the poor little creature wince. But she forced herself to think: He is so kind. My darling is so kind. He always thinks of me.

She said: "I will, dearest. Tonight, perhaps."

She rose when he moved towards the door, following him like a frail white shadow. On the threshold, he stopped again, to touch her cheek lightly. He opened the door, and went out. She closed it slowly.

Her palms flattened against the polished wood. Her lips almost touched it. Then, very slowly, they came into contact with the door. She stood there, pressed against the wood, as if crucified against it, as if fainting against it, unable to move away for fear of falling into utter darkness, forever.

CHAPTER XI

Just before dinner, Annette went to the apartments of Celeste and Peter.

Her assumed sprightliness had now become involuntary habit, and she moved quickly on her thin little legs and tiny feet, hardly seeming to touch the floor in her tread. Her blue-and-white print frock emphasized the childishness of her figure, and the fair ringlets about her pale face enhanced her apparent immaturity. Nothing could have been sweeter than her smile when, after her soft knock, she entered her guests' sitting-room.

She found Celeste sitting near Peter, as they awaited the dinner bell. Celeste, in a white frock, appeared all coolness and freshness, though the day had been extremely hot and breathless. Peter, as usual, was drained and exhausted. Annette's quick and perceptive glance touched them uneasily. Was it her imagination, or was Celeste abnormally pale and drawn of eye and lip? Certainly she had a sterner look than ordinarily, and her round dimpled chin was set with a grim obstinacy. Had the darlings been quarrelling? As always, at the hint of a disturbed or violent atmosphere, Annette's heart rose on an arch of disquiet and fear. Her smile became even more tender and eager, and her hands lifted a little, as if to implore, to soothe.

"Hasn't it been too dreadfully hot?" she prattled. "No, no, dear Peter, please don't get up. I'll only stay a minute, until dinner. It is almost time." She reached out, and took Celeste's hand, as she sat down, and gazed at her with pleading and speechless earnestness. Were they tired of her? Did she annoy them with her foolish impotence? Did she bore them?

Celeste, who had always known so much about her niece, felt a nameless pang. Did the poor little creature sense the cold and angry and protesting words which had been uttered just before her arrival? Did such words leave a ringing discord in the air? She forced herself to smile affectionately.

"It *has* been hot," she said, her conscience aroused. "But we hardly feel it at Robin's Nest."

"We didn't go away this summer as usual," said Annette, pathetically grateful for Celeste's smile and the pressure of her hand. "Henri thought we ought not to, with things as they are in Europe. He wanted to be at home, in case of 'developments.' But I hardly think there will be 'developments,' do you? It would be so stupid, so terrible— One doesn't dare think of it."

Peter glanced swiftly at his wife. But she would not look at him. She was all attentiveness towards Annette.

"Well, I'm sure we couldn't find a pleasanter place than Robin's Nest, darling," said Celeste. "It was so kind of you to invite us. We are so very grateful." She paused. Her lips tightened to a thin line. "But, it must be very tiresome for you, to have us underfoot all the time. That's why I've just been arguing with Peter that we ought to look around and find a place of our own."

Annette was immediately alarmed and distressed. She held Celeste's hand tightly with both her own, and leaned towards her. "Henri thought you might have that in mind," she said, her voice breaking. "I couldn't really believe it. You don't know how happy you've made me, dear, just being in the same house with me. It has been such a difference. I've been so lonely, at times. I—I've thought you might stay indefinitely. It would break my heart if you should leave."

Celeste was silent. Her lips became grimmer than ever. She averted her eyes. But Peter lifted himself a little in his chair. He said: "That is what I've been saying to Celeste, Annette. We ought to stay a little longer." He appeared a little confused, and a faint color rose to his gaunt cheekbones. "I've been outlining my work. I wouldn't want an interruption just yet. But Celeste believes we've been inconveniencing you."

"I still believe it," said Celeste, in a hard tone. She looked at her husband directly. "It is too much for Annette. You ought to realize that, Peter." But her eyes continued their angry argument with him. He had declared, just before Annette had entered, that he must remain, that he needed to remain, that once out of that house he would learn nothing from Henri. He had learned so terribly much that morning. He had to know more. He, he had said, simply could not understand Celeste. She had become morbid, over-sensitive, even hysterical. Why on earth did she insist upon leaving? She had been silent at this question. But she had looked at him strangely, with a kind of speechless and desperate fear. One never said to one's husband: "We must leave this man's house, for our own sakes. Do you not understand that I've never forgotten him, that for all these years he has been in my mind, like a plague, or an obsession, or a disease? I have believed that I hate him; I've thought one never forgets the people one hates. I don't know. Do I hate him? Does he repel me? Do I loathe him? I don't know! I only know that I can't stop thinking of him, that I hear his voice everywhere, that when I see him I can hardly breathe, and that I lie awake at night with his face before me in the dark. That when he touches me, even in passing, or by accident, I turn to fire. It was like that from the very beginning, when I first saw him. I still don't understand. I only know I am in danger, perhaps more so from myself than from him. For your sake, my darling, we must leave here."

No, one never said this. One only got up at once and fled. She looked at Peter, and the danger seemed hovering around him, to destroy him, and all that danger came from herself, and not from Henri.

In her desperation, she spoke again, loudly, to drown out Annette's imploring voice: "We must leave, Annette. I can't impose on you any longer. All these nurses, this inconvenience, this upsetting of your routine. You've had to consider us before making plans of your own. You've had to adjust your life to ours. It isn't fair to you."

Could one say to one's dear hostess, whom one loved: "I've got to go away, before I destroy you? Can't you understand that it seems frightful to me to see you as Henri's wife, that at times I hate you, my darling, and that I am afraid that some day I shall hope you will die? Can't you help me to save myself from this awful thing? Each time that I see Henri—there are terrible thoughts in me. Help me to save you, and myself, also."

Thinking these things, filled with terror, she looked from Peter to Annette. For the first time she saw the mysterious resemblance between them. They were both pure of heart, both tender and vulnerable, both gentle and chaste and too honorable to understand the fierce and shameful things that could invade the hearts of others. She felt dark and violent of spirit, twisted and atavistic of mind before their purity of heart, their truth and faith. She felt unclean, degraded, corrupt, all heat and humid darkness, all tempest. She was not prostrated at this. Rather, she felt strong and most aware, vital and warm of breast and trembling of thigh. The danger in herself was all voluptuousness, full of hot languor and a desire to which she dared not give a name. And they could only look at her with their pellucid light-blue eyes, and be disturbed and distressed, as at a wilful and selfish child.

Then Annette rose, bent over her young aunt, and kissed her tenderly. There was a soft catch in her voice: "O darling, how can you say such things? How can you be so cruel? I love you so, Celeste. If you go, I can't tell you how terribly I'll miss you."

The burning tears were heavy in Celeste's eyes, though she averted them. She said: "But, we won't go far. We'll stay in Windsor."

"But where, dear?" urged Annette. "You'd have to build. I thought it was understood that you were to remain here until you had built a house of your own."

Celeste was silent.

"We've already been looking at plans, and blueprints," said Peter, coldly. "We've almost decided on the kind of house we want. And now Celeste wants to leave, before anything is settled. It will only be a little while."

Annette looked down at her aunt, at that hard white profile. She could hardly keep back her tears. She bent her head so that she could see Celeste's face clearly, and her mass of bright fluffy hair fell over her cheek in a most touching manner.

"Darling, look at me. Don't you love me any more? Are you tired of me? Do you really want to leave me? Have I bored you so much?"

Celeste lifted her head swiftly, her lips parting. But when her eyes met the swimming blue purity of Annette's, and she saw their pleading, their hurt, their pathetic guiltlessness, she could only be silent again. She kissed the frail cheek so near her own, and tried to smile. Finally she said:

"How—how can you be so silly, Annette! It is only that I thought we were all too much for you. There's Christopher here, and Edith. I've thought of your health——"

"Oh, I'm really very wiry, very vigorous!" cried Annette, very quickly as always when her physical state was mentioned. "I'm very deceptive. The doctor says that people like me live forever. 'Runts have so much vitality,' he told me. I may be a runt," she added, with a little catching laugh, "but I'm as strong as steel wire. You've no idea. Henri often tells me I quite exhaust him. He says he wouldn't be surprised if I buried him a half-century before I died, myself, and ended my days as an ancient little old woman in a chimney corner. Sometimes I quite believe him, though he is so extravagant. Every year I get more strength. Really." She smiled radiantly, and put her little thin arm about Celeste's shoulders, and invited Peter to laugh with her.

But, thought Celeste, your heart would break, and then you'd die. And surely, we'll break your heart, and Peter's too, Henri and I, unless you let me go. I haven't your strength, my darlings. I haven't your goodness and faithfulness. You don't know what I am! I didn't know, myself, until lately.

Then she thought: Can't I trust myself a little longer, for their sakes? Haven't I the decency and the self-control? Surely, I'm not so weak, so depraved, as all that!

She said: "I see you've both overruled me, so I suppose there's nothing more I can say. Peter," and she turned to her husband with her old gentleness, "you'll really make up your mind tomorrow about the plans? You've been so indecisive."

Now that he had conquered, Peter was all eagerness to appease her. "Of course. And we'll consult Annette, too. There's got to be a room or two for Annette, when she visits us." He smiled at Annette, and she returned his smile joyously. She clapped her hands and almost danced with her delight.

"How lovely! And, oh yes, I'm to give a dinner party for

you two! Henri spoke of it. He is always so considerate. Won't that be just perfect?"

CHAPTER XII

While Annette was engaged in her loving persuasion of Celeste to remain at Robin's Nest, Armand Bouchard, father of Annette, brother of Celeste, arrived for dinner with his son, Antoine, "the reincarnation of Jules Bouchard."

Armand was now a widower. He lived with his unmarried son in his enormous and almost ludicrously palatial château on the Allegheny River. It contained nearly two hundred rooms, and, as some wry wit declared, it housed enough servants to form the nucleus of a flourishing village. Mrs. Armand had attempted to overwhelm the châteaux and palaces of the other Bouchards by sheer weight and size and majesty of proportion, and had succeeded in producing a vast pseudo-mediæval monstrosity of ostentation. She had had no real taste. Armand, though allowing her to have her way in the matter of the château and the furnishings, had had the prudence to call in the best landscape gardeners in America for his grounds. As a result, the ridiculousness of the château was in great measure modified by the beauty, magnificence and luxurious splendor of the surroundings. To minimize the tremendous proportions of the building, the gardeners had installed terraces that slowly descended to the river, had transplanted giant elms and oaks to shade those terraces, had made long grades that swept, park-like, to gray stone walls, where a "lodge" guarded the high iron gates.

In the midst of all this lived the diabetic and obese Armand. Henri had appointed him Chairman of the Board of Bouchard & Sons, which demanded little of Armand except an occasional pompous appearance and an earnest and judicious manner during meetings. There he would sit, in his great plush chair, thrusting out his fat underlip, looking sharply from face to face with his tiny beady eyes, uttering deep

103

growls under his breath, and, in the meantime, jingling a collection of small silver coins in his untidy pocket. Whenever he heard that jingling, he would smile with pathetic pleasure, and would hum deeply in his throat. Sometimes he would pass his hand over his large round head with its cropped gray hair, or rub the back of that hand vigorously over his pudgy nose. And again, sometimes he would relieve himself of a weighty opinion of no importance at all. Everyone treated him with the utmost profound courtesy, inclining respectful heads whenever he spoke, and something dimly resembling a smile would gleam coldly in Henri's pale eyes. Thus Armand would be allowed to believe that he was still a power among the terrible Bouchards. He was an old man now. It was little enough that Henri had granted him, though the Bouchards often expressed slight surprise that he did even this, Henri not being conspicuous for charitable actions. Few ever noticed that the fat old man's hands, in repose, had a chronic and tremulous motion, impotent and tragic, like the hands of the blind. They were more engrossed in contemplating the ruin of one who was once all-powerful, and had been so completely undone by his son-in-law. They wondered what his thoughts were, if ever he had nights of frantic and futile rage, or great sadness.

Sometimes they even pitied him, contemptuously. He had never been a favorite, had been derided even in the days of his power. For he was untidy, gross, none too clean of habit and person, despite a battery of valets. Freshly pressed trousers had a way of wrinkling across his fat thighs; vests puckered, immediately became stained; shirts became mussed and soiled.

Only his brother, the vitriolic "Rabelaisian Trappist," Christopher, had the shrewd insight sufficient to enable him to guess at the thoughts that might occasionally come to the old man. Christopher knew that Armand had, all his life, been tormented by an obscure integrity, that he had a stunted conscience of sorts, that, at the final moment, there were things he would not do. They were not many, these things, but they were enough to arouse the risibility of the Bouchards, and their amused scorn. In consequence, Armand, even when most weighty, had had an air of bewilderment, fear and hesitation about him.

Therefore, Christopher had the penetrating idea that Armand was enjoying some measure of peace since his removal as a power. At times, when discussions became very secret and full of intrigue, a vague look of fright and uneasiness would come over that florid and puffy countenance, and after a few moments, preceded by much throat-clearing, jerking of head, rubbing of nose, sniffling, and blinking of eyes, Armand would rise with dignity and plead indisposition, or an appointment. Then he would waddle from the Board room on his short swollen legs, his pace quickening as he reached the door. He had every aspect of flight, and they would watch him go, grinning covertly. Sometimes it was a trick of theirs, to get him to leave prior to really serious discussions. They did not wish a witness to these proceedings, especially not such a witness as Armand.

Christopher also guessed that Armand had really only two interests in life now: his beloved daughter, Annette, and his diabetes. For one of his self-indulgence in the matter of food, the disease was a catastrophe. He had always been a gourmand, rather than a gourmet. For years, when confronted by the necessity for a nefarious decision, which he must make for the fortunes of the Company, or repudiate for the sake of his conscience, he would suddenly and temporarily abandon the imminence of the decision for a session at the table. His chefs would be commanded to labor to produce the most exquisite and the richest of dishes, and Armand would sit before them in desperate concentration and eat, literally for hours. There was something orgiastic about these occasions. Armand would not speak; often, he would be alone in the vast cathedral spaces of his dining-room. He would tuck his "bedsheet" of a napkin under his chins, lift his shoulders, grasp knife, fork, spoon, and fill the echoing silence of the room with the sound of loud and frantic munchings, swallowings, gluttonous chewings. His great puffy face would become more florid by the moment, congested, filmed over with a greasy sweat, and his ears would turn purple around the rims. Later, he would subside in his apartments in a semi-coma of tortured digestion, and, involved in physical miseries, would forget his mental agonies. A valet would bring him various sedatives for his gut, would apply hot packs to his swollen belly, and later call a physician. When he would finally sleep, a look of deathlike peace would rest on his mauve features.

Now he had his diabetes, which threatened his life if neglected or ignored. He had his insulin needle, which had become of engrossing interest to him. In these days, he had little to disturb him, and only occasionally resorted to the pleasures of the table to soothe his psychic conflicts. He never sat down to a meal without his dietary list before him, a document which was now more important to him than any paper formerly connected with the Company. He carried his list with him to every home where he was invited to dinner with his relatives, and when the conversation threatened to turn upon the affairs of the Company and its various subsidiaries, he would loudly break into the midst of it with earnest admonitions about certain dishes which had been placed upon the lace cloths. "Now that," he would say, pointing with his knife or fork, "is practically poison. Full of sugar. Full of albumen. Too much protein. You haven't the slightest idea, I see, what that can do to your pancreas. My doctor was saying, only the other day——"

As a result, Armand was very seldom called by his name among his gay relatives. He was designated as "The List." He occasioned great mirth among them because of his learned discussions about the necessity of "simple meals, wholesome, full of minerals, plain and sustaining, well fortified with vitamins." Sometimes he would gravely call upon the chefs of his family in their very kitchens, and exhort them upon the matter of too much butter, too much sauce, too much wine, too much seasoning. He would fill his plate with mounds of tasteless salads, a slice of lean meat, a raw sliced vegetable, and assure the others (whose gold-rimmed plates were full of "poison") that they were digging their graves with their teeth. He would then watch them devour the "poison" with gusto, his own face expressing his wistfulness. Once, with pathetic ingenuousness, he had even invited some of his relatives to watch the administration of his insulin needle, but this had been declined.

Beyond his health and his needle, he had only one other passion, his daughter. For his son, Antoine, now Secretary of Bouchard & Sons, he had only fear and secret hatred and frightened detestation. At times, Antoine fascinated him, by his resemblance to his own father, Jules. On occasion, he had dreams when he saw the old Jules, subtle, smiling, sardonic, full of the old Machiavellian laughter. And then he would see it was not Jules at all, but Antoine, and would awake in a trembling sweat, and would avoid Antoine for days.

Yet, Antoine was all respect for his father, listened to him with courteous gravity by the hour whenever Armand would discourse upon diet, asked his advice upon minor matters connected with the Company, and would even amuse him by pungent comments on other members of the family. For Antoine was witty, a maker of epigrams, an accomplished conversationalist, personally elegant and debonair—the perfect portrait of the French gentleman of the old regime. There was a portrait of Jules in Armand's panelled library with the gaunt echoes, and sometimes Armand would stand before it, gazing at it with the sadness, the instinctive dread, the uneasiness and disquiet and aversion that he had felt for his father in the latter's lifetime. Then, with growing if obscure terror, he would mark out all Antoine's features in that dark narrow countenance with the subtle black eyes, the sleek small skull with its black hair, the mobile satirical mouth with its lifted left corner, the long slender nose with the sharp nostrils. All the intellectual qualities, the refined ruthlessness, the cruel delicacy, the living deviltry, the vital alertness, of that face had been reproduced in Antoine, even to the slanting eyebrows with their quizzical look. It was Mephisto's face, fascinating, sparkling with sadistic amusement, perceptive and lethal.

He had sighed with nameless relief when Antoine, some years before, had declared that he was not in the least interested in the Bouchards or their precious rascality or their net of subsidiaries. He was a poet, he had declared, with a smile that laughed at himself as much as others. ("God! Are we going to have another François in the family?" asked Christopher, remembering the tragic father of Henri, who had killed himself in the face of a raucous world.) So Antoine, after a brilliant career at Harvard, had studied in England, France and Germany, had travelled almost constantly, had spent well but discreetly, and seemed to have decided that the career of the accomplished and polished dilettante suited him admirably. He had published a thin volume of exceptionally ribald but intellectual poems, which had been hailed delightedly all over the world. He was a connoisseur of the various arts, but only with lightness, for his own amusement, and his taste was impeccable. At one time he gave it out candidly that he was considering the stage, at another time he was interested in futuristic painting, at still another time, in miniatures. His knowledge of music was superb, and he was a fine pianist. Even his vices were distinguished by a native elegance and refinement, his ladies as highly bred and accomplished as himself. He was still not married, though he was in his thirties.

This flower of the Bouchard family was very popular, even among his own people, which was no mean compliment to his graces of temperament and personality. The ladies of the family competed for his presence at their tables, for no party could be dull with Antoine Bouchard. They, the ladies, were all more or less a little in love with him, and even his male relatives would brighten with anticipation at his appearance. He was a ne'er-do-well, they would say, a fool probably, but he was decorative, and added distinction to the family.

Then, five years ago, this graceful, this accomplished, this vivacious and witty young man, had calmly announced that he intended to identify himself with the family fortunes. "Don't hurry," he said with a smile, and extending his hands in that remembered gesture of Jules'. "I'm not impatient. I'll recline placidly at home while you boys compete for my services. When you have something solid to offer me, bring it on a silver platter. The highest bidder gets the incomparable services of Antoine Bouchard, guaranteed to add color and liveliness to the dullest office."

They had not taken him seriously, at first. But Christopher had apparently done so. Within a week, he had written to Antoine, offering him the position of secretary in his own company, Duval-Bonnet, the airplane manufacturers in Florida. The position carried a most excellent salary. But Antoine had quickly refused. "I can't endure the climate," he had said, in an amiable note to his uncle. Then, still assuring each other that they were fools to pay the slightest attention to the brilliant and useless Antoine, they all made him offers. Francis, Jean, Alexander, Emile, even Nicholas, came forward discreetly, with suggestions. Hugo, the Senator from Pennsylvania, suggested politics. Antoine affected to investigate each friendly proposition, but finally regretfully declined. "He's not really interested," said Francis. "What could you expect?" Then Georges, the publisher in New York, made the young man an offer, which all were certain he would accept, considering his poems and his familiarity with the publishing business. To their surprise, this was also refused.

"He's full of nonsense," was the family verdict. "He likes to play with ideas."

But there was one who was not at all sure of this, and this one was Henri Bouchard, his brother-in-law, and cousin. And Henri, alone, made no offer. It was Henri who listened, and watched, with a tight inner smile, and silence.

For it had been Henri, in his vengeance, his greed and relentlessness, who had stripped Armand, father of Antoine, of his power, who, out of obscurity and impotence, had suddenly seized the throne of the Bouchards. Antoine had been very young at the time, a schoolboy, and therefore indifferent and unaware of the glacier that had moved inexorably over the family, a glacier rising from a hidden source, gathering force and terror in silence, irresistible in its strength and remorselessness. Antoine had grown to manhood, he had gone all about the world, pursuing his pleasure, smiling, full of *savoir faire*, graceful and indifferent, spending his own enormous fortune, showing interest in nothing. Then, all at once, languidly smiling, shrugging, spreading his hands, he had announced his casual interest in the affairs of the Bouchards.

So it was that Henri watched, grimly amused, tight of lip. So it was that he was not in the least surprised when Armand, diffident and confused, had accompanied his son to Henri's office and had announced that Antoine had finally decided that he might like to enter the "business." "He's thought over all their propositions," said Armand, with vague apology. "Nothing appeals to the boy. Then—then I suggested you, Henri. He said he's open to coercion."

They had sat at Henri's desk, father and son, facing the formidable man with the pale eyes and brutal heavy lips. Henri sat at Armand's old desk, before the vast expanse of mahogany, his square hand with the broad colorless nails grasping a pen. And Armand sat on the other side of this desk, the very desk where he had formerly made all the plans for Bouchard & Sons, almost a suppliant now, an impotent and sick old man, completely undone by this younger and more terrible reincarnation of Ernest Barbour.

And then Henri had slowly turned his eyes upon Antoine, sitting so gracefully, and with such a dark sparkling smile, beside his father, utterly at ease, full of elegance and composure, apparently only amused, apparently only casually and amiably interested in his father's supplication. He met Henri's eyes blandly, his own gleaming and full of light mirth, a cigarette in a long gold holder hanging from his thin dark fingers.

So! thought Henri, moving the pen about in his hands, very slowly, very precisely.

Antoine's smile widened. It was a very attractive smile, which ladies found irresistible, so charming and amiable it was.

"Nothing exhausting, you understand, Henri," he said, and he had Jules' mellifluous voice, full of musical undertones that threatened to break out into laughter. "Nothing too confining. I've got bonds and stock in Bouchard, and the subsidiaries, and God knows what else. Very confusin'."

Henri's mouth had compressed itself, until it was a pale slash in his pale face.

"Do you know anything at all about Bouchard?" he had

asked, his heavy and ponderous voice in granite contrast to Antoine's. "After all, you've been a kind of playboy, haven't you? What assurance have I that this isn't just a new and temporary interest that will peter out in a few weeks? This isn't a circus, you know; it isn't a carnival, with a carousel and a band, and dancers. I've got to know a little more."

At his tone, sardonic, contemptuous and patronizing, Armand was suddenly aroused from his sick sloth, his comatose inertia. He had raised his ponderous bulk in the chair where other supplicants had sat during his own tenure. For a moment or two there was a wild and enraged clamoring in him, a confusion, a fury. That was his chair, in which this frightful interloper now sat! It was his son, to whom this interloper addressed such condescending and taunting words! His son, who ought now to be sitting there, the power of the Bouchards! His son who had been so appallingly robbed of his birthright!

His fat face turned purple. The little jetty eyes glittered. A long trembling passed over his body, over his belly, like a visible ripple. He stammered, in a choked voice: "Henri, I'm sure that Antoine—realizes. He—he isn't a fool." He paused. His blood rushed to his head. He cried out: "This is my son! My son!"

His words expressed all his outrage, his sudden comprehension, his complete hatred and despair.

Henri turned his massive head and looked at him with Ernest Barbour's formidable face. He said nothing; he only stared expressionlessly. Armand had felt the impact of that look, like a murderous blow from a stony fist.

Then Antoine had laughed lightly. He had glanced at his father with humorous surprise. The old boy, then, must have some affection for him, under the instinctive fear and hatred and aversion. Armand caught that glance. His father had looked at him with just that mirthful surprise on his deathbed, when his son had incoherently, but with painful sincerity, protested that he did not want Jules to die. Armand was completely undone. He felt an enormous urge to weep. All the years, the foolish, fruitless, impotent, ruined years! he thought, confusedly. And now, he was back again where he had been, face to face with Jules, with Ernest Barbour, and he was tired and sick to death.

"Look here," said Antoine, "don't let's be sentimental. This is Henri's concern, Father. He has a right to ask questions. If he doesn't want me—and God knows there hasn't been much in my life to make anyone want me—that is his business."

Jules and Ernest! Armand passed his plump and shaking hand over his eyes, rubbed his nose with trembling frenzy. He looked at them, facing each other, and the past was one with the present. He wanted to get up, to run away into darkness and forgetfulness. What a most terrible family this was! What murderers, thieves and liars, what brigands and monsters! He saw it all now. He could not endure it.

"I'm a sick man. I don't know anything," he muttered aloud.

They had ignored him then. He had sat there, collapsed in his chair, his hands gripping the arms, his filmed eyes staring blindly before him. He knew nothing of what transpired; he only heard the echoes of Henri's calm voice, the light easy tones of Antoine's. Later, Antoine told him that Henri had made him an offer. He was to enter Bouchard & Sons as a sort of chief clerk, a secretary, in order to acquaint himself with the affairs of the Company. Henri had promised him an assistant secretaryship if he proved himself serious.

Three years later, Antoine was Secretary of Bouchard & Sons.

From the very beginning, the Bouchards were astounded and incredulous. "It won't last," they said. "He'll be off again soon." But it lasted, and Antoine was not off again. Moreover, to their amazement, he proved exceptionally brilliant, audacious and perceptive. Henri expressed his approval of his new Secretary. Slowly, during the years, an apparently great confidence grew up between them. Antoine never presumed; he gave way before all Henri's decisions. He suggested, but never insisted. Under that graceful and elegant exterior was a mind of flashing steel, as opposed to the iron club of Henri's mind. "The Neanderthal man and the dancing swordsman," said Christopher, watching intently through the years. "The man in bearskin, and the man with the embroidered cloak."

The Bouchards, very discreetly, tried to inveigle Antoine into a discussion of his inexorable relative. But Antoine was all loyalty, all admiring enthusiasm, all deference. What he thought, they did not know. But Henri knew. He was not audacious or too imaginative by nature. He was the man of force, and knew that men of force are the most powerful. But he understood what went on under Antoine's narrow dark skull with the sleek hair like a wet seal's. He knew that he had, in his office, the most ruthless enemy he had ever known. At times, he was highly and grimly amused, an amusement tinged with brutal disdain. He knew who was the stronger. In the meantime, it diverted him.

Between the two men was a subtle understanding, an admiration for each other. They did not "have to write books" to make themselves clear to each other. Insofar as it was possible for him to do so, Henri made a confidante of Antoine. He can wait, he would say to himself, of his wife's brother. He knew that during his own lifetime Antoine would dare nothing catastrophic or startling; at least, he believed he knew that the young man was completely aware of the hopelessness of any such action. But after his own death, what? Antoine was much younger than himself. Antoine would probably marry, and there would be sons. As for himself, he had no children, would never have them by Annette. The sense of dynasty was very powerful in Henri Bouchard. He lusted for sons, who would maintain his power when he was in the grave. His virility was like a great and tumultuous river restrained by a dam. He understood that Antoine never forgot that it was he who ought to be occupying Armand's throne. He understood that in Antoine burned an unremitting vengefulness and lust, and a determination. They were enemies. But they were also admiring friends. They hated each other. But they also had a deep if traitorous affection.

Antoine was a frequent visitor at Robin's Nest. Henri enjoyed his company vastly. Antoine never failed to entertain him. He even found himself becoming subtle in Antoine's presence, and they had secret jokes together. It surprised him that Antoine had a peculiar tenderness for his sister, Annette, a curious protectiveness, and that the Jesuitical face would insensibly soften at the sight of her. This was all the more strange because Annette, though apparently fond of her brother, exhibited a faint uneasiness in his presence, a chronic alarm.

Henri even looked about for a proper wife for Antoine. One of the family, if possible. Jean's little daughter, Dolores, perhaps, an apparently inoffensive young girl with an angelic fair face and a cloud of fair hair. Just the sort to appeal to the dark and devious Antoine. He often had Annette invite Dolores.

It pleased little Annette that Henri invariably expressed pleasure when he knew that Antoine was to be a guest at dinner. His heavy equanimity would lighten considerably, and that stony quality of his would become almost jocular.

He was the first on the cool terrace this evening to greet Armand and Antoine. Annette and Celeste and Peter and Christopher and Edith had not yet come down. However, Christopher soon made his appearance, and the four men had an extra drink while they waited. Henri, who had inherited his great-grandfather's aversion to alcohol, would drink only a small glass of sherry, with no enjoyment, while Christopher and Antoine drank whiskey-and-soda. Armand, watching them greedily, drank his fruit juice, and shook his head at the whiskey.

Between Christopher and Antoine was a deep and fundamental hatred, though they understood each other perfectly. Christopher was gloomily, as always, fascinated at the astounding resemblances between Antoine and his own father, Jules. Sometimes he stared at him for long minutes together, hearing again the voice that had been stilled since Armistice Day, seeing in every gesture, every turn of the sleek small head, every smile, every lift of the "devilish" eyebrows, the ghost of one he had hated and feared. When they talked together, it was like the light dancing of rapiers.

"How's Pete?" asked Antoine, with his dark and glittering smile. "I haven't seen him for weeks. Any improvement?"

"Considerable," said Henri. "He's getting restive."

"Still intransigent?"

Henri shrugged, glancing calmly at Christopher.

"Our white knight in silver armor is sharpening up his pike," said Christopher. "There are the sounds of trumpets. The tournament is about to begin."

"And Celeste?" said Antoine. "Is she tying the blue ribbon on his arm again, as usual?"

"What do you expect?" remarked Christopher, guardedly. He might ridicule his sister himself, but it annoyed him when another did so. He had loved her with profound passion; he had been her guardian after their father's death. Sometimes it appeared odd to him that Antoine should make poisonous thrusts at Celeste, he, who was so like his grandfather, Jules, the father of Celeste, whose one adoration had been his daughter.

"There's been a change in Celeste these last years," said Antoine, lighting one of his interminable cigarettes, with his gold monogram upon it. "I was only about sixteen when she married Pete, but I remember her quite clearly. There was a kind of 'virtue' about her, an innocence. If I wanted to be florid, I'd say that it was a sort of 'purity.' More of the mind than anything else. That's all gone. She's a hard piece now. She's a Bouchard at last. Now, I'm not insulting my little auntie. In a way, I'm complimenting her. But something's gone out of her, which is probably all to the good."

"I'd say she was bitter," said Armand, fumbling in his vest

pocket for his dietary list, and screwing up his fat and congested face in a momentary apprehension that he had forgotten it. His face relaxed; the list was there. "Embittered. That's the word for it. She was always such a soft little piece."

Christopher turned the stem of his cocktail glass in his delicate fingers. He said nothing. Henri was all blandness.

"Perhaps she's just grown up. She was almost a child when she married Peter. What did you expect? After all, she's over thirty. Not even very young."

"What a hell of a life she's had!" said Antoine, with pitiless humor, and a light laugh, as if the thought gave him a perverse pleasure. "It was to be expected, from all I've heard. Why didn't someone stop her from marrying him? What was the matter with you, Henri? You were engaged to her. Why did you let her go so easily? You aren't the type."

Henri only smiled. He accepted one of Antoine's cigarettes, though he had no real taste for tobacco. But he had found that smoking, the acceptance of another's courtesy, sometimes bridged an awkward moment. He allowed his Secretary to light it for him. For one instant, as the lighter flamed on his granite face, the eyes of the two men met, Antoine's subtly and cruelly amused, Henri's as expressionless as polished and colorless stone.

So, thought Antoine. He hasn't forgotten. The sphinx isn't so invulnerable, after all.

"Why bring up such a tactless subject?" asked Christopher. He allowed the butler to fill his glass again. "We've more interesting things to talk about, I'm sure."

"Especially as your own sister is now Henri's wife," said Armand, reprovingly. He turned his round cropped head, with its almost white hair, uneasily from one to the other. "Not a nice topic of conversation."

"By all means, let's converse about diet," said Christopher, with a smilingly vitriolic glance at his brother. "How's the pancreas, Armand?"

His ridicule was lost on the infatuated Armand, who appeared grateful. "My doctor has told me that I can reduce the insulin to one shot a day. Something new. Concentrated, I believe. Very convenient. No more fuss about asking for boiling water, when I go out to dinner. Sometimes people stared."

He beamed at them, as if he had accomplished a meritorious act, which they must applaud. Henri watched the curling of his smoke; Christopher drank quickly and deeply. Antoine smiled at them all.

The french door opened and Celeste appeared. They rose and greeted her. "Well, Auntie, you are as ravishing as ever," said Antoine, taking her hand and kissing her cheek with an air. He adored pretty women, even when they were his relatives. He studied her with cunning amusement. An assured piece. She sat down and accepted one of Antoine's cigarettes, and he lit it for her. Stony, he thought. But stone cracks under repeated blows. He closed his lighter with slow and thoughtful movements.

"Peter will be down directly," she said. Over those deep-blue eyes there was a kind of veil as she looked at them. "He won't need his day-nurse any longer, he believes," she added, though no one had asked about her husband. "He thinks it silly, and I do, too. Miss Tompkins may go the end of the week. He sleeps well at night, he says, and hardly coughs at all. Tomorrow, he wants to go for a drive."

She leaned back in her chair, and her white hands tightened only a little on the arms. She smiled. She looked at Christopher.

"You've been very bad, Christopher. You agitated him terribly this morning. You might have been kinder, considering everything."

"Good God, is he a child?" asked Christopher. "You know very well that he's argumentative. He always was belligerent and accusing. Then, he never liked me. What did I do to him? He asked me some questions, and I answered them. Celeste, you aren't his mama, you know."

"You forget how ill he's been," she replied. "Well, never mind. You two never were congenial." For all her calm, there was a pent restlessness about her. Antoine, watching her closely, saw that she never looked directly at Henri, who appeared bored. He had averted his head. He was looking out over the long roll of green grass, which was turning mysterious in the twilight. The sky was heliotrope, the tops of the great trees burnished in the failing western sun. The penetrating sweetness of the rose-garden came to them in the warm evening wind. The birds whistled with melancholy notes in the high branches. There was a great and shadowy peace all about them, yet Antoine, with his acute perception, knew there was no peace on this quiet terrace.

"Is he going to write again?" he asked.

But Celeste only moved her head slightly.

"Another exposé of the Bouchards," mused Antoine. " 'The War-Mongers.' What does he think we are doing now? He'd be surprised."

At this, Henri turned to him, and something in that immobile broad face, impelling and implacable, caused Antoine to pause. There were times when he forgot the power of Henri Bouchard, when he could chaff his brother-in-law and impudently challenge him. But he had the infuriating impression that these occasions were only by Henri's consent. An agile monkey might torment a lion, when the latter felt indifferent or indulgent. But there were other times when it was extremely perilous. This was one of those times, Antoine saw. He subsided. But his fine fingernails pressed against his palms.

"Nothing about the family would surprise Peter," remarked Celeste, bitterly. She stopped, abruptly. Peter and Annette were coming out upon the terrace, Annette laughing softly, Peter walking slowly and with deliberate firmness. Behind them appeared the thin dark face of Edith, and her smart frock.

Chairs were drawn up for the ladies, and Antoine, with many gestures, drew one also for Peter, whose sunken face flushed at this ostentatious courtesy. Antoine gracefully asked about his health. The silent Edith accepted a cocktail. Annette began to prattle in her sweet and breathless voice.

"Isn't it nice, Henri?" she asked. "Celeste and Peter have decided to stay with us a little longer, until they build their new house. I had such a time persuading the darlings," she added, with a fond glance at her young aunt. "She believed she was 'imposing' upon us. Now, wasn't that absurd?" She looked at them all, radiantly.

So, thought Antoine, Celeste wants to run. Very interesting. In the neat dossier of his mind he entered another fact.

Dinner was announced, and they all rose. Antoine felt that he had gathered much diverting and useful information in the past five minutes, information which he believed might someday undo Henri Bouchard.

CHAPTER XIII

Armand set up his list near his plate, and anxiously consulted it whenever the butler held a dish at his left. He would adjust his glasses, peer forward to study the list, after a reproachful glance at the dim candles, and then either accept what was proffered, or shake his head. The windows stood open; a cool and scented breeze invaded the charming room. Somewhere, a thrush sang to the approaching night. Over the garden wall a crescent moon rose, sweeping like a silver scythe against the electric blue of the evening sky.

Annette was all happiness. It was beautiful to her, to have her relatives about her. She dwelt on each fondly, from her place at the foot of the table. Never had she felt such peace and contentment. That moment against the door of her room was forgotten. Somewhere, out in space, the abyss waited, but here all was candlelight, flowers, the shimmer of silver, the sparkling of water in crystal glasses, the faces of those she loved. Sometimes she leaned forward to study her father's list with him; he sat at her right. As her bright soft hair caught the candlelight, and her gentle rosy mouth pursed in profound concentration, Armand would forget his diet to scrutinize that sweet and fragile profile with a strange and desperate aching in his frightened heart.

"Papa," she said, reproachfully, "it says you can have fruit salad. You refused it. And such delicious fruit, too."

"But cantaloupe disagrees with me," he replied.

"And fish. You can have that too. But you didn't take it."

"Not when there's meat. Too much protein."

Peter was absorbed in some somber meditation of his own. He sat near Edith, who watched him with considerable thoughtful sadness. How much he had suffered all his life! she thought. But he was one of those who are born in pain, live in sorrow, and die in anguish. It was better for them to die quickly; it was even better if they were never born. Die

117

soon, poor Peter, she thought. That is the most merciful thing for you.

She saw his tired hands, listlessly holding the silver. His thin cheek had a febrile flush upon it. He struggled to restrain impulses to cough. Celeste watched him closely, as always, and as she did so, the worn expression about her eyes increased, and the corners of her lips sank deeply with a drawn look. It was she who filled his plate silently, though he shook his head automatically. And then, at her anxious look, he would smile at her briefly and tenderly, and obey her silent urgings.

It was Antoine, and Christopher, who alone saw how Henri watched these two, without appearing to do so, and how the brutal somberness increased on his face. Christopher observed this with inner satisfaction, and Antoine smiled internally.

Celeste had feared a certain constraint after the morning's affair, but Christopher was amiability itself, especially to Peter, who responded with reluctant curtness. Edith was distrait; she watched her husband with a curious line between her nut-brown eyes, and then her glance would touch her brother quickly. Annette chattered sweetly; Armand studied his list, and admonished his daughter about the probable amount of albumen in her parfait. "But I'm sure there are no eggs in it, dear," she replied. He tasted the delicious mixture cautiously, shook his head, laid down his spoon with resolute finality. "Certainly, there are eggs," he said. Annette lost her appetite.

In the meantime, Christopher had become engaged in a conversation about gasoline with Henri. "We are experimenting with a new airplane engine at Duval-Bonnet," he said, "which promises to be exciting. But it requires a high test gasoline beyond any which has now been developed. We have, of course, been using the principle of catalysis. But one of our chemists thinks he has developed a fluid catalytic cracker, which, as you might know, is really a very fine powder, and can be piped and pumped and handled exactly like a liquid. You may not think that very dramatic, or important, but I assure you it is one of the most spectacular discoveries of this century."

"Have you used it in the gasoline you employ in your planes?" asked Henri, with an interest apparently out of proportion to the subject. But Peter suddenly raised his head alertly, and listened with intense eagerness.

"Yes." Christopher paused, and looked at Henri significantly. "We've built forty crackers, full size. It was an expensive experiment. It succeeded."

"And the engine design?" asked Henri, casually. "To use the new gas?"

"We have an offer. An exceptionally splendid offer. We'll probably accept it. The offer includes the new cracking process."

Peter laid down his fork. He looked at Henri, and Christopher.

"Would this famous offer come from Germany?" he asked.

They turned to him, Christopher with arch surprise, Henri with that immobile look of his.

"Good God! You certainly have an intense imagination!" exclaimed Christopher with a light laugh. "No, the offer did not come from Germany. It might, you know, have come from our own blessed Government. That's all I can tell you."

Henri smiled a little. He took out his cigarette case, tamped a cigarette on the cover, lit it. Through the smoke, his eyes gleamed like cold agates.

You lie, thought Peter, with desperation.

Christopher, after a long smile at Peter, turned to Henri again. "As you know, we've been experimenting with butadiene—adding styrene and various other things. We've hopes of it. That it will eventually free us from the East Indies' rubber. There's a lot of work to be done. You ought to see our new plant, and laboratories. There's chemical history in the making, there."

"Why," said Peter, "is it necessary for you to experiment with this—this butadiene? You aren't expecting aggression from Japan in the Indies, are you?"

Christopher laughed again. But Peter's eyes were ablaze; a muscle jerked in his cheek.

"Christ!" said Christopher, softly. "You are a monomaniac, Pete. We expect nothing, not even a war in Europe. We aren't interested." He repeated, even more softly: "We aren't interested. At the present time, our sole interest is in making America self-sufficient."

Peter said nothing for a moment, then he spoke with intense quietness: "I've heard that Germany has already perfected a process for synthetic rubber. It wouldn't be your process, would it, Christopher?"

Christopher was quite amazed, and overwhelmingly amused. "How should I know? After all, brains aren't confined to America. It is possible that German chemists are also experimenting."

Peter's face was grim, as cold as ice. "I have heard it is called the 'American' process. Two of your men were in Germany eight months ago, Chris, and they spent six weeks with German chemists."

For an instant the bright metallic mask over Christopher's delicate features dimmed. He met Peter's eyes, but Peter was indomitable. He returned Christopher's look with bitterness and contempt, and great desolation.

"You are misinformed, Pete," said Christopher at last, very gently. "You've been had. No one from Duval-Bonnet has been in Germany. Who told you that?"

"Their names," continued Peter, as if he had not heard, "were Carl Brouser and Frederick Schultzmann. Would they be familiar names to you?"

Christopher smiled. But his fingers clenched about his fork, as if it was a weapon. Henri dropped the hand with the cigarette, and looked slowly from Peter to Christopher. The smoke curled from between his square strong fingers in a long spiral. Antoine, for some reason, found Henri more interesting in these tense moments than Christopher. Edith, lifting her dark head alertly, stared at her husband, her lips pinched, and Celeste could only sit in silence with her violet eyes shining brilliantly in the lamplight. Armand, oblivious, was studying his list with the aid of his anxious daughter. Their heads were together.

"Brouser and Schultzmann have never been away from Duval-Bonnet for more than a few days, for the past four years," said Christopher. "Someone has been telling you fairy tales."

Now Henri spoke, and he looked only at Christopher. "Have they?" he asked, with profound quietness.

Was it fear that betrayed itself in the light eyes of Christopher, thought Antoine, and defensive hatred? For a moment, he was speechless.

"Have they?" repeated Henri, in a louder voice, but still quietly. However, there was something terrible and violent in his tone.

"Good God! What is this? Certainly, it is a lie. Carl and Fred are our most trusted chemists. They have families in Florida, also. They are American citizens. Like most gifted chemists, they are absorbed in their work. They spend twenty hours a day, sometimes, in the laboratories. Nice chaps. Devoted. Geniuses."

"Very interesting," commented Henri, breaking rudely into Christopher's speech. "Nevertheless, I'm not in the least interested in their families or their poetic consecration to Duval-Bonnet. I only want to know if they were in Germany, as Pete says."

He did not move; the smoke from his cigarette rose tranquilly between his fingers. However, he gave an impression of cold and colossal violence as he sat motionless in his chair.

Christopher apparently was astounded, and could only stare at his brother-in-law. Still looking at him, Henri said to Peter: "Pete, where did you get this information?"

Peter turned to him, and studied him with frowning bewilderment. He saw that large and stony profile, with its deadly lack of expression. Was it possible that Henri was acting, that this was a play to throw him, Peter, off? But, when he glanced at Christopher, and saw the spectral tightness of his mouth, the drawn and glittering eyes, he was not so sure.

He said, very slowly: "I've ways of finding out. I won't tell you, Henri. It would endanger the men who told me. The Social-Democratic Germans who form the Underground in Germany. Two of them are employed in a chemical concern in the Ruhr. That is all I can say. You've probably heard of the Gestapo, haven't you?"

"I tell you," said Christopher, with unusual emotion, "that it is a lie! Brouser and Schultzmann have never been away from their posts for more than a day or two." He paused. His delicate nostrils flared. "I'm positive of their loyalty. It is possible, however, that there are spies, even in Duval-Bonnet, but I can hardly credit this."

"Brouser and Schultzmann were in Germany. Photographs were shown me," said Peter.

"You have those photographs?" asked Henri, still watching Christopher.

"No. Certainly not. But I could identify the men if I saw them."

A dark purple vein rose in one of Christopher's bloodless temples, and beat visibly. Edith had turned very pale. She stared at her husband with dilated eyes.

"It is easy to get photographs of anyone," said Christopher. "To fake photographs, too. It is very possible that your ridiculous spy obtained such photographs directly from Florida, and passed them off to you dramatically as being taken in Germany."

"Goering was in the background. His hand was on Schultzmann's shoulder," said Peter, quietly.

Christopher burst out laughing. "Christ! Do you think, if

121

that were true, that such photographs would dare be taken, dare be distributed, dare be made accessible to anyone?"

"It was a secret photograph, taken by one of the Underground Germans. He had developed a camera small enough to be enclosed in a ring. I might add that there is no need to search for that camera. It is destroyed now, or successfully hidden. The photograph was shown me, and one or two others, for a certain purpose. The spy wished this information to be laid before American authorities."

Christopher, though still smiling, struck his clenched fist lightly on the table. But his eyes were malignant as he looked at Peter.

"It was a faked photograph. I insist that it was. Any amateur could do it."

"The spy," said Peter, "talked freely with Schultzmann and Brouser. Don't have your friends look for him, however. You won't find him."

There was a sinister silence around the table. Armand, feeling the portentousness in the atmosphere, forgot his list. He looked slowly at them all, apprehensively silent. He had not heard the conversation; he only knew that something quite terrible was happening. He moistened his dry fat lips.

Then Henri moved a little, and smiled. It was like a basilisk smiling.

"All nonsense, of course," he said, serenely. "I'm sorry, Pete, but the dramatics aren't convincing. If Brouser and Schultzmann were really there, Chris would be the one to know."

Christopher drew an inaudible breath into lungs that had been tightly compressed. "I most assuredly would know. However, I'll question the boys very closely, when I return." He smiled amiably. "What damned nonsense."

Peter thought: Is it possible Henri didn't know, that he is enraged, that he will do something to find out? And if he didn't know, why does he care? He is tied up with the I.G. Farbenindustrie; it would be the most natural thing in the world for him to arrange to give the Germans the cracking process and the design for the new planes—for a round sum. It would be natural that Christopher had his approval. Under the circumstances, why should it enrage him, make him look at Christopher in that deadly way? They've been doing those things for a century—the Bouchards.

He was enormously perplexed. It was not in the nature of things that Henri didn't know, that his approval had not been obtained first in this frightful transaction. It had been

Peter's conviction, from the first, that the power of the Bouchard family had arranged this matter. Who would dare do anything in the family without Henri's consent?

But Henri was regarding Christopher with that cold and appalling steadfastness, even as he said: "I agree it is nonsense." He stirred in his chair, as if to rise.

Christopher was silent. But under his hooded eyelids his eyes were like a serpent's.

Why should the implacable, the monstrous Henri care, so long as great profits were assured? thought Peter. Unless he had other plans?

Then Henri turned to Edith, and said tranquilly: "How is Galloway coming along with that arm of yours? Is it definitely arthritis?"

Edith started. She stared at her brother, bemused. Her thin lips were livid. It was a moment or two before she could answer, and then she said: "No. It isn't arthritis, thank God. A strain. At tennis, a few months ago."

All at once the hard brown of her eyes was dim with tears. She rose, glanced at Celeste and Annette, who rose also. "Girls, let's powder our noses," she said.

Peter rose also. He was trembling so greatly that he felt extremely ill. "I will have to be excused," he murmured. And left the room.

After the women had gone, Henri was silent while port was poured into glasses, and cigars lit.

Then he looked at Christopher, and said: "You are an accomplished liar. I've always known that. I still don't know if you are lying. You can deceive even me." His hand lifted a small salt-cellar and closed about it. His pale eyes studied Christopher in the candlelight, and there was something frightful in their expressionlessness. "I hope you aren't lying. It would be very bad for you, if you were. You know that."

Christopher flushed, and his face became evil with his rage and impotence. And with fear, thought the deeply absorbed Antoine. But more than anything, his humiliation at Henri's tone and manner poisoned him.

"Duval-Bonnet is mine," he said, in a neutral voice. "I want you to remember that, Henri. I made it; I built it; I have it."

"That is interesting," said Henri, with a smile. "Have you forgotten I own thirty-five percent of the stock?" He puffed at the cigar a moment, removed it from his mouth, regarded it with profound distaste. "Outside of that, I can ruin you, you know. I can do a good job of ruining. Anybody. In a few months, it will be very dangerous should the Government know about the planes and the cracking process. Leavenworth is a very disagreeable place, I understand. Later, if we are in the war, I shouldn't wonder if firing squads might not be employed."

Christopher's impotent humiliation made every vein in his temples swell. "Good God, are you fool enough to listen to the drivelling of that imbecile? Do you take his word against mine?" He thrust his chair away from the table. Now he was beside himself. "You know what he is. Yet, you have the audacity to listen to him, the stupidity! You know the tripe he writes. You know what he's after. Everything is grist to his mill, lies and half-truths and other idiocies. He will say anything, do anything. Look here, send an investigator down to Duval-Bonnet. Have him check on Brouser and Schultz-mann." He paused, almost choking in his restrained wrath. "I'm not without resources of my own. If that idiot should publish a calumny, I'll sue him. I'll take every penny away from him."

Henri was silent. Behind that broad stony brow he was thinking rapidly. All at once he began to smile, easily. But Antoine saw his eyes, and grinned to himself.

"Why all the excitement?" asked Henri. He pushed his chair away from the table. "Let's forget all this shall we?"

He rose. Christopher and Antoine rose also. They had forgotten Armand, who had been staring at them all as if fascinated and horrified. His swollen face was lard-like in color. He could not rise. He could only sit in his chair, with his hands clutching his list.

"Forget it?" asked Christopher, coldly. "That is easy to say. Do you think I can forget your threats so easily? Your contemptible threats?"

Henri was unperturbed. "I don't threaten lightly. I'm not a bully, I hope. I only like to have things straight. I only like to know what is going on. And somehow, there are certain things I don't like. I hope these 'lies' aren't one of them."

He put his hand on Christopher's shoulder. "Whenever you have a plan in mind, let me know, will you? Then we'll all be satisfied. But the plans, I'm sure, don't include letting the Nazis have plane designs, cracking processes, and synthetic rubber. That's all. Shall we find the ladies and see if they have anything more interesting to talk about?"

He walked away from them. Christopher and Antoine looked at each other. They did not even glance at the paralyzed Armand, sitting like a lump of putty in his chair. Antoine raised his eyebrows humorously at Christopher who, balked and infuriated, stared back at him.

Christopher did not speak. But slowly, he began to smile. He touched Antoine's arm, and the two of them followed Henri out onto the terrace. Antoine began to hum musically under his breath.

Christopher thought: I've got to get away immediately. I ought to be able to get them on long distance.

CHAPTER XIV

Celeste spent an unusually exhausting half-hour with Peter, before she could persuade him to go to bed. He was highly excited, confused and vehement.

"I tell you, there's something here I don't understand!" he cried. "There was this morning—and now tonight. They were fairly obvious, a few years ago. What is it all about? They said they didn't want war. I believe that now. Things have fallen into a pattern. Hugo worked to invoke the Neutrality Act against Spain, when he first became Assistant Secretary of State. You'd have thought he would have opposed that—I know that by nature the Bouchards would be fascists. But they'd never overlook profits, and opportunities to stimulate wars. They've been very ardent about nationalism, for a purpose. But there's something here." He paused, and a stark expression of horror stood in his eyes as he gazed at his wife. "I'm thinking of France," he muttered, in a choked voice.

Celeste gave him a strong dose of sedative. "You'll be thinking of nothing, if you keep on injuring yourself with speculations like this," she said. "Wait until you've thoroughly recovered, dear."

"What is Henri up to?" he continued, restlessly, not having heard her. "I can see they're afraid of him. He rules them like a dictator. What is it they're trying to hide from him?"

"I'm sure you are imagining things," said Celeste, soothingly, fanning herself with her handkerchief. The evening was sultry, almost unbearable. She lifted her arms a little, as if to aid her breathing. All at once, she was stifled with her sadness, her imprisonment, her hopelessness. Peter threatened to have a bad night. She could go nowhere; she could not escape even for a few hours, and at a time when escape became the most exigent necessity of her life. If Peter would only sleep for an hour or two, it might be possible to wander through the grounds, sit quietly under some great tree, and be alone. She glanced at her watch. It was almost ten. She had been over an hour in an attempt to calm Peter, who insisted upon talking with gathering confusion and despair. Annette would have retired. Armand had left at half-past nine, Christopher and Edith had accepted an invitation for the evening, and Antoine had joined them. No doubt Henri had left, also. The great house was filled with warm and rustling quiet. It would be beautiful in the garden, with the silver curve of the moon over the cool trees.

But Peter, with his terrible preoccupations, saw nothing of her weary face and the strained brightness of her eyes. He quarrelled with her when she insisted upon helping him to bed. Once or twice he even struck away her patient hands. But she pressed her lips grimly together and refused to be put aside, to listen. When he was once in bed, she would not bring him his writing pad and his pen. When her hands touched his flesh, she felt its thin heat. At last, she was forced to call Miss Tompkins, who came in with a sharp professional smile, and, after a quick glance at Celeste's drained and sinking face, ordered her out of the room.

"I'll read to Mr. Bouchard," she promised. "He'll soon sleep. Invalids who are recovering are often fractious." She plumped up Peter's pillows, and he glowered at her despairingly.

"What shall I read to you?" she asked him brightly.

"Nothing. Just go away," he answered her, with tired rudeness. "I've things to say to Mrs. Bouchard."

The nurse shook her finger at him archly. "Now, we're being very bad." He looked at her with disgust. "Mrs. Bouchard is very tired. It's a nasty hot night. We mustn't overwork the little lady, must we?"

For the first time Peter looked at Celeste and saw her.

She hesitated, and approached the bed again. "Perhaps it would be better if I read to Mr. Bouchard," she said. "I've nothing else to do, and he prefers me to read to him."

Peter was silent. He saw how strained she was. He saw

126

that she had become quite thin, and that her luminous pallor had been reduced to white exhaustion. There were dark indentations about her eyes. He was filled with fear for her, and remorse. He made himself smile.

"No, darling. Do go away, and rest. I'll be perfectly all right."

He held out his hot and tremulous hand to her, and she took it. He kissed her lingeringly. I'm killing her, he thought. I'm obstinate and selfish. I expect too much of her. I've made her my servant, my audience, my slave, my confidante. It's too much. But, who else have I?

He was overwhelmed by his loneliness, and his desolation. He felt quite ill again, and lay back on his pillows and closed his eyes.

Celeste slipped through the lamp-lit silence of the house, emerged upon the terrace. It was strange how her heart was beating, with such stifling pain and despondency. She stood on the terrace a moment, looking over the dark and murmurous grounds. A wind was blowing through the tops of the shadowy trees, but no breeze moved across the earth, which flowed with a pale and spectral light that could not come from the thin edge of the moon. The sky had a curious hot pallor about it, against which the pointed tops of distant poplars moved in sharp black outline. The stars were dim, though no clouds touched the brilliant curve of the moon, and the scent of disturbed grass, roses and leaves, rolling in advancing and receding tides towards Celeste and away from her, presaged a coming storm. Sometimes, against the dark and ghostly sky the plumes of a willow tossed, and then subsided, like the giant skirts of a ballet dancer, and sometimes there was a silent flash of lightning illuminating some restless backdrop of foliage.

Celeste knew that in the rose-gardens there were white iron benches on which to sit under the bordering trees. She began to walk over the grass. Suddenly the crickets began a vociferous chorus, and from the lily pond far to her left came the baritone answer of bullfrogs. Fireflies darted at her feet, in the close air all about her, and there were the spectral brushings of tiny wings near her. The wind was coming closer to the earth; she felt its hot breath on her damp cheeks. It lifted tendrils of hair from her neck, molded her thin skirts about her thighs. But it did not cool or refresh.

The roses were in full lush bloom, and she saw the confused blur of their whiteness in the dark dusk of the night, and smelled their over-powering fragrance. She found a seat under a tree, and leaned back, overcome with her weariness. But it was beautiful to hear no voices, and to know that there was no one here but herself. The night, the silence, the chorus of crickets, the deep mysterious murmur of the trees, the sudden flash of the voiceless lightning, the isolation and uneasy peace, the air of the solemn and mystical night, gave her quietness and sanctuary.

It was so seldom that she dared think. She kept her thoughts grimly at bay, fending them off as one fends off raging dogs with a whip. Almost always, she was afraid to be alone, because of those fang-toothed thoughts. Even when she did think, she would allow her mental wanderings to become mere shadows of emotion, refused to face them.

As she sat there in the darkness, she said to herself: I'm old. And, somehow, I don't care. It doesn't matter to me whether I live or die. There is nothing for me, nothing in all the world. I must understand at last that Peter will not live long. I must face it. How shall I face it? What will there be for me then? An empty and useless life. I'm drained. There's nothing in me. Nothing to console and fill up the endless hours and days and nights. Nothing matters, or promises to matter.

She saw everything so clearly now. She had lost the capacity to feel keenly. A vast dull inertia pervaded her. She lifted her hands and looked at them in the wandering pallor of the flowing sky-light. They were empty and useless. She had no desire to fill them. All at once their emptiness seemed part of her very soul. Her undesire was deathlike. She could feel nothing in her heart or her mind that could inspire life or joy or pleasure or usefulness. She was formed of substanceless mist. And in that mist was a core of pain and sorrow. She turned away from herself as one turns away from a heavy weariness, with sickness and aversion.

All these years she had helped and nursed Peter, and wandered with him. Until recently, she had been one with him in his terror and indignation and despair. She had been his echo. Now, she was not even an echo. She simply did not care. She wanted to lie down, to press herself into the earth, to die, to forget. For she knew that she still dared not think, that if she really allowed herself to think she would be destroyed, and others with her. The core of pain and sorrow in her began to glow, to become incandescent like a threat of blazing and destroying fire.

She felt her involuntary tears on her cheeks, but did not wipe them away. Years ago, she had sat like this, alone in the night, and all about her had been the distant thunder of promise, the promise of her life. She had been so young then, so ardent, so passionate. And so innocent, and stupid. So stupidly eager and lustful of living. She could remember how she felt, like the memory of a dream. This wind, this dark richness of night, ominous though it was, this tide of rose-scent and fragrance of warm grass, were memories, rather than present events. "I see, but do not feel, how beautiful it is," she quoted to herself. She sat, not in the present, but in a memory of the past. In herself, there was only windless chaos, formless nothingness.

How could one endure the endless coming years of one's life, feeling only the memory of emotion, smelling nothing but the memories of a dead hope, experiencing nothing but recollections of vanished events? Whatever was to happen in the world of tomorrow held no significance for her, not even pain, not even terror. She would be a ghost in that world, desiring nothing but death, unmoved by any shape of catastrophe. She was already dead.

The pain in her became huge. But, I am not old! she cried to herself, soundlessly, in the last frantic movements of despair at the threat of dissolution. There ought to be a promise of joy in the future, or at least, a promise of active life, of passionate insecurity. But even as she thought this, she did not care.

The wind in the trees increased like a multitude of hoarse and sinister voices. She listened. She had heard those voices with Peter, once, in such a dark garden and dark night, and they had solemnly excited her. She had clung to him, and had turned her face with courage to the voices, defying them, lifting her breast against them. Now, they only vaguely frightened her. The lightning was becoming stronger, and mingled with the wind was the hollow echo of approaching thunder. But the brilliance of the moon did not lessen. Now the scent of grass and flowers was smothering, as blade and petal stirred with increasing uneasiness.

She looked towards the house. It was hidden in trees, except for one far-distant window, gleaming with pale yellow light. Was that Peter's window? She half rose from the bench, with the old accustomed habit of going to him when he could not sleep. But even as she stood up, the light went out. The great mansion was now not even a shadow in the night.

She stood there, under the trees, her hands fallen to her sides, her face as still as stone. She did not move. She had no desire even to take a single step.

There was a sharper rustling near her. She turned her head

listlessly in its direction. A sleepless squirrel perhaps, or a snake, or a hopping toad. The rustling came nearer, and she had the sudden and inexplicable sense that someone was approaching her, though she could see nothing. Some instinct out of the primordial wells of instinct made her stand perfectly still, her ears suddenly preternaturally sharp, her eyes probing the darkness. The rustling stopped. Yet the sense that someone was near her was keener than ever.

She knew, too, that whoever it was had felt her own presence, and was as warily silent, feeling for her in the atmosphere. She felt her heart begin a quickened thumping, as of fear. But, this was absurd. Some servant, perhaps, unable to sleep in the hot night. Or, perhaps a marauder. But Robin's Nest was surrounded by high walls, patrolled by two watchmen, with dogs.

She started violently as a low voice said: "Is someone there?"

It was Henri's voice, calm and slow as ever, though alertly interested.

Celeste did not move. But all at once a sheath of fire enwrapped her, so that she felt incandescent, burning in the darkness, as visible as a pillar of flame. She felt that her face had become an oval of light. Her heart began a tumultuous beating. Suddenly the lifeless confusion of the night, all meaningless sound, all heavy inertia and appalling formlessness, took on a wild and universal significance, became as close and roaring as stormy breakers, and was all imminence. She had become the core of the vortex, and her hearing, all her senses, were assailed by tumult. She experienced an awareness of herself such as she had never experienced before, and a consciousness of everything about her.

She could not have spoken even if she had wished to. She could only stand there, blown upon by strong winds. A flash of lightning lit up the sky, and revealed her there, in the cave under the tree, motionless, as still as the trunk of the tree behind her.

"Celeste!" exclaimed Henri, with genuine surprise. Now it was dark again. The wind suddenly fell, though the dim roaring stirred the top-most branches. A hot breath ran over the grass. The thunder murmured far off in space. Celeste could feel, rather than see, that Henri was approaching her. Now she saw his dark silhouette against the lighter darkness.

She forced herself to speak, and her voice was faint: "It was hot. I came out for some air."

She moved now, and was unaware that she had taken a step towards him. It was an involuntary step, and her hands rose like shells upon a wave, then dropped. Her whole body was like a shell also, as fragile as a puff of down, effortlessly blown. A dreamlike state fell upon her. Whether Henri sensed this or not, he gave no indication. He only stood and peered at her, seeing the floating white oval of her face.

"Yes," he said, very quietly. "It *is* hot. I came out, too, to see if I could get a breath of air."

He came closer to her. "You aren't going in? Let's sit down a few minutes. I think there is a storm coming. It's bound to get cooler. The house is like a furnace."

She found herself sitting on the bench again, and he was beside her. The dreamlike sweetness, mingled with a nameless terror, increased within her. She was becoming languidly numb, and resistless. She saw a dim flash in the darkness. Henri was opening his cigarette case, and extending it to her. With fingers that had no feeling, she took a cigarette. When he lit it for her, the flame blinded her eyes, so that she closed them momentarily. He saw the full whiteness of her lids, her clear pallor, the sad vague redness of her lips. He lit a cigarette for himself, and leaned back on the bench, and stared into the darkness.

"I wanted to have an air-conditioning plant installed, but it seemed foolish, considering that we were always away for the summer," he said, in the most casual and indifferent of tones. "Now, I think I shall do it."

She heard his voice, but not his words. Now all about her was a strong warmth and poignancy, a languor and an odd beating that appeared to come from the air itself. She was trembling somewhat. She asked herself nothing, thought nothing, was only experiencing. She drew a long deep breath.

"Yes," she murmured. The glowing tips of their cigarettes were like fireflies in the hot gloom. Her lips formed words, and she listened to them vaguely as to the voice of a stranger. "Has Annette gone to bed?"

"Yes, long ago. And Peter?"

"He was restless, and I left him with Miss Tompkins. I saw his light go out."

He heard her voice, and noted its dreamlike toneless quality. He did not answer. They sat in silence. Celeste's breathing was becoming more difficult. Her body suffused with heat. Emotion filled her so that every vein sang and hummed, and she heard a prolonged roaring in her ears. But she had no desire to move. She wanted only to sit like this, forever, never moving again, only feeling.

"I think he is much better," said Henri at last, quietly. "The rest is doing him good."

Celeste's confusion increased. She forced herself to understand Henri's words. Of whom were they speaking? Peter! She sat up, rigidly, sick with a kind of shock. Now she was completely aware of herself, of Henri, and full of dread and sharp terror. She made a motion as if to get up, and he caught her arm, though he appeared not to move. She felt the strong grasp of his fingers. They slowly descended, had taken her hand. Her own hand was trembling and burning.

"No," he said. "Stay here with me for a few minutes. What are you afraid of?"

She was speechless, her heart swelling. If I stand, she thought, I'll fall. I'll surely fall!

"I've never had a minute with you alone," he said, still grasping her hand firmly. "After all, we are relatives, you know. You're my guest, yet I only catch glimpses of you, going in or coming out. Like a ghost."

She could not speak. She could feel the sweet and heavy languor stealing over her again, and she tried to resist it.

At last she faltered: "There are so many people to see. I've been away so long."

"Too long," he said, gently.

He released her hand. Immediately an appalling desolation fell over her, a sense of loss, acute and aching. He was leaning forward, but away from her, his elbows on his knees, his quiet hand lifting the cigarette to his lips.

"Do you remember a day, a very long time ago, when you first came here, and we all walked in this rose-garden?" he asked. "That was when Edith and I came home. Old Thomas was with us then. He died in Florida, when he was with Edith and Christopher. It was a hot afternoon when I first saw you. You came with your mother and Christopher, and you were such a little girl then. Wasn't it in July, 1925?"

"I think so," she whispered. Her hand was aching from a grasp that was no longer upon it. Her heart was devoured by a strange hunger.

He laughed softly. "Such a little girl! With a big hat and a white dress. You even had blue ribbons! What a romanticist Chris was, in those days, I couldn't believe you, when I saw you. He must have kept you under glass. You were a little girl, too, unbelievably nice." He paused. "You've changed, Celeste. It's not just that you're older. It's something else."

I must go away from here, at once! she thought. But she

did not stir. She felt his strength, his power, though he was so still, and they kept her motionless. The emanations from his body and his personality were like heavy chains upon her arms and legs, and she could not struggle against them.

Now she felt, rather than saw, that he was turning to her. "What is it, Celeste? What's happened to you?"

She pressed her fingers tightly together, and spoke almost incoherently: "I've grown older, that's all. I'm not a child any more. I'm not even very young now. Does anyone remain the same?"

He was silent for a few minutes. She felt his eyes upon the dim shadow of her face.

"It's something else," he repeated, at last, and she started at the sound of his voice in the windy darkness. "You had some quality of freshness and simplicity, of faith and strength. It's all gone. I'm sorry about that."

She did not answer. Ponderous silence was all about them, except for the wind. Even the crickets were still. A long rolling passed far in the distance. A sulphurous smell ran over the invisible grass.

"You should have married me," he said, and his tone was most casual, and very light.

She could move now. She cried out: "You mustn't say that! You must never say that again—" And could say nothing more. But her throat tightened; tears sprang to her eyes; they fell over her cheeks. Her heart was strangling in her breast.

"Why not?" he asked, reasonably. "After all, it doesn't matter now." He paused. He took her hand again, and held it tightly. "It doesn't matter now. Does it?"

She tried to pull her hand away, then surrendered it limply. "No," she whispered.

"We got what we wanted," said Henri, in an amused tone. "You—Peter. I—Annette. We're very happy now. And contented. We ought to congratulate each other."

"Don't!" she cried again, as if in unbearable pain.

"Why not? It's true, isn't it?"

She wrenched her hand from his. She put both her hands to her face a moment, pressing them against her eyes. She was sick with a queer anguish.

"Do you remember the day you kicked me out?" he asked, gently. "I came, and you gave me my ring." He was silent a moment. "And then I went away. But you looked after me, through the window. I saw your poor little face there, all the way to the gates. Why did you look after me, Celeste?"

She wrung her hands, twisted her handkerchief. "How do I

know? It is such a long time ago. Perhaps I was—sorry. Sorry I had hurt you."

But he said remorselessly: "I know why. It was because you really loved me, Celeste. You knew it, at the very last. It wasn't Peter you wanted, really. Perhaps you had persuaded yourself that you did; it was what he said, which was so novel and unique, that had appealed to your poor little ingenuousness. He was a hero. He fought the Bouchard dragons. You didn't like your family. They frightened you. They made you feel foolish and small and inferior. Peter fought them; he was such a hero. And so romantic. I wasn't romantic, I am afraid."

Her voice was trembling, but hard as iron now: "You mustn't talk like this. It's stupid. Very stupid. You are unfair. You were always unfair, Henri. Anyway, what does it matter? It was a long time ago. I was only a child. Nothing matters now. We've come a long way. We aren't young any longer."

But he said, as if she hadn't spoken: "You were good and sweet and had a peculiar kind of 'virtue.' So, Peter appealed to you. In a way, perhaps, you really did care for him. But you loved me. You always did." After a moment, he added: "You always have. Even now. Is that why you're afraid of me, Celeste?"

Terror overwhelmed her. She sprang to her feet. He stood up, also, but much more slowly. She faced him, and cried: "I'm not afraid of you, Henri Bouchard! Do you know what I think of you? I think you are a coward. A cheat! If you weren't, you wouldn't talk to me like this! Haven't you any shame? Don't you think——"

"Of Annette? Of Peter?" She was startled, and terrified, at the sudden change in his voice, which had become rough and brutal. "Shall I tell you something about yourself, Celeste? You are a fool. You are over thirty now, but you are still a girlish romantic, full of idiotic dreams. When you hear the truth, you shy away, daintily. You don't like the truth, do you? Shall I tell you something else? I despise you."

His voice, his words, shocked her so profoundly that she could not move, nor speak, and could only stare at the shifting outline of his face above hers, in the thickening darkness.

"Yes," he said, "I despise you. You aren't what I thought you were. I never thought you were a liar, and especially not that you would lie to yourself. But, you are a liar; you do lie to yourself. You think you are noble and honorable, don't you, when you lie like this? All loyalty and pride, dedication and duty. You think: 'What would the world be if one renounced duty, or were unfaithful, or looked at the truth?' And so, let me tell you that such principles as yours have made the world sick. It's made it what it is. The maudlin folly of people like you has done more to prevent any progress than any other one thing you can name. I tell you, you've got to look at the truth, and live accordingly. If the world is to survive, it's got to look at the truth."

The shock still made all her flesh vibrate. She cried out scornfully: "And you, Henri Bouchard, think that you've looked at the truth! Don't you know that I know what you are? Have you really thought I was so blind, and dumb, and stupid, that I didn't know? You've said you despise me. Well, let me tell you that I know you are a liar, a mountebank, a malefactor, a cheat on a colossal scale. You're a scoundrel, Henri. A beast. When the world rids itself of such as you, it will be a better place, a cleaner and a safer place—" She paused, smothering with her impotence and her rage.

But even in that impotence and rage, she became aware that he had listened very intently, and that he had come a step closer to her. "Yes?" he said. "Who's told you these things? Peter?"

"Do you think we've been blind all these years, in Europe?" she cried, bitterly. "Don't you know that Peter has been studying, interviewing people, reading, searching?"

And then she heard him laughing uncontrollably. She stopped, abruptly.

"O God!" he exclaimed. "If that isn't the damnedest rot! And you've been trailing him around the world, listening to that, faithfully recording his idiocies! I had an idea there was something like this. But I didn't realize the full extent of it all."

He seized her hand and pulled her towards him, roughly and strongly. "You're a fool, Celeste. A romantic, drivelling fool. I don't blame you too much. Look at your associates! You're still a little girl, the little girl I first saw. I put a flower in your hair that first day; do you remember? That was pretty and romantic, wasn't it? Enough even for you! I ought to have known then that you'd never really grow up."

She struggled with him briefly. But he caught her face in his hands and kissed her brutally upon the lips. He took her in his arms, and kissed her over and over, until she was blinded and stunned, and could not resist.

"I love you, my poor imbecile darling," he whispered, against her ear. "Do you know that? I've always loved you,

135

and wanted you. Now, you've come back. Do you think I'll ever let you go again?"

She pressed her hands against his chest. "Let me go," she said, through her clenched teeth. But her knees were weak beneath her. If he had released her, she would have fallen. Her lips burned as if stung by flame.

"No," he said, softly, kissing her again. "I'll never let you go again. You never wanted me to go. You're a shameless woman, aren't you, darling? I've watched you these last weeks. I knew I had only to reach for you, and you'd come. You knew that, too. I've reached; you've come. It's as simple as all that, isn't it?"

She had grasped his arms, to push them from her, but now her hands dropped away. She burst into tears, as he held her. He bent his head and pressed his cheek against hers, though she tried to turn her face away.

"Hush, dear," he said, with great tenderness. "I'm sorry that I had to say that to you. But it had to be said. I've known all about it. Don't you know how I love you, Celeste? Don't you know that nothing matters but you? There are things I'd like to do, but they would hurt your miserable kind little heart. So, we'll have to wait. No, we won't wait for love. And not too long, for other things. We've waited a long time. I've a lot of patience, dearest. But not too much."

He smoothed her hair, murmuring in her ear. He pressed her face closer to his. She was all anguish, all wretchedness, shame and resistance. But suddenly she was overpowered by a delirious joy. Without her own volition, she clung to him, devoured by hunger and the first desire she had ever felt. Her lips bloomed and softened under his own. Her eyes, opened wide, and stared at the stars, which shrunk and brightened to points of flame. The wind, the trees, the thunder and the distant roaring of the gathering storm, sang exultantly with atavistic passion and ecstasy. She felt the spinning of the earth under her feet, and its wild rotation invaded her body when he lifted her in his arms and took her away into a darkness which was hot and clamoring and impenetrable, and full of singing voices.

Christopher and Edith sat in the smothering heat of the great drawingroom, with every lamp burning. They heard the gathering storm, which, though rain had not yet come, was shaking the windows with subterranean sound.

Edith was wiping her eyes in silence and sadness, and

Christopher was immobile. From time to time, he glanced at his watch.

"I don't understand it," he said, in his neutral voice. "They said she didn't go out. At least, she didn't order a car. The butler saw her on the terrace, over an hour ago, without a hat. He was under the impression she had gone for a walk. And no one knows where Henri is. He didn't go out for the evening, either."

Edith sighed. Then she said, wearily: "It's a hot night. Perhaps they're out on the grounds somewhere, together, trying to get a breath of coolness."

"No doubt," answered Christopher.

Suddenly, he got to his feet, and went to one of the black and shining windows, which reflected every lamp hotly. A flash of lightning lit up his face, which was like a plaster mask, gaunt and suddenly evil, sunken and dark under the bony cheeks. His back was to Edith; she saw only the contour of his thin shoulders, but she felt something violent and repressed in him.

"Do you think we ought to go and look for them?" asked Edith, restlessly. "After all——"

Christopher was silent for a moment. Then he said, not turning: "No. They'll be here shortly. Where could they go?"

"I'm afraid—for Celeste," said Edith, pressing her handkerchief to her eyelids again. "It'll be terrible for her, Christopher. She and Adelaide were so attached. She'll never forgive herself."

Christopher turned, and now she saw his face, and in a sudden fear she half rose from her chair. Was it possible, she thought, that he could have had a secret affection for his mother, that it had been quite frightful for him? His plaster pallor, the colorless glitter of his eyes, were alarming to her. Or (and this must be the more logical explanation), he was concerned for Celeste, afraid of her frantic grief——

But there was something in his look which was incongruous with her surmise of softer sentiments, something which increased her instinctive fear and confusion.

"What is it, Christopher?" she cried, involuntarily.

But he did not hear her. He was listening. She turned her head, and listened, also. She heard the terrace door opening, but no voices. Now, there was only silence. Edith stood in the center of the room, near her husband, and the heart under her thin breast began to pound uneasily. Christopher caught her wrist, and so unexpected, so vicious was his grasp, that she almost cried out. He was not looking at her; he was staring at the great empty archway of the room. Then he swung her behind him so that she almost fell into her chair, and he moved towards the archway as soundlessly as a feather floating. She watched him go, in the daze of a nightmare.

She saw him stand rigidly on the threshold, as he reached it. But she did not see what he saw: Henri and Celeste pressed together in the silent abandon of passion, in the shadow near the stairway. Edith wanted to go to her husband, as he stood there, seeing what she could not see, but something in the rigid contour of his shoulders, the carved motionlessness of his gaunt pale head, held her still in her chair.

Christopher thought to himself with brilliant clarity: Bitch!

He could not have summoned any will in himself to move, or speak. He could only watch, and feel a dry and dusty disintegration within him, a dusty wind of hatred, accompanied by stabbing pangs of bitterness and grief. And mingled with these was a horrible kind of humiliation and personal debasement.

In all his life he had loved only one creature with complete purity and tenderness, with absolute softness and gentleness. And that had been his sister, Celeste, who, from her birth, had been his self-dedicated charge. Even when she had married against his will and desire, and had gone away for so many years, he had never forgotten her for a moment, had willed her return with a kind of cold desperation. He had considered her something apart from other women, something pure and untouchable, clad in a chastity and integrity and nobility which nothing could destroy. That was his sentimentality, his naïveté, and now, his shame, his degradation.

He had known for so long that Henri Bouchard would never relinquish Celeste, no matter how long he would have to wait. But Christopher, with a curious kind of simplicity, had believed that it would be Celeste who would pronounce the period of waiting, and set its limits. Its limits would be the death of her husband, the divorce of Annette by Henri.

During these past months he, Christopher, had lived in a kind of airless vacuum of indecision, doubt and gloomy anxiety. So much depended upon what transpired between Henri and Celeste, upon what was decided by his sister. Now, as he stood there, devoured by the most frightful hatred and rage and self-abasement, he made his decision. His degradation was none the less, but only increased, by his acknowledgment that he had been a naive and sentimental fool, a Victorian fool. He had only vengeance left. He thought: She is no better than any of the others. She is filthy and corrupt, foul and disgusting. She had surrendered so easily, so supinely, without even a struggle. In another man, these thoughts would have wildly amused him, furnished him with ribald comments upon the simplicity and absurdity of human nature. He found nothing amusing in himself.

He thought: Now, I know what I must do. How I would like to go to him, and murder him! How I would like to show him what I know! But he dared not do this. He dared not let Henri Bouchard even know what he had seen.

So, it had not been enough for Henri Bouchard to have humiliated him, Christopher, fourteen years ago, to have stripped and degraded him in the face of all the family, to have publicly betrayed and destroyed him, to have sent him away into virtual exile. (And then, triumphant, Henri had seized the power of the Bouchards, which Christopher had so malignantly and unremittingly coveted, had, like Napoleon, set the crown on his head with his own hands.) No, it had not been enough for him. It had not been enough until he had taken Celeste and had disgraced her, under this roof that sheltered her own brother and her own husband. And her brother stood there, feeling the final deathly humiliation and impotence.

Deep within the heat of the maelstrom, Christopher was aware of the hot core of unbearable pain, which he could not analyze and could only feel.

The concentration of his eyes, the violence of the emotions that were almost destroying him, must have reached the consciousness of Henri Bouchard. For he lifted his head and turned it in Christopher's direction.

For a few instants, the two men regarded each other in an intense silence. Then Henri relinquished Celeste, gently.

"Yes?" he said, quietly, with that brutal directness which always intimidated others. Celeste, now stood beside him, with a remote and rugged expression in her eyes, which were dim and suffused. Her hair was dishevelled, a mass of black curls about her cheeks and neck.

Christ! thought Christopher, looking at her. He had an impulse to go to her swiftly, and strike her again and again across her pale cheek, until she fell down.

Edith appeared in the archway. She came forward a step or two, glancing first at her brother and then at Celeste. And then her thin face flushed darkly red.

But she said, very quietly, to the bemused Celeste:

"Celeste. We've bad news. We came back—just a little while ago. And there was a message. Your mother has just had a stroke, at Emile's. You're to go there, at once." She paused, and her tears came, helplessly, with obscure anger: "We've waited for you. Celeste, you must go at once!"

CHAPTER XV

Henri glanced at his watch. It was three o'clock. He resumed his restless pacing up and down the lighted and empty room, unnaturally bright and silent in this early morning. The crickets no longer shrilled outside in the warm grass; the crescent moon had slipped far down behind the great trees. The storm had been brief, had passed with as swift violence as it had come, leaving behind only the cool and passionate scent of the earth and of foliage heavy with water.

At one o'clock Christopher had called briefly from Emile's home to announce that Adelaide Bouchard, his mother, had just died, after only a moment or two of consciousness. Did Henri intend to inform Annette, grand-daughter of Adelaide, at once? No, Henri had replied. There was no necessity to disturb her. It would only shock and upset her. Better to let her know in the morning, after a good night's rest. In the meantime, he, Henri, would wait for the return of Christopher, Edith and Celeste. He was not in the least tired, he replied impatiently, at Christopher's suggestion that he go to bed. He, himself, would have gone to Emile's home had he not been afraid that Annette would awaken and miss him, and be alarmed. As it was, he frequently went to her door to see if she still slept. At this, Christopher smiled darkly to himself, and hung up, after Henri had belatedly expressed his regrets at the death of his wife's grandmother, his own aunt.

Henri, who rarely smoked except in company with others, and who was noted for his precise and compactly neat habits, had filled several trays with the remains of cigarettes during these past hours. He would eye them with startled aversion when he encountered them, as though this had been done by a stranger without fastidiousness and orderly manners, and then would light another cigarette and smoke it restlessly. Sometimes he would sit down, and run his broad fingers through his crest of hair that was neither light nor graying, but rather bleached in appearance, and he would stare with excited gloom before him. He thought of Celeste, but he thought of many other things, also. He had long ago discovered that one's thoughts could be preternaturally sharp in the early hours before dawn. His light straight brows drew together in concentrated scowls.

It was not his way to taste in retrospect fruits already eaten, nor did wine already drunk intoxicate him. "Let him take who is able; let him hold who can," had always been the philosophy upon which he had lived, and would continue to live. Tomorrow, he was to have visited Jay Regan, the aging but still potent financier. Now, that was impossible. Even he could not overlook the amenities necessary after a death. He was annoyed. Adelaide could not have died at a more inopportune time. It was not the habit of Mr. Regan to send quiet and secret summons to any of his friends unless something grave portended, something imminent and of the most profound importance. For once, Henri was puzzled. He speculated upon Regan's communication, and cursed the mischance of Adelaide's death. A miserable attenuated old woman, who ought to have died years ago! She had distorted, practically ruined, several lives with her confounded nobility. What evil the good can do!

Henri reflected that there is in all men a lust for power, but in the "good" there is a greater lust than in the "wicked." Moreover, the wicked can sometimes be made to pause at the demands of reason, but the good are without reason. Therefore, they are the most destructive, the more dangerous. The most wicked man lacks a complete conviction; the good are made brazen by it. What had happened tonight was the long result of Adelaide's "goodness" and nobility of character. He frowned again. He hoped that Celeste would not react to her mother's death in a ridiculous fashion. If she did, it would make it a little more difficult for him. But that was all. He liked to have events occur in an orderly and progressive fashion, and thereafter be filed away for future reference. To have them bulge untidily from the files and blow all about was distasteful and angering to him. During the fourteen years of Celeste's marriage, in which he had seen her at irregular periods, he had made no attempt to reach her. He had waited for the proper hour, when the act could be accomplished, and laid as a foundation for future events.

In these years, he had had to consolidate his position. Not even for Celeste would he have jeopardized that position. Now, when everything was safe and secure, he had moved to take her. It would be very annoying if she again became temporarily inaccessible. It would take up time, and time, now, was very important to him, and ought not to be wasted upon a silly woman who must be seduced all over again. For a moment, he contemplated abandoning his pursuit of her. Why not let her go in her foolishness and simplicity? He had more important things to engross his attention.

It had always been incredibly amazing to him that powerful men were frequently destroyed by their lust for a single woman, or, sometimes, just women. It was still amazing to him. He could think of no occasion when his passion for Celeste might be irresistible enough to make him turn aside from larger issues and drivel over her with complete abandon. "Like a damn libidinous dog," he thought, with disgust. Women were the rewards of power, the ultimate rewards. And only that. But in adolescent America (who, in the midst of her very adolescence, was rotting and aging at the top), the reward was considered the only thing of value. That was the influence of women, and drivellers, who believed the rump that perched on the knee of him who sat on the throne was more important than the throne. God! The world was full of eager rumps, and there were actually men who seized on one and let ruin fell them during their preoccupation! His disgust mounted.

If his pursuit of Celeste at any moment threatened to endanger himself, then he would let her go. He had always known that. Yet, at the thought, he was seized by such an astounding and protesting despondency that he felt new disgust, and even alarm, for himself. He stood up again, and began his restless pacing once more. There was no reason for abandoning Celeste. It was only irritating that he might have to begin the pursuit again just when it was more important that his whole mind be engaged in imminent issues. He must bring things to a climax in his private life very shortly. He had confidence in himself, that he could juggle his private life without endangering the great motive power of his existence.

So preoccupied was he that he was completely startled when he saw that Edith and Christopher and Celeste had returned. He went to meet them. Celeste had not wept, he discerned, after a quick and penetrating glance at her. Her face was marble white, and her eyes unusually wide and brilliant. She was very still. She looked at him blindly, as a statue stares, and did not seem to know what to do next. Edith had one arm about the younger woman's waist. It was she, rather than Celeste, who betrayed the signs of sorrow, for her eyelids were swollen. Christopher was pale, but as inscrutable as ever.

"Well?" he said. He regarded Henri without expression.

"I'm sorry," said Henri, looking only at Celeste. "But she was very old. We've got to remember that."

Why did Celeste look at him like that? He frowned.

"I think," said Christopher to his wife, "that you'd better take Celeste to bed."

"Come, dear," said Edith, to Celeste. "You're so very tired."

Then Celeste opened her white mouth, and still gazing at Henri, spoke like a sleepwalker, in a toneless high voice: "I can't forget what she said. She said I must go away, at once. That was just before she died. She said: 'Go away from that bad man, where he can't reach you, and kill you. In the name of God, go away and never see him again.'"

And then, after saying that, she stood there, rigid as stone, staring at him with the blind bright blueness of her eyes.

A dull scarlet passed over Henri's grim face. Christopher smiled faintly, touched his lips with his bony and delicate fingers. Edith was acutely but sternly embarrassed.

Henri looked slowly from one to the other, saw Christopher's smile and Edith's cold anger when she met his eye. He clenched his fists. He lowered his head like a bull and the nostrils in his short nose dilated. This was ridiculous, humiliating. He turned to his sister.

"Take her to bed," he said, shortly.

"Yes. One must never remember what the dying say," said Christopher, nodding curtly to Edith. "The girl's not responsible."

"I must go away," said Celeste, and she stepped out of Edith's grasp and stood apart from them, with a sudden wild desperation on her face. "I must go away at once! You can see that, can't you?" Now her voice rose on the arch of a cry, and she struck her hands together with a loud sharp noise.

"She's hysterical," said Christopher, coldly. He seized his sister's arm, and said slowly and clearly: "Go to bed, Celeste. Do you want me to call the doctor and have him put you to sleep like any other fool of a woman? Behave yourself. You aren't a child any more."

She looked at him, her face all wild white tremulousness,

and tried to withdraw her arm from his painful grasp. But he held her remorselessly.

"You don't understand," said Celeste, in a tone of such agonized mournfulness that Christopher's inhuman eyes strangely softened. She held out her hand to her brother with a pathetic gesture. "I never forgot him. I couldn't forget. I stayed away, ran away, for years. It was all so terrible. There was nothing I could do but stay away. And then, I came back. And then, there was tonight—" She paused, and cried out in a loud and aching voice: "You don't know about tonight! I knew then that it was all useless, my running away, that I couldn't stay away from him! What am I to do? Christopher, tell me what to do!"

In spite of her sadness, Edith was disgusted. "What a scene! The family has always been known for its luscious family scenes, but this is the most revolting. Celeste, haven't you any shame, for yourself? Don't you know what you are saying? Please, Chris, help me to put her to bed immediately, before she has every servant listening and peering."

She turned to her brother and said: "Well, say something, damn you. Don't stand there like an image of a charging bull. What have you done to her? O God, this is disgraceful!"

"I agree with you," said Henri, quietly. His color was still high. He moved to Celeste, and said, in a hard and penetrating voice: "Nothing happened. You are hysterical, my girl. Go to bed. You've had a bad night and aren't responsible, but for God's sake, try to control yourself a little."

At the sound of his voice, she started violently. She stood rigid, but trembling, in her brother's grasp. She gazed at Henri with a kind of nightmare horror. Then, all at once, she began to cry, the tears running down in a river from her distended eyes. "Henri," she said, brokenly, and took a step towards him. Christopher released her. She lifted her hands to Henri, and he took them very gently, trying to control her with the power of his eyes.

"Yes, darling," he said, softly. "I know. Go to bed. Rest. We'll talk about all this another time."

But Celeste said through quivering lips: "She said I must go away from you, Henri. You know I can't do that. Never again. Henri, why can't I die? Why did I ever come back? But you wanted me to come back, didn't you?"

Henri was silent. Edith retreated a few steps with an expression of contemptuous loathing and renewed embarrassment. But Christopher watched intently. He saw that Henri and his sister had forgotten him and Edith. Then Henri said: "Yes, Celeste, I wanted you to come back."

He held her to him, and she dropped her head on his shoulder. He smoothed her head gently and tenderly. The violence of her weeping began to subside, as she clung to him, grasping his sleeves with desperate hands. When he kissed her, she pressed herself closer and closer to him, her black curls falling over his strong fingers.

Edith looked at her huband, who appeared to be very calm. She said, quietly: "Well, this is a nice, shameless thing, I must say. A beautiful scene. One forgets, of course, that Annette and Peter are upstairs sleeping like woolly lambs. This isn't very pretty, you know. High, fine and romantic! I think it's just untidy and nasty and revolting. I wash my hands of the whole thing."

She lifted her dark head, straightened her shoulders, and walked from the room. Christopher smiled thinly after her, and then stood in silence and watched his sister and Henri. The girl was quieter now, sobbing softly, while Henri murmured in her ear words that Christopher found inaudible, however he strained to hear them.

Once he had used his sister to entangle and secure Henri for his own purpose. Now, he reflected with exultation, he could use her to ruin Henri. The stone basilisk had his spot of vulnerable flesh, through which he could be struck to the heart. Christopher had hoped for much, but not this much. His exultation rose to the pitch of delirium. Over his dry and bleached features ran a flash of murderous light.

Henri was releasing himself from Celeste's clinging. He was saying gently and slowly: "And now, you must go to bed, and rest. You know that, don't you?" He looked about for his sister. She had retreated to the reception hall outside the room, and was waiting at the foot of the stairs, very pale and grim. He led Celeste like a child to Edith, who waited and watched, her mouth compressed, her eyes full of contempt.

"She'll do now. Take her to bed," he said, and at his look, implacable and yet expressionless, she felt the old fear of him, and put her arm about Celeste again. Henri watched the two women go slowly up the stairs, then he returned to the great lighted room where Christopher still waited.

Christopher opened his case, and said, casually: "Cigarette?" Henri stared at it as if he was in doubt as to what it was, then accepted. Christopher lit it for him, lighted one for himself. He said: "The funeral is Thursday. It was unfortunate that my mother didn't die before we got there. She lived just long enough to see Celeste. Must have waited for her. The poor girl was put through some bad paces."

Henri sat down, and looked directly at Christopher with his pale eyes, which had regained their old surface gleam. "Who else heard?" he asked, abruptly.

"Only Edith, and Celeste, and I. We were only admitted in groups of two or three to see the old lady. Good luck, there. Not that anyone else would have understood. They would probably have thought that she meant Peter." He laughed silently.

Henri glanced at his cigarette, threw it aside. "Sit down," he said.

Under Christopher's thin high cheekbones there ran a line of color. In all these years he had never become accustomed, as almost all his relatives had, to Henri's hard dictatorial commands. His venomous hatred became a metallic taste in his mouth. Nevertheless, he sat down. He could wait, endure, a little longer.

Outside, the birds had begun their morning chorus of awakening song. The wind was rising. The sky, in the east, was slowly turning gray. Henri sat in his chair, his hands resting on the arms, and regarded his brother-in-law in a long and meditative silence.

Was there amused contempt in his eyes, understanding? One could never tell, with this formidable bastard. Inwardly writhing with his impotence, Christopher could hardly restrain himself. There was a voluptuous quality in his helplessness, so that he felt suddenly weak and undone. But his hatred was more malignant than ever.

He waited. Surely, the swine must say something, do something!

But Henri said only, with a peculiar smile: "May I offer you my sympathy on the death of your mother?"

Christopher was silent. It was Henri who waited. He studied Christopher's mask of a face, now enigmatic and closed. He smiled again. He rose with his usual compact ease and went calmly from the room.

CHAPTER XVI

Jay Regan sat in the vast and sacred gloom of his cathedral office and watched Henri Bouchard walk firmly and evenly across the dim and polished floor towards him. The great mahogany desk was like a dusky mirror before the fat old man, so ponderous and so somber, and it threw glimmering reflections on his immense tired face with its cropped, almost white, mustache. Behind that desk, in that dusk, he was almost invisible, but even Henri was impressed, as always, by the air of formless and shadowy power that he exuded. This mighty buccaneer of finance seemed, in his age, no bravo, no adventurer, but a power that by a lift of a hand might cause empires to crash, at the merest sound of whose deep quiet voice the heads of world parliaments must turn towards him in helpless hypnosis. Here was the real emperor of the world, the real dictator. Hitlers and Mussolinis, for all their trumpets and insane bombasts, must, in the end, listen to him, and cower before him.

Yet, he was old now, and approaching the time of his death. During all the years that Henri had known him, he had never felt in him a lust for power, or exultation that he possessed it. He was a simple and natural force, without apparent enjoyment for the knowledge that terror and ruin could be invoked by him. Nor had he ever been a spectacular force, a dramatic and theatrical force, loving publicity and a train of attendants. Whenever he moved, he moved in abysmal silence and darkness, and only the long reverberations of the earthquake, moving away from the silent center of him, gave evidence that the Titan had stirred or spoken. There would be flashes of significant lightnings in the press; there would be Congressional Committees, or meetings in offices similar to this, on Wall Street, or a gathering of the thousands of members of the American Association of Industrialists, or presidents would confer and statesmen put their heads together. And, far off, in Europe, in Asia, in

147

South America, the winds would stir uneasily in the breath of the earthquake, and white palaces of Government would hum like hives, and the bronze doors of the Bourse, the Reichsbank, to the Bank of England, the banks of Italy. Roumania, Hungary, Scandinavia, would catch yellow sparks of sunlight as they opened and shut in feverish activity. But always, he moved behind a wall of shadows, in velvet silence, and not even the keenest ear heard the ponderous echo of his step through the colonnades of the world.

This was the man who had moved the marionette, Mussolini, and had breathed into his wooden breast the very breath of life. In 1927, this miserable posturer and impostor, this little mountebank, this wretched and third-rate actor, this paranoiac with delusions of grandeur, had been at the point of collapse, laughed down and derided by his own realistic countrymen, who, loving true art and adoring a true actor, had found his gestures and his voice absurd and ridiculous, and without artistry. Italians forgave anything, so long as it was art, and a murderer of grace and dexterity, of voice and manner, inspired their admiration and applause. They would cheer a Borgia, if he poisoned with an air and had the proper drape to his sleeve as he lifted a dramatic hand to instill the venom in a jewelled cup, and displayed a certain heroic grandeur of profile. They loved the emphasis on grace, the resonance of a rounded period, in a world that they knew was dull and frequently without beauty. But this maker of legs, this graceless mountebank, had no splendor, no beauty. He could not even act. If a man had no true appreciation of the elegant gesture, no awareness that a phrase must be uttered with certain rich intonations, no subtlety of posture, then he was worthless, and most probably a fool.

His "march on Rome" had interested the vivacious and intelligent Italians, with their adoration of the proper artistry. It revived memories of Cæsar's entrances, with pageants, trumpets, the blaze of red banners against the burning blue sky, the tramp of white horses and the flash of helmets in the sun, the fire caught on the tips of spears from the immortal clarity of Italian light, the thunder of victorious armored feet. For a while, their interest remained. But, they soon recognized that this Cæsar was bogus, ridiculous, a syphilitic fool, and that even his pursuit of women lacked the grand air and was only the waddling of a middle-aged Pan at the heels of dressmakers' dummies. He sickened them. Those behind him, the great industrialists and financiers of Italy, were dismayed. They displayed their Cæsar over and over to the jeering and ribald mob, affixing to his head an absurd fez with tassels, inventing flamboyant uniforms for him, rehearsing him in his speeches, finding for him more and more spectacular beauties with which to cohabit publicly, arraying his cohorts in purple and gold and arming them with carved swords. The Italians' amusement increased. The Affaire Mussolini became, for the civilized Romans, the invasion of a countryman's dream of grandeur, and they were insulted.

"Bad opera," they would say, shaking their heads. To an Italian, "bad opera" was the supreme crime, and nothing could be forgiven it.

Jay Regan understood all this. Where art failed to beguile, he said, money could be used as a club. It was in that portentous March of 1927 that he lent $100,000,000 to the lurking fascists behind Mussolini, and the amazed Italians discovered that, "bad opera" or not, this malignant third-rate actor stood over them with a poised dagger, and compelled them, not only to watch his disgusting performances, but to applaud them also. They watched him strut across the stage of history, and were nauseated by his raucous voice, his lack of technique, his ignorance of even the most elementary gestures of true art. They shrugged their shoulders fatalistically, and went about their business, hoping that universal contempt would soon quiet this spear-carrier forever.

But the spear-carrier, who would have sunk into oblivion at the behest of the Italian people, had friends who were no such lovers of art as they. He had Mr. Regan, in America. He had the Bank of England, and the silent movement of golden hands towards him. He had the bankers of France, who hated their country. But he did not have Germany. The German Republic watched him with alarm and gloom, and its confused protests were lost in his violent shoutings, the stamping of his flat feet. The Germans were not quite sure about what they were protesting, except that their instinct, always so elemental and primitive, smelled danger. Some there were who condescended to explain to them that Mussolini was really valuable. "He made the Italian trains run on time," they would say, with solemn nods of their heads.

"But," inquired a great German liberal, whom Mussolini never forgave, and who was later tortured to death in a Nazi concentration camp at the mountebank's behest, "what have prompt trains to do with the human spirit, with human enlightenment, with human liberty?"

Such gross ignorance, such naive stupidity, was properly ignored. The Germans continued to ask, and no one answered. In the meantime, the heroic background of history bore upon it the posturing and prancing shadow of a lunatic created and sustained by a hundred secret hands that manipulated him. And that shadow grew larger and larger, and the swords that followed it were not spectral, but made of steel forged in America, in England, in France.

At last, even those Germans who, under certain circumstances, had a proper regard for the promptness of trains soon had a problem of their own, and they temporarily forgot Mussolini. For another mountebank, who did not even wear a fez with tassels, and had not even the rank splendor of uniforms to commend him, had lifted his raucous voice in their own midst. There was, in the German, a love for the heroic in stature, for helmets, for the clanking of swords, for the Nibelungs, for winged and armored feet, for Wagnerian voices. But this miserable little man, this clerk with the nasty face, this jumping Toad of the Ages, had nothing to commend him, not even a knowledge of "bad opera." But, he had a Voice, and that Voice echoed in the cathedral silence of Jay Regan's office, in the austere walls of the Bank of England, in the feverish Bourse. The German people listened, exhausted by the languor of wretched years, and turned aside with hesitant weariness. Only their enemies listened in their own country, the fools, the lunatics, the perverts, the greedy, the vicious, and the mad. But others listened, and bent attentive ears across oceans, across mountains, across the ragged edges of boundaries. And after they had listened a little while, they moved, and the vast machinery of doom began to murmur, to rise to a secret roar.

For the Toad of the Ages had promised that he would kill the Man with the Red Beard who lay like a supine giant beyond the Ural Mountains, ever watching the world of men and stroking his beard in silence. No one knew what the giant was thinking, or what he was contemplating. The world of men can endure anything but silence, and is maddened by it. They only felt the fiery blue eyes turning slowly from nation to nation in profound meditation, and they became hysterical at the threat that they believed lived in him. Let him once rise from his contemplative motionlessness behind his mountains, they said, let him stand erect like a colossus, and ramparts would fall at the shout of his voice, and governments would crash into dusty ruins at the very echo of his feet. Let him walk, and at the very shadow of him against the sun the enslaved peoples of the world would rise up like a black tide and inundate their masters.

The Toad of the Ages had as yet only a voice. But he soon had money. With the golden swords there came an army of murderers, liars and thieves, there came long and deadly whispers from every corner of the world. And the Toad of the Ages soon eclipsed a bad actor, though possessing not even bad art of his own. The Toad, with his croaking voice, the Italian posturer who could only awkwardly manage his cloak, stood before amazed multitudes, armed with swords forged in secret in other countries. They looked at the Man with the Red Beard, squeaked their defiance of him, and rattled their swords at him. And now the Church listened, the Church that hated the new liberation of men. In the cool purple dusk of cathedrals, in the musty dankness of little wooden tabernacles, a storm of voices rose, squealing, screaming, filled with venom and fear and hatred, and resounded and echoed in every nation in the world. The Man with the Red Beard was the Supreme Enemy of orderly government, of orderly law, of morality, of marriage, of established authority, of God, the Bible, woman's virtue, children's obedience, commerce, the little red school-house, and the corner grocery store. The Toad and the Bad Actor were twin Messiahs that protected the beds of good women, small bank accounts, labor, government, the dollar Bible, and the little church with the clapboard steeple.

The seduction of the Common Man had begun.

The seduction, as the Masters had very well known, was not very hard. One had only to enlist the Church. Year by year, the Common Man himself had gathered in the sticks and the straws of prejudice, stupidity, ignorance and fear and hatred, and was sitting on this wretched tinder waiting for the spark that would set the rubbish aflame. The Church had this spark, already tended and guarded for the hour. Always, through the centuries, it had this spark, sheltered by its sinister hands. The bonfires were set ablaze. By their frantic light, every man was convinced that he saw the crouching shadow of the Man with the Red Beard, poised to spring over the boundaries of the world.

The work was done. The fire was spreading. The world entered a universe of crimson clouds.

In the meantime, the Man with the Red Beard maintained his silence. But, he knew. He began to move behind his mountains.

The Common People, enamored of legend and fairy tale,

always believed that the man of destiny burst like an exploding comet against the skies of the world. They jeered, always at the implication that men of destiny sat behind acres of polished desks in vast quiet offices and talked together in words of the vernacular. Who, among the distant Italians, the distant and frightened Germans, knew that their Cæsars were controlled by men in rumpled tweeds, in creased and untidy trousers, in New York, in Berlin, in London, in Rome, in Paris? Who knew that the fires of destruction smoked at the ends of good cigars about mahogany boards heaped with neat papers? Who knew that the voice of destruction did not bellow from the echoing spaces of time, but whispered quietly in Wall Street, in the Bourse, in the Reichsbank, and that often that voice had an English or French or American accent? The day of the hero was gone. The terror wore a vest and pampered a swollen belly, and used tonic on a balding head.

Not even anguished Spain could awaken the Common Man, nor could her cries enter the mean little walls of his house, nor the light of her burning cities strike on his dull eyelids.

So, as Henri Bouchard approached his old and potent friend, he saw in him all the great and subterranean power that now heaved with increasing strength through the world. Yet, it was only an aging sick man who sat there, with ambushed eyes, a cropped white mustache, and quiet hands, and a peculiarly charming smile.

He had a great fondness for the younger man, and an indulgent admiration. Before him, on the desk, was spread an enormous sheet of paper upon which appeared something like a spreading family tree. Mr. Regan had been studying this paper for hours, moving its crackling width from time to time. It was indeed a sort of family tree. At the top was Bouchard & Sons, and from it extended the multitudinous subsidiaries controlled by that company, the names of the presidents and other officers.

He gave Henri his hand, and shook it warmly. "I was sorry to hear of the death of your aunt," he said. "I intended to attend the funeral, but something came up. You received my telegram?"

"She was an old woman," answered Henri, sitting down. "Quite unimportant. Besides, her death prevented me from coming to you, at your suggestion."

They smiled at each other. Mr. Regan rubbed his chin. He said, as he invariably said when seeing Henri: "I can't help but be amazed at the resemblance to your great-grandfather. I can see him now, sitting just where you're sitting.

The last time he came to this office was when he was seventy-five years old. But still potent. You've got his eyes."

"And his other virtues, I hope," said Henri. He was always amused at this preliminary. He knew that Mr. Regan was subtly impressing on him that he must act as his great-grand-father had acted, that he must consider what Ernest Barbour would have done in the face of certain imminent circumstances.

Mr. Regan swung about in his chair, and opened a drawer, from which he drew a silver carafe and two goblets. This was the usual ceremony. They drank together from these little goblets. Mr. Regan lit a cigar for Henri, who did not enjoy cigars. Beyond the heavy carved doors there was a constant activity, but no sound of it came here. The windows were so heavily draped that little light came through. It therefore surprised Henri when the great old man ponderously lifted himself from his chair and went to one of the cathedral windows and looked absently through it. He would peer, bend his head, seem very interested, then disinterested. His vast and pudgy profile loomed against the new brightness that invaded the office.

"Yesterday," he said at last, "an honest man walked down the Street."

"And that's unusual," said Henri.

"Very unusual," agreed Mr. Regan, with a smile. Again, he rubbed his chin, and continued to peer.

"Do you expect him now?" asked Henri.

"Unfortunately, no. But I hope to see him often. In the White House."

Henri lifted his eyebrows in surprise. "I didn't know he [mentioning the name of a certain gentleman who, it had been agreed, was to be the next President] was in New York. Is he? I'd like to have a little talk with him on this trip."

"He isn't here," said Mr. Regan, calmly. He came back to his desk, seated himself once more in his mighty chair of carved wood and velvet. "Besides, he isn't the one I mean. You know him slightly. Wendell Wilkie."

Henri stared, genuinely astounded. "Commonwealth & Southern!" he exclaimed. "You're joking, Mr. Regan." He burst out laughing.

Mr. Regan smiled. The light from the window was behind him, but Henri had the odd impression that something strange was on that gigantic face.

CHAPTER XVII

"I'm not joking," said Mr. Regan.

"But, good God! The man hasn't the slightest notion of politics! No one has ever heard of him, except the Street. You can't be serious!"

"I am," said Mr. Regan, quietly. He folded his hands on his enormous belly and leaned back in his chair. "You see, Henri, I'm sick at the stomach. Ulcers in the spiritual belly. That's why I called you in."

Henri hardly heard him. He stared again, his pale eyes gleaming in the half light. His face was grim. "Not Wilkie," he said, softly. "A nobody, as far as the people are concerned. Who would want him? He isn't a man for us. He never was our man."

"That's why I want him for President," smiled Mr. Regan.

"I don't understand, Mr. Regan. The man we picked is our man. Another Coolidge; a second Harding. Even a Hooverian echo. Safe. We've got to have him. Next year. The machinery has gotten under way." His astonishment mounted. He leaned towards his old friend. "I still don't believe you are serious. 'An honest man.' Do you know the last quotation on Commonwealth & Southern?"

"I do. That isn't Wilkie's fault, you know. He didn't create the TVA."

Henri was silent. He sat motionless, except that his strong fingers began to beat a tattoo on the arm of his chair. Then he said: "My ignorance is terrible. Would you enlighten me why you are so in love with Wilkie all at once?"

Mr. Regan's pinpoints of eyes began to sparkle, but his face was somber. He touched the immense spread of paper on his desk. "Henri, do you know what this is?" With a deft motion of his pudgy hand he spun the paper towards the young man, who looked at it attentively.

Henri smiled. "Yes. I see. What has this got to do with Wilkie, your 'honest man'? And, if he is so damned 'honest,'

154

what do you want with him? Haven't we had enough honesty in the White House since 1933? I thought you'd had your bellyful."

Mr. Regan said tranquilly: "I never liked Franklin, even when he was a young man. For many reasons. Besides, he's not the man—for the coming years. We need youth and strength and virility. So—Wilkie's my man."

"The man for your money?" asked Henri.

Mr. Regan was silent a moment. He looked into space. "No," he said, softly, "not the man for my money."

"The Party won't have him. Even you can't do that, against their wishes. They've already decided on our man, for the nomination next June."

"What you are implying," said Mr. Regan, arousing himself from a strange preoccupation into which he had momentarily fallen, "is that this time you, and the others, will not put up my man."

"What I am implying is that we've already listened to you, Mr. Regan," said Henri, smoothly. "The other was your man. We've been building him up, by your very orders of less than a year ago. We can't change. For a sudden and inexplicable whim."

Mr. Regan clasped his hands on his belly and contemplated Henri for a long moment or two. "First of all, we'll talk about a number of other things, son. Later, we'll come back to Wilkie. How old are you now, Henri? Forty-one? Forty-two? A good age. You are at the height of your mental and bodily vigor. I congratulate you. Henri, you and I have been in agreement for the past year—about certain developments. I think we are still in agreement."

Henri did not answer. He gently bit his index finger, and did not turn his implacable eyes from his old friend.

"We've changed our opinion, I believe," continued Mr. Regan. "About some things. Henri, what is your stand today?"

"You know what it is. Hitler has kicked us in the backside. I discovered that, myself. That's why I went to Europe this year."

"And—well?"

"Frankly—and simply—we've been had. We're fools, Mr. Regan. It is a humiliating idea. It doesn't fit my conception of myself at all!" And Henri smiled slightly. "You see, in our discussions with Hitler, we forgot German geo-politics. We forgot German geo-politics that for over one hundred years have been more or less openly declaring that Germany should, and must, conquer the world. Hitler was the professors' dream of the military Messiah, but a Messiah who would accomplish the conquest without war or bloodshed. These professors, and the other milky ones—the German intellectuals—believed that modern conquest was through economics, and through German 'superior mentality.' Can't you see them, in their musty libraries and laboratories, in their crumbling universities, getting all lyrical over the robust idea of 'Strength through Joy'? There's nothing an attenuated and downy intellectual loves so much as a flexing of muscles— in another man. I've seen them stroke such muscles; a fact. And with adoring looks. To the casual masculine American eye, that would have been indecent, shameful; to one with an elementary knowledge of psychology, it was significant, and not in the least homosexual."

"Go on," said Regan, as Henri paused. The great fat old man leaned forward, his elbows on his desk, his hands clasped under his chin.

"Yes, we forgot German geo-politics, the idea of Pan-Germanism which is over a century old. I believe the American Founding Fathers were aware of it. But few others seemed to be. Now, I find that very significant, too. Why wasn't the idea given publicity, except to Germans? That seems to me the most important thing today—this Pan-Germanism idea. We overlooked it. We thought we could do business with Hitler. Or rather, with German economists who know that war means ruin both for victor and victim, and prefer profits and markets to territorial expansion. So—the economists, the Reichsbank, the intellectuals, were all in one enthusiastic camp—conquest without war. They were well on the way to it, too. Intellectualism and economics—these were able to overcome the intrinsic war-like psychology of the German people, in those who were clever. But there were many who weren't clever—the German mass, the pipsqueak people, whose prototype, whose hero, whose god was the Pipsqueak of the Ages—Hitler. And Hitler, I've discovered, doesn't give a damn for intellectual-economic geo-politics."

Regan frowned. "I'm afraid I'm losing you, Henri."

Henri laughed. "Wait a bit. I'm not finished. As you know, during the period 1933–38, there has been an unending struggle between Hitler and the German economists. Hitler organized every phase of German life, including industry and economy. We all know that Germany did not have gold with which to purchase raw materials; the people in charge of the economic structure set out to create German credit all over the world. Hjalmar Schacht, the leader and organizer, inaugurated the barter system. They came into the market whenever there was a surplus, and traded, taking whatever raw materials they could buy, whether it was coffee, steel, copper, etc. They paid for them with the finished products, such as typewriters, and gimcracks and cheap gadgets of all kinds, and flooded other countries with them, and especially America. In pursuance of their commerce, they created and controlled the major airlines of South America, as you know. Incidentally, Duval-Bonnet, Christopher's concern, furnished most of the planes.

"So, Germany was able to compete on a grand scale with us and Britain in Europe, and in South America, until we found various markets closed to us. It is getting very bad, as you know. Both we and Britain saw that things were getting very bad. Schacht and his friends had planned a slow and gradual economic conquest, first by infiltration and trade, and, second, by actual control of finances. They urged Hitler to have patience. They believed that gradually through competition and by exploitation of German workmen and satellite countries, they would reduce us to nothing. Complete conquest, because they would control finance, trade and industry. They whined that they were a 'have-not people,' so that fools in America and England would not become suspicious, and they even created for themselves a wide sympathy among imbeciles and sentimentalists. But during those years they were never short of raw materials, for which they can thank Bouchard and the subsidiaries, I am afraid. They expected to become so potent economically and financially that within fifteen years Germany would not need to go to war for markets."

"Ah," said Regan, softly. "And that left us all—where?"

"Two years ago," continued Henri, "I saw this clearly. I didn't yet pay much attention to Germany geo-politics, and the militarists. So, I began to cut down on shipments to Germany, whether through South America, to evade the Versailles Treaty, or directly, through cartels. Germany could have a certain amount of material, yes. But no longer were we to supply her with things which might jeopardize ourselves, such as latest plans for airplanes, new processes, and a dozen other things. It was my plan to integrate all American production as far as armaments were concerned, get ready, increase shipments of arms and material to England and France, through South America. A slow steady diversion of the flow away from Germany. We got our politicians to increase sentiment in America for a cash-and-carry plan, which would redound to the advantage of France and England. We made long-range plans, quietly. For, we saw what was coming—Germany would seize all markets, and, perceiving the military weakness of other nations, would defy them to take those markets away from her."

"Go on," said Regan, as Henri paused a moment to examine his hands, and frown at them.

The younger man lifted his head and fixed his inexorable eyes upon the great financier's face.

"But you know all this. We've gone over it before."

"But I like a synopsis." Regan smiled.

"We went along with Germany, we industrialists and economists in England and America. Because we were taken in by a very super-clever rascal—Hitler, who not only deluded us, but even Schacht, himself, and all the other financiers and economists in Germany. Hitler had promised to protect German capitalism, in which we are all interested, from Communism and organized unions. He was to be our buffer state between Russia, and Europe, which was very satisfactory, considering our subsidiaries and other investments, in Europe. He was to protect our European investments and commitments and our financial control there. So, we played along with him, agreeably. That's where I kick myself.

"I thought that a strong economic and financial control in Germany would assure all Europe freedom from Communism, and America, too. And then, I read *Mein Kampf*, and took up the serious study of German geo-politics. Originally, as you know, old German geo-politics intended the military conquest of the world by Germany. The modern geo-politicians intended it by market conquest, and economics. I thought the old idea was dead. I discovered it was very much alive.

"For I suddenly discovered that Hitler despised modern geo-politics, and Schacht, and all the professors and intellectuals who hated blood. That he was an anachronism, a military geo-politician. He believed in short cuts—by the sword. He was beginning to show a vast contempt for financial and industrial masters, and now that he had been able to delude them into helping him, in Germany, in America, and in England and France, he was a powerful military force. Behind him, he had the Junkers. He had the mass of the German people, who could never understand the subtleties of the new geo-politics, and wanted excitement and murder and force and blood. Pipsqueaks love violence. Hitler was the emperor of all the pipsqueaks all over the world, not only in Germany."

"In short—?" murmured Regan.

"In short, he wanted war. For its own sake. Modern geopolitics was slower, and safer, and had for its object the complete subjugation of the markets and the finances of the world. That isn't enough for a pipsqueak. He wanted triumphal arches, covering slave-states, trumpets, banners, thrones and crowns—all the paraphernalia of operatic military conquest. He wanted the visible signs of conquest. It wasn't enough for the conquerors to sit urbanely in international banks. He wanted to march into capitals through a sea of blood. He wanted to be God, not the protector of bankers and industrialists and all the chromium-plated machinery of dull commerce and profits. There would be no exultation among the German pipsqueak-mass if their own bankers and industrialists could lyrically explain that they had driven America and England out of the typewriter, the airplane, the manufacturing and the financial markets of the world. What did that net the average German in his miserable office, and on his little farm? He wanted other clerks and other farmers to kiss his feet, hail him as super-man, cower before him, serve him, while he trampled them. That is the true German psychology, which we overlooked while we dallied with Schacht. That is the German brute-spirit— the hatred for all other men, the desire to physically gouge them, crush them, whip them, torture them, kill them. And that's what we're up against now. The German spirit."

"And, now you're left with a fine economic machinery on your hands, —and Hitler, and the German people."

"Yes. That is where I now rise and let someone kick me in the backside. And I imagine that hundreds of others like me, all over the world, are rising for well-placed kicks, too. For, we can't do business with Hitler."

"What, then, do you intend to do?"

Henri got up and slowly walked up and down the vast room. Light struck his large pale face, and then shadow. His step was heavy. Then he stopped before Regan's desk, leaned his hands on it, and said quietly:

"We'll have to let Europe go. Hitler will strike soon. We know that. We'll have to let Europe go—to him. We can do nothing else. We've brought it about—all of us. But, we can cut our losses, and salvage what we can. In America. In South America. A bad business. But we have no other choice."

"And how do you expect to accomplish that, my dear Henri?" Regan smiled somberly.

"By making ourselves too strong for attack. Hitler won't attack us, when he finds that it will be too costly a struggle. But—we can't have war. That will ruin us all. It will be the end of capitalism and industry as we know them today. There will be an internal economic revolution in America, as well as bloodshed and bankruptcy, if we go to war. In the meantime, while we regain our own strength, which we lost through American god-damned sentimental disarmament ideas, we've got to support England and France, make them strong enough to resist Hitler for a little while, at least. We can't do business with Hitler. We can't have war, either. We've got to become strong enough to resist both the doing-business-with-Hitler idea, and the war-mongers." He smiled suddenly, and lifted his hands from Regan's desk.

"So," he continued, "I've given orders to all our subsidiaries to cut sharply all shipments of material to Hitler, and to our banks to stop German credit. We've got to hurry. Time is of the essence, now."

Regan rubbed his chin. "Patriotism, of course, has nothing to do with this?"

Henri ignored this as an absurd joke between them. "We've been had," he repeated. "Our noble defender against Communism, against organized labor all over the world, has kicked us solidly and is thumbing his nose at us. We ought to have had more intelligence, before we got ourselves, and America, and England and France, into this confounded mess. We didn't have the intelligence. Now, we must salvage what we can. We made Hitler. Now he's stalking us with the very arms we gave him to defend us."

He paused. "As you know, we've long had another plan, which apparently isn't doing so well since Munich. We thought we'd turn Hitler's militarism against Russia. After all, we thought reasonably, that's what he really hated, wasn't it? Russia? Russia was his enemy, and ours. Russia, with her damnable proletarian revolution. Another form of pipsqueakism. The rise of the Common Man. We had to prevent that. Now, I've lost hope that Hitler will leave Europe alone, and attack Russia. We're all in it."

There was a long silence in the room, while the two men stared at each other somberly. Then Regan said:

"You know, I don't think it is going to work, Henri. I think we'll be in the war, too."

Henri struck his fist solidly on the desk. "No," he said, grimly. "We won't. We won't allow it. We've already made plans. That would be the final ruin—for us. American war-economy would be so colossal that we'd be destroyed. It would give Roosevelt his strongest chance to overthrow us, and bring about a form of socialism in America, in which our present system of profits, capitalism and industry, couldn't survive. We 'economic royalists,' as he has so nicely designated us, would find ourselves taken over, controlled, regulated, and put out of business. That's why we can't have war—for America. Our masters would be the American pipsqueak-masses, the common man, the little miserable clerk and farmer and factory fellaheen, the bellowing unions."

Regan put his hand over his mouth, and spoke in a muffled tone from behind his fingers. "And your large family, Henri —what is their attitude?"

"They don't want war, either. We're all agreed on that. We won't allow it, any of us. But—they disagree with me on the idea that we can't do business with Hitler. They think we can. They've got a very clever idea, which I confess at first appealed to me. They have long believed that Big Business can move from the control of industry and finance to actual power over the destiny of the people. They are willing to concede, as benevolent autocrats, certain privileges and benefits to the masses, but are determined on supreme power for themselves in politics, to gain not only the sphere of influence in America, but international control of raw materials all over the world,—their manufacture, distribution and allocation. In other words, the revolution of business managers. As I said, that once appealed to me, too. I had no objection," and he smiled wisely, "to being economic dictator of the whole damned world.

"They, the Bouchards, believed that no matter what happened in Europe, they could strike a bargain with Hitler. They said that he simply couldn't 'do without them.' They believe we can buy a dozen Goerings. So, they wished to continue to supply Hitler with everything he wanted, through cartels in South America, and have been building up sentiment for Germany, encouraging native fascists and appeasers, and are busy with plans for the creating of various peace societies all over the country. They are incredulous when I tell them about the ancient German geo-politics. They are obsessed with the idea that a Hitler-controlled Europe is our best guarantee against Communism in America, or radicalism, or New Dealism, or unionism. They laugh at me when I tell them that Hitler wishes the military and physical conquest of the world. Even if he did, they argue, his intelligent economists and financiers and industrialists would control him. So—they wish to keep up their financial and material support of him. He wants only Europe, they say. Let him have it, with our blessing.

"But, I say that he wants the world. And I'm going to stop him. But not by war. I've put the brakes on our companies. We aren't selling Hitler anything we need ourselves. We are keeping our patents and our new and innumerable processes at home."

"Then, Henri, you and your family are all determined on peace. But you are determined to make America strong so that Hitler can't attack us physically. You aren't interested in building up America. You think it unnecessary?"

"I think that covers it, Mr. Regan."

Regan was very quiet for a long moment or two. Then he said, almost inaudibly, but with strange penetration: "Henri, did it ever occur to you that your family really wants Hitler to conquer the world, literally, as well as in other ways."

Henri stared at him. His light eyes gleamed stonily. He did not move, but his hands slowly clenched. Then he said, with utmost contempt: "Ridiculous."

"Not so ridiculous, Henri. Let us look at the facts. Suppose Hitler not only conquered Europe, but us. He would need strong native men in America, powerful men, to keep American industry moving and growing, supplying him with what he needs. Under such a system, such men would have more power under Hitler, over the destinies of the American people, than they have under our present independent Government. Yes, they could well do business with Hitler, then! They could reduce American labor to serfdom, produce an economy of kings and slaves. Masters not only of finance and industry, but masters of men. Under Hitler domination, of course. But, that would not matter very much."

Henri was silent. Then he leaned forward, and said, softly: "You don't speak without reason, Mr. Regan. And you've got some evidence, haven't you?"

"I have, Henri," replied Regan, in a slow grave voice.

He rose ponderously and wearily, and went to a safe concealed in the panelled wall. He brought out a thick sheaf of papers, which he laid before Henri. The younger man took them up in his hands and began to read them quickly. There was a prolonged silence in the great room, disturbed only by the swift rustling of papers. Regan watched Henri as he read. That pale and massive face showed no emotion, no rage. It remained as still as stone. It was the face of Ernest Barbour, all frozen savagery and inhuman calm.

"Newspaper owners—famous 'military' heroes of the last war—clergymen, women's societies for peace, muck-raking writers, traitors, liars, fools, Senators, politicians, lunatic-fringers, plotters, spies—they're all there, aren't they, Henri?" said the old man at last, as Henri laid the papers down slowly. "They've got them all tentatively organized, haven't they? And not for the sake of 'peace.' Not just for the sake of 'doing business with Hitler,' as you believed. And you've seen the tie-up there, haven't you, with foreign Nazis and fascists? Not a pretty picture, eh, Henri?"

Henri did not answer. But his face was frightful, all the more so because it expressed absolutely nothing.

"They don't see, as you see, Henri, that domination of Hitler over America means the real end of capitalism, private enterprise, industry. They forget Thyssen, for instance. That is their egotism. Henri," and now he beat his hands gently on the desk, "I've discovered something. Only in a democracy can capitalism flourish, serve itself, serve the people."

But Henri only said: "And so, against my orders, they are continuing to supply Hitler with our very life-blood. They have defied me."

He stood up.

"They are out to ruin you, Henri," said Regan, in the gentlest of tones. "Because you won't play with them. They'll have your scalp, Henri. There's nothing they won't do. They are preparing to hand America over to Hitler, lock, stock and barrel. And you, too, most probably."

"Last month," said Henri, glancing at the papers on the desk, "they shipped a tremendous amount of Canadian nickel to Hitler. When we so desperately need nickel—" He paused, and caught his breath in an ominous sound.

"And last week," said Mr. Regan, reflectively, "your brother-in-law, Christopher, had a pleasant luncheon with certain gentlemen, among whom was your brother-in-law, Emile, your relatives, Jean and Nicholas Bouchard, Herr Doktor Meissner of the Reichsbank, the German Consul General, the president of your own organization, the American Association of Industries, the son of Mr. Hiram Mitchell, pious little automobile manufacturer to millions of pipsqueaks, Mr. Joseph Stoessel of the Nazareth Steel Company, competitor of your own steel company, Sessions, four presidents of four of your largest American subsidiaries from various parts of the country, two resounding Senators who are on record as hating England and loving the fascists, your relative, Hugo Bouchard, Assistant to the Secretary of State, Bishop Halliday, that sonorous anti-Semitic, anti-labor, anti-Roosevelt, anti-British and anti-liberal radio bastard, Brigadier-General Gordon MacDouglass, owner of one of the most influential chains of newspapers in America, Count Luigi Pallistrino, Italian chargé d'affaires, Mr. Horace Edmund, vice-president of your British associate and vassal armaments company, Robsons-Strong, Mr. John Byran, my esteemed competitor on the Street, and others of more or less importance. Yes, there was also that gentleman whom we had named for the nomination on the Republican ticket next year, and a certain infamous gentleman whom we shall not name at the present time, but who was once our man, also. Incidentally, one of Mr. Roosevelt's closest associates was there, too, a fact which would surprise the President excessively, and cause him to scrutinize his Cabinet a little more closely than he seems to be doing."

"And?" said Henri, quietly.

Mr. Regan marvelled at his equanimity. He said: "They discussed what I have already told you. They also discussed you. It seems that Mr. Hitler doesn't like you, Henri. Not at all. The Consul General delivered himself of some measured and poignant quotations. The consensus, finally, was that you had to be got rid of, and soon. You were an 'obstructionist.' Those were Hitler's orders." He smiled grimly. "Have you ever had a heart attack, Henri?"

"Let's not be melodramatic," replied Henri, seating himself with immense calm. Then he was silent, his lips compressed, his eyes staring before him with a terrible expression, his hands clenched on the arms of his chair.

"I assure you I'm not in the least melodramatic, my dear boy. Do you think they'd stop at anything, to get rid of you? You are one of the most powerful men in America, and your obstructionism can be fatal to them. We're up against the most deadly foes the world has ever known. Machiavelli, Metternich, Napoleon, Torquemada, Richelieu, et al. were mere dabblers in boudoir intrigue compared with these. They play, not only for territories and markets, Henri, but for all the peoples in the world. And—they've just about got what they want. Do you stand in the way? Well, a heart attack, or an assassination by some intransigent 'bolshevist,' are quick ways to die."

Henri, with more agility than he usually displayed, stood up again, and began to pace up and down, his head bent, his arms folded tightly across his chest. So, that stony imperturbability could be shaken, and shaken to its base. That broad face had become ugly with passion, and dangerously suffused. The broad forehead was visibly damp.

He stopped abruptly, and looked at Regan. "And so, because of your loans to Mussolini, and your arrangements of loans to Hitler, and the Bouchard shipments of materials, the cartels and assignments, we've come to this."

"We're all guilty, I admit, Henri. But—you and I had the same idea: to build up Hitler as a buffer state between Europe and Communism, between America and Communism. It wasn't a bad idea—then. In fact, under other circumstances, it would still be a good idea. And, there's our State Department. It did a good job for France, at our instigation. To a certain extent, it is still our Department, though your buff-colored relative, Hugo, is busily undermining it."

Henri stood before him, staring at him fixedly without really seeing him. Mr. Regan shook his head. "It's no use, Henri. You can't keep them in line, now. The stakes are too big. You can't do it alone."

Now Henri turned purplish red with the most violent rage he had ever felt. His egotism was mortally stricken. Before this mortification, this fury, he realized the full extent of his degradation and impotence.

Mr. Regan got up and approached him. He put his hand on his shoulder, and from his tremendous height looked down upon him, his little glittering eyes very piercing. "You want to stop it, don't you, Henri? For your own sake. I do, too. For the sake of the disease that's eating me alive."

"How about publicity?" asked Henri, more to himself than to Regan. "How about laying the facts before the President?"

Mr. Regan shook his head slowly and heavily. "No use. I've an idea the President has some inkling. It can't be exposed. There would be a revolution. Perhaps what the devils want. In the confusion, in the uproar, they could seize power. Moreover, they've got their men sprinkled thickly all through Congress, too, and in every Department. It is a scandal that dare not be betrayed, for fear of the consequences, even if it could be proved. And, Henri, we cannot expose anything, you and I, without fatally involving ourselves. Would you like Leavenworth, Henri?"

"Then," said Henri, somberly, "we are helpless before blackmail?"

"Would you," pursued Mr. Regan, "be willing to sacrifice yourself for your country?"

When Henri did not reply, the older man continued: "Even under the best of circumstances, my lad, you would be ruined.

You, an 'economic royalist.' Mr. Roosevelt might find in your confession the great chance of his career: to destroy the real masters of America."

"We could strike a bargain with him," muttered Henri, chewing on his lip.

Mr. Regan laughed drearily, and pressed his hand on the other's shoulder.

"One doesn't strike bargains with Franklin. Do you remember how we tried it, a few years ago? No, Henri, we're between the devil and the deep blue sea."

They looked at each other. "Henri," said Mr. Regan, "I think I can trust you. I think I know of a way out. There are a few like you, who don't want what the Bouchards want, either. The Amalgamated Carbide Company, for instance, your competitor in the manufacture of various synthetic products. The American Motors Company. Several others I can name. And, myself. Besides, we've got some Congressmen of our own too, you know." He paused. "Will you have dinner with me next week, Henri? A quiet little dinner, with a few guests?"

Henri was silent. His light brows had drawn themselves together in fierce concentration. He said, finally: "And, in the meantime, I'll do what I can do."

Mr. Regan was alarmed. "Henri, they're not to know what you're up to, you understand. If they get the smallest inkling, we're lost."

The full weight of the looming catastrophe suddenly impressed itself upon Henri Bouchard. The veins in his forehead swelled. "God!" he exclaimed, softly. "The bastards dared defy me! They dared do this to me!"

Mr. Regan gazed at him with something like surprised scorn.

"So, you're a childish egotist, too, Henri. I had hoped for something better than that. Never mind. I still have faith in your power, your personal strength. Please God, we'll come out of this."

He went back to his desk and fell into his chair as if exhausted. His mighty head dropped on his chest. He gazed blindly at his desk, and sighed over and over.

"You see, Henri," he said, "how it is. That is where Wendell Wilkie comes in. Even under Roosevelt, we've got a chance to break this thing. But, under Wilkie, who knows so much more about the intrigues of the masters, we've got a still better chance. Moreover, we'll have the better and more intelligent people behind us, with Wilkie. The smaller business men, of comparative integrity, for instance, besides the rabble. The sound middle class. Roosevelt doesn't have them. Wilkie is a realist. We can lay the whole thing before him, and he won't leap at our throats with cries of joy, as Roosevelt would do. America will come first with Wilkie. When I said he was an honest man, I meant a great many things. And all of them are complimentary to a great realist, a great American, a great man of affairs."

He lifted his head, and extended his hand to Henri.

"Well, Henri? We're in this together. Do we go on together?"

Henri took his hand. He smiled, and that smile, in his congested face, was ugly to see.

"We go on together," he said.

They sat in silence for some time, while Mr. Regan refilled the goblets with brandy. He was not surprised, and smiled only a little, darkly, when Henri drank with swift abruptness, and allowed his goblet to be filled again.

Then, as the room became duskier as the day sloped to sunset, Mr. Regan began to speak with grave slow softness:

"Henri Bouchard, I'm an old man, and I'm going to die soon."

Henri, who had been thinking of many things, was momentarily startled at this odd change in the conversation. But he said politely enough: "Surely not. You aren't in bad health, Mr. Regan?"

But Mr. Regan only regarded him in a strange steadfast silence for some time. "No," he said meditatively, "it would be no use. No use at all."

Henri was only indifferently puzzled. And then he smiled, a most disagreeable smile, and rose.

After he had gone, Mr. Regan thought to himself: Yes, you'll go on with me, you son of a literal bitch. Yes, you'll go on, you great-grandson of a colossal dog. But not for the reason I had sentimentally hoped. In fact, your precious relatives' idea would have had considerable appeal for you, under other circumstances. Perhaps, if they had reverentially discussed it with you. Yes, I am sure of that.

But you'll go on with me because they dared challenge your sovereignty, even if it was a challenge uttered in private. You'll go on because they are trying to destroy you, unseat you, throw you out. And that is one thing you'll never forgive them; one thing your monstrous egotism can't stomach— that they dared think they could do this to *you*. For that, you'll stop at nothing.

CHAPTER XVIII

Henri Bouchard remained in New York for several days, locked in his private suite at the Savoy-Plaza. During that time he had the "quiet little dinner" with Mr. Jay Regan and certain others. Had he been a true adventurer, he might have enjoyed what was said at that dinner, what plans were laid in the face of the precarious enormity of the situation, might have felt much excitement and exhilaration at the prospect, and at the thought of confounding and ruining his enemies.

But he was no true adventurer. He was a plotter on a gigantic scale. However, like his great-grandfather, he had no audacity. He believed in force, in the attainment of power which allowed him to use force and coercion like a knotted club.

He studied many papers. He gave especial care to the study of his brother-in-law, Christopher Bouchard. For long hours, he gnawed the nail of his index finger, and thought. Then, grimacing with disgust and cold rage, he put in a call for Christopher, who was still at Robin's Nest.

"Something has come up," he said, in a confidential tone, his fist curling on the table near the telephone. "I'd like to talk with you, privately. Right here. How soon can you come? It must be practically immediately. Incidentally, I may say that it will be of tremendous importance to you."

Christopher was astonished, and wary. The razor-profile sharpened keenly as he thought. Was it possible that the forbidding and stony devil had gotten wind of something? But, that was incredible. He wished to hear Henri's voice again, to judge by its tone, to catch a hint, so he said, amiably: "Certainly, I'll come at once. By plane. I'll be there before midnight. Is that too late to see you?"

"Not at all," said Henri, making his tone sound pleased and friendly. "The sooner the better. As I said, this is very important." With an effort, he let his voice drop, become increasingly friendly. "By the way, how is everything at home?"

Christopher laughed a little. He knew Henri very well. The swine was no good at dissembling. His voice always gave him away.

"Well, this isn't going to please you, I am afraid, but Celeste packed up Peter and baggage very abruptly today, and decamped."

Henri's eyes narrowed, and he smiled somberly to himself. But he said, echoing Christopher's laugh: "Not so good. Well. Where did they go, in the flight from Herod?"

"I've let them have Endur, which Celeste always claimed she disliked. They had a time with Annette, who's bathed in tears, with Edith comforting. Celeste explained that as Peter has now begun to write his muck-raking, he needs complete quiet. Peter seemed somewhat surprised at this, but evidently the little fox had taken him over the coals previously about leaving, for he said nothing. They cleared out very quickly. Evidently to get away before you returned. Celeste managed everything with dispatch, and with a high hand. Never thought she had it in her. When I tried a little discreet protesting, she turned on me like a small fiend and told me to mind my business." He coughed, gently. "Incidentally, she looks like hell. Haunted, I believe the word is. Refugee from a concentration camp. She appears to be taking my mother's death rather hard."

"Eh?" said Henri, before he could catch himself. He had forgotten all about Adelaide. "Oh, I see. Yes, of course. That was bad for her."

He added, after a moment: "I'll look for you, then, before midnight?"

After he had finished his conversation with Christopher, he resumed his study of the papers. Sometimes he stared into space, as motionless as stone. He must be adroit, now. He must wind, and watch, play delicately: all things that he despised. Sometimes he turned white with his mounting rage against his family who had so dared plot against him. He was no sadist, like Christopher, who loved revenge for its own exquisite sake. He must revenge himself, he must crush, subdue, destroy, but only for his own protection, and the teaching, once and for all, that he was supreme, must never be plotted against, or opposed in the slightest manner. His outrage was the outrage of a Napoleon, upon learning that his mediocre and treacherous little brothers and sisters had dared dream that they might overthrow him.

When Christopher arrived, a considerable time before midnight, Henri was as calm and contained as ever. Christopher darted a sharp glance at him, but could find nothing in that large harsh face to arouse any uneasiness in himself. Henri was quite at ease, ordered whiskey and soda for his guest, laughed, as he said: "I suppose this is somewhat raw, calling you in at this time of night. But it happens that I must make a certain decision tomorrow, and—I need your suggestions, and your own decision."

Christopher was immediately alert and intrigued. He sat near Henri in the coziest sort of intimacy, and no one watching that "ravenous, chromium-colored wolf," as his brothers called him, would have suspected the secret malignance behind the amiable smile he directed at his brother-in-law.

"I'll be glad to help," he said, with great cordiality. He passed his hand over his narrow and delicate skull.

Henri sat back in his chair and surveyed him with saturnine humor. "Do you mind if I review your own history for a moment? It's a very interesting one. I don't mean to offend you, of course, but a freshening of memory is necessary."

Christopher smiled, and shrugged. "Go on," he said.

Henri put his fingers together and stared at them meditatively. "I'm sure it's agreed that you were given a dirty deal by your colorful father, Jules, when he left control of Bouchard & Sons to Armand, and made you a petty, subsidiary officer. Your own personal fortune, as Bouchard fortunes go, was comparatively meager. I think he did that, deliberately. Well, no matter. But, you've done well for yourself. You've got Duval-Bonnet, your own creation. Has anyone ever congratulated you on it?" and he smiled quizzically.

Christopher laughed. He allowed Henri to refill his glass.

"Yes," continued Henri, with frankness, "you've done well for yourself. With assistance. My assistance," he added, pursing his lips humorously. "And I think you know that I never back anyone without reason. You've lived up to expectations. I've watched you over a number of years, Chris, and you've never made a mistake."

"Thanks," said Christopher, drily. He studied Henri with eyes as bright as a serpent's, and as wary. A faint pulse of fear began to beat in him, fear of this formidable and ruthless man who could still crush him and stamp him out with one lift of his heel. And his hatred grew with his fear. Mixed with these was an icy rage at the bland condescension in Henri's voice, amiable and affectionate though it was.

Henri was silent for a moment, as he studied his broad and powerful hands. Then he lifted his pale inexorable eyes and fixed them on Christopher.

"You'll allow me to be a little sentimental, eh? Well, we Bouchards have always been great breeders, until the dynasty descended to our generation. Now, we haven't done so well. One or two children, at the most. That's bad. Let us look at Bouchard & Sons, for instance. Armand, who is out, and so doesn't matter much, has only his son, Antoine, to contribute any flesh to the Company. And, somehow, I don't find much pleasure in the thought that Antoine's children might inherit Bouchard & Sons. In fact, I've already taken care of that part. You understand that this is in strict confidence?"

Christopher felt a sudden fierce excitement. He laid his glass down carefully, and gave all his attention to his brother-in-law. The pulse of fear had been superseded by this new emotion.

He smiled. "Antoine won't like that," he said, softly. "Antoine—has ambitions."

Henri returned his smile with an inclination of his head. "Yes, I know that. And I love to spike ambitions, when they don't fit in with my plans.

"So, Armand has no one else but Annette, his daughter, my wife. I don't need to tell you that Annette will never have any children, and what that has meant to me for the past few years. When you married my sister, I had some hopes. But, you and Edith seem about as sterile as others in the family. You haven't even produced a girl!"

But Christopher was as rigid and intent as bright metal. "Do you mean, that if we'd had children, they might have been your heirs?"

Henri waved a hand negligently. "Why not? Edith's my sister. I'm very fond of Edith, as you may have discovered before this. But the time for Edith to have children is past. Inconvenience of nature."

Christopher relaxed suddenly in his chair, and now his sudden volatile hatred turned against his wife, whom he, in fact, truly and deeply loved. He remembered what she had said upon their marriage fourteen years ago: "No, Chris. No children. I'll not be responsible for bringing any more Bouchards into this world!" He had not cared, particularly, then. He had only laughed. It was enough for him that he had Duval-Bonnet, and Edith. In truth, he detested children. The sense of dynasty was not in the least strong in him.

Henri saw his look, and smiled internally. He spread his hands, and shrugged. "So, here we are, I with Bouchard & Sons and no heirs, you with Duval-Bonnet, and no heirs. Do you like the idea of Bouchard & Sons—though you are no longer actively connected with the Company—going to your lovely brother Emile's son, Robert?"

Christopher had a quick inner vision of Robert, Emile's personal secretary, Robert, the short, the black, the surly and vicious, the ever silent and chronically resentful. One was hardly conscious of that young man, with his snarling voice and beetling black eyes, so like his father, except that Robert had nothing of Emile's false geniality and fat sparkle. But now Christopher saw Robert clearly, and his narrow lips tightened.

Henri inclined his head. "That's how it is," he said. "Who else have we got?" He added, when Christopher did not reply: "I don't admire Robert. Yet his father has already planned it."

So, thought Christopher, that's his game. Never a whisper out of him, yet while he's been plotting with us, he had his damned son in mind all the time. He regarded the inner vision of his nephew, Robert, with loathing and fury. But nothing appeared on his emaciated mask of a face. He only nodded, very slowly.

"Of course, that seems logical," Henri conceded. "I can see that. Emile has a right to plan. After all, he is vice-president of Bouchard & Sons. It is natural that he should have ambitions for his son. Besides, Robert's little wife, Isabel, looks as if she is going to present a crown-prince to Bouchard very shortly. A great breeder, by the looks of it. How long have they been married? Less than nine months, but the egg is practically ready to burst, isn't it? Too, she is a Catholic, and Catholics aren't notorious for restraint in breeding. Yes, it all seems to be working out by plan. Emile is entrenching himself. His own personal fortune is enormous. He owns a large block of stock in Bouchard, and larger blocks in the subsidiaries. His wife, Agnes, is a very rich woman, too. Then, little Isabel, grand-daughter of our foul automobile manufacturer, Mitchell, will inherit considerable shekels in her own right, for all her grandpapa was quite a Ku-Kluxer and bible-worshipper and didn't approve of his son, Edmund, marrying a Roman Catholic. I understand our Isabel is quite his pet." He stared at Christopher with affectionate immobility. "You don't mean to tell me, Chris, that you haven't thought of all this before?"

Christopher was silent. His meatless fingers clenched with a quick and lethal movement. He had hated his brother, Armand, but now merely despised him since his descent from power into the intricacies of The List. For his brother, Emile, he had an enormous natural hatred, congenital and bottomless. Now, when he saw the "natural plot," he was seized with a sense of impotent suffocation, a sensation as of drowning.

Henri shifted in his chair, sighed with humor, and raised his brows. Christopher, at the slight sound Henri made, visibly started, slowly fastened his eyes on Henri's face. He said, very quietly: "You. You've thought of something, haven't you? You aren't letting Bouchard go so easily, are you?"

"No," said Henri, frankly, after a moment. "I'm not. That's why you're here, if you didn't know it before."

At this, Christopher felt such an enormous wave of relief that he became actually weak. He had never depreciated the power of Henri Bouchard. He would have called it naïveté in another man, this belief in the omniscience of his brother-in-law. His voice was hoarse, when he said: "Yes. Go on."

He could hardly contain himself. He stood up, quickly, walked back and forth for a moment or two, passing his hands over his small and bony skull. Then he sat down again, as sharp and alert as a lean and silvery wolf. His eyes had begun to sparkle with swift and smiling malevolence. "Go on," he repeated.

"I've long thought of a way out," continued Henri, genially. "I've planned a way out, from the beginning. Celeste."

At the mention of his sister's name, Christopher straightened in his chair with a movement of almost violent energy. He stared at Henri with cold but furtive ferocity.

"Yes, Celeste," he muttered. He drew a deep breath. "But there's no hope of children, there. You know that." His eyes began to leap in their elongated sockets.

"Perhaps not there," said Henri, very softly. "Not with Peter. No. But with me—yes."

Christopher could hardly breathe, after this astounding statement. He leaned forward, clutching the arms of his chair. His features were alive, fluid, shining. "You mean?"

"I mean," said Henri, with equanimity, "that I soon intend to divorce Annette. And marry Celeste. After that coughing rabbit, Peter, dies. And he'll die soon, as I told you."

Christopher fell back in his chair. Then suddenly he was shaken with a grim and terrible joy. His little Celeste! It was all right, then. Everything was all right! He forgot everything, in the thought of Celeste. And then he remembered Emile, and his son, Robert, and he suddenly laughed aloud, a quite shrill and vicious sound.

Though Henri was well aware of Christopher's passion

for his little sister, yet he was newly astounded. And a compassion rare with him stirred him a little. He had always believed that there was something more than a trifle incestuous in Christopher's love, a great deal of the paternal. But he had not fully realized the extent of all this. He knew that Celeste loved her youngest brother, but also feared and suspected and disliked him, especially since her marriage to Peter. And so, Henri's compassion. It seemed pitiable to him, who rarely pitied anything, that so much love, so much ferocious protection, so much single-heartedness and relentless devotion, could have poured from so deadly and serpentine a man upon a sister whose love, these past years, had only been lukewarm. Every man had his soft spot of potential death. Christopher's was Celeste. Again, Henri felt pity.

He had another thought: Perhaps, now, it was not necessary to go on with his plans. Perhaps Celeste was enough. He eyed Christopher fixedly. No, it would do no harm to appeal to his rapacity, also. Love and rapacity: an invincible combination.

He said, in a kind tone: "Why are you so surprised? Surely, you know I never give up?" He assumed affront. "You must have known that I've always wanted Celeste, and intended to have her some day." He smiled faintly. "And my intentions were always honorable, I assure you. Once, she thought she hated me. She never did, really. She came back, quite willingly. When Peter's dead, there'll be no difficulty. But, of course, all this is very confidential, as you know. Celeste and I had a little talk, that night her mother died. It's all arranged."

Henri continued to watch Christopher closely, his eyes narrowed. It had been so very easy. Again, his pity stirred. He had no intention of divorcing Annette and her fortune, so long as Armand lived.

He shifted to a more comfortable position in his chair, refilled Christopher's glass. Christopher, still gloating, took it automatically, and drank.

"And now," said Henri, with a deliberately quick change of tone, "we've settled the sentimentalities. Of course, there wasn't any need of all this explanation. You must have known it all along. I didn't call you to New York to discuss any such obvious thing. It was something quite different, something immediately important."

Christopher came out of his dream of triumph and joy with a start, and a new wariness. How could he have forgotten! With trembling fingers, he fumbled for his platinum cigarette case, lit a cigarette. But the cigarette hung drily from his lips, as he thought. He might lift a murderous hand against his wife's brother; he might rejoice, with a deadly and virulent rejoicing, at the fall of Henri Bouchard. But, Celeste's husband was another matter. All his triumph and his joy flowed out of him, congealed. He felt suddenly very ill.

Henri saw all this. Yes, he thought, he had been quite right. Love was not as invincible as rapacity. He saw now, from the constant vibration of Christopher's eyelids, that he was suddenly plotting again. It would not be beyond him to try to keep Celeste from Henri, for the furtherance of his own schemes. The thought was causing Christopher real agony of mind. But behind it was his rapacity. Henri knew the exact moment when Christopher's love lost the struggle with his over-powering greed. It was then that Henri moved again, and his pity was entirely gone, replaced by stony malignancy.

"We'll get down to business, Chris. It's after one o'clock, and we still haven't come to the real thing."

But Christopher was sunken deep into his private chaos. Henri had to raise his voice harshly to bring him back. He started. The chromium-colored eyes had lost all their gleam; they were actually haggard. Bemused, he hardly heard Henri's opening words:

"We'll pare down to essentials. We know that Hitler will move against Poland in a few months, perhaps sooner. There'll be war. England and France will attack Hitler. They'll have to; they're frightened out of their wits this time. It's now or never. But, you know all that."

Christopher said nothing. But he was all alertness now. He had had a shock. He had forced his own recovery.

"It has been my firm belief, at least it has become my belief recently, that we can't do business with Hitler," resumed Henri. "You, Chris, and some of the others, haven't agreed with me. I presume you still disagree?"

Now Christopher forgot everything in the intensity of his listening. The thin vague pulse of fear returned to him, but stronger now, beating heavily in his chest and his temples. He regarded Henri in fixed silence for a few moments, before smiling easily, and lifting his hand with a deprecating gesture.

"I still think we can do business with Hitler," he said.

Henri shook his head slowly. "And I know we can't. But that's an old story. We've gone over it a dozen times. I won't argue with you. The only thing we have agreed upon is that America is not to enter any war cooked up in Europe."

Christopher nodded. "We'll see to that."

"As we've all agreed before, war will ruin us. Roosevelt is bent on government ownership, or at least a strong form of socialism. The war, if we get into it, will be his God-given chance. America will become the besotted empire of the Common Man. In this barnyard, civilization will be trampled down under hoofs. Not that we don't appreciate the good services the Common Man has done us, and will continue to do in the future! You can always rely on the Masses to go grunting and trampling and chewing wherever you drive them. Swine!"

"Yes," said Christopher, smiling reminiscently. "Every time our holy reverend Halliday sends forth his sonorous venom over the radio, a pogrom threatens, the Polacks in Detroit get ready to pull Jewish beards, the aristocratic Oakies of the South fondle ropes and dream of lynching Negroes, and Mitchell, Halliday's guardian angel, slaughters another union in his cheap automobile plants. The mob never learns, thank God."

"Thank God," echoed Henri. "And so, if we have a war, the mob will follow Roosevelt into socialism, and bellow for our scalps. We've done a good job in the past with the masses. We can't rely on continuing an equally good job if we get into the war. When it becomes a choice with the fellaheen of gorging themselves, or hating others, they prefer the gorging. Roosevelt fills their bellies; we gave them hatred. They prefer their bellies."

"Nevertheless," said Christopher, "the masses instinctively love fascism. We can rely on that. They love the boot and the whip. It gives them a kind of orgasm—a voluptuousness. The Germans aren't the only perverts. The masses love to murder and torture. Give them the chance, and they'll run for it, screaming with joy. That's why fascism is so popular. Why it would be popular here."

Henri contemplated him a moment. "However, fascism, though it appeals to me personally, wouldn't do in America. I'll be servant to no master. And, I believe, you agree with me?"

"Certainly," said Christopher, smoothly.

The fear was strong in him now, a metallic taste on his lips. Henri appeared to grow before him, to become terrible and gigantic and threatening. Yet, Henri was laughing, lightly.

"Not that there is any danger of real fascism in America.

We know the limits. For our own survival. But this isn't getting down to business, I'm afraid.

"When the war comes, we'll have our greatest chance. In South America. When Germany is involved in the war, she will be unable to control her damned airlines in South America; we'd then have an opportunity to get control."

Christopher moved imperceptibly in his chair, but he gave the impression of leaning forward, watching Henri with narrowed eyes.

"I now have the chance to gain control of the Eagle Aviation Company," said Henri, with impassive calm. "It has been offered to me. The stock is down to five dollars a share. Yet, they have the plans and patents all ready for large passenger planes that can easily be converted into bombers."

Christopher said nothing. He was whiter than ever.

"Now," said Henri, with a casual wave of his hand, "your company, Duval-Bonnet, makes only fighter planes. Eagle Aviation also makes fighter planes, and possesses fine patents for pursuit planes. While you, yourself, have perfected planes for speed, you haven't the facilities for making large ships, nor the motors for them. Our own subsidiary, Giant Motors, are making such a motor for the planes planned by Eagle Aviation."

Christopher felt that he was smothering. He put his hand momentarily to his throat. But otherwise he betrayed nothing of what he was thinking. Through a bright haze, he saw that Henri was smiling blandly.

"If I purchased Eagle Aviation, I could put Duval-Bonnet out of business. But quick," he was saying. "A very unfraternal thing to do, of course. And, naturally, I haven't even given that a thought, as you can well imagine. But I have had a very nice thought, which will appeal to you.

"And this is the thought: I will purchase Eagle Aviation. You will merge Duval-Bonnet with it, under the name of Eagle Aviation, with you, of course, as president at a very good salary. That ought to appeal to you. Your personal fortune, as Bouchard fortunes go, isn't very large, thanks to your delightful father. And, as president of the merged companies, you will be in control of the most powerful airplane manufacturing combine in the country."

Christopher, dazed, his ears ringing, his heart roaring, could only stare at him. Suddenly, he could not contain himself. He literally shot to his feet. He began to move up and down the room, his face chalky, his eyes newly glittering.

And Henri watched him, smiling grimly to himself. Christopher stopped before him, abruptly.

"What do you want?" he asked, in a low and shaking voice.

"Sit down, Chris. I've never seen you so agitated." Henri was smiling calmly. "Good God, is it always a question of a deal between any two of us?"

"Yes," said Christopher, in a tone that informed Henri that he was at the breaking point. "It is always a question of a deal. What do you want?"

"Sit down, I said. That's better. Now, we can talk reasonably. What do I want? I want Eagle Aviation. I want you as president. After all, you're my sister's husband. By the way, you know I still control Edith's bonds and shares in Bouchard. You've thought that ungenerous of me, haven't you? You've wanted to control them, as her husband. Unfortunately, I've thought differently. No bad feelings, I hope?"

Christopher did not answer. He sat on the edge of his chair, his bony hands grasping his knees. He could not look away from Henri.

"Of course, this is still in a state of discussion," continued Henri. "I may change my mind—tomorrow. I only wanted your reaction to my suggestion."

"You only wanted—" repeated Christopher, with a faint and ghastly smile. And then could say nothing more.

"In the event the deal is consummated, and you are willing to merge Duval-Bonnet with Eagle Aviation, and become its president, say at about four times your present salary, I will retain fifty-one percent of the preferred stock of the combined companies, which will give me the controlling interest. You realize, of course, that I will have to supply you with Giant Motors and Spark instruments."

"That will give you control, then," said Christopher, in a stifled voice, "of Duval-Bonnet, too, my own company."

"Only," interjected Henri, smoothly, "figuratively. I'm not overly interested in aviation. I've got Bouchard & Sons, and we'll be very, very busy soon, manufacturing armaments. Incidentally, did I tell you that on next Monday I purchase the Concord Arms, too? A fine little company! I intend to merge it with Kinsolving Arms, after I've had a talk with Francis."

Christopher was speechless. Only once before in his life had he been so enormously shaken. His rapacity clamored in him exultantly. He could hardly restrain himself. Yet, he held himself motionless, forced his eyes to battle with the pale eyes of the terrible Henri Bouchard.

"You want something," he whispered.

There was a brief silence in the room. Henri leaned back in his chair and surveyed his brother-in-law with calm intentness. "Yes," he said quietly, "I want something. I want you."

Christopher heard these words with immediate terror. He thought: Does he know? Is it possible he knows? How could he know? It was incredible that this formidable swine could have heard the slightest whisper. But, if he knew, then he would move. There was still time. There was still time to crush the plotters, and Christopher had no illusions that he, himself, would be spared.

The two men stared at each other in that silence. There was a singing sound in Christopher's brain, a sickness about his heart. He tasted the bitterness of complete fright and dread. He tried to pierce behind that large expressionless mask of Henri's face. But he could read nothing there.

Mingled with his terror was the rising shout of his exultant rapacity. He was over fifty now, but compared with the other Bouchards (whom he knew laughed at him in private) he was nothing. His enormously wealthy wife's fortune was still controlled by her brother; her husband could not touch it. Edith's mother had given that control to Henri, out of her malice and hatred for her daughter. Christopher, in exile in Florida, was a nonentity in his relatives' eyes, even a ludicrous figure, thanks to Henri Bouchard. Now the opportunity had arrived to give him power equal to any held by any other member of the family, save Henri. It was the fulfilment of a dream dreamt during hundreds of sleepless and gnawing nights of hatred.

He cried out suddenly, over his suspicions and his terror: "What do you want?"

"Good God," said Henri, mildly. "I've told you. Perhaps I've had a change of heart, too. After all, Edith is my sister. I'd like to see her more often. Then, as I told you before, you've impressed me with your ability. I've watched you for years. Who else would I naturally choose for Eagle Aviation, but you? Who else is there, so familiar with the aviation business? Can you name anyone else in the family?"

Christopher was silent. But his eyes bored into Henri's, with renewed fear and confusion.

"There's another thing," said Henri, in the gentlest of tones. "It's a matter of precaution. Not that I don't trust you implicitly, of course. But, to protect my own interests, I'll have my own men in the company—to assist you. Only to assist you, naturally."

He knows! thought Christopher. And immediately was numb with fright.

"I want you to come in with me," said Henri, even more gently. "But I want to trust you. You know, I didn't like Peter's story about Brouser and Schultzmann. Even though, I am sure, it wasn't true. Nevertheless, it disturbed me. I don't like—lies."

Christopher rose again, walked up and down, passing his hands over his head in that old gesture of his, so like his father's. And Henri watched him without expression.

To accept all this would mean the abandoning of the plot, his association with the others, his dream of power and vengeance. But, he thought, in his fever, there was no need of vengeance now, because of what Henri proposed to do with Celeste. And, plots can be discovered; plotters can be sought out and ruined—destroyed. The plot, though the plotters were themselves powerful, was still precarious, full of mortal danger. This, that Henri was offering, was sure, and certain. But, to accept, would make him Henri's man. He could not move against Henri without destroying himself. He knows! he repeated to himself, savagely.

Here was a means of escape from a plot of which he had always had his inner doubts. It would bring him power, wealth, triumph, this escape. It would force him to betrayal, but the betrayal of his relatives would not annoy him in the least! It would be his personal triumph over them, after years of ridicule and none-too-secret laughter.

He stopped abruptly before Henri, and Henri saw all the polished evil of this man, his cruel exultation, his wild and deadly decision.

But Henri said, "I repeat, I must trust you. And," he added with a smile, "you dare not let me distrust you."

He looked at his brother-in-law, and waited, impassively.

Christopher drew a deep breath. "May I offer you a suggestion?" he asked, in a peculiar voice. "Get rid of Antoine, my sparkling nephew. At once."

So, thought Henri, it is done, then.

"Yes?" he said with quietness. "Antoine? And who else?"

Christopher sat down again. His breath was still coming in quick and audible gasps. "I think we ought to have a little talk," he said.

CHAPTER XIX

Peter wrote, feverishly, swiftly:

"This is a story told to the middle class of America, of the world. The powerful do not need to be told. They know the story too well. The Masses are incapable of enlightenment, due to a biological immaturity of mind which only centuries of evolution can eradicate. Though they suffer in these days, they suffer as animals suffer, blindly, dumbly, without question, without even a desire for change. The forces of reaction, the strength of the status quo, do not reside in the mighty, as popularly believed, nor in the cautious middle class, as they believe, themselves, but in the Masses. Therefore an attempt to enlighten the Masses is a failure. The old aphorism of Cæsar's, that the mob desires only bread and circuses, is still valid. If Cæsar can contrive to make those circuses bloody, resounding with the cries of the dying, the Masses are happy, contented, satisfied, and will return to their hovels and their gutters without a single wish to improve their own lot. Thus, the purpose of circuses.

"Therefore, this book is not dedicated to the illiterate Masses, who are actually the greatest sufferers at the hands of their masters. For it is not the Masses that reform government, that destroy the tyrants, that overthrow the oppressors. The men who lead the Masses, men of good will, of compassion, pity, justice and indignation, have come, in most cases, from the enlightened and intelligent middle class. Nor do I desire the support and the anger of the intellectuals, those milky and impotent eunuchs who know little of government, much of dead books, and nothing at all of men. Their vinegar indignations are impotent. Their cries are the cries of acid children. They are ignored by the tyrants, rightly, and regarded with contempt by vigorous and healthy men generally.

"This book, then, is dedicated to that class still least corrupted: the middle class of the world. For this is the class that has given to every republic, every democracy, the soberest soldiers, the best art, the strongest and most decent government, the greatest social improvements, the firmest stability, the cleanest spiritual morals, the most judicious indignation, the soundest reforms, the most advanced science. When this class is destroyed, the whole nation perishes, whether it be destroyed by the mighty (who are endlessly conspiring against it) or the Masses (who endlessly envy and hate it). It stands alone, sane, strong, sometimes bewildered, often stupidly enraged, almost always healthy, and upon it, and its enlightenment, depend the whole structure of civilization, the whole progressive evolution of man, the whole hope of the future.

"The Masses are easily kept in subjection by the oppressors. In truth, they prefer subjection, strong paternalistic government and autocratic guidance, for they lack the organs with which to think, weigh, judge and plan.

"In America, today, the conspiracy against the middle class has already been hatched, its doom pronounced, its destruction planned. This was done in Germany, by Hitler. If these things are allowed to come to pass in America, we shall see the end of civilization, a reducing of the earth to a habitation of slaves and princes, which condition, though beloved of the Church, sought after by the masters, is so horrible, so repugnant, so appalling, that the last of the men of good will must put nooses about their own necks and die in despair.

"To you, then, the great, sound, healthy and enlightened middle class, I give my salute, all my hopes, all my prayers, knowing that you alone can save the world of men, knowing that you can change America from a royalistic Republic to a Democracy, knowing that only by your own will can you perish, and all of us with you.

"This, America, is the story of your enemies.

"You believe you have many enemies. It is this dull and stupid politician, or this one. It is 'Communism,' perhaps. It is this man who would keep you isolated from the world of men, or the man you bitterly denounce as a 'war-monger.' It is this President, or this ex-President, it is Hitler or Winston Churchill or Stalin. It is this religon, or that race. You do not like this man with the long nose? You do not like the English, or the French? Perhaps the Jews annoy you? Perhaps the Italians irritate you with their ferocity, or their gaiety, or their laughter? You have been told by your priests and your teachers that all men are brothers, and that God is your father. But someone has told you, has he not, that this is absurd, dangerous, fantastic, the dream of fools who would lead you to war and death and economic ruin?

"Yes, you have many enemies. But the ones you have been given are non-existent. They have been conjured up for you by your true foes, by your masters in America who know no race, no nationality, but who conspire with their secret fellows in every country in the world, not only against you, but against all your brothers under every sun, and against their own people.

"Do you think your American enemies and masters hate and fear and despise their fellow conspirators in Germany, in England, in Italy, in Japan, in South America, in Russia? If you do, you are naive, and stupid. You are dangerous in your ignorance. And in your danger, America may die.

"Should there be war—and there will be, God have mercy on our souls—do you think your American enemies will sternly refuse to do business with your enemies across the seas? Do you think the masters, the banks, the industries, will automatically put up walls against each other? Again, you are naive, and stupid. While you die, while you starve, while you struggle, and pray and hope and sacrifice, your American masters will gaily be meeting their co-conspirators in Switzerland, perhaps, or some other 'neutral' spot, and financial and utility and war-matériel exchanges will be happily arranged, money and credits passed, all in a spirit of the fondest fellowship, and your ultimate fate decided in an atmosphere that has transcended nationality, race and boundaries. You will probably be in a death-struggle with Germany. But while Britons and Americans are fighting, knee-deep in mud and blood, against Germans and Italians and others, American bankers, British bankers and German bankers will be quietly and fondly meeting together to discuss exchanges of credits in some anonymous little spot. Do you think your newspapers will tell you of this? Again, you are pathetically naive. No report will reach your ears. The black curtain will be drawn over the conspirators and you will never know.

"While America will be feverishly arming herself and her allies-to-be, your American masters will be arranging for shipments of vital war-necessities to your alleged 'enemies' through international cartels. And these war-necessities, translated into guns and bullets and bombers, will be directed against the lives of your sons, your children and your friends.

"Was it Hitler who invented fascism, or Mussolini? Look closer, my brother, into those great offices behind the smoking mills and factories, into that boudoir, into that suave dining-hall where the lustrous ladies and their benefactors sit and devour the riches of the world, into that mighty bank with the bronze doors, into those rooms of the international stock-exchanges, and behind those towering cathedrals in the midst of starved cities. In these places the plot against mankind was invented, planned, carried into world-wide action.

"When Manchuria was invaded, who directed that the matter be reported obscurely, that your antagonism be subtly aroused against the Chinese? When Ethiopia was tortured, who inspired the newspapers with admiring comments that Mussolini had 'made the trains in Italy run on time'? When the Spanish Republic was attacked by the hirelings of reaction, slavery and exploitation and ignorance, who was it that told you that the Republic was 'Communistic,' criminal, a murderer of innocents and priests? Who was it that deafened your ears against the cries of the tormented and the helpless, and dulled your conscience when your brother was dying? Who was it that distorted news from Russia, that inspired your distrust and hatred, that threatened vague calamities unless Russia was check-mated and restrained, that denied shipments to Russia unless paid for immediately in gold, while other shipments were sent to Germany through international cartels —without gold? Who called Russia 'godless, atheistic, plotter against the world, against order, against God, against morality'? Who, when the world of sane and civilized and decent men was betrayed at Munich, hailed the senile Chamberlain as a great man, a hero?

"It is not too late. You have only to look, to understand, to learn. You have only to draw aside the rich curtains and see your despicable enemies whispering together in secret. The men of all nations, who invented Hitler, Mussolini, Franco, and their abominable conspiracies against mankind.

"Among these men your American enemies are the most powerful. These men have decided what form of government every country shall have and maintain, betrayed them to their eternal enemies, robbed them of the natural resources of their homelands, elevated madmen to power and authority over subjugated peoples, enlisted priests and princes of the Church in their secret army of destruction, extended their rapacious hands to the farthest corner of the world, decreed how you shall live, what you shall read, eat, wear and think, what politicians you shall support, what good men you shall murder, what victims you shall torture or ignore, what armies you shall maintain or not maintain, whether you shall live, or die in agony and hatred.

"For these men have such undisputed and sinister control

of the destinies of the American people, and the destinies of the world, that they can decree what shall be sold, how much shall be sold, how much produced, and at what price, anywhere on earth. They can decree what man shall be elected President of the United States, what our foreign policy shall be, what modifications shall take place in our government, or even decide its overthrow! Who shall sit on the thrones of Europe, who shall control the chancelleries, who shall march, who shall retire, who shall die? These decisions lie in the hands of these men.

"Their hirelings and henchmen in Congress, their labor-baiting organizations, fascist in character, their paid clergymen, satellite businessmen and industrialists, their suborned newspapers and treacherous publishers, their political machine, have, for their ultimate object, the superseding of the political power of the American people, and the establishing of themselves as the supreme dictators over all phases of the life of the world.

"You, the people of America! What agonies you have endured at the hands of these men, in wars, in starvation, in despair, in hopelessness and in poverty, in exploitation and loss of liberty! What agonies you are still to endure—unless you look behind the walls of newspapers, politicians, churchmen and silence, that they have built up about them to hide themselves.

"For, they have decided that you shall lose your freedom, your franchise, your civil liberties, your dignity, your honor, and your manhood. They have created Hitler as a rampart against 'Communism.' If the rampart is now threatening to tumble on our own heads, your enemies will look beyond the ruin to the future. They have not wanted war with their creature, Hitler. They have hoped that he might assist them in subjugating and enslaving you. If he will not—if we, the American people, must rise and destroy this monster they have created—then they must swiftly change their plans, they must plot that fascism be not utterly destroyed in Europe, they must make certain that the future bugaboo is Russia, that no man of good-will shall enter the White House, that a form of hateful and dangerous Naziism be instituted in America. They will work to these ends, sleeplessly, whether there is war or not.

"This book is written to tell you what you do not know. It is planned to cause you to look up from your circuses and your gadgets and your cheap toys, and to fix your eyes upon your real enemies."

The pen slowly slipped from Peter's fingers in a gesture of utter exhaustion. He leaned his head on his thin hand and closed his eyes. He often had such waves of weakness, which came from his soul even more than from his wasting body. Behind his eyelids he saw circles and balls of dull fire, whirling nebulæ of blue and crimson and yellow. He pressed his hands against them. Now a familiar faintness overwhelmed him, during which all his thoughts swirled together in a spiral of mist, formed of pain, and floated away from him.

In the midst of this blowing disintegration, he had only one clear thought: How was it possible to encompass, between the narrow pages of a book, the whole incredible and gigantic story? He could only touch here and there, like lightning glancing on the highest peaks of mountains, but which left the deep clefts of valleys, the oceans and the clamoring rivers, in complete and shadowy darkness. He could make audible only a few thundering voices, coming from various distances. His picture, therefore, must seem disjointed, incoherent, and by reason of this, more and more fantastic and incredible. The people believed only little ordinary stories. They regarded the echoes of giants, the shaking of their steps, their looming silhouettes, as fantasia, the awesome chimera created by writers of fairy stories or epic legends. They might even find such vast images to have a semi-divine or heroic quality, which their meager souls must admire. The people lusted always for heroes, for the superman, for Olympian gods. He, Peter, must be exhaustively careful that he presented no such images to the public mind, for its childish adulation. The images must be terrible, but also hateful. It must be shown that they were only little men after all, but more endowed than most with lust for power, with mercilessness, with cruelty and rapacity and treachery. But how to do this, when only the tallest peaks could be shown forth by lightning, when only the most stupendous heights could be revealed, in the compass of a book?

He opened his eyes and looked about him. His table was heaped with data, hundreds of pages of it, and letters, and books. He must write a veritable library if he was to give even a two-dimensional story. Moreover, he could not name names, for fear of libel suits. He must give only hints, endow his true characters with strange appellations, twist more than a little, highlight out of proportion, sink other facts into a dark background. He must do all this, if only to have the book published.

His sister-in-law, Estelle, wife of Francis, had urged him

to write "something that would attract the attention of Hollywood, Peter, if you really wish to deliver a 'message.'"

How, then, was one to awaken this huge American mob, this singing, sports-loving, eager, selfish, stupid, generous and ignorant mob that loved only mean little pleasures? When he thought this, Peter was seized with an anguish of love and anger and suffering. How great could be America, how noble and strong, if it would but hear and understand and leap to its feet with a shout of indignation and fury?

His impotence overwhelmed him. So much to say, so much to tell and reveal, and it must all pour out through the thin squeak of his pen and the dribble of vapid ink. The stark and terrible story must be reduced to scrawls which probably would attract the eye of only a small minority. And hour by hour the doom approached more swiftly, unseen amid the glare of Main Streets, unheard amid the darkened delights of moving-picture theatres.

The Walpurgis Night was closing over mankind, but the prophet gesticulated alone in the deserted bazaars, and his voice echoed back to himself from the empty places. The sellers and the buyers had flocked to listen to the brittle voice of some trollop in the city.

Peter lifted a letter from the pile near his hand and reread it. It was from his relative, Georges Bouchard, the publisher:

"You will remember, Pete, that your book, *The Terrible Swift Sword*, was not well received by the public. They aren't interested in non-fiction, at least, not yet. (Personally, I believe the day is coming when they will be.) They are still not receptive to such books as yours. They are only troubled and disturbed by them, and finally they are incredulous. They don't want to be annoyed.

"You will tell me that if I had allowed you to use your real name instead of a pseudonym, the book would have attracted more attention from critic and public alike. But, as I told you, there were many drawbacks to this. Bad taste, in the first place, though you won't agree with me, as usual. The public doesn't like men who betray their families, even in a 'good cause.' Then, there was the libel angle. I still don't cotton to the idea of my family falling heavily on me, *en masse*, nor will you, if you give the matter just a little thought.

"Now that brings me to your proposed new book, *The Fateful Lightning*. I've looked over your outline, and given it long and serious thought. And, frankly, it quite terrifies me. What do you expect to accomplish by it? Do you actually think the American public would care for it, consider it, weigh it, be aroused by it? As a publisher of some years and some standing, I must disagree with you. It will be called melodramatic, insane, turgid and impossible. Besides, there have been whole floods of books written on this very subject before, and they didn't stir up even a breeze. Then, candidly, your idea of using your own name on it frightens me.

"I'm in a bad position, too. I'm a Bouchard. I simply can't see myself publishing such a book."

He had added wryly (and this Peter could not forgive): "It is too bad that we no longer have publishing connections in Germany. I'm sure Goebbels would appreciate *The Fateful Lightning*. Your book, *The Terrible Swift Sword*, was very cordially received by him."

Peter compressed his pale lips. He continued to read the letter:

"However, if you are really hell-bent on publishing such a book, under your own name, I recommend that you see Cornell T. Hawkins of Thomas Ingham's Sons. This is a strong and conservative old firm of great prestige, and highly respected. In the past, they've gone in for the more decorous literature and churchly text books, but it seems that a new spirit has recently come to life there. I think that is the influence of Hawkins. You must have heard of him, at least, though you never mentioned meeting him. A great man; a great editor. I might even say, a great democrat and aristocrat, though that sounds paradoxical. Though his background properly would seem to be the austere panelled white walls of some New England mansion, filled with frigid shining furniture and bookcases of old classics, he has a cold yet passionate modern spirit and an astounding intellect. If he does nothing else, he will listen to you sympathetically, and give you the soundest advice. You can trust him. And when I say that, I want to assure you that I've rarely said it of another human being."

Peter threw aside the letter, and covered his aching head with his hands. His exhaustion became insupportable. Had he been a woman, he would have burst into terrible tears. After a long time, he dropped his hands and stared through the window.

He winced, as always, at what he saw. From the walls of the house, Christopher's Endur stretched away, a plain-like sheet of green grass, to distant walls and polished gates. Everything was utterly stark and glaring brilliantly in a hot and sterile wind and under a sun like a blazing ball of glass. No trees cooled those vast lawns, except where, on each side of the immense acreage, two identical rows of pointed poplars stood as stiff as painted wood against a colorless summer sky, their sharp purple shadows as rigid as themselves. The radiant scene was empty, unbearable in the intense heat, for Christopher had an aversion to flowers. The view matched the interior of the square white mansion, with its glassy and chromium furniture standing in its own reflections against walls of glass or white wood.

No curving light of a bird's wing softened this stage-scene of emptiness and burning radiance. Only the unhampered winds, as dry as air surging from ovens, made any audible sound about the house or grounds. That wind was almost constant. It exacerbated Peter's nerves. The windows were wide and clear as laboratory windows, and the narrow draperies were set against walls instead of glass, so that one could not escape the blazing austerity of the view.

As sterile, as dead, as passionless as the owner, himself, thought Peter. He loathed Endur. Its bleakness, its lack of merciful shade, its openness, which seemed the wary openness before a fortress where no enemy can hide, was eloquent of Christopher's character. But here he must stay until his own home, on Placid Heights, had been completed.

As he stared so bitterly through the window, Georges' letter in his hand, Peter thought suddenly of his father, Honoré Bouchard. It was very strange that he so often thought of his father in these days, and each time the vision he had of Honoré was clearer, sharper, more urgent, more kind. In all the years since Honoré's death on the *Lusitania,* his memory had remained with his youngest and favorite son, like the gentle melancholy over an autumn landscape. It was in 1932 that Peter first began to have these warm visions, full of substance and clarity, as though Honoré, in the flesh, stood before him, speaking. He had been only a young collegian when his father had fallen into the gray chasms of the Atlantic, and over the years Honoré's face and form had become diffuse, uncertain, his voice dimmed and hollow. It was exceedingly strange, then, that Peter saw him again so clearly now, and heard his voice so strongly.

CHAPTER XX

It seemed to Peter, as he remembered his father now, that Honoré had always been afflicted with a kind of desperate melancholy, silent, patient, gently smiling, and abstracted. He had never complained, had never been pettish or irritable or distracted, though sometimes given to inexplicable gestures of soundless violence in the very midst of some casual remark. His three older sons, Francis, Hugo and Jean, had found this somewhat amusing; his wife, Ann Richmond, had found it very annoying. But Peter, when he saw these gestures, saw how his father's kind smile suddenly became fixed, almost a grimace, would feel his heart lurch with a nameless fear and frantic compassion. The Honoré who spoke, who maintained a firm and considerate exterior, who listened attentively and with sympathy, was not the Honoré who lived beneath the surface of the flesh, tormented, desperate, despondent and without hope. This, Peter knew, even when he was still very young.

No small part of the present success of Bouchard & Sons was due to Honoré Bouchard. Peter, in spite of anxious searchings, could find nothing that might justify his hope that his father had been less unscrupulous, less inexorable, less venal and rapacious than Jules Bouchard, his cousin and friend. It was true that he had been kind and compassionate, that his charities had been large and practically secret, that he had been sympathetic and gentle to all, even to his greedy and vicious wife who must have sickened him often, and that, in a strange way, he had had integrity and character. Nevertheless, he had followed all of Jules' advice, so far as Peter could see, had listened to Jules, acknowledged his shrewdness and genius. Peter's searching revealed nothing objective that would lighten his heart and console him. The record of Honoré Bouchard was open to his eyes, and there was no instance where Honoré had set the welfare of America above profits, or the safety of mankind above the rising power of the Bouchard dynasty.

Yet, Peter could not shake off the memory of his father's brown deep eye with its expression of desperate melancholy and abstracted brooding. He remembered that round bullet-head with its cropped gray hair, the sturdy, rather short figure, the broad and solid shoulders, the somewhat crooked nose, and the kind and thoughtful smile. There had been a strange stillness about Honoré, as if he were listening to something no one else heard.

Sometimes Peter had even hoped that his father had been weak, too weak to resist the pressure of his cousin, Jules, and the others, that he had been too kind to oppose them, or that there had been a spiritual or physical listlessness in him which had prevented him from struggling with the other Bouchards. But there had been no weakness, no listlessness, in that strong and homely face, Peter had had to admit with later sadness. He might have a distaste for the greedy and the exigent, the selfish and the cruel (and he had demonstrated this quite vigorously many times in Peter's presence), but when it became a matter of the Bouchard fortunes and power and profit, he was as relentless as his cousin, Jules.

What distortion of soul had been in him which had made this usually reserved man voluble when he discovered some personal viciousness, rapacity or cruelty in a member of his immediate family, even to the point of inflicting physical punishment on his young sons, yet which had kept him silent, acquiescent or cooperative when it was a matter of Bouchard wealth, Bouchard profit or Bouchard aggrandisement? No matter, then, if multitudes suffered, if national honor was betrayed, if plots were set in motion against the peace and welfare of a whole nation or a whole world! Peter sometimes saw a gleeful pleasure in his relatives at the success of some abominable scheme, a gloating, a chuckling delight. But he never saw these in his father. Instead, he had observed that the melancholy deepened in Honoré's eyes; he would become more silent, a little grimmer, a trifle more solitary than usual.

Peter was eternally tormented by the enigma which was his father. The clearest memories he had were of Honoré's deep kind voice, his gentle and affectionate hand, his sweet and thoughtful smile, his meditative philosophy and wry embittered wit. Honoré, of all the Bouchards, alone was scholarly. He had had an immense library, and would spend endless evenings reading under his quiet lamp. Of all his relatives, oddly enough, he seemed to prefer Jules Bouchard, his cousin, and in Jules' light and debonair presence he would become almost gay, his laughter unusually ready, his face lighted with real pleasure and comfort.

Was there something fundamentally alike in these two? Peter would think, in miserable distress. Surely everything that was good and wholesome and decent in Honoré must have been violated by the suave Jules. Yet, if it was violated, there was no sign of it.

Then Honoré, sent by Jules on some dangerous and secret mission to a Europe suddenly plunged into chaos, had died on the *Lusitania*.

Peter remembered that night well. Now, as he remembered, he lifted his hand from his eyes, and raised his aching head. His blue eyes narrowed, became intent, as he stared sightlessly through the blazing window of his room. Something seemed to be forming before his eyes, something significant, something which was about to explain the enigma of his father to him. His hands tightened slowly on the paper before him, as with desperate quietness he tried to concentrate. He saw his father's face so clearly now, grave, kind, weary and hopeless. He saw his father's lips move in silent but urgent explanation.

The news, he recalled, had come to Jules first, by some mysterious route. And Jules had been stricken, at the moment, with the first of his terrible heart attacks. Peter remembered that Leon, Jules' brother, had come to Honoré's home that night, to tell the newly made widow of her husband's death. Leon, the surly, the bulky, the somber of voice, had entered the house, quite undone, his face gray and shaken. He had given the news somewhat incoherently, and Peter remembered that his greatest concern, his greatest preoccupation, had been for his brother, Jules, and that over and over again he had exclaimed, in the midst of the widow's tears, that "this will kill Jules!"

Peter, so young then, had listened to Leon, had heard him through a wavering mist of grief. He had felt a dull and aching anger against Leon, that he had dared so to exclaim about Jules. He had felt no wonder that those surly and sunken eyes had been filled with curious tears, that the strong square hands had literally wrung themselves together in a kind of distraction. He had known that Leon had had for Jules a reluctant but deep affection. But it was certainly odd that his sole preoccupation had not been for the tragic death of Honoré, but for Jules' condition, for Jules' grief, and that, at the last, he had risen in distraction and declared that he must return at once to his brother.

Peter had accepted it as grief, as had everyone else. But now, as he sat there thinking with such painful concentration and urgency, he wondered. Jules, it is true, must have felt the profoundest sorrow of his life at the death of his beloved cousin. But, Peter thought, there had been a queer meaning in Leon's words, in his manner.

"My God!" he groaned, rubbing his forehead with his knuckles. Something stood there before him, full of explanation, if he could only see and understand. He forced himself to be calm. He saw his father's face again so sharply, and he tried to read the silent words on the moving lips.

Then he remembered something else, and it came up from the gray and shadowy depths of his memory like a mist which slowly took form.

There had been a witness to the death of Honoré. The lifeboats had been rapidly filled to capacity after the death-blow of the German torpedo. There had been one empty place, and a ship's officer, slavishly mindful even then in the midst of the catastrophe of the Bouchard power, had urged Honoré to take that place. But he refused. The witness said Honoré had stood on the tilting deck, and had shaken his head slowly and quietly. And that he had smiled in the strangest way. His face had taken on a mysterious look of peace and content, withdrawn and aloof. He had looked about him at the hundreds of frantic and terrified people who would not be saved, who must die. And he had tightened his hands on the deck rail and lifted his head. He had died with them, refusing to live.

What had caused that terrible heart attack of Jules'? Merely grief? Merely the thought that it had been he who had sent his cousin to his death? Peter now believed, with passionate conviction, that it had not been these.

Slowly, with blinding clarity, with shaking heart, Peter knew that Jules had known that Honoré had died because he could no longer bear to live.

It was this, then, which had stricken Jules down.

Peter's eyelids burned. But his spirit was suddenly and painfully lightened. His heart ached with renewed grief for his father, but also with exaltation. The enigma was solved. Honore's self-decreed death had been a final repudiation of his life, of all the things he had done, of all the things he had been persuaded to do. It had been a deliberate expiation.

Then, he must have hated his life.

Things began to fall into a pattern. Peter remembered an odd conversation he had had with his father on the eve when he had first gone away to school. He had been only fourteen then. Honoré had called him into his library, and had taken his hand awkwardly in his own. He was not given to demonstrations of affection, and the young Peter had been very touched, so starved of heart had he been, so lonely and afraid in the midst of his terrible brothers. He had known, of course, that he had been his father's favorite, but Honoré had never before touched him so gently, or smiled at him with such open grave affection.

"You are going away to school, my son, and will be alone," Honoré had said, with that queer French inflection in his voice which had always puzzled Peter. Honoré, the son of the French-born Eugene Bouchard, had been born in America, but had nevertheless acquired his father's accent. And that accent gave to his voice a kind of warmth and dignity, an adult overtone.

"Yes," Honoré had repeated, "you will be alone. But that won't matter to you, will it, Peter? You have always been alone. Just as I was once alone."

And then he had gazed into his young son's eyes with deep and melancholy concentration. "We have always understood each other, have we not, my son? And so, some day you will remember that if a man is to remain as God intended him to be, he must strive always to be alone in his heart. Once that heart is opened to the things of the world, whether those things are power, or ambition, or greed, or even great love, then that heart is lost forever. The glass is broken. It will never hold water again."

And then he had added, looking away from his son, though holding his hand still more tightly: "There is no mending the glass. There has never been a cement invented that will mend it, or conceal the cracks. It will never hold water again."

All this, then, Honoré was trying to explain to Peter even at this late hour. And this explanation was the answer to the enigma. The soreness in Peter's heart abated. He felt nothing for his father now but grief, passionate understanding, and deep unmuddied love.

All at once he felt strong and integrated again, almost exultant. His exhaustion vanished. Honoré's face faded from his inner eye. But he could feel his smile, tender, at peace.

Peter picked up his pen. The words came more smoothly now. There was no longer any conflict, any pain, in him. He could work. He could have faith. Nothing mattered any longer but his work, not even Celeste. He was invulnerable as he had never been invulnerable before.

CHAPTER XXI

"What shall I play?" asked Annette, pushing back the cloud of fine light hair from her forehead, and smiling at her young aunt. She sat at her harp, her thin little fingers softly stroking the shining strings, her small white arms casting a shadow over the carved gilt.

"Something of your own, darling," replied Celeste. She sat in the cool dusk of the great drawing-room, her lap filled with the lush roses from the gardens of Robin's Nest. All her figure was in that dusk, but her face had borrowed a luminous quality from it, so that her features had the pale and polished look of a marble mask, austere and stern. There was a petrified quiet in the very contour of her forehead, a still rigidity about her lips.

Annette's fingers struck the strings with muted gentleness, and the notes rose like golden butterflies expanding in the sunlight. Celeste could see those butterflies, catching the pure light on their wings, dipping, circling, blowing like brilliant leaves, dancing in a sudden puff of bright air, their movements murmurous with the softest harmony, hardly heard but sweet as an imagined melody. It was music heard in a dream, chaste yet gay, sinking to a whisper, rising on a thin and exquisite single note, suddenly scattering in a burst of poignant sound, frail and fluttering, to sink again to an incoherent caprice of radiant motion, almost inaudible.

Celeste was entranced. The taut hands that lay on the roses relaxed. Her eyes were fixed on the innocent and illuminated vision the harp had evoked. Under that bright and innocuous harmony there was the sweetness of melancholies, of delicate sadnesses. Then she heard, under the murmur of butterflies' wings, a rising wind, dimly ominous, dark with shadowy portent. The light on the dancing wings became stark and hard, like the sudden light piercing through dusky clouds.

Faster, faster, blew the butterflies, now in a faintly discordant frenzy, struggling against the voice of the gale, which had become hoarse and threatening. Now the butterflies were pale ghost shapes, without gold, without brightness, and the wind had a shape, curling, gray, coiling like smoke, rising in vast form like a wall of darkness. And in the midst of the vortex fluttered the cold colorless feathers of falling and frantic little wings.

Now the notes became louder, bleak and harsh, as if coming from over long stretches of black ice from regions of thunderous death. The last wing sank and disintegrated. Chaos had the world. Celeste discerned wild cries in the midst of the vortex, lost cries of lost souls. A last whirling of discordant sound, a sudden crash of strings, and there was only silence now, ringing and breathless.

A heavy inertia lay over Celeste's body. She stirred, sluggishly, looking at Annette, who had become very pale, and was gazing before her with empty wide eyes. Celeste began to speak, then closed her lips. She stared at Annette for a long time. Annette's hands still touched the strings, but flaccidly, like dead and bloodless hands. Her small face was extremely quiet, the expression tragic in its immobility.

The blazing sunlight lay on the broad windowsills in aching radiance. The green shadows of trees cast waving reflections into the quiet room. Somewhere birds called sleepily in the heat, the summer breeze was filled with the scent of cut clover, warm and sweet, and heavy roses.

Then Annette suddenly smiled. It was a gentle smile, gay as always. But her large light-blue eyes, so beautiful in their shape and color, remained empty. She looked at Celeste.

"I haven't a name for it, yet," she said, dropping her hands upon her knees. "Do you like it, darling?"

Celeste hesitated. Then she said in a strained voice: "It—was terrible. Yes, terrible. How can you think of such things, Annette?"

Annette's fingers laced themselves together with a convulsive movement. But she still smiled, though the smile was fixed.

"Did you think it was terrible? But it was true, wasn't it? Everything innocent and lovely, gentle and pure, is finally destroyed. That is what I meant to say."

Celeste stood up, abruptly. The roses spilled to her feet. She stood behind them, as behind a barricade. "Don't say that, Annette," she said, in a low tone. "It isn't true. It can't be."

But Annette looked at the fallen roses, and did not move or speak. Celeste bent down, and fumbled at the flowers. Thorns pricked her fingers. Her eyes were dim, and her heart beating with sorrow and fear.

She stood up at last, the roses in her arms. She saw that Annette was gazing at her now, so gently, so tragically, and with such tender quiet.

"You are so beautiful, Celeste," she said, in her sweet low voice.

The fear sharpened in Celeste, and the pain.

"Some day, I'll write a serenade for you," said Annette. She smiled a little.

Celeste looked down at the roses. She thought: I ought not to have come today. But Annette's pleading had finally broken down her decision to remain away forever from Robin's Nest. She had come today to have luncheon with her niece. It was in this very room that she had heard of her mother's illness, and here, later, had occurred that scene which she could not remember without shame and anguish. Now, as she remembered again, the very dusky warm air was permeated with Henri's personality. Celeste lifted her head with sudden and unbearable misery, and saw that Annette was regarding her with a still and sorrowful smile. Was it possible that Annette knew? It could not be! She, Celeste, could not endure it if Annette was aware.

Celeste stammered: "Don't bother writing anything about me, darling. I'm not in the least interesting." The foolish inane words struck with a sound of imbecility on her own ear.

A maid entered with tea. Celeste glanced at her, and explained: "No. I must really go. It is almost four o'clock. Peter will be wondering—"

Annette rose with the light and effortless movements of a child from her stool. The strange and sorrowful look was gone from her little face. She was eager again, and coaxing. "Please. I haven't seen you for so long. You always refuse our dinner invitations. Now I'm not going to let you go so soon."

She sat down on a sofa, before which the maid placed the tray and the cups. All her air was light and gay again, and full of innocent happiness. Her little hands moved swiftly amid the tinkle of china and silver. She filled a cup, and extended it smilingly to Celeste, who stood awkwardly near by, the roses still in her arms.

"Oh, come," coaxed Annette. Her eyes were brilliant in the dusk, and gallant.

197

For the last three hours, Celeste had felt only the heavy and apathetic inertia which had lain over her since her mother's death. She had the vague knowledge that this inertia was self-induced, a protection against thoughts which would have been unendurable. She had forced herself to move with the slow and careful movements of a drugged man, for any quick gesture, any quick word, would have broken open the thick scars which covered her wounds with a brittle crust. Careful, careful, her mind had whispered. Do not think. Do not remember.

But now the crust had been broken. Her mind and her body throbbed in painful unison. She was ill with her sorrow, her despair, and her fear. With these was a sick and over-powering shame. She wanted only to run from this room, from the sight of Annette's frail and pretty face with the wide and intelligent eyes that knew so much, had never filled with hatred, and were so wisely gentle always.

She accepted the cup Annette gave her, and stared down at it dully. Annette had been speaking. Several minutes passed before Celeste became aware, with a vague start, that there had been silence in the room for some time. She looked up. Annette was regarding her with a singular expression, full of reflective but deep compassion.

"I'm not very good company, I'm afraid," faltered Celeste.

"I know," said Annette, softly. She put her hand over Celeste's. "Mama and I weren't as close as you and Grandmother were, dear. But still, it was very terrible for me when she died."

Celeste was silent. The wide blueness of Annette's eyes was too close to her, so that she saw nothing else. Her heart sickened, huge with suffering.

In order to avoid Annette's look, she glanced away, and her own eyes encountered the portrait of Ernest Barbour over the white fireplace. All at once, such an agony of longing and desire and passion swept over her that she trembled. She put her hand to her cheek, and pressed the fingers deeply into her flesh in a spasm of sharp anguish. She forgot everything, and saw only that painted face which had taken on the aspect, the third dimension, the color of living flesh.

She turned to Annette, and put aside her cup.

"I must go," she said, abruptly, and in a voice more than a little hoarse. Now she was seized with terror. At any moment Henri might return, Henri whom she had not seen for nearly a month. Annette did not move. She only looked up in a great and wordless silence, and her face, foreshortened and still, fallen in shadow, was unreadable. The cup stood on her thin knee, its amber contents catching a single ray of sunshine so that it seemed formed of liquid gold.

Celeste turned away and gathered up her roses once more. The powerful scent nauseated her. "Peter will be so grateful," she murmured. "There are no flowers at Endur."

"I know," said Annette, softly. "It must be very awful."

There were footsteps on the terrace, light and swift. Celeste, with renewed terror, turned her head alertly and stiffly in the direction of the steps. Her suddenly thundering heart sent the blood to her face, so that its pallor was inundated by a wave of crimson. Then she glanced at Annette, who sat so still and motionless, and who was watching her with the strangest intensity.

But it was not Henri who entered. It was Antoine, Antoine of the dark and glittering smile, the sleek small black skull, the elegant and graceful carriage. He brought with him that air which Christopher had declared belonged to the "Internationale des Salonards." His subtle black eyes gleamed sardonically at the sight of his sister and his aunt, and he gave them an elaborate and exaggerated bow.

"Ah, ladies!" he exclaimed. He blew them a light kiss. "Just in time for tea, I see. Or, could I have a whiskey and soda, my pet?" he added, bending down to kiss Annette, who put her fragile hand to his cheek in an affectionate gesture.

"Of course," she said. "Do ring. I didn't know you would drop in today. One never knows when one will see you again. How is Papa?"

"Papa?" repeated Antoine, giving a subtle accent of light ridicule to the word. "Oh, Papa, as always, is engrossed in The List. Last night he had sweetbreads, and is closely watching the reaction. You know: the old Chinese superstition that like cures like. The magical stone in the toad's head cures kidney stones," he continued, at Annette's questioning look. "The brains of dogs cure brain fever, or brain tumors. Livers cure bad livers. And so, dear Papa believes that the pancreas of innocent cattle will normalize his own pancreas. We watch and wait."

"You are nasty," said Annette, with a fond smile. She sighed. "Poor Papa. When I can't supervise him, he gets the most exotic and dangerous ideas. Is sweetbreads on The List?"

"I've never studied that interesting document," replied her brother. He turned gallantly to Celeste, who still stood near by in stony silence. He thought: She gets thinner, and paler. She is gaunt, the pretty little bitch. Itching, no doubt. What a devoured and devouring look she has, in her eyes.

He said: "Well, Celeste, how is our genius?"

She started a little, and looked at him with stern stead-fastness, hating him, repudiating him.

"I suppose you mean Peter?" she answered, with quiet scorn. "Peter is well. He is very busy."

The maid entered with the whiskey and soda. Antoine bent over the tray and filled a glass with a very large amount. He sniffed it delicately. He shook his head with sadness. "Your esteemed husband, my pet, has execrable taste in whiskeys. One of these days I'll give him some excellent advice. This smells like Prohibition bathtub brew!"

"You're very rude," said Annette. "You know Henri drinks hardly at all."

Antoine nodded his head several times, slowly and wisely. "He should, my dear. He really should. I think that's what is the matter with him. A man who doesn't drink is a dangerous man. And sometimes a vulnerable one, too."

He drank deeply, and grimaced. "A man who doesn't escape from reality occasionally will eventually go mad," he remarked, lifting the glass and turning it about in his thin dark fingers. "Hitler doesn't drink. Ergo, he's mad. Henri doesn't drink. Ergo——"

Annette laughed. The sweet and musical trilling of her laughter was like the note of a bird.

"Ergo?" she repeated.

"Ergo, he's your husband," said Antoine, lightly. He turned to Celeste again. His black eyes sparkled upon her evilly. "Am I right, Celeste?" he asked.

She looked at him. "You talk nonsense," she said. She hesitated, and added: "Darling, I really must go."

But Annette reached out and clasped her hand warmly and lovingly. "Oh, don't run off just yet, dear. Antoine's just come."

"Filling the air with brightness and gaiety. Such fun," remarked Antoine. "I'm a fascinating devil, aren't I, Celeste? Not like our heavy villain, Henri? Is it true that ladies prefer devils? Or do they prefer glaciers like our own Iron Man?"

"Antoine!" protested Annette, with a laugh. "Don't call Henri that."

"Well, how is old 'Stone Face,' then?" he asked, ruffling the airy bright hair on her head. His hand was unusually tender. She looked up at him with a sudden melting of her small features.

"You are so naughty," she said. "You have a name for

everyone, haven't you? What do you call me, you wretch?"

He paused. He looked down at her with a strange changing of his dark and elegant features. Then he said: "'Lady of Shalott,' perhaps. You remember? She sat in front of a mirror, and spun great webs of silvery cloth. She didn't dare turn away from the mirror and look at the real world it reflected." He was silent a moment. He swung back to Celeste so quickly that she stepped backwards as if to avoid him. "You remember, don't you, Celeste?"

"No," she said, coldly, her arms tightening about the roses.

"I don't, either," said Annette. She leaned back against the sofa, and smiled. "Do go on, Antoine."

He refilled his glass, but did not drink. He stared down at its contents, and smiled in a peculiar way.

"There was a curse on the Lady of Shalott. She was doomed never to look directly at the world, but only at its reflection in the mirror. She saw the green river through it, near her castle, and the wooded slopes, and the traffic on the water, and the towers of the distant town. She saw Lancelot in the mirror, and she fell in love with him. And then— she turned away from the mirror to look at him clearly."

He lifted those gleaming and dancing black eyes of his and looked at Celeste, but spoke to his sister: "And when she saw Lancelot, not in the mirror, she died. And the mirror cracked from top to bottom and fell about her in a thousand silver splinters."

Annette was quite pale, but smiling. "Was she beautiful, the Lady of Shalott?" she asked.

"So beautiful that she was a legend," replied her brother, turning to her again. "I'm a fanciful devil, aren't I, pet? Always the poet. Never mind. Don't look away from the mirror. It will crack. It always cracks." He added, suddenly to Celeste: "Has your mirror cracked yet?"

But she countered with a hard smile: "What do you call *me*, Antoine?"

He stared at her meditatively, and pretended to concentrate upon her. "Once I would have called you 'Innocents Abroad.' But, somehow, that doesn't suit you now." He stretched out his hand and patted her on her shoulder, merrily. "I'll find a name for you, don't worry. Did anyone ever tell you you had eyes like delphiniums, Celeste? No, I'm wrong. They're blue stones. Blue daggers. That's better."

Celeste said, looking at him fixedly: "Do you know your own name? They call you 'Understudy.'" She paused, and looked him up and down with deliberate contempt. "But, I don't know. You see, my father, your grandfather, was a gentleman."

Antoine's black eyes narrowed until they were gleaming slits in his brown and diabolic face. Celeste's smile was unpleasant. She turned to Annette, whose distress was very marked.

"Good-bye, darling," said Celeste, kissing her niece with sudden gentleness. "I'll call you soon. You must have luncheon with me."

She left the room, walking swiftly and erectly. Antoine stared after her, with a virulent smile. Annette cried: "O Antoine! How could you be so cruel? Now, you have hurt her, when I love her so much. I've had such a time persuading her to come today, and now she won't come again."

He sat down beside her, put his arm about her childish shoulders. He pressed her to him. Now he was very grave and sincerely quiet.

"Pet, may I give you some advice? Keep away from Celeste. Let her alone. It will be best for both of you."

Celeste, moving with numb and awkward feet, got into her small car and deposited the roses beside her. She drove away down the winding parkway of Robin's Nest, and then out into the hot and lonely road. Then she drew up under a great tree, stopped the car, rested her arms on the wheel. She stared before her with dry eyes for a long time, before she started the car again and returned home.

She found Peter resting after his day of writing. He greeted her eagerly from his deep chair. But before kissing him she felt his forehead and his hot thin cheek. Her hand was gentle and anxious, and full of tenderness. She sat down near him, after placing Annette's roses in deep water.

He asked if she had enjoyed her day. But she saw that he was only being polite and affectionately solicitous. He wanted her to ask him about his work. She did so, and he leaned over to his table and took a sheaf of papers in his hand. Now his exhausted eyes were pathetic in their uncertain exultation.

"It is very hard to condense things," he said. "It is a matter of sorting and weeding, choosing the highlights, discarding and curtailing. When I wrote my first book, I had a single theme: the making of wars by armaments manufacturers and their bought politicians. The field of their activities was necessarily narrow and well defined. The cleavage between nations was distinct. But now, there are no boundaries, no frontiers. Even in the field of industry, one concern extends into another in one large and intricate root-system of subsidiaries. The industrialists are now the real rulers of the world. I can't narrow anything down. When I begin with the Bouchards, I find the root-system extending into the Bourse, the Reichsbank, the Bank of England, and then into the I.G. Farbenindustrie, and into a multitude of other industrial concerns all over Europe, all over the world. It is a sinister web. I pull on one small end, and the whole fabric moves. I would need to write a dozen books, and then it would only be the beginning."

Celeste took the sheaf of papers from him. She felt drained and sick to death. In a moment he would notice. She said, in a loud clear voice: "May I read this, dear? Now?"

"Of course," he replied, eagerly, and touchingly pleased. He watched her face as she read the closely written papers with every appearance of concentration. After a long time, she put them down and stared at him unseeingly.

"The story is so horrible, so fantastic, that it won't be believed, Peter. That is their safety: the enormity of the truth is incredible. Yes, I had an idea of it all, from what I have heard, and what you've told me. But even I find it incredible. How, then, will it be accepted by the people?"

He leaned towards her with sudden passion. "In these days, Celeste, moderation is overlooked, prudence is boring. Everything is oversized, gigantic, clamoring. If I wrote with restraint, played down facts, droned on conservatively, the book would have no value, and no audience. As I said, I have highlighted the highlights, exhibited only the larger crimes, revealed only the larger criminals. Perhaps you think that sensational. But only the sensational attracts the attention of the American people. This isn't a text-book on criminology, Celeste. It is an exposé. One doesn't remember the revolutionary principles of Luther. One remembers best that he threw an ink-well at the devil."

Celeste laid down the sheaf of papers. "Will Georges publish this, Peter?"

He hesitated, became gloomy. "I'm afraid not. But he gave me some advice. He suggested that I talk to the editor of Thomas Ingham's Sons, in New York, Cornell Hawkins. You see, Georges has suddenly become squeamish about the Family. Besides, he's getting old. And cautious." He added: "I'll go to New York on Monday, and see Hawkins. Frankly, I haven't much hope. I shall be told, of course, that American readers aren't interested. Or rather, that American women aren't interested. And American women compose the majority of the readers in this country. They prefer 'simple love stories' and other trash, especially if there is an 'adorable' heroine."

His voice had become thin and bitter. He pushed the papers away with a suddenly desperate hand, and then covered his eyes for a moment.

"I would be interested," said Celeste. "Surely the American women, whose husbands and sons are to die, will also be interested. It is women, now, who listen to the voice crying in the wilderness. Men are too busy trying to make money. They'll countenance anything if they are left to peace long enough to accumulate a bank account, or buy gadgets. It seems to me that gadgetry has replaced political interest in America. If the American colonists had been interested in a daily new flood of gadgets, we'd never have had a Revolution. Technological progress has killed the average man's desire to participate in government."

"Because it panders to the average man's childish love for toys," said Peter, with quickening urgency. "And playing with toys destroys adulthood, the capacity to think. You know, there might be a profound and sinister design in that."

Celeste was silent. She gazed through the broad bright windows. Only at sunset was Endur endurable. Then the empty grounds, devoid of foliage and other natural obstructions, offered a wide immensity of view, uncluttered, broad and solemn, of the western sky. That sky was now a lake of palpitating flame, in which floated the red and incandescent sun. The smooth and empty grass was touched with a rosy shadow, like a reflection of the heavens. On that side of the house, the cavalcade of pointed poplars stood against the scarlet sky, sharply black and motionless. The silence was huge, as if all life had been suspended.

Celeste spoke hurriedly, in a light and toneless voice that was full of repressed pain: "Tomorrow let's drive up to Placid Hills, Peter, and see how our house is coming along. I hate Endur. It's like a desert. Besides, you've noticed that Edith and Christopher are in no hurry to go back to Florida. Edith hinted, this morning, that they might want to return to Endur. Of course, they'd be delighted to have us as permanent guests, she said." Celeste's mouth twisted with some bitterness. "I never could endure this place."

Peter hesitated. He was about to say that he wished to work tomorrow, and that he was not particularly interested in the rising house on Placid Heights. But something in Celeste's voice kept him silent. For the first time he saw her clearly. For weeks, now, he had been so engrossed in his thoughts, in the plans for his book, that he had not really seen his wife. Now he was alarmed. He raised himself in his chair a little, and gazed searchingly at her profile. Was it only the stark and ominous sunset light that made her appear so thin, so ill, so distraught and pent? Her features were very sharp, almost pinched. There were mauve shadows under her broad cheekbones, and her lips, usually so blooming and full, were dry and pale. Her nostrils, always delicately flaring, were now so distended that it seemed as if she was perpetually striving for breath. He saw that her fingers were clenched together in an attitude of determined self-control.

"Celeste," he said, in alarm. "My dear, you look ill. What is the matter?" He reached out and covered her taut hands with his own. He felt their hardness and coldness. But her smile, when she turned to him, was quite calm, full of tenderness. However, there was an opaqueness in her eyes, and she did not look at him directly.

"There's nothing wrong, darling. Perhaps I'm tired. It's been so hot, you know. I can't tell you how anxious I am for us to have a home of our own."

She stood up suddenly, gently pushing his hand away. She laughed a little, tensely. "Do you know something, Peter? I'm afraid I can't stand seeing the Bouchards much more. They—smother me. That's a horrible thing to say about one's family, isn't it? Antoine came in today, just when I was leaving Annette. He's a horrible creature, full of innuendoes and malice. He never liked me, and I'm afraid, now, that I hate him."

" 'Innuendoes'?" repeated Peter, slowly, looking at her intently. "What 'innuendoes,' Celeste?"

She was frightened. Peter's eyes, fixed on her, were so clear and steady, so perceptive. She could not move or speak in her fear, and Peter's regard seemed to strip her, to examine her. She looked at his emaciated and intellectual face, at his veined temples and thin light hair. He was defenseless, this good and honorable man, who loved her, and whom she had so betrayed. Who would compare with Peter? Peter, who thought never of himself, whose sole passion and concern was for all mankind, and its suffering, and its despair? She felt unclean, degraded, unfit to be seen by him. Remorse was a metallic heat in her mouth, a blazing pain in her heart, which she could not endure. She gazed at him speechlessly, her eyes wide with her torment, the sockets strained.

"You mean, 'innuendoes' about me?" he went on. He smiled a little sadly. "Does that matter, darling? I never cared, you know. I don't like Antoine. He reminded me, in a way, of your father, and Jules and I were always at odds. There, I've offended you," he added, as the torment increased in Celeste's eyes.

"No," she whispered. "Oh no, Peter. You could never offend me."

She dropped on her knees beside him, but did not touch him. Her look implored him, passionately, despairingly. He was both alarmed and puzzled. Then he smiled again, with infinite love, and gently touched her hair. She dropped her head to his knee, and was very still.

CHAPTER XXII

"No, you misunderstand me," said Peter, with that feverish urgency which was increasing in him. "I have tried to show that all this villainy, all this ruthless and rapacious plotting, all this interrelated industrial empire which knows no national boundaries, no loyalties, no idealism, does not operate apart from the rest of mankind. I have tried to show that it is the world's indifference, private greed and stupidity, lack of humanitarian values, which has permitted, and is permitting, the growth of this industrial international empire which is bent on enslaving all other men. If these monsters and villains, these plotters, finally succeed—and I am ominously afraid they might—the guilt will lie with all men everywhere, not with only a few.

"You have only to look at America. At one time, in the early days of the Republic, politics was the chief concern of the young American people. That is why we elected the Washingtons, the Adamses, the Jeffersons, the Jacksons, the Lincolns. Each candidate was scrutinized by his constituents. We had an illustrious parade of Presidents. But now we have abandoned politics to the politicians. Politics operate above and beyond the people, who don't want to be disturbed, but wish to be left to enjoy their mean and childish sports and pleasures, and their multitudinous toys which have been given them to distract their attention. Since Lincoln, what President have we had who was a nobleman, a statesman, a man concerned with the welfare of his people and the welfare of the world? You might name Wilson, Mr. Hawkins. But it was the American politicians who killed him. Had the people been awake, aware, and not stupid and dull and entranced by the stock-market and easy little profits and toys, Wilson would have succeeded in his plans to regenerate the world, to awaken it to moral and spiritual responsibility for its neighbors. How can a hero succeed if his people are ignorant, selfish and blind and deaf? And, it is the plan of their new masters to keep them so. So it is that what is to happen to all mankind in the near future is the guilt of the American people, the British people, the French people, not only of the German people."

"You mean," said Mr. Hawkins, "that the people create their own destroyers and oppressors?"

"Yes," replied Peter. He was silent a moment, pressing his hands on the brief-case which held part of his manuscript. His expression darkened. "And then, there is another matter, which I have thought of. In the early days of the Republic, the American people were a homogeneous race. They had inherited the political awareness and interest of their British forebears. And this, combined with the 'high thinking and plain living' of the Puritans gave them a sense of national responsibility and a universality of perception. They were the best of peoples: simple but intelligent men of idealism and rationality. They understood that the world could not live half-slave and half-free. That is why they enthusiastically supported and aided the French Revolution. For instance, if we had Negro slavery still in the South, I doubt very much that the American people could be aroused, in these days, to indignation, to a crusade against that slavery.

"Why? Because we are no longer spiritually homogeneous. A great part of our population is composed of immigrants from slave-nations, who have bequeathed their slave philosophy, their spiritual ignorance and sloth, to their children. Education in our public schools has not enlightened them, or increased their passion for freedom, for American ideals. The children of dull German slaves, Slav peasants, Italian starvelings, cannot have in themselves the burning joy in liberty. They cannot, and never will, feel that bright enthusiasm for the rights of man which the early Americans found the most precious thing in life. They did not come to America, as did the American Colonists and Puritans, because they could no longer endure the antagonism of Europe toward their single-hearted hatred for oppression, their desire for freedom. They came to eat, to devour, to ravish, to destroy. And, to betray."

He added, somberly: "When the final testing hour arrives for America, how can this slave-mob be aroused to defend our country, to die for it, if necessary? In the hour of our danger, is it not possible that this mob, through the influence of their priests, their masters, their exploiters, will desert, betray and destroy us?"

"That's a gloomy prospect," remarked Mr. Hawkins, thoughtfully. "You believe it could happen, Mr. Bouchard?"

"Certainly. You have only to look at our various foreign-invented organizations. The German-American Bund. The various Italian Fascist organizations. The 'White' Ukranians. The organizations which have given aid and comfort to Franco. What will these do in the final hour? How can the American people survive them? They have bought members of our State Department. They are financed by our great financiers and industrialists. As the tempo rises, after war is declared in Europe, they will become more active, and more dangerous. And as they do so, the people will become more apathetic, more isolationist, more disunified. That is our danger."

Mr. Cornell Hawkins was silent. He leaned back in his ancient swivel-chair and stared at Peter with his frosty blue eyes. This descendant of New England Puritans, of disciples of Thoreau, of Emerson, was a lean and lanky man in his fifties, gray, hard and thoughtful. His quiet and reflective face, rather pale and sunken, expressed a greatness of intellect which already had acquired fame among scholars and artists. His was not the showiness and brilliance of lesser and more explosive men. His intellect had that sparseness, that starkness and cold austerity, of a New England landscape seen under clear winter skies. There was no fuzziness, no confusion, no doubt, in his quiet and penetrating eye, the color of shadows in the hollows of snow. He possessed that stillness, that awareness, that patrician detachment, which is the sign of the aristocrat. His smile was slow and wry, but gentle; his speech, low and hesitating, but pungent. He laughed only silently, and infrequently, and then his disillusioned mirth lit only his eyes with a brighter and bluer gleam.

He was both disingenuous and kind, thoughtful and wary, courteous and unswerving. He had the aristocrat's indifference to sartorial elegance, that mark of the plebeian. He rarely removed his somewhat battered hat, and he had no poses. His hand, eternally holding a smoking cigarette, was lean and beautifully formed. When he heard a phrase that interested or stirred him, all his gaunt features came alive, touched with cold light, brilliant with real pleasure.

Peter, as he sat at the untidy desk of this great and renowned editor, felt peace. His urgency was no longer hot and confused. He was understood. His incoherencies became coherent under that kind if icy eye. He believed that his fumbling words were disregarded, that his thought was perceived. The dusty windows of the large bare office let in a flood of summer sunshine, sparkling with golden motes. Here was no pretense, no thick rugs and fine furniture to impress the vulgar. Heaps of manuscripts lay on the splintered desk, overflowing ash-trays, disorderly piles of letters, scattered pens and pencils. The floor was grimy, and discolored. Chairs with squeaking legs were thrust back against the mildewed walls. Yet, out of this disorder, this untidiness and indifference to elegance, had come some of the world's finest and noblest literature. There was an air about this man, in this casual room filled with stark hot sunlight, of greatness and simplicity. One knew instinctively that the veriest tyro of a frightened author would be accorded the same courtesy and consideration as the most gilded and popular writer who could boast ten or twenty "large printings."

Peter knew that Mr. Hawkins was not overcome by the presence of a Bouchard in his office. He was seen as a man, as a passionate author, only. If Mr. Hawkins believed his work had value, integrity and color, then he could be certain of a hearing, and perhaps of publication. If Mr. Hawkins believed him stupid, amateurish, worthless and emptily violent, no other considerations would have weight with him.

Something tight and defenseless and fearful in Peter relaxed. He thought: I should like this man for a friend. He has no deviousness, no cruelty, no cunning. There is a mystical quality in him, a philosopher's doubting and searching. I have never had a friend! If he only likes me, then I shall be free. If he considers my work, then I shall know it has value.

Mr. Hawkins, in his turn, simply and openly studied Peter, weighing him. Peter had sent him the first quarter of his manuscript a few days before. He had found time to read it, among other swarms of manuscripts. He had been impressed by Peter's passion and sincerity. Now he laid his hand on the sheaf he had read, and thoughtfully ruffled the pages.

"You say your cousin, Georges Bouchard, won't consider publishing this?" he asked.

"No," replied Peter, shortly, coloring a little. "There are family considerations, you know."

Mr. Hawkins smiled bleakly. "And libel, of course."

"But, I have the proofs, the documents!" cried Peter, with new despair.

"Nevertheless, truth is no guarantee against a suit for libel," said Mr. Hawkins, wryly. "If Jesus were alive today, and making His remarks about certain Pharisees, He would be sued for half a million dollars. In those days, they could only crucify Him. Of course, libel suits are one form of crucifixion. We've got to be careful, you know."

He rubbed his wide thin lips with his hand, thoughtfully, and regarded Peter with the fixed cold blueness of his eyes.

"You haven't thought of publishing this, yourself, Mr. Bouchard?"

Peter's color heightened. He answered, stiffly: "No! I've thought that was cheap. There's a stigma in publishing yourself. As if no one else found your work worthy of the risk. My relatives will be highly amused, and gratified, if I don't find a publisher."

"But Georges Bouchard did publish your first book, *The Terrible Swift Sword?*"

"Yes, anonymously," said Peter, with grimness. "Besides, the family wouldn't have sued him. That would have brought the stink out into the open. Especially as my anonymity would have been exposed."

"And it is only family considerations which prevent him from publishing this? Why, then, did he publish your first?"

Peter was silent for some moments. He bit his lip. Then he said, hesitatingly, "Frankly, I don't understand. I've thought that some pressure had been brought to bear on old Georges. Only that could explain it."

Mr. Hawkins' chair creaked as he gently rocked in it. He lit another cigarette, and puffed on it meditatively. Peter watched him with deep anxiety.

"Look, you've got to tell me one thing, Mr. Hawkins: has my book, outside of its revelations, anything to recommend it? Is it amateurish, badly written?"

"No, it isn't amateurish," said Mr. Hawkins, slowly. "It has drama, and fire and color. And those are rare in reportorial writing. I'm an old newspaper man, myself, and we were supposed to exercise restraint in our work. We had to acquire an aversion to adjectives." He spoke incisively, in his quiet if hesitating voice. Then he smiled. "However, I like adjectives. I don't like modern stark writing, which substitutes exclamation points and obscenity for good craftsmanship. There's no exuberance or passion among modern writers. They think it vulgar, or something. Richness of phrase, and opulence of adjective, are 'Victorian.' Too lush, they believe. Personally, I regret it. Starkness can be decadent, you know, especially the modern self-conscious starkness. Only when starkness is pure and sincere is it healthy, and possessed of beauty."

Peter listened, his sense of ease and freedom growing. "Then, you might consider publishing this?"

Mr. Hawkins smiled wryly once more. "I'll be frank with you, Mr. Bouchard. Your name is a consideration, of course. On a book, your name will increase the chance of large sales. I want you to understand that, so you won't feel we took your book—if we do—under false pretenses. Publishers are merchandisers, too. We sell books. We must make a profit, or go out of business. That is what is so hard for the average author to understand. He rosily believes a book should be published on its merits (and his own book, of course, always has a lot of merit, mostly 'artistic'). He loftily disregards the fact that his book probably won't sell. If you mention that, he favors you with a glance of superb contempt. What does that matter? he asks. The public needs books of merit crammed down its throat, for its own good. He believes publishers should be crusaders in a noble cause. Super-castor-oil-givers to a public that loves lollypops. Fortunately for their stockholders, publishers disagree with this opinion. We publish books we think, or hope, will sell; then everybody from the printer to the author is happy."

He paused. Peter's emaciated cheeks flushed a dark crimson with mortification. Mr. Hawkins watched him closely. He smiled a little, though he was touched by Peter's expression.

"I'm not speaking personally, of course. Money is no consideration in your case. You are a crusader. But you have written interestingly, and with power. What you have to say is grave and momentous; better still, it is well-written. I think it might be popular. I can't guarantee that. But I think it might. Again, your name will arouse preliminary interest among critics, and the public. I think the day has come when the public will be more interested in non-fiction than in fiction. My competitors don't agree with me there. They think the love story is the most important thing in writing. They call it 'human interest.' As if there were no human interest in anything but a pair of adolescents and their feeling for each other."

He was silent a moment, then continued more strongly: "I believe there is human interest in what you have written. The most terrible and foreboding human interest. I also believe American readers are growing up. I believe that Americans must now be told who are their enemies, and why they must defend themselves. You see, I am an American."

He smiled again, a little sadly. But the frost of his eyes melted into kindness. He stood up. "Let's have lunch. We'll talk more about this. I've got to discuss your book with Mr. Ingham, first, of course. I'll let you know in a few days."

As Peter accompanied the editor down the creaking elevator, he felt once more that sense of liberation, of comfort, of peace, which so many had experienced in the presence of this great and simple man who had only kindness for the sincere, and sympathy for the earnest, but the utmost contempt for the poseur and the fool.

Book Two

THE BEGINNING OF SORROWS

"For nation shall rise against nation, and kingdom against kingdom: and there shall be famines, and pestilences, and earthquakes, in divers places. . . . All these are the beginning of sorrows."—Matthew xxiv:7,8.

CHAPTER XXIII

Armand was alone in his great and echoing house. He was always so much alone. He would wander through the immense rooms, which were dimly lit, the corners thick with shadows like cobwebs, his fumbling feet making no sound on the rich rugs. He was a man undone by an integrity which had never been enough. Somewhere, in the vague sick recesses of him, he knew this, but was only bewildered. He had gone far, and done much that was evil. He had cavilled petulantly only at the little things, and then with a shrill vehemence. He had felt a soothing of his conscience then, a slackening of the tight tension in him. So, he had deceived himself for many years, that he was better than his family, that he was intrinsically a good man. At heart, he would say to himself, I am really a good man.

But now the incantation was no good at all. He repeated it over and over, now that he was old, but it brought him no comfort. He was face to face with himself, but still he could not look at the remorseless mirror held before him.

Once he had cried to himself: If only I had been complete! But he meant only that he desired he might never have had even that small integrity which had so tormented him all his life and had brought him nothing, not even the smallest peace.

No one comes to see me now, he would think, as he would go restlessly from room to room. Even though I still own fifty-one percent of Bouchard stock. He had not yet come to the place where he could smile at this, or burst into bitter laughter. It was still a matter of querulous and lonely wonder to him. He would repeat over and over to himself, the whisper coming from between his fat and pouting lips: "Fifty-one percent." And then he would jingle the coins in his pocket and listen with childish eagerness to their tinkle.

"Fifty-one percent," he would whisper, after the jingling of his coins had soothed him a little. And he would smile.

He would square his fat bent shoulders and look about him challengingly, though nothing but cold and silent walls met his eye. He was still potent, then. The fifty-one percent stood between him and a horrifying reality. In these more sanguine moments he could deceive himself that it was jealousy and envy that kept him so solitary in his vast and empty house. His relatives hated him for his golden power. They vented their resentment by avoiding him.

Sometimes he peered through the dark windows, which reflected the scattered lamps, and he would stare down the silent lighted road that wound away through his park. Sometimes he would strain his ears for the sound of a car, the whisper of tires on the asphalt. But there would be no sound but the wind. He would wander on again to another room, look through other windows which revealed the black and glimmering river and the distant twinkling of lights on the opposite bank. A steamer would whistle; the trees near the window would rattle drily. Often he would hear the hooting of a desolate train, the hollow echo of its passage if the wind was in his direction. The loneliest of white cold moons would lie on the window-sills or touch his fat and despondent jowls with a silver light. It was a specter's face that peered hopefully through the polished panes.

The servants, moving on cat's feet through the great carpeted halls, caught glimpses of this fat old man sidling from room to room. He would glance at them without seeing them, would purse his lips, scowl a little, and move on. They would watch him go, see how he would start as he thought he heard the tinkling of a telephone, or footsteps on the walks outside. But no one but his daughter called him, and then usually earlier in the day. Sometimes he would open the door of his room and come into the hallway, persuaded he heard a voice. And then the door would close again, and silence would surround him.

He had no friends. In earlier years, he had often been invited to dinner at the homes of his relatives, or of acquaintances. But that was when he was president of Bouchard & Sons. His conversation had never been brilliant. He was a shy and suspicious man, dull and unimaginative. Like most men of his temperament, he gave the impression of fearfulness, even of cowardice. No one had ever cared enough to discover why he was afraid, or what so terrified him. He did not know himself. When asked for an opinion, he would search the questioner's courteous face with his little beetling black eyes, as if conjecturing what sly villainy, what desire to trap him, what double motive, had inspired even the most innocent and polite of queries. And then he would reply cautiously, minutely watching every expression on the other's face which might reveal to him that he had made himself vulnerable or ridiculous. In consequence, his words were always meatless, dull, without color or vitality. If he sometimes forgot himself, and replied spontaneously, in the surge of some rusty emotion, he would spend later lonely hours anxiously going over his answer to see whether he had said anything which might be used against him. Even in earlier days he had rarely discussed politics, believing, in his pathetic and dingy egotism, that his words were weighed and gravely noted, and later quoted at conferences as a key to "a trend." There was no solace for him in books, for his sole absorption in his youth had been his Company. He understood no music, had never cared for it. It was effeminate stuff, fit only for those decadent Europeans who had no "Company" to engross them. Nor had he liked even golf, that last resort of the ignorant American businessman, the "corporation fool."

He read only the newspaper owned by his family, the *Windsor News,* and the New York *Times.* Out of the latter newspaper he might have derived some knowledge of the world; out of its tremendous library of news he might have gleaned some awareness of the world of men, of politics, of history. But he never read anything but the Stock Market reports, the financial news, the obituaries, and one or two of the dullest and most conservative editorials which the more enlightened avoided. Now that he was removed from his own active Company, he read hardly anything but the financial and business sections, and then only to watch the Stock Market and to gloat over the rising prices of Bouchard stock, or to despair over their decline.

For a while he had been quite excited over Europe, prior to the Munich fiasco. He had gone, uninvited, to his relatives' homes, and there had seized upon the male members and exhorted and argued and fumed by the hour. But they soon discovered that his knowledge was meager, his prejudices ignorant if vehement, his excitabilities childish. Even the younger and female members found themselves unable to keep from laughing in his face. Since then, he knew practically nothing. He sealed himself up in his loneliness and misery, and watched through windows. He had nothing to give anyone now. He had no power with which to bribe or coerce. He had no gifts of person or conversation which might make him desired for his own sake. He had no love or warmth of temperament, no concern with other men, which migh endear him. He had only his jingling coins, his "fifty-one percent," his diabetes, to keep him company in the long days and the endless nights.

His "court physician," despite his enormous retainer, found him insupportable these days. For Armand had been driven to the last extremity: he called his physician on the telephone at least four nights a week, to discuss with him gravely some suspected new development in his malady. The conversations lasted at least half an hour each time. At these times that flabby and bloated old face would come alive and alight, his eyes would glow. He would sit on the edge of his chair, gripping the telephone, his voice trembling with absorbed eagerness, and even fanaticism. What of that new concentrated insulin of which he had read in the last issue of the American Medical Association's magazine? Was there anything to it? The magazine said it was predicted that only one shot a week would be necessary. What's wrong with you fellows? What's wrong with research? Were they letting the whole thing die?

The physician, a really brilliant man interested in research, had actually been able to coax many thousands of dollars out of Armand's tight pocket for a certain research laboratory in which talented and devoted young physicians, undistinguished for private means, labored night and day to discover new cures and new drugs to alleviate the agonies of such men as Armand Bouchard. The money, however, had not been quite enough, for the physician had informed Armand, in the first months of hope, that the laboratory needed millions. Armand could not understand this. He would complain querulously about the "greediness" of these young researchers. Why were they not contented to labor selflessly for the sake of humanity? Why did they not understand that they were really "dedicated"? Why should they care for "fat" salaries? Was it not enough to serve mankind? When the physician explained that the young men had families, or obligations, Armand was outraged. Families and obligations indeed! How dared the gifted priests of medical science have such things? They were traitors, exploiters. Medical science should be a monkish fraternity, where heaven-endowed men ought to spend their lives in devotion, thinking of nothing but service. Service, Armand would repeat, grudgingly writing another small check and hurling it at his physician. When the latter mentioned the Rockefeller Foundation, Armand would smile sourly and say, thank God, *he* had nothing on his conscience.

At this, the physician would eye him somberly, and ask silently: No?

The physician was a venal and luxurious man, and no selfless saint. But sometimes he would stare at Armand for a long time and wonder if the lives of such men were worth the labor of the brilliant-eyed young researchers in that hot and meager laboratory. He thought of their exhaustion, their thin and eager hands, their passion for analysis, their joy in discovery. Was all this primarily designed to extend the useless and miserable existence of fat old men with diseases induced by fatally stricken psyches? "Who can minister to a mind diseased?" he would quote to himself. For he was coming to believe, reluctantly, with many angry repudiations, that the diseases of the flesh were only the outward and visible manifestations of diseases of the soul. He had discovered, only too often for his own peace of mind, that the sufferer from heart disease, from diabetes, from cancer, was sick of the world, sick of life, sick of self. Were these diseases only a subconscious desire for death, for the obliteration of a mind that endlessly accused itself, for the eternal stilling of a sleepless despair? The flesh struggled to survive. But in the eyes of the sufferer the physician would often detect the agony of a soul that wished nothing but darkness and nirvana, and escape from consciousness. The crippling diseases, too: were these not the index of a soul that dumbly prayed to be relieved from active participation in a world that feverishly labored for nothing?

It was conscience, or despair, or grief, that sickened the soul, and sickened the flesh. This, the physician was beginning to believe. He was revolted, derided himself for becoming a dupe of Christian Science, or other "superstitions." But the evidence was growing. He found himself, quite against his will, fumbling with a very new Bible he had recently bought, and angrily reading the New Testament's accounts of the healings of the sick by Jesus. "Take up thy bed and walk," Jesus admonished the crippled man. "Take up thy bed, have courage, have manhood, and face the world of reality and fight it with bravery and faith," He must really have meant.

The world, to the physician, was becoming filled, despite his "enlightened" resistance, with millions of anguished and despairing souls that could not endure existence in such a frightful place. He observed, too, that as the tension among nations increased, and hatred bloomed like a bloody flower in every habitat of man, and fear blew like a poison gas through every city, disease increased. Death, and the desire for death, were striking the souls of men as blight strikes fruitful trees, blackening them, withering them, killing the flowering branch.

Once he was on the point of saying to Armand: "Give millions, not thousands, to my research laboratory, understanding that you will help science to discover new methods of curing disease, not only for yourself, but for millions of other men. Then, perhaps, you will be cured." But he knew that his words would be met with greedy indignation, or a stare of utter incomprehension. He would arouse himself from these speculations with an angry word, or a gesture of contempt. He would go to his research laboratory, and cautiously and in circumlocutions, he would hint at his speculations. He found, to his great surprise, that the young physicians knew all about this, and did a great deal of speculating themselves.

So it was that with more gentleness than his usual custom he would listen to Armand's eager questions, his suggestions, his long and meandering discussions of his disease. Under this flow of self-absorbed words, he would search for a hint of the real cause of this old man's suffering, the real cause of the refusal of his glands to operate. Finally, he had a hint. Armand lived in chronic fear. Of what was he afraid? Of himself? Of others?

The List was now Armand's gospel, the magic which extended his existence. But it was not extending it, the physician knew. Daily, he was becoming weaker. Death, the desire of his soul, would soon end the life of his body. Why was this?

The physician might have received a hint on a certain night when Armand, in his lonely apartments, was listening to the radio.

Armand detested radios. A few years ago, he would never have listened to the flow that moved heavily through the ether. But now, in his lonely extremity, he listened. Out from Europe, out from the capitals of the world, came anxious voices, exultant voices, terrified voices, exhorting voices, all concerned with only one thing: the debacle of civilization, the approaching and inevitable war, the tortures and agonies of mankind face to face with its self-wrought dissolution. Some of the voices blamed Hitler, urged the rising of the world against this madman who had been created by the powerful, the lusters, the haters of men. Some of the voices declared that it was the British or the American or the French "war-mongers," who were bringing this doom upon all. Others decried the self-seekers, the exploiters, the crafty, the conspirators, the ambitious. The pacifists who had kept America unarmed were blamed; the "armaments manufacturers," others declared, had plotted the coming horror for the sake of profits. None cried out that it was every man everywhere who had conceived, allowed or consented to the rising catastrophe. None asserted that it was in the souls of men that the guilt lay bloodily. The German madness had been there for every man to see, but no one had revealed it to the sight of all the world. Some few had seen, but they had been silent, hoping to profit by the disease.

Now only turmoil came from the air, and through the millions of radios in defenseless homes. But no voice cried out: "You, who listen, are guilty of this."

Armand listened, crouched in his dark rooms, bending his ears toward the instrument, the dull light that came from it the only light about him. And, as he listened, his face puckered, pursed, his gray brows drew together. In himself he could feel a sudden weakness and disintegration, a dull fever and nameless anguish.

He suffered as an animal suffers, with wild dull surprise at his own voiceless pain, with incomprehension. And with it was a sick horror and formless guilt. Sometimes he would stare about him in the diffused darkness, and say to himself: Where have I been all this time? What has been happening?

He was without imagination, without the ability to analyze himself or others. Yet, within him, the enormous sense of guilt grew, so that he felt his blood hurry faster with a kind of terror. Where was his guilt? He did not know. But the sickness increased in him. He began to see the face of Jules Bouchard, in the illuminated dial of the radio. It was a smiling face, darkly exultant, subtle and ironical.

When some commentator hysterically cried out against the "armaments manufacturers," Armand started to his feet and shouted: "Damned nonsense! As if a handful of men like myself had anything to do with this!" He felt the verity of his own words, and was momentarily, if indignantly, comforted. What folly to believe that a few men actually set out to create wars for their own profits! How dared the fool mouth such idiocies! Worst of all, the ignorant and the stupid might believe it.

He sat down again, trembling with the first hot rage he had felt in many years. He turned off the furious rash of words, and sat panting in the darkness, clenching his fists and beating them on his fat knees. Where were Henri, Christopher, Antoine, Francis, Emile, Nicholas—the whole damned family?—Why did they allow this infernal nonsense? And then he saw their faces, passing slowly before him, and was silent.

He began to speak aloud, slowly, dully, incredulously: "Yes, of course. They are guilty. We are all guilty. Not just us—not only the Bouchards. But people like us, in Germany, in France, in England. People like us, who made Hitler, who armed him, who shipped him matériel of war, who lent him money, who plotted with him, against our own countries, our own people. Why did we plot?"

His brows drew together, and he gnawed his lips in the darkness. There was a vast trembling in him, so profound that he vaguely thought the whole house was swaying in a vast agitation. He clenched his fists under his chin, and crouched forward on his chair, a stout grotesque figure with a large head partly covered by sparse gray curls. He might have been a fat gnome there, in the darkness, concentrating as he had never concentrated for many years, his mind aching and throbbing, his heart shaking.

He remembered all those years when he had been Chairman of the Board of Directors, after he had relinquished the presidency of Bouchard & Sons to Henri. Even now, in retrospect, he felt the profound wincing, the sudden sweat, the dry-mouthed impulse to flight, which he had felt during his attendance at the Board meetings. He remembered how his ears had suddenly rung, become deafened, dull, so that the words and statements of others were a blur, and meaningless. But, he had heard, in spite of himself, and what he had heard came back to him now so vividly that they seemed written in letters of fire on the dark walls of the room. His subconscious mind had heard and recorded, and it was like a hand, now, opening inexorable books for him to read.

Faces, haloed with sinister light, floated before him. He saw their smiles, their lifted eyebrows, heard their low voices. Lips moved soundlessly, then suddenly roared loudly so that he caught every distinct and ominous word before it faded again into silence.

The voices told of money, food, oil, cotton, pouring into Franco's Spain, after the collapse and ruin of the Republic, a constant flood which had been denied the starving and valiant people who had thrown off the crushing power of Church and State exploitation. He heard the voice of his relative, Hugo Bouchard, Assistant to the Secretary of State, urging that precious ores and matériel of war be sent to

Franco, a request which was granted by the Bouchards and the presidents of their subsidiaries. "Of course," said Hugo's voice, shrillingly loud and clear in the hot darkness of Armand's room, "there will be the question from certain vicious radicals why Franco needs such enormous quantities." Hugo smiled; there was a dim echo of laughter all about him. "It will even be asked if most of this matériel does not find its way to Mussolini and Hitler. Now, we boys employ very expensive public-relations and publicity men, and it is up to them to put the quietus on the thing. They can do it. They've done bigger and better jobs than this. They'll be fools, or worse, if it ever gets out about the real amounts we are sending to Franco. What the hell! We've been helping Franco since 1936, you boys in active positions, and I and any friends in the State Department. We're not stopping now. Hitler needs—" and the voice sank to a murmur, was lost, for it was at that moment, years ago, that Armand had muttered something incoherent, and had fled from the room, followed by the derisive and laughing eyes of the others.

Now Christopher's voice, vitriolic and incisive, rose in the darkness: "We aren't deceiving ourselves, I hope, about the immensity of the coming struggle in America, whether or not there is war in Europe. Labor is rapidly getting out of hand, under this Administration. Dogs and swine! We've got to get busy, and that without delay. Francis, what are you doing about unions?"

Emile's voice: "Hitler must win the coming war. Tell me, you fellows, just what have been your shipments to Hitler, through Holland & South America? I have my own figures here, from Bouchard & Sons, but I'm not very familiar with your work. Henri, what about those cartels? What are the production figures?"

Jean's voice: "I tell you, fascism is the only protection we have against labor. Some of you have wondered about the American masses' reaction to such a regime. But I tell you now the people don't want to think. They want to be led, regulated, thought for, even driven, if driven firmly and strongly, 'for their own good.' Do you think the American mob is any more intelligent than the German or Italian? If you do, you're fools."

Alexander's pompous parson's voice: "We've got to have a government by Managers in America, Business Managers. Why, I've got Biblical approval of this——!"

The voice of the President of the American Association of Industrialists: "I tell you, it isn't going to be very easy. It's

223

fine to say we've got to destroy democracy in America. But you must remember there is a noisy if minority group which is all for Jeffersonian democracy, and if they are eloquent enough, there'll be trouble here. Especially if there is war. We're strong, I admit that. But what are we doing in a practical way?

"Look at the facts: Kiss-mammy idealists. Marxist college professors, New Deal politicians, vociferous and ideal-drunk newspapers are already bellowing and breaking down public trust in our business structure. We're 'fascist, conservative, reactionary, and Tories.' They've got a following, and that can grow among stupid masses. Look at labor gains, since that rascal has been in the White House! Do you think that labor is going to relinquish its rights so easily, and quietly let us destroy its goddam precious democracy? You're confounded asses if you think so!"

Jean's soft and smiling voice again: "We can give them something more colorful. We've already organized strong minorities, reactionary and safe. What is that new organization of yours, Chris, when war breaks out in Europe? The America Only Committee? We'll have five million members overnight, all sound blimps who will hate anything we tell them to hate: 'war-mongers,' Jews, radical statesmen, snotty-nosed idealists. Anything. While they are hating so vigorously, we can bring out our own Guardians of America, the lawful and white-washed successor to the Ku Klux Klan. Don't forget, too, we've got the American Legion with its hatred for Communists. All we need now is a few good slogans, and our publicity boys ought to be able to find them. We have sufficient committees, I believe, to befuddle and disorganize the stinking masses long enough to let Hitler win in Europe and keep America out of the mess. Then, when Hitler has cleaned up the balance of Europe, we'll demand that he assist us here. It's the least he can do, after all we've done for him."

Then Antoine's voice, accompanied by his dark and glittering smile: "I've seen enough in France, among my elegant associates, to know that France, with all her fervent patriotism, and her 'devotion' to *liberté, égalité, fraternité*, will fall easily during the first few months of German assault. It's all settled, there. A faint show of resistance, to throw off public suspicion, then an 'insupportable' situation which will end in immediate capitulation. The French leaders have done their work excellently, even in such a homogeneous country where the masses profess to adore France. It will be easier in America. Who loves America? The descendants of Germans,

Italians, Poles and God knows what other human scum? The American people, too, are the most stupid and ignorant in the world. They will allow fascism to gain dominance here much quicker than the French will allow it. I agree with Jean. A few active committees and organizations, all hating something or other with that single-hearted delight that animates the American-Neanderthal man, a few induced lynchings, black-mailings, libelling, and a good splash of rich vulgar ridicule, and the work is done. Labor? Labor is too illiterate, too greedy, too gross and animalistic to lift a hand, labor leaders to the contrary. When we take over the Government under the new Nationalism, labor will simply love to work twelve hours a day for just enough to keep its gaunt belly filled.

"Besides, haven't we the Church to rely on in America, with its gospel of work, propagation, family, obedience and ignorance, for the masses? God knows, we've subsidized it enough! Then, we've got our newspapers, our chains. I think they will justify our faith in them."

The voices came quickly now to Armand's shrinking ears, vicious, gloating, laughing, conspiring. And now the voice of Mr. Douglas Flannery, publisher of the Detroit *Clarion* which boasted four million readers not only in the Detroit area, but far beyond it:

"My paper has gained over a million readers during the last six months. Doesn't that signify anything to you gentlemen? I've slashed everything, from the New Deal to Britain, France and Spain, from labor leaders to Communists, and I'm proud of the record. I've emphasized that we need in Washington sound and conservative business men who will put the needs of America before the Marxist needs of European radicals. I'm not afraid!" continued the pompous and rumbling voice triumphantly. "I'm the only newspaper in America that dares to attack the Jews and the Negroes, and in the event of any dissatisfaction or confusion in America, which might interfere with the plans of you gentlemen, a pogrom, an epidemic of lynching, can easily be arranged. These will distract the public mind. Look at my columnists! I can truly say these boys are doing their work excellently. If Roosevelt has the audacity to seek a third term, which he won't do of course, we'll rip him wide open. We can quote Washington with the best of 'em!" he added, on a roar of laughter.

In the darkness, Armand suddenly clapped his hands to his ears, and rocked desolately on his chair. His wrinkled forehead was wet and cold as ice.

Now the voices became a confusion in the hot silence of the room, voices of conspiracy against America, against the world, against all mankind. Voices of greed and cruelty and rapacity and immense cunning. Voices that told of the re-armament of Germany, of fellow conspirators in England and in France, the conservatives, the Tories, the plotters on English country estates and on the French Riviera, of vast loans to Hitler, of the intricate maze of international cartels that would restrict the arming of America, and the conversion of her economy into effective war-production, of the division, under these cartels, of South America between German and American companies, of the suppression of competition, under these same cartels, and the monopolizing of the markets of America, of the exchange of vital patents with Hitler, of propaganda throughout the world which served as apologia for Naziism and eulogized the gains made in fascist countries over labor and "decadence," of arrangements for shipments of vital war matériel to Hitler in the event of war, through South America and other neutral countries. The voices rose like a storm, like a hurricane, so that the sick man listening to them as he rocked desolately on his chair thought that the very dome of the sky echoed with them, threw them back to the duller echoes of earth.

And then, they faded away on a last shrill note. But the air of the world vibrated with them, quivered like plucked strings, which though now silent, still trembled with unheard reverberations.

Armand lifted his head from his chest and stared about him, blindly. His mouth had fallen open, and he was panting. His sickness was devouring him like a tiger.

The years of his life marched before him, those confused, frightened and formless years, filled with shrinking and fear. He had had such a small and wounded integrity, which had never been enough for anything but to induce this lethal disease in him. All those years, when he might have done something! Instead, his weak conscience had gnawed at him, devouring the cells of his flesh, petrifying the vital forces in him, delivering him up at last to this desolation and this feeble despair, this loneliness and lost hopelessness, this bewilderment and torture.

He did not regret; he merely suffered. What could I have done? he whimpered to himself. I never really cared. Why, then, was I tormented? Why did I run away?

He stood up, and his whimper broke from his lips: "I

really was a good man! I hated it. I was better than they. I really had the capacity——"

Now his terror inundated him, and he clasped his fat hands together convulsively, and glared about him, affrighted.

He had never had any patriotism. His sole loyalty had been to himself, to his family. He could not understand. Even now, he consciously felt no fear for America, no concern for the world. He was only aware of a terrible and engulfing dread and horror.

"I was really a good man!" he cried again, to the somber darkness.

And then he knew that all his life he had wanted to be good, to be simple, to be kind. But he had been a coward. This very desire had been part of his cowardice. It had never been enough to overcome his native rapacity and avarice. He saw that he was an even greater criminal than Henri, than Christopher, than all the rest of his ominous family.

He had never had any faith in anything. He opened his mouth now, and whispered: "God." But the word meant nothing to him at all. It was an incantation without magic. His heart was beating with slow thick strokes, as if it were drowning.

Now he felt that the rooms of his house were crowding about him, the walls overhanging him like the walls of a cliff, that he was about to be crushed. He dropped his mouth wide open, and gasped. He said aloud, with fainting wonder: "My conscience was only fear for myself, fear of any possible consequences that might come on me because of the plottings and conspiracies of myself and others."

His mortal terror increased. He felt death in him. He glared about him like an animal. When a branch of a tree brushed the window he started with a cry, and trembled violently.

And then he heard the distant opening and closing of a door, the footsteps of his son ascending the great gilt and marble staircase.

A great sweat broke out over his body. He ran to the doorway of his rooms, stumbling, staggering. He flung open the door, caught at the frame to uphold himself. He cried out, over and over, in a voice that ran through the corridors like the voice of a tortured man in flight:

"Antoine! Antoine! Antoine!"

CHAPTER XXIV

Antoine, who had just had a most delightful and intriguing evening, and was now bemused in very pleasant thoughts, was considerably startled to see his father standing thus, with such a distraught and frantic face, with such a trembling pot-bellied body, in the doorway of his apartments. It was some time since Antoine had entered his father's house.

The light in the lofty corridor was very dim and soft, and its uncertain diffusion gave an eerie and unreal quality to the apparition that confronted the young man. But he was amazed at the eyes, glaring, starting, catching the suffused light on their distended balls. He saw how his father clutched the frame of the doorway, how his knees were buckling. He saw his terror, which was overwhelming and frenzied, saw the open gasping mouth and heaving chest.

He went to him quickly, exclaiming with unusual roughness: "What is it, Papa?"

But Armand did not move or speak. He only regarded his son in a kind of hypnotized horror, watched his approach in complete silence.

He thought in numb anguish: This is my son. But he is like my father. I have never seen this so clearly before. It is my father, looking at me, and I hate him. How can he help me? He would only destroy me if I told him. He would laugh in my face. My God! There is nothing I can say or do.

There was an appalled terror in his eyes as Antoine continued to advance towards him, and though he still did not move, he appeared to shrink, to dwindle.

Antoine, slightly alarmed now, took his father's arm. It was rigid as wood under his hand, and trembled constantly. "What's wrong? Are you ill? Let us go in. You must sit down."

Armand stumbled as his son led him back into the great hot room, so dark and heavy. Antoine was forced to support him. He brought his father to a chair, and with unusual thoughtfulness lowered him into it. He turned on a few lights.

228

Armand watched him, crouched on the edge of the chair, his shaking hands, overgrown with thick curling auburn hair, clenched on his fat knees, his head sunken in his shoulders. He resembled an old sick animal, gasping and undone.

"Shall I call Dr. Billingsley?" asked Antoine, standing near him and eyeing him with reflective penetration.

Armand whispered: "No. No. It is nothing." He lifted his hands and pressed them against his face. He sighed. The sound seemed to come from the very depths of him. When he dropped his hands his expression was stark, abstracted.

Antoine hesitated. He drew a chair near to his father, and sat down. Still watching the old man, he lit a cigarette, put it with slow and delicate gestures to his lips, and blew the smoke thoughtfully upwards. That narrow black head, so sleek and small, that brown smooth face, those glittering black eyes and that subtle mouth, impressed themselves vividly on Armand's tormented consciousness as they had never done before. Yes, it was his father who sat before him, not his son. This was Jules' sleek elegance and fastidious composure, and now, as Antoine smiled a little, it was Jules' smile, secret, faintly amused, quietly cruel.

"There must have been something," said Antoine. "You looked like the devil, for a minute. What frightened you?"

What frightened me? said Armand to himself, still staring at his son. He thought: It is you.

Despair choked him. He put his hand for a moment to his chest, and gasped again. He said: "It was just that I was alone."

"Ah," murmured Antoine. His eyes narrowed. They pierced Armand like thin black rapiers. He thought, contemptuously: The old fool. Wandering around this mausoleum like a dirty fat ghost. He never had any guts. What does he want? Something has frightened the life out of him.

He saw that Armand was still staring at him rigidly, and something in that fixed regard made him momentarily uneasy.

"You look like my father," said the old man.

"So I've heard," replied his son, smiling. He added: "Did that frighten you?"

Armand answered with sudden quietness: "Yes." Then his rigidity dissolved, his features twisted, his eyes were wild with terror again. He cried: "I'm sick! I'm dying!"

Antoined frowned. The smoke from his cigarette floated before his face, and his eyes gleamed through it, evilly, thoughtfully.

"Nonsense," he said, quietly. "Billingsley told me only last week that you were doing splendidly. He did say, however, that you needed some interest in your life. You think too much of yourself, dear Papa. You've never had any hobby, or any amusement. You've gotten moldy in this house. Green with mold. Yes, I can see you're lonely. What can you expect? You live for Annette's call every morning, and then you subside into inertia again. You never go out, except to visit her, and the family has long given up inviting you. You almost invariably refuse invitations. I understand that you don't even take a drive in the mornings, as you formerly did. You've become so damned engrossed in your List that you've abandoned even those few interests you once had. Too introspective. You ought not to have retired so soon."

His voice, silken, soothing, yet filled with smooth Jesuitical cruelty, held Armand's distraught attention. He listened, not looking away from his son, rubbing his knuckles against his fat reddened nose or against his shaking mouth.

There's something here, thought Antoine. His feral instincts were alert. For he had seen the sudden vividness in the old man's eye at his last words. He repeated, watching him closely: "You ought not to have retired so soon."

"No," whispered Armand. He dropped his hands again to his knees. His head fell forward on his chest. His voice came to his son, stifled, almost inaudible:

"No one tells me anything. I never know. I've been listening to the radio. They—believe that Hitler will march soon. On Poland. There'll be war. We'll be in it——"

Antoine shifted slightly on his chair. He dropped the hand that held the cigarette, and it was tense and still, the smoke curling slowly.

"No. We won't be in it. Did that worry you?"

Armand was silent.

"Then, you have no need to worry," continued Antoine, smiling again. "I can give you my personal assurance. You never did like the idea of war, did you? Well, then, you need have no fears whatsoever. America won't engage in any European mess. 'Keep our boys from fighting on foreign soil.' That's our slogan. For the first time in history the Bouchards aren't interested in war for America."

Armand lifted his head, and again he stared at his son motionlessly.

"Yes, I know that."

"Then, why were you worrying?"

But Armand said, gazing at him with the strangest fixity: "I never believed in anything. We were never religious, we

230

Bouchards. We have never been Americans. Isn't that very queer—never having been Americans?"

The fool's in his dotage, thought Antoine. He smoked again, to hide his irrepressible smile.

Armand's voice was faint and toneless as he continued: "French schools. German schools. We've never been Americans. We had nothing to do with America, or for America."

"We've built up a vast industrial net-work," said Antoine, again watching his father closely. "In a way, we've helped develop America. We're in everything. That ought to make you proud. You used to be proud. I remember that, when I was a child. Steel, mining, armaments, chemicals, copper, cars, railroads, aviation—we're in it all. Really, we're American, after all."

Armand looked away from him and regarded the radio with dumb steadfastness. "And that, too, of course."

Antoine frowned. "Radio? Probably."

Armand had begun to nod his head slowly. The nodding continued. He did not seem to be able to control it.

Then a rush of words came from his dry lips, a whispering rush so faint, so choking, that Antoine had to lean forward to catch the sounds:

"Tell me something about it. No one ever tells me. I don't know anything. What will happen? If Hitler wins—over there what will happen? To America? What is happening in the world? You've got to tell me."

Antoine was silent for a few moments. The glare of terror was again in Armand's eyes. He had begun a soft pounding of his knees with his clenched fists.

Antoine shrugged. "Don't you read the newspapers? You listen to the radio, don't you, Papa? Then, you know as much as we do. Suppose Hitler takes the Corridor, takes Poland? That's no concern of America's. Europe has always had its confounded quarrels. And always will. Britain may attack him. I don't know. Incidentally, I'm not much interested. Just now, we are concerned with America."

And then he noticed a heap of newspapers beside his father's chair, all open at the financial pages. He laughed lightly. He pointed to the papers with his thin brown finger. "Is that what was worrying you? The Stock Market? Well, I agree with you it's in bad shape. However, we are expecting a rise." Armand said nothing. Antoine continued in a curious silence: "Naturally, you would be concerned. After all, you still own fifty-one percent of Bouchard stock. So, if the Market has been disturbing you, I can assure you, personally, that it won't disturb you much longer." He waited a moment. He said, more quickly: "It has been worrying you, hasn't it? The Market?"

"Yes," said Armand. The strangeness of his look increased. "You think the Market will rise? It usually drops for a while, after the outbreak of war. Why do you think it will rise?"

He actually knows nothing, thought Antoine, smiling internally. He shrugged lightly. "Why shouldn't it? We're bound to make money. It is really very simple."

"The Neutrality Act?" said Armand, again in a whisper.

Antoine laughed. "Oh, come now. You can't be that ignorant, Papa. There's South America, and Holland, and half a dozen other avenues."

"For Germany?"

Antoine paused. He narrowed his eyes intently. "Yes. Who else? There'll be nothing for Britain, or France, either, if we can help it."

Armand moved even farther to the edge of his seat. There was a passionate intensity in his regard. "We've never done that before. We've sold to both belligerents, in the past. Why Germany now, and not—the others?"

"Because," replied Antoine, slowly and carefully, "we want Hitler to win. I thought you knew that, dear Papa. Hitler is our only hope, all over the world." He spoke as one speaks to a dull child, choosing simple words. "We've got to get rid of democracy, or Communism. They amount to the same thing. Labor is getting out of control, under this filthy New Deal. We've got to have a new outlook, a new philosophy, in America. Not just business as usual. We want the business of controlling America absolutely. We'll get it, too. With Hitler's help." He reached over and patted his father's knee. "Then watch your stocks rise!"

"You mean, fascism in America?" murmured Armand.

"A nasty word!" smiled Antoine. "Let's say, rather, the control of America by businessmen. By managers. That's only sensible, isn't it? Hitler has promised to assist us. The yellow weasle has given us his word, for all it's worth."

"How can he 'assist' you?" Armand's voice was clearer now, and louder.

Antoine hesitated. "There are ways," he replied, pleasantly. He stood up. Armand still sat in his chair. His uplifted eyes were very bright as they contemplated his son.

And now he hated Antoine as he had never hated anyone before, not even his father for whom he had had a peculiar frightened regard under the hatred. He was frozen with his

232

renewed terror. He pressed his hands together, and a long shiver passed over his body. He thought: It's too late. I can't do anything. I don't even know what to do, or whether I want to do it. It's all very confused. I ought to have kept up, known what was going on. No one ever tells me. I don't know anything.

Antoine was smiling down at him. "I'd advise you to go out more. Annette and I have our own interests. We aren't children any longer. I heard you refused Estelle's invitation to dinner on Saturday. Why don't you reconsider it?"

"I will," said Armand, obediently. "Yes, I think I will."

When Antoine had gone, Armand sat crouched in his chair, his head thrust forward, his teeth gnawing his lips. There was a frightened struggle raging in him. Though he did not move for nearly an hour, his forehead, his balding skull, were damp and glistening. Finally he stood up, almost fell, so weak had he become. He fumbled for his telephone, and though it was nearly midnight, he called his lawyer and made an appointment for the next day, in New York.

CHAPTER XXV

Henri Bouchard sat alone this hot August day, at his desk in his great Bouchard offices. The heavy doors were shut, and he had told his secretary that he must not be disturbed for at least an hour. The bronze-colored curtains were partially drawn against the blinding light that radiated through the windows, and there was a somber, almost pious, hush in the room. Here and there a sunbeam struck with hot golden silence on the edge of some metal on the desk.

Henri was smoking. He rarely smoked alone. It was his only sign of some profound inner uneasiness and perturbation. He sat at his desk, not moving, dressed in his favorite dark gray, which had earned him Antoine's name of the "Iron Man." He stared before him, his large pale face stony and immovable, his pale eyes fixed. He lit cigarette after cigarette, but hardly put them to his lips. They burned out slowly between his fingers. Sometimes his eyes dropped momentarily to the neat heap of papers before him, and would remain there for long moments in a kind of somber trance.

At the end of each fifteen minutes, he would take up his telephone, his private direct wire to Wall Street, and listen carefully to the swift metallic voice which informed him of late developments in the European situation. He would replace the receiver, not a muscle in his face moving, would light another cigarette, and stare again at the papers.

One report had reached him that morning: "The American people remain apathetic, during this mounting crisis in Europe. Only among certain groups is there any deep interest. It is the consensus of experts that the inertia of the people is due less to fear of future events than to a static ignorance and indifference. One expert believes that the indifference can be laid at the door of past efforts on the part of professional pacifists and isolationist Senators. Others, more informed, more attuned to the public mind, believe that Hitler has made himself so exceedingly popular with the American people, with his anti-Semitism, anti-democracy, and ruthlessness, that they couldn't be aroused against him except on the occasion of a direct attack upon America. Hitler, no doubt, understands this, therefore he will refrain from such an attack, aware that in its absence he can rely upon the American people's apathy to place no obstruction in his path of conquest."

At this, Henri had smiled grimly. He smiled again, as he recalled the report. But what could one expect of a nation of first and second-generation European slaves, who must feel abysmally uneasy in the presence of a liberty created and loved by a handful of Britons in the far and bitter past? How would George Washington deal with this cringing nation of swine and slaves? Would he recognize, in these sullen Teutonic faces, these dark swarthy Mediterranean wretches, the people whose blood he had shared, whose language he had spoken, and with whom he had fought and suffered? If he could come among them today, would he not despise them, understanding the threat implicit in them for America, and the survival of America? Rome had learned the deadly lesson, that one dare not admit among a free people the children of besotted and superstition-ridden slaves. The vandals at the gates of Rome had not been the Goths and the Visigoths.

These were strange thoughts for Henri Bouchard. He smiled contemptuously when he thought them. But he could not dispel the uneasiness in him, the hatred, the aversion and

234

anger. What was America to him? It was true, that except for the slight strain of French blood in his own blood-stream, he was of the race and, outwardly, of the religion of those who had founded America. His heritage was British. But never in his life had he known one thrill of patriotism or passion for America.

He lifted the sheaf of papers, stared at them, thrust them away from him. Jay Regan, the aging and dying financier, had sent them to him by special messenger. He told himself that it was his rage against his relatives who dared conspire against him that so disturbed him now. Was patriotism, after all, only jealous fear and envy and ignorant hatred? He finally concluded this must be so.

He lifted the telephone again, and now the sharp metallic voice was shrill and breathless with excitement. "There is a rumor that Russia and Germany will soon reach some form of accord, after which Russia will not oppose any territorial ambitions on the part of Hitler, so long as Russia, herself, is not attacked!"

Russia! This was not impossible, of course. Henri remembered Munich, when Russia's offer of assistance had been ignored, when she had been shut out from the shameful conference at Berchtesgaden. Was this her revenge, then, born of her bitterness against those hypocrites who had mouthed of peace, those cowards who had sold the treasure of ages to a murderer and a liar, those plotters who hated their own struggling people? Henri smiled suddenly. He felt a harsh sympathy for Russia. When the attack against the hypocrites, the cowards and the plotters began, it would be a just judgment upon them. Then their people would shriek that they had been betrayed, blaming "the industrialists and capitalists" or "the politicians," not understanding that before death can overwhelm them the disease must first destroy them internally. When the final hour arrived, the people, of course, would not be aware that the rottenness had first been in themselves, whether they lived in mansions or in the gutter, that their own brutish hatred, ignorance and lack of values had betrayed them to their enemies.

Even the Bouchards, and all their friends, could not destroy America if America was not ripe for destruction. Diseased seeds could grow only in diseased soil. The soil of America was diseased.

Henri rose and walked heavily up and down the room. He was not subject to any malaise of the spirit, to any uneasiness. All his life he had known what he wanted, and had seized it.

His mind had been single and integrated. Now he could not understand his own heavy and somber thoughts. He listened to the loud words in his own spirit as to the voice of a stranger which he could not shut out. He was impatient and disturbed, as he had never been impatient or disturbed before.

Was this fear for himself, or revulsion against relatives who conspired against him? He believed it was both.

There was a soft tap on his door, and angrily he called: "Come in." His secretary entered apologetically, and cringed at his glare.

"I am sorry, Mr. Bouchard, but Mr. Armand Bouchard is here and wishes to see you. He says it is very urgent."

Henri scowled. "Please tell Mr. Bouchard that Mr. Antoine is not in at present." Then he paused, abruptly. What the hell did the old sot and fool want with him, Henri? He had not been in these offices since he had made his appeal for his son. All at once, a curious excitement struck at him. His instinct was awakened.

He sat down at his desk. "Please send Mr. Bouchard in at once." While he waited for Armand, he tapped on the top of the desk with his blunt fingers. What the devil possessed the miserable old cringer? What had he heard?

He despised Armand, rarely thought of him, and then only with contempt. Armand was done, old, destroyed by some chronic inner disease which Henri had already suspected was not of his big-bellied body. But he was still latently potent. He, Henri, knew enough of Armand to believe that there must be moments when his father-in-law would remember this.

Now all his uneasiness of the last hour or two, all his smoldering rage and disgust, concentrated themselves upon the vision of Armand, and his intrusion. He was annoyed at himself for this childishness, but the cold emotion remained. He held the greater part of Bouchard bonds but his dominant rôle in Bouchard & Sons was only by consent of Armand and his precious fifty-one percent. It was a situation which had long enraged Henri, and which had impelled much of his caution. The situation had sometimes become almost untenable for him.

So it was that when Armand, already disorganized, already shaken to the very frightened depths of him, already confused and terrified and sick of soul and flesh, encountered Henri's cold and formidable look he winced as if Henri had struck at him with his clenched fist. His first impulse was flight. He stood far from the desk, and actually trembled, moistening his dry and swollen lips, staring at Henri in utter silence and disintegration, his hat in his hand like a beggar.

Henri rose slowly and reluctantly. He placed a chair for his father-in-law. What was wrong with the old fool? He looked as if he had heard the most frightful news, and was on the verge of collapse. Now Henri forgot his anger and frustration. He was suddenly alert, and he could even smile.

"Well, this is pleasant," he said, in his heavy and toneless voice which denied the pleasantness of this visit. "Sit down, Father. You perhaps didn't know that Antoine isn't here? I wish you had called up first, and saved yourself this trouble."

Armand sat on the edge of the chair. Now the visible trembling invaded his knees, which shook in their untidy trousers. Henri, seating himself again, saw the soiled collar which was hardly more than a stained cloth about Armand's fat neck. The lapels of his coat were sprinkled with white flakes. His vest was badly buttoned, and a tuft of shirt protruded through it. The big round head, with its crop of gray tendrils, shook faintly, as if the old man had been seized with a palsy. But it was his face, the color of tallow, the staring little black eyes, the uncontrollable twitching of his facial muscles, which focussed Henri's attention. It was evident that Armand was sick with despair and fear. He kept touching his mouth with a tremulous hand. He could not speak for a few moments, and then he said, almost inaudibly: "I didn't want to see Antoine. I came because I knew he wasn't here."

"Yes?" said Henri, in a smooth and quiet tone. "Well, then, is there anything I can do for you, Father? Are you ill?"

Armand gazed at him mutely for long minutes. Then his lips moved again in a whisper: "Yes. Yes, I am very ill."

He looked down at his hat as if he had never seen it before; then, with odd timidity, he placed it on the desk which had once been his. Henri watched all his fumbling and uncertain movements. Then, as his eyes met Armand's, he was shocked and startled at the brilliant terror in them, the sudden overwhelming despair. He half rose from his chair, then sank down again, in alert silence.

Something was up. Of that, he was very sure. He saw no accusation on Armand's face, no querulous protest. Could it be that there was actually a plea in those tormented eyes, in those aimless fat hands, overgrown with auburn hair, which kept lifting and dropping themselves?

"What's wrong?" asked Henri. "You seem disturbed. You know, if I can help you, I'll be only too glad to do so."

He thought: He's had a shock.

He saw that Armand did not know what to say, that the chaotic and terrified thoughts in his mind were too huge for speech, for orderly beginning. It was a mortally-stricken old animal that sat across from him, trying to stop the shaking of his lips with his stained and yellow teeth. And Henri saw that this was no new thing, but a manifestation of a life of fear, of cringing, of nameless anguish. He was surprised. He had never given sufficient thought to Armand in the past to conjecture about him, yet the cumulative evidence that had been stored in his subconscious now neatly fitted together and revealed itself as a visible pattern to him.

His surprise grew, and with it, a cynical compassion for Armand, so bedevilled, so undone, so confused and tormented. He studied him with an alert and rising curiosity. He saw that Armand, in his turn, had fixed his eyes upon him with sudden penetration and passionate eagerness, and that he had straightened in his chair as if this business was so urgent that he could hardly force it into the orderly confine of mere words.

His words broke from him, in stammering and discordant confusion, and he leaned towards Henri, putting both hands upon the desk and pressing upon it so that the cords sprang up visibly through the hairy flesh:

"There are so many things I remember lately!" And now he spoke in French, which his father had insisted upon, though it had been laughed at as an affectation by the other Bouchards. Henri had to listen acutely to understand. What frantic stress must the miserable old fool be enduring that impelled him, in his distraught frenzy, unconsciously to use the language of his childhood?

Armand's hands were moving with strong jerks in the air, as if to ensure full comprehension for his own incoherent words and make them understood. His eyes were bright and feverish, and as he uttered each word he mouthed it as a stammerer mulls over the painful sounds he cannot control:

"All the things—over the years, that I remember, Henri! My father. Jules. He was a terrible man. I always knew the terribleness. It frightened me very much." Henri, even as he listened with strong interest, remarked to himself that this language, pouring from Armand's shaking lips, was not rusty, as might have been expected from one who had not used it for years, but was strong and naturally accented, though hoarse with peasant inflections as if Armand's very flesh remembered its ancient blood. These, too, were ancient peasant gesticulations, and even over his face there came

238

a subtle mask, coarse and vital and earthy.

Now the words came faster, so that Henri lost many:

"You see, Henri, it was always very dreadful to me. I never realized it until just recently. Yet I must have known. There was something in me, rebelling." He struck his chest firmly, though his eyes never left Henri's. "I had no words for it. I was dumb. Speechless. But it grew, like something in my heart. They only laughed. They saw it in my face, perhaps. It was very ridiculous to them. Do you understand? Well, there was nothing I could do, not even for myself. I could not understand it. It was so excessively absurd. You find it absurd, my son?"

Something made Henri say quickly: "No, I do not find it absurd." He spoke in English, and a curious restlessness passed over Armand's face for an instant.

He continued: "I do not undertand even yet. I only know I am ill. The needle—it does not help me. How can I tell the doctor this? He cannot understand. No one knows. But it is there. And now I know it will kill me."

He was silent. But the hands pressing on the polished desk spread an aura of dullness about them, as of sweat. He leaned even closer to Henri and searched his face with those starting and pathetic eyes.

Henri regarded him thoughtfully, leaned back in his chair, and said nothing. To what a pass this tortured soul had come in this gross and unwieldy body that it must cry out even to a man such as himself, thought Henri. There had never been much friendliness between Armand and the man who had married his daughter, never any confidence or sympathy, or kindliness. In fact, Henri could not remember that there had ever been any of these between Armand and another human being, except Annette. Armand's mean and peevish little wife, his brutal brothers, his subtle and vicious father, his inadequate and sorrowful mother: among all these he had never had a friend or a confidant. He had lived alone in his body, which had been awkward and lumbering even in his youth, and if he had ever wished for communication with another man he had never indicated it.

This is a hell of a day! thought Henri, uneasily, remembering the thoughts which had preceded Armand's coming. And now this old tragic fool sat before him, increasing his incomprehensible uneasiness!

Out of his irritation and rusty pity, he said, slowly picking his way through his stony French: "There is something troubling you. If I can help, I will. What is it? You have said that you have 'rebelled.' I will not pretend that I fully understand you. You have told me enough to indicate to me that your conscience is making you suffer." He pressed his lips strongly together to keep from smiling at the ridiculous word.

Armand stared at him, then slowly lifted his hand and rubbed his mouth heavily. He whispered: "My conscience. Did I ever have a conscience?"

He drew a deep breath, and spoke with long spaces between his words, as if it had become a matter of terrible importance to him that Henri should understand:

"You see, it is all so confused. Once or twice, I thought: I cannot go on, doing these things, plotting. But I went on. Why? Because I was greedy. I was weak. I was afraid of appearing ridiculous. Sometimes Christopher suspected. He would look at me with the most wicked and cunning eyes. I could not endure his suspecting."

He paused, and asked: "Will there be war, Henri?"

Henri was silent a moment, then replied judiciously: "I am no prophet, Father. How can I tell? But I am firmly against war. For the first time, the Bouchards want no war."

Armand nodded, and smiled wretchedly. "Yes, I know. That is what is so terrible to me. You understand?"

Henri stared, frowning. Then, he understood. The old fool, then, was not entirely a fool. He smiled. "Yes, I understand."

They looked at each other in a long silence, and then a strange sympathy wove itself between them. Henri was aware of a growing excitement in himself.

Armand looked down at his trembling fingers. He spoke hesitatingly: "Long ago, I hoped you would be my son. You see, I have no son."

"No son—" repeated Henri. And then he said nothing else. He looked into Armand's eyes, so bright and tragic and haggard.

"Antoine is really like my father. No man could be father to a Jules, Henri. I am so terribly afraid. Antoine is to marry the daughter of Andrew Boland."

Now Henri forgot everything in his dismay and apprehension. "The devil! You mean Mary Boland?" So, Antoine had done well for himself to pick out the daughter of that pious old serpent, Boland, "Aluminum Emperor," and owner of one of the most powerful oil combines in the world.

Armand saw Henri's perturbation, and nodded somberly. "You see how it is. We must move very fast, must we not?"

Henri said nothing. But as he looked at Armand, his excitement grew, and he felt a quicker beating of his heart.

Armand gave the impression of drawing closer to the younger man. Now his words came in a tumbling rush:

"I remember many things about you, too, Henri. You are not a good man, are you? You are rapacious and ruthless—like all the other Bouchards. You would do anything for power and profits. But, I am not condemning you. How could I? You, at least, never had a conscience, so nothing could be expected of you.

"I remember the legends of old Ernest Barbour, your great-grandfather. He was never really cruel, or subtle or vicious. That was because he never had the slightest conscience. He was a force. A natural force. One does not blame the glacier or volcano. It cannot help itself. Sometimes, it can be admired. You are like that, Henri.

"I did not quite understand that until I heard your conversation with my brother, Christopher, when you warned him of his plottings with the Germans. Then I recalled other things, also. They made a whole. Tell me, Henri, what you wish, what you intend to do, in America."

Henri did not speak for several moments, though he studied Armand intently with his pale and inexorable eyes. He knew he must move cautiously.

He began to speak with heavy slowness: "I thought you knew. It is not that I have had a change of heart," and he smiled. "I am thinking of what is best for America—because what is best for America is really best for us. Things have changed. The world, after all, belongs to the people who inhabit it, and not a chosen few, not even to the Bouchards. When strong men devour everything, they starve the weaker who prepare the food for them.

"The war that is coming was brought on by the greed of industrialists and bankers to perpetuate the status quo. And this war might be the very weapon that will destroy the system which they have laboriously built by the manipulation of everything that could be exploited. Now, I believe that every man, even a Bouchard, can operate best in a system such as ours—capitalistic democracy. It can only be saved in the future by evolving methods to give the people as much as possible, stopping short of destroying working capital. After the war, we'll undoubtedly have newly created markets in the world. 'Production for use!' We must inaugurate a higher standard of living all over the world, not only in America. This will steadily increase markets for peace-time products, and will be the greatest force against future wars.

"Our relatives do not agree with me. They are complete fools. They see themselves as a family of potent Hitlers, operating in America. They do not realize that tyranny devours itself, in the end. They do not understand the people at all. They will fight to the death for the status quo, with their European allies. It is their greatest dream to reduce the world to mediæval ism again, supported by a supine State and a rampant Church. They do not see how ridiculous they are. The world is filled with a different breed of men now."

Armand had listened with the most painful attention. He had nodded eagerly once or twice. He had relaxed sufficiently to be able to sit back in his chair.

"And Antoine?" he said, now in English, as if some unbearable strain had been removed. "He doesn't agree with you? He is plotting against you?"

Henri was surprised. He frowned, and said nothing. How the hell could this old fool have known this, absorbed as he had been in his infernal List?

"I know all about it, though nobody has told me anything," continued Armand. "Yes, he is really my father. I can see that."

His face was a better color, and firmer and more resolute. "I knew what you believed, and wanted, Henri. That's why I came here this morning. You see, yesterday I was in New York, with my lawyers." He took out a crumpled paper from one of his untidy pockets. His hands were no longer trembling. He was, for this hour, the old Armand again, fumbling but compact, awkward but practical. He looked down at the paper, and said:

"I've made a new will. But no one shall know of it but you, myself and my lawyers. I have created a trust fund with my fifty-one percent of Bouchard stock, for you and my little Annette. I shall collect the income during my lifetime, but I am giving you now power of attorney to vote the stock as you see fit on any occasion. After my death, the stock and income will belong to you jointly. They will eventually pass to the survivor, of course."

He looked at Henri, with a deep smile. Henri had turned singularly pale. He sat as motionless as granite in his chair.

"As for Antoine, my son, I am leaving him only my minority shares in other corporations. He will have nothing to do with Bouchard. That is the danger I've eliminated."

"Let me think about it for a moment," said Henri, in a curiously stifled voice. "The trust fund has already been created? And I now have power of attorney?"

He stood up, and began to walk up and down the room. The nostrils of his short and powerful nose had dilated, because breathing had become so difficult. Exultation filled him like a bright and expanding gas, threatening to burst its confines. He could not believe it! He lifted his head and clenched his fists. Now, he had everything, and not merely by the grace of Armand Bouchard. His power had been the slothful Armand's, only. Now, it was his own.

He stopped by Armand's chair and looked down at the fat and shapeless bulk sprawled in it. Armand's face was lifted. It wore an expression of complete peace and content. The eyes were closed. Henri, who had been about to speak, was silent. He slowly and thoughtfully bit his index finger.

CHAPTER XXVI

Peter's book was developing with a feverish rapidity and fluid ease. He was like a man who works swiftly and anxiously the while the sky darkens and he glances over his shoulder at the first intimations of thunder, and the first red flashes of lightning. Despite his reason, which told him that men rarely cogitate, almost never understand, he had that intoxicating faith of the crusading author that the printed word might divert the fury and calm the ignorant passions of mankind. Only when he wrote like this did he even for a moment believe that the pen was mightier than the sword. Was it not Voltaire's pamphlets which had destroyed the oppressors of France? Was it not his word that had overthrown the golden throne and set up the guillotine in the market-places? Behind the cry of his written and impassioned sentences came the rumble of the tumbrils, and a whole continent awoke from its slumbering lethargy at the blazing trumpet of his soul.

Then Peter experienced bottomless despair. A nation enchanted by baseball and comic strips, by painted Hollywood trollops and automobiles, could not possibly feel the ancient and mystical urge of an ideal. Such a nation is by nature timid and conservative, suspicious and dull, easily hating the weak, easily submissive to the strong. Only among the New Englanders, perhaps, and among the decaying aristocracy of the Southern States, could there be found a man similar in feature and mind to the noblest forebears.

Should he awaken and disturb such men (and how few there were in America!), what could they do? For the first time in his life Peter had a sickening doubt of democracy, where the voice of the ox is as important as the voice of the wise man. He might arouse a hundred thousand enlightened men to the terrible danger that was blowing up like a hurricane over the rooftops of the world. They might rise up, crying aloud. What could they do, in a nation of one hundred and thirty millions of dolts and ignoramuses who would gape without comprehension at stern and portentous faces, and listen apishly to warning cries? He had no illusion that these few men possessed any considerable power in America in politics and in public places. American democracy, itself, held ability and mental aristocracy suspect, was inimical to superiority, and placed in power only those gross charlatans, those bumbling clowns, those sly and inferior minds, that most resembled the majority of the people.

All his adult life Peter had disliked the policy of the Roman Church, which had apparently kept millions in mental serfdom, and elevated only a few (in those countries in which it was potent) to positions of power and authority. Now he began to wonder if the Church was not possessed of a subtle and ancient wisdom, and if it did not fully understand that the majority of men are still in the dark dawn of civilization, and that any attempt to thrust them into the full light of significant history threw a whole world out of perspective and made for grotesque chaos and fury and misery.

But, fascism was not the answer to the bewildered and brutish ignorance which seemed so integral a part of democracy. Nor was the passionate affirmation of foolish idealists that men needed only bookish "education" to make them walk on their hind legs, valid and adequate, or even intelligent. What, then, was the answer? How could a way be found so that superior men, of integrity, compassion, purity of mind and heart, subtlety and ability, would be elected to fill the powerful halls of Congress and the seats of authority? The greatest obstacle was that such men lacked that theatrical dash, that roaring basso, that agile buffoonery, that cheap and colorful noisiness, so beloved of the masses.

At these thoughts, Peter's pen would grow so heavy in his thin fingers that it would drop impotently to his desk, and he would stare wretchedly into space for a long time. Impotence would paralyze all his muscles. There was really no solution, he thought. Many brilliant men had acknowledged this, with sadness. His warning of danger would be heeded only by those who already knew the danger. And they, too, were impotent.

He would tell Celeste of his thoughts. She would listen gravely, mutely. Then one day she said to him: "You can only do what you can. And if every intelligent man did what he could, it would be of value, whether he was a clerk in some obscure office or a philosopher in a great university, or a single politician, or a lone industrialist. It's your job, Peter, to make them see this value, and how, in the aggregate, they might have considerable potency. Even minorities can have some measure of strength."

Peter's egotism as an author, the desire for power which lurks even in the most selfless men, his despair and feeling of inadequacy, were not comforted at this observation. But it was all he could do. Perhaps the imponderabilities of chance might operate sufficiently to place a few scattered men in positions of authority and power. It was his only hope. He recalled that a few Senators and Congressmen, a few politicians, were already as aware as he of the blackening danger, and though they were attacked as "war-mongers, internationalists and interventionists," by the suborned press and by crafty enemies of the people, they would not be silenced. He must show them the way, must encourage and hearten them.

He continued to write.

In his preoccupation, he was only vaguely and irritably aware that Celeste was becoming excessively pale and silent and abstracted. He was one of a gregarious nature, but he suddenly became conscious that he and his wife rarely accepted any invitations, never took small vacations, or had any other diversions. He remembered, too, that while he and Celeste had lived with Annette and Henri, Celeste was almost always absent and attending some festivity. Now, she lived immured with him in that horrible Endur.

So it was that one hot August morning, Peter felt that life had become, all at once, acutely unbearable. He had listened for hours to the excited and ominous stream of voices pouring over the radio, crackling with rumors, with accounts of the gathering of German divisions near the Polish border, with the pompous statements of American "authorities," and the fearful whimperings of cowards. A flat and crushing sense of despondency, of dry weariness, of aversion and disgust, overwhelmed and stupefied him, rendering him unable to think, and awakening in him a passionately hungry desire for some refreshment, some little gaiety and release. All the vague pains and prostrations of his illness came back to him, and though he did not recognize it as such, the last hopeless surging of the will-to-live tormented him.

He dressed with trembling fingers, conscious of his nameless urgency, his sick desire for escape. When Celeste, as usual, came with his breakfast tray, she was surprised to find him dressed, and standing near the window, looking out with restless gloom at the blazing expanse of grass. The tall poplars of Endur were bending like giant plumes in the hot summer wind, ruffling and whitening and tossing. He closed his eyes for a moment and turned to his wife.

"No," he said, irritably. "I'm not such a damned invalid." He added, more gently: "I'll go down with you, darling. I can't write today. In fact, I might say: I can't write." He tried to smile.

Celeste said nothing. She laid the tray on the bedside table, then straightened and scrutinized Peter. He was so thin now, so haggard, that all his flesh appeared translucent and fragile. She suppressed the pang that struck at her heart, and returned his smile.

"How nice," she said. "You've worked too hard, dear. Frankly, I'm tired of eating alone. Shall we go down now?"

His irritation continued to grow during the meal, which sickened on his tongue. He thrust back his coffee cup, and said with that vague heat and painfulness that distinguish the nervous:

"Look here, Celeste, what have you been doing? We never go anywhere. No one comes to see us. Are we pariahs? I know we've never been the darlings of the family, but good God! we can still pay our way. We're not beggars, my pet. We're not poor relations. I've never loved the family, I know. But why this thick silence?"

Celeste slowly replaced her coffee cup. An anxious and secretive look came over her face. She glanced about the breakfast room, so stark, so blazing with glass and chromium, so emptily sterile, and shivered a little. She said, not looking at Peter: "I didn't know. I thought you wanted to be quiet, while you worked."

"I didn't want to be shut up like some damned monastic eunuch!" cried Peter, with unusual irascibility. She saw how gaunt was his hand as it lay on the table, so that every bone and vein could be discerned. "There, I'm sorry, darling. I suppose it's my fault, too. So, I must be quiet, eh? The stern and serious author shut away from the world while he writes his momentous claptrap, which is bound to change the face of something or other. What does it matter whether I write or not? Who cares? Maudlin egotism to believe anything matters, in such a frightful time, except wickedness and ruthlessness and greed. Here I sit, like some infernal Lady of Shalott, spinning my idiot webs—" He paused abruptly, for Celeste had started, and was staring at him with the strangest expression in her eyes.

"What's the matter, Celeste?" he asked.

"Nothing," she replied, after a moment. "I just remembered that you told me that Mr. Hawkins had a high opinion of what you've written. He didn't seem to think it claptrap, did he?"

"O hell, I'm not interested in what anyone thinks!" he exclaimed, with increasing exasperation. "Wait until he sees the last batch of manuscript. He'll hold his nose and send it out to the incinerator. Of all the cursed egotism, to believe——"

Celeste was silent. She had dropped her eyes. She sat utterly still. He felt annoyance with himself for hurting her, and perversely his irritation strengthened.

"Yes, it's my fault. I gave you the wrong idea. You're still young, darling, and here you've sat, day after day, like a disciple at the feet of some miserable little messiah. And, of course, you've never considered that I might want some change. How many weeks have we been shut up in this metallic prison? Without seeing a single soul?"

Celeste regarded him quietly. "What would you like to do, Peter? Shall we have a dinner? And whom would you like to invite? To tell the truth, I'm very pleased to have you come to life like this. It's a sign your health is returning."

"I don't care, dear. Two or three of the family. My brother, Francis, perhaps, and his horsey Estelle. Not my brother, Jean, though. That poisonous mushroom. Have Christopher and Edith gone back to Florida? He's your darling brother, so I suppose you'd like to have him. He's in New York, now? Well, that's a relief. You might invite Annette and Henri, though I could well endure it if he couldn't come. But I'm fond of Annette. I thought you two were such friends? Is she off us, too?"

"Annette has called up almost every day, but I thought——"

"Yes, I know. The great changer-of-the-face-of-the-world

mustn't be disturbed in his history-making labors. So, Henri and Annette ought to be invited. Look here, haven't you any friends outside of the family?"

"A few." Celeste began to count on her fingers. "I think it would be nice to have a small dinner. It is more congenial, I think. I don't care for formal dinner parties." Her gestures and voice were lifeless, and too quiet. "How about a week from Saturday night?"

"Nearly two weeks! And in the meantime, of course, we'll continue to stagnate. I can't write, I tell you. I'm dead inside. I don't want your consolations and your inspiration, Celeste. Not today, thank you." His look and manner were frenetic, and she saw, with alarm, that he was frantically afraid of something. "Can't you make the dinner sooner?"

"I'll try." Her anxiety increased namelessly. She wondered whether she ought to call Peter's physician. If she did, he must not know, in his present state.

"I suppose it would be highly improper if you called someone and suggested that we would appreciate a dinner invitation within the next night or two, or perhaps for tonight?"

She had never heard him direct such crude sarcasm to her before, and her fear quickened. "For one thing, you know, Peter, I'm supposed to be in mourning. And Armand and Christopher, too, and other members of the family. Never mind, we can have quiet dinners. Would you like to go out for a drive this morning?"

He agreed, with sullen eagerness. Celeste sighed. A car was brought and she and Peter were driven about the hot brown countryside. The wind was a breath from the infernal regions. They passed wilted fields, corn standing brilliantly in the glaring sunlight, meadows where cattle drowsed. Though Peter was quite still, staring through windows rapidly becoming coated with dust, she felt his aching excitement and wretched exhaustion. But, later, that afternoon, he could not rest in his shaded room.

He was about to rise from his hot tossed bed, when Celeste softly entered. The shades of the room were drawn, arrows and slivers of golden fire darted through the slats of the Venetian blinds. Yet, even in that hot gloom he could feel a tense strangeness about her, a rigidity.

"Are you awake, dear?" she asked. "Annette and Henri have dropped in, to invite us personally for dinner tomorrow night. Shall I tell them you are too tired to see them just now?"

"No!" he cried, with alarming violence. "For God's sake, Celeste! I'll be dressed and down in a minute or two." He got up, and forgot the peculiarity of Celeste's appearance and manner. She left the room in silence.

But he found himself unusually weak when he descended the empty stairway to the rooms below. He was forced to pause halfway down. The great white and gray and silver hall below was like a hot vacuum to his swimming eyes, and the unshaded sunlight that filled it stung his vision. His wet hand slipped on the chromium balustrade, and he felt himself reeling. It took all his will power to retain his consciousness. He felt an acute nausea at the very sight of the bleak glassy splendor about him.

When he entered the large living-room, the nausea was strong upon him, and he hated every inanimate object that met his eyes. Here, too, all was white and gray and pastel hues and chromium and polished silver, from the pale rug to the blinding pallor of the walls, from the round glass tables to the faint blue divans and dim coral chairs and frameless motionless mirrors. How could he and Celeste ever have endured these weeks within this appalling house? Not even a flower stood in the twisted glass and silver monstrosities that perched on the tables. He looked away from it all to Annette and Henri, waiting for him. He hardly saw Celeste at a distance, sitting on a small blue chair, her hands in her lap. For a few minutes he had heard no voices. But when he entered, Henri rose, smiling, as harsh and calm and unshakable as ever.

"Hello," he said. "We thought we'd come unannounced, so you couldn't hide from us. How are you? You look much better."

His voice was genial and friendly, his pale eye thoughtful and penetrating. He shook hands with Peter, who, relieved of the horror of the house by a human presence, was returning his smile with astonishing pleasure.

He found it delightful to see even Henri, in spite of what he knew, in spite of the years of violent hatred and enmity between them. He was like a man who has lived for a long time on a desert where the silence has been unbroken except for the cry of a predatory bird and the rush of wind, and then, at last, hears a human voice, and is overcome with joy, even though that voice was once revolting to him. He turned to Annette, and took her soft little hand. They regarded each other with intense fondness, their similar large light-blue eyes shining and moved. Such a dear gentle little creature, he

249

thought, so ingenuous and kind and understanding. Her thin blue dress made her small triangular face almost vivid, and reflected itself in her eyes. The bright fine tendrils of hair curled up about a round white hat like a skull-cap. Her air was at once defenseless yet strong, sweet yet firm, intelligent yet innocent. She pressed his hand, answered gently his inquiries about her health, and asked about his own.

"Oh, I am doing splendidly," he replied, with unusual buoyancy, almost feverish in its animation. "Celeste can tell you that my cough has practically gone. Work seems to agree with me."

Henri smiled to himself. Out of the corner of his eye he glanced at Celeste. But she sat in some petrified and abstracted dream, staring before her, her lips very pale and carved in her drawn face. She seemed to hear nothing.

"We're so interested in your new lovely house on Placid Heights," said Annette, smiling at Peter radiantly as he sat down near her. "Have you been out there lately, to see how the work is coming on?"

No, Peter said, with some reserve. He had been so busy, and hadn't felt like it. He understood that Celeste had gone frequently, however. At this, Celeste stirred, lifted her head sluggishly, and turned her face towards him as if she had only half heard. She said: "I was out there a week ago. We expect it to be ready by Christmas."

Annette was all shining enthusiasm. She glanced archly at her husband, and exclaimed: "You'll think us prying, or curious, of course, but Henri and I have often gone out, and Henri was quite stern with the workmen and the architect. There was something about copper gutters."

"You have to watch these people," remarked Henri, with bored ease. "It's a good design, Peter. Simple, effective, and not too large. We're looking forward to the house-warming."

"The view is delicious," remarked Annette, moving to the edge of her chair animatedly. "The hills all about, and then the valley and the rolling countryside. It will be marvellous in the autumn. I envy you. Not that I don't love Robin's Nest, of course," and she gave Henri a look of touching adoration. "But new houses always excite me."

Celeste rang for tea, then subsided into her profound dull silence. She literally seemed unable to move without a terrible effort. A lock of her bright black hair fell over her petrified white forehead, and another ringlet lay against her colorless cheek. Her shoulders were bent, her whole body had the appearance of heavy collapse.

Henri and Peter talked pleasantly, but Henri was aware most acutely of Celeste. He saw her flaccid white hands in her lap, the fallen curve of her thigh and calf, the sunken line of her breasts. She seemed ill. He smiled to himself again. She sat so near him that he could have touched her, and he knew that she was aware of him as he was of her, and that she dared not look at him directly.

Annette turned to her young aunt, and exclaimed: "Darling, you look so tired! You know, I'm really provoked with you, refusing my persistent invitations. And so, we've come to insist upon you and Peter having dinner with us tomorrow night. Or tonight would be better."

Peter looked from his wife to Annette, and smiled unpleasantly. "Celeste thinks I'm a monk, I'm afraid. I only found out today that the reason we have been so apparently ostracized is because she has barred the doors and pulled in the shutters. But, I suppose it's my fault, too. I must have given her the impression that I was a Trappist at heart."

"I see," said Annette, softly. She gazed at Celeste's motionless profile with the strangest expression, compassionate, sad, and very mournful, though she smiled brightly a moment afterwards, and sighed. "You don't know how happy this makes me to know that you two are coming out of your retirement. I was going to be very disagreeable today, if you had refused our invitation. Tonight, dear? Or tomorrow?"

Celeste said listlessly: "Tomorrow, if Peter prefers it."

"Yes, tomorrow," he answered, quickly. That horrible weakness was assailing him again, however sternly he fought it. He could not have brought himself to leave the house tonight. He drew a deep breath. "It will be good to get out of this place! Not that we aren't grateful to Christopher and Edith, of course. But it's an appalling house, isn't it?"

For the first time, Celeste appeared fully aware of the conversation. There was even a dim flush on her cheeks now, and her eye flashed with sudden blue fire as she regarded her husband.

"I don't think that is very kind, Peter," she said, and now her voice thrilled with its old resolution. "I never liked Endur, but it was once my home, and Christopher was very thoughtful." She thought: He is not himself. He doesn't know what he is saying. He is frightened and distraught.

"Of course, darling," Peter replied, with feverish contrition. "I'm sorry. But I can't help it if it depresses me. It reminds me too much of your brother."

The tea was brought in now, and Celeste, without the slightest quiver of her hands, filled the delicate cups with topaz fluid. Her thin black dress made her white throat and arms gleam like polished marble. She gave a cup to Annette, and one to Henri, who accepted it with a casual smile and an inclination of his head. She did not look at him. She said: "Peter, oughtn't you to have your eggnog instead of tea?"

"O God!" groaned Peter, giving her an impatient look. "Wouldn't you prefer it if I asked for a bottle and rubber nipple, Celeste?"

She studied him a moment or two, and her fearful alarm made her heart beat fast. She momentarily forgot Annette and Henri. Henri was laughing with a sound that was not pleasant, and Annette appeared embarrassed. But Celeste was seeing only the hectic pallor of Peter's face, his too brilliant eyes, his dry hot lips. All at once he began to cough violently, and Celeste winced visibly. After a moment or two, she filled a cup for him and gave it to him, as if nothing had happened and she had not heard his remark. Her air of haggard dignity and calm pride hurt Annette's gentle heart, and her eyes filled involuntarily with tears. She remarked brightly, to Peter: "How is the book coming along?"

The old hauteur and uneasiness of Peter's appeared again at any mention of his work. He hesitated, shot a furtive glance at Henri, then replied with restraint: "Not too well, I'm afraid, Annette. I'm getting dry and dull and uninspired. Perhaps I've been too close to it."

"Or rather," said Henri, blandly, "perhaps you don't know enough about your subject matter."

"Henri doesn't mean to be rude," murmured Annette, in distress.

But Peter ignored her. He regarded Henri with his old cold aversion and dislike. "No, the trouble is that I know too much, have too much material. I can't seem to organize it. I'd like to put everything in. It's so enormous, so grim and portentous. I would really have to write a documented library to do it justice. When I see how impossible it is to do more than suggest, condense, telescope together, I feel pretty desperate. It reads like a nightmare, and the innocent and uninitiated would hardly believe it." Now his look at Henri was harsh and somber, and full of contempt.

But Henry smiled. "Oh, come now, we aren't as bad as all that. In fact, if you wrote the history of any industry or enterprise in America, whether it was dry goods or butchering or steel-making or brewing, it could be so presented, so highlighted, so exaggerated and colored, that it would sound like the tale of Ali Baba and the Forty Thieves. For, you see, the human element is there, inescapably, and whatever the human element touches is likely to have a bad odor or some skulduggery. The end result, however, is usually quite harmless, and in the meantime quite a number of people innocently and happily prosper."

"I presume," said Peter, in a shaking voice, all his feverish color gone so that his face was once again translucent and full of gray shadows, "that the 'number of people' who have profited from your companies and subsidiaries have been only the Bouchards? What of the rest of the world? What of the world which is coming? Can you truthfully say it, too, will 'innocently and happily prosper' in the kind of civilization you are creating for it now?"

Henri laughed lightly. His pale eye shone on Peter indulgently. "Frankly, I don't know. I have my business to attend to, and that takes too much time for me to have any odd minutes for philosophizing.

"But, I can say this to you now: You cannot honestly declare to a people, 'Look, here is your oppressor, you are the victim.' The victim, by the way, creates the oppressor. Nothing is apart from the rest of the world. The world as we know it now, and have known it in the past, is the visible result of total human nature, its work and its will. For instance, the German people invented Hitler. He was their desire made flesh, to paraphrase the Bible. So, if certain 'bad' men have gained control of America, which I deny, it is because Americans have been too slothful, too greedy, too stupid and mindless, to prevent it, and so they have tacitly allowed it. They do not exist apart from their 'exploiters,' nor do their 'exploiters' exist apart from them."

Peter forgot everything now but his burning passion, his loathing and hatred and rage against this man. "You make it sound very simple," he said, his voice now trembling so much that he could hardly control it. "But it isn't simple. Granted that the stupidity and sloth of the people make tyrants possible. That does not make the tyranny virtuous, or inevitable. Criminals take advantage of the trust of the helpless, or of the defenseless. That is your crime."

Henri was silent. But he still smiled. He looked at Annette, who had turned quite pale in her distress, and was twining her fingers together. He looked at Celeste. But she was staring at Peter, with a white still face, and was listening intently.

Henri frowned thoughtfully, and tapped his fingers soundlessly on the arm of his chair.

"Yes," said Peter, in a quieter tone now, "I agree with you about one thing: that nothing exists apart from anything else, and that one must remember the human element. But there is an element, perhaps, that you don't know anything about, Henri, and that element is the deeply buried desire of every man to believe that he and his work are important. The desire may be conscious or subconscious, but it is there, demanding that he believe that he, and his efforts, are necessary to his fellowmen and their welfare. You may think that very silly. I think it is the only noble thing in man. When that belief is killed in a man, and modern industry is fast killing it, by its monotony, its automatism and deadly mechanical pattern, then a man loses his will to live, which is always very precarious even in the strongest of us.

"The men of power have either not known of the piteous human desire to be of significance to the world, and to improve it by work and voluntary effort, or they have not cared about it. It is nothing to them that this desire has the profoundest promise of good for the world, a promise of universal harmony and greatness and kindness, and that it has the power to cure much of the sickness and ruin of mankind."

He paused, and said in a lower tone: "Perhaps you are right in another thing. A long time ago you told me that war is one of the strongest instincts in man. I am beginning to believe it is. For war is the expression of the will-to-die of whole masses of people. The problem is to make life so adventurous, so vital, meaningful and important to every man that he will not, in his desire for death, resort to mass-suicide."

"And how do you propose to do that?" asked Henri, with the same bland and infuriating look, as if he were talking to some raving fool.

Peter hesitated, and now his look was stern and steadfast. "Perhaps, as I said before, by letting men believe, again, that they are important to the world. Religion has a strong hold on man only in direct ratio to the amount of importance it confers on him. You wish me to be practical, I see. Can you show me how modern industry allows a man, for a single moment, to believe he is of importance and that he, and he alone, gives some peculiar touch to his work that no other could? Our machines have removed the personal joy from handicraft, from individual workmanship, from creation. What joy is there in making castings or strips of metal identically the same, at an identical machine, by an identical human robot? When modern industry removed the personal element from its giant shops and plants and factories, it began to destroy man's will-to-live, which is based on his individual sense of importance. And so, it laid the groundwork for devastating wars. I believe that is why fascism inevitably leads to war. It is the last convulsion of a despairing people."

He added: "War, in the end, is delightful to people, because war is now the only thing which allows a man to believe he is individually important, and that something depends on him, personally."

His thin and exhausted face was suddenly illuminated by passion, by pity and sorrow. "It is a terrible thing," he said, in a still lower tone, as if to himself.

Now, he looked only at Celeste. She was smiling at him, and her eyes were dilated and shining. Henri stared at each of them, slowly, in turn.

"You are putting all that in your book, too?" he asked.

Peter became aware of him, after that long exchange with his wife, and he frowned a little. "There is so much," he said. "Yes, I am trying to tell it. The whole thing is so—enormous."

He was listless again, exhausted, the brief and burning fire gone from him. He was desperately ill once more.

Annette spoke now, and her voice was trembling, her hands twisting in her lap: "O Peter! I wish there were something I could say now, that would let you know how you've stirred me. I never have the proper words for anything. But I know you are right." Her lashes were wet, her lips tremulous.

"It ought to be interesting at any rate," said Henri, with that superior and pleasant condescension which is so enraging to any author, and which puts him nicely in his place. "You can count on me for a copy. Ingham's are to publish it?"

"Yes," said Peter, curtly. He drank his tea with abstraction; it was cold and nauseating to him. His despair was a bleakness and windlessness in him. How impotent he was! How clearly Henri had shown him his impotence, in the face of his own great power and physical strength and compactness.

During his abstraction, he was unaware that Henri was scrutinizing him intently. It would have amazed him to know how important he now was in Henri's thoughts, and that the other man was engaged in rapid reflection.

"Look here," said Henri, with abruptness. "You say you have too much material. Are you aware, for instance, with your damned documented proof, that a certain group of men in Washington, and other places, are determined to overthrow the Government and install fascism in its place? With the actual help of Hitler?"

Peter looked up with such a start he almost dropped his cup. He could not believe what he had heard. Henri was nodding, with a grim smile.

"I assure you it's true. And I'm not one of them, I promise you. That surprises you, doesn't it? I imagine you've had your suspicions. How would you like verification?"

Peter was astounded. His glazed eyes looked instinctively at Celeste. But she was gazing at Henri with a rigid expression of shock, and fully for the first time.

"I imagine," said Henri, regarding on'y Peter, "that you have given some vague intimations in your manuscript. But vague intimations can always be attacked and disproved. Facts can't."

But Peter was without the power to speak.

Henri leaned back in his chair comfortably, and raised his eyebrows with a quizzical expression. But his eyes were fixed with unusual intentness upon Peter.

"I mean, it is an actual plot, which has only recently come to my attention. I'll be frank with you. I've wanted America to keep out of the coming war because war will destroy the status quo, and I'm rather attached to the status quo. I don't give a damn what Hitler does in Europe. But I want to keep him out of America. Unfortunately, there are some men, and it would surprise you who they are, who want Hitler here, or at least, want his influence here. They're working for it. A gentleman very close to some of us said only recently: 'We need Hitler, and his efficiency. Put the damned mob back in its place. I say: Bring him over!' You may think that very brash and crude. But it isn't. They've drawn up the actual plans."

Peter pulled himself out of his paralyzed lethargy of amazement, and stammered:

"Why do you tell me this? Now? You?"

Henri shrugged. "Because," he answered, blandly, "I don't want Hitler here. I'm very well satisfied with things as they are. I'm not too interested in what Hitler does in Europe, but I'm determined he shan't do it with any of our matériel— if I can help it. I'm not sure I *can* help it. I'm working towards that, of course. I have coerced," and he smiled a little, "or better, persuaded, some others to join me, for I am sure that I have no desire to be any Thyssen to Hitler. It's not patriotism. I'm only giving you an outline." He paused, wondering if he was being indiscreet, stupid and naive. "I may succeed. As it looks now, I might not. You can imagine the rest."

Peter suddenly got to his feet, and in a deep silence, he walked up and down the room with shaken steps. He kept putting his hands to his face, and then dropping them with a quick gasp. The two women were frozen in their chairs, Celeste watching Peter, Annette watching Henri. Annette's cheeks were bright red, her eyes too bright.

Then Peter stopped before Henri. His lips moved with an effort. "Somehow, I believe you. I don't know why. I understand, though, why you've told me. It's not—not patriotism, or decency. You want to protect yourself. That doesn't matter. What can I do?"

Henri was very grave and serious now. He leaned towards Peter. "Your book will be finished too late, I'm afraid. Suppose it is published a year or more from now? It won't do much good. The damage will aready have been done, probably irreparable damage.

"However, I have just had an idea. Suppose you write for the radio. You can't, of course, deliver any such addresses, yourself, for reasons which are very obvious. But, I can have such addresses, warning the people, delivered by two or three competent commentators. I have such commentators in mind. Two have recently been removed from the air for lack of 'sponsors.' I happen to know why they haven't any sponsors now. I think you can guess that, too. They don't need sponsors. I will pay for the broadcasts. None of the chains will dare to keep these men off the air when I give the word. They'll have plenty of facts, too, which I will give you. Remember, there's an election coming up next year," and the grimness of his face relaxed for a moment. "Frankly, I don't care if Roosevelt or any other man equally of his opinion is elected. I am thinking of a man who was mentioned to me lately, by a certain old gentleman. He may not be nominated. If he isn't, and the Republican Party puts up some dolt, some ventriloquist dummy, then, we must have Roosevelt. That surprises you, doesn't it? But I tell you now that not even the greatest of the New Deal's asininities are important any longer. The only important thing is the preventing of those schemes of which I've just told you. Everything else can wait."

He continued, when Peter again could not speak: "Go on with your book. But these addresses on the radio are more necessary, more immediate. What do you say?"

Peter's eyes were blazing in his gaunt and sunken face. He was alive again, burning and passionate. He almost cried aloud, exultantly. After a little, he said: "My God! I can't believe it. Of course, I'll do it! You have only to give me the facts, a lead now and then!"

He could hardly breathe with his newly awakened sense of potency. All his senses were awake, crying out. But Henri was quite calm, his smile smooth as ever.

He rose. "Good. You'll be discreet enough, of course, not to give the slightest hint where you get your information. That would be disastrous. I must work behind the scenes. I must find out all the plotters, and do what I can, myself, to stop them in their tracks. In the meantime, you might arouse quite a portion of the people to their peril. Study the commentators who are subsidized by the American Association of Industrialists, one of our own organizations. Wright Benson is the ablest. You can get many leads from his propaganda, which is very adequate, to say the least. You'll see the fine Italian hand behind what he says. Study the newspapers, especially that powerful rag in Detroit. You'll have your work cut out for you, and it isn't going to be easy."

Peter pressed his hands to his throbbing temples. Celeste stood beside him now, seeing only him. He turned to her and read the wordless anxiety in her eyes. "My God, darling!" he cried. "Nothing matters but this. Can't you see?" He put his arm about her, and she dropped her head to his shoulder.

"I'll send you some material by special messenger tomorrow," said Henri, holding out his hand to Peter. Peter stared at the hand, then took it. "And another thing," said Henri, smiling as if with deep amusement, "don't be scholarly in your attack. Use words of one syllable, if possible. Remember, the majority of the people are pretty ignorant. They have a natural suspicion for what they call 'college professors.' Keep it simple, telling, violent, and spectacular. Nothing measured and restrained. They'll only turn you off, otherwise. Listen to Bishop Halliday, that pious swine. Copy his style, and improve on it. He's a good rabble-rouser. Be a rabble-rouser."

Peter smiled convulsively. Henri saw that his mind had already flown off into an excited and turbulent realm, and that he was already formulating what he would write. He did say, however: "It'll be fantastic, working with you, Henri. I still can't believe it."

"Believe it," replied the other. "I'll give you some very interesting facts tomorrow night, after dinner."

Annette was silent. But her little hands clutched Henri's

solid arm, and she was smiling radiantly, seeing nothing but his face.

And so it was that no one saw that Celeste, too, was looking at Henri, her lips fallen open, her eyes dark and strange.

CHAPTER XXVII

Peter had purchased ten acres of land on Placid Heights for his new home.

The land embraced a whole low hill, and behind it rose the mauve folds of taller foothills so that it seemed enclosed in the ring of an immense and circling fortress. The house, now in the process of being built, stood on the tip of its hill. The grounds were to be adequately landscaped, but at this time, in late August, the hill was brown and scorched, with here and there a bent and sinewy tree and spindling second-growth timber. Therefore, the house had an exposed and vulnerable look in the brawling sunlight, its strong gray walls somewhat grim, its red roof too bright and raw.

But the hill sloped gently down to a narrow cleft between the hills, a valley filled with radiant and translucent mist, so that the trees scattered through it stood motionless in a silver light. No other house was visible. There was only the pale brilliance of the sky, the purple folds of the hills, the dream-like valley, as far as eye could see. There was no wind, no sound of a bird in that vast and widespread quiet, under the universal cataract of the sunlight. Only the sawing of wood, the clamor of workmen's hammers, an occasional rough voice, or the clump of a footstep on rough new flooring. The smell of fresh sawdust permeated the hot and sterile air.

A short way down the slope a small blue car was parked, and near it, on a smooth stone, sat Celeste, her red dress a splash of color against the yellowed hillside. She did not look up and back at the house. She stared before her down at the valley, her hands motionless beside her, a lock of her hair lifting and falling faintly as the slightest of breezes sometimes touched it. The stern quiet of her face had relaxed; her lips were softer, more blooming, more gentle, than they had been for some time. Once or twice she smiled, quickly, with a caught breath, then sighed, and for an instant or two the old rigidity would tighten her features, to pass away once more in a vivid flash of renewed sweetness.

She had come out to discuss the panelling for the library with the architect. He had gone. She was all alone. The diamond on her hand flashed in the sunlight like a round prism. She had sat like this for nearly an hour.

No one looking at her could have guessed the feverish excitement that filled her, the sudden gusts of black despondency that followed, which were followed in turn by a wild bright quickening that made her clench her hands together, and pierced the swelling of her heart with voiceless ecstasy and deep passionate sadness. Then, as if exhausted by her own emotions, she would become very limp and still, to begin the cycle of emotion again within a few minutes.

She had been dead so long.

Since last night, when Henri had proposed his plan to Peter, the latter had been so violently excited, so exultant that Celeste had been unable to restrain him. Any suggestion that he calm himself was met by an outburst, by his crying that she did not understand him, that she was trying to quell the first joy he had felt for months, even for years. So, she had finally said nothing. She saw that Peter, too, had been dully desperate, full of impotence and fear and hopelessness. Now he had been given an opportunity to reach millions, who must be awakened.

Celeste would think of the man who had made it possible for Peter to live again, to feel once more that terrible bright exultation of the potent. And she would feel a trembling in herself, and would catch her breath. So many years had passed since she had experienced this shaking emotion. She became aware, after so long, of the acute sharpness of the world's imminence, its passionate violence, its urgency and wonder and vivid color. She had been given again that clarity of perception, that exhilarating keenness, which she had once felt in existence, and which she had forgotten had ever been. Now, as she thought of Henri Bouchard, her awakened senses observed everything with such vividness that it was almost painful. The small rubble at her feet took on significant shapes and forms. The shadow of a twisted tree near her was full of meaning, and as its great leaves bent in the faintest of winds, she could hardly endure the poignancy of the sunlight upon them. She would lift dazed eyes to the sky, and it seemed to her that the drifting outlines of pale clouds were more than she could bear.

So absorbed was she that she did not hear the grunting struggle of a car as it climbed the roadless hill, nor the slam of its door. Nor did she at once see the strong broad figure that began a slow ascent towards her. When she discerned who it was that was approaching her, it seemed only the continuation of her dazed and radiant dream. She could only sit there on her stone, dimly smiling, her face towards the climbing man.

Then, all at once, she became aware of him, and it was like a shock through all her body, a wild awakening. She could not rise. She could only sit there, her hands gripping the sides of the stone, her face white and set. When he lifted his hand in a friendly salute, she did not answer. She was paralyzed; her heart appeared to stop.

Now he halted for a moment some fifty feet below her, and wiped his damp face with his handkerchief. "Hello!" he called.

Her lips and throat were dry. She was still unable to move. He climbed slowly and easily towards her, then halted again some ten feet distant. "Peter here?" he asked.

Her voice was a hoarse rustle, projected with infinite effort: "No."

Now she could stand up. He was smiling at her in the friendliest fashion. "He's not ill again, is he?"

Her lips formed the negative, but no sound came from them. "At the last minute, Annette decided it was too hot, and so I thought I would run out myself," he said.

Celeste was silent. They faced each other, and now he, too, did not speak. His large head was inclined gravely, his expression serious. She awaited what he would say next, with an agonizing acuteness of all her senses. But he only said at last: "Well. And how are things coming along here? You know, we often come out."

"Very well," she replied, again struggling to speak. Her limbs were heavy and throbbing.

He turned away from her, and smiled again. "I'd like to see for myself," he said, and climbed up and away from her towards the house. She watched him go, mutely. After a long time, she sat down again on the stone, quickening with a desire to run away, to get into her car and turn it down to the valley. The desire was like a blowing flame in her, but she had no will to respond to it.

She did not know how long he had been gone, but he was

suddenly beside her again. He was not looking at her; he was gazing down at the valley with a contented expression. "Very nice," he remarked. "And not too far from the city. You know, I saw the old Sessions house a few times, when I was a brat. You've heard of it, Celeste? If I recall it rightly, the plan of the interior was similar to this, and there was an exterior resemblance, too." He laughed a little. "It ought to have been preserved as a family monument. There's a story that it inspired old Ernest Barbour all his life. Then it was finally abandoned by the family, after my great-grandmother, May Sessions, died, in 1910. By then it had become surrounded by slums, but she still stayed there. Must have been a fascinating old devil, my great-grandfather, eh? The house was slowly falling into flakes, but she stayed there, thinking of him. When she died, though, the family pulled it down so it wouldn't degenerate into a rooming house, or worse."

He laughed again. His strong broad teeth flashed in the sunlight, as she gazed up at him, dumbly. "You know, I'd have liked the final irony—the old Sessions house becoming a bordello. There's an epigram in that. The thing that at first inspires a man finally becomes his degradation. I'm clever, aren't I?"

Now she could smile, painfully. She stood up, brushed off her dress. "I must go," she murmured.

He lifted his hand easily and closed it softly, but firmly, about her arm. She started, and then hardly controlled a humiliating impulse to tear her arm from his grasp. So she stood, becoming very still and cold. But a sudden sharp heat spread from the fingers that grasped her, spread all down her arm and then into her body. Now her eyes widened, fixed themselves upon him, blazing with vivid blue light, proud, bitter and incandescent.

"Hello, Celeste," he whispered.

Any movement on her part, she thought, despairingly, would make her ridiculous, increase her wild humiliation. So she did not stir. But her heart was rising on a swift arch of exquisite pain and tumult. And he watched her closely, smiling, that pale and polished gleam of his eye narrowing between its lids.

"Let's walk down there a little way," he said. He dropped his hand to her own hand, and held it strongly. He drew her after him, and she followed, stumbling, seeing only the floating ground at her feet, too engrossed with her shame to resist.

They moved along the slope at an angle, so that a rising

262

hump of ground hid them from the sight of any curious workman at the house above. There was a short squat tree here, with thick shade. They stood under it. Here, Henri dropped Celeste's hand, and they faced each other in silence, a silence almost violent in its unspoken power.

Then Henri spoke very gently, and slowly: "Its time we had a talk, don't you think? And made up our minds what we are going to do."

Celeste smiled bitterly, and flung up her head. "Are you actually considering divorcing Annette?" she asked, with harsh mockery, her look very direct and bright.

She expected him to hesitate. But he slowly and gravely shook his head. "No. Not yet." His voice was reflective and firm. "For a reason I can't tell you about just now. It came up very recently. It makes it impossible for me to divorce her—at present. The opportunity will come later. Not very late, I hope.

"And now, you. Are you going to wait until Peter dies before we begin to live?"

The audacity of him, inexorable as it was, and now grim, stunned her. She could only stare at him, dumbfounded for a long time. Then incoherent and furious words rushed to her lips in such a flood that she stammered over them, as one stumbles, falters, runs and staggers in flight: "Oh, you are contemptible! How can you—! You are a ghoul! There's nothing I can say to you but this—leave me alone. Stay away from me. Haven't you hurt me—and Peter—enough? Do you think it's easy for me to look at him? Now? I've got to make it up to him—How can I bear looking at him, every day, every night? You could never understand that. There never was a decent impulse in you, no honor, no fidelity, no kindness. You would kill poor little Annette, easily, if it would help you in any way. Sometimes I think you are killing her; she has such an awful look in her eyes lately. What am I going to do? Nothing! Never! Never, never."

She turned away from him, and took a few rushing steps. But he caught her at once, and pulled her back. He shook her with hard violence.

"Celeste. You fool. Stop struggling; you are ridiculous. Look at me, Celeste."

She was weeping loudly now. But at the vicious contempt in his voice, the implacable command, she stopped, sobbing under her breath, regarding him with mute and intense hatred through her wet eyes. He dropped his hands from her shoulders.

"There, now, that's better. You act like a child, a stupid and unreasonable and romantic child. We aren't children, you little imbecile. We aren't even very young now. This is a matter to be faced, understand, and decided upon. Yes, you are hating me now, aren't you? You've made a fine mess of our lives, yet you have the impudence to glare at me as if I were the one to blame, and not you. A fine defense mechanism, but a cowardly one, like all defense mechanisms. Or is all this beyond your intelligence?"

A flood of scarlet ran over her face. She was very quiet now. She said, looking at him fixedly: "Yes, perhaps I'm a coward. I always thought I was. But that doesn't matter now. I'm Peter's wife. It may surprise you to know that I don't want Peter to die! You see, I love him."

"And so," he interrupted her, ironically, "you prefer to discuss this matter after Peter is dead? You have that in mind? You can't see the nastiness of that? Bah, you make me sick, Celeste. Why can't you be honest? The fact that you have decided to think about matters after you are a widow doesn't enhance your fine honor, your smug virtue and righteousness. It doesn't undo any 'wrong' you've already done to Peter. It doesn't exonerate you because you won't face things until your husband is dead. The thought is already there."

She was silent a moment, still staring at him. Then she drew a deep breath, and said softly: "All right, then. I'll decide now. Whether Peter lives, or dies, there'll never be anything between us, Henri. Never. Not even if you divorce Annette. Not even if Annette should die, and you do want her to die very badly, don't you?"

He began to smile. "Annette die? Yes, I wouldn't mind that. I've no real dislike for the little thing. In fact, I'm fond of her. But it would simplify many things if she died soon. Soon, but not just now."

"I'm sure I hate you now," said Celeste, with a kind of wonder. "Yes, I'm sure of it."

His smile became a laugh. "That's better. I like you to hate me. And you haven't really decided, have you? You are a wordy little wretch. Didn't Christopher feed you milk toast and romanticism all your life? I think I remember that. You are an untidy little romanticist. Your hair is all disorder. I'm speaking figuratively, of course. You see, I have to be very careful in choosing words that aren't beyond your limited intelligence. You've thought yourself quite a high and noble intellectual all these years gypsying around Europe with Peter, haven't you? You've sat and listened to the masters at every international tea-table. So now, you have a Mind and a Soul. Yes, my love, you make me sick."

He added: "I never liked sickly romanticism. I asked you, believing you might have acquired just a little sense, to discuss with me what we are going to do now. And you come out with Jane Eyre."

He moved a foot or two from her, and inclined his head towards his car below on the slope. But his harsh and cruel eyes did not leave her face.

"I've never pursued women. Frankly, I don't like women. I don't like you; I never did. But I've loved you. I'm not too sure, just at this minute, whether I love you any longer. Fools make me puke. You are quite a fool, you know. But, I've loved you. I might even love you again.

"But just now, I'm not sure. I'm not even sure I want you. I'm almost sure I don't."

He paused. Her face was as white as bone, in the shadow. She could not look away from him. She said nothing. But her heart went down into the blackest depths of despair and desolation, of an anguish so acute and immense that it seemed her heart must stop. He watched her narrowly.

He lifted his hand slowly, and pointed at her, and his finger was like a dagger. "I'm going to start to walk, Celeste. And at any time before I reach my car, you may call me back. But once I get in it, and go away, that's the end. Think about it for a moment, honestly, like a decent human being. When I go away, that's all there is. There'll never be anything more. 'Never, never,' " he added, with quiet disgust.

He waited a little while. But she stood there unmoving. He smiled grimly. With infinite slowness and resolution, he turned away from her, began to walk in the direction of his car. She watched him go.

He had reached a little mound of rocks. She thought: He is really going. He won't look back. He'll never come back.

Now all her pulses were like separate hearts in her throat, her temples, her hands, her knees. She could feel their sickening bounding and leaping, tearing at their confines, forcing a taste of salt into her mouth. He was within sixty feet of his car now. He walked very steadily, never faltering for a moment, never hurrying, never pretending to delay. She saw his broad gray back in the sunlight, the back of his large and brutal head. He seemed as unaware of her as if she did not exist.

Now a huge pain took hold of her with iron teeth, so that she literally felt their tearing in her flesh, their clenching in her vitals. No! she cried in herself. O no! O Henri, no!

The strong figure moving so inexorably in the sunlight had shut out everything else in her consciousness. It was a nightmare, a dream that dragged each horrible moment to its ultimate conclusion, never hurrying, never pausing.

Now the iron teeth had fallen on her last living defense, and she felt a soaring of agony in her body and her spirit which was unendurable. It was this that made her cry out, a great loud cry that was less an act of her will than pure torment, which had become beyond her power to fight.

He heard that cry. Through a wavering and darkening mist he came back to her, not slowly now, but walking with quick and rushing feet. She did not know that she lifted her arms to him.

And now she was held close to him, passing her hands over his shoulders, his arms, weeping wildly and terribly, clutching him as the drowning might clutch. He did not comfort her, but held her more tightly. He felt the smothering beat of her heart, her suffering. When he tried to release her frantic hold upon him, to calm her, she became less controllable. He was alarmed, and looked about him uneasily. Someone might have heard that awful cry she had uttered in her extremity.

He released himself forcibly. He took her convulsed face in his hands, and by looking into her eyes he forced her to be calmer. She was weeping again, but with more quietness. She lifted her hands and clasped them about the wrists so near to her cheeks, and her fingers were like iron, biting into his flesh.

"Henri!" she cried, hoarsely. "You wouldn't have gone away? Not really?"

He held her again to him, tightly. "Yes, my love," he said, very softly. "I would have gone. Really." And then he added, more roughly: "Don't do that again to me, Celeste, not ever."

CHAPTER XXVIII

It was on that day in September, 1939, when a world ended and a strange, new and terrible one was born, that Antoine Alexis Barbour Bouchard was married to Mary Eloise Boland.

The wedding was very quiet. As was pointed out in a hundred adoring newspapers, young Mr. Bouchard had only recently lost his grandmother, the late Mrs. Jules Bouchard, and young Miss Boland had been bereaved of her mother some two months ago. The marriage took place (for "reasons of family tradition," sang the newspapers) in the beautiful little old chapel of the Episcopal St. Mary's-on-the-Hill in Windsor. The chapel, which was not very old, had a very ancient and Norman look, all heavy gray walls and ivy and strong squat towers, to match the parent building, aggressively Norman and stately. The stained glass windows were excellent, with just reason. They had been lifted bodily from a real Norman church in France, and transported, at enormous expense, to their new setting by old Ernest Barbour, who had built the edifice. Here, he, himself, had lain in that rainbowed and mysterious light cast by the windows, and here other Barbours and Bouchards had slept on their cold satin pillows before they were carried to their last narrow niches in the cemetery. Here infant Bouchards had been christened, had later made their confirmations, had been married, had shifted in their solemn pews, yawned, stretched, dozed and plotted, had indulged their peculiar thoughts and their sadnesses, had pondered their lusts and hatreds.

The Family was extremely delighted with Antoine's choice. No member ever married inappropriately. Antoine had carried on the tradition, in spite of past uneasiness about him. The Bouchard males had always had a penchant for great ladies. Miss Boland was a great lady. She was also, happily and appropriately, very stupid. Her figure was rather short and plump, like a dainty squab's, and she possessed very tiny and pretty little hands and feet, plump also, and white as

267

milk, dimpled of knuckle and beautifully tended. Like many young women of her figure, she had a round soft white breast, and swelling hips, and a short narrow waist. Her face, too, was round and soft and dimpled, and she smiled almost constantly with the sweetest of tempers, the dimples appearing delightfully in cheek and chin and about her lips whenever she smiled, which was practically always. She had a round pink mouth, a little round tilted nose, naturally rosy and blooming plump cheeks, and very large bright gray eyes surrounded by bronze lashes. From her low forehead rose the soft fine waves of her auburn air, to blend into a gleaming knot at the nape of her short white neck. She was very pretty; she was very charming; she had the sweetest of tinkling laughs. She never said a thing of any significance, but neither did she ever say a word that was not tactful, gracious or proper. She was twenty years old and she was also a virgin. She had never had a thought that was original or acute, pertinent or profound, unchaste or compassionate.

Best of all, she was a great heiress. And she adored Antoine. All in all, therefore, the family could do nothing else but approve his choice. She was a typical Bouchard woman, and so, perfect.

Miss Boland was the only child of her father, a ruthless old bandit who had had three previous wives before marrying Mary's mother. None of these wives had borne him children, and so he had discarded them. Mary's gender had at first infuriated him, but she had finally won him with her charm and sweetness and imbecility. She had not been more than a year old when he had begun to look about him for a suitable husband for her. When Antoine had appeared on the scene, he had been highly gratified. He was seventy years old now, and had begun to worry about his daughter.

To his father, Armand, Antoine had said: "She is really a delightful and satisfactory little creature. Her mother came of a family of prolific breeders, so you will probably be a grandfather half a dozen times over."

All in all, Antoine's choice was universally approved.

The wedding, though quiet, was perfect. Miss Boland looked like a rosy cherub in her filmy white veil, her embroidered satin gown with the train six feet long, her bridesmaids with their demure faces and their aquamarine gowns of buoyant tulle. Her cousin, the ambitious second vice-president of the Morse National Bank, was best man. She stood at the altar with Antoine, and through her veil her round and stupid and pretty face shone like a rosy moon.

Because of the sinister and ominous event which had exploded in the world, the honeymoon was short and quiet. The happy couple returned to live in the great gloomy castle of Armand's.

Within less than a week, Armand was passionately fond of his new daughter. As for herself, she "loved" all the Bouchards, considered them the most brilliant, the most soigné, the most endowed and superior creatures in the world. She was very grateful to them for taking her into their closed clan. This did nothing to abate their approval, though after five minutes they found her tedious.

She set herself to be indispensable to Armand, for she was really quite kind, provided she was not puzzled or compelled to think a situation through. She saw that Armand was sick and old, and this aroused some pity in her. Her own father was as tough and twisted and dry as an old and weathered tree. Here was a creature she could mother, and the maternal instinct was very strong in young Mrs. Antoine. It was enough for her that he was sick and neglected, that everyone laughed at his "List," that no one considered that "List" as important. Mrs. Antoine found it very important. She spent hours each day with him, bent over the despised paper, seriously and gravely discussing with him various menus, and personally seeing that only those articles selected appeared on the table. "My love, I haven't diabetes," protested Antoine, when another dish of sweetbreads or lean thin meat or broiled chicken appeared at dinner. "Neither have I an aversion to potatoes. And I loathe limp vegetables cooked in water and flavored with mineral oil."

But young Mrs. Antoine was very firm. As a result, Antoine ate dinner at home not more than twice a week. He was hardly missed. Armand and his new daughter spent a happy dinner hour discussing the menu for the next day. It was no wonder that he began to adore her.

Within less than two months, she was happily pregnant.

In a world that was sick to death, that lived in a nightmare of constantly shifting backgrounds of fury and madness and confusion and hatred, that was so twisted and blown by a thousand rumors, that presented a multitude of rising and falling faces lighted by the glare of a wild Walpurgis Night, that resounded with the shrieks and cries of faceless madmen, young Mrs. Antoine lived a placid and insulated existence.

"You are so restful, my sweet," Antoine would say to her at breakfast, as she prattled away on some pretty asininity. "You haven't the brain of a mouse." He knew many women without the brains of mice, but they never seemed to realize it. They were full of seriousness, and discussed many problems with an air of intellect. It was delightful to find a woman who happily accepted the fact that she was a fool, was content with her rôle of amiable rump, and had a pretty little laugh that strove for no significant meaning.

The gloomy castle on the river began to take on an air of festivity and gaiety, incongruous to its character. "Like an ancient giantess wearing a foolish little hat over one eye," Antoine would say. But sunlight now invaded the immense dark rooms. Potted flowers appeared on every vast window-sill. Antoine said nothing until his cherished Rubenses and Goyas suddenly disappeared, and he discovered that his cabinet of ancient and curious snuff-boxes had been tossed into the store-house over one of the garages.

"But those little boxes were so nasty, darling," said young Mrs. Antoine, quite red of cheek, and with tearful eyes. "I looked at them. Some had such horrid little pictures on the lids. So musty and old, and not pretty at all. Besides, no one ever uses snuff now, so why do you want them?"

The cabinet reappeared in the library, and Antoine kept the key. Mrs. Antoine put a vase of flowers on it, and re-arranged the draperies at the windows so that the cabinet was in constant shadow.

And then, of all the Bouchards, Antoine suddenly found his wife unbearably fatiguing.

He had always admired his relative, Rosemarie Bouchard. She was a woman of wit and malevolence and swift vitriolic mind. He knew of her embroilment with Henri Bouchard, but he also knew that she had many other interests. She had some talent for writing, and small vicious "profiles" of prominent people written by her often appeared in the "smart" magazines, and even in the newspapers. At the present time, Rosmarie was in Washington, where she had many friends among the wives of Senators and officials of the State Department. She was writing casual columns for a newspaper syndicate now, and Antoine was delighted by her wit, her pungency, her subtle and perceptive remarks on the national and international situation. He visited her several times. It annoyed him that she was still so engrossed with Henri, but he slowly began to have hopes for himself. He returned from these visits much elated and soothed in mind, and was able to treat his little wife quite affectionately thereafter. After a stimulating dinner, a sweet frappé could be enjoyed.

Rosemarie, in her turn, began to look forward to Antoine's

visits with increasing interest and pleasure. Their similarity of temperament and mind, even their physical resemblance to each other, piqued and amused her. Besides, she was very useful to him. She could inform him of the slightest rumor, the slightest change in opinion of the powerful in Washington. He began to take notes in his small artistic hand, as he sat with her in her smart apartment. He discussed with her many matters of importance, and though well aware that she was vicious and treacherous and greedy, he knew he could dispense with considerable caution during these evenings alone with her. They wanted the same things. They understood each other. They could help each other. By the early spring of 1940, they were in love with each other. She no longer saw Henri, even during her brief visits to Windsor, but she could tell Antoine many things about his hated kinsman which were of extreme value to him.

Because of her free access to the salons of Washington, she was also able to tell him many other things. Acting as his spy, she sought out politicians, newspaper owners, prominent lobbyists, powerful women, and, finally, was able to get on excellent terms with the gravely excited and highly placed men of the "New Deal." They all thought her merely a brilliant and intellectually inquisitive woman, charming in appearance, of excellent taste, and great sympathy. What they told her, in their soothed egotism, was relayed to Antoine, with Rosemarie's own subtle and excellent footnotes.

When the America Only Committee suddenly burgeoned into prominence, Rosemarie appeared among the organizers, but only sub rosa. She was too clever to allow her name to be used. She knew that one faction of her family was supplying the huge sums necessary for its existence and its expansion. Because of this, she was sought after by the officers of the Committee. She wrote much of the propaganda which appeared in its smooth pamphlets. She wrote many of the radio scripts which were shouted over the ether by bought, suborned and traitorous speakers. Antoine supplied her with certain information and suggestions. It was understood, of course, that the Bouchard name must never appear in any fashion.

Rosemarie, it was, who brought many Senators into the America Only Committee, by way of large checks, promises or even delicate blackmail. Rosemarie never appeared at the German Embassy, and was even heard to express her contempt and disgust for the Third Reich, and Hitler. Nevertheless, it was rather odd that much of Goebbels' choicest propaganda appeared in her scripts, cleverly changed and disguised, but still virulent.

"Remember, the motif must always be Americanism, and very patriotic," Antoine had cautioned her. "And play up 'Constitutionalism.' Everything must be very dignified and solid and respectable. You can let the clergymen be as vociferous as possible. Everything is excused under the name of religion. By the way, you must impress upon them that their own motif is 'Christianity,' as opposed to atheism, Judaism and Communism. Also, it is necessary that we secure the services of some national hero, some prominent man. Look around for him."

Therefore, it was Rosemarie Bouchard who found the "national hero" who could act as spokesman for the America Only Committee.

CHAPTER XXIX

Captain August Jaeckle was of old German-American stock, and had been born in Wisconsin on January 2, 1900. He was now only approaching his forties, and was of considerable comeliness. He had that indestructible adolescence of face and figure so irresistible to women, for he was rather short and slight of build, and had fair thin hair on a boyish skull and a rather stupid and immature cast of feature. Even in old age, he would still possess that rather wizened adolescence; the mind behind that sloping smooth forehead had petrified into a school-boyish fourteen-year-old. He was a great athlete, was frequently quoted on the necessity of teaching youth physical stamina and muscle-building, and his remarks on the classical trend of American schools were very strong and contemptuous. "That's Europe," he would say, with profound scorn. "We've got to teach our youth to revere the body."

As his remarks were always distinguished by profound stupidity, the American public considered him a very oracle. They delighted in photographs of him. His vapid serious countenance, with the small and somewhat effeminate features, his lock of light hair falling over his forehead, his air of innocence and grave dedication, his large pale blue eyes shining with fanaticism, he appealed overwhelmingly to American women and to a certain type of American man. It did not matter to them that he was a fool and an ignoramus, that he was a poseur and a passionate seeker after the cheapest publicity (in spite of his loudly declared aversion for "the press"). He was a hero. He personified "American youth."

He was a hero, indeed!

For August Jaeckle, at the meager age of seventeen, had nobly lied about his birthdate, and had enlisted in the American Army in May, 1917. Two of his brothers were already serving in the Navy. "I used to cry, after Mother had kissed me goodnight," he was fond of saying with a sweet reminiscent smile, and that shy air of his which convulsed middle-aged women with tender ecstasy. "I couldn't stand it, thinking of George and Heinrich standing foursquare on their battleships with the wind in their faces, while I was wasting my time in the Shinehaha High School. Mother tried to console me. I was her youngest, her 'little boy.' She couldn't bear to think of me joining my brothers in the defense of our country. It was even worse for her when George was killed at sea. She used to cry. But there was something in me (perhaps it was my father's voice—he had been killed in the Spanish-American war, you know, just before I was born) that kept urging me to serve my country. George Washington and Lincoln had always been my heroes. So, one day I kissed her good-bye. She had no idea that she wouldn't see me again for nearly two years. But I knew. She thought I was going off to my classes. But I went to the recruiting station."

At this, he would smile again, lovingly, with great tenderness for the vision of that valiant schoolboy marching off to the wars, with his mother's kiss still damp on his boyish cheek. His eye would become moist. His voice would tremble. He would draw a deep shaking breath into his immature chest, still unmanly at the age of thirty-nine. He would almost whisper: "Mother!" At this, it was not unusual for susceptible ladies to control sobs. Everyone knew by now that Mrs. Jaeckle had died of pneumonia, during the great influenza epidemic, without ever seeing her valorous young son already in the trenches of France.

Everyone also knew that August had become a hero almost overnight. Single-handed, he had wiped out a machine-gun nest of fifteen Germans (also boys), had taken twenty prisoners, and had marched them back to his own lines with a stern and exalted look upon his face. No one but August knew that it had been a little Jewish sniper, caught with him and ten others in a shell-crater, who had really wiped out the machine-gun nest and died a few minutes later of a bullet in his heart. Happily, a hand-grenade from another isolated shell-hole had demolished the other witnesses to this act of supreme marksmanship and heroism, leaving August quite alone, and quite mad with terror. He had risen from his own shell-hole, screaming, and in his rush to his lines had come across the twenty Germans cowering in still another shell-hole. Exhausted, starving, diseased and hopeless, they had surrendered to him with cries of joy. For a few feet, in fact, they had literally pursued him, begging him to take them prisoner. He had finally come to his senses, and had obliged his "captives."

Always, there lived in his craven and stupid and frightened heart the fear that someone, somewhere, might know of the little Jewish sniper. In consequence, and by virtue of the involved mechanism of self-defense which operates so darkly in the human soul, he had become a rabid anti-Semite. He had never been at all religious during his school days. But now, he became a militant "Christian," a vicious and fanatical enemy of everything that was irreligious. The defense mechanism operating vigorously, Russia became to him a symbol of "anti-Christ." He hated all things that smacked of Communism, which, in some peculiar fashion, was a symbol of Judaism to him. Sometimes, at night, when the face of the little Jewish sniper would rise up before his inner eye, stern, reproachful and contemptuous, he could not sleep. He would walk the floor, sweating, weeping, wringing his hands, his whole being afire with hatred. It was then that he would give vent to the foulest and most obscene cries, in a low and whispering voice intense with madness.

For he loved his heroism. He loved his publicity. He wore his medals with passionate egotism, for all his publicized "modesty and shyness."

At the age of thirty, he had married a wealthy buxom widow some ten years his senior. Some fatuous ladies declared she was a "mother symbol" to him, and indeed he was often heard to admit shyly, with a deep look at his wife, that "Emma resembles my dear mother so much." Within a year after their marriage, he began to call her "Mama," though she had never borne a child. The widow was a woman of no small intelligence, and possessed considerable shrewdness.

However much she resented the "Mama" appellation (for she was handsome and had great style), she never betrayed it. She, too, loved publicity, and she had never been blessed with it before. Her first husband had been merely a fat businessman of remarkable skulduggery, and there had never been anything about him to inspire rhapsodies in the press. Indeed, as he had made his money by supplying inferior blankets to the Army, he preferred obscurity. So Mrs. Jaeckle wore her new fame proudly, made over a considerable fortune to her "boy" husband, simpered over him in public, often ostentatiously smoothing back his incorrigible lock of light hair, and posed with him girlishly for press photographers. She also gave out interviews to lady reporters in which she carolled over dear August's "sweet boyishness, simplicity, profound and scientific mind, and lovable shyness." This spoke well for the woman's histrionic ability, for she knew only too shrewdly her husband's meanness of mind, stupidity, ignorance, avarice and tiny petulancies. She knew, too, that he was capable of only one largeness: hatred. She despised him. But she was grateful to him for lifting her from the anonymous mass, for she was a clever woman, of talents and accomplishments.

But the public, however adoring, has a new hero every day. August could not compete forever with pretty male Hollywood actors, ball-players, radio singers and the newest colorful gangster. Mrs. Jaeckle saw the cloud of worshippers thinning away into air. The shine of the medals was no longer bright enough to dazzle the capricious public eye.

Mrs. Jaeckle was indeed clever. Moreover, she had an authentic regard for truly great and noble men. Among her friends was a scientist of supreme achievement, a Belgian count who was, at that time, teaching trigonometry in some obscure New Jersey college. Apparently he was doomed to pass his life away in this backwater when he suddenly discovered some new system of mathematics which lifted him, for a time, to almost the same precarious fame as the latest Italian murderer in Chicago. Only a few brilliant men even pretended to understand this latest system in the realm of that most classical of the arts, mathematics. But the mystery and the newspaper acclaim made the public conscious of this new hero, though where his heroism lay the average man could not tell.

Then, one man understood, one man among the five who pretended the system was no mystery to them. Of course, this man was Captain August Jaeckle, now almost forgotten.

Fame does not always bring lucrative rewards. The Belgian count was only too well aware of this bitter truth, and he did not hesitate much more than an hour before he accepted Mrs. Jaeckle's check for ten thousand dollars, a permanent annuity of two thousand dollars a year, and a small new house near the campus of his college. For this quiet reward, he let it be known, very reluctantly, that Captain August Jaeckle had long been studying with him, Captain Jaeckle, in his shyness, never before having allowed the public to guess at his secret addiction to mathematics. "It was always a kind of vice with me," August admitted, with blushes and blinkings of his vapid shining eyes.

Two of his elderly former teachers in the Shinehaha High School were greatly amazed at all this, but understanding acutely that there was no fame in rebuttal, they allowed themselves to be interviewed, with photographs, and declared that "dear little August was always the boy-genius of mathematics in their classes." They were very grateful for the substantial checks sent to them by the more grateful Mrs. Jaeckle.

The fame of mathematics was good for one year of new and heightened publicity for August.

Mrs. Jaeckle was indefatigable. The lust for notoriety was a disease in her fifty-year-old body. She searched feverishly, while the new fame began to decline, for new fields for August to conquer. She hinted at divorce. The newspapers went wild. She denied the rumor. This was good for two months. She and August would adopt two children. Photographs of a multitude of orphans appeared in the newspapers, with large captions asking pertinently: "Is this the one?" August, in turn, became famously interested in aviation, mechanics, economics, social problems. He was an authority on President Roosevelt, whom he hated. He gave lectures. (Mrs. Jaeckle wrote the lectures.) He travelled about, speaking on practically every subject, always shy and modest and boyish.

During this time, Mrs. Jaeckle's fortune began to show symptoms of attrition, due to the new social theories of the Administration. This induced a vast and hysterical hatred in her. She found its echo in August, who feared nothing more than poverty and obscurity. August began to speak on "American bolshevism," "the new American Communism," "Roosevelt dictatorship," "international plotters against pure Americanism." Somewhere, American womanhood, and the Home, were hinted to be under attack by nefarious conspirators in the background. August was famous again.

August was invited by the German government to visit the Third Reich, and to see for himself how the new order was operating in Germany, how private property, private enterprise and initiative were rewarded and encouraged, how pure Womanhood was protected, how the youth were trained in physical culture, how the Home was revered. August, accompanied by "Mama," went to Germany, was fêted, photographed, followed by loving crowds (carefully herded by Stormtroopers into strategic positions for photographers), and personally decorated by Hitler. He returned to America, dazed with adulation, his meager and vicious little heart swelling with pride and emotion. He was consulted by State Department officials on the "truth" about Germany, and his remarks delighted their hearts. His first lecture, after his return, was in the nature of an apology for German anti-Semitism. His second stated that Germany was invincible in the air, on land, and on sea. His third, that Hitler was a demi-god.

"We must learn that there is a new and burgeoning spirit rising in the world!" he cried, to an audience of fat middle-aged ladies who loved to hear of the masculine contempt of Hitler for everything female. "We must learn that the stream of human evolution cannot be damned by foolish idealists and outworn democrats! We cannot escape the dynamic revolution of the human soul, as it is expressed in politics. Politics are history. In Germany, one hears the rumbles of a mighty new birth of the world. However we shut our ears, the thunder will penetrate. The Future is in Germany. We cannot silence its voice. We can only ride in its train, if we are cowardly. Or, we can march in the vanguard, with Hitler, if we have courage and pride and the spirit of true America in our hearts."

Always, he spoke with authentic passion and noise, for lately the face of the little Jewish sniper had a terrible way of meeting him every night when he was alone.

August was famous again, more famous than ever. The indignation and laughter and furious contempt of his enemies only made him the more famous. Violent controversies took place all over America, in the press, in public forums, in parlors and in kitchens. Bishop Halliday gave a series of radio addresses on this "vibrant young American hero who has heard the call of the Future." Subversive organizations, already forming in the dark, and bearing heroic names such as Friends of the American Constitution, Guardians of America, Soldiers of Washington, and so on, invited him to speak.

The war gave August his greatest opportunity. He lectured inexhaustibly on the folly of "intervening in European conflicts," and of giving aid and comfort to Russia, the arch-enemy of Hitler. Hitler was the bulwark against universal bolshevism. Moreover, the war was none of our business. Hitler had never, at any time, dreamt of attacking America. That he intended to do so was the lie of "interventionists, Communists, anti-Christians, international bankers, war-mongers who want profits from the deaths of our boys, first-generation Americans, 'Moors' [a euphemistic term for Jews], New Deal politicians, who want a war to keep them in power," and practically everyone who disagreed with August. His slogan, "The Coming Thunder," inspired a small and best-selling volume written by Franz Haas, who was later indicted as an agent of the German Government.

The American public, sweating in secret and terrible uneasiness since the ghastly attack on Poland by Hitler, finally became wildly vociferous and excited. Many sections, heretofore adorers of August, began to despise him, to laugh at him, to call him a "pipsqueak," a fool, a trumpery hero, a masquerader, a petty mountebank, a bumbling numskull, a solemn idiot, an ignoramus and a faker. In their ire, they saw their hero as he was, and their fury against him was a fury against themselves for having been part of his adoring train. His pretensions to learning were unmasked. One of his school-teachers, who had never ceased to regret her duplicity, and who had an ancestor who had fought and suffered with Washington, now declared her folly and her seduction at the hands of Mrs. Jaeckle. But, as no one had ever understood the fame of mathematics anyway, this one trembling voice was hardly heard.

Serious and intelligent men attacked August in the press, in the pulpit, and over the radio waves. They stripped him naked. They exposed him to the jeers of their enlightened listeners. One by one, they demolished his foolish arguments. They denounced him as a dupe and an imbecile, a two-penny actor, and cast doubt on his ancient claim to heroism, and on his alleged aversion to publicity.

However, as these men were intelligent gentlemen of learning, wisdom and understanding, the American people disliked them intensely. They preferred the screamers who defended August, for these screamers were violent, colorful, dramatic and vicious. Their lies were extravagant and monstrous, and inspired the delight of the masses. They preached the vilest hatred, and the masses squirmed with sadistic lust. "Lie to the people, tickle them in their prejudices, make them itch for blood, especially the blood of the defenseless, make them hate, make them long to destroy and murder, and you can do with them as you please," said Bishop Halliday, who was a very astute servant of Christ, and also a dear friend and servant of Baron von Teckle, Chargé d'Affairs at the German Embassy.

In the South, where lived Americans of old British blood, August was anathema. In most parts of the West, this was also true, except in those regions infected with German strains. August's great following was among the populations of the large Northern cities, whose peoples stemmed from Poland, Italy and Germany, and Ireland. After one telling lecture by August, many Jews were attacked on the streets of New York. Bishop Halliday was delighted.

All this, however, while making August very famous, or infamous, did nothing to increase his fortune, or rather, Mrs. Jaeckle's fortune. August was ripe for subsidy.

Rosemarie Bouchard knew Mrs. Jaeckle quite well, and she sought her out very discreetly. The details were never known. But, suddenly, August became an officer in the America Only Committee, and under its auspices acquired a high and solid respectability. Rosemarie polished his scripts, wrote many of his public addresses. He, who in the past had adored no one but himself, began to adore her, to follow her about, to touch her hand shyly, to dream about her. This dark and vital woman, who in no wise resembled "Mama," nor Mrs. Jaeckle (now quite fat and shapeless and mustached), wildly disturbed his senses. He would have worked for her for no reward at all but her smile, and the promise in that smile.

Captain August Jaeckle became one of the most momentous and dangerous figures in contemporary American history during the first year of the second great World War.

Rosemarie Bouchard had found her hero for the America Only Committee. Antoine's faction was highly pleased.

CHAPTER XXX

Antoine, with those deft and graceful gestures, that insouciant manner, which he had inherited from his grandfather, Jules, poured another measure of cointreau into his Uncle Christopher's delicate glass. He smiled as he did so. Christopher leaned back in his chair, held his glass to the light, appreciatively, and smiled also.

"So, you've got Eagle Aviation, too," remarked Antoine, seating himself again, and lifting his glass in a light salute. "Good judgment on old Stone Face's part. Give the devil his due, he generally picks the right man. You won't be returning to Florida, then?"

"I'll be commuting between Windsor, Florida and Detroit. We have plans for building a large plant in Buffalo, also, and perhaps Los Angeles. Henri has hinted that the British Government has already approached him with an offer to assist in the building of the plants. The cash-and-carry plan will soon be in operation. There's always a way of getting around the Neutrality Act, and good old Hugo is working on the State Department to that effect."

Antoine laughed. "Playing both ends against the middle—the usual Bouchard game. In this war, we'll do it for a while. Not that I approve of it, of course. We have our plans. Britain mustn't be supplied with too much. That was our original idea. You still agree?"

"Of course," replied Christopher, gravely. He turned the glass in his fleshless and transparent fingers and regarded his nephew fixedly with his silvery gray eyes, so enigmatic and motionless.

The two men were sitting together very cozily in the great gloomy library of Armand's castle. A red fire burned on the black marble hearth, and a dim gray snow was falling softly outside, this early December day.

"I think we'd better call a meeting, Chris," suggested Antoine, after a thoughtful stare at the fire.

"The sooner the better. Hugo is coming home for Christmas, and I understand he is bringing Senator Briggs with him, and one or two others. We must move fast, now. I have it on excellent authority that France will collapse in the spring. That will be the beginning of the end."

Antoine's glittering smile flashed in the darkness of the warm room. "The end! The end of the British Empire! You know, I've always hated the British. Perhaps it is the French in me. So, I've a personal reason. How long do you conjecture it will be before the Lion is smashed to a pulp?"

Christopher was silent for a few moments. Then he said, softly: "Have you thought about Russia?"

"Russia! Good God! Stalin's signed a pact with Hitler, hasn't he?"

Now Christopher smiled his curious icy smile. "I'll tell you something else. Hitler will attack Russia some time next summer."

"Impossible!" But Antoine was staring piercingly at his uncle. "Not until England is done. You think England will be done by then, though?"

"No," said Christopher, placidly, "I don't. And because England won't be smashed, Hitler will turn east. That's always been his mission, you know."

Antoine rose swiftly to his feet and began to walk up and down the room. He was frowning intently. "I don't like this. You never speak without knowing what you are talking about, Christopher. If Hitler attacks Russia before England is done——"

"Then," said Christopher, very softly, "he is done."

There was silence in the room, as Antoine moved silently up and down over the thick rugs. He glanced repeatedly at Christopher's gaunt and sunken face. But he could read nothing there, though the red fire flashed up on the fragile taut bones and made vivid holes of the eyesockets.

"He must be stopped," said Antoine, at last, pausing before his uncle.

"How?"

"I'm going to New York next week. Von Teckle will meet me there."

"That's dangerous, Antoine. If you are seen." .

"I won't be. Will you go with me?"

Christopher hesitated. Then he said: "Yes."

Antoine sat down again on the edge of his chair, his sinewy thin arms folded on his knees. He regarded Christopher in a long silence, smiling in a peculiar fashion. "I'd like to be sure of you, Chris," he remarked, very softly.

Christopher shrugged. "My dear Papa used to say: 'Never trust anyone but the devil.'"

"You are in this with us very deep, Chris," said Antoine, reflectively, turning to the fire again with a gentle expression.

Now Christopher was smiling his enjoyment. "Are you blackmailing me, by any chance?"

Antoine, smiling in return, made a Latin gesture with those agile brown hands of his. "Of course not! Certainly not! But, as my dear grandpapa said: 'Never trust anyone but the devil.' You aren't quite a devil, Chris. But old Stone Face would be hard to convince."

Christopher studied him oddly. "You are still afraid of him, eh?"

Antoine flashed him a shrewd glance, full of light hatred and ire. But he said, humorously: "You must remember that my darling papa is Annette's papa, too. And while that fact remains, Henri's got Bouchard. I've been thinking."

"Yes?" prompted Christopher, softly.

But Antoine turned his black and jerking eyes upon him penetratingly before he answered. "Do you think the Gray Glacier has forgotten his penchant for our little Celeste?"

Christopher did not move. But every nervous muscle along his body tightened. He said: "I don't know. Has he?"

Antoine rose again, and moved to the windows. He gazed out upon the snow. Without turning, he asked: "And—if he hasn't—what is your position?"

Christopher placed his glass carefully on the table, very neatly, very precisely. "My position? I haven't any. Celeste can manage her own affairs, for all of me. She isn't a child. What she does is her own choice. I can tell you this, however: she won't divorce our dying Galahad."

"But, after he is dead?"

"Henri knows on which side his bread is buttered. He won't divorce Annette. Can you imagine him doing anything so indiscreet? So disastrous?"

"No," admitted Antoine, turning from the window. He thrust his hands in his pockets. This gesture did not in the least disturb his elegant appearance or rob his slender quick figure of its grace. Now his face was in such shadow that Christopher could not see it. But he felt its malignant alertness.

"You know, of course, that our angel Celeste has been meeting the Iron Man in some cosy rendezvous in New York, quite regularly?"

For the first time Christopher showed some perturbation.

His hands tightened on the arms of his chair. But he said calmly: "Has she? Who is your informant?"

He felt, rather than saw, Antoine's wicked smile. "I can't tell you that. But I know the source is authentic. Is it possible you are disturbed, Chris?"

Christopher deliberately relaxed himself. "No," he said. "As I've remarked before, it is Celeste's affair. But what is all this leading to?"

Antoine came back to his chair, sat down, leaned towards his uncle, his smile very broad and sparkling. "Yes, you're in with us very deep, Chris. Henri might be interested to know just how deep. We've kept minutes, you know. Incidentally, he still hasn't the slightest idea?"

"I can vouch for that," said Christopher, keeping his voice neutral. "If he had, don't you think he would have moved before this? He can still smash us. Yes, as you've so subtly pointed out, I'm in this deep. But, as I asked you a moment or two ago: What is all this leading to?"

"Just this," replied Antoine, in a sweet tone. "If my little sister should hear of these delightful rendezvous, I imagine she will divorce the Gray Glacier promptly. And—if there is a divorce—" He threw up his hands swiftly, pursed his lips as if blowing away a feather.

"Henri is done," concluded Christopher. "Well done. My fat brother will throw him out of Bouchard, bonds or no bonds. Of course, in that event, Henri might be moved to wreck Bouchard. Have you thought of that?"

Antoine was silent. His brown face puckered drily. His eyes fastened on Christopher's bloodless face, in which the mouth was smiling ever so slightly.

"The plan—your plan—smells," said Christopher, still in a very gentle tone. "We can't risk the smashing of Bouchard. Ever heard of Samson? There's something about Henri that reminds me of Samson." He paused, then continued:

"If he wrecked Bouchard, he'd wreck himself, you'd say. And what of you? You're Secretary of Bouchard. Would you enjoy being part of the wreckage?"

Antoine did not answer. He began to rub his puckered mouth very daintily with one forefinger. It was not a usual habit with him. Christopher saw the gesture, and suddenly it was as if there had occurred an appalling explosion in his chest. He remembered that gesture, delicate, reflective; it was his father's very own. Now he was alive, burning, quickening, with the most fantastic and irresistible hatred for Antoine. His hands clutched on the arms of his chair, and his transparent nostrils dilated. By some trick of the firelight, playing on Antoine's features, so brown and taut and narrow, it was Jules' face that was turned to Christopher.

"You wouldn't enjoy the wreckage," he repeated, in a strangely hoarse voice.

Antoine began to smile. "So. You are still involved with your darling, eh?"

The explosion of uncontrolled hatred in Christopher was still shaking him. But he said, calmly enough: "Suppose we leave my sister out of this? I've merely pointed out to you that you can't polish off Henri without ruining yourself. Do you want to risk it?"

He was surprised when Antoine said thoughtfully: "I'd like to see the old fool's will. Of course, Annette will have her share. There is also my share. There will be provision, naturally, for Henri to be retained as president of Bouchard. Nevertheless, I'd like to know the exact terms of the will. Have you any idea? Papa is your brother, after all."

"We've not been very devoted, you will remember," Christopher pointed out. His triumph was hardly less disastrous in its physical effect on him than his hatred. "He'd hardly confide in me."

"You've got the same firm of lawyers. You could find out, Chris. A few discreet questions."

Christopher was silent. But he was smiling again. He gloated inwardly. For the first time, he had exulted over his father in exulting over Antoine.

Antoine sighed, flung out his hands again. "Yes, as you've remarked, the plan smells. I was very fond of it. There were personal implications, too. I'll keep it in mind, however. If we are forced to use it, you won't object."

"Why should I?"

Antoine was suddenly relieved as he thought of something. "We'll keep things quiet for a year. By that time, most probably, it won't matter. Old Stone Face won't be in a position to smash Bouchard. Still, I'd like to know about that will."

He studied Christopher intently. "I'm rather fond of my own sister, too."

Christopher laughed a little. "You know how she adores Henri. Annette's no imbecile. I wouldn't be at all surprised if she had some idea of Henri's frequent little depredations. Wives always know by some damned intuition. If she hasn't made any objection in the past, she won't, now."

"She might be forced to."

Christopher lit a cigarette. "I wouldn't rely on that. And

now, shall we drop that subject? We have more important things to discuss, I think, than the state of women's hearts."

Antoine began to laugh amiably. "How do you like our hero, Jaeckle? He's costing us five thousand dollars a month, but he's worth it."

"It was a clever move," admitted Christopher. "Five thousand dollars? Out of whose pocket?"

"The general fund, of course. Rosemarie managed it very nicely. At our next meeting, I suggest a considerable increase in the funds for the Committee. It now has three more subsidiary committees, too, which need financing. Especially in the South, among the Ku Kluxers. We're taking up the Negro angle, there. Negroes in the South, Jews in the North, Mexicans in the South-west, labor in the East. A very neat program, if I say it myself. We can so disorganize the damn country that it will stop staring at Europe for a while. We need that, while we complete our plans. Hitler must have a clear field; he mustn't be annoyed by alarmed preparations in America. Disunity must be stimulated. It won't be hard. The mob hasn't the brains of a louse.

"Rosemarie is a very bright girl. The Family hasn't appreciated her enough. She is now organizing a pacifist society to be called 'Mothers of America.' All the mamas in the throes of libido will join with enthusiasm, to protect their 'boys.' We've begun to subsidize Halliday, too, as you know. Three thousand a month. Our next step will be to organize the middle class. Have you heard of that Irish scoundrel, Patrick McHenry, of New York? He's been clamoring for years that Roosevelt is out to liquidate the middle class, but no one has listened to him very closely because he lacks funds. We intend to supply them."

Christopher had been listening keenly. At intervals, he had nodded his head with an air of grave approval.

"We'll give Roosevelt enough to think of right at home without troubling his tender heart over Europe," added Antoine. He paused. "You think all this very crude? It lacks finesse? When has it ever been necessary to use elegant tactics with the masses? Especially the American masses?"

"I haven't said I've thought it crude," said Christopher.

Antoine thought of something else. "By the way, have you heard the latest commentator, Gilbert Small? We're outlining a plan for Jaeckle to denounce him as a Communist, a tool of Stalin, a war-monger, an interventionist and hireling of the New Deal and dupe of Britain. We have a dossier on him. It's unfortunate that he isn't a Jew. He isn't even a New

Yorker, which is always good for our brand of propaganda. He's a Middle-Westerner, and his mother is a native of Martin Dies' own State. All this has disarmed us, temporarily. He, too, again unfortunately, is a war hero. We tried to find a connection between him and the Spanish Communists, but I must admit that his dispatches to his former newspaper, the New York *Times*, were fine examples of neutral and dispassionate reporting. Moreover, as you know, he wrote a book on Russia which has forever barred him from Stalin's bailiwick. Nevertheless, for public purposes, he is a Communist. We've put pressure on the broadcasting chain which allows him to spill his trash on the air. But for some mysterious reason they are resistant, in spite of threats. And, mystery again, he is acquiring a huge following in America. Have you heard him at all?"

"Yes," said Christopher, thoughtfully, "I have. His scripts are excellent. Just the right amount of fire, and very logical. Simple, too, and moving. Not his style, which was always rather dull and reportorial. I wonder who is really writing his scripts?"

"We've tried to discover that, too. But it remains a mystery. He's dangerous to us. He's connected with the American Freedom Association. I'd like to know who is financing that Association, too. None of our boys, you can be sure of that."

Christopher's face was properly serious and interested.

"Of course," continued Antoine, "our America Only Committee has over three million members to date, while the American Freedom Association has less than two million, if that. And our Committee is growing larger every day." He laughed. "The Association has made the mistake of hiring gentlemen and scholars, with the exception of Small. Whereas we concentrate on clever hoodlums, rabble-rousers and liars. Consequently, we shall always be more potent in America than the Association."

His spirits were rising. His love for intrigue was rampant. Christopher watched him closely.

"Have you been to see your revered father-in-law, Boland, recently, about shipments of oil and aluminum to Germany? And what about Canada? The shipment of nickel?"

"I'm to see him while I am in New York, Chris. Italy has almost enough aluminum for Hitler. But the petroleum and the nickel are other matters. The nickel problem will be settled next week. Our subsidiary in Canada has its orders. It is just a matter of quiet ships to South America, and that is being arranged, also. But more important than this: I'm to see Phyllis's husband and father-in-law, the Morse National, next week. Hitler needs huge funds in the near future. Loans can be arranged through the banks in South America, not to mention the Banque de France and the Bank of England, and others. Dr. Schacht will meet our representatives in Switzerland sometime during the next three months. By the way, Rosemarie's little sister, Phyllis, is organizing the Catholic Wives and Mothers of America, to assist our Committee. We expect it to be a potent organization."

There was a soft tap at the door, which opened slowly, to reveal the rosy round face of Mrs. Antoine. "Tea, dears," she chirped, fondly. "And darling Annette is here, too, Uncle Christopher. Have you finished your very, very important business?"

CHAPTER XXXI

There was a great hot fire in one of the vast drawing-rooms, and there, as though crouching about heat and light in the immensity of some primordial cave, full of looming shadows and shadowy carved ceiling far overhead, sat young Mrs. Antoine, Annette and Armand. The firelight sparkled rosily on the pale silver, picking out the elaborate curve of handle or lid, and lying in pink reflection in the waiting shells of teacups. Behind them lurked the dim shapes of heavy furniture and the glimmering backs of long tables, like prehistoric animals, half-seen in the flickering light. The draperies had been drawn on windows that reached from floor to ceiling, and were the shape of cathedral apertures. But the wind roared and bent against them like a strong resistant presence, and in quieter intervals one could hear the dry hiss of snow. Sometimes the fire flared up to show the dark gilded portraits on the walls, their spectral faces seemingly coming alive and growing vivid for an instant.

Antoine and Christopher joined the group about the fire. Antoine was all affability, his sparkling smile quite radiant and full of laughter. Mrs. Antoine, serenely pouring tea, glanced at him fondly from time to time, her round rosy face blooming with health and placidity, her short plump figure already betraying signs of approaching maternity. Dear Tony is such a wit, she thought to herself. He quite brightens up even such a day as this. She was very happy.

Armand had spread a huge white napkin over his fat knees. His clothing, as usual, was crumpled and soiled. Between the spaces of his thin gray curls his big round scalp gleamed. He had become very old these last three months, but calmer, almost contented, since the marriage of his son. Behind his glasses, his tiny black eyes were less frightened, less apprehensive. Nevertheless, when he saw Antoine and Christopher, his pudgy features tightened, and he said, in a strange voice: "Winter's come early this year."

Christopher lifted his head alertly and turned his enigmatic eyes upon his brother. But Antoine said lightly: "Wars always bring early and hard winters."

"What've you two been plotting about, again?" asked Armand, wiping away crumbs from his thick lips. He smiled, but again that smile was uneasy, and fearful, and cunning.

"Would you like to know?" countered Christopher, and now a cruel and amused gleam passed over his attenuated face.

Armand lifted his hands and fluttered them. The plate tilted precariously on his knee, and he caught it just as it was about to slide, with its contents, upon the floor. "No, no," he said, very quickly, and with another frightened smile. "I'm done with all that. I only want to be left in peace."

He rubbed a drop or two of tea from his vest. Christopher saw that his hand was shaking. The old man, his eyes searching for refuge, encountered his daughter, Annette.

"Tony never plots; he's too gay," said young Mrs. Antoine, gracefully filling cups for her husband and "Uncle Christopher."

"She means, the darling, that I haven't the brains to 'plot,'" said Antoine, deftly kissing the plump little hand that gave him his cup.

Mrs. Antoine smiled comfortably. "How you change the meaning of my words! I never meant that, Tony. I only meant you are just too sweet and happy to care much about anything except your books and your pictures. And some are such ugly pictures! Especially that—that Renoir. Such fat women; no shape at all."

"In the sunlight, your body would look just like a Renoir,"

said Antoine, gallantly. "All rosy plumpness and mother-of-pearl shadows."

Mrs. Antoine giggled and blushed. "How would you know, you naughty boy? You've never seen me in sunlight."

Annette, beyond greeting her brother and uncle with a faint smile, had said nothing. She sat near her father, her black wool dress making her appear more fragile and wan than ever. Her little triangular face was quite haggard, and seemed to have dwindled lately. But the great pale-blue eyes, so full of light, were gentler and more profound than they had ever been. The firelight sparkled in her cloud of fine light hair, so that her head was haloed.

Antoine's vivid glance dwelt on her musingly for a moment. Then he said: "Where's the Iron Man? Didn't he come with you, Annette?"

"No. He had to leave for Washington this morning. I presume you mean Henri?" replied Annette, with her quiet bright smile.

"I think Henri's a darling," prattled Mrs. Antoine, looking about her contentedly, and loving her relatives. "He says the nicest things to me. He told me last week that I was just what I was made for, and that you deserved me, Tony. Wasn't that sweet?"

"Very," answered Antoine, wryly. Christopher was laughing, his silent and virulent laughter which made his death's-head of a face quite startling in the firelight. Antoine again turned to his sister. "You came alone, rabbit? Why didn't Celeste come, too? I thought you were such friends."

Annette stirred her tea, and accepted a tiny sandwich from the gilt plate which Mrs. Antoine was pressing upon her. Her face was very calm and still. "Celeste's in New York. Last minute discussion with the decorators. I understand there are a pair of silver lamps on Madison Avenue that she wants, and the decorators are quite violently against them. She intends to settle the argument, and bring the lamps back with her."

"So," said Antoine, slowly, looking at Christopher, and smiling evilly, "you and Peter are alone in your tombs. You in your warm tomb, and Peter in his glass and chromium mausoleum. You ought to have invited him, Mary."

For an instant Mary was uneasy and embarrassed. "Oh, I've invited both Uncle Peter and Aunt Celeste very often, dear! But they never come. They haven't been here since October. Dear Uncle Peter depresses me so; he looks so ill. And Dr. Gordon doesn't think I should be depressed."

Christopher was no longer smiling. His features had the color and texture of plaster again. He sipped his tea thoughtfully. But Antoine was grinning diabolically. He hummed very softly under his breath.

"Celeste hopes to have the new house completely ready by Christmas," remarked Annette. "She has already invited us for Christmas dinner. All of the family who will be in Windsor at that time. There are only a few things to do to complete the house."

"Such as the lamps, from Madison Avenue," agreed Antoine, smiling at her.

For a long moment brother and sister regarded each other in a suddenly rigid silence. Annette's little face was pale and shining, her eyes resolutely bright. "Such as the lamps," she agreed, at last. Her hand did not shake as she held her cup.

As he stared at her, Antoine's face lost its evil look, became dark and closed and brown in the wavering light. There was a peculiar pain in his chest, a most unfamiliar pain. He turned away from her, but he knew that she still gazed at him, indomitable in her fragility, and at bay. She knows, he thought.

"Have you listened to any newscasts today, Papa?" he asked Armand.

Armand hurriedly chewed and swallowed a hard little nugget of a cake before he replied. "No. I never listen to 'em. Too depressing. I've had my fill of troubles. I'm letting the world wag along by itself." He smiled uneasily, and again his eyes sought refuge.

"I listened to William Benson, this afternoon," chirped Mrs. Antoine. "I always think one should keep up. And things are so thrilling now, so exciting. It's so easy to be frightened. But Mr. Benson is so reassuring. He says we must be calm, and sensible. We must just look on, and hold our peace. Europe is none of our business. Hitler isn't threatening us. There're three thousand miles of water, he says, and the war-mongers can't get around that."

"Perhaps airplanes can," said Annette, looking affectionately at her brother's wife.

But Mrs. Antoine was quite superior. "Mr. Benson went into that, Annette darling. No airplane could make a round trip. Besides, Hitler isn't interested in us at all! This is a European quarrel; they're always quarrelling, those strange creatures with the outlandish names. It has nothing to do with us. Mr. Benson is so clever. He had a lot of arguments which I didn't quite understand, but I know they were clever.

He understands so many things, more than poor little me does."

Christopher looked at Antoine. "Isn't Benson the new commentator for the Green Network? And isn't he the American Association of Industrialists' man?"

Antoine was very arch. "I wouldn't know that. So far as I know, he is on the Limey Lemonade half-hour. Limey Lemonade! God! You've got to admit we Americans have an unconscious sense of humor."

Armand was exhibiting every sign of uneasiness. "Do we have to talk about the war? Haven't we pleasanter things to discuss?"

There was real fear and distress on his fat and swollen face.

"Such as The List?" suggested Antoine. He turned to his wife. "What is it tonight? Liver?"

Mrs. Antoine bridled. She shook her little pink finger at him, with a smile. "Now, now, Tony. It's Thursday, and we always have liver on Thursday. It's so good for Papa. Full of vitamins, and blood, I think. It's good for you, too."

Antoine shuddered elaborately, and the others laughed. "What are you having for dinner tonight, Annette?" he asked his sister.

"I don't really know," she smiled in answer. "I think it's capon. Our housekeeper mentioned it this morning, I believe. Or perhaps it's capon for tomorrow. Why?"

"If it's capon, or anything else except liver, I'll drive home with you," he said.

Mrs. Antoine's face was puckering as if she was about to cry. "Oh, Tony. How can you be so bad? You haven't had dinner with us since last Friday. You aren't really going away tonight? I think there are onions for you, if you want them, with the liver."

He patted her hand. "If Annette isn't having capon, I'll stay for the liver," he promised. "I'm mad about capon. They call me Capon in New York."

"I doubt it," said Christopher. "I really doubt it. I could give instances."

Even Armand laughed at this. But Mary looked from one mirthful face to another in great puzzlement. "I never understand your jokes," she complained. "Please explain it to me."

"Uncle Christopher was just being vulgar, pet," said her husband, patting her cheek. "I wouldn't soil your ears."

Christopher was glancing at his watch. "It's almost six. If you don't mind, Antoine, I'd like to listen to our mysterious Gilbert Small tonight."

"The radio?" exclaimed Armand. "Do we have to listen to that thing blare?"

But Christopher had already risen, and was making his way to a tall Chippendale cabinet which housed the radio. The dial sprang into light. A moment later a quiet masculine voice invaded the great room. "This is your KLDB announcer speaking. We are glad to bring you again at this hour Mr. Gilbert Small, authority on European affairs. Mr. Small's opinions are not necessarily those of this Station's. He has no commercial sponsor, and therefore speaks frankly, as he chooses."

There was a short wait. Armand's teacup clattered irritably on his saucer, and he sighed and shifted noisily in his chair. "I don't know why—" he mumbled. "May I give you some more tea, dear Papa?" asked Mrs. Antoine. She began to chatter brightly and clearly as Mr. Small's grave firm voice emerged from the radio. Antoine turned to her, and said softly: "My pet, will you please shut your mouth for a moment?" She stared at him blankly, her mouth falling open, her eyelids blinking. She glanced miserably at Annette, but Annette was leaning forward a little in her chair, her eyes fixed on the radio. Christopher stood near the cabinet, his head bent.

"Today," said Mr. Small, "the Nazis murdered ten thousand men, women and children in Poland. Today, one thousand Czech students were shot to death in Praha. The oldest was seventeen. Today, in a pogrom in Munich, two thousand little Jewish children were dragged from their mothers' arms and pushed aboard cattle trains for shipment into death. Today, twenty Austrian intellectuals were murdered in a cellar in Vienna.

"There is a great calm in America. Tonight, in a New York stadium, two famous pugilists are fighting for a purse of fifty thousand dollars. Tonight, in a New York theatre, a crooner is drawing an audience of six thousand titillating women and girls, who will sigh and swoon all over each other as his sweet voice thrills them to their toes. The streets of America are filled with men and women carrying bundles of Christmas presents. In Hollywood, Marianne Vincent has announced she intends to divorce her fifth husband very shortly. I said we were calm. No. We are very excited. We have such important things to think of. But not one of these things concerns the events in Poland, Czecho-Slovakia, Munich, or Vienna. You see, Poland, Czecho-Slovakia, Munich and Vienna are so far away, and the people are so strange. They are not really our brothers and our sisters and our children. They are creatures apart."

"Too true," murmured Mrs. Antoine, happily, forgetting her husband's snub. She looked about her for the usual affectionate smiles. But every face was grave, turned away from her. Armand's head had fallen on his chest; his hands were slack and flaccid as they hung from the ends of his dropped arms.

"Tonight," continued Mr. Small, "when I heard these things, I had the most curious vision of a certain garden standing in the sunset. A quite mythical garden, you will agree. It is very silent in the garden; over the great dark trees the sunset is red as fire, and burning vividly. Even the birds are quiet, and the river near by flows onward without a sound, its surface blazing with crimson light. There is peace in the garden; the flowers bend their heads.

"But all at once (and this is only my vision, you understand), I see a dead man lying there, a very innocent young man. His sleeping face is covered with blood. It is very sad. He has never wronged anyone; he has never injured a living soul. He has only been happy, and has only wanted to live peaceably with his brother. Nevertheless, he has been done to death by a brutal and savage hand. Where is the murderer? He is hiding somewhere among those trees, crouching in their black tangled shadow, his hands covering his sweating face.

"The sunset darkens. And then, all at once, a terrible and furious wind blows through the trees, bending them, whitening them, throwing them up against the red sky. The birds cry out in the branches. The flowers turn pale as death and hang their heads, falling to the ground. And out of the wind comes a great Voice, echoing from space: 'Where is Abel, thy brother?'

"Somewhere, out of that cavern of twisted tree-trunks, out of the fury and turbulence of wind and the cosmic Voice, comes a faint whisper: 'Am I my brother's keeper?'"

Mr. Small's voice was suddenly still. But the air vibrated with its memory. Christopher lifted his stark and motionless face and looked at Antoine, who was smiling widely. Armand did not stir. He might have been dead, or asleep, sprawled in his chair. Annette's little hands were clenched on her knees. Mrs. Antoine sat gaping near the fire, blinking her eyes, bewildered and confused.

Then Mr. Small's voice rose on a loud arch of accusing sound: "I hear the Voice again (and again I must warn my listeners that all this is just a dream of mine). And the Voice cries out: 'What hast thou done? The voice of thy brother's blood crieth unto Me from the ground.' "

He paused again, with passion, and then resumed: "You will say to me, my listeners, that you are not Cain, that you did not slay Abel in the peaceful garden, that it is not his blood that cries out against you. But I tell you that you are Cain, that you did slay Abel, that it *is* his blood that is crying out against all of America, against all of the world. If we did not actually lift our hands today, in Poland, in Czecho-Slovakia, in Munich and Vienna, we gave our consent to the real murderer. We gave the consent of silence. We knew the garden of death was there. But we were off in the town, celebrating and adoring our pugilists and our crooners, our Hollywood strumpets. If we heard the Voice that cried out from space to us, we merely told the latest band maestro to beat his drum the louder, to call on his trumpeters to shrill more deafeningly. It was none of our business. Cain was not threatening us. There was the river between the garden and the town, and the river kept us safe from him. It was too far for him to swim. Besides, it was just a local quarrel between Cain and his brother, and was no concern of ours. We've always known that the two brothers have fought for years, and it had become very boring.

"We did not hear the Voice when it turned from Cain and cried out to us: 'And now art thou cursed from the earth, which hath opened her mouth to receive thy brother's blood from thy hand.—A fugitive and a vagabond shalt thou be in the earth.'

"And that, my friends, is what America has become today: a fugitive and a vagabond in the earth, hiding and whimpering in theatres and stadiums, while Abel lies dead in the garden. It must be a most horrible sight to God, to see us here. He must be quite sickened. Once, I imagine, He was proud of us. Once, we were valiant and strong and brave, and full of indignation against oppressors and murderers. Now we condone them. Now we finance them. Now we send them weapons to kill more innocents. Now we silence those who would warn us that Cain is at our very door, the Cain we have admired, financed, condoned, for half a dozen years. In future broadcasts, I shall tell the names, outline the machinations, of the men who have done these things, who have conspired against you, who are opening your doors to Cain. They have been very active. They will become more active in the future, lying to you, lulling you, deceiving you, so that you may not rise up and demand arms against your enemies, and revenge for the death of the innocents who were murdered today, and the greater number who will be murdered tomorrow. You see, they believe Cain can be their weapon against a free America. They do not want a free America. They want a nation of slaves. You. And you. And you.

"Will they succeed? Will the sleeping soul of America brighten once more into reality and power and passion? I don't know. Only you can give the answer. I, myself, am very afraid. I am afraid that America has sold her dream for a handful of lollypops.

"There is a couplet of Wordsworth's which I should like to quote to you now:

> " 'Whither is fled the visionary gleam?
> Where is it now, the glory and the dream?' "

He spoke the last slowly, loudly, clearly, and then his voice dropped into profound silence. Christopher turned off the radio, and then stood by it. He and Antoine exchanged a sharp look.

"Melodramatic claptrap," said Antoine. "If that's the best he can do, he'll be no danger."

"I don't know," mused Christopher. "I'm not so sure of that." He came slowly back to the fire. "Remember: melodrama appeals to the mob."

"But not if bayonets are at their backs. They're deaf to any appeal which urges them to fight, or endangers their bellies. They'll listen more readily to a man who urges them to hide in the cellar, and promises them full bellies if they keep their mouths shut."

Now Annette spoke, her light voice quite vibrant and swift, her blue eyes flashing strangely in the firelight. "You have a very low opinion of the American people, haven't you, Antoine?"

"My dear," he replied, easily, "it isn't just an opinion. It's personal knowledge. There are some fools who believe that Americans can still feel the impulse to rise to an ideal, to sacrifice that others may live, and all the other trash. I don't believe it. As our Mr. Small so poignantly pointed out: they prefer Hollywood strumpets, lollypops and prize-fighters. A nation like that has no mind, no spirit, no decency, no pride or intelligence. You see, I'm very frank."

Annette was silent. But her small thin body was taut as bent steel.

"I think Mr. Small is horrid," prattled Mrs. Antoine. "He's just a war-monger, like Mr. Roosevelt. He wants our boys to die on foreign soil. Just for the Jews, or the Czechs, or somebody. Did you hear Captain Jaeckle the other night? He says nobody wants to attack us, and besides, we've got three thousand miles of water between us and Hitler. Somebody ought to put that silly Mr. Small off the radio. He wants to get us into war, and we won't! The mothers won't let the war-mongers take our boys away to die."

Antoine gestured towards his wife, but grinned at Christopher.

"There speaks the voice of the American people," he said, sardonically. "What more do you want?"

No one noticed Armand. His eyes were closed. He appeared to sleep. Even when the visitors got up to go, he still lay immobile in his chair.

Later that week, Christopher was shut up with Henri. He had talked for an hour, while Henri had listened, sometimes jotting down a note or two.

"Yes, I think it's a good idea for you to go with him to that conference," said Henri. "This is very interesting, indeed. He has no suspicions, of course?"

"He hinted I was 'in very deep,'" said Christopher, laughing. "He has a light hand with blackmail, but a candid one. By the way," he added, curiously, "there is something about Small's broadcasts which sound familiar. You wouldn't have any idea who writes his scripts, or who is buying him time on the network?"

Henri regarded him blandly, with a faint smile. "No. Why should I?"

CHAPTER XXXII

Hugo Bouchard, second brother of Peter, and Assistant to the Secretary of State, lived magnificently in Washington with his handsome wife, the former Christine Southward, whose father had been "Billie" Southward, Chairman of the Republican Party in Pennsylvania. Hugo had inherited this lofty position after the death of the rotund and affable Billie, and because of his own personality, which was bluff, amiable, easily moved to laughter, and possessed of those extrovert qualities of fellowship, good humor, open sympathy and expansive reasonableness, had become even twice as popular as his father-in-law, which was quite an accomplishment. A lawyer of considerable parts and acumen, he still received a large salary from Endicott James of New York (publicity agents and attorneys for Bouchard & Sons). His own private fortune, augmented by the million and a half of his wife's, was gigantic, a fact which he, for many reasons, kept modestly to himself. His brother, Jean, had declared that he was a club in brown velvet with a gold handle, a remark that was not without its astuteness. For Hugo Bouchard was large and solid of frame, without flabbiness or bulginess, and had a commanding presence which inspired confidence rather than timidity. He had a big buff-colored face, bright golden eyes full of laughter and friendliness, a blunt and amiable nose, a big gay mouth with excellent flashing teeth. His hair, once buff-colored also, was now a silvery mass of thick shining waves, though he was only in his early fifties. All this, combined with a certain splendor and warmth and solidity, made him the ideal politician, trusted by many, disliked by few, even his enemies, and admired by almost everyone. With all these admirable assets, a certain hearty bluffness and a rollicking affectionate voice, very few discerned that here was a consummate rascal, an avaricious and relentless man, a man without scruple and without conscience. Even his wife hardly knew this, for he was quite moral in sexual matters, and was a devoted father to his three young daughters, Elsie, Alice and Joan. The only one who really understood him, and disliked him without reservations, was his youngest child, his son, Hilary, now almost seventeen years old.

No man really likes to be "understood." Hugo was no exception. He had taken an almost immediate dislike to Hilary, when the child had been hardly a week old. For Hugo was of that thoroughly masculine nature which tends to adore daughters and feel an indifference to sons. He doted on the three girls. Christine doted on Hilary. This annoyed Hugo. Hilary was small and brown and puckered, "like the damned Jules line," Hugo declared, contemptuously. (He did not admire his relative, Antoine, as he decidedly had not admired Jules, his second cousin, and Antoine's grandfather). As Hugo had a hearty admiration for the "Aryan" type of physique, which he fondly believed tended to the tall, the robust, the solid and clumsily masculine, accompanied by fairness and "openness" of countenance, Hilary's elegant smallness, his delicate features and hands, his sharp black eyes, his slight smile, subtle even in early childhood, his wryness and Latin's grace, affronted and repelled him.

Moreover, Hilary displayed an unusual and brilliant intelligence, and an endless zest for knowledge. He also loved all things of beauty, and so worshipped his handsome mother. Christine, a not very bright woman, yet possessed the intuition of love, and so all her presents to her son displayed exquisite taste and thoughtfulness. She filled his room, even in childhood, with objets d'art which she had sedulously fettered out in New York, Paris, Vienna and London. She was speechless with passionate admiration for his wit and grace, and found no music sweeter to listen to than the praise of Hilary by his tutors. At sixteen, he was admitted to Harvard. Hugo, in spite of himself, and in spite of his contempt for learning and all the intellectual arts, was moved temporarily to reluctant pride. Hilary's forte was mathematics, that great and classic art. Hugo wanted the lad to study law, and often jokingly declared that Hilary would soon be invaluable to the Bouchards. He also remarked that while Antoine was an adequate "Understudy" to Jules, it would be Hilary who would inherit the subtle fame of Jules Bouchard.

This remark betrayed Hugo's profound ignorance of his son. For Hilary, though possessing a remarkable resemblance to Antoine, and to Antoine's grandfather, and showing all those apparent traits of character: keenness, wryness, cynicism and wit, which had been the outstanding characteristics of Jules, had a quite different form of spirit, which few ever discerned.

For, amazingly, this young replica of Jules resembled his Uncle Peter in character. He was honorable, brave, steadfast and compassionate, and exquisitely perceptive. But, unlike Peter, who was inclined to be blunt, angry, aggressively honest, and somberly quiet on occasion, Hilary was shrewd, skeptical, cynical and disillusioned, by nature. Moreover, he possessed an enormous and delicate tact, and a highly developed sense of humor, a balance of temperament which was incredible in one so young, and a keen awareness of the necessity of keeping his own counsel practically always. There was little of the dreamer in him, but, oddly, much of the mystic. His conversation was delightful; his air very "soigné," to quote the infatuated Christine. "He looks too much like Goebbels to suit me," was Hugo's disparaging remark. "All the damned Latin Bouchards look like Goebbels." This remark, when quoted to Antoine, and others of the faintly "Jules line," did nothing to endear Hugo to his relatives.

Hilary, very early, took an unremitting dislike to the Family, with few exceptions. He had seen Peter only a few times, and though understanding this particular uncle, and feeling a great and sad compassion for him, he considered him, regretfully, something of a fool. In Hilary's opinion, only fools disarmed themselves, made themselves vulnerable, by reason of their very integrity and honesty. Hilary believed that one's character should be known only to oneself and to God, and, preferably, only to oneself. One should show the world only what one desired the world to see, and as virtue was always suspect, and integrity derided, these traits should be guarded like a golden treasure and unlocked only upon extreme occasions. As a result of this philosophy, very few of the Bouchards knew anything at all about Hilary, and he was unanimously declared to be Jules' complete replica, even more so than Antoine.

Hilary had a deep affection for Annette, a casual fondness for his three sisters, who worshipped him in spite of their beloved father's aversion, a complete indifference for practically every other member of the family, and, very strangely, a mysterious attachment for Henri, whom he called "Uncle Henri," having disdained to disentangle the ramifications of relationship. He was too balanced and too cool to hate very strongly, but he truly hated his father, thought him a bumptious fool, a complete liar, a dangerous scoundrel, and a treacherous dog. As Hilary was too egotistic to conceal this fine opinion of Hugo, and too indifferent to him as a man, Hugo's initial dislike could scarcely be expected to have diminished with the years.

There was another deep and subterranean reason for the hatred between the two. Though Hugo adored all his daughters, who were fair, pretty and vivacious, and very fond of him, his youngest daughter, Alice, was his darling. The two older girls were, like their comely mother, not very "bright," though amiable and charming. But Alice was witty and intelligent, full of laughter and sudden seriousness, and possessing a bright zest for living. She was scarcely more than a year older than Hilary; they had grown up together. Unlike Hilary, she was inclined to be tall. She had his gracefulness, his tact and perceptive keenness, his ingratiating mannerisms, his elegant gestures. Moreover, he very early learned that she had integrity and honor; the two older girls were too complacent, too amiable, too happy, to have any character at all, except delightful selfishness and charm. It was Hilary's pressure on his mother, who in turn pressed determinedly upon Hugo, which resulted in Alice's going to a fine university and studying law, instead of to the fashionable finishing-school which Hugo believed was more in keeping for Bouchard daughters.

Alice was very healthy, but not aggressively so. She did not have that sweaty, wholesome appearance, that repulsive exuberance of animal spirits, which so often distinguishes the robust American female. Like Hilary, she loathed sports. Her skin, all milky whiteness and softness, with an apricot bloom upon her firm young cheeks, needed no artifice. She had her father's golden eyes, and long bronze lashes, and their expression was alive and eager, yet profound. Her mouth, overlarge, was yet sweet, firm and strong, and brightly colored, so that the size was overlooked. Her hair, a lighter gold than her eyes, was heavy and straight, and hung in masses on her wide shoulders. Everything about her expressed exquisite strength and fineness; her figure was excellent. "Grecian classic," Hugo would say, proudly. Moreover, she had taste, and a natural simplicity in dress, which enhanced her beauty.

Hugo, though never a subtle man, and sly, rather than perceptive, yet very early saw that there was some passionate bond between his darling, and his hated son, Hilary. When they had been children, they desired only each other's society. Hugo had attempted to send Hilary away to a military school. "Make a man of the little pipsqueak," he had said. But Christine had violently opposed this. Hugo waited. He waited until Hilary had gone to Harvard. But long letters passed between brother and sister. Alice did not mourn over her brother's absence. But she became more serious. When she went away, herself, to the university, she saw to it that her choice was not far from Harvard. Hugo knew that his son and daughter spent many week-ends together in New York, in a state of complete happiness and gentle rapport. To counteract this, he often visited New York, himself, and met Alice, and took her with him, leaving Hilary alone in wryly smiling silence. Hugo did not even descend to the politeness of asking Hilary to join them.

Hugo, like many men of his temperament, had a certain rugged obscenity of mind, and a crude vulgarity. On the infrequent occasions when he was aroused, he displayed a violent brutality, lasciviousness of tongue, and ugly ruthlessness. He was careful to hide these traits from his peers; his inferiors knew them only too well. He always suspected the worst of everybody. In his private opinion, no woman was virtuous. All women (except his wife and daughters) were trollops, complaisant rumps and filthy of mind and desire. (Of men, he had a slightly higher opinion, though he cast upon them his own reflection.) Sincerely convinced of the vileness of womankind, and the venality of men, he suspected the foulest of implications in an exchange of smiles between the sexes, in the slightest gallantry or the most innocent coquetry. He had a fund of vicious stories. All of them emphasized sexuality in its crudest form, and the worst did more than hint at perversion.

With such a mind, and with his bottomless hatred and aversion for his son, he pretended to be convinced that Hilary's love for Alice was perverted, unclean and dangerous. (Alice, of course, was the pure damsel without the slightest suspicion of the hideous yearnings of her brother.) In the end, Hugo no longer pretended to be convinced. He believed he knew. Now his hatred took on a maniacal quality, born of his jealousy. It never occurred to him that he needed a psychiatrist to probe into the dark pits of his own mind.

Hilary, of course, knew of all this. His disgust had been so intense that he had been physically, as well as mentally, nauseated. He had felt indifference for his father, and disdainful amusement, rather than hatred. But now he hated. He was also extremely alarmed for his beloved sister. But he knew he would never dare to enlighten her. For his own part, he made his letters shorter and more infrequent, when he wrote to Alice. He was often very busy when she suggested meeting him in New York. On his holidays, he forced himself to strike up more intimate relationships with friends. This lad, hardly seventeen, found himself engrossed in a dreadful problem from which he could see no escape, either for himself or his sister, or his father. For he saw that by gently relinquishing Alice's hold upon himself, he was clearing the way for his father's obsession.

Too, he saw that Alice's best hope of escape from an embroilment in an appalling situation was through marriage. Therefore, on every occasion, he asked her if she had become interested in some young man or other. When he did meet her in New York, he often brought mature classmates with him. None interested Alice, until her brother introduced her to a young man named Charles Miles.

Charles, unfortunately, came of an obscure farming family

from upstate New York. In his high-school years, he had displayed such brilliance in scientific research that he had won a scholarship at Harvard. However, he was so badly needed at home that he had been unable to avail himself of this opportunity, and it was not until he was twenty-four years old that he felt himself free enough to take advantage of it. At the time Hilary introduced him to Alice, Charles was twenty-seven years old, unusually mature, thoughtful, grave, clever and intellectual. He was also penniless.

Alice immediately fell in love with him. This dark, lean young man, who, she thought fondly, resembled her dear brother, dazzled her, won her. His gentleness, his humorous thoughtfulness, his kindness and interest, at once inspired her respect and affection. After six meetings, three of them alone after the discreet withdrawal of Hilary, they became engaged.

The uproar that ensued on Massachusetts Avenue could be heard three houses away. It took no great astuteness on the part of Hugo to discern the fine Italian hand of young Hilary. Hugo's hatred became murderous, insane. He threatened Alice for the first time in her life. But the girl, appalled, white of face, stood her ground resolutely. She had been forewarned by her brother. She would marry Charles Miles, she said, no matter what happened. Christine, though not very intelligent, was a shrewd woman. Her vague suspicions became strong in her. She stood by her daughter. If Hugo cut her off, she, Christine, would see to it that the young couple did not starve.

No one had ever opposed Hugo Bouchard before. He was like a wild incensed bull. He raved, shrieked, threatened the most obscure and frightful things. His family, with pale faces, withdrew from him. Christine shuddered over and over in her pleasant apartments. Her two older daughters crept about the magnificent house, hiding from the sight of their father. Alice went to New York to stay with her relative, Mrs. Phyllis Morse, who was fond of her.

Hugo was demoralized and full of terror, as well as full of rage and hatred and jealousy. Now he felt his impotence. He wanted to kill. He stayed away from the State Department, even in these momentous days. He was sick to death, torn with agony, frustrated, anguished and mauled by the most nameless of passions. He had rationalized them, of course. Charles Miles was a servile and contemptible nobody, a beggar, a starvling, a fortune-hunter; a cur and a swine. It was horrible that such as he should dare to lift his eyes to a Bouchard daughter, this penniless scoundrel, this farming lout, this creeping snail. He would not permit Charles to come to the house. He threatened to kill him, to have him thrown out of Harvard, to expose a probable police record. He went so far as to write the president of Harvard, demanding the expulsion of Charles. If this was not done, he threatened, there would be no more Bouchard money pouring into the coffers. He notified the university that Hilary would be immediately withdrawn.

But Christine again stepped in. Hilary would remain. She, Christine, would pay his tuition. Quite quietly, she wrote to the president and in her own turn demanded that Charles be allowed to remain, explaining that "Mr. Bouchard was only temporarily excited and would get over it shortly."

Into this disordered and furious household, Henri appeared one late December day. He had heard rumors of the uproar, but in his characteristic fashion he hardly believed that a sensible man could be truly distraught over any affair which involved a woman. Hugo knew this opinion of his relative's, and composed himself long enough to shut himself up with Henri just two days before Christmas. He had the greatest fear and respect for Henri, and wished nothing more than his good opinion.

CHAPTER XXXIII

Henri did not underestimate his relative, Hugo, nor was he persuaded that that hearty bluff smile, that genial affability, that loud rollicking laugh and goodfellowship, were the attributes of a fool. He knew that Hugo, as a man, a politician, and a Bouchard, was one of the most powerful men in the State Department. Hugo, it was, who had brought the most intransigent into the camp that supported, condoned and apologized for Franco, who had prevented the shipment of food, medical supplies and materials of war to the desperate Loyalist cities. Hugo, it was, who had distorted American public opinion into the belief that the Loyalists were "Reds, dangerous Communists and radicals, priest-murderers and ahteists." Later, after the fall of the Spanish Republic, it had been Hugo's influence which had speeded shipments of oil and scrap, food and munitions, into Franco's enslaved and anguished Spain. If much of all this found its way to Hitler, that was palpably none of Hugo's business, nor the business of the State Department, which had acted in good and virtuous American faith.

It was Hugo, who had a profound regard for conservative British politics, who had induced the State Department to proceed with caution in European affairs, and who had inspired admiration for the Men of Munich. When American public opinion cried out indignantly at the shipments of scrap iron and oil to Japan, it was Hugo who inspired the newspaper releases apologizing for the little yellow men, and hinting that China was hardly the virtuous and noble democracy so sweetly imagined by Americans. Most of the men of the Department were much like Hugo, cautious, expedient, conservative, fascistic in thought if not in intent, career men of family and polish and craftiness and greed. One thing they possessed in common: a profound and aristocratic loathing of the "common people," "the cattle without brains or guts." (Though "guts" were implied rather than said, the gentlemen being so excessively refined.) Hugo was more robust than many of the milky patricians of the State Department, but he was much more dangerous. They at least believed they were protecting their "class." Hugo, and others like him in the Department, cared only for the status quo, their wealth and their power, which they were grimly determined should remain intact. A still closer circle believed that it might be necessary, some near day, to enlist the aid of Hitler in subduing the American masses, which were showing alarming symptoms of beginning to think for themselves.

It was Hugo who helped vigorously in the formation of a policy of distrust and hatred toward "Red Russia," who had been behind the demand that Russia pay for her shipments in gold. Out from the discreet and fastidious purlieus of the State Department came the releases which minimized Russian strength, which "scorned" the pact between Russia and Germany, which hinted at the dire designs of Russia upon the peace and safety of the world. Most of the gentlemen of the Department had the highest regard for Mussolini; two had medals bestowed upon them by that very clever mountebank. When General "Billy" Mitchell had warned the American people of the necessity of a powerful air-arm, it was the State Department, led by Hugo, who had besmirched and destroyed and broken the heart of that valiant and tragic soldier. The milky patricians fearfully believed that for America to be safe it was necessary only that she remain unarmed and refrain from provoking hostile gestures from Hitler and Mussolini. But there was an inner circle, composed of Hugo and the more ruthless and savage realists, who wished America to remain unarmed for their own monstrous reasons.

And it was the State Department who catered timorously and with maudlin respect to a certain religious organization which was the most terrible enemy of democracy and liberalism in all the world, stronger and more terrible than Hitler, himself. Because of this organization, the State Department was adamant in its pressure on the Government to refuse visas and passports to a tortured and dying German Jewry. The gentlemen of the Department, who had a dainty dislike of all those who were not Harvard graduates and who could not boast an early-American ancestry (even though that ancestry might have been composed of London whores and jail-birds swept up from the gutters of English cities for transportation to America), had a terrified aversion to people who could not speak English without an accent, or whose features were not correctly in line with the prevailing type of features extant in the State Department.

It was Hugo, in short, who was most powerfully behind the timorous, class-conscious, fascistic, crafty, liberal-hating, Red-baiting and witch-hunting elements of the Department. Never were they vulgar, even in their contempt and hatred and suspicion of Mr. Roosevelt. Everything that was released by the Department was shining with gentlemanly restraint and polished phrases and bloodless elegance. The more earthy statements of Hugo were cleaned and deodorized before being made public. But the conspiracy was there, nevertheless.

The State Department, on occasion, protested in plaintive tones to France, to Russia, to China. But never, never, did it protest to England, to Italy or to Mussolini. On occasion it reproved some more honest and valiant English statesman on his indignant remarks anent the feebleness of America's timidly annoyed sentiments towards Hitler. These statesmen, who were young, honorable and realistic, were anathema to the royal circle within the State Department, and were disdainfully stigmatized as "war-mongers, who are desirous of embroiling America in European conflicts." The royal circle could not, in truth, scorn these Englishmen as not being "pukka sahibs," for the majority of them were scions of old and noble British families. But they inferred, with regret, that they were not upholding their "class," the arch-crime of all.

Henri Bouchard knew that Hugo's clique formed only one segment of the State Department, and that it was ruthless, vulgar, expedient and coarse. Nevertheless, it influenced very perilously the other cliques, and, in their combined power, they could override the very Secretary himself. The Secretary could do nothing against the libel that Mr. Roosevelt was dominated by the "Jews" (instead of by the State Department, which was proper), or that the New Deal was composed of brigands, starry-eyed theorists, "bright young men from New York, of dubious ancestry," and Communists. The Secretary apparently thought all this very querulous and funny. He, too, was a gentleman, and he was convinced that gentlemen were not very effective.

In the meantime, during these early days of war, the State Department was in quite an aristocratic dither. Its natural bent for England, and reverence for English politics (and the late English policy of appeasing Hitler and supporting him) caused it to feel a very natural sympathy and concern for Britain. Nevertheless, the old habit of appeasing, placating, apologizing for and supporting Hitler, was still very strong. On this seesaw, therefore, they were quite understandably sick at the stomach, bouncing affrightedly in the air, coming to earth with strong bumps, and thus disorganizing their delicate nervous systems.

However, Hugo and his very earthy and realistic clique had no sympathy at all for Britain or for France, a fact they carefully concealed from their pallid and exquisite colleagues. They had their own designs, their own plans.

And these designs, these plans, were very well known to Henri Bouchard.

Henri, who had discounted many of the rumors reaching him of the frantic fury in the Hugo Bouchard household, nevertheless was now impatiently aware that many of the rumors must be true. Hugo was as genial as ever in his greetings to his kinsman. His laugh was still rollicking. But Henri saw that the buff-colored ruddiness of Hugo's face was somewhat less than usual, that his laugh was forced, that his handshake was damp and alarmingly tremulous, that his yellow eyes were sunken and feverish. His big body, too, was less rounded and firm, under the expensive tweeds. There was a haggard look about him, a distraught nervousness, even while he grinned and smoked, and delivered himself of a few of his choicest jokes. He had always been a prodigious drinker, but now he swallowed glass after glass in a kind of frenzy.

One of Henri's attributes was the ability to take cognizance of prevailing conditions and study how to take advantage of them. He could do this on an instant's notice. Even while he talked amiably with Hugo, his mind was busily at work, plotting, conjecturing, feinting. He encouraged Hugo to drink, but kindly refused to have his own glass refilled more than once.

Hugo burst into a loud rough laugh. "Always keep your feet on the ground, eh, Henri?" he shouted. "Always the Iron Man! You're a cute devil, but I know all about you. You never fooled me."

Henri smiled easily, and said: "I never cared whether I fooled anyone or not. Besides, you know very well I don't drink much. Weren't you the one who said my whiskey was swill, last Christmas?"

Hugo laughed even more loudly. He reached out and slapped Henri's thigh with affection and cunning. He's drunk, thought Henri, but more drunk with his damned emotions than with whiskey. Now Hugo lifted one index finger and wagged it archly.

"What're you up to, eh? You didn't come down to Washington and leave a certain— Well," he added, with a broad wink, "we won't mention that, so stop scowling, you sly rascal. I mean to say, this isn't a casual visit, is it? You're after something, as usual. What is it? Aren't the boys satisfying you, lately?"

Henri smiled again, comfortably. He watched Hugo closely. Hugo, in spite of his noise and his riot, had the air of a man who listens for something at a distance. Sometimes he started nervously, cast a quick look at the massive wooden door of the library.

Henri felt his way, his pale motionless eyes fixed on Hugo's twitching face: "I do have a commission. From Annette. We'd like to have you and your family down for New Year's. You know, you refused the invitation for Christmas, on the ground that you had a previous commitment. Now Annette won't be satisfied until you come down to Windsor."

Hugo opened his big loose mouth to speak, then closed it grimly. His body appeared to tighten under his clothing. His large coarse hand tapped on the long oaken table beside him, increased in momentum while he stared at Henri. But he said, quietly enough: "I'll speak to Christine. How long are you staying with us? Until tomorrow? She'll let you know. But you know, of course, that Alice won't be with us?"

Henri raised his eyebrows. "No, I didn't know. How should I? Where is the girl? She's somewhat of a pet with me, you know."

Hugo made an uncouth sound. "Come off! come off! You aren't immured down there in Windsor. You must have heard something."

"I'm not interested in family private matters," said Henri, with impatience. "They're none of my affair. I expect the same respect for my affairs as I accord to others."

Hugo paused. He scrutinized Henri with suspicion. "Well," he said roughly, "Alice won't be with us. She's staying with that damned Phyllis Morse in New York for the holidays. Prefers it, it seems. Children are the god-damnedest waste of time. You ought to be thankful you haven't any. Well. Perhaps we'll come, Christine, Elsie and Joan, and—'' Suddenly he stopped. His face became evil with its coarse wrinkling and twisting, full of hatred and fury.

So, thought Henri, his mind swiftly working. He lifted his glass and pretended to drink. He said, elaborately unaware of his kinsman's expression: "And Hilary, of course." He put down the glass. "I've often thought how closely he resembles Armand's Antoine. Haven't you seen the resemblance, yourself?"

Hugo uttered an involuntary oath. His tapping fingers clenched; he lifted his fist and beat it heavily once or twice on the table. Henri knew very well with what aversion, dislike and contempt Hugo regarded Antoine, and how often he had smarted under that gay young man's dexterous thrusts and light ridicule. He hoped, devoutly, that his manœuvre had been a clever one, and had not merely served to enrage Hugo against himself.

When Hugo spoke again, in an incoherent and thickened voice, Henri knew that the manœuvre had been very clever indeed. "Yes, damn it, I've seen the resemblance! It goes deeper than that. He's like that swine in character too. Smirking, lying, twisting, bowing, scheming. A fine son for Hugo Bouchard! A stinking pig. The only son I have, and he has to—he has to—'' His voice was suddenly choked off, and a purple tide ran under his ruddiness. His eyeballs glared in the lamplight.

"Oh, come now, Hilary's only a boy," said Henri, watching him acutely. "It's true he resembles Antoine remarkably. But Antoine's no fool, you know. He's a damned brilliant plotter. Just now," he added, after a pause, "he's doing some very devious plotting indeed."

Hugo's expression changed. It became coarsely sullen and uneasy. He lifted his big hand and plucked at his lip. He stared at Henri, and his opaque yellow eye narrowed. "I don't know about that," he mumbled, uneasily. Now he passed his hand over his thick waves of white hair.

So, thought Henri, it's as I suspected. And knew.

Henri had an aversion to intimate gestures of any kind, and never indulged in them with others. Yet now he forced himself to lean towards Hugo and pat him on the arm. "Hugo, you and I have always been friends. Once we acquitted ourselves with glory. Remember? Against the Armand faction; in other words, against the Jules Bouchard faction. I haven't forgotten your help. I couldn't have accomplished anything without it. You've served me; I've served you. That's a big bond between men like ourselves. Especially when we serve ourselves while serving our friends."

Hugo, though resisting uneasily for a few minutes, could not withstand this not-so-subtle flattery. His fear of Henri, and his respect, had grown with the years. He smiled tentatively. His fist relaxed on the table.

"I've never underestimated you, Henri, my lad. I knew whom I was helping. I've done as you suggested, while in the Department, and before. You can always rely upon me."

Henri leaned back in his chair, and allowed his large stony face to darken. "I believe I can, Hugo. But, it's very serious this time. I've said Antoine has been plotting. Dangerous plotting. I'm not sure what it is, exactly. But I need your help."

So great, now, were Hugo's alarm, perturbation and suspicions, that he momentarily forgot his private tragedies. He began to sweat. He pulled out his handkerchief and passed it over his high broad forehead, the statesman's forehead.

"What is this damned 'plotting'? I don't believe it. What would he plot? I haven't heard anything."

"I haven't heard much, Hugo, I confess. But I am psychic, perhaps," and Henri smiled pleasantly. "I feel things. I feel something in the wind. Perhaps you can tell me."

But Hugo shrugged with gathering sullenness, and looked at a point a little beyond Henri's eyes. "Imagination," he muttered at last. "What would that smirking idiot plot?"

"Don't underestimate Antoine," warned Henri. "He's clever. Like your son, Hilary."

At this, Hugo started with quite extraordinary violence. His eyes, turned upon Henri, became full of a yellow glare. He clenched his teeth; his big coarse nostrils distended like the nostrils of an ox.

Now Henri had quite a regard for Hilary, but he knew this was not the moment for softness. He added: "You've underestimated Hilary in the past. I've always known that. And I've always known he resembles Antoine more than just physically.

"I flatter myself I understand men. That's my business. I understand Antoine. I don't know what he's up to, but I have the vaguest of ideas. You see, I'm being very confidential with you, Hugo. I know I can trust you."

Hugo's fists doubled on the arms of his red leather chair. He breathed audibly. The yellow glare increased in his eyes. Henri watched his agonized uncertainty with unswerving closeness.

"What do you want?" asked Hugo, in a stifled voice. "You always want something. You don't fool me," he repeated.

"Yes," said Henri, quietly. "I do want something. I want your help. I want you to use your influence to stop shipments of scrap and oil to Japan. Immediately."

Hugo started, again. His teeth glistened between his lips. But his voice was curiously quiet and still when he said: "No."

The two men regarded each other in a profound silence. Henri seemed unperturbed. He did not stir a muscle. His expression was placid and controlled. Hugo was like a huge bull at bay, ready for the assaulting plunge towards his enemy. He waited for Henri to speak again, but Henri was silent. Then Hugo said: "Why?"

"Because," said Henri, tranquilly, "I don't want Japan to be made stronger. I think her ultimate victim is America. I have a regard for America, if only as a field for profitable business."

Now Hugo grinned, very unpleasantly. "Claptrap. Why should Japan attack us? She's got China on her hands. China will take her a generation to digest. If ever. What does it matter to you?"

"I don't share your optimism, Hugo. I think we are next on the agenda. Japan will turn westward. She doesn't like us, you know. Besides, there are her commitments with Hitler. It's very involved, I admit. But, as things go along, Hitler will become very annoyed with us. He might induce Japan to attack."

"She won't attack!" exclaimed Hugo, with unwarranted violence. He turned in his chair, fiddled with objects on the table, then swung around roughly to Henri. "That's pure rot. Besides, she'll have no reason. We aren't going to help Britain. That's certain. I can assure you of that."

"And I," said Henri, quietly, "can assure you we will. We have cash-and-carry now. We'll have something more important, soon. How do I know? I can't tell you that. But I assure you I shall use all my influence."

"You!" ejaculated Hugo. He burst into a raucous laugh. "Since when have the Bouchards been so damned patriotic? Since when have they come out on the side of 'freedom, God, and the right'!"

He waited again for Henri to speak, but Henri did not oblige him. Then Hugo lost control of himself. He began to shout. "Let me tell you something! We don't want England to win, in Europe! You know that! My boys don't want it; even England doesn't want it! She wants a negotiated peace, and quick, too. Why should she destroy Hitler, and open herself to bolshevism from Russia? She needs a strong Germany in Europe to protect her. As always. That's always been her game. We know it in the Department. We've always known it. Just as we know that France will collapse in the spring. It's all arranged. Yet here you come, breathing sweetness and light and 'in God we trust,' and want us to throw all our plans overboard. No, my boy, it won't do, it really won't do."

Now Henri spoke, in a sharp penetrating voice: "And now, I'll tell you something. What you say about England is true, in a measure. But only in a measure. You speak for the so-called ruling class in England. But let me tell you this: Chamberlain will soon be out. Eden or Winston Churchill will take his place. The 'ruling class' will have diarrhoea very shortly, out of sheer funk and terror. Because the British people are now aroused. I'm not just prophesying when I say that England won't sign a negotiated peace with Hitler. She'll fight to the bitter end. It's sink or swim, now. It's Hitler, or us. Do you want Hitler in America?"

Hugo stared at him, and slowly paled. He said nothing. Henri nodded grimly.

"I've a suspicion, I really have. I really think you've been duped by Antoine. You're a clever fellow, Hugo, but not as clever as Antoine. He hasn't told you all of his plans, has he? Perhaps you think he is a very amiable chap, Hugo. Perhaps you think he is 'all for one, and one for all.' I have another suspicion: I believe that Monsieur Antoine is working only for himself. He hasn't a very high regard for you, Hugo, nor does he think much of your intelligence."

Hugo still was speechless. "I believe," Henri went on, grimly, "that Antoine has convinced you that England will cave in, sign a negotiated peace with Hitler, and that Hitler will then dominate Europe and do excellent business with us. Am I right?"

But Hugo was silent. He stared at Henri with bulging eyes.

"I give you the credit of not having been completely duped by our fine manipulator, who has been using you for his own ends, Hugo. I give you the credit of keeping your own counsel. Now, am I right or wrong?"

He knew his approach and attack had been crude, calculated to have effect only on the most brutal and exigent form of mind. His contempt for Hugo grew as he saw the wild and violent uncertainty, the stung egotism, in those fixed yellow eyes.

He spoke very, very quietly now: "Hugo, how much do you trust Ignatius O'Connor, and Francis O'Malley, in the Department?"

For a moment Henri thought that Hugo had not heard him, so unchanging was his expression. And then Hugo said, coming to himself, and speaking gruffly: "Why? What have you got against Iggy and Frank?" But a wily tight look appeared about his big loose mouth.

Henri smiled. "A nice trick, answering a question with a question. But I know all about that trick; I use it myself." He made his face change to one of gloomy gravity, and lifted his hand for a moment, dropping it thereafter with a gesture of resignation. "All right, then. I see we're getting nowhere. I must admit I'm disappointed. You and I have always been friends; better, we've worked together. I came to talk to you in confidence—but I see it's no use at all."

He took out his cigarette case, extracted a cigarette, lit it with calm thoughtfulness, as though his mind had become occupied with another matter. Hugo watched him, truculently, one clenched fist on his desk. He sat on the edge of his chair, his big thighs spraddled; he resembled a tawny and overfed and dangerous lion, treacherous though aging.

Then he said, belligerently: "We aren't getting into this thing, I tell you! The people don't want it. Sentiment's against us tangling ourselves up in Europe again, Roosevelt or no Roosevelt. No politician in America is strong enough to drum up a valid reason for attacking Hitler. Besides, Hitler's too popular here, due to his persecution of the Jews. Do you think you can get the American mob to fight for 'liberty'?"

His look now was one of grinning loathing. "What does the mob want with liberty, anyway? I tell you, if Hitler appeared off the coast of New York, the gutter rats would be meeting him with flowers and paeans. They love him, I tell you. Liberty's never sat very well on the American stomach—the people have too long a memory of happy and irresponsible slavery."

Henri allowed himself to smile. "You're quite the psychologist, aren't you, Hugo? You know, in a way I am forced to agree with you. I don't give a damn for the mob. But I do give a damn for myself, for Bouchard, for all our subsidiaries. Do you trust Hitler?" Hugo's expression changed, became more sullen, but he said nothing. However, his eyes narrowed to pinpoints of baleful yellow light.

"Frankly, I don't trust him," continued Henri, ruefully. "I'm candid enough to admit that if I thought we could, I might consider—certain things. But I know we can't trust him. I don't want him here, the loving and adoring American mob to the contrary. We're powerful in America—we Bouchards. I'd like to keep that power. You know enough about what he's done to the industrialists in Germany to get some idea what he'd do here.

"I'm not interested in England, or France. Let Hitler take the British Empire apart, and the hell with it. Who cares? But I don't want him here. And he'll be here, inevitably, unless we stop him. How? That's why I came to see you, to discover if we could work out some program."

Hugo began to rub his chin, but he still regarded Henri watchfully.

"What did you mean, asking me if I trusted O'Connor and O'Malley?" he demanded, sullenly.

Henri hesitated. "Well, frankly, it's just what I've been reading in the newspapers. Weren't they back of sending Myron Taylor to the Vatican? Aren't they back of trying to discredit the so-called 'liberals' in the Department, who've taken a stand against Franco, and who've been agitating to keep shipments of scrap and oil from going to Japan?"

Hugo laughed roughly. "So what? We aren't in a position to annoy Hitler and Japan. We've no army, no arms—nothing. Call it appeasement if you like, or diplomacy. I presume you mean the inner campaign against Sumner Welles, who's always liked Russia? You can't blame Iggy and Frank; they're Catholics, you know."

"Since when," said Henri, meditatively, "have we predicated our foreign policy on Catholic sensibilities? Do you remember your history, Hugo? Very interesting reading."

Hugo struck his meaty fist savagely on the table. "We're getting nowhere!" he shouted. "What are you getting at, anyway? Trying subtlety for a change, eh?"

Henri made his face suddenly hard. He leaned towards Hugo. "All right, then. I've told you I care nothing about what happens in Europe. But I do care what happens here. I happen to like my position. I've decided to do anything to maintain it. I'm willing to risk anything." He paused a moment, then continued: "I have no real basis for my suspicions, I admit. But I know a few things. I know that our dear Antoine lately met the German Chargé d'Affaires, and O'Connor and O'Malley were with him. I wonder what they discussed?"

It was a bold stroke. He watched Hugo narrowly. He had spoken in order to discover whether Hugo had known of this meeting, though he had not been present. And then he felt a sudden weakness of relief in himself. Hugo's blank expression of shock, his falling mouth, the sudden glare in his eyes, convinced Henri that Christopher had been correct in his surmise that Hugo had not known of the meeting.

Why had he not known? Christopher had been doubtful on the point, thought he had his ideas. O'Connor and O'Malley, he believed, were playing their own game, with their own Catholic clique. Hugo, in spite of his leadership, his plottings and conspiracies, his cooperation, was not really one with this clique within a clique. He had not been fully trusted; he was a Bouchard, and wealth, at the last, is almost always conservative and fearful, delicately taking alarm when danger breathes too closely.

"I don't believe it!" stammered Hugo, his face swelling and suffusing. "They wouldn't dare! Why should they do that, without telling me, without my knowing and—" He stopped, abruptly. Without your being present, finished Henri, to himself.

Henri shrugged. "I don't care whether you believe it or not, my dear Hugo. It happens to be a fact. May I warn you? If you speak of it, they'll deny it; they'll know there has been a leak. They won't like you, Hugo. They'll believe you have been spying on them. I have an idea they don't trust you completely. They'll trust you less, if you tell them. And, you'll be outside the pale, then, and Antoine, and the others, will rule the Department, sub rosa. Do you like the thought of being glorified office boy to Antoine's fine Italian presence in the background?"

Now all Hugo's hatred for his kinsman, Antoine, all his subconscious loathing of him, both for himself and for Hilary's resemblance to him, all his natural suspicion and jealousy and love of power, roared to his head. He was literally speechless, as he sat opposite Henri, swelling with insane fury and rage. But his mind worked rapidly. He remembered many things which had puzzled him, which had eluded him, lately, in the State Department, but he had been so engrossed with his private upheavals in this house that he had thought of them only vaguely, though his instinct had been aroused. It was the memory of these intangible things which convinced him that Henri was telling the truth.

"So," he muttered, through clenched teeth, "they're playing their own little game, are they?"

"Against us," said Henri, gently. "Do you think they love the Bouchards? Do you think Antoine loves us? I can tell you this: when Armand dies, Antoine won't be so very pertinent in Bouchard affairs. I happen to know it. Perhaps he suspects. In revenge, and in his own desire for power, he'll do anything, against us, against our interests."

He looked at his cigarette, and said: "I don't know why I'm telling you this. You could do me harm by repeating it. But, as I said, we've always been friends, working together. I thought you might work with us now."

"Who do you mean by 'us'?" demanded Hugo. He was breathing with obvious difficulty.

Henri eyed him blandly. "I suppose there's no harm in telling you. Antoine must have been suspecting, and so he probably told you. Alex, Jean, and Emile—perhaps. And—some others, not connected, except remotely, with the Family."

Hugo turned aside his head and stared at a photograph of his beloved daughter, Alice, which stood on the desk. Henri could see his profile, vicious and hugely violent. "How about Christopher?" Hugo said, at last, in a mumbling tone.

Henri waved his hand. "Well, perhaps Christopher's working with Antoine, too. I don't know that, however. I've just my suspicions."

Hugo swung back to him with violent swiftness. "All right," he grunted. "What do you want?"

Henri felt a vast relaxing in himself, an almost weakness of relief. He looked at his kinsman, felt his fury, his jealousy, his savage suspicion and hatred for those who had betrayed him, for those he now believed had been using him. When

Hugo thought of Antoine doing this to him, his gorge rose to maddening heights.

Henri said, feeling his way cautiously: "Let me go into this further for a moment: I've just come on a piece of information. Some of our—less patriotic citizen-financiers have just met Dr. Schacht in Switzerland. You didn't know that? Well, among the arrangements made, the Bouchards were not included. Why? Have you any idea?"

Hugo appeared even more stunned than ever, if possible.

Henri continued: "I thought you didn't know. But Antoine did. I believe he arranged it. You see, he doesn't like us at all. Incidentally, while perhaps you have misguidedly believed that the conquest of the world by Hitler might have nothing but beneficial results for the Family, Hitler doesn't intend that in the least. You see, I happen to have a little inside information. Hitler's far more fond of South America, with its Catholic-Falangist upper-class, than he is of America, where so many of us are of Anglo-Saxon origin. He doesn't believe you can trust the Anglo-Saxon. Then, Franco is one of his trained seals, and Franco has already sent one hundred well-trained Falangist priests to South America to pave the way for an ultimate conquest of that continent by the fascist forces. The South American industrialists, who have complete control of labor, with the assistance of the Church, will make admirable servants of Hitler, and he knows that. There is much propaganda already started there, that South America's destiny is one with the destiny of Spain, her 'mother.' What will be the inevitable result, if—certain—contingencies arise which make Hitler dominant in America? I will paraphrase the old saying 'Westward the course of Empire!' I will say: 'Southward the course of Empire.' With everything that that means. What will become of us, then?"

Hugo gnawed his lip in acute silence, staring fixedly at his kinsman. His brow had a series of deep leonine wrinkles. It was evident he was thinking swiftly.

"I think Antoine knows this," said Henri, softly. "He is already heavily invested in South America, and deeply interested in the Nazi cartels there."

Hugo struck the desk again and again in fulminating silence.

"He is playing, even now, on the strength of his 'Latin' blood," added Henri, with an amused smile.

He waited for Hugo to speak, but Hugo maintained his silence. Henri shrugged imperceptibly.

"I'm well informed, Hugo. You know, I never go off the

deep end. For instance, do you know there is a plan afoot to produce the name of a certain fascistic newspaper owner from New York State at the coming Republican convention? I don't like that man. I prefer another. One Regan suggested. I also suggest that you run for Vice-President. That can be arranged."

Hugo started. He swung fully upon Henri. Now his eyes were glittering. But he said again: "Who is the man?"

"Wendell Willkie, of Commonwealth & Southern."

Hugo shouted with sudden turbulent laughter. "Willkie! Who ever heard of Willkie, except on the Street? Who are you going to get to vote for him? And, why Willkie?"

"For the peculiar reason," said Henri, with a smile, "that he is an honest man, an American, sound, wholesome and intelligent. I've investigated him closely; there's nothing dirty in his career. He's a better man than the wily Roosevelt, who turns like a weathercock in every wind. His policies, I believe, will be conservative, realistic, and honorable. I've found nothing in him which leads me to believe he will betray America, and everything indicates that he will fight for America, if elected. There is nothing elusive or unpredictable about him. If America is to survive, she needs him, not only during war years, but later. I shall put up your name for his Vice-President."

He spoke with power and authority, and Hugo's tendency to ridicule subsided. "Who's behind Willkie?"

Henri smiled again, very wryly. "An old man heavy with his sins, perhaps. Who wants to save America from the ruin he formerly plotted. A very, very powerful man."

He coughed, then resumed in a sprightlier tone: "Just to change the subject momentarily: isn't Christine's fortune heavily invested in the United States Chemical Products Company?"

Hugo blinked his eyes at this abrupt change in pace. "Well?" he said.

"Nothing very important. But I understand the American Carbide Company has some thought of buying up that company. They intend to do that to remove a competitor. All this is confidential, though."

Hugo turned quite pale. "You are certain of this?" he muttered, in a strained tone.

"Quite certain. I thought you might be interested. Now, it's never been my policy to interfere with other companies; enough to do at home. But I can tell you this: American Carbide has asked me to help finance the sale. They offer me a very attractive block of stock in return."

Now the eyes of the two men locked like grim antagonists. Hugo was breathing stridently. All his ruddy color had faded; it was replaced by a mauve and apoplectic tint. His clenched fists fell open on the desk, and he seemed to dwindle. And before his eyes Henri seemed to expand, to become more terrible and ruthless.

"You wouldn't do that—to us?" he whispered hoarsely.

"Did I say I even considered it?" asked Henri, mildly. "Even though I'm interested in American Carbide, myself, not only for financial reasons. Their president happens to be a close friend of mine."

Hugo got suddenly to his feet. He towered over Henri. His breathing became more difficult, and his eyes were violent.

"What do you want?" he asked.

Henri studied him for a long and penetrating moment.

"I want—several things. I want the shipments to Japan to stop. I want a curtailment, or even a stoppage, of the huge shipments of oil, steel and food to Franco. I want supervision in Spain, for the distribution of these things, if smaller shipments are sent, by trusted Americans, who don't like Franco. Just to see that none of the shipments go to Hitler. I want your clique to align yourselves conservatively with the liberals in the Department. Sumner Wells is very popular in South America; I want a sort of 'good friend' policy to be initiated in the South American countries. For many valid reasons, South Americans don't like their big northern neighbor. They must be made to trust us, and it can be done, if they see we are sincere. They must join with us in a continental bloc against Hitler, no matter what happens in Europe. A little later, I want investigation of those American companies who have cartel arrangements with Hitler, and who are furnishing Hitler with matériel. I want the investigation to be given wide publicity in the newspapers. I want a more friendly attitude towards Russia——"

Hugo drew a deep breath, and grinned, though he remained definitely lavender in tint. "Ever hear of the German-Russian pact, my fine Machiavelli?"

Henri snapped his fingers. "I'd like to prophesy that Hitler will soon attack Russia. In the meantime, lay the groundwork in the Department. You'll have to withdraw from the more dangerous elements in your clique, and bring the uncertain ones with you, by hook or crook. I also want a deeply sympathetic attitude towards China."

Hugo walked back and forth over the thick rug of the

library. "And that's all you want, eh?" he said, viciously. "Just a few trifling little things."

He swung back on Henri. "What about the European cartels in which you are personally interested?"

"I'm blocking them from Hitler." Henri added: "If you, and some of your clique who trust you, throw in your weight with the liberals in the Department, we can do all these things."

He stood up now and faced Hugo, all his casualness gone. His large pale face was grim and more terrible than ever, and inexorable. His pale and stony eye held Hugo in sudden fearful fascination. "I tell you, Hugo, I'm serious in all this. If you can't—do—this, then I'll move. And things will start moving, also. You won't enjoy what will happen, personally. I'd be sorry for that, but there are bigger stakes in this than your own welfare, even though we've always been friends. You see, I know a great many things which you don't suspect I know."

"Are you blackmailing me?" asked Hugo, incredulously, but with terror.

"I'm advising you," said Henri, quietly.

Hugo, after a moment, pressed his hands over his eyes. "Let me think," he said, almost inaudibly.

Henri waited. He said, after a moment: "The Department has always admired England. But lately, the admiration has cooled. I want it revived."

Hugo dropped his hands. He looked old and haggard.

"You've got me," he said, with exhaustion. "You ought to have come to me before."

Henri smiled grimly. "I wanted to make sure—about certain things. And now you've got to move fast, Hugo. Very fast indeed."

Hugo was silent.

"Move cautiously," said Henri. "Don't do anything too sudden. Talk it over with those members of your clique whom you can trust. And—you might keep me informed. You might let me know your own—opinions."

"You are asking me to spy on my friends?"

Henri laughed derisively. "Bah. Don't be a fool. What man has 'friends'? You've changed your mind about many of the objectives of your clique. Every man is entitled to change his mind. But don't let your change become suspiciously abrupt. You see, I need to know a few more things before you abandon your intimates."

"My God," muttered Hugo.

Henri put his hand genially on the other's trembling arm. "You have much to gain, and nothing to lose. A little later, I'll inform the American Carbide I'm not interested in their proposition. Incidentally, I have a few tips for you, direct from the Street, and a little later I'll discuss them with you. By the way, you haven't said how you'd like to be Vice-President. Or, perhaps, something even more important can be arranged."

Hugo drew a deep and strangled breath. He said, weakly: "What do we do now? Sing the Star-Spangled Banner?"

CHAPTER XXXIV

Peter Bouchard sat with Mr. Cornell T. Hawkins in the warm and comforting seclusion of the Ritz dining-room. The last of the manuscript of The Fateful Lightning lay on the white table between them. Mr. Hawkins thoughtfully sipped his cocktail and stared at the pages. Then he looked up and politely scrutinized Peter's haggard face with its blue tint and white lips. He saw the ringed and sunken eyes, the feverish pulsing of the thin nostrils. Something of what he was thinking, in his cool compassion, must have communicated itself to Peter, for he said, with a wry smile: "I'm glad it's done, Cornell. I've a feeling I won't see its publication. I've just been to my doctor this morning, before I saw you."

Mr. Hawkins said nothing; his silence implied a concerned questioning. But Peter, with a restless movement of his head, dismissed the subject.

"I'm working on other things, now, which will occupy all my attention. This book—you have no idea when it will be published?"

Mr. Hawkins shook his head. "In about six weeks, perhaps, you'll get the galleys for any corrections or deletions or additions. Then, later, the page proof. After that, we usually allow some time for the critics to read the book. Then, publication. It all depends on our list at the time. We want to make this a big thing. We'll do our best, but there is no predicting what the public's reaction will be. We base our advertising on prepublication sales to the various distributing agencies. That's all I can tell you, Peter."

"I'll be willing to pay for lavish advertising," said Peter, eagerly. Then he flushed, for Mr. Hawkins' frosty blue eyes were twinkling. "Please, don't misunderstand me. I'm not trying to log-roll. But, you see, it is so very important to me, that the public read this book widely. I've even thought of free distribution."

Mr. Hawkins' eyes continued to twinkle, though he did not speak. He turned his glass about in his fingers. Mr. Hawkins had a deep and reserved cynicism, which he could not always control, and like all men with this particular brand of cynicism, he had a kind and sensitive perception of others, and a treacherous compassion which frequently made him uneasy and distrustful of himself. He looked steadfastly at Peter's febrile expression and dying face, and that compassion made his heart contract very painfully.

Now Peter, with a look that begged forgiveness in advance, spoke hesitatingly: "My first book, *The Terrible Swift Sword,* was mysteriously squelched right at the height of its popularity. I've told you that before." He paused. "They—might try to intimidate you——"

Now Mr. Hawkins' own expression changed, became cold and tight. He said, with hard and quiet reserve: "No one has ever intimidated me yet." He added, curiously: "What you told me about Mr. Henri Bouchard is very interesting. He was very frank with you. He knows about this book, of course?"

"Yes." Peter became uneasily reserved, himself. "In fact, he gave me material for it that I wouldn't have known, otherwise. He's very hard to understand. I don't trust him, even now. He wouldn't be doing all this, and arranging for the radio programs, if he wasn't very vitally concerned, himself, and if he didn't have a stake of his own. He believes, very firmly now, that the continued advance of capitalistic-industrial democracy is the only climate in which all the people can be safe—and America can be safe. I believed that once, myself. Now I know that we must go still further—we must have a kind of socialism in America, in which competition is eliminated, and every man serves his neighbor rather than himself."

Mr. Hawkins was very surprised. He stared at Peter with astounded disbelief. "But, you would first have to change human nature. And thus far, in human history, I haven't discovered any sign of that change. It seems to me that we must predicate all social advances on the fixed facts of human personality. You can't go against the grain, you know, even if your ideas are sublime and beautiful. Unless," and the frozen light-blue of his eyes was wintry, "you can use force."

"We've used force to do evil things. Why can't we use force to accomplish good things?" demanded Peter.

Mr. Hawkins paused, and there was a curious expression about his mouth. "It seems to me I've heard that before, somewhere. Didn't Hitler say that?"

Peter flushed darkly. "I'm afraid that you don't understand, Cornell."

But Mr. Hawkins merely lifted his glass and drank appreciatively. It was the most damnable thing, but there really was little difference between good zealots and evil zealots, he reflected. They were equally dangerous to human welfare. Both were inimical to the slow and torturous advance of human society through free will and gradual liberty. They left no margin for choice.

"I've always hated coercion, of any kind," said Mr. Hawkins, meditatively. "Whether that coercion was for good or for evil. Even 'good' coercion is an insult to human dignity. That's why I've never approved of Mr. Roosevelt's methods."

Peter's face had become stiff with irritation. But Mr. Hawkins was tactful. He changed the subject. There was no use arguing with a fanatic, even if that fanatic was a virtuous man. Mr. Hawkins was becoming even more distrustful of virtuous men than of amoral ones. He regretted this, for it increased his cynicism. He was fast coming to the point where he would affirm nothing and believe nothing. He realized, that if such an attitude brought eventual peace, it would also bring inertia, a spiritual stupefaction. It was necessary to life to believe in something.

He said: "When do you believe there will be real activity in Europe? So far, the Germans and the French just stare at each other over the Maginot Line."

Now a dark tint, as of imminent dissolution, spread over Peter's features. His hands began to move aimlessly and weakly among the silverware. He was like a man who cannot rid himself of an eternal nightmare. "I don't know," he muttered. "Who knows?" Suddenly, he lost control of himself and put his hands momentarily against his eyes, pressing them in deeply. "I can't stand it," he said, inaudibly. "There is something terrible——"

He dropped his hands, and said: "I have a friend in France.

He's in Paris, now. Baron Israel Opperheim. I was able to help his son out of Germany. I've tried to get Israel to leave. In his letter to me, he hinted he was almost persuaded. But one never knows about Israel. He is a cynic."

Mr. Hawkins' interest was aroused. What Peter had said was provocative. But he said no more. Yet Mr. Hawkins, with sudden clarity, felt Baron Opperheim's mysterious "cynicism" all through his own consciousness, though he could not put it into words. He was filled with comprehending sadness, a kind of strange communion with that unknown Opperheim in threatened Paris. And he had another peculiar sensation: he believed, implicitly, that Baron Opperheim must have gazed at Peter with Mr. Hawkins' own and present reflectiveness.

Outside the tall and shrouded windows a wet and January blizzard was falling, and the air was gloomy and dim. Mr. Hawkins watched the large and heavy snowflakes dropping inexorably. There was something of the mystic in him. He felt the death and implacable sorrow of the mournful day all through his flesh and spirit, and the sick hopelessness of the perceptive and intelligent man was like the taste of dry ashes in his mouth.

CHAPTER XXXV

Celeste wandered restlessly in the conservatory of the great new house on Placid Heights. She carried a basket with her, and under the truculent eye of the gardener she cut hot-house roses. She did not particularly like hot-house roses; they gave her the vaguely gruesome feeling that always attended on her contemplation of the unnatural. These thorns were weak and flaccid, a simulation of defense, as if the flowers knew instinctively that there was nothing against which they need defend themselves. They were meticulously tended; their natural enemies would never attack them; all danger of a hostile environment, which would have strengthened them, given them vigor and lusty life, had been eliminated. No wonder, then, that they were feeble, too delicate and too decadent. That hostile environment of the fields, coupled with the struggle for existence and the competition natural among all forms of vital life, made roses colorful and full of resistance and health, made their thorns weapons of sturdy defense, made their branches sinewy and fibrous with the urgent determination to live and survive, made them exude the heavy and intoxicating scent which these vapid weaklings would never possess.

Celeste found the thought very interesting. She paused in her cutting to gaze unseeingly through the cloudy glass to which the wet and heavy snowflakes clung. Suppose the idealists and the theorists had their way, and human life were bereft of the necessity to struggle for existence, and all vigorous competition were eliminated. Suppose humanity were protected from the natural forces that threatened it, and a hostile environment. Suppose, since that hostile environment was removed, that the weak could then survive. Would not humanity, like these hot-house roses, become flaccid, possessed of a decadent and feeble spirit, lacking color and vitality and health and vigor? Would it not become uniform, without interest and variety, in such a society? Would not the surviving weaklings, coddled, pampered and inherently inferior, yet possessed of their strange ability to procreate lavishly, finally outnumber and inundate their superiors?

As such a dangerous soft environment was artificial, it would not survive under stress. And stress eventually came. When it arrived, would not these enfeebled men die at once, having been robbed of their natural weapons of defense, their health and toughness and sinewy resistance?

Yes, it was an interesting thought. Celeste's smooth black brows drew together in her concentration. She would argue this out with Peter. Once, he had believed this, as she, herself, now believed it. But lately he had become excited and querulous, and had vehemently pleaded the cause of the hot-house rose. Man had a right to be protected from his natural enemies; he had a right to demand from his rulers that his environment be made easy and sweet and comfortable. He had a right to insist that "unfair" competition be removed. In other words, thought Celeste, with cool disgust, it was man's right that he should be spoon-fed with pap, that he should recline in unearned comfort, and cling, like a fat vulnerable slug, to the stem of the social order. Why? Simply because he was man! And, because he was man, he was inherently superior to the lesser beasts that struggled naturally and healthily with a hostile environment, and derived vigor from that struggle!

Did Peter now, once possessed of some measure of realism, plead this insane and foolish premise because he felt the deathly increase of weakness in himself, felt the stronger pangs of dissolution? Perhaps it was always the weak and dying rose that pleaded that his stronger fellows were wronging him in crowding him out and stretching towards the light with all the passion of their unblighted stems. And demanded, also, that those unblighted stems be cut back, that the bright and colorful bud be lopped off in order that the worm-eaten bloom be given an opportunity to unfold its diseased petals without competition, and fill the garden with their sick and decaying scent.

Celeste, despite her love and pity for her husband, felt the strong stirring of dissent and impatience in herself. Then, she decided not to argue with Peter. He would be so exhausted when he returned from New York. She sighed, turned away from the roses, and laid the cut blossoms on the gritty wooden table. She did not want them. If they stood on her tables, she would be reminded of the argument, and would feel again that stirring of passion and anger and impatience.

She felt changed and much older. She remembered herself as a young girl, and her mouth twisted with irritability. Was it always the ignorant that espoused the cause of the weaklings? The untried, the innocent and the deluded? She did not know. Some thought nagged her, with its vagueness. Was Henri influencing her? She felt a warm tremor over her tired body, and a quickening of her heart.

She went into one of the hushed dim drawing-rooms and drew aside a curtain. The grounds had not yet been landscaped; that was a project for the spring. The winter had fallen all about and over the new graystone house, had forgotten and ignored it, covering the long slope to the valley, as it had done for centuries before, with a heavy and glimmering wave of snow. The driveway was still only gravel; its sunken path was faintly visible in wet dark streaks and smooth scalloped edges of whiteness. The ancient trees had not yet been moved or cut down, and as they bent under the snow they were like old gaunt men bending under the weight of time. The early winter twilight stood over the house, the white dropping hills and the twisted iron trees, like a fathomless depth of gray still water, in which dimension, distance and substance were lost and all objects had acquired the wavering and indistinct forms of dreams. The valley at the end of the long slope was lost in a kind of gray opaque mist. Nothing moved or stirred in that smothering silence except the dropping flakes of snow. There was no wind. Isolated though the house was, stranded like a desolate hulk on petrified and rounded white waves which extended endlessly into space and time, Celeste yet had the dismaying sensation that it was really enclosed in a vast glassy ball filled with drifting fog which rolled in upon it from every surface.

Behind her, as she stood at the windows with their diamond-shaped panes, the house extended, as shapeless, as dreamlike, as empty, as the outer world. It was a house of shadows. She heard the crackling of a fire on a distant hearth in the great still room, but it had no verity for her. Through all her senses she felt the unreal curving of the tremendous staircase in the hall beyond the room, the upper corridors, the rooms opening off them, the dining-room and the library, the morning-room and the terraces. Yet, she could not believe in their existence. It was all a dream. Nothing really existed except her trapped consciousness in a dull universe without form or substance. Somewhere, in the depths of the house, servants moved noiselessly. But still Celeste could not believe in their existence.

A curious and frozen fear pervaded her, a sort of alert lifelessness and awareness. She felt herself longing desperately for a human face, a human voice. Peter was still in New York. She had only to order a car, she thought, to be in the city within a short time. But the thought brought her no relief. A heavy lethargy was upon her. She could not make herself believe there was any city beyond that shadowy mist below.

Finally, she could not even believe in her own existence. The diffusion outside diffused her. She felt her personality silently and softly disintegrating, so that all its cells moved and prepared to drift away. Yet deep in herself was a hot core of drugged pain.

She was only dully surprised to discover that she was weeping. The pain in her heart strengthened, but she did not know what caused the pain. She dared not analyze and examine it. She only knew that she could not endure this house, that she had never been able to endure it, that she had dreaded it from the moment the first stone had been laid. She had hoped, vaguely, and from the very first, that she would never have to live in it, and when the day of entering had arrived, she had been ill with a kind of inexplicable horror. Its beauty was, to her, the fantastic beauty of a nightmare, grotesque and unreal. Yet, it was a simple and majestic building, and she had chosen all of its furnishings herself, had made all the arrangements. But she had done all this in the depths of a fantasy, and without joy.

Without joy. Yes, all her life had been without joy, until she had known Henri. And that joy had been one with pain and suffering. Her tears came faster now. But she was not weeping for herself. She could not have told why she wept. The snow fell swifter and more inexorably beyond the window. It did not glitter. It was only a pall of death. She felt its death all through herself.

She thought of the war, the "phony" war, where terrible antagonists gazed at each other in speechless silence, and waited. Even the war was unreal to her. She could not feel its imminence, its reality. She thought of Peter; he, too, was a shadow. However, the pain leapt in her heart like a startled thing.

She was not aware, for some moments, that she had been staring at a pinpoint of light twinkling far below the house, a pinpoint that wavered from side to side, and was increasing in brightness. When she was fully conscious of it, she could hardly believe it. Who would be coming up here on this desolate winter day? She was expecting no one. Her relatives and friends always called up first before visiting her.

She watched the light coming closer. Now, far down on the slope, she could see the struggling black shape of a car, leaping on the ruts, falling, swaying, its lights piercing the foggy gloom, and surrounded by a dim aura through the snow. She pressed her face against the cold panes of glass. Could it be Henri? But Henri was in Washington. He had called her only that morning.

The wheels of the car had found the gritty driveway, and it was plowing heavily upward. Celeste could hear the laboring of the motor, its muffled roaring. It was having a hard time negotiating the frozen ruts and the slipping gravel. Then, with a triumphant hoarse heave, it had swung about before the house, and had stopped.

It was a large black limousine, like a hearse. And now Celeste recognized it. It belonged to her brother, Emile. But why should Emile, who was perfectly indifferent to her, and for whom she felt nothing at all except a dull dislike, be visiting her? The chauffeur was climbing out of the car. He was opening the door. The tall black figure of a woman was alighting with difficulty, for the car was tilted to one side in the drifts. It was Agnes, Emile's wife.

Agnes Bouchard! Agnes, whom she had always dreaded and avoided, the cynical hard Agnes with the cruel amused eyes. Why should she be visiting her young sister-in-law, whom she openly disdained and found excessively boring?

Celeste turned on the lights, and the great quiet living-room sprang into warmth and pleasant stillness. Even the fire took on courage, and leapt upward. The snow and the death were lost behind windows suddenly dark and protecting. Now the whole house became real and tangible, solid and strong, no longer a diffused and misty outline of walls. Little as she liked Agnes, Celeste yet felt a pleasure in this approach of another human being. She heard Agnes' voice in the quiet hall, a brisk clipped voice with its undertone of wryness and humor. That voice no longer made her shrink. She advanced towards the archway with a welcoming smile.

Agnes appeared. Though she was no Bouchard by birth, but only by marriage, she had all the attributes of the "Latin" Bouchards. She was somewhat tall, and possessed a compact and excellent figure, very chic and slender. She was now about forty-nine years old, but there was a briskness and avidity about her which made her appear much younger. She moved with swiftness and lightness. Her narrow white face, with its long "harpy" nose and patrician thinness, had a cruel and alert look, cynical and shrewd, and there was no gentleness in the thin thread of her twisted lips, so violently painted. Her hard and bold black eyes had a predatory gleam in them, disingenuous and malicious. Agnes Bouchard had no faith in human nature, nor in any of its "virtues." She did not believe that it possessed any altruism or kindness or justice or mercy, or even decent honesty, nor that it had more intelligence than a monkey. She found it rather regrettable, but amusing, too, that the only good men she had ever encountered had been fools, and impotent. "The children of darkness are wiser in their generation than the children of light," she would quote, with conviction, and no sadness at all. She found no difficulty in adjusting herself to such a dark and menacing world, and was constantly mirthful about it, because she was a clever woman of considerable intellect and much knowledge. In many ways she was much like her younger relative-by-marriage, Rosemarie Bouchard, except that she was a wiser woman and possessed of much innate integrity and forthrightness and open disdainful courage, and that there was no sadism in her such as there was in Rosemarie. She had for her husband a kind of affectionate scorn and indifference, and a cold and vicious contempt for her dull but dangerous son, Robert, the familiar and slave of Antoine Bouchard.

She brought briskness, coolness and movement into the room with her. She had not removed her smooth black fur coat; it fell back to reveal her smart black dress and scarlet scarf. There was a Russian hat of the same fur on the perfect white coiffure with its silvery waves. She was removing her black kid gloves; it was evident, however, that she was not remaining very long.

"Agnes," said Celeste, extending her hand, real pleasure shining over the ivory planes of her face. "I'm so glad you came. But what an awful day."

Agnes' piercing eyes flashed over her young sister-in-law, and there was a minatory brightness in them. The scarlet thread of her lips curled. "You won't be so glad I came in about five minutes," she said, with hard and disdainful curtness. She moved to the fire, rubbed her hands, stared about the room. "A nice place," she commented. "I probably won't be seeing it again."

Celeste was startled. All her life, she had felt dread at the sound of cruel and relentless voices, and the old shrinking, the old tension, made all her nerves tighten defensively. "Why, Agnes? What is wrong?"

Agnes continued to rub her hands. The act made a dry and rustling sound in the room. She had begun to smile, her predatory profile outlined against the fire. Then she turned her head again and stared at Celeste with brutal curiosity, as if the younger woman had been an object which aroused her amusement, contempt and wonder. The inexplicable dread in Celeste increased. She retreated involuntarily. Agnes moved away from the fire and sat down in a chair, her excellent back straight and alert. Celeste seated herself also, and waited, her hands pressing one upon the other.

"Celeste," began Agnes, in a cold and curious voice, "do you know anything? Anything at all? Are you a complete fool? I always thought you were, you know. I thought it from the moment I first saw you. You were about five, then, weren't you, or a little younger? You had black pigtails and big dark-blue eyes and a stupid little red mouth. You were always afraid. People always spoke of you as a tender little creature who must be protected. Women never felt that way about you, even when you were a nasty little brat. It was always men."

Celeste was silent. Her white face was very still and taut.

But her eyes fixed themselves expectantly upon Agnes. Agnes nodded with a cynical smile.

"Yes, you were always good at that attitude. They thought it was defensiveness. But I know it is invulnerability. You always took exceedingly good care of yourself. You still do."

She paused, and humorously lifted her hand, and began to check off the fingers. "First, there was your father, Jules, who ruined the lives of his sons, because of you. 'Little Celeste must be protected.' He never thought the boys really ought to be protected against *you*. They weren't loving sons and brothers to begin with; but Jules' distribution of his estate, to 'protect' you, did nothing to increase the loving kindness between Armand, Emile and Christopher. Probably they would have feuded, anyway, and plotted against each other, but not with the ferocity they have exhibited because of you. Did Jules know that? I often wonder. He never did like his sons. He was a very subtle man."

Celeste's white lips parted, and she said, quietly: "This is very interesting. But family history bores me, I am afraid. I am not to blame for my father's will. Also, I must confess that I don't see how all this concerns you, Agnes, or how it is your business. Emile's done very well for himself, hasn't he? Or, do you want more? You always were very avaricious."

Agnes still kept her hands in the air, in the attitude of counting, but over them she regarded Celeste with narrow gleaming eyes and a malevolent smile. "So, you do have fangs," she commented. "I always knew it. No one else ever seemed to."

She continued with inexorable animation: "Now, let's see. Jules was the first man to come under your 'spell.' After that, there was your brother, Christopher. He was not born a saint, but your existence made him a devil. He fought for you with your father. They fought for you from the very minute you were born. You knew, of course, that Christopher was in love with you for many years, Celeste? So much in love that he could never care too much for any other woman. Not a nice story, is it? A little ugly? I've always been very sorry for Edith, Christopher's wife."

A look of horrified terror, repudiation and sickness flashed over Celeste's face. She stood up, catching at the back of her chair. "You are a dirty woman, Agnes," she said, and her voice was only a hoarse whisper. The sockets of her eyes stretched with her sickness and loathing, so that they were filled with blue flame.

Agnes nodded with smiling grimness. "Honest people are

always nasty, my dear. No one loves them. They are out-casts. They say such devastating and improper things. I'm being an honest woman now. For the sake of your soul. For the sake of things so much more important than you, you miserable white little wretch. I'm not blaming you for your brother's passion for you. You couldn't help it, I suppose. You were lovely and soft and innocent, a combination that does mad things to men. But because Christopher loved you, and still does, I am afraid, you ruined his life. He's quite insane, you know. He would kill for you, destroy everything for you, even his life. Under certain present circumstances, that is very fortunate. But I will come to that later. What I am saying now is that your very existence made a fiend out of him, instead of just the average bad Bouchard he would have been. He hated his brothers; they all hated each other. But you made the hatred worse."

Celeste stood by her chair, clutching it with wet hands. Her breast, under the blue wool frock, rose and fell with passionate agitation. Her white forehead, her pallid upper lip, gleamed with moisture.

Agnes continued with hard serenity: "Now, let me see. Henri came next, you remember." She paused now, and waited.

Celeste did not move, but she appeared to dwindle and shrink, become smaller. However, she gazed steadfastly, and in petrified silence, at Agnes. Agnes was smiling again, with renewed viciousness.

"What you did to Henri! Oh, of course you couldn't help it! You never could. It wasn't your fault that Henri came back to America, that he tried to regain what had been stolen from him. He would have done that even if you had never existed. I grant that. But he came and saw, and you conquered. Of course, you were young and inexperienced, and you had a right to change your mind. Henri was a bad man, to begin with; all the Bouchards are. It's part of their irresistible charm. Henri, however, was the worst of them all. Nevertheless, he wouldn't have been such a monster, if it hadn't been for you, if he had never seen you. For it seems, unfortunately, that you have the ability to bring out everything that is evil in everyone. I know you do that to me,"— and she laughed curtly.

"I thought Henri had escaped, when you finally threw him over and married Peter. I thought he would then become just a naturally bad Bouchard, a normal Bouchard. You went away. And then, you came back."

She stopped, for Celeste had moved, just a little, but even that slight movement was as if lightning had struck her.

"I'll come back to Henri, later," said Agnes, with cruel softness. "We'll go on now to poor Peter. In some way, he seemed to have escaped the pestilential nature of the Bouchards. He was a 'good' Bouchard. There haven't been many. I can't recall any other, in my own experience. Yes, he was a 'good' Bouchard.

"It wasn't your innocent little fault that Peter had been gassed in the war—by Bouchard gas, at that. It wasn't any of your doing that Peter returned here. You didn't know anything at all about Peter until he arrived. He was sick, but he was still alive. He still had courage and strength and purity. He married you, and you both went away. I am not saying that he might have been happier, or healthier, with any other woman. At least, until you came back. But, he is dying now. And he is dying in misery and hopelessness. Perhaps that has nothing to do with you. I've heard that you have been the tenderest wife, and he seems devoted to you. I'll give you that credit. But—sometimes I wonder—You never gave him any peace, or any real happiness, for it is not in you to give happiness to anyone, only passion and madness and despair and ruin."

She stared remorselessly at Celeste. For Celeste's control had suddenly and violently broken. Her face, her eyes, expressed supreme terror. She had stepped behind her chair; she had lifted her hands, palms outward, towards Agnes, as if to fend off some brutal and lethal attack. She cried out, incoherently: "Go away! I won't hear another word! Get out of my house, now, right away!"

But Agnes was unperturbed. She regarded Celeste with shrewd and significant thoughtfulness. "I see," she said, reflectively. "I see a lot of things. You aren't outraged, so much, by what I have said about Peter. You are only afraid of what I am going to say next, aren't you?"

Celeste was silent. But she was shaking strongly. She dropped her hands. Then she whispered: "My God. Go away." She moved backwards, towards the door.

"Come back, Celeste," said Agnes, quietly. She stood up. Her smile was gone. Her features were stark and harsh. "Come back. Sit down. I didn't come out in this beastly weather to give you a lecture on your little kitten morals. You can sleep with a dozen men, for all of me. You can curl up in a dozen beds, and I'll only shrug over it. That's your business. I suppose, too, you have *some* fastidiousness."

Celeste had stopped retreating, but she did not return to her chair. The two women faced each other across the wide and gleaming carpet in the silent room. Celeste seemed no longer to be full of terror and dread. She was as still as frozen ice, and as expressionless. Her eyes were empty, as if the shock she had undergone had driven the soul out of them.

For a moment, Agnes experienced a rare qualm of pity, and a deep curiosity.

"Celeste," she said, in a changed tone, "I'm sorry for you. You were very young and inexperienced, when you married Peter. That was Christopher's fault. He wanted to save you for himself. Perhaps you've been sinned against, too. Perhaps it isn't all your fault. 'Victim of circumstances,' maybe. When you came back, you were a woman at last, not a child. You had always loved Henri, hadn't you? You had never forgotten him. I can see that now. I thought you were just bored by your sick husband, and looking for a last adventure. Henri must have seemed very romantic to you, I thought. Besides, he hadn't forgotten you. None of the men who loved you ever could. I thought, wrongly, probably, that you knew this, and were taking advantage of it. I am mistaken. And so, I'm sorry for you."

Celeste tried to speak. And then, with a gesture infinitely pathetic and full of tragedy, she put her hands over her face. Agnes watched her. Her own face darkened, twisted, and those hard black eyes were suddenly gentle and sad, as they had never been before.

"My poor child," she said, compassionately. "It is all so terrible."

After a moment she laughed a little, and there was a tremulous and bitter note in that laughter. "I'm so sorry for you, my dear. And, believe it or not, I'm sorry for Henri, too! That's incredible, isn't it? Being sorry for a man like Henri?"

Celeste dropped her hands. Her face was wet with mute tears. Her lips were trembling. "Does Annette know?" she asked, in a painful and dwindled tone. "Does Peter know?"

If Agnes had any last doubts about Celeste's true emotions, these selfless words destroyed them. She hesitated. Then she went to Celeste and put her arms about her with a tenderness alien to her nature. "Come, dear, sit down. I've got so much more to say to you." She led Celeste back to her chair, and with her own scented handkerchief she wiped away the younger woman's tears.

"No," she said at last, thoughtfully, "I don't think Annette and Peter know. But practically everyone else does, I'm afraid."

Celeste shivered. She leaned forward and clasped her hands over her folded arms, and crouched forward in an attitude of utter collapse and anguished cold. Her head dropped forward. Her bright black hair fell over her face.

"I can't believe that Henri was so naive that he really expected not to be found out," said Agnes. "I think there is another explanation. I think he believes, in his egotism, that no one would dare to talk about him, or whisper about him openly, for fear of reprisal. So long as people knew, and kept quiet about it, he didn't care. He knew everyone was afraid of him. He probably knows everyone is talking. That doesn't matter to him. So long as they don't try anything inimical. He can cope with enemies. And circumstance. But let them try to injure him, or you, because of this—matter, and he will smash them—he believes. The trouble is, they *are* trying. And might even succeed. And that will be very bad." She paused. "I'm not thinking of you, Celeste, or even of Henri, when I say it will be bad. I am thinking of things much more important."

Celeste stirred sluggishly, in the depths of her collapse and despair. She lifted her head. Her hair clung in disordered ringlets about her wet cheeks. Fear and panic were alive in her eyes; her face was gaunt with them.

Agnes sat down near her, and leaned forward, speaking with a quiet intensity. "Celeste, my darling, don't you know anything at all?" she asked, with surprised pity. "Hasn't Henri told you anything about what he is trying to do? Or, are you only his favorite harem wife, kept in purdah, behind screens and veils and walls? Does he think you are a moron, who wouldn't understand?"

Celeste's haggard expression changed. "He has told me quite a little," she murmured.

Agnes leaned back in her chair and contemplated the young woman for a long moment or two. Her own expression was dark and somber. "I see," the muttered. "Yes, he must have told you. He is a very clever man. He knew that he lost you once because he was repulsive to you—his ideas, his intrigues and his plans were repulsive. Perhaps you came together, once or twice, out of sheer irresistible attraction, when you returned from Europe. But he knew that was not enough to keep you. That was it, wasn't it? So, he had to tell you. I have no doubt he dressed it up a little, quite artfully, so that he acquired a kind of stern nobility in your eyes, even a selflessness, God help us! Imagine that, of Henri! It would be quite amusing, if it weren't so damnably ominous. Frankly, can you imagine Henri doing anything heroic and noble because of patriotism or change of heart or virtue or greatness?" She laughed harshly.

But Celeste said nothing. She only waited.

"Nevertheless," continued Agnes, changing again to somber intensity, "what he is doing now is the only chance for America—for all of us—to survive. You know that, don't you? And you know who his enemies are, and what they are trying to do?"

"Yes," whispered Celeste. "I know. He's told me."

"They're very terrible enemies." Agnes went on. "There is only a feeble chance that he will win. He is determined to win. He has brought some of the Bouchards with him, because they are frightened, because he has intimidated them, bribed, threatened, coerced them. No matter. You know," she added musingly, "if I were a younger woman, I'd make tracks for Henri, myself. There is something about him. He's quite a man."

Again, Celeste's face changed, became intense with passion and tragedy. She fixed her eyes upon Agnes, and waited, her very breath suspended.

"I don't wonder you love him," said Agnes, with stern gentleness. "He has everything. There aren't many like him now, in America. He has a frightful fight ahead. Emile's in with him. Even if Emile is my beloved husband, he's a bloated black rat. Henry did a good job in bludgeoning him. Christopher's in with him, and Alex, and Francis. But there's another faction, and a very pestilential one. You know that?"

Celeste nodded dumbly.

"Antoine, that sparkling bowing friend. And others. Others, not only a few Bouchards, but others just as powerful, in politics, in the newspaper field, in industry. The lesser Bouchards are just milling uncertainly along the fringes of both factions. Henri is trying to boot them into line. Antoine is trying too, with much more finesse. And behind them both is a confused and amorphous America. Things are very bad, Celeste, my dear. You know that. What of the future? America will trundle along behind the winner. We want Henri to win. You and I. And so many others, too. We'll live—with Henri. We, and America, will die with Antoine."

She stood up, as if the pressure of her thoughts was too much for her. She began to pace up and down the room, this elegant and assured woman, clasping and unclasping her hands.

"I've never been patriotic. I've never been an 'American.' How many Americans are there in America? So terribly, terribly few. How many love America? I am afraid to answer that. I only know that America is inert, stupid, mad, dull and dead. We've got Antoine's kind to thank for that. A nation of belly-filling morons is very necessary to them. And a nation of lunatics. Do you know about the organizations he is backing. Filled with insane women, with haters, with the greedy and the cruel and the stupid and the criminal? We've got the makings here in America of a robust Nazi party. Hate is their God, and Jaeckle is their prophet. They've got priests behind them, murderers, thieves and liars, and madmen. That's the outlook, in America, and that's the outlook Antoine is fostering. You know why."

She drew a deep breath. "It's funny," she murmured. "But I believe I'm an American now. Because of America's peril. Because of the madmen."

"I know," whispered Celeste.

"The America Only Committee," continued Agnes. "Half of them are sincere fools and imbeciles, who perhaps even love America, and don't want to get her embroiled in what they call 'foreign' wars. As if there were ever any 'foreign' wars! You'd think America was a planet rolling around serenely in her own orbit, instead of part of one world. It's as if a man had cancer in a remote part of his body, and his mind asked him what it had to do with it. It was only in his belly, wasn't it? What had that to do with his arms, or his eyes, or his heart or his lungs? By some miracle, such a man tells himself, he can ignore the cancer in his belly. But there comes a day when all of him will die. He forgets that.

"And then, hovering around the fringes of the America Only Committee are the lunatic organizations, the orgiastic women who would like to tear little children apart with their naked hands, who would like to torture other women, who would like to sleep with their own sons, who would like to stand, breast-high, in the blood of the murdered. Why do you shudder, Celeste? Don't you know anything at all about mankind? I do, unfortunately.

"And then there are the murderous and avaricious priests, who would like to torture the helpless, who would like to steal their possessions, who would like to enslave the world, who are bloated with hatred and madness. And then there are the criminals, who want to rape and torment and kill,

336

and see an opportunity to do these things without punishment. Yes, there is much madness in the world. And much of this madness is behind Antoine."

She stopped now. She stood near Celeste. The snow whispered at the windows. The winter wind rose on the long arch of a bowl.

Agnes suddenly cried out in a loud voice: "How frightful it is! How can one endure it? The Walpurgis Night of fury and death is upon us. And waiting, in their quiet rooms, are the lusters after power. Waiting in Washington, waiting in their great factories. Waiting for the ruin of America."

She pressed her thin white fingers against her cheeks. "Madness," she said. "Madness. The whole world is mad. There are only a few sane men left. Only a few like Henri. What does it matter if he is thinking only of himself? He can save us, all of us."

She turned quickly to Celeste. "Does Henri think we'll get into this war?"

"He doesn't know," sighed Celeste. "A few months ago he was certain we wouldn't. But, not now. He is trying to keep us out. He was sure it would mean the end of America, as we know it, if we were drawn in. Now, he almost believes it will be the end of America if we aren't."

"Does he still hate Roosevelt?" asked Agnes, with a brief smile.

"I don't know. The President once irritated him, terribly. But now he is indifferent. He says this thing is much bigger than politics. However, he thinks the Republican party has a fair chance of winning the election if it can find a good and spectacular man who will appeal to all elements. Of one thing he is certain, though: Roosevelt will run for a third term, against precedent, prejudice and tradition, and the Republican candidate will perhaps be defeated."

But Agnes seemed not to have heard this. She sat down again near her sister-in-law. "And now, Celeste, all this comes back to you."

"To me?"

"Yes. You and Henri. Henri's enemies will stop at nothing to destroy him. They know, now, what he is trying to do. I don't know what other things they have in mind, but they are ready to expose you. They'll do it, too. You think the American people won't be interested? Well, then, you must remember that bigger men than Henri have been destroyed by a peccadillo. The vast mass of American people are very childlike, easily swayed. They believe they are very virtuous, statistics to the contrary. Henri's enemies can make such a national uproar over this—this little affair—that anything he tries to do thereafter will be smeared. You think that is childish? I assure you it isn't. Every enemy clergyman in the country will harp on Henri's 'infidelity,' until the fate of America becomes a small affair in comparison. Of course, the more intelligent men will only laugh. But the mass of puerile, and fornicating, Americans won't laugh. In their stupidity, they will argue that a man who sleeps with another man's wife must be a complete rascal, must not be trusted, and is capable of the most heinous and treacherous crimes, that everything he does must be suspect. Many a hero has failed, many a great leader of the people has been discredited, because his pleasant little private eccentricities were exposed, exaggerated, and branded as infamous. That is the way of the mob. And Henri's enemies know it."

Celeste was as white as death. "I don't believe it!" she cried. "The American people can't be so stupid and ignorant."

Agnes nodded her head gravely. "I assure you they can. Like so many of our class, you believe that your mind, your reason, your intelligence, are shared in equal quantities by all other people. That is our fatal mistake. The little laborer, the little shopgirl, the little storekeeper, the little artisan, whose lives are in jeopardy in these days, will be titillated, made indignant and furious, because the man who is trying to save them from death and enslavement sleeps with another man's wife occasionally. You think this incredible? I only ask you to look at history. Not only Cæsar's wife must be above reproach, but in America Cæsar himself must be a eunuch. That is our Puritan heritage."

She hesitated. "And, of course, there is the matter of Armand, too. Have you forgotten that Annette is his daughter? What if she is told, and she divorces Henri? Don't shrink so, my dear. You must think of all this. If Annette divorces Henri, then Armand will go out to smash him. Armand is a bulbous sick fool, but he is very malignant, also, and he loves his daughter. Remember, Henri is only president of Bouchard because of Armand's power. Once he is thrown off center, then the work he is trying to do is ended."

She stopped and waited. But Celeste said nothing.

"You have only to wait a while," urged Agnes, putting her hand on Celeste's shoulder. "Only until Armand dies, perhaps. At the worst, only until Henri has swung matters to a conclusion. It is a small thing, really, compared to all of America, isn't it?"

"What can I do?" said Celeste, hopelessly. "Henri wouldn't listen to me. He would say that it is ridiculous, that I must let him take care of things, himself. He would laugh me into speechlessness."

"Yes, I know, dear. That's why you mustn't tell him what I have told you. He is such a damned egotist. Frankly, I don't know how you'll manage it. Tell him anything else. Tell him Peter needs you. Tell him you can't see him again while Peter lives. It's up to you now, Celeste."

Celeste was all resignation, all renunciation. She sighed, over and over. She murmured: "If he goes, he might never come back. He told me that once, himself. He will never come back. I know that. Once I send him away— Later, when he understood, he might not want to come back."

"That's what you must risk," said Agnes. "I know how you feel, darling. But all this is nothing, compared to the larger things."

She stood up, and began to draw on her gloves. She looked pityingly down at Celeste, so broken now, so despairing, so drained and lifeless. Then she bent quickly and kissed the younger woman's forehead.

"Oh, my dear, my dear," she said. And went away.

Celeste listened to the laboring of the car as it roared away into the early night. She listened with intensity, as if to shut out her own thoughts. Then, when everything was silent again, except for the wind and the crackling of the fire, the wave of desolation and grief and agony which swept over her could hardly be borne. In the extremity of her pain she could not move. She could only stare at the fire until her eye-sockets were a glare of reflected light.

It was a long while before she could rise and climb heavily and weakly to her room. She turned on the lights. She heard the soft pealing of the dinner gong. But she sat down at her desk and drew a sheet of paper towards her. She began to write, and every word was like a knife in her heart.

She began without salutation: "I have come to the conclusion that we cannot meet again under present circumstances. Please believe that this time my decision is final. Don't try to see me, please. It is useless. Perhaps some day you might be able to understand."

She sealed the letter, addressed it to Henri at his office.

Book Three

THE ABIDING EARTH

"One generation passeth away, and another generation cometh; but the earth abideth for ever."—Ecclesiastes, 1:4.

CHAPTER XXXVI

Annette Bouchard suffered from the common sadness of the gentle and unassuming: she was consistently neglected and forgotten, even if she was loved by many. For even the cruel and the malicious had nothing evil to say of her, and if they were guilty of disparaging remarks about her patience and sweetness, they made them with regret and pity.

Her mind was unworldly. It was not that she was unaware of suffering and wickedness and all the foulness that is inherent in mankind. But she had a steadfast awareness of the flow of eternity. And she was endlessly compassionate and understanding.

The late February day lay over Robin's Nest like a gauzy gray curtain of smoke, in which everything was indistinct. But there was a warmth and peace in the great old house which had never known the birth of a child. So old and strong a house, she would think, with so many rooms upstairs which might have been made into nurseries! Could there be such a thing as a sterile house? Children had lived there, yes. Henri and Edith had played in these grand still rooms, had run up and down the wide spiral staircase, had seen Christmas trees in one corner of the larger drawing-room, had watched the rain running in quick-silver drops down the diamond-paned windows, had slept in quiet rooms, had fought, wrangled, laughed and wept within these walls. But only two children, after all. Annette had wanted to adopt children, but Henri had been enraged at the very idea, and had given her such a malefic look that she had never spoken of it again.

It gave Annette a wistful happiness to know that she lived within the house where Henri had had his early childhood. She liked to think of him as a child. She tried often to think of it. But her efforts evoked no image in her mind. When she tried to imagine him as a little boy her uneasy thoughts returned to the portrait of his great-grandfather, Ernest Barbour, which hung in the larger drawing-room. Then a curious compulsion would come over her; wherever she was, in whatever part of the house, she would be compelled to go to that room and look up at the portrait. Several times this compulsion had come upon her after midnight, and she had had to creep downstairs, light a lamp, and gaze at the painting for a long time.

She remembered that when she had first come to that house as a bride the portrait had seemed to regard her with cold and indifferent curiosity, even remote enmity. Those pale basilisk eyes would stare down at her with a strange fixity, and once or twice she thought that they were contemptuous. Later, they were merely indifferent. When she believed her heart was breaking (and this was often) she imagined there was an alert liveliness in those eyes, as if the painted face harbored thoughts and interest. But never had she imagined pity in them, or kindness. Fury, yes, icy anger, evil disdain, and sometimes aversion and contempt, but never pity. Sometimes they appeared to understand her, and to scorn what they understood.

She had never, in the beginning, believed what others maintained: that Henri was a replica of his great-grandfather, that the eyes were identical, the planes of the large colorless face, the crest of the virile rising fair hair. Sometimes she would concede that there was a physical resemblance, but the expression was different.

But now, in this last year, she had, with fear, been forced to acknowledge to herself that Henri was now precisely as Ernest Barbour had been. There was the same deep thick furrow between the eyes, the same heavy indomitable folds about the brutal mouth, the same blunt strength in the short nose, the same look of inexorable determination. Sometimes she was sure that the portrait slowly turned its head with Henri's own gesture, and sometimes it seemed to her that the lips tightened as Henri's did, just before he opened them to speak in his monotonous voice. Ernest Barbour had been about Henri's age when the portrait had been painted, and there was the same shadow of premature gray in the light dull hair.

For some mysterious reason, this growing resemblance frightened her. Often, she had the confused thought that it was no longer Henri Bouchard who lived in this house with her, but Ernest Barbour. She would then wander through the quiet and empty rooms, feeling a stranger, a strange woman who had no right here. The curtain would part, and May

Sessions, Ernest's first and last wife, would appear, in her thick crimson velvet gown, bustled and looped, her auburn curls high on her head, a jewel on her white plump throat, her pretty round dimpled face about to break out into the pleasant and gracious smile which was a legend in the family. (There was a small portrait of his great-grandmother in Henri's room, and it had such a kind expression, so humorous, so twinkling and perceptive, that Annette had felt a nostalgic grief that she had never known this great lady.) Ernest had divorced May, who had loved him with such strength and passion, and had married her cousin, Amy Drumhill, widow of his brother, Martin. There was also a portrait of Amy in one of the bedrooms at Robin's Nest, and she had been lovely, Annette thought. Amy had had a sweet and gentle face, dreamlike and unearthly, with large soft eyes and brown ringlets. The portrait had been painted when she was a girl, and the slender white shoulders were fully revealed above the faded ivory satin of her gown. But she had no reality for Annette. Annette was glad that, after Amy had died, Ernest had remarried May, and that they had both died in the old Sessions house that had been the inspiration and the ruin of that terrible man. The old Sessions house had long been rubble, had long been carted away in ignominious ruin, and May had never lived at Robin's Nest where her daughter, Gertrude, had known such agony. Nevertheless, it was May that Annette always expected to see, entering through a shadowy arch, gliding up or down the great staircase. If Ernest Barbour was the evil and sleepless haunter of this house, May was its kind and beneficent spirit.

Annette would sigh. She would think, mournfully, that Henri ought really to have married a woman like May Sessions, always gracious and beautiful and strong and lively. A woman who would have given him children. No wonder then, that the portrait looked down upon her with inimical contempt, and that the pale fixed eyes were often minatory.

It would have amazed Henri had he known of Annette's thoughts. For in her weary and idolatrous love for him, she had often pondered over the thought of giving him a divorce, of enabling him to remarry and have the children she would never have. (She could often hear those shadowy children racing in the upper halls, laughing in the distant rooms, hurling themselves down the staircase, demanding, caressing, crying.) Then it was that her pain became unendurable, and she would be thrown into fits of weeping that made her ill for days. But after a year or two of her married life, she knew she could not give Henri a divorce. Not while Armand was alive. Annette knew so much that no one else knew, or of which no one else dared to speak.

Once she had heard her cruel relative, Rosemarie Bouchard, say to her sister, Phyllis: "That horrid little twisted creature will never divorce poor Henri. She has her claws in him very properly. She knows that he can't divorce her, because of that smelly bloated old Armand. So, she gloats smugly over him, knowing she has him trapped."

Annette had been terribly ill for six months after that, so ill that she had almost died. No one knew why; her physicians were puzzled. It was only the thought that if she died Henri might be ruined that had brought her back to life. Shortly after she had been able to rise from her bed, she had visited an obscure lawyer and had made a will leaving to Henri everything of which she might die possessed, and had enclosed a sealed letter to her father in which she prayed that her share, or more, be left to her husband, that Armand would remember him and do justice to him. But she still feared that with her death Henri might be destroyed.

It had been only a few months ago that Armand, taken ill again, had whimpered the truth to her, from what he considered his death-bed. She had felt such joy, such release, that she forgot her fears for her father. Later, doubt and fear came to her again. If Henri divorced her, or the capricious sick Armand changed his mind, the threat of ruin would remain. Armand had forgotten that he had told her in his semi-delirium, but Annette did not forget. There were three, now, who knew: Armand, Henri, and his wife.

It was only lately that a strange and terrible thing had occurred to Annette: she hoped, with sad impatience, that her beloved father would die, and that with him would die the threat to Henri. With horror, she caught herself searching for signs of dissolution in Armand's sick face, and she shuddered inwardly when the hope of his immediate death invaded her thoughts. Time was so short, she would say despairingly to herself. Henri was no longer young; if he was to marry a real woman, and have children, he must do it soon. And Armand lingered on with his needle and his List and his complaints and his misery.

Her horror at her thoughts, her impatience, her sorrow and sadness, were eating away her last strength, were making her flesh more transparent, her large light-blue eyes more haunted and weary. She felt that all evil was in her. But she could not control her passionate desire that her father would soon die.

Though the Bouchards pitied their daughter for a bemused and invalid fool, Annette had never been unaware of Henri's frequent derelictions. She had followed the courses of his love affairs with painful and absorbed interest. Oh, not that one, she would say to herself, with terror, when one affair or another seemed to be unduly prolonged. Not that woman with her shrewd little green eyes and avaricious mouth, not that woman with her cruel sweet laugh and her fluttering stretching hands, not that woman who loved no one but herself. And, dear God, never never Rosemarie Bouchard, that svelte smart Parisian evil! Even if Armand died, she would never give Henri a divorce so that he could marry one of these. They would bring him only wretchedness and hatred.

Each time that he began another affair, she would manage to meet the woman, to study her. And in all these years, she had never met one to whom she would relinquish Henri. Not until lately.

Always, from the beginning, she knew that Henri had loved Celeste, that he would never forget her. But when Celeste had returned, Annette had experienced only anguish. For Henri could not marry Celeste. Celeste was Peter's wife, and Celeste would never divorce him. Never did she dare admit to herself, not even in the dark recesses of the night, what she already knew. The thought was too much agony. Henri would marry no other woman, this Annette now understood. But he could not marry Celeste. And Annette, with the guilt of the hope that Armand would soon die, could not extend this same hope to include poor Peter, whom she loved tenderly.

Had the liaison brought Henri joy Annette would have derived a sad contentment from the fact. But it was bringing him no joy. Often, she would study him from a distance, and she could discern no new freshness in him, no new vitality or pleasure or life. Instead, these last two months, he had become grimmer, older, more savage, more coldly violent. And it was not because of the unremitting work he was doing; Annette understood that. It was something else.

She had realized, for the last few weeks, that he was not meeting Celeste any longer. She was confused and bewildered and frightened at this. She could not believe he had tired of Celeste, nor she of him. Why, then, was this?

Sometimes she would think to herself with sad surprise

and humility: Perhaps they are disturbed about me. Perhaps they think it is "wrong." She took a strange and inexplicable comfort from this, felt a sudden aching of her heart in tenderness, all of which she could not understand though she was past-mistress in the art of self-analysis. There would be a sudden relief in her, a softening and dissolving that would bring tears to her patient eyes.

For sometimes, in the past, during all Henri's brutal and indifferent derelictions, she would start from her trance of serene self-control with a dazed sensation as if being awakened from a drugged sleep. Then she would experience the agonizing pain and despair and repudiation of resignation. Her own human desire for love and peace and security could not be controlled on these occasions. She would ask herself, with frantic misery and rebellion, why she should have been singled out for lovelessness and detestation and ignoring. What had she done? Was she not a woman, who desired only to serve and to love, and to be possessed of just a little peace? Why must all the self-abnegation be hers, the self-withdrawal? Could not Henri have spared for her a little affection, a little consideration, a little tenderness?

It had been so much worse when Celeste had returned. She did not confess even to herself how frenziedly she had hoped that Henri and Celeste would not come together. That was because she had always so loved and admired Celeste, so trusted her. Celeste, she would argue childishly, but with faith, had too much integrity, too much honor and kindness and sense of duty, to betray her niece and her husband. If Celeste became faithless, then Annette's last defense against a monstrous world would be gone.

But Celeste and Henri had come together. Annette guessed quite accurately at the struggle which must have tormented the older woman. Her pity was deep and profound. Nevertheless, her heart was assailed and torn apart with bewildered pain. If only it had not been Celeste! Annette could not explain, even to herself, why she should feel such wild despair. She would watch Celeste, note how she averted her eyes from her niece, see how her pallor and silence and coldness increased daily, how her every word was distrait and incoherent or sorrowful. At these moments, Annette's despair and anger would soften, and she would feel only compassion. Once or twice she had to restrain herself from crying out: "It doesn't matter, darling! Don't suffer so. I'm really glad." But some virtue in the poor little creature's soul would ooze and bleed like a separate and wounded organ, and her last faint hold on life, her last faint faith in mankind, would loosen and sicken.

And then, she understood that Henri and Celeste saw each other no longer. After her first confusion, she was sharply overjoyed. Celeste could no longer betray her. Her faith and her hope were renewed again, her courage and her tranquility.

She was waiting for Henri today. The warm quiet room was fortified with lamplight and fire against the gloom and grayness of the twilight, against its cold and deathlike menace. Annette wore a soft yellow wool dress and her bright fine hair was swirled about her head in ringlets. Her whole appearance was gentle and childlike, and her large blue eyes shone brilliantly. She heard Henri's approach, and the old painful throb began in her throat. She turned to him, smilingly, and held out her hand.

"Hello, dear," she said, softly, searching his face with inner anxiety.

He looked at her in silence, his expression lowering. Then he said, briefly: "Good evening." He spoke with an effort, when he added: "A miserable day, isn't it?"

He sat down heavily, near the fire, propped his elbow on the arm of his chair, cupped his chin in his hand. He stared at the fire. He had forgotten her. She saw his gloom and abstraction, and was impotent. If only he drank, as other men did! If only there could be the pleasant tinkle in tall glasses, the pungent odor of whiskey, the heartening hiss of soda! But, Henri Bouchard had no solace, no escape from reality. He desired none. Was that a weakness, or a strength? Annette did not know. She only knew that alcohol was loathsome to him, that the taste and smell revolted him. Once he had remarked that he wished they dispensed it in capsules, so that one need not taste it, but could get the effect nevertheless. But he had not really been serious. He desired no effect.

Annette timidly sat down near him, a fixed bright smile on her little three-cornered face. She clasped her hands tightly together, and said in a light tone: "Would you like a capsule, Henri?"

"Ah?" he said, gloomily, turning his head slowly to stare at her. He scowled. "A capsule?"

She felt a fool under that long and inexorable look which condemned her for her inanity. She stammered, still smiling fixedly: "You know, dear. You've often spoken of capsules.

349

For alcohol. It's such a horrid day, and so much flu about. I thought perhaps you might like a drink."

She waited for his abrupt and annoyed refusal. But, to her surprise, he began to smile. He dropped his hand. He regarded her with an almost friendly look.

"That might not be bad. All right, then. But not Scotch and soda. That's too extended a drink. Something concentrated—and strong. I don't know what."

She was dizzy with excitement and happiness. It had been so long since he had condescended to speak to her casually, or to notice her. He was staring at her now with a curiously thoughtful expression, and there was a quickening in the colorless and inexorable eyes that were regarding her intently. She jumped up at once and rang for a servant. She gave the order for two Manhattans. "But very strong, please," she whispered. She returned to Henri and sat down again. Her smile was wide and strained.

She knew very well that she had intelligence and eloquence, but with Henri she had always been mute and absurd. She wanted to say, as always, bright and subtle things to him, brilliant things which would inspire his admiration. But the words that came from her were always dull and awkward, and without vitality. She loved him so terribly, and feared him even more. She could only gaze at him with the light and brilliant blueness of her eyes, and wish desperately that she could approach him, that he would speak to her fully of what tormented him in these wild and dreadful days. She was sure that he would be amazed at the extent of her knowledge.

Though Henri was not a subtle man, he was astute and penetrating. He knew much of what his wife was thinking. Annette was quite mistaken: he did not consider her a fool. In many ways, he considered that she was superior to Celeste; her mind was pellucid, more mature, more civilized. Often, he was very sorry for her, and angered with himself for his own brutality, for no one, he knew, could hurt this poor pretty little creature without suffering some hurt in himself. He was not given to compassion, but he had felt more pity for Annette than he had ever felt for another human being.

Though his look was still curiously thoughtful and alert, as he stared at her, he allowed himself to relax a little. When the cocktails were brought, he gave them a brief glance of distaste, put the glimmering glass to his lips and gulped hastily. He made a grimace, wiped his mouth hastily with his handkerchief. Annette sipped hers slowly, hoping and praying that the rigidity in her body would lessen, and that she would be able to speak to him in casual tones. All her married life, she had dreamt of an hour when she and Henri might talk together easily, might reach friendliness and intimacy, might laugh together in the firelight. Was this the hour? She had never been with him before when he was so thoughtful, so ready. The cocktail created a bright and glowing warmth in her, and the tense trembling of her muscles relaxed. It might have been her imagination, but Henri appeared less stony now, and his broad strong hands lay quite easily on the arms of his chair. Her heart became an enormous and quivering lump in her chest, and there were sudden tears in her eyes.

"Was that good?" she asked, in a shaking tone. "I mean, the capsule?"

"Yes," he said, in a friendly tone. "Not bad at all. Except for the taste. Why don't they invent drinks that aren't repulsive to the palate? That would be a god-send. I feel warmer now. I've been cold all day."

What can I say that will interest him? thought Annette, desperately. But she could find nothing to say. She heard herself speaking: "I heard from Papa about an hour ago. He's been ill again. He's terribly frightened. And he's gained twenty pounds, which is very bad."

Why should he be interested in Armand? But to her surprise, he was interested. "He eats too much," he commented. "What about the List? Has he been neglecting it?"

"I don't know. I think he's just unhappy," said Annette, her tone lowering sadly.

"Why should he be unhappy, Annette? He never liked the business. It's been a relief to him that he isn't connected actively with it. Is he lonely? He never cared much for company."

Annette said, without forethought, and with pain: "He's sick in his soul, Henri. I don't think even he knows why."

Henri was silent. But his eyes remained on hers, thoughtfully. Then he said, after a long moment: "Yes. Yes, I can see that. It's too late for him. It was always too late."

His paleness was less. There was even a flush about his eyes, as the alcohol took effect on his unaccustomed stomach. He said: "Sometimes I think it is always too late for all of us. Perhaps I'm sentimental. But you know what the Chinese say: 'Each man lives a life of quiet desperation.' " He smiled a little.

It was the alcohol which made Annette say impulsively, leaning towards him: "Henri, do you live such a life? No one ever knows anything about you. Do you? Do you, Henri?"

He did not answer her for a moment, but only stared at her. Then he said, with strange quietness: "Yes, I do."

She clenched her hands together, and cried out: "Let me help you, Henri! I've always wanted to, you know."

He lifted his hand and half concealed his mouth. Over his hand he regarded her with a strange intensity. "Why?" he asked.

The tears were thick on her golden lashes. She said, with sad humility, dropping her head: "Because I love you."

There was a sudden thick silence in the room. Henri saw that fair bent head, the trembling of the little immature breast, the tense white hands on the childish knees. He saw her desolation and misery, and hopelessness. He frowned, and his lips drew together in a hard and puckered line, as if he was greatly ashamed and embarrassed, and unendurably touched. He sighed. She had never heard him sigh before, and the sound pierced her heart. She looked up, and exclaimed in a trembling voice: "Oh, Henri. Henri!"

And now he saw her piteous face, its pain and weariness and loneliness. "Don't!" he said, quickly and abruptly, and turned away. He pushed himself to his feet. He began to walk up and down the room, his hands clasped together behind his strong back. His steps quickened. He seemed to have forgotten her. She watched him through a splintering dazzle of tears.

And now he began to speak in a low tone: "You oughtn't to have married me, you know. That was a long time ago; there's no use speaking of it now. I had my reasons. I thought I might find time to be kind to you. I haven't found the time, or, perhaps, the inclination. You knew what I was. There has never been time in my life for anything but——"

He halted. She rose involuntarily, and stood near her chair, grasping the back. She cried out: "Yes, I know everything about that, darling. But I always did love you so terribly. Don't reproach yourself. You've made me so happy, really, just being married to you."

He turned his head over his shoulder and stared at her incredulously. He stood, now, below the portrait of his great-grandfather, and it was two identical faces that looked at her with granite disbelief. A wave of dim confusion rushed over her. Her heart was beating wildly.

He was smiling again. He came back to his chair and sat

down. He looked up at her. "Sit down, my dear. Don't be so tense. You are quite a romantic, you know. I can't imagine that just being married to me has given you very much."

"Oh, it has," she whispered, through pale lips. She sat down on the edge of her chair. Her eyes were glowing, filled with light. Her humility, her sincerity, made him acutely embarrassed. He lifted his hand and bit his index finger, and averted his face from her.

His embarrassment increased, and his uneasiness. And again, he felt repulsion for her. It was as if she had touched his flesh with urgent loving fingers, and all his body tightened in repudiation. He regretted this involuntary sensation, but he could not help it. If only she would not look at him like that, if she would not be so intense, if only she could be casual! But she would never be what he wanted, and so, all these years, he had repelled her for fear of her intimacy.

The alcohol had dulled his normal reactions, however, and so after a moment, he could control his embarrassment and his pity. He said, not looking at her: "You've asked me, Annette, whether you could help me. I think you can."

"Yes?" she cried. "Please tell me." She could not believe that she had heard him rightly. She leaned towards him. Her little hands fluttered as if to touch him. Again, his muscles tightened, and he was ashamed of their tightening.

"Do you know what is happening today—in America?" he asked, quietly, denying her eagerness and intensity. "You live such a secluded life, my dear. I've often wondered whether you were aware of what's going on and what it all means to us."

She shrank, and flushed. But she made her voice as quiet and impersonal as his own: "I'm not entirely a fool, Henri. I read, and listen. Yes, I know. I feel terribly impotent and frightened about it all." She added: "I go to the public meetings of the American Freedom Committee." She hesitated: "Please don't be angry, but I'm a member. One of the Charter members. And one of its largest contributors."

"No!" he exclaimed in surprise. But there was no annoyance in his look, only interest. "I didn't know that. I'm not angry, my dear. In fact, I'm pleased. You see," and he hesitated only a little, "I'm the *largest* contributor. I also finance Gilbert Small, its radio speaker."

A wave of delight and excitement flooded her. This was intimacy beyond any of her hopes. She was drawn into a conspiracy with him. She could hardly control herself. She began to laugh incoherently.

"Do you know anything at all about what I am trying to do?" he asked, when she was calmer. He leaned towards her over the arm of his chair, and he was very grave. "Anything at all, Annette?"

"No," she said. "Can't you tell me a little?"

He was silent. He regarded her with narrow penetration. Then he spoke briefly and quickly. She listened, hardly breathing, the light welling in her eyes, her little face very pale and intent, forgetting everything but what she was hearing. Once, only, did she whisper, as if she could not control herself: "I didn't know!"

He slapped his hand heavily on the arm of his chair, and shrugged. "Well, you know now," he said, flatly. Then he was silent, staring at the fire. She watched him.

"And now," he continued, after a long moment, "there is a way you can help me. If you are willing to do it, without question. Things are very ominous; they are coming to a crisis. I haven't given you anything, except a brief outline. Now, I need your help."

"Yes?" she whispered. "Anything, Henri. You have only to ask me."

"It might not be easy. You might wonder," he warned. He was silent a moment, and now he looked only at the fire. "How much do you love your brother, Antoine?"

"I love him very much," she said, simply.

"I was afraid of that. You don't know, of course, that he is the head of the faction that is opposing me?"

She was dumb with miserable amazement. At her silence, he turned his large head and regarded her with tense grimness. "Yes," he said, slowly, "that's right. That's why I still want to know if you will help me. And, in helping me, probably destroy your brother, and the others with him. That's probably why I ought to shut up now, and not say anything more."

She could not speak. All her joy was gone, and there was only terror and anguish left behind. But she looked at him resolutely.

"Your father knows," he said, with cunning astuteness. "He knows all about it."

He saw how she struggled to draw a deep breath. She lifted her chin. She was very white, and the bright rings of hair on her little head were like a shining crest, curiously strong, but curiously piteous and vulnerable, also.

"Tell me what to do," she said, in a low firm voice. He saw the pulsing of her small white throat, so thin and soft, and he felt new respect for her.

"I will tell you, then," he said slowly, watching her. "Tomorrow, visit Antoine and Mary. Just a casual call, you know. You wondered how they were getting along, and you wanted to see your father. Then, express regret that Christopher and I seem to be at odds. Speak impulsively, as if you were sorry and confused. Tell Antoine, but very casually, and in distress, that Chris and I have had a violent quarrel. You don't know what it's all about, of course. But it worries you. Everything worries you."

He paused. Annette was looking at him in silence. The firelight glittered on that lifted small head with its indomitable but defenseless curls.

Then she said: "Is Christopher——?"

"Yes," he replied impatiently. "But you've promised not to ask questions. I can only tell you that Antoine suspects something, and he must not suspect. If he does, then we'll learn nothing more of what he is doing under cover, from Christopher. But look, I'm wasting time.

"And then, you must confess that I've been borrowing money from you. A lot of money. That I seem very worried. That I went to New York to see old Regan, and that I came back in a very gloomy and depressed condition. You are very concerned about me. You wonder what it is all about. You wish I would give you my confidence." He paused, and smiled grimly. "All this sounds very foolish to you, doesn't it? And silly?"

"No," she said, steadfastly.

"Well, then, you can infer that old Regan wouldn't see me, or something. You gathered that, you'll say. Then, you can add that I've quarrelled with Emile, and Nick and Francis about something. Very violently. You are very bewildered. You don't know what it is all about. You wish you did. You want to help me."

"Yes," she said, simply.

"And here's another thing," he said, with gathering intensity. "Before you talk like this to Antoine, who will be very sympathetic and interested, by the way, you must see your father. You must tell him this: that he is to pretend that I've tried to borrow five million dollars from him, with my bonds as collateral. And that he has refused me. Bring him down, then, to Antoine. Have him remark about it pettishly

355

and tell Antoine that he has refused. Your father will understand. You will, in front of Antoine, beg him to lend me this money. He is to refuse, very angrily. He is to complain about me, that I seem to be losing my grip, and that he is beginning to have doubts about me. He is to say some nasty things. No doubt he can think them up on the spur of the moment," and Henri smiled grimly with amusement.

But Annette did not smile. There was a strange whiteness about her lips, which were rigid and still.

After a long time, she asked, steadily: "Will all this finally hurt Antoine? Very badly?"

"Yes," he said ruthlessly, watching her. "Very badly, indeed. It will ruin him."

She did not speak. She only looked at him with anguish.

"If you do this, it will encourage Antoine to be a little less cautious. He will move more quickly, and openly. That is what we want. He is concealing too many things. Time is short. We can't wait. He's got to lay himself open."

She was silent. He hated himself, strangely, for what he said next: "Look, my dear. I won't need to tell you what my success means to America, to the world, to all of us. You've got to imagine it. Coming down to a deceptively simple statement, it means this: Either I go under, or your brother. You understand now. You've got to decide between us."

She felt the enormous implication of the things he had left unsaid. It seemed to her that the great warm room was full of significance, ominous and most terribly important. And in the midst of this vast implication, this universal grimness and fury, she heard his words again: "Either I go under, or your brother."

She felt such a huge pain in herself that momentarily, and with abstraction, she wondered whether she could endure it and live. She was very still. She saw Antoine's face before her. A whole lifetime ran before her inner eye. She remembered herself and Antoine as children. He had been so gay and glittering and full of amusing ways. She had been so neglected, and only Armand and her brother had cared for her. Armand had been too old; he could not understand much. But Antoine had understood. He had torn himself away from his delightful affairs very often, in order to amuse her and encourage her, and make her laugh. She saw the gay little things he had brought her, to make her smile in her many illnesses: a monkey on a stick, that had squealed and run up and down with a flirt of its tail, a mechanical dog that squeaked and turned over in the most absurd way, a music box that tinkled, that opened to reveal tiny dancing figures, a little book that had no leaves inside, but exploded when opened, a little mechanical man that strutted when a key was turned, and presented arms. When she had been too listless to read, he had sat beside her for hours, patiently plowing through classic romances, patiently helping her with her French, and telling her naughty but sparkling anecdotes in that language. She never saw him, even now, without smiling at the remembrance. He had always made her laugh. He had never sympathized with her. He had always pretended that she was "faking." When she would force herself to rise and sit in her chair, Antoine brought her no flowers, but only the silliest of gay magazines filled with the most improper cartoons. When she attended dances and parties, he was always there to escort her, to bring her corsages, to pretend that she was the most beautiful girl in the room. He had bought her records of her favorite arias, and had sung them with the great singers, in a voice that was remarkable for its depth and feeling. She could see him so vividly now, his dark sparkling smile, his extravagant gestures, his dancing eyes; she could hear his voice, resonant with real beauty and feeling.

She closed her eyes on a spasm. She was not unaware that Antoine was an evil man. But she had forgiven him that, always. Because she had loved him, because he had loved her. She had pretended that real evil could not truly live in such a laughing and vivacious young man, that what he did he did out of sheer deviltry and gaiety of spirit. Now, she saw him.

She opened her eyes sluggishly to see Henri watching her intently, with a gloomy and cynical look.

"Never mind," he said. "I see it's too much to ask of you. But I want you to forget what I've said to you. You owe me that much."

He stirred heavily, as if to rise from his chair. But she was quicker than he. She sprang to her feet. She knelt down beside him. She clutched his arm, in the rough sleeve, with desperate hands.

"No!" she cried. "I'll do what you want, Henri! It doesn't matter. I've got to do it. It isn't only for you——"

She could say nothing more. All the strength went out of her. She sagged on her knees. She dropped her head on his arm, less in surrender or love than in utter prostration.

Henri looked down at the little head on his arm, and his

face tightened with compassion and sadness. He lifted his hand and placed it gently on that head. She did not stir; she seemed to have fainted. He felt the soft ringlets under his fingers, so childlike and defenseless, and their softness crept into his nerves and touched his heart with a poignant sorrow.

CHAPTER XXXVII

As when the young Henri Bouchard had walked towards him across the rich and somber carpets of his office, and old Jay Regan had had the startling and confused thought that Ernest Barbour (long dead) had come to life and was approaching him, so now the old financier had a similar and equally confused impression that this present young man was Jules Bouchard, resurrected, subtly flamboyant, glittering and smiling.

He had seen Antoine Bouchard fleetingly on many occasions, but only at a distance, and had exchanged not half a dozen words with him in the past. He had been troubled, then, at the resemblance between the young man and his dead grandfather, Jules, but never so startled, so instantly frightened and ominously depressed, as he was now.

My God, he thought, it isn't possible! Yet, here was Jules again, suave, graceful, dexterous and subtle, with the well-remembered small skull on which the hair resembled that of a sleek seal, the narrow dark face, brown and somewhat puckered, the dry wily lips, smiling now to form the sparkling dark smile which was a replica of Jules', the Machiavellian eyebrows, tilted and quizzical, the small sharp ears close to the head, the light swift walk and the whole air of mocking ingratiation. And, most of all, the vivid evil eyes, so full of laughter and gaiety and cruel refinement.

Jay Regan was not in the habit of rising to greet guests, for he was too old now, and had always been too formidable to bestow this honor upon lesser giants. But now his surprise, and his strange, ominous, and suppressed terror, caused him to rise involuntarily. It was as if a ghost had invaded the cathedral purlieus of his office. He stood there, leaning on his polished desk, staring, immovable as a mountain is immovable. He was at once a younger man, and an ancient one, feeling his age, his weariness, his disgust and fear, all through his flesh, which had awakened to an earlier middle age.

He and his father had been so intimately connected with the Bouchard family that he began with no formalities: "It's Antoine, isn't it?" He hesitated. Then he lifted his large and solid hand, veined but like heavy meat, and extended it to Antoine.

Antoine was all deference, all old-fashioned grace and admiration. "I've never really known you, Mr. Regan. I've seen you only a few times, casually. It's been a long time since we met, hasn't it?"

Regan was silent a moment. His shelved and ambushed eyes studied the young man somberly. "Yes," he said, with strange slowness and emphasis, "a very long time."

He sat down again. He placed his hands, palm-down, flat and heavy, upon the desk. A dull aura, as of heat and perspiration, spread out about them in an outline, on the darkly polished surface. His mountainous bulk appeared collapsed and full of weight. His chest and belly became one huge round mound, and the great domed head was set upon that mound like the head of some ruined and immeasurably ancient Buddha, overcome by the centuries, overcome by evil.

Antoine sat down. He gave off an atmosphere of elegant but deadly vitality and delicate exuberance. Everything about him appeared to crackle. "He will explode, one of these days," the irrelevant thought came to old Regan. The young man was very gracious and deferential. He allowed a thoughtful look of admiration and respect to increase the sparkle of his eyes. Seeing this, Regan smiled to himself. What was the devil up to? For the first time in a long while he felt an answering alertness and aliveness; his old sluggish blood quickened, his old piratical instincts stirred again, refreshed.

"I will be frank with you, sir," said Antoine. "Very frank. I owe that to you, for I know you have no time to spare for elaborate preambles. So, I am prepared to be candid."

Aha, thought Regan, happily. "I will be candid," had been one of Jules' most dangerous expressions, calculated to make the serpent coil upon itself in cautious expectancy. Regan said, abruptly: "Your grandfather and I were great—friends.

You remind me very much of him. We did a lot of business together."

Pleased with this opening, Antoine said quickly: "Yes. So I know. And that is why I hope we can do—business—together, as you did with my grandfather. Very serious business."

He paused, delicately. He assumed an expression of embarrassment. Regan leaned towards him, delighted, feeling young again.

He put on that large aspect of paternal benevolence which was considered very charming. "And how is little Mary, Antoine? I had luncheon with her father only last week, and he spoke of the coming event."

Antoine assumed husbandly indulgence. "Mary is splendid, Mr. Regan. We expect the event about June. I haven't yet decided whether it is to be a boy or a girl. Frankly, I prefer a girl."

"What? No dynastic ambition?"

"I'm thinking of the brat's intelligence," said Antoine, with another of his gay smiles. "Sometimes Bouchard males aren't very bright, you know."

Regan paused. But his whole great old face broke into a thousand secret laughter lines, as if a mirthful web had been spread over it. "Such as," he suggested, gently, "Robert Bouchard?"

In spite of his insouciance, Antoine was startled. He betrayed this by the merest narrowing of his black eyes, the merest tightening of his mouth, and then only for an instant. Then he was smiling again. "You are omniscient, Mr. Regan, as well as omnipotent."

Regan spread out his hands in gentle deprecation. "To both allegations I enter my complete denial. I am, let us say, only —observant, and affectionate. The Bouchards and the Regans have been very closely knit."

But Antoine was very thoughtful. He studied the immense old man opposite him. His insouciance was shaken, and for a moment or two he felt gauche. The old fiend, then, was not in his dotage, nor fumbling nor easy, as Antoine had hoped. The power of Wall Street was still a terrible power. Antoine saw that his planned campaign would have to be considerably revised and adjusted to the real Jay Regan. He revised rapidly in his mind. In the meantime, Regan, who understood so many things, understood this also.

"Bob and I are great friends, even if we are relatives,"

Antoine said, and despised himself immediately for this naive witticism. Nevertheless, he also immediately saw that this apparent naïveté might deceive Regan, and make him less cautious. So he added, with a sprightly air: "After all, the younger generation is coming up. We'll inherit Bouchard eventually, you know, and we must pick our companions in advance."

"And your henchmen, and vassals, and allies, too," added Regan, with the most affectionate and friendly of airs, as if he felt the most kindly feeling for this young man.

Antoine laughed. "Well, yes. Of course! I'm not impertinent, I hope, in suggesting that I'd like to have some assurance that the great Mr. Regan might be an ally, later?"

Regan was silent. Very slowly, he fumbled for a cigar in the silver box near his hand. He cut the end, put the cigar in his mouth. Antoine, without haste, rose and struck a light for the old man. Regan puffed with concentration for a few moments. Through the gray smoke his Buddha-eyes stared at Antoine with timeless wisdom and unblinking shrewdness.

"I believe in striking directly at a thing," said the devious Antoine. "So, I might as well tell you now, Mr. Regan, that I've just heard that you've refused my brother-in-law, Henri Bouchard, a considerable loan."

He leaned back in his chair, and smiled elegantly. Regan took the cigar from his mouth abruptly. He held it in his fingers, and the smoke coiled near the sides of his head like incense. He was immovable. The tiny ambushed eyes glittered for an instant under his brows. What the devil! he thought to himself. He did not stir, but there was a sudden huge tautness about his body, and a stillness.

"May I ask who gave you that—information?" he said.

Antoine lifted his hand airily. "Now, that would be violating a confidence, sir. Please forgive me, but I can't tell you. I only know that I received it. Could I ask you, without impertinence, whether this is true?"

But Regan was silent. He was like gray granite in his chair. His mind darted, conjectured, wondered. Had Henri disseminated this lie, and, if so, for what purpose? He said, finally: "It isn't impertinent for you to ask, Antoine, but it would be indiscreet of me to give you any definite answer, wouldn't it? Suppose, now, that you go on from there?"

Antoine leaned towards him with sudden seriousness. "You know my situation, Mr. Regan. I am Secretary of Bouchard. My father, though retired from active participation, is still

361

the power of the company. You will see, then, how this concerns me. If there is anything—wrong, it becomes vital for me to know, you see."

"I'm afraid, then," said Regan softly, "that I'm not the one to ask. Did you really believe I'd tell you, Antoine? Come now, you can't really believe I'd tell you who negotiated a loan with me, or why, can you?"

He went on, smiling humorously: "Why don't you ask Henri? After all, he is your sister's husband. I presume you are on good terms."

"Oh, excellent terms, certainly," replied Antoine, stinging all over his body, and cursing himself for ineptness. "But, it's a delicate matter. As I told you, however, it is a matter of vital concern to me, and if I was stupid enough to ask you that question, I hope you will understand that it was only because of my natural anxiety."

"Very natural," acceded Regan. He waited a moment, then cautiously picking his way in the complete and midnight darkness, he added: "If there is any way I can assist you, Antoine—If there is anything that is giving you anxiety, I'd be glad to help. Naturally, I am interested in—er—all sides of the question."

And now he allowed himself to look disturbed. He allowed his hand to drop and betray just the slightest tremor. He allowed a look of old distintegration to creep over his features. He said, slowly: "I've always had a deep admiration for Henri. When I was a very young man, I saw his great-grandfather, Ernest Barbour, in my father's offices. I—I had thought he resembled Ernest. Sometimes I'm not so certain. The physical resemblance is there, but——"

The "but" hung in the air with tremendous significance. Then, thought Antoine, exultantly, it is true!

He laughed lightly. "I never knew old Ernest Barbour. But, judging from the stories I've heard of him, any resemblance between him and Henri is purely coincidental. Or, I should say, physical. It seems to me that old Ernest's pure and simple plan was to benefit old Ernest, and the hell with the rest of the world. He had no senile patriotisms, no sentimentalities, no fears or qualms, or hazy idealisms. He knew what he wanted, he set out without fear to get it, and he always did get it. And the devil take the hindmost. Now, Henri, unfortunately, isn't like that, though he occasionally gives that illusion."

"You mean, Antoine, that he does consider the hindmost?

Well, I, for myself, have never known an occasion when the hindmost ever benefitted the superior man, or ever showed him the slightest gratitude. Come, now, I don't believe that of Henri. He hasn't gone sentimental."

Antoine's spirits and cunning were rising. Now Jules, thought Regan, would begin to feel some wariness, and would begin to think. But this young rascal has an even stronger strain of Latin blood in him, which leads him to believe that practically everyone is a fool. Or, could it be a Teuton strain?

"Not sentimental," said Antoine. "I can't accuse him of that. I'd say that he was scared to death. He was one of the great instigators of the plot to rearm Germany, in violation of the Versailles Treaty. Through international cartels, through his association with I.G. Farbenindustrie. But I know that you understand all that. He thought, and quite correctly, too, that it was necessary to build up a strong and dictator-controlled Germany against the spread of bolshevism, and Hitler was his man. He was, and still is, the man for us, and will soon attack Russia. That will rid us of the Communist threat. Later, we shall deal with labor, especially after Roosevelt is disposed of neatly.

"I'm sure you know our plans. The business of the world, and the world's business, is inevitably in the hands of the great industrialists and corporations. That is why labor must not, and cannot, have any voice in the future. Hitler will win this war, he must be helped to win it. We have given him promises, and he has given us his own promises."

He stopped, delicately. "You agree with me, Mr. Regan?"

Regan assumed an expression of embarrassed concern. He stared at Antoine with reluctant and furtive admiration. "I'm not committing myself, my boy. Go on." He said to himself: Jules would have known better.

"A democracy controlled by labor simply cannot exist any longer," Antoine said. "After Hitler has signed a negotiated peace with Britain—after he has attacked Russia, and conquered her, we will enter into certain agreements with him. In the meantime, we shall have come to control labor, have elected our own choice as President, and shall see our way to a fascistic sort of government in which labor shall have no part, and shall be compelled to obey our orders. That is our plan. But you have known this for some time."

"Yes," said Regan, thoughtfully. "But, I've lived a long time, and I've been thinking. There is a certain imponderable something in human life. What if Britain refuses to sign a negotiated peace, no matter what happens? What if Hitler gets bogged down in Russia? What if we enter the war, ourselves? You know, there are quite a number of 'warmongers' here. All of this, of course, is only speculation."

Antoine smiled slightly. "Don't think we have overlooked the imponderables, Mr. Regan. Suppose, then, that Britain does not sign a peace, and that Hitler encounters extreme difficulties in Russia? Suppose we enter the war, under pressure from irresponsible politicians, or in some other way? We have our plans, too. For instance, Bouchard & Sons made a net profit out of World War I of two hundred and fifty million dollars. We then bought twelve million shares of a certain motor corporation, and now completely dominate it. We have an extremely large branch in Germany at the present time, and we are supplying motors to Hitler, and very excellent motors, too.

"Now, my father-in-law, as you know, controls one of the largest oil cartels in the world, supplying Germany with oil at present. Too, he controls a certain extremely good synthetic rubber patent. Incidentally, answering part of your question, America will have a hard time gaining control of that patent to make synthetic rubber, in the event the Indies' supply is cut off for us. My father-in-law will make certain that we do not get it, on the ethical ground, at first, that Germany has been granted it. War or no war, that patent will remain in the hands of Germany, and our motor branch will still continue to turn out motors for Hitler, even should the remote possibility occur that we enter the war, ourselves. My father-in-law plans a delaying action in America, which will keep us from manufacturing synthetic rubber for a long time. All of this will have a bad effect on our own preparations to fight Hitler."

Regan was slowly nodding. He gave the impression that he was endeavoring not to show much interest, but that he was really extremely excited. Antoine noted this with gratification.

"Then," said Antoine, "my father-in-law is one of the directors of that certain aluminum company which has a cartel arrangement with Germany. This arrangement will permit Germany to acquire all the aluminum she needs for airplanes, but will enormously limit the supply for America. Again, this will have a bad effect on our preparations for war. At the very least, it will have a delaying action while Mr. Roosevelt's muddle-headed school of professors prepare to get around to the matter."

Regan turned his cigar slowly in his fingers, and stared at it reflectively. "Where," he asked, "does Henri come in on all this?"

Antoine laughed. "Henri *was* in on all this. At first. Then, all at once he had a change of mind. It seems that he doesn't trust Hitler. Hell, who does? But Hitler, and we, know that it is to our mutual advantage to work together. He is to win the war, with our assistance, and the assistance of the great British, French, and other corporations, and, in consultation with us, be assigned a sphere of influence. Then, in America, we shall put over a fascist form of government, with all the trimmings to satisfy the fatuous and donkey people. That will be the end of democracy, which cannot co-exist with us.

"Henri was quite agreeable. In fact, he thought up most of the idea, himself. Then, he had a change of mind; he didn't trust Hitler. He believed that Hitler might set out on the conquest of America. That is quite true. We planned for that, also. After Hitler has conquered America, we will take over the industrial control of it. There is where we split with Henri. He believes that Hitler won't let us seize the control. He can't see himself dominated by Hitler. We can."

Regan leaned back in his chair and gazed at Antoine with strangely blank eyes. "The whole plan is bold, and just a little terrible. Plans have a habit of back-firing, you know. You deprecate the American people. I'm not getting into any discussion with you on the subject of their intelligence. Incidentally, let me ask you this: Are you, and your—associates, still supplying Hitler with oil, motors and other matériel? I understood Henri had stopped that."

"Henri," said Antoine, delicately, "does not know everything."

And then, while Regan listened with the most painful attention, Antoine told what had been done to circumvent the orders given by Henri Bouchard. As Regan listened, he allowed a smile, half of incredulity, and half of amazed admiration, to appear on his mouth. Once or twice he said to himself: Jules would have told no one, no one on God's earth! A half hour went by, and Antoine's soft voice continued.

And then, when he had done, there was a long silence in the immense and shadowy reaches of the room.

Regan began to speak, and he made his voice shake: "I see. I see. I'm an old man, and I've had my hands in many plots, but now I'm astounded. This is the biggest, and the most incredible. I can see your viewpoint: this war is no longer a struggle between nations, but a struggle between one Idea and another. The struggle of the people, in whatever nation, against those who are determined to master, control and rule them. Yes, I see. Frankly, as you would say, the Idea has occurred to me many times in the past, but I gave it up as fantastic. Now, I see that it has possibilities——"

And now he allowed himself to appear enormously excited. He rocked back and forth in the chair. He rubbed his mouth over and over with a hand that did not shake too obviously. He gave the effect that he was trying to control himself, that he did not wish to let Antoine discern how much he was agitated, or how grimly exultant.

He also, very convincingly, gave Antoine the impression that he, an old man, had become cautious and careful. He said: "I must come back to the American people. What of them? Can you keep them subdued, while Hitler wins, and unarmed, until he gets around to them?"

Antoine laughed again. "It isn't very hard. We've got Jaeckle, who's very potent here, and has a huge following. We've got the America Only Committee and a dozen subsidiary committees, in which the more violent lunatic fringe can have their little excitements. We've got the Church, with its hysterical bellowings about 'International Jewish Communists, and international Jewish bankers.' The banker business was a neat touch, wasn't it? You think it too obvious? I'm afraid, Mr. Regan, that you've never fully investigated the abysmal stupidity of the American people. They believe anything, provided it gives them an opportunity to hate something. We have our plans for race riots, for Negro lynchings, and are organizing very strong pacifist organizations in conjunction with the others. We have picked speakers who appeal to the timorous and hoarding middle class, who hate labor anyway. We have our newspaper columnists who harp on the iniquities of labor unions, our radio commentators, our Senators, our Congressmen. We have our plans for nationwide confusion and disunity, if the people begin to show any disturbing tendency to interfere with Hitler. It won't be hard to discredit Roosevelt; we've already done excellent work there. He'll never be elected again. We have our man picked——"

"I've heard of Willkie, Wendell Willkie, mentioned as a possible candidate," said Regan, abstractedly.

"Willkie?" Antoine laughed with extreme merriment. "I've heard that rumor, too. He'll never be put up by the party.

We'll see to that, I can assure you. Not that I've anything against him personally, but he's an unknown factor, whereas our own man knows what we want and what we plan. You can be easy on that point, sir."

Again, there was silence in the room. Then, after a long moment or two, Regan said thoughtfully: "You know, I can't help remembering that it was the British masses, against the will of their government, who insisted upon war with Hitler. What if that happens here? You see, there really is such a thing as a vast, dumb and amorphous conscience in peoples, and that is the greatest of the imponderables."

"Not in America, Mr. Regan. There is no national or racial conscience. Only forty percent of the people are of British stock. The others hate Britain. Moreover, the people generally are too unintelligent to think logically. Even more than the German people themselves, they are amenable to lies and to skillful propaganda. We don't consider them for a moment."

He paused, then continued: "There is no chance of our failing, either now or in a post-war world. And that is why I've come to you today."

Regan did not remove those piercing and ambushed eyes from the young man, even though he neatly moved and rearranged articles on the polished expanse of his desk. "Yes?" he said softly.

"It was good news to us, Mr. Regan, when we learned that you had refused a loan to Henri. It might interest you to know, too, that he's borrowed large sums from my poor sister, and he approached my father, who refused him. He needs quite a lot of money to circumvent us. He won't get it. We want assurance from you that he will continue not to get it from you."

Regan lifted his hand and massaged his lips again. A sharp and curious look pointed his eyes. He said: "I don't finance lost causes."

Antoine smiled, and the dark sparkle of that smile invaded all his face. "Thank you," he said, in the gentlest of tones.

With a graceful inclination of his head, very deferential and warm, he lit a cigarette, and the two men smoked in quiet amity for a little while.

"And now, I come to another small matter," said Antoine. "Lord Ramsdall's brother, James, is a director, as you know, of Logan Hollister, your London banking counterpart. James is a cautious devil, but old Georgie has let me know, very discreetly, that James is watching you closely, to learn your next move, and that he, himself, is holding back on permits to allow the Venezuelan Oil Products Company to ship oil to Hitler through South American ports. He controls Venezuelan Oil Products, as you know, and is also a director of the Argentine Property & Industries, the Argentine South-Eastern Railroad, the Buenos Aires Waterways Dock Company, the Uruguay Railroad Systems Company, and one or two others. We need their full cooperation just now, very urgently, in the matter of supplying war matériel to Hitler. James, like all the British Tories, is determined that Hitler shall not be overthrown in Europe, or if the war does go against him—which isn't very likely—that a negotiated peace be signed with him in which he retains political power in Europe. The British Tories, like ourselves, dare not let democratic or liberal ideas survive. However, James is watching you, waiting for your next move. If you can give him the proper signal, the pace of the war will be immeasurably quickened, and Hitler's conquest of Europe completed in short order. The British Tories are much more afraid than are we of what we have called the 'imponderables.' "

" 'The imponderables of the peoples' conscience,' " murmured Regan, almost inaudibly.

"I beg your pardon?" asked Antoine.

"Nothing. I just remarked to myself on what is possibly nothing at all," said Regan. "So, James is waiting for my word, is he? He'll get it. I can assure you of that."

He opened a drawer in the desk and brought out the mounted decanter and two small glasses. He filled them delicately. Antoine watched the golden liquor rising in the glasses. "Napoleon?" he asked.

"Napoleon," agreed Regan. "I always use it to seal a bargain."

He smiled now, affectionately, and with grim charm. He watched Antoine as the young man appreciatively sipped.

"I've said," remarked Regan, a few moments later, "that I never finance, or associate myself with, lost causes. I'd like to know the names of a few men who are in this with you, the heads of the corporations. I understand, of course, that they have to move circumspectly, but none has been to see me. Who are they?"

When Antoine had left the office, after the warmest of handshakes, Regan put in a call for Henri Bouchard, in Windsor. He spoke quickly and tersely: "Look here, when you do a little important lying hereafter, why not inform me beforehand? I had a few bad minutes an hour or so ago when your relative, our little Antoine, called in. However, I got the drift. Incidentally, it is very important that you come in to see me tomorrow, no matter what you have to leave. By the way, he isn't like Jules at all." He added, irately: "He thinks I'm in my dotage."

After the call to Henri, he called a certain great man in British politics, and during the conversation much was said about James Gordon, brother to Lord Ramsdall, the powerful newspaper owner.

CHAPTER XXXVIII

Richard Morse, President of the Morse National Bank, rolled back to his massive leather chair with a grunt of satisfaction, after he had closely studied the news bulletins which had come in on his private news service. He sat down, his legs so short that his feet swung clear a full five inches from the floor. He felt about with one foot for his leather footstool, and smiled grudgingly at Antoine.

"Well, perhaps you didn't do any harm, shooting off your mouth that way to old Regan," he said. "Our friends couldn't have moved so fast without that Venezuelan oil. Moved up their timetable a bit. Fact is, though, I could've murdered you in cold blood, at first. You had no real assurance that Regan wasn't pumping you and distributing the information where it would do us the most harm."

But Antoine only laughed. "I know enough about the dear human race to understand that an old pirate like Regan doesn't become religious and soft and conscience-stricken overnight. It takes time. And indigestion, gout or ulcers. He doesn't have any of those, so don't feel any urge to save his soul. What has he done during the last five years which would have made us doubt him? He financed Mussolini in 1927; he made it possible for Hitler to obtain credits in the most unlikely places; he put pressure on the Bank of England and the Banque de France; he extended credits to Japan and advanced money to exploit Manchuria. He and Dr. Schacht are old friends. As late as November, 1938, he met Schacht in Berne, where profitable arrangements were made for German credits all over the world."

"That's fine, fine. But what has he done lately? Nothing. During your precious five years he has sat on his swollen rump in his office and glowered. He always did have a soft spot for England. Yes, yes," added Mr. Morse, testily, "I'm remembering the meeting with Schacht in November, 1938, but that was only to safeguard his own investments. You took a long chance, Tony, a very long chance."

"But you must admit it was a good one. He promised to give the signal to James Gordon. The signal was evidently given. The oil moved on from Venezuela almost immediately. And now," and Antoine made an expressive gesture with his narrow brown hands, "Norway. Denmark. Holland. Couldn't have been done without that huge supply of oil in a hurry."

Richard Morse grunted, puffed at his cigar. He was a very short fat man with a huge red face, deceptively good-natured and benign in expression except for the piercing blue of his little piglike eyes. His white hair was cropped closely about his big round head, but at the top there was a riot of snowy curls, very beguiling. He had little white hands, daintily kept, and he wore a large diamond on the left hand, a gaudy piece of jewelry which, however, did not detract from his solid appearance. He affected soft gray as his most becoming color, and he was fastidious down to the last detail.

The two men sat in thoughtful silence for a little while, a rich and satisfied silence. Then Mr. Morse spoke, and his expression had become less satisfied: "What'll the reaction of the country be to these new invasions? I've had an uneasy feeling. Whole country may be damned well stirred up, y'know. Maybe it'll have the hell scared out of it. Especially after Hitler's constant reassurances that he planned no more conquests in Europe. How many people, d'you think, will swallow the new stuff he'll put out, that he had to 'defend' Norway, Denmark and Holland from British aggression, when even the goddamnest fool in America knows that Britain hasn't the planes, tanks or men to protect herself, let alone invade any other country on the Continent?"

"I've told you over and over, sir, that the American people don't think. I can assure you that the only real reaction of

Americans will be a more fearful impulse towards isolationism. Getting into a hole and pulling it closed after them. The word has gone out to our organizations to step up the activity. Bishop Halliday, for instance, is to give a radio broadcast tonight urging even more violently that we mind our own business, that Hitler has no designs on us, that all the frightened rumors and warnings of the 'war-mongers' are inspired by 'International Jewish bankers.' "

He paused, for Mr. Morse had lifted his hand abruptly, and was scowling. "Y'know, I never did like getting mixed up with religion like this. 'Leave religion out of business' has always been my golden rule. You can't depend on religion. It's an explosive. It's an insanity. It's a drug, a disease. Unreliable. You can buy it one minute, and can't buy it the next. It's—it's the one big imponderable in human affairs, and I've kept my skirts clean of it. Oh, I'll grant you it's been serving our purpose very well, lately, and as yet shows no indication that it won't continue to serve it. But, I don't trust it. An awful mess can be stirred up here in America. Outside of a few Protestant ministers who hate England and the Jews and democracy, the big majority of the American people, who are Protestants, haven't forgotten the blessing that the Pope bestowed on the Italian Army when it went out to murder Ethiopia, and they haven't forgotten the Concordat between Hitler and the Pope, and they haven't overlooked the fact that Hitler's satellite countries and allies are Catholic. And now, the countries he has invaded are Protestant countries. Protestant pulses all over America are going to be uncomfortably stirred, y'know. They're going to scrutinize Halliday and his gang just a little more closely, and the leaders of the America Only Committee, and the rest of 'em."

"Jaeckle, our best man, is a Protestant," reminded Antoine, smoothly. "And one of the leaders of the America Only Committee is a Jew. We've kept the active Catholic leaders in the background, because of the probability of just this emergency."

Mr. Morse struck his desk irritably with the palm of his hand. "I repeat: I don't like this getting mixed up with religion. Look here: Protestants in America are going to do a little thinking. I've never quite subscribed to your theory that all Americans are donkeys and morons. A few do think, and when they think they get mad. They're going to ask themselves a lot of questions. How come Hitler's allies and satellites are Catholic? And what about the Pope's rôle in Europe during the past year? It won't take much to convince them that this is really a religious war, under the surface, a last final deadly struggle between the forces of Catholic reaction and Protestant liberal progress. Y'say it's fantastic? My boy, it's the fantastic element that always comes up inconveniently, when you least expect it."

"But that's nonsense, sir. Idiots though the American people are, they won't come to that conclusion. It isn't true, and you know it. Why, the three most potent leaders of the American Freedom Association, our worst enemy, are Roman Catholics. Archbishop Mueller has denounced Halliday a hundred times, and has urged us not only to prepare to defend ourselves, but to declare war on Hitler. The Catholics are as much divided on this war as are the Protestants——"

"Nevertheless," said Mr. Morse, loudly and rudely, "that propaganda can be spread. What if we have religious riots in this country? In the confusion, the people will begin to think, in a rudimentary fashion. It won't serve our advantage, I can tell you that. We've got to have a nation determined on peace, let hell break out anywhere else. A bad thing, getting mixed up with religion."

He added, with sudden explosive rage: "And there's my son's wife, that miserable, tight-mouthed ——. Organizing the Catholic Mothers of America, which is printing anti-Semitic, anti-democratic, pro-German propaganda by the million. A fine bunch of relatives you have, in certain places! What d'you think the majority of Americans, the majority that is Protestant, is going to think about the Catholic Mothers of America and their tripe when it finally gets around to thinking?"

"When it does get around, if it ever does, it will be too late," said Antoine.

Mr. Morse rocked violently in his chair, and glowered. "I tell you, I don't like it. Catholic this, and Catholic that—all hating something. Getting too damned bold, they are, forgetting that they're really hated and feared under the surface, forgetting that they are still less than one-fifth of the American people. God damn it, I hate 'em, myself! Dragging my four grandchildren into the Church, in spite of what I said, and made clear. My son's a——" and he expressed his opinion of his weak and timorous son in such words that Antoine, despite his alarm, had to smile.

"Phyllis means well," he said, demurely, for he detested that female relative, and despised her frightened husband.

"She's a damned danger to us!" shouted Mr. Morse, turning quite purple. "One of my ancestors fought with Cromwell, and did a good job, too, driving the Irish swine into the sea. God damn it, I wouldn't mind a few thorough anti-Catholic riots in America, and if they don't shut up soon, they'll have 'em——!"

He struggled for breath. "Look here, we've got to have a nation unified for peace, until Hitler is in a position to help us. No more damned Catholic societies messing things up. Have I made myself clear?"

Antoine nodded soothingly. "Of course. But that isn't in my province, exactly, Mr. Morse."

Mr. Morse pounded the desk with both fists. "She's a cursed cousin of yours, isn't she—that Phyllis? Tell her to shut up. My son's wife is not going to mess things up for us. That's my final word."

Antoine was amused. "You can't blame the Catholic Church, or the Bouchards, either, for Phyllis."

Nevertheless, he was extremely uneasy, despite his debonair expression. It was the most damnable thing! He had always had the highest respect for the ruthless and venal Richard Morse, who could always be depended upon to be avaricious and expedient, without dangerous emotion or doubtfulness. Yet, he had given vent to the most primitive of hatreds, and had exploded into emotional vilification of a Church which had, paradoxically, done much to promote his interests. In the final wild hour, then, it was not reason, it was not even self-interest, that made the decisions that shook the world. It was emotion, primordial passions, and the deep inexplicable pulse of the amorphous human heart.

Jay Regan had murmured something which he had believed inaudible, but Antoine's quick ear had caught it: "The imponderables of the peoples' conscience." (In Morse's case, it had been the imponderable of instinctive hatred for the stranger.) The imponderables of the peoples' conscience! For the first time in his life, Antoine felt apprehension and doubt. What if, in the final wild hour, the conscience of the American people exploded into terrible being? What if they started from their beds, their desks, their machines, their tables, with one loud and frightful cry of rage and indignation? What, then, would happen to their enemies, the men secretly sworn to betray and enslave and despoil them?

Incredible, thought Antoine. However, his apprehension became deep uneasiness. This mongrel race of men called

Americans, this spawn of the gutters of Europe, this bewildered, stupid, ignorant horde, bedevilled by Church and by hatred and by lies, could never have one unified voice, could never compel its diverse pulses to beat in unison. Their masters, their betrayers, were too strong, too cold, too ruthless, too clever, for them.

The news machine began to tick furiously. Muttering profanity, Mr. Morse pulled himself from his chair, reached the machine, lifted the long thin white ribbon spewing out in frantic haste. He read swiftly. And then his red face turned the color of old dough, and his mouth fell open. He stood with the ribbon in his hand, and did not move.

Antoine rose swiftly, and went to him. Mr. Morse could not speak. Antoine took the ribbon of paper from his paralyzed hand.

"The Honorable James Gordon, of the British banking firm of Logan Hollister, has just been arrested on a warrant charging him with treason against the Empire——"

The two men looked at each other in an enormous silence. The machine increased the tempo of its clicking. Numbed, Mr. Morse lifted the ribbon again, and read:

"Information in connection with Mr. Gordon has been furnished Washington, in the belief that American associates of Mr. Gordon——"

Antoine said: "Yes? Well, we're still neutral. It's bad about Gordon, but they can't do anything to us."

Mr. Morse spoke thickly through stiff lips: "Except that matériel and oil will be curtailed in South America, for Hitler." He began to swear in a low steady voice, numbed and incoherent.

The machine clicked on. Stupefied, they read: "Mr. Gordon's brother, George, Lord Ramsdall, the London newspaper publisher, has also been taken into custody for investigation in connection with certain subversive articles which appeared in his publication, which, it is charged, have for their purpose the hampering of the British war effort. More serious charges, it is expected, will be preferred by Scotland Yard against Lord Ramsdall."

"Curse them!" cried Mr. Morse. "Don't they know they're done? Don't they know the Empire's finished? Don't they know Hitler will invade them in a matter of months, and smash them? God-damn fools!"

Antoine said nothing. He stood near Mr. Morse, his dark and puckered face very pale. He said at last: "I don't know. Are they finished? I don't know!" He heard again, with sudden sharp fear: "The imponderables of the peoples' conscience."

Mr. Regan was chuckling as he sat at his desk and telephoned Henri Bouchard in Windsor. "Well, they got Gordon, and Ramsdall. Our little manœuver was a great success. Hah! Hah!"

CHAPTER XXXIX

From all over America, immediately after the invasion of Norway, Holland and Denmark, came a curious sound, like a gigantic breath sucked in, and held. It was as if a man had sat at his peaceful table, idly watching the light of sun and shadow lying on unthreatened fields outside his window, and then became aware of a far-off but terrible sound, doomful and sinister. It was not thunder, for the sky was still serene, the aerial blue still soft and shining, the shadows and the light still held motionless in the tranquil peace. The full plates still steamed fragrantly on the white cloth of the table, the silver still shone brightly, and the birds in the trees outside still twittered and brushed the leaves. Not a thing had changed, after that terrible sound had gone, except that the silence was somewhat deeper, somewhat more intense, somewhat more waiting. The man could hear that waiting; it reminded him, with sudden horrid unease, of an animal crouching, burrowing into the gound soundlessly, drawing himself together, after the shadow of an eagle's circling wing had passed restlessly and seekingly over him. The wing had gone, but the terror and waiting of the animal remained, and its heart continued to pulse in swift horror and dread.

That was the waiting and the fear that made America draw in her breath in one universal convulsion, and hold it. She strained her ears. The sound did not come again. Her heart still pulsed; she felt its unease, its rapidity, through her whole body. From the space from which the sound had come there was only silence now. But it was no longer a serene and sunlit silence. The peaceful light on her fields had a brazen look in the sunset; the blue spaces of heaven seemed less tranquil than foreboding. When the birds sang their last song to the evening there was a strange shrill sound in the notes, sharp with nameless fear. And the very trees, standing so motionless on the grass, seemed less dreaming in the evening glow than hushed in the gaunt and hollow silence that lies at the heart of a hurricane.

It was some days before a hundred voices, shocked into speechlessness for a while, began their wild screaming, their hysterical shrieking, again. They cried again that even this was not America's business, that what America had heard was only the echo of a storm that had passed harmlessly far from her.

But millions of Americans, now, once dulled, once too greedily frightened, once too indifferent, too cruel, too stupid, too ignorant, impatiently and absently brushed aside those dangerous and inimical voices as one brushes aside clouds of gnats with a wave of his arm. And these Americans looked toward that shining space in the heavens from which the terrible and ominous sound had come, and their faces were pale, their eyes staring, in the too bright light of the brassy sunset. For, they were listening.

The green gauze of April's fragile garments was caught in a thousand trees on Placid Heights, near Windsor. In the valley the river was fresh clear silver, running free and swiftly through new fields. The slopes of the hills brightened. The sky had a faint but pellucid clarity that touched the heart with mysterious hope, and from the ground rose the strong breath of the young earth.

Workmen were busy about the house which Peter and Celeste Bouchard had built. They had stripped away the undergrowth down to the rich brown soil, and upon this soil they were sowing grass seed. New young saplings had already been planted. Low mounds of various shapes would soon be flower-beds. Evergreens were suddenly massed together where only straggling timber and weeds had grown. Paths were gravelled; there was a smell of pungent tar in the clear cold air, for the driveways were being laid. In the air, also, was the odor of clean sawdust, the sound of many voices. The conservatory was being built, behind the house.

376

The voices echoed back from the brightening hills. The winds of spring bent the trees, moaned gently in the pines of the slopes that fell away from the house.

Peter, from his window, watched the activity. He had been very ill again. He sat in a wheelchair now, for he had only been allowed to get up from his bed a few days before. It would be several weeks, he had been warned, before he would be permitted to walk outside. To himself, he said: It will be never.

How many days have I left? he would ask himself, anxiously. He had been ordered not to work, at least not for long. But his desk had been pushed between the windows, paper had been placed upon it, and his writing utensils. His doctors no longer objected. Enforced idleness, they saw, would kill him quicker than work. For some reason they could not discern, he must work.

He wrote broadcasts. Under an assumed name, he wrote articles, embodying the information received from Henri, which "radical" and painfully obscure magazines published without recompense. A few times, the pressure of an unseen hand forced more prominent magazines to publish his articles. His book was finished, was soon to be published. He knew he could not begin another. He had no more time. What he must do now must be swift, pungent, telling, like a warning cry lifted in darkness. It must be sharp and loud, so that the sleepers might be awakened.

He was writing an article now, called "What Is Our Hour on the Timetable?"

But he felt that he was pushing blindly against a wall that had no gate in it, though behind the wall lay a threatened and slumbering city. His voice was so feeble. Could it carry beyond that wall?

He was one of the first voices that cried out that Japan, like a great carrion bird, was already circling over the city. His articles, upon pressure from that unseen hand, had been published reluctantly in two or three prominent magazines. As a result, "William Conrad" was now being vigorously attacked not only in enemy newspapers and by public speakers, but on the very floor of Congress, itself. His identity was demanded. He was denounced as a war-monger, a liar, a trouble-maker, probably in the pay of armaments-makers and the "international bankers." He was accused of endeavoring to create strained relations between America and Japan, "our good friend and excellent customer."

Nevertheless, an embargo on oil and scrap was placed on shipments to Japan.

He worked on. He counted every hour of the life that remained to him. He felt death in every part of his body. He thought of nothing but his work. That was all that mattered. Celeste, himself, his life, were nothing now. The last straw of self was blazing in the bonfire of his terror for America.

Celeste, understanding all this, did not urge him any longer to conserve his last strength. She only comforted him when his pain was too great, and only nursed him. She saw how terrible was his agony. She could do nothing to minimize it. When Henri came, she brought him to Peter, and left the two men alone together.

She hardly saw Henri these days, though he came very often, sometimes alone, sometimes with Annette. Her consciousness was removed from him. And from herself. She dared not think of herself, for, if she did, she feared she would go mad. For a most frightful contingency was upon her, which she did not think of, even when she was alone. Peter, she knew, must die soon. In his death was her only safety. Yet she did not think even of that very often. All her life and her efforts were centered on her husband.

When Henri came, and she met him, she looked at him as from a far and empty distance, not seeing him. He was always courteous and cold, and indifferent, passing her on the threshold of Peter's room, as if she had been a servant. Sometimes, but only very rarely, there was a faint far twisting in her, like the dulled memory of a pain stifled under a narcotic. But even he did not matter now. As for himself, if he saw that there was a thin white line running from her brow back over her black hair, which had not been there a few months ago, he did not even glance at it directly. If he saw how haggard and gaunt her face was now, how pallid her lips, and how deep the bluish shadow about them, he gave no sign at all.

It was Christopher who saw, of course, and who suffered, for all his malignancy. All the other relatives had been asked, tactfully, not to call upon Peter and Celeste during these last days of Peter's life. They called on the telephone, they invited Celeste for dinner, but that was all. Christopher and Edith came, and Henri and Annette.

It was Christopher who knew before even his wife knew, or Annette. And certainly, before Henri. Despite all that

Christopher was, his love for Celeste had always been a great and pure thing in his life. So, it happened, that on a particularly bright soft April day he came to see her, and her alone.

CHAPTER XL

Celeste was resting in her room, after a morning of ministering to Peter. She had almost fallen asleep, out of deep exhaustion, when a maid, softly entering, told her that Christopher had arrived, and that he wanted to speak to her upstairs, alone.

Celeste stirred sluggishly, out of the depths of her anaesthesia of suffering and weariness. She was lying on a yellow velvet chaise-longue, and she drew the silk coverlet a little higher over her body before Christopher entered. He shut the door behind him, and then came to her. She looked up at him, and smiled wanly, stretching out her hand. He looked down at her hand as if it were some curious object, then, with the strangest and most convulsive of sighs, he caught and held it so tightly that she felt pain. But she forgot the pain immediately, for her heart began to pound with a sick premonition.

He had not said a word as yet. He sat down on the edge of the chaise-longue near her knees, and looked at her. He still held her hand. He could feel its frail chill, its thinness. He looked down at it, and automatically began to rub it in his dry cool palms, which yet were warmer than her fingers.

She had always loved him so much, she thought, dimly. He was always her brother, her father, even when she had feared him the most, and hated him the most. That narrow razor-like profile, those cold and enigmatic eyes, those tight and colorless lips, at once so crafty and so subtle, were ageless to her. He was still her young brother and protector, and her friend. If his thin sleek hair was gray now, with only

379

a few faint streaks left of its once smooth brown, that had no meaning for her.

There was something in his quiet attitude, in his stillness and silence, now, that seemed to loosen the anguished tenseness in her, and she whispered: "Christopher." And she sighed, over and over, as if something stirred in her heart with unbearable relief, but also with unbearable suffering.

He was very grave. Slowly, then, he bent towards her, and kissed her cheek. "Poor Celeste," he said, gently. "Poor child."

She flushed when he said this, as though he had said something embarrassingly indecent, or tactless or absurd. She drew her hand away, dropped her eyes, and answered: "Why?"

When he did not speak, she glanced up quickly, and saw that he was smiling just a little. But the silvery eyes were not smiling; they were very gentle, and unusually soft. She had not seen this softness since she had been a child, and she was poignantly touched. Her indrawn breath was almost a dry sob. Again, she colored.

"Celeste," he said, "it's been a long time since I asked you to trust me, hasn't it? And the last time, you had no reason to trust me. But I'm going to ask you to trust me now. You see, I know so much about you that you think is hidden from everyone. It isn't hidden from me, darling."

She had listened to his first words with an attitude of cooling withdrawal, but at his last words she started, looked up swiftly with raw fear white on her face. But she said, calmly enough: "I don't know what you mean, Christopher."

He was silent a moment or two, then he said, heavily: "Yes, my darling, you do."

He waited. She did not speak. Her face was whiter than ever. When she lifted her hand to push away that white-streaked lock from her forehead, he saw that her hand was shaking.

"I'm not a child, Kit," she said, unconsciously using the nickname for him which she had not used since childhood. And as she used it, he winced a little, as if in pain. "I have my worries; you know that. But so do many other people. Have I been whining?"

"No," he replied, abstractedly. He sighed. "So, you aren't going to trust me, are you, dear? I don't know how I could help you. Now. But I thought it might be some relief——"

He was surprised when she suddenly burst out with tight but uncontrolled passion: "Nothing can ever help me again!

No one can ever help me! O God, I wish you'd leave me alone, Kit!" And she pressed her hands suddenly against her face, palms-out, and moved violently on the chaise-longue.

He waited, not touching her. After several long moments, she dropped her hands, and showed him her face, starkly, and it was haggard and convulsed. "Go away, please, Kit," she whispered.

He stood up, as if to go, but instead, walked slowly up and down the room, his head bent, as if thinking. She watched him, drawing her breath in and out very quickly, as if she were weeping. But her suffering eyes were dry and watchful. Her hands were clenched together, the nails whitening under the pressure.

Then he stopped beside her, and he was suddenly stern. "You've got to trust me, Celeste. You've got to talk to someone. Who have you, except me? Do you remember how you used to come to me for everything—" He paused, for she had begun to smile with such bitterness and darkness, and the eyes that were fixed on him were bright and hard.

"Still," he said, quietly, "it would have been best if I had succeeded, fifteen years ago, when I tried to make you marry Henri, wouldn't it? You see, I do know that you are thinking how I almost succeeded in keeping you from marrying Peter."

What he said was brutal, but Celeste met it with bitter relentlessness. "If I had married Henri then, it would have been all up with me. You knew it. If Mama hadn't interfered, you might have succeeded. You didn't think of me."

His natural cruelty flared up in him, and he lashed at her: "It's rehashing old garbage, all this, isn't it? But I want to remind you, my dear, that it hasn't 'been all up with you' since you came back. Has it?" He added, when she only stared at him in terror: "You see, I do know a great deal, my pet. I do know that you haven't thought it was endangering your immortal soul, or something, to cavort around with Henri for some time."

She sat up, stiffly, and her face was gaunt with desperate fright. She could not speak. Her hands fell limply on her knees. He could not endure seeing her like this, and sat down quickly beside her. He took one of her cold and rigid hands. But she only looked at him, speechlessly.

"Celeste, you've got to trust me, my darling," he urged. "Can't you see there's no one else? Do you actually believe that I'd be treacherous to you, now?"

He waited. But she still could not speak. He could feel her shivering.

In the gentlest of voices, he went on: "You see, I've known about you and Henri for a long time, from the beginning——"

But she interrupted him in a hard loud voice: "What I'd like to know is: Who doesn't know about it?"

He frowned, startled. "No one, I hope, except you, and me, and Henri."

"Then, disillusion yourself, Christopher," she said, in that unnaturally loud bright voice. "It seems practically everyone does."

He let her pull her hand away from him. He was enormously disturbed. "No, you are wrong, Celeste. I know it. The people most concerned, for instance, Annette and Peter, don't know. That's all that matters, isn't it?"

"Who told you, then?" she said.

He waited a moment or two, then said, very quietly: "Henri."

She stared at him with blank incredulity. Then, forcing her voice through her stiff lips, she cried: "I don't believe you! He wouldn't——You are lying!"

"But he did," said Christopher, inexorably. "From the very beginning. We discussed it."

Now her haggard face turned crimson, and her eyes were suffused. "You—you discussed it!" she repeated, in a stifled voice. "You, my brother——"

"Stop being a romantic, sentimental fool!" he exclaimed. "Of course, I discussed it with him! When I found out. After all, you are my sister, you know. If you were going to trollop around, I wanted to find out why, and I wanted to keep you from getting hurt. I knew what he was; I've always known. I've always known, too, that women aren't important to him, even if he always did want you. I know he is vengeful, and seducing you (nasty, Victorian word!) would make him feel quite high and satisfied, after you had kicked him out some years ago. I wasn't going to stand by and see you hurt, not if I could help it. So—we had the discussion."

Horrible shame swept over her. She put her hands to her throat, and averted her head. He put out his hand to touch her, then withdrew it.

"Let's be sensible, my dear," he said, more gently. "You know, of course, that he's always hated all of us. Even you, too, probably. He came back to smash us. I had a little smashing I wanted to do myself, to the family. He wanted you, and I saw if you married him, I'd have an ally of sorts, though he's a damned treacherous swine. You spoiled my plans, and married Peter. Then, you came back. I soon saw that something was up between you. Perhaps you'd grown up, and saw that you really wanted him. I'm not blaming you. But I knew you would probably be hurt. I didn't want you to be hurt. That's why I forced him to discuss it with me."

"You forced him——" repeated Celeste, and now he saw that she was smiling contemptuously. And at her smile, his face darkened spitefully.

"You're not telling me the truth," added Celeste. When he did not speak, she turned to him, and her smile was very malevolent. "You're not, are you?"

And then he saw that he must be truthful with her, if he was to relieve her agony and secure her trust. He pressed his lips together for a moment, then looked at her directly: "No, not quite," he said. "That is, I'm not telling you everything. But what I'm not telling you doesn't matter. Let us say, for instance, that I found out, and talked to him about it."

She was partly disarmed by his words. She turned her face away from him again. "What did he tell you?" she asked, almost inaudibly.

"He said," continued Christopher, with renewed gentleness, "that he intended to divorce Annette, after Armand died, and marry you. And I had reason to believe that he was telling the truth." He added: "You see, he wants children. It isn't only you, my dear."

She was silent. But now all the bitterness and hardness had gone from her expression, and it was heavy and mournful. She sighed, pressed her fingers to her eyes, dropped them, and looked steadfastly at the windows that opened out on the wide April air.

"And then," he went on, "I found out that you haven't seen him since January. No, he didn't tell me. He's a close-mouthed devil. But I found out, perhaps by intuition." He paused. "Why, Celeste? I know it isn't his fault. It's yours. Was it because of Peter?"

"No," she said, clearly. "It wasn't because of—Peter. I know you think I'm hysterical, but I don't begin something to end it emotionally, without a reason. If it had been—Peter, I'd have never begun it."

He said, with increasing gentleness: "Then why, darling? You weren't tired of the affair, were you?" When she did not answer, he said urgently: "I've really no way of knowing, but I have an idea you didn't tell *him* why, either. You didn't think enough of him to tell him?"

She still did not look at him, but her profile became rigid and very pale. She twisted her fingers together. She said, quietly: "I didn't dare. There were too many other things to consider, things more important than us."

He was baffled at this, opened his mouth to question her, then did not speak. He fixed his attention on her profile, and his own face tightened, became extremely thoughtful. He was a subtle man, and excessively intuitive and discerning. As his thoughts progressed, he became incredulous, shook his head once or twice as if arguing with himself, then, as he read his sister's face with increasing clarity, his incredulity vanished.

He said, reflectively: "I don't think anyone would have tried to injure him. They wouldn't dare."

Yet, even as he said this, doubt and alarm quickened in him. He stood up, and began to walk up and down again, with accelerated steps. Finally, he stopped at the foot of the chaise-longue, and said: "Perhaps you are right. I can see that. But, why didn't you tell him, instead of breaking it off like that?"

She said, in a dull voice: "Who could ever tell him anything? He's too brutal, too egotistic. Who would ever dare to lift his hand against the powerful Henri Bouchard? Yes, he'd think that. He's always thought it. He forgets that every man is vulnerable, especially a man who sets out to destroy his enemies."

Christopher sat down quickly beside her again. "Celeste," he said, with low urgency, "just how much has he told you?"

She shrugged, restlessly. "A great deal. Does it matter?" She added: "I knew if I told him, it would do no good at all. He wouldn't listen. He has such enormous conceit. So I had to do it myself." Now a look of extreme pain came into her face, and she sighed, again and again. "And now, I suppose, it's all over, for him. Even if I explained, after a while, when it was safe, he wouldn't care."

But Christopher only sat and scrutinized her keenly.

Her caution, her control, were gone now. She went on, in a louder, swifter voice, rubbing her hands together, drawing herself together as if she were most frightfully cold: "I knew we couldn't—see—each other again, while Armand was living. It would be fatal to him. I couldn't see him until he had divorced Annette. And he couldn't do that, everything considered, until Armand died. There were so many things—People are so vicious——"

She was speaking incoherently. Then she could say nothing more, and was silent. Feeling her impotence, she flung out her hands in a gesture that was full of speechless desolation.

Finally, she whispered: "I'll tell him, some time, when it's safe. But he won't care, then. I wrote him. He never tried to see me again. He told me, once, that if I ever sent him away, he'd never come back. So, he won't ever come back."

Christopher was overwhelmed with pity for her. He put his hand on hers, and said: "Yes, he'll come back. All you have to do is send for him. I know it."

But she shook her head with profound and dreary conviction. "No, he won't." She added: "Even when I explain, he won't come back. He will be furious. He will feel I've insulted him by suggesting that he had ever been vulnerable. You see, I know all about him."

Christopher began to speak, then stopped. His colorless and narrow face suddenly flushed a little. He shook his head slightly, to himself. Then, with resolution, he put his hands on his sister's shoulders, and turned her forcibly to him. He looked into her desolate dull eyes. He said, softly: "You don't think he'll come back—when it's safe, of course—because of the child?"

Now the dullness of her eyes vanished in the sudden frantic lightning of terror which flashed into them. She tried to pull herself backwards from his hands, but he held her inexorably. Her mouth fell open blankly, and he saw the white shining of her teeth.

"Celeste!" he said, sharply, frightened for her.

But now she had a frenzied strength. She pulled herself free of him. She swung her feet to the floor, and stood up, trembling as if she had been struck. She cried out: "How did you know? Does everyone know?"

He stood up. He knew he had to calm her, for she appeared ready for wild flight, and God knew what excesses, in her terror. He grasped her arms and held her again, with hands that were both gentle and firm. But he could hardly bear to look at her poor distraught face.

"No, I'm sure no one knows, except me. Who comes here, anyway? You haven't seen Annette for a month, and as far as I can see, Henri doesn't look at you when he does see you. Edith hasn't been here for some time, either. So, I'm the

385

only one. And I wouldn't have known, so far as any sign is concerned. It was just—call it my intuition," and he smiled slightly, a smile which was intended to reassure her. "Sit down, dear. You'll fall, if you don't. There, let me help you."

But she suddenly turned to him and clung to him with desperation, dropping her head to his shoulder. She began to sob, wildly and without control. He put his arms about her, letting her weep, knowing it was the only relief for her. He pressed her head against his shoulder, murmuring words of tenderness and compassion and understanding such as his wife had never heard from him, nor anyone else. And for the first time in many years, he felt the old sad melting of his heart for his sister, the old sick throbbing and protectiveness.

It was a long time before she relaxed sufficiently to let him put her again on the chaise-longue. Beyond the windows heaven had darkened immediately overhead, but in the west the sky was all static, hollow blue, with one small fixed cloud in it, touched at the rim with pale cold fire. Celeste was shivering so violently that Christopher closed the window, lifted the coverlet from the couch, and placed it gently over her shoulders. She sat, huddled together, her head bent. Then he sat near her once more, and studied her with grave pity.

"Why didn't you do something about it—before?" he asked.

She said, hardly audibly, and without lifting her head: "I might have. But, Peter took ill, right after—right after I sent Henri away. He was sick for nearly three months. He almost died, you know. I didn't have time—to think. I had a vague idea something was wrong—in March. But everything was so confused. There were so many nights when we thought Peter would die. And I was so exhausted. No time to think, at all. And, when I did, I couldn't leave him, not even for— that. I kept waiting, thinking each day that I could leave him. I knew it would have to be for about three or four days, at least. But he kept getting worse. I couldn't leave him." She drew a gasping breath. "Then, last week, when I could leave him for a few hours, I went to a doctor in Philadelphia." She paused. Her head dropped lower. She whispered: "He said it was too late. He couldn't do anything for me. No one could."

Christopher could not help saying, with alarm: "Did the doctor know you?"

"No. I just picked him at random. I didn't give him my name, of course."

"How long—?" asked Christopher.

"Over four months, now," she whispered.

Now that everything had been said, Christopher was appalled. He fumbled for a cigarette, lit it, stared at it blindly. Then he offered Celeste a cigarette. She took it, and he lit it for her. The tears ran down her pale cheeks in childish rivulets. But he saw that she was calmer, now.

"You must have some plans, Celeste, haven't you?" he asked, after a little. "How do you expect to explain this? To Peter," he added, hesitatingly.

She said, in a voice completely without expression: "Peter's doctors say he will die almost at any time."

Despite what he was, he was sick at her words. He frowned involuntarily. "And," he said, inexorably, "what, after that? When Peter is dead? How will you——"

"I can't go away," she said, calm with despair. "Everyone will be sure to find out, eventually. So, as far as anyone will know, it will be Peter's child."

He could not help exclaiming: "Do you expect them to believe that, Celeste?"

When she shrugged heavily, he saw how completely she was undone. "It won't matter. They won't dare deny it to my face. If I went away, they would have reason to talk about it, openly. If I stay, and I will, they won't dare——"

"But, we all know that you and Peter——"

She lifted her head and smiled darkly and fully at him " 'You all know.' But none of you will dare to say it openly."

She looked at him with the hard straight eyes and the cold smile that are the products of cornered despair. He felt painful compassion for her, intense and wretched.

"You've got courage, my pet," he said, staring at her with incredulous and sad admiration. "Yes, I can see what you mean. No one but the family will doubt. But they won't talk about it, except in whispers. There's family pride, you know, and even though we hate hell out of each other, we put up a solid front to everyone else. And after a while, if you keep your mouth shut, and your head up, they'll pretend with you. A kind of perverted family loyalty. Yes, you can get away with it, if you stick it out and look them in the eye."

And he smiled at her affectionately. "And Edith and I, of course, will stand with you, for what it's worth. And you and Peter have so few friends that no one knows anything about your affairs."

Then he had an alarming thought: "But what if Peter doesn't——"

She said, very quietly: "In that event, of course, I'll have to go away, before it's too obvious to him. I've got to spare him that, you know. No sickly confessions, and all that, even though he'd stand by me, I know."

There was a long silence between them. Celeste finished her cigarette in the heavy serenity of despair and resolution. But Christopher's cigarette burned itself away in his fleshless fingers.

Then he said: "There's another thing: Henri will eventually know. Have you thought about that? What do you think he will do?"

"That's another reason for my staying, and facing it out," she replied, tonelessly. "When all of them see that I expect them to believe it's Peter's child, he won't dare say anything. Even he wouldn't dare say anything. Did you actually think that he would strike an attitude and shout to the world that it's his child? Not if I know Henri!"

"I see. Of course, you're right. But there's another thing: don't you think he might rush matters, then, about a divorce from Annette?"

She looked at him with sharp fright. Then, she shook her head. "No. Not under present conditions. No. He'd know that he wouldn't dare do that, while Armand is alive. While it isn't safe for him to do it."

Then she said, drearily: "I think he'll be glad he's out of it, anyway."

She was suddenly crying again, her lip trembling childishly. "I'll have the child, anyway," she said, with simplicity. "That's something."

For some time Christopher amused himself with certain vicious thoughts. Then he became aware of Celeste again, with renewed compassion and love. He took her in his arms and held her close to him.

"Poor darling. You're a brave little devil, you know. You always were, God help you."

She drew away from him a little. "Not so brave," she said, steadfastly. "I've thought of killing myself, sometimes."

That night, at Endur, Christopher told Edith, without emotion, and with an air of indifference. He knew her strength and lack of emotional upheavals. But even she listened, aghast, though she said nothing until he had finished.

"My God, how terrible," she said. And, characteristically: "How terrible for Henri."

Christopher smiled unpleasantly. "You mean, how terrible for Celeste, don't you? Or do you still have a brother-fixation, sweet?"

She looked at him, her nut-brown eyes filled with an expression he had never seen there before, so ruthless, so minatory was it.

"Aren't you mistaken, Christopher?" she asked, quietly. "You're speaking of a sister-fixation of your own, aren't you? Never mind. We'll get nowhere, bickering." She looked at him fully, and now her eyes were dim. "You've never really loved me, have you, Christopher?"

He was about to say something, out of the virulence of his nature, but remained silent. Then he said, reflectively: "I believe I have. Yes, I believe I have."

She swallowed stiffly. She sat before him in her smart plainness, her slender legs crossed. Her brown hair was streaked with silvery lines, but her dark profile was still lean and firm and young. "You are a brute, you know," she said. "But I've told you that so many times. What do they call you? 'The white snake.' I've never thought that about you. Sometimes I've thought you loved me."

He repeated, still reflectively: "Yes, I believe I have."

She said: "Yes, I think you are telling the truth. You know, I've always hated Celeste a little, because of you. I don't think I hate her now. I'm glad you told me that you love me, Christopher," she added, simply. "You never told me before, not in so many words."

He was touched. He went to her and took her hand, then bent and kissed her. "You're a fool, Edith. But you're the only bright woman I've ever known, too. I like bright women."

She lifted her arms and put them about his neck, pulling his head down so that she could kiss his lips. Her smile was soft and tremulous, despite the habitual stern lines of her mouth. "You hurt me all the time, you pig," she said. "But you can't help hurting everyone. I understand you, you see. Well, thanks for small favors, my pet. I know you never told any other woman you loved her."

She pushed him away from her, with a little laugh, in which he joined. Then she frowned thoughtfully before her. "Your darling little sister has courage," she admitted, grudgingly. "I never noticed that, before. So, we're in a conspiracy of silence, eh? You don't think there'll be trouble with Henri?"

"No. It's obvious there won't. And when Peter's dead, and

pray God that's soon, Celeste will be treated tenderly, outwardly, at least, by the family. With you most tender, in the forefront. The family is a little afraid of you, my soft little angel. They won't dare laugh in your face."

CHAPTER XLI

Peter knew that each day that he lived was a day borrowed reluctantly from death. He had known that with his mind, but never with his full consciousness of body and spirit together. It was like a fact established by the cold intellect but never accepted by the senses and the emotions.

But on this early May day he awoke very early in the morning, just before dawn. Though it still was very dark, the darkness had that thrilling quality of the earth immediately preceding the rising of the sun. It was an aliveness, an awareness, that quality, as if he stood in a dark ante-room looking at a closed and massive door behind which teemed great life and great movement, unseen, and unheard. He had awakened, and though he was aware of an immense lassitude and numbness in his body, his mind was abnormally clear, vivid and alert. When he moved his hands, he could hardly feel the motion, so numb was his flesh, and he was quite amazed to discover that the pressure of the bed under him was barely perceptible to his body. He listened to the darkness, to its clear and hollow substance. The windows of his room could not be seen. Everything was impenetrable, and filled with peace.

Then, in that vast and hollow peace, that breathless and motionless peace, came the first faint murmur of the winds of dawn, soft, whispering, like the woodwind notes of an orchestra. They murmured solemnly, hardly stirring. Slowly they deepened, became stronger. The newly-leafed trees moved and lifted up their branches and their voices, strengthening the light far notes. Now, from far and wide, from over the dark moveless hills, from over the distant valley and the far river, other voices advanced and rose. The tremolo of the bird took up the song, until all the dim air fluttered and was pierced by golden notes.

Peter lifted himself heavily in his bed and drew aside a drapery. The earth still lay under a black and airy sea, but beyond the eastern hills there was a line of pale bright fire, throwing those hills into silhouette. That fire ran electrically over the rims, and above it the sky slowly pulsed into a tremulous rose, streaked with thin flame. Now the chorus of the thousand voices deepened exultantly; the wind increased the tempo of its cello notes; the sweet fluting of the birds became of such crystal poignancy that Peter felt the tears in his eyes.

He had never regretted the necessity of death. He had always been so busy, so anxious, so tormented, that he had never felt that death might overtake him, personally. At least, he had never felt this with his emotions. Now, he felt it. He was filled with sad and active regret, with immeasurable sorrow, with a nostalgia that was like an unbearable pain in his heart.

Concerned, as he had always been, with the agonies of men, with injustice and cruelty and madness and fury, he had been too absorbed to withdraw into himself and indulge in contemplation. He had rarely thought of God. When certain men had spoken to him of God, he had listened with inner impatience. What had "God" to do with the immediate and terrible problems of mankind? It was an apotheosis to be indulged in only by metaphysicians, by those who had no real regard for their fellows. At its worst, "God" had been the abracadabra of the wicked, the foolish, and the tyrants. If Peter had thought of God at all acutely in his life, and particularly in the past years, it had been with rage and hatred and detestation. If there was "God," how had He been able to stand by in complacent or evil silence through these years, through the last decade, and see what there was to be seen? How could He have beheld the degradation and violence of mankind, the torture of the innocents, the death and tears and despair of the defenseless, the multitudes who had died with hands uplifted to the mute heavens, and not have moved in His eternal might and destroyed their enemies? How many countless prayers must have risen from the ghettoes of convulsed Poland to that silent and heedless God! How many anguished cries for help must have started from the bloody cells of the concentration camps, from the burning walls of churches and synagogues, from the turgid gutters where children died in torment, from blasted homes and shattered fields!

Yet the heavens had remained mute. There had been no sign from Him who had declared that it were better that a millstone were hung about a man's neck and he were cast into the sea than that he inflict suffering upon one of these "little ones." Thousands upon thousands of these "little ones" had perished, their mouths stopped with their own blood, their arms reaching for the mothers who were not there—and God had slept, or had not cared. The innocent had died unsuccored and uncomforted, in agony, torn asunder by man, deserted by God.

Out of his thoughts, then, out of his anguish for the helpless for whom no one cared, there had arisen in Peter a profound hatred and loathing for any "God" who might exist. He had felt his spirit standing naked and alone on a desolate mountaintop, cursing God for the horror He had inflicted on men. There was no excuse; the apologies and explanations of churchmen were foolish and outrageous mouthings, the mutterings of imbeciles who must have their idiot-magic even in the face of the desperate agonies of the world. There were some who declared that God was "testing" mankind by this horrible spectacle of human depravity and human suffering. There were some who promised that those who died helplessly, and in torture, would enter a "better world."

But to Peter no "better world" was worth the last fluttering, dying gasp in the throat of a little child. What eons of eternal bliss could ever erase the final memory of that death, that hopelessness? If the enemy paid and paid throughout eternity for his cruelty and his madness, it would not be enough to take from the records of time the glazing of one child's bewildered and suffering eye, as it died in loneliness and pain. There was simply no explanation, no excuse, for the last pathetic lifting of a dying child's hand, for the last wild shriek of a mother searching in ruins for a little body ruthlessly murdered, for the last groan of a man in a concentration camp. There was no forgiveness for the men who did these things. There was no forgiveness for the God who permitted them.

Peter's hatred and loathing for "God" extended to the vile creatures He had created, to all the world.

Now, as he watched the morning rising over the hills, he

was overwhelmed by his pain. A universal suffering pervaded him. He felt the universal sorrow of the earth. And at last, in him, the hatred ebbed away, leaving only tears and sadness behind. He saw that the tormentor suffered equally with his victim, that in the end he died in equal anguish. So, Peter's sorrow, too deep for despair, too profound for words. He felt the universal aching throughout his spirit, felt a grief too enormous for anything but prayer, for anything but compassion.

And with this, he knew, with all his emotions, that he was about to die.

The realization, all at once, brought him a solemn and bottomless peace. He watched the dawn brightening, heard the louder triumphant voices of the earth. But he felt no joy with his peace, no fulfillment. He could not deceive himself that he "understood." He only accepted. He was glad that he was about to die. He hoped only that there would be no remembrance. How frightful to carry into eternity the memory of the horror of men, of the indifference of God, of the mysterious hopelessness of the world!

When Celeste came softly into his room at half-past seven, she thought Peter was asleep. But when she approached the bed, she saw that his face was turned speechlessly to the window, where he could see the morning sunlight on the tops of the trees. He turned to her when he became aware of her, and smiled.

She said to herself: He is dying.

And then it seemed to her that there was a great rending pain in her heart, suffocating and shattering. She knelt beside the bed and touched his hand. She felt its coldness, the skeletal hardness of the fingers. She could not speak. She looked into his eyes, and they remained like this for a long while, looking deeply into each other's souls and thoughts.

Finally, Celeste laid her head beside her husband's on the pillow, and knelt like that, hardly breathing, not thinking.

At last, she felt his hand on her head, gently and slowly smoothing it. When she looked up, her eyes dry and burning, she saw that he was smiling again. His voice, weak and calm, came from his quiet lips:

"My darling, you look so tired, so exhausted. Will you do something for me? Go out today. Go somewhere. Go for a walk. Look, the sun is shining, after a week of rain."

"No," she said.

"You must, dear," he said, with great urgency. "It would

please me very much. I'm much better, you know. After a while, I'll get up and work a little."

"No, Peter, you mustn't work today," she answered. "You—look so tired. You didn't sleep much, did you?"

He did not answer for a moment, then said, turning his head away a little on the pillow: "No, not much. But then, I get no exercise. Lying here, and sitting in the chair—that isn't very much."

She gazed at his profile, so attenuated, so delicate and drained now of every emotion, of every longing. Yet, it was not a peaceful profile. It was one of profound resignation and weary patience. The pain in her heart quickened so that she pressed her hand to her breast, and she was blind with suffering.

She saw at last that he had turned his head again to her and was regarding her with deep and penetrating love and compassion. "Celeste," he said.

"Yes, darling?" she whispered.

His hands moved restlessly on the light blanket which covered him. "You know, dear, and I know," he said, "that I haven't much longer to live. I'd like to know that when you are free, you will be happy, that you will find happiness. Somewhere." His voice was very gentle and very calm.

"Peter," she began. And then could say nothing else. But her tears came now, very slowly, dropping over her cheeks. He raised his hand heavily, and, with a smile and a faint sigh, and with infinite tenderness, he brushed those tears away. "Hush, dear. Don't cry. Why should you cry? In many ways, we've been very happy together. I like to remember how happy. It's been no life for you. I'd like to think that you might be really happy again—sometime."

And again, they looked at each other in that deep and unspeaking silence.

Celeste was sick with her pain. She lifted his hand and pressed it to her cheek.

"You're still young, my dear," he said, more faintly now. "Life won't end for you. You've had a lot of misery, with me. I hope you'll forget that misery, and remember the pleasanter things. The things we saw together, the talks we had, the walks, the times we laughed, the new places we visited, the friends."

"If I remembered all that, I'd never be able to live," she said, inaudibly.

And then it seemed to her that her heart broke and divided

on an immense and tormented cry. She pressed her face against the bed. She burst into wild sobbing. "Forgive me, Peter!" she groaned. "Forgive me!"

Her hands clutched the sheets and blankets, pulled at them, writhed among them. Her sobs shook the bed. She forgot everything but her anguish and despair and remorse.

It was not for some time that she realized that Peter had neither moved nor spoken, and had not replied to her. When at last she lifted her ravaged and tear-stained face, she saw that he was looking at her with grave and stern gentleness, and with such sad and passionate understanding. And then he raised his hand and pressed his fingers on the long white streak that ran backwards from her forehead. He lifted that streak and moved it between his finger-tips.

He said: "I never saw that before, my darling."

She opened her shaking lips to cry out against herself, but he shook his head. He said again: "I never saw it before. I've been so blind, so inexcusably blind."

And then he moved his head so that he could kiss the white brand of her long suffering. She felt the pressure of his lips, and closed her eyes on a spasm of agony that struck at her consciousness, and made all things faint and dim about her.

When the doctor had paid Peter his daily visit, he went down to see Celeste, who was waiting for him. He said, gravely: "He is very weak. You know, of course, Mrs. Bouchard, that he may go at any time. He is resting now. He asked me particularly to tell you to go out for the day." He paused, seemed about to speak, hesitated, then said nothing.

"Did he say why?" asked Celeste, dully.

"There are some people," replied the doctor, "who want to be alone when they—realize. They want to think about it. You see, I don't think he fully realized all this before— not completely. He does, now. He wants to think about it. He's in no pain. He seems much better, mentally, than he has been for some time. Physically, of course, he is much weaker." He studied her intently. He remembered what Peter had said to him at the last: "I feel it's come. I want to spare her. I want to be alone. She mustn't be here." Of course, that was nonsense. Sick men often felt like that, the doctor argued to himself.

"I'll come in again, in about two or three hours," he added. "His nurse is with him now. I think it would please him if you were to go out for a while."

He went on, when she did not speak: "Mr. Bouchard is right, of course. You look very tired and ill."

With more compassion than he usually felt for those he served, he saw how haggard she was. Her eyelids were red and swollen, her lips white and parched. She was still young, but she looked old, especially now, when the bleached lock of hair fell in disorder over her forehead.

"It would do you good," he urged. "It does no good, making one's self ill in caring for an invalid. This is the first nice day in a long while. Suppose you go out for a few hours, Mrs. Bouchard."

Celeste nodded, but he wondered, when he went away, if she had heard. Something nagged at his consciousness, the consciousness of a doctor. There had been something about her which he had overlooked, in his preoccupation with Peter. He shook his head, impatiently, puzzled.

Then, at last, it came to him, and he was profoundly startled. Yes, there had been a heavier fullness to her breasts, a richer outline to her figure. It was strange that he had not noticed all this before, he exclaimed to himself. How tragic, then, for the poor young creature! He wondered when —He recalled, with greater bafflement, that he had been in personal attendance upon Mr. Bouchard for over six months. During that time, his patient had been very ill, completely bedridden.

The doctor pulled himself up sharply, shook his head, grimly. One must not think these things. A physician, especially, must not think these things, and more especially, not of rich and powerful patrons!

It could have happened! he exclaimed to himself. What other explanation is there? After all, he was not so terribly ill, in the beginning. Stranger things have happened! Why, there was that case of Mr. Jonathan, who had been bedridden for two years with a failing heart, who had not been allowed to lift his head from the pillow. Yet, his wife had produced a fine bouncing baby two days after her husband had died! So, it was not inconceivable——

CHAPTER XLII

At two o'clock, Celeste, dressed in a black broadcloth suit and loose furs, and a small black hat with a gay red feather springing up from it, came in to tell Peter that she was taking his advice, and going for a drive. She had powdered and rouged her face, and painted her lips. She looked quite merry and composed. Peter gazed at her, sighed inwardly, and returned her kiss when she bent over him. The nurse smiled benignly.

"Don't hurry back," he said, pressing her gloved hand. "Are you driving, yourself?"

"Yes, I'd like to be alone, in the country, darling. You are certain that you won't need me?"

"Not at all," he answered, with immense gaiety. "Miss Broder is here. She is going to read to me for a while. Then, later perhaps, I'll sit up and do some writing. There is to-morrow's broadcast, you know."

She gazed at him, and thought: He is surely better. He looks more rested. There is even some color in his face.

She kissed him again, and left the room. He listened acutely until he heard her drive away. Then he raised himself a little and watched her small red car going rapidly down the long driveway. At the bottom of the incline, it turned, wheeled away towards the valley, was lost among the greening trees and shrubbery. Then he fell back on his pillows again, and sighed, over and over. A gray shadow moved across his face, and his light-blue eyes sank deeply into their sockets.

Miss Broder brought him his morning's mail, sitting beside him and slitting open the letters, which she gave to him. He read listlessly, dropping the sheets from his hand, as if they were too heavy to hold.

"Why, here is a foreign letter!" she exclaimed. She peered at the stamp. "A French letter!"

He lifted his head eagerly, and took the envelope from her

397

hand, and scrutinized it. "It's from Israel," he said. "I haven't heard from him for two months. He's so damned obstinate. I suppose this is in reply to my letter demanding that he get a visa and come here."

He tore at the envelope with eager trembling fingers, waving away Miss Broder's offered assistance. A thin sheet of paper, covered with delicate blue writing, fell out. Peter began to read, his eyes leaping over the page:

"My dearest, dearest friend," said the letter, "when you receive this, I shall no longer be in France. I shall be in Germany. I have heard that the German Government have taken two dear friends of mine into custody, as hostages against my return, for trial, they say, for heinous crimes against the Reich. My dear friends are innocent good people. One of them was a professor of physical science in the University of Berlin. Such a dear, kind old man, who had never harmed anyone, who had lived in some gigantic and mystical world of his own, in which he had moved with God. Unfortunately, his God has been unable to protect him, for he is a Jew. The other friend is the writer, Emil Meyer, who wrote those delightful, fantastic, semi-fairy-tales of ancient Teutonic gods. It appears that he had no right to weave his stories of those gods, for he, also, is a Jew. Both my friends are in Dachau. I have been promised that when I return, they shall be released. I do not know whether these promises will be kept, for there are no men in Germany any longer, but only mad beasts. However, it does not matter. No doubt, I shall be confined to Dachau, also, but there I shall see my dear friends, and comfort them, for the time that will remain to all of us.

"I ought not to have left Germany. I ought not to have left my friends who suffered. There is an obligation upon mankind to suffer with its fellows, not to flee, not to desert them in their extremity. The agony of one is the agony of all.

"Do not sorrow for me, my dear friend. Be glad. I am an old man, and I cannot live and look upon the things which are done in these days. Be glad that I have died. Let me quote to you the words of Faust:

"Eh bien! puisque la mort me fuit,
Pourquoi n'irais-je pas vers elle?
Salut! O mon dernier matin!
J'arrive sans terreur au terme du voyage;

398

> Et je suis, avec ce breuvage,
> Le seul maître de mon destin!"

Miss Broder, who had been watching her patient with that smug and loving kindness almost exclusively reserved for the rich, was acutely alarmed at the ghastly grayness which suddenly appeared on Peter's face. His features became pinched, his pale lips blue. The alarm of the nurse was greatly increased when Peter looked at her with a dazed and empty expression, the paper slipping from his hand to the bed. Yet, when she bent over him, he said, very quietly:

"Miss Broder, I'd like to be alone a little while, if you please."

"Are you ill, Mr. Bouchard?" she asked, anxiously, her warm hand reaching out to touch his forehead. But he moved his head away from her, and repeated, very gently: "Please. I'd like to be alone."

She left him, then, demurring, with long backward glances of anxiety. She closed the door behind her, but stood by it. Finally, she went to telephone for the physician.

Peter watched his nurse leave him. Then, as the door closed, he lifted Baron Opperheim's letter and read it again, every word, slowly and carefully. At last, his hand dropped; the letter fluttered to the floor.

Peter turned his head and looked at the bright May sunlight streaming in through the windows, touching the rug, the posts of the bed, the side of a chest of drawers, the gay backs of books in a small bookcase near the fireplace. He looked at the intense warm blue of the sky, and the pattern of green leaves that flickered against the windows. Everything was silent except for the swift rustling of the trees, the drowsy whirring of a grass-cutter on the wide lawns about the house.

He felt no pain in his heart. He felt only a complete deadness, a complete and heavy desolation that was like the crushing weight of great stones upon him. Under that weight he could not breathe nor move. Sorrow was too small a word for what he was enduring. It was as if the last frail hope, the last little peace, had gone from him forever, leaving him face to face at last with the heart-breaking and speechless agony of eternity. "Hail! O my last morning! I arrive without terror at the end of my voyage!" Faust had said, and Israel had quoted him. "I am, with this draught, the sole master of my destiny!"

But Peter could feel none of the nobility and grandeur of

the words. He felt only the dread waste, the fearful and useless anguish, the immortal hopelessness.

All at once he could not endure it. He raised himself on his pillows and cried out furiously, and in dying agony, to the sunlight, to the immeasurable blue sky: "Israel! Israel!"

His body strained in repudiating hatred against the sky and the sun, against the God who had lifted no hand to prevent the tragedy of all the ages. Vast chaos tumbled before his dimming eye. Vast mountains rose into tumultuous being, collapsed into red mist; thousands of brilliant fragments exploded before his vision. He lost all sensation of integration; he was a spark of burning malediction whirled about in heaving and limitless space, a spark that lamented and cursed and implored in a wild gale of imprecation and dying despair.

Somehow, in that immense confusion he felt the taste of hot salt in his mouth which increased to a choking flood. He felt himself falling through emptiness, down into a huge darkness filled with pain.

He opened his eyes slowly, as if heavy stones lay on the lids. The sunlight still streamed into the room. There was no sensation in his body. He was only feeble consciousness.

Then he became aware that Annette was sitting beside him, holding his hand. Her bright fine hair was a halo of soft light about her tear-stained face. Her large blue eyes were fixed upon him, and her lips were trembling. He saw her through a haze. Beyond her were diffused shapes. He was not curious about them, though vaguely he understood that they were two of his brothers: the gray and frigid Francis, with the ice-blue eyes, the little dark Jean. Emile, "the bloated black rat," and Armand, and Christopher, Celeste's brothers, were there, also, and Agnes, Emile's wife. Beyond the door, waiting and concerned, was Estelle, Francis' wife, and Alexa, the poor fat stupid wife of Jean, and other relatives, and several friends.

The doctor was there, also, and the nurse. But Peter saw no one clearly but Annette. As he looked at her, she smiled sweetly, pressed his hand, and bent towards him. "My dear," she said, softly. "It's Annette."

"Yes," he whispered. He looked at her, and there was a sudden sharp intensity in his eyes.

"We're looking for Celeste," said Annette, tightening her hold on his hand. "She'll be found soon."

But he still looked at her with that brightening intensity which appeared under the glazing of his eyes.

He felt no pain now, not even sorrow, not even despair. He was only supremely aware.

He gazed at Annette, and saw, with sudden profound knowledge, that here was another like himself, vulnerable, gentle, compassionate, and despised. The last strong flowing of his spirit went out to her in recognition and brotherhood. And she gazed back at him, her blue eyes widening, and deepening, welling and flowing, with understanding of his recognition. She moved even closer to him; she bent over him. They communicated in silence, in sorrow, and tenderness.

"Yes," whispered Annette. "Yes, my dear."

She touched his cold sunken cheek with her lips. Tears ran over her cheeks. When she could see him again, she saw that he was smiling at her.

His eyelids were so heavy. I will sleep a little, he thought. It surprised him, vaguely, that there was no sensation in his flesh.

The darkness behind his eyelids was soft and thick, yet full of waiting life, like the hour before dawn. He gave himself up to the darkness. A strange comfort was creeping all through him, the sweetest of consolations, as if a friend had smiled and spoken. He heard a voice, faint as from a distance, but strong and clear. It called his name. He tried to answer, and he heard his own voice echoing back to himself in the night, as from a thousand resounding places. He was suddenly frightened, filled with horror. Then the call came again, nearer, stronger, reassuring. There was the dimmest light visible now, the sound of approaching footsteps. Someone, in the dimness, which was now a silvery haze, took his hand, held it firmly and warmly, and he felt the presence of someone beloved.

He knew, now. He was flooded with light and joy and peace. He clutched the hand that held his own. He felt himself moving through space, peering through the shining haze at the face of his friend. "Israel," he said.

From far behind him in the darkness he had left he heard the sound of weeping. He hesitated, drew back from the drawing power of his friend's hand. The weeping lacerated his heart.

"Come," said his friend, urgently. "Come. The morning is here."

CHAPTER XLIII

Cornell Hawkins looked long and thoughtfully at his visitor. So, this was the most formidable and the most terrible of the Bouchards, this strong stocky man with the light-gray crest of vital hair sweeping up from his broad and brutal forehead, and the pale implacable eyes which were as opaque as polished stone. Mr. Hawkins had long wished that he might see this man in the flesh; he had had much curiosity about him. That wide and heavy face rarely appeared in newspapers, and rarely was there a mention of his personal life. He had moved obscurely and invisibly, as the gods move, only their portent sensed, only the vaguest of gigantic shadows thrown on the vast horizon of events.

In his turn, Henri Bouchard regarded Mr. Hawkins with equal curiosity, hidden and unperturbed. But he thought: I wonder how much that poor wretch has told him, about me, about the family? From his first look at Mr. Hawkins, he knew that here was a man it would be useless to attempt to cross-examine, however dexterously it was done. Henri knew his New Englanders, their classic reserve, their cold aristocracy, their restraint and icy subtlety. Any question, no matter how delicate, would be met with frosty evasiveness or rebuking silence. For this, then, Henri admired Mr. Hawkins, and his face brightened faintly with friendly interest. Above all things, he admired that aristocracy of spirit which the other man personified, an aristocracy which was never venal, never small or mean, never malicious or petty.

"Of course, I knew that Peter was very ill," said Mr. Hawkins, in a low and reflective voice. "He told me, once, that he couldn't live very long. But one never knows. I've seen many people live to a hearty old age, always 'dying,' and making last wills and testaments, and summoning relatives to their deathbeds. I—I had hoped that might be the case with Peter."

He smiled slightly, but his expression was sad.

"Had we known that you and he were such friends, we'd have invited you to the funeral," said Henri. "But we thought the relationship between you was purely that of author and publisher. And publishers aren't very often friends with their authors, are they?"

"No," replied Mr. Hawkins. His smile was a little grim, as he thought of some of his authors. He thought also he might like to attend the funeral of some of them, provided, of course, they had first delivered one or two last lucrative manuscripts to be published posthumously. He saw some of them now, in his mind's eye. Miserable, conceited and exigent wretches! Who ever had invented the legend that authors moved dreamily far beyond the realm of ugly finance? Someone, evidently smarting from recent encounters with authors, had remarked that the average author could outwit and out-bargain the longest beard in a Levantine bazaar. Mr. Hawkins had met only one or two great authors in his life, and they had been kind and modest men, without affectation or pose or greed. But the average author, who only considered himself great, was a noxious species with a peculiarly penetrating and demanding voice, an enormous vanity, and deliberately affecting much temperament. Or he was sometimes a fat and untidy beast, with a lofty expression, a taste for bars and rowdy women. These were bad enough, thought Mr. Hawkins. They were exceeded in unpleasantness only by women authors.

He said: "Peter and I were very good friends." And again, his expression was sad. "Where is he buried?"

"In the family plot, in Windsor. Near his mother. His father, you know, died on the *Lusitania*. There is only a memorial to him. Peter was very fond of his father."

"I know. Peter told me about him." Mr. Hawkins looked beyond Henri. The early June sky was gray, thick with rain-clouds, but between some of their folds a faint radiance was streaming in long wide bars.

Now there was silence in the office. Mr. Hawkins had some idea of what had brought Henri Bouchard to him, but he had no intention of making the approach easier for this inexorable man.

Henri was laying an envelope on Mr. Hawkins' desk. "We found this letter, addressed to you, among Peter's effects," he said. "I'd have brought it sooner, but I was named the executor of Peter's estate, and there were some matters to attend to."

"Thank you, Mr. Bouchard. But you could have sent it, you know." Mr. Hawkins touched the envelope gently.

"Yes. But I wanted to talk to you about Peter's book," said Henri, after a slight pause. "I understand it is to be released next week?"

Mr. Hawkins nodded. He watched Henri acutely. "I saw the proofs," continued Henri. He smiled indulgently. "He has a lot of excellent information there, from sound— sources. But he writes melodramatically."

Mr. Hawkins' eyes became reserved and withdrawn. "There's a fallacy, you know," he said, dryly, "that a thing is only true when it is dry and hard like a moldy crust. When all the life has evaporated from it. And, perversely, if a thing is colorful and strong and vehement, the tendency is to believe it is fiction. Why? Are only dead dull things true, and the living and bright, lies?"

"You approve, then, of his flamboyant style?" Henri's glance was somewhat derisive.

Mr. Hawkins was annoyed. "I never could see that it was necessary to dress truth up in grave-clothes," he said. "I might even say that the dead things are not true. If they were true, they would still live. And truth, like a beautiful woman, deserves color and passion."

Now Henri's smile was also derisive. But Mr. Hawkins suddenly saw that this was a pose. He said, abruptly: "We have all the intention in the world of giving this book, *The Fateful Lightning*, every chance to succeed. That is what you want to know, isn't it, Mr. Bouchard?"

Henri was surprised at this penetration. Like all men of his kind, he underestimated the intelligence and perception of other men. He said: "Yes. That's what I wanted to know. I want that book to succeed, Mr. Hawkins. I want it to have all the publicity it can get. I want it to be widely, persistently, advertised. I want every newspaper to carry large and striking advertisements, every day, for months. Perhaps for years."

Mr. Hawkins was silent. He waited. Deliberately, then, Henri brought out his cheque-book. Mr. Hawkins still waited, watched while Henri took out his pen and slowly uncapped it. Mr. Hawkins began to smile.

"Why?" he asked, quietly.

Henri did not pretend to misunderstand him. "I don't know very much about the publishing business," he said, with an answering smile. "We're not in it. Except for newspapers. But I understand that it costs considerable to launch a book. Is there a large advance sale, by the way?"

"I haven't talked with Mr. Dalton, our sales-manager, lately," said Mr. Hawkins, still watching him. He felt quite perverse. "I understand it is about ten thousand, however, though it may be more or less."

"That's not enough," interrupted Henri, with a frown.

Mr. Hawkins did not speak. Henri put his pen to a cheque, and looked steadily at the other man, his pale fixed eye very intent. "How much, Mr. Hawkins?"

"For what?"

Henri's light thick brows drew together again. "To give this book proper launching, and wide publicity?"

Mr. Hawkins leaned back in his chair, which creaked. Mr. Hawkins lit a cigarette and puffed at it. Through the smoke his frosty blue eye sparkled a little, but Henri could not tell whether it was with amusement or anger.

"Mr. Bouchard," began the editor, after a long silence, "you've said you don't know much about the publishing business. I agree with you. I suppose it has never occurred to you, has it, that sometimes publishers publish books just because those books have an intrinsic value, above the consideration of sales?"

"No," said Henri, smiling, "it hadn't occurred to me. Does that ever happen?"

"Quite often. It would surprise you. Let us say, perhaps, that we do it for the good of our souls. Even if we lose money on it, which we often do. Sometimes, you know, we get sick of publishing trash, even though that trash runs to three hundred thousand copies, and the movies buy it. You haven't thought that some of us possess integrity, have you?"

"No," repeated Henri, frankly, and with a wider smile. "Who has?"

There was a dull and angry burning in Mr. Hawkins' chest. He sat up, abruptly. "We don't need your money, Mr. Bouchard. We'll do the best we can for Peter's book. We have a large appropriation for it."

Henri put away his pen and cheque-book. Now he looked at Mr. Hawkins somberly. "I'm afraid you don't understand. It is very important to me that this book be widely advertised, and widely bought. I don't think it is necessary to tell you why. That is my own affair. I wasn't trying to buy you. I was only trying to assure a big audience for the book."

He paused. But Mr. Hawkins did not speak.

"I suppose you wouldn't have too much objection if I saw to it that the book was commented upon by certain prominent radio commentators and speakers?" he asked, sardonically.

"None," replied Mr. Hawkins, coldly.

"And if reviewers gave it prominent notice?"

"Do you think you can buy reviewers, Mr. Bouchard?"

"I can try." Henri was smiling again, disagreeably. "Now, don't tell me they have 'souls,' too. Perhaps some of them have. And again, perhaps there are even more who haven't. I've been reading book reviews, lately. Some of the reviewers become quite ecstatic over the damnedest love-sex trash written by nasty women, or by men who ought to have been women. I've even read some of the books they've wildly recommended. American literature is in a bad way, isn't it, Mr. Hawkins?"

"American literature, Mr. Bouchard, is patronized mostly by women," said the editor, and now he also smiled.

"Do you think that is the explanation for emphasis on women and 'lahve,' then?"

"Women like to read about women, I admit," said Mr. Hawkins. "They also like to believe that men are engrossed with women, and run their business with a bemused aside, an absent flick of their hands. Something they hurry through to get back to women. When men begin to read extensively, then perhaps we'll have better literature in America, something concerned with the stuff of life. A Thomas Mann, a Feuchtwanger, a Wassermann, won't be popular in America until men read. Perhaps you can suggest how we can get men to read, Mr. Bouchard?"

When Henri did not answer, Mr. Hawkins continued: "When American men stop thinking that making money is the only thing for which they were born, then the arts in America will have a new lease on life, a new vitality, and a real immortality. Then we'll have a vital and valid literature, and true greatness in books. But so long as men don't read in America, our literature is bound to be a reflection of the stuff that appears in the women's magazines, with the emphasis on 'women's love and marriage problems,' and the cavortings and skirmishings of adolescents—books dealing with romanticized sex-encounters. And worse. We have a few great women writers, but they aren't too popular. The popular writers are writers like these," and he lifted a volume from his desk and handed it to Henri. "This has already sold three hundred and fifty thousand copies. Hollywood paid two hundred thousand dollars for the picture rights, yesterday. It is going to be a play, also."

Henri examined the book distastefully. It was entitled: *The Angry Four*. By Ralph Coniston.

"It is about the love and sex problems of four women," said Mr. Hawkins, with a disagreeable smile. "We published it. What few men there are in the story are all shallow cardboard, in two dimensions. Like paper-doll cut-outs. Very unimportant creatures, with no life of their own except when they come to violent sex-encounters with the four engaging ladies. We have just received another order for thirty thousand copies. The women love it."

He added: "American men don't love it. They don't read it. At least, we've got to credit them with some taste. But I can tell you this, and it is very encouraging: men are beginning to buy non-fiction books about Europe, and the war, in steadily increasing quantities. We published another book recently, called *Thirty Days in Germany*. An RAF flyer wrote it. He was shot down over German territory and some simple obscure German peasants helped him to escape from the Nazis. It is very popular, among men. American men are taking a new interest in the world, beyond American concerns. This is very encouraging."

He went on: "You won't be able to buy all reviewers, Mr. Bouchard. Strange to say, many of them have integrity. That is a good thing for the future of American literature."

Henri said: "Well, let us see, then. I'll have a number of prominent radio commentators mention Peter's book. I'll have a greater number of newspapers mention it editorially, and in other ways. No objection?"

"None," said Mr. Hawkins. "We also like to sell books, you know. And I should particulary like to see this book extremely popular, and not for the money's sake, either."

Henri ignored this, and Mr. Hawkins' thin lips tightened. "I'll want a thousand copies for myself," said Henri. "For personal distribution, discreetly, of course."

He rose, and smiled. "Will you have lunch with me, Mr. Hawkins? I'd be very glad if you would."

Mr. Hawkins hesitated. Then all at once he felt the urgent need for a drink, for several drinks. He pulled his battered hat over his forehead, and rose, slowly.

"How about the Ritz?" asked Henri.

407

But Mr. Hawkins shook his head. It was sentimental, of course, but he could not sit with Henri Bouchard where he had sat with Peter. It was very foolish, but if he sat with Henri, there, he would see Peter's face too clearly.

CHAPTER XLIV

Annette entered the cool dusky-blue of the hall of the house on Placid Heights, and was met by Edith Bouchard, wife of Christopher, who greeted her with more affection and warmth than she usually extended to members of her family.

"Dear, you shouldn't have come, especially after you have been so ill," said Edith. "How are you now?"

"It was just the grippe, really, Edith, and it affected my nerves," replied Annette, removing her white gloves, and taking off her small hat. The June day was warm and close, with a hint of coming thunder in the air. Annette smiled. Her little triangular face was wan, but her large blue eyes were steadfast and shining. "How is Celeste?"

Edith hesitated. Her expression became closed and reserved. "Well, she still won't see anyone or go anywhere, except to the cemetery. We try to tell her she's morbid, but she doesn't seem to care. She hasn't been out of the house for days, now, and only goes into the garden in the morning and just before dark. Lots of her friends have come to see her, but she hides from them. Of course, she will get over it eventually, but there is no use pressing her just now. That's why I don't think you ought to have come, darling. I doubt if she will see even you."

She led the way into the quiet living-room, whose french windows opened onto the green slope of the lawns. Roses filled every vase and bowl. Speckles and bars of sunlight made bright spots and little pools on the rugs and furniture, and glimmered on the polished tops of tables. The two women sat down, facing each other, and regarded each other in grave silence. Then Edith said: "Christopher and I are staying with her, you know, until we feel it is safe for her to be alone."

"Safe?" murmured Annette, in distress.

"Well, I might say, until she is more herself. She hardly speaks, you know. Seems dazed and abstracted. She doesn't grieve in the usual way, poor thing. I haven't seen her shed a single tear, not even at the funeral, or afterwards. Just walks around in silence, and we have to speak twice to her before she answers. Her doctor is very worried about her, and suggests that she go away for a while. But she won't, of course." And now Edith's dark face was more taciturn than ever.

"Poor, poor darling," sighed Annette. Her pretty eyes filled with tears, and she swallowed over a thick lump in her throat. "I've always loved her so, and I believe she loves me, too. Are you sure she won't see me?"

Edith's lips drew together thoughtfully, and now her nut-brown eyes fixed themselves consideringly upon Annette. Damn it, she thought, it has to come out sometime, and it might as well be Annette who spreads the news. Yes, there could be no one better than poor little Annette. They wouldn't dare laugh in the poor little creature's face, and she has such a delicate high courage.

"Celeste might see you," said Edith. "I'll ask her. Of course, things were bad enough, without this other——"

Annette lifted her head in alarm. "What do you mean, Edith?"

Edith stared at her with lifted eyebrows. "My God, Annette! Don't you know?"

"Please tell me!" cried Annette, half rising from her chair in her distress. "Is she ill? Oh, I knew it! Something told me!"

"You mean to say," said Edith, incredulously, "that she didn't tell you? I thought you were such friends, my dear. Didn't she tell you she is going to have a baby?"

"A baby!" repeated Annette, in a dazed voice. She sat down again in the chair. It was a large chair, and she was like a thin weak child in it, her little feet dangling some inches from the floor. Her hands, so frail, white and small, lay on the arms. Her bright fair head reached only part way to the top.

But it was not a child's face that stared at Edith. It was the face of a still and suffering woman, very white, quiet and

409

unmoving. And it was in shadow, that face, and very translucent. But the eyes widened, shone out of the shadow like blue strong light. The mouth fell open a little, and that was all.

Edith wanted to look away from that stark and overwhelming pain and shock. But that would not do at all! She forced herself to regard Annette with a faintly puzzled look. "How like Celeste that is," she remarked, irritably. "But, of course, we can excuse her. Peter was so ill, you know, and she nursed him constantly. She told me from the beginning, however, just before he took that turn for the worse."

Annette was silent. She was like a wax figure in the chair. Her eyes stared out at Edith unblinkingly. Blue lines of suffering appeared about her mouth, and there were bluish shadows under her cheekbones.

"How long?" she whispered.

Edith shrugged. "About six months, now, I believe. The baby is due in September. It's very terrible for her, you know." She spoke casually, but slowly, gazing at Annette with calm deliberation. "You remember, Peter seemed quite a lot better, the early part of the winter. He and Celeste went to New York quite a few times, together, and we all had hopes that he might recover, in spite of the doctors' verdict. At least, he appeared much happier and stronger, then. That must have been because the baby was started, and he had finished his book, and the future looked brighter for them, poor things."

Her voice was cool, indifferently compassionate. But it was a frightful effort for her to continue looking at Annette, who sat there so still, like a stiff and artificial doll opposite her. She repeated, with an air of surprise: "She really didn't tell you, Annette?"

Annette's pale stiff lips parted, and she said, almost inaudibly: "No. She didn't. We didn't see much of each other then, and then, in February, Peter took so ill."

"Yes, of course. She didn't have time to think of herself, after that. We try to cheer her up," continued Edith, in a bright tone that seemed pretense even to herself. "We try to tell her that at least she'll have Peter's baby to console her. That's something, you know, after all these years. Sometimes," she added, on a sad note, "I think the poor girl would die if it weren't for the baby. She realizes that, subconsciously, and takes some care of herself."

"Yes," whispered Annette. And now her eyes moved slowly

from Edith and stared blindly at the blazing light that poured through the window near her. Edith saw her profile, shrunken and dwindled with anguish, but very quiet. Annette's voice, when she spoke again, was strong and clear, a startling contrast to her face. "Poor Celeste. But she has something, now, to live for. I feel very hurt that she didn't tell me."

Her little fragile hands moved suddenly and violently on the arms of the chair, as if they had been jerked. They lifted, palms up, stark and stiff. And then they dropped, slowly, heavily, the fingers spreading outwards on the damask arms, and grasping as if in a convulsion of agony. But her profile remained calm, like a plaster mask. Her fair rings of hair rose and fluttered gently in the warm breeze that came through the window, and somehow, the sight of that bright fluttering was like an iron blow on Edith's tight cool heart. God help you, my dear, she thought, with rare compassion and sadness.

Annette, now, turned her face back to Edith. She smiled a little, very gently. "I'm so glad, Edith," she said, with sweet softness. "So glad for Celeste. She'll realize, when the baby is born, how wonderful it is. I can hardly wait, myself."

Edith tried to speak, but her throat was dry. She pressed the palms of her hands together. She dropped her eyes. There was a limit to what even she could stand, she thought.

"I'd like to see Celeste," said Annette, and her clear sweet voice was very composed. "Do you think she'd see me?"

Edith rose, in relief at a promised escape. "I'll see her. She's in her room. I'll try to bring her down." She hesitated, then added: "You might be easy with her, if she sees you, Annette. After all, it isn't a happy thing for her to be reminded that Peter won't ever see his child."

"I'll be careful, darling," promised Annette, softly. How blue and steadfast her eyes were, how shining and still!

Edith turned to the door, then stopped, abruptly. Celeste stood on the threshold, as silent and still as stone. Annette, seeing her, rose involuntarily. And then her gentle heart contracted in a spasm of pain. Was that really Celeste, there, that gaunt drained woman with the frozen face and loose hair? Annette uttered a faint cry. She held out her hands, and now tears gushed to her eyes, spilled over her cheeks.

"Celeste!" she cried faintly. "O Celeste, my darling!"

I hope to God that she heard what I said! thought Edith.

Celeste did not move, not even when Annette came up to her, and took her cold hand. Her full black dress accentuated the ghastly pallor of her face. The white lock fell over her forehead. Even her dark-blue eyes were less blue, and shallow and glazed.

She stared at Annette as if she did not see her. Annette began to weep, pressing her young aunt's hand. Celeste looked down at her. Then she said, in a low dull voice: "Annette."

"Yes, dear. I had to see you, even though you didn't want to see any of us." Annette was smiling now, though her tears still fell. "Do you mind very much, my pushing in on you like this?"

"No," said Celeste, still staring at her with that far blindness. She drew a deep, harsh breath. "I'm glad. I've wanted to see you."

Oh, my God, thought Edith, in great alarm. And she said, in a slow firm tone: "Annette has just told me you never told her about the baby, Celeste. She was very hurt about it, weren't you, Annette?"

Annette looked steadfastly into Celeste's eyes. "Yes, dear, I was very hurt. You ought to have told me, you know." She added, clearly and strongly: "I've always loved you so, Celeste, and I thought you loved me. You ought to have told me. But never mind. I'm so happy for you, darling. You have something to live for now. You'll have Peter's child."

And now her look, more steadfast than ever, more compelling, fixed itself stanchly upon Celeste. Celeste's lips parted convulsively; her hand trembled in Annette's.

Annette said, even more loudly and clearly: "You mustn't grieve because Peter won't see the child, darling. You must think how wonderful it will be. Nothing matters but the baby now. Nothing matters, Celeste. You must think about the baby."

Her voice, strong and penetrating, finally reached Celeste's consciousness. The wildness passed from her face. She looked at Annette in silent anguish, as if pleading.

"Nothing matters but the baby," repeated Annette. "There's nothing else."

Edith's heart, which had been beating with unusual rapidity, began to quiet. She moved over to Celeste, and put her hand on her arm.

"Annette's right, Celeste. You mustn't think of anything but the baby. It wouldn't be fair to the child. You—don't matter. Poor Peter doesn't matter. No one does. The child has a right to his life, you know. You have no right to interfere with it."

Automatically, dully, Celeste turned her head and looked at Edith. She looked at her a long time. Then she again turned to Annette, who was smiling.

"Yes, I can see," said Celeste. "Nothing matters."

She smiled, darkly and mournfully, lifted her hand, and pushed away her hair.

"The family will be very surprised," said Annette, in a rallying and affectionate tone. "And probably as hurt as I was because they weren't told. Do you mind if I tell them, darling?"

Celeste was silent for a little. She regarded Annette long and somberly. "Please do, Annette. I'd be glad if you did."

Some thought struck her, and over her pale face ran a sudden inflamed color, and she turned away. "I'm tired," she murmured. "I think I'll go and lie down, if you don't mind."

She walked away, moving slowly and hesitatingly as if she were blind. Annette and Edith watched her go, in silence.

"It's frightful, isn't it?" murmured Edith, after Celeste had disappeared. She motioned Annette to her chair, and sat down near her. She drew a deep breath. "I think, though, it's done her good to see you. In a few days I'll invite Agnes and Estelle to come in for tea, and you too, dear. Celeste simply must go about again. She broods horribly, you know."

"Yes," said Annette. Edith rang for tea. She was deeply relieved. But still, she could not look directly at Annette, sitting so resolutely yet calmly in her chair, and smiling so gently.

When Annette had gone, Edith went up to Celeste. She found her sitting by the window, staring unseeingly out upon the gardens and the trees.

"Celeste," she said, abruptly, "this isn't going to do at all, you know, brooding and sulking about here, like a damned recluse. I've invited Agnes and Estelle, and Annette, for tea on Tuesday. You need company. You need some diversion. I'm taking you to New York next Friday, to see some plays, and to buy what you need."

Celeste turned her blind face to her, and cried out, violently: "No! I won't have it! Why don't you leave me alone, all of you?"

But Edith, unmoved, pulled a chair close to her sister-in-law. "You are such a fool, Celeste. You heard what Annette said: you've got to think of the child. Peter's gone. You knew he would go, soon. It was a blessing for him; he'd suffered so. You knew for a long time that he couldn't live. Do you think it would make him happy if he knew that you were deliberately trying to kill yourself?"

Celeste put her hands over her face.

Edith continued, inexorably: "I don't know what you have on your mind, if anything, Celeste. But it doesn't have any significance now. Life goes on. It didn't end for you, in Peter's grave. Celeste, I thought you had some courage, some resistance, and pride. But you haven't. You're behaving like a hysterical Victorian woman. You're committing a refined kind of suttee." She waited. Celeste did not speak. Her thin and transparent fingers shut out her face.

Edith went on, in a lower tone: "I wonder what the family is going to think, with you hiding away like this, like a criminal, or something."

Celeste dropped her hands abruptly, and stared at Edith with a distraught look. "What do you mean?" she asked, hoarsely.

Edith shrugged. She looked away at the window. "I'm wondering if they won't think you've gone insane. And, they'll wonder——"

It was not for some time that she turned to Celeste again. Celeste was sitting quietly, her hands in her lap. But she was quite composed. "You're right, Edith. Invite anyone you want. I'm sorry. This has been hard for you, hasn't it?"

Edith, with inner thankfulness, said, briskly: "Damned hard. I don't like being a recluse. I've had the feeling I was a private nurse caring for a mental patient. It hasn't been delightful for Christopher, either. He ought to be in Detroit now, instead of relieving me of my nursing duties."

She could hardly believe it when she heard Celeste laugh. It was only a small laugh, but it was not without mirth. And now her dark-blue eyes were shining with the first tears she had shed since Peter's death. Very moved, Edith rose and put her arms about the younger woman's shoulder.

"There now, why don't you have a good cry? It'll do you worlds of good, I know. And I know that you haven't gotten over not being here when Peter died. He sent you away; he knew it was coming. He wanted to spare you. There, now, cry. Cry harder, darling. Harder."

Later, when Celeste slept peacefully, as she had not done since Peter died, Edith went to the telephone and called Christopher, who she knew was in conference with Henri.

414

"Look, my pet," she said. "Annette's been here. She knows. And, I think it would be a good idea to tell Henri, before he goes home. No, everything's all right. Celeste is sleeping like the proverbial babe. See here, I resent that ultra-concerned tone. Remember, I'm your wife."

CHAPTER XLV

Christopher returned to Henri. They had been discussing, with grave concern and understanding, the collapse of France. Books were open on Henri's desk, to which they had been referring. As Christopher sat down, Henri said: "It's gone according to schedule, and order, though a little earlier than Hitler expected. Everything is going fast, now. What is the latest?"

Christopher said: "I just looked at the report. The British are retreating towards the coast. Everything is in disorder. Frankly, I don't know what the hell we are going to do. Are you going to Washington tomorrow?"

"Yes. I talked to Hugo this morning. He's quivering like a damned leaf. Sometimes I think he'll burst with the pressure we're putting on him. He can't seem to settle down to anything since Alice ran off with her Charlie, and married him. Not that it's a bad thing, for us." And he smiled, grimly. "I've harped enough on Hilary's resemblance to our little darling, Antoine. And it was Hilary, as you know, who engineered the elopement."

"We keep getting our women mixed up in our concerns," said Christopher, restlessly. He began to tap on the desk with his fleshless fingers.

Henri uttered a short harsh laugh. "Yes, I know. You were a past master at that yourself, Chris. Only, it didn't work, did it?"

Christopher smiled bleakly. "It wasn't my fault." He seemed abstracted. Now there was a rough flush on his cheekbones. "You're right. It's a mean thing, mixing up our women with

415

ourselves. And a humiliating one. Why do we need women? Like a rotten cheap movie. I wish we could keep them out of things."

Henri watched him. Then he said, abruptly: "What's up, Chris?"

Christopher shrugged, turned back to his brother-in-law. "That was Edith calling me. About Celeste."

Henri said nothing. He leaned back in his chair. His pale eye was inscrutable. Finally, he said: "Well, what's the matter with Celeste? Still brooding about Pete?"

Christopher lit a cigarette, then stared at it gravely. "It isn't only that. She's physically sick, too. Some women are like that, when they're pregnant."

He continued to stare at the cigarette. Then, casually, he looked up. Henri had not made the slightest gesture. He was leaning back in his chair, his eye fixed immovably upon Christopher. There was no expression on his broad pale face, except for a curious tightness about his mouth.

"Pregnant?" he asked, without the faintest inflection in his voice. "I didn't know that. How long?"

"Six months," said Christopher, indifferently. "You didn't know? I thought everyone did. A posthumous child usually excites some interest, and sympathy."

They looked at each other in an intense silence. Henri's hand lifted an object on his desk, dropped it softly.

Then Henri said: "Pete, of course, didn't know?"

"No. I think Celeste hardly knew, herself. There were more important things. He was very ill, as you remember. Expected to die almost daily. She nursed him all the time. Otherwise, she might have done something about it. It isn't the most pleasant thing for a woman, I suppose, to have a posthumous child. Not," he continued, looking calmly at Henri, "that we won't all be there, to help her, and give her what consolation we can."

Henri shifted to another spot the object he had lifted. He regarded it with absorption.

"Annette visited Celeste today," said Christopher, with a sympathetic air. "She was very upset because Celeste hadn't told her. One can rely upon Annette."

Henri swung his chair about to face the windows. "Yes," he said, in a neutral tone, "one can always rely upon Annette." He continued, without the slightest change in his voice: "I didn't know. I haven't seen Celeste for some time. Alone."

"Yes, I knew that."

"It explains a lot of things," said Henri, musingly.

Christopher was about to speak, then said nothing.

Then Henri said, "I wonder how long it will be before that damned old Armand dies?"

Christopher laughed unpleasantly: "He's gone reckless, I hear. Stuffing himself. It ought not to be long."

But Henri said, absently: "The family. How many know about Celeste?"

"You, now, and Annette. Frankly, even Edith and I didn't know until just lately. It's about time, though. Of course, one can understand. Celeste was too concerned with Pete to care about anything else."

Henri turned back to him. The old implacable look was heavy on his features. "Yes, I understand a lot of things, now. Celeste is quite a fool, you know. I think we've always agreed on that."

Christopher answered, with an evil glinting in his eye: "I'm not sure she's been a fool. Just think of it a little, for a minute."

Henri thought of it, grimly. He sat like stone in his chair. Then he said: "Yes, I see." His expression changed slightly.

"And it wouldn't be very safe, let us say, for you to see her alone at any time," Christopher remarked. "Not yet, anyway."

Henri got up, abruptly, and walked up and down. Christopher watched him with a malignant satisfaction he could not control. Then Henri said: "How long is Edith going to stay with her?"

"I've got to return to Detroit. You know that. Edith will stay as long as necessary. But she's my wife. She just reminded me of that," and Christopher smiled.

"She's also my sister. If I ask her to stay, she will."

Christopher's narrow face flushed. "I think I need to remind you, too, that she's my wife."

"And Celeste is your sister." Henri suddenly smiled. "Come on, now. We're bickering. You won't mind if Edith stays?"

"I'd damn well mind if she didn't," said Christopher.

Henri sat down again. He clasped his hands together on the desk, and the two men stared at each other intently in silence.

CHAPTER XLVI

Antoine watched his father, Armand, as he surreptitiously wiped up the thick brown gravy on his plate with large gobs of bread. Armand, bent clumsily over his plate, his gray, auburn-streaked thin curls glimmering in the candlelight, thought himself unobserved. All his motions were greedy. He ate, as always, with avid haste, almost gobbling. The peasant strain, so deep and strong in him, assured him with its unreasoning instinct that a man must eat, and eat fast, if he was to nourish himself and fill his belly adequately. Three generations of family wealth and power had not extinguished that animal instinct, so avaricious, so bestial, so enormously hungry for constant sustenance against a time of famine. Armand was not aware of the instinctive urge which had made him a glutton, a voracious devourer of provender. He had always had, he would say, a hearty appetite. In later years that instinct had been his only comfort, his only defense, against a world grown horrible, threatening and full of spiritual pain.

He had early discovered that his more fastidious relatives thought his stuffing offensive and disgusting. He had tried to learn nicer manners. He had warned himself, over and over, that he must not fall upon food like a famine-stricken Chinese, or a wolf. But he had only learned to be furtive, to eat a little more slowly, while inwardly he trembled with primordial panic at his enforced restraint.

During the past few months, when each day brought new terror and new despair to him, he had frenziedly abandoned The List. The impact of events had forced him to desert that List, and he had fled to the table once more in unreasoning fright and passionate desire for consolation. The warnings of his physicians were nothing to him now. Nothing was left but his hunger, at once physical and spiritual, and he ate as a dying man on a desert gulps water which he knows is poisoned, but which offers him a momentary surcease from his torment before death seizes upon him.

In his need, in his despair, he had served an ultimatum upon little Mary, Antoine's wife, that he would eat no more spinach, no more liver, no more unseasoned vegetables and glutenous bread. If he could not have the "right" food in his own house, he would go elsewhere, he had declared, even in the face of Mary's tears. Mary, herself, then approaching the end of her term of pregnancy, felt too enervated to struggle with her father-in-law, and finally surrendered. The rich and luscious dishes again appeared on the table, and Armand fell upon them with such avidity, such delight and mad hurry, his brow glistening with sweat, that Antoine, the delicate, was revolted. Nevertheless, with his usual subtlety, he understood.

So, this night, as always, Antoine watched his father. Mary was not at the table. She was still at the Doctors Hospital in New York, where she had given birth, a week ago, to a fine boy, who was to be christened Stuart. ("No more damned French names in the family, as far as I am concerned," Antoine had declared.) Antoine had observed his father closely and curiously throughout the elaborate meal, none of the items of which were calculated to contribute to Armand's health. Armand had gained much weight; he was bloated now, covered with soft dough-like flesh. His ruddy color had gone permanently. Suety dull folds of flesh had distorted and minimized his features, so that he had the expression of a diabetic old boar, filled with chronic fear. Three thick chins bulged below his normal one, and had an oily bristling look. As his health and life declined, as his girth and weight increased, he lost the last vestige of personal pride. He often did not shave for two or three days at a time, so that there was always a gray-red shadow over his chins and cheeks. His clothes were deplorable, stained and crumpled. His disintegration was almost complete. Because he could not force his swollen feet into shoes, he wore bedroom slippers constantly, and shuffled about in them through the house like an enormous and uneasy ghost, searching with dull desperation for something he could not find. Never a fluent conversationalist, he would sometimes not speak for days, not even to his son.

As Antoine observed him closely, his tilted black eyes glinted, and a faint smile touched his satiric mouth. Not very long now, he thought, with satisfaction. As he thought this,

419

his father suddenly dropped his silverware with a clatter upon his plate, gasped, turned a sudden bright purple, and struggled to rise. Antoine, with every indication of alarm, got to his feet and went to Armand, who was flapping his fat shapeless hands in the air and fighting for breath. His eyes, so sunken now in folds of flesh, fixed themselves in agony upon his son.

It took Antoine and two male servants to drag Armand to his bed. Armand's physician arrived very promptly, and administered a hypodermic to the sick man, his lips tight and grim.

"You know, of course, Mr. Bouchard, that your father is killing himself?"

"Yes, doctor, I am aware of that. But he prefers to die in his own way, it seems. I think he would rather die after a gorging meal than 'starve to death on cow-food,' as he puts it. We've found it is useless to try to do anything with him."

"Then, he must go to a hospital for some time," said the doctor. "Where his diet will be closely watched and planned. Otherwise, he cannot live. I can say freely that he may die at any time, this way."

Antoine considered. "I will talk to my sister," he said, finally. "She is the only one who has any influence on him at all."

Antoine called Annette, and asked her to come to her father's house at once, if she could. In the meantime, the doctor appointed three nurses to care for the sick and desperate old man panting so stertorously on his bed, struggling for each breath of life.

Annette arrived shortly, alone, breathless and distracted. A thunderstorm was crashing violently outside, the lightning invading the great dusky rooms with ominous flashes. Little beads of perspiration shone on Annette's pale face, and there were tears in her pretty and poignant eyes.

When Antoine took her up to her father's room, they found Armand asleep at last, a mountain of flesh heaped up on billowing pillows. The nurse whispered to them that he was "much better," and ought not to be disturbed. Annette went downstairs again with her brother to one of the drawing-rooms, where she sat down and wept quietly.

Antoine thoughtfully and slowly lit a cigarette. Then he sat down near his sister and took her hand. "Don't, darling," he said, gently. "You know how Papa is. There's no use. We're hoping you might persuade him to go to a private hospital for treatment and care. While he is at home there's no hope for him, you know."

"But why should he want to die?" implored Annette, looking at her brother with wet and mournful eyes. "He does want to die, Antoine. He is committing suicide."

Antoine was silent. He narrowed his eyelids and watched the smoke he expelled from his pursed lips creep towards the molded ceiling.

"Perhaps things are too much for him," he murmured, reflectively.

"Yes, I know," cried Annette. "I know so much about Papa that no one else seems to know."

"One of the things that are too much is you and Henri," said Antoine, as if he had not heard his sister.

Annette removed her handkerchief from her eyes, dropped her hands to her lap and clenched them rigidly on the little lace-edged square of linen.

"What do you mean, Antoine?" she asked, in a shaking voice. "What is wrong with Henri, and me?"

He turned to her. She was very pale. But her eyes met his with high and valiant courage, and steady calm.

He hesitated. Then he put his hand over her cold taut fingers, and pressed them gently. "Darling, I know this is terrible for you. But have you really swallowed the fiction about 'Peter's baby'?"

Annette's nostrils dilated, and her upper lip lifted tensely. But her eyes did not leave her brother's. Now they were deep with fear, though the courage brightened in them strongly. She said, very calmly and quietly, "I don't know what you mean, Antoine."

Antoine did not speak, though he regarded her piercingly. Then he simulated weariness and sad disgust. He turned away from his sister as if the sight of her affected him with unbearable compassion. He said, with pent anger: "My dear. My dear."

Annette said nothing. He waited. But there was no sound from her. Then he pretended great repressed anger, and swung to her again. "Annette," he said, "you must know, of course, that that isn't Peter's child."

Annette was very still. He could see the shining of her eyes, so gallant, so steadfast. "Antoine," she said, "what a horrible, cruel thing to say about Celeste, your own father's sister. And how unspeakably outrageous and cowardly. You wouldn't dare say that to anyone else."

He laughed shortly, and ruefully. "My sweet little pet, everyone in the family talks of it, in the closest of whispers, of course. Family pride, and all that. You must have heard," he added, incredulously.

"I never listen to lies, especially not vulgar and cruel lies," she answered, in a firm, unshaken tone. Now her eyes were vivid with scorn and indignation. "And I'm horrified, Antoine, that you should help spread them."

He smiled at her in elaborate disbelief, shaking his head slowly. "Never mind," he said, quietly.

Annette's lips felt cold and thick as ice. She said: "Go on, Antoine. I want to hear the rest of the lie."

He shrugged fatalistically. "All right, then. I'll tell you. We all know that the child is Henri's, your dear husband's."

Annette did not stir or speak, but only looked at him fixedly.

"You must know, my dear, that he has been meeting her for months, in nice little rendezvous in New York, and elsewhere. You didn't know, darling?" he went on, with quickening compassion, which was not entirely simulated now.

"I didn't know," she said, steadily. "And, no one else knows, either. Because it isn't true. Henri's enemies are just trying to injure him."

Antoine studied her with meditative pity. Her face might be wizened, her gentle mouth withered and blue with pain, but her look remained clear and unshaken. Then he frowned a little. "His enemies? What do you mean, darling? Isn't he the Iron Man, Old Stone Face Bouchard? Who could injure him? Hasn't he quite openly declared that Gibraltar is a piddling little rock compared to him, or words to that effect?" His mouth jerked in amused contempt, but his eye was suddenly watchful.

Annette's mind rose above her aching heart, and she studied her brother intently before answering: "Men like Henri always have enemies. You know that, Antoine. So, when something criminally libelous is said about such a man, one always wonders who hopes to gain by it, or what enemy is trying to ruin him."

"Do you actually think I'm Henri's enemy?" asked Antoine, with affectionate disdain and indulgent amusement. "What would give you that idea, Annette?"

Now she could not endure looking at him, at the dark sparkling face which she loved. Tears as heavy and salt as blood filled her eyes, and her throat throbbed. But she said, softly enough: "I don't want to think you are Henri's enemy, dear. I only believe that someone has been lying to you, out of malice or malignancy, and that you are trying to keep me from getting hurt."

When she looked at him again, she saw that his sleek black head was bent and that he was examining a ring on his finger with immense concentration. She could not see his face.

Then he said in a changed voice, not looking at her: "Yes, sweet, I am trying to keep you from getting hurt. You were always my little pet. I wouldn't lie to you, or tell you malicious rumors. That's why I investigated the thing, first. Do you remember when they came back last spring—Peter and Celeste? It was just a short time after, that their gay little affair started. He always wanted her, didn't he? They were engaged once; I remember that. Then there was that split-up. Then she and Peter went to Europe, you and Henri married. You were very happy then, weren't you?"

Annette's thin, white throat tightened, but she lifted her pointed chin higher. "Yes," she said, "I was very happy."

"But she, and he, had no scruples at all about destroying your happiness, darling. None at all. I don't know when the affair started, but I don't think it was very long after Peter's and her return. It doesn't matter who told me. I was told. I investigated. I wanted to be sure, first."

Annette's head was still high, and her smile gallant, gently incredulous.

He sighed, and the sigh was not all hypocrisy. "Their meetings were very frequent. You know, the Iron Man is quite a fool if he thought he could hide permanently. He never has his photograph in the papers, so he thought he was safe. Celeste, too, has been away a long time, so she wasn't easily recognized. But such things, like murder, will out."

Annette drew a deep but repressed breath. "Do they still meet, Antoine, according to your kind informants?"

He frowned, flashed her a black and glittering look. "I think they stopped meeting sometime last January. At least, that is what I'm told. Why, I don't know, except that Peter became ill, and I suppose she wanted to play the devoted wife again for public consumption."

Annette asked quietly: "You had some object in telling me these lies, Tony. What do you expect me to do now?"

He was relieved. He became alert and vital once more,

423

taking her hand and holding it strongly. "I want you to divorce him, Annette. Go to Reno, if you want it that way. Or, better still, get a divorce in this State on the grounds of adultery." He watched her with intense keenness now.

But Annette was not shaken. "For adultery," she repeated. Her eyes were strangely brilliant as she looked at him. "Naming Celeste as corespondent?"

Antoine's eyes narrowed on her, fixedly. Suddenly, he saw Christopher's face before him, evil, razor-sharp, deadly. He hesitated. "Well, no, perhaps. That would be too much of a scandal. But, when you told him you were going to divorce him, you could threaten that you would bring in Celeste if he tried to fight the suit. That would stop him."

"But you have said that Henri and Celeste haven't met since January, Antoine. You couldn't prove anything now, could you?"

He was puzzled, even in his inner excitement, by the sharp note in her tone, her intensity. "No," he admitted reluctantly, and with obscure uneasiness. "You are right, there. We couldn't use Celeste very easily just now. They're guilty, just the same, and this child is Henri's. But you needn't let him see that you know you can't use Celeste. If you threaten him with her, threaten to drag her, as well as him, through a divorce court, he won't cause you any trouble. I can assure you of that."

He heard her slow, deep breath, saw how she relaxed in her chair. She began to speak, very firmly and softly:

"Antoine, I never thought you were really cruel, or merciless, or vicious. I don't want to think so now, even if you are trying to make me think it. You seem to have forgotten that the Bouchards aren't merely relatives by marriage, but relatives by blood. Celeste is our aunt, the sister of our father. Henri is my husband, your brother-in-law, but he is also a blood relative of ours. His father was our great-uncle; our grandfather, Jules, was Henri's uncle. Papa is Henri's first cousin; Henri is our second cousin.

"Wait," she said, as Antoine began to smile with hard malice. "You'll say all that doesn't matter. But it does. And, I believe you know it does. Even if you don't, I do. I have family pride. I have family affection. Even if what you told me were true—and I don't believe it—I would remember first of all how closely we are all bound to the family. I believe you would remember that, too, unless you had some more important motive."

She paused. Antoine had suddenly drawn closer to her; his eyes fastened upon her alertly. "What motive could I have, my dear, except wanting you to be protected?"

Careful, she thought to herself. She forced herself to smile, to lay her hand on his. "Darling, you and I have always loved each other, haven't we? I'm grateful, Tony. But do you honestly think it would make me happy to be dragged through a divorce court, to see my relatives smeared, and to give Henri's enemies a chance to hurt him? Even if Celeste were not hurt? You see, dear," she added, and now her voice shook a little, "I love Henri very much. I wouldn't do the slightest thing to injure him."

He was silent. His dark and narrow face was gloomy, and there was a vicious expression about his mouth, as if he had been furiously disappointed and frustrated.

He put aside her hand, stood up, looked away from her, and said, steadily: "All right, Annette. If you aren't interested in protecting yourself, I shall have to do it without you. I've some family pride, myself, pride in you as my sister. I'll tell my father what I know about your Henri, and his sister."

Annette sprang to her feet. She caught her brother by his arms and held him with astonishing tightness and strength. Her eyes, more brilliant than ever, looked at him with indomitable power:

"Antoine, if you do that, I will tell Papa that you are lying, that you have some ulterior motive. And I know you have; you must have. It isn't your sister that makes you want to do this. I will tell Papa to investigate your reasons. I will investigate them, myself. I will tell Henri that in some way not known to me as yet you are trying to injure him. Do you know what I will ask Henri to do? I will tell him to sue you for libel, and make it a lot of money. I will tell him what you've said to me today. Henri hasn't the family pride we have. He doesn't like you, Antoine, I can tell you that. He wouldn't stop for a minute out of any consideration for you as my brother.

"And, do you know something else? Papa will listen to me. He has always loved me so much. He likes and admires Henri. Do you think he will stand with you, and your lies, against my faith in Henri, and my love for him? Do you think he would do anything to break my heart? The only thing you would accomplish, Antoine, would be to ruin yourself. Papa would throw you out. Henri would sue you for libel. What would you do then?"

He stared at her with naked hatred and rage. He struck her hands down. Now she saw all his evil, his relentlessness. But his voice was very quiet: "Don't be melodramatic, Annette. I wouldn't go to my father without proof that Henri and Celeste met for months, before the mysterious January when they severed diplomatic relations. My father has pride, even if you haven't. He will do something, I assure you."

"Not if it will make me miserable, or break my heart," she answered, as quietly as he. "Not if I tell him I know you are lying, and if Henri tells him so. And we will. He would rather believe us than you. Your proof means nothing. Even if it did, it still wouldn't mean anything."

His hatred was a frightful thing to see. "I believe you are as nasty a trollop as your lovely auntie. You must be, to protect her like this."

Annette did not speak. But she began to smile, a gallant white smile, undisturbed.

Now his control broke. "Why do you want to protect her, and him? You haven't any decency, Annette. No self-respect or pride. You know he despises you, that he would be glad if you were dead, so long as you died after your Papa died, and so didn't inconvenience him. He has had a dozen women, since you were married. He pushed them in your face. Do you think he ever cared a damn for you? He married you to get back the power of the Bouchards. I've seen him looking at you, and I've wanted to smash him in the jaw."

"Why didn't you, Antoine? Because you know he would have smashed you out of existence if you had raised your hand against him. And let me tell you something else: if I go to Henri and tell him what you've just told me—these lies—and what you have proposed I should do, that would be the end of you. Wouldn't it? Henri wouldn't stop at anything to ruin you. He'd go to Papa, with me. And then, Papa would move, too, if Henri asked him."

He could not speak. He could only look at her with the face of an evil stranger, hating, terrible in his still rage. His black eyes glittered, and there was a dull sallow pallor under his dark skin.

Annette waited. Her heart felt squeezed with anguish at his look. A light cold perspiration broke out on her upper lip, and a dimness floated before her. But her resistance against the fainting of her body was still unbroken. However, her voice was weaker when she began to speak again, though it did not falter:

"I'm not as cruel as you, Antoine. You see, I love you, too. I won't tell Henri what you've said to me today. We can both forget you said it. You've forgotten Christopher, too. He would join with Henri, and Papa, to ruin you forever. I will try to forget everything."

She picked up her gloves and bag, and moved towards the doorway. He watched her go. Such a small frail figure with such a high brave head and steady step!

He was mad with rage and disappointment. His plan of months was destroyed. He clenched his fists. Annette, reaching the door, turned her head and smiled at him, gently, piteously. She lifted her hand in a soft gesture, and went away.

He could see the blue shining of her eyes long after she had gone, and the most curious constriction tightened in his chest.

CHAPTER XLVII

On the trivial, noisy, bickering stage of American preoccupations and concerns broke the great and disordered drama of the fall of France. Far and wide were scattered the little squealing men and women, the trumpery furniture of a cheap comedy of errors, the ribboned lamps and bowls of artificial flowers. The orchestra, which had been blaring forth gay discord, shrieks and thumps, was drowned out by the sudden thunder of the death of a nation, as the rocks of its great foundations dropped into the sea. Now the colored lights faded in the lightning, and showed the silly human creatures pressed against their gaudy and substanceless backdrop, their mouths fallen open, their eyes astare with terror. They felt the shaking of the earth, its long shuddering tremors that slowly rolled away. The thunder that had sharply roared in the serene skies at the fall of Norway, Denmark and

Holland, had startled and frightened. It had swiftly passed, leaving only a faint rumbling in the distance, which had soon died, also.

But this thunder shook the very walls of America; this wind beat against its every window; this lightning filled every room, showing the cowardly, the stupid, the ignorant, the frightened or treacherous faces. Here and there the flash struck on a fearful sad face, a stern face, a warning face. But these were few.

"It is a good thing," remarked Antoine Bouchard, cynically, "that we've a Republican Convention coming up to take the cattle's minds off France, or God knows what might happen. They might even force Congress into declaring war on Germany!"

This fortuitous circumstance, and the renewed and febrile activities of the infamous organizations supported or invented by the Bouchards and their associates, served to distract the frightened and quaking souls of the American people. Despite the heroic epic of the evacuation of Dunkirk, despite the triumphant and gloating perfidy of the French men-of-power (who had long plotted this frightful debacle), a perfidy that was quite open and quite dreadful in its cynicism, despite the last desperate call upon the men of compassion and justice in the world made by a few noble Frenchmen, the Bouchard organizations were soon successful, through their agents and their newspapers and speakers, in convincing the American people that in some mysterious fashion all this was "propaganda" designed to make America the victim of British "imperialism," or to enrich "war-mongers and international bankers." Certain clergymen completely ignored the awful tragedy which filled the air of the world with its cries, its dissolution, its falling walls, and with a dexterity amazing in its bold impudence, imputed the death of France to British "imperialism," and even darkly hinted that perhaps the fate of France had been conspired for the sole purpose of "putting American boys on foreign battlefields."

Nothing was too vulgar, too stupid, too fantastic, for certain clergymen and their brother plotters to impute or openly declare. Nothing was too foul, too obscene, too degenerate, too wild, too insane, for certain newspapers, speakers, Congressmen, radio commentators, to broadcast on the shivering air of America. There were some, like Mr. Cornell Hawkins, who declared that the very enormity of the lies of the traitors and the maniacs would make the

American people burst out into angry and cleansing laughter.

But the American people did not laugh. The majority eagerly believed the lies. More especially, now, because the Bouchard-supported organizations boldly spread out the black flag of anti-Semitism. Here, now, was a victim that could be tormented and destroyed without the shedding of a single "American boy's" blood. Here, now, was a scapegoat on which the American mob could expend its terror, its fear, its soul-deep agitation, which had been aroused at the spectacle of the collapse of Europe, and be diverted from the affrighting truth.

While thousands of young Britons struggled, drowned and died on the beaches of Dunkirk, while the iron treads of thousands of German tanks rolled over the dead bodies of the betrayed, the noble August Jaeckle, his fair lock of hair falling over his mad and shallow blue eyes, raved from a public platform in Chicago:

"We can't shut out from our ears the thunder of the future! Germany is invincible in Europe! Britain will soon fall!—Hitler has no designs upon America. He has said this over and over. Three thousand miles of water separate us from the old bloody battlefields of Europe. Don't let our international bankers and foreign agitators and war-mongers betray us into a war that can only end in a stalemate, in ruin and bankruptcy, and cost us the lives of a million American boys!"

There were some men, like Mr. Hawkins, who were struck dumb with shame at the spectacle of a vast American public wallowing and writhing in an orgasm of fear and hatred, shouting out, not against Hitler, but against a few courageous Americans who were heroically trying to arouse their countrymen to face the enemy boldly and resolutely. In New York, and other large cities, grave-faced scrawny young Communists paraded about with signs on which were printed: "No foreign wars. The Yanks are not coming!"

"The imponderables of the people's conscience!" said Antoine Bouchard.

His faction, his friends and associates, were confident that their "man" would be nominated as the Republican candidate for President of the United States. The Republican Convention was held in Philadelphia in June, 1940.

Some members of Antoine's faction had uneasily observed that there had been considerable talk of "Willkie for President" since the latter part of 1939. Articles, apparently out of the blue, had appeared in prominent magazines for the past several months, in which Mr. Willkie, his career, his courageous struggle against the strangling TVA, his intelligent defense of private ownership and private enterprise, and his brilliant and amazing record as president of Commonwealth & Southern, were all extolled and discussed. Though Mr. Willkie conceded that the excesses of Big Business in the nineteen-twenties deserved no defense, he contended that only private industry had the inspiration, initiative and spontaneous invention to overcome periods of depression and assure the prosperity and soundness of the future. His arguments for the case of private enterprise appeared in many publications, especially in those magazines and other periodicals bought and read by the more intelligent and solvent segment of the public. More "homely" portraits of him, not too sentimental, appeared in the periodicals bought by those nonchalantly designated by the unthinking as "labor."

Even all this would not have disturbed Antoine's faction, or even aroused the slightest awareness in them, had it not been for a certain other thing, also.

Mr. Willkie had once been a Democrat, and a firm supporter of Mr. Roosevelt. But, as he said wryly, "the party had left him." He was too honest a man, too intellectually honest, to abide blindly by the decisions of a group of men whom he considered had betrayed the very principles on which they had been elevated to power. He did not consider it virtuous, or loyal, to declare: "My party: may it always be right, but, right or wrong, my party." Such an attitude, he believed, was excessively dangerous, and inimical to the welfare of America. Its stupidity was beyond question.

A pungent and vigorous writer, he refused a "ghostwriter," and wrote a series of articles, himself, for the leading magazines, in which he contended that a more minatory enemy than Big Business threatened America, and that enemy was Big Government. These articles attracted the attention of the thoughtful and the intelligent, those concerned with constitutional government and the maintenance of American integrity and sturdiness of character. He also wrote an article for a great and solid periodical, entitled "We, the People," which aroused a tremendous discussion of the possibilities of his nomination as a candidate for President of the United States.

Mr. Willkie, however, declared, with some bewilderment,

that he seemed to be "in front of a trend." With considerable bemusement, he tried to trace the beginnings and the outline of the strange, obscure "trend" that had sent him pushing before it. It was there, huge but amorphous, seemingly impelled by an irresistible force, invisible but inexorable. Mr. Willkie had accepted the first flurry of the trend as merely the interest he excited in defending private enterprise. He went along, faintly incredulous, and dimly bemused, on the wave of what not even he or his supporters as yet saw as a gigantic and definite determination. The trend had grown into an enormous flood, fed by a thousand streamlets, before Republican politicans were aware of it, and then they became aware with amazement. The managing editor of an esteemed and brilliant magazine resigned to devote all his energies to the Willkie movement. Had anyone noticed it at the time, he would have observed that long and enthusiastic comments about Mr. Willkie were appearing all over the country in increasing numbers and prominence, and that there seemed to be some predetermined plan behind all this, some pattern.

Advertisements from non-political sources appeared in newspapers all over the country, and petitions were circulated urging his nomination, also from non-political sources.

The majority of Antoine's faction, though observing this mysterious phenomenon, merely laughed at it. "The barberless Hoosier," as they called him, had long ago bored them with his earnest and simple honesty and stubborn integrity. They had once thought him colorful and potent, in the days when he had been engaged in a David-and-Goliath struggle with the Government (without, however, the happy dénouement of the Bible) but they had watched him with cynical detachment and fatalism. Also, they had admired him for his ability to wrest from the Government $30,000,000 more than the original price offered for the Commonwealth & Southern subsidiary, the Tennessee Electric Power Company. But as a candidate for the Presidency of the United States, in opposition to the "man" already chosen as that candidate by the powerful Bouchards and their friends, Mr. Willkie was not even taken seriously. Antoine declared him an "impudent bumpkin, a clodhopper Don Quixote, Diogenes looking for the White House with an oil lantern, the comic relief." He was annoyed, was Antoine, at the sudden and apparently sourceless burgeoning of Mr. Willkie's name in public newspapers and public discussions, and some instinct crept warningly along his nerves.

The "man" chosen by the Antoine faction, and confidently expected to secure the nomination, was a smallish fat man with a dull cherubic face, a duller smile and fixed light eyes. He had had a wide political career, and in every office he had distinguished himself by his unremitting antagonism to any liberal idea, his dogged conservatism, his endless hatred for "the alien element," and especially those progressive doctrines to which he believed only that element was attached, his aversion for labor, his adoration of the powerful, his servile worship of tradition, and his really remarkable record for economy in public expenditures. This alone would have endeared him to the Bouchards and their friends. But when to all this was added the attraction of an old and established American ancestry, an obstinate and unimaginative and blatant honesty, a rough and truculent manner (so beloved of the people), a connection with the American Legion, who adored him, a loud hatred for "foreign ideas as opposed to one-hundred-percent Americanism," a loathing for "New Deal extravagance, boondoggling and spending," and an avowed passion for "the American way of life, with every American a two-fisted fighter," the Bouchards felt that heaven was indeed doing very excellently by them. The man had the affection of the people; he was already a puppet in the hands of his masters. Nothing could have been more satisfactory.

They had carefully built him up over a period of months. He had had a third-class reputation in the country, but he was suddenly brought to first class position in the public attention. The Bouchards and their friends were clever enough not to have him mouth any isolationism or anti-British sentiment, for they had already discerned an uneasy stirring in the American people. They allowed him to speak with gravity in reproof of Naziism, in a voice that expressed more sorrow and lofty scorn than anger. His favorite phrase was: "Between brown bolshevism and red bolshevism we in America can discover no difference." That disposed very neatly of the fears of those timid souls who hated either "bolshevism." But on one thing was this candidate for the nomination very firm: No American boy would ever die on foreign soil!

When some obstreperous heckler demanded what the esteemed gentleman would advise in the event of an attack on America, the candidate laughed coldly. "Do you actually believe that any nation, anywhere in the world, would have the audacity or madness to attack us! You forget, my dear sir, the three thousand miles of water on one hand, and the six thousand miles of water on the other! No matter what happens to the rest of the world, no one would dare attack us, for they would know it would mean certain death and defeat. Therefore, there is no necessity for military peacetime training of our young men, as urged by the more excitable elements in our country. There is no necessity to build up a large reserve of armaments, as our war-mongers and munitions manufacturers would like us to do. We have more than enough battleships and airplanes—However, I do urge an attitude of watchful waiting and careful preparedness." This, then, disposed of those who were firmly pacifistic in tendency, and those who desired "adequate means of defense."

The candidate received the passionate support of the America Only Committee. His speeches about "American boys" caused American mothers to writhe in ecstasy. They were convinced he stood between their sons and war like a rampart of iron.

In the meantime, as Mr. Willkie was observing with considerable bewilderment the huge and resistless trend that was pushing him forward to that June in Philadelphia, Henri Bouchard and his faction watched with grim sleeplessness. "Wendell will be nominated," Mr. Regan had assured Henri. "Stop your nail-chewing. That stuffed flabby fish of theirs hasn't a chance."

But "the flabby fish," now represented as the sturdiest example of America's sons, was doing very well. If his resounding phrases were empty and without substance, the people did not know it. The petty bourgeoisie, the little shopkeeper, the small tax-payer, regarded him with delight through their myopic glasses. "American traditions of individualism, American hatred for imperialism, American soundness of politics, American economy in government, American dislike for bureaucracy, American belief in the principles of personal independence and sturdiness of character," fell from his lips like golden pellets. That they signified nothing tangible was discerned only by a few. Had the gentleman been asked to define a single term, he would have been at a loss, and would have retired to greater vaguenesses.

Nevertheless, he won 310 votes on the second ballot during the Republican Convention. Mr. Willkie had few delegates; none of the seasoned politicians believed for an instant that he had a chance for the nomination.

Mr. Willkie was a fighter. He might have only a confused idea as to how all this began, and no idea at all of the powerful forces that were really behind him, but now that he incredulously saw he had a fighter's chance to win he threw himself into the struggle with gusto and hearty joy. He went everywhere; engaged in debates in hotel lobbies; shook hands with thousands. Once, speaking to the Convention, he cried: "Democracy and our way of life is facing the most crucial test it has ever faced in all its long history. I expect to conduct a crusading, aggressive, fighting campaign to bring unity to America, to bring the unity of labor and capital, agriculture and industry, farmer and worker and all classes to this great cause of the preservation of freedom."

His square passionate face, his disordered hair, his vivid fighting eyes, appeared hugely in national newspapers.

Antoine's faction was apprehensively annoyed at this sudden and impudent intrusion into their plans. "This has gone beyond a joke," said Jean Bouchard. "Someone's behind all this. Let's smoke him out. I don't like it, I tell you."

But look where they would, they found no footprint behind Mr. Willkie, no echo of a portentous voice, no shadow.

There was none to suspect. On the subject of their "man" all the Bouchards, of both factions, were apparently in the heartiest of agreement. Christopher had reported to Antoine that Henri was to contribute an enormous sum towards the nomination of the preferred candidate. Henri and his faction were financing the advertising in every newspaper in the country in behalf of this man. If, in the same newspaper, appeared even larger photographs and better-written and more intelligent articles about Mr. Willkie, the fact was regrettable but not likely to arouse suspicion. If radio commentators in behalf of Mr. Willkie seemed to have more time to speak of him, their sponsors could not be detected. If a noisy crowd in the gallery at the Convention suddenly rose as one man with shouts of: "We want Willkie!" not even the subtle Antoine could have suspected for an instant the power behind all this. If magazines and periodicals were filled with stories, photographs and eulogies of Mr. Willkie, no one seemd to have an explanation.

Mr. Willkie gained steadily at each ballot. Now Antoine and his faction became alarmed. At the fifth ballot, they were desperate, dumb with enraged bewilderment. When the results of the sixth ballot were known, they were speechless. Mr. Willkie had been nominated as the Republican candidate.

When Antoine and the other Bouchards gathered together in Windsor, it was to sit for grim black hours facing each other, talking, pacing the floor, cursing, plotting, suspecting, hating. But there was nothing they could do. Something stronger than themselves, or more subtle, or more determined, had won.

All they could do now was attempt to salvage what they could from the ruins.

"At least," said Antoine, with bitter sarcasm, "we'll be backing an honest man for once. See what you can do with him."

"He has some color and vitality, which is more than you can say about that gray bladder of ours," commented Jean. "God! He always seemed to me to smell of wet stiff leather."

It was then that the full and incredible enormity of the thing staggered Antoine. How had this thing come about, while he and his friends had waited so smugly in Windsor for the final returns of the balloting? Never for a moment had they doubted the final result! Nothing had been overlooked, ill-planned or neglected.

It was useless to call in the managers and upbraid or threaten them or to demand from them an explanation. For the explanation evaded them all. The delegates had had their instructions. They had listened for hours to the speeches of the various candidates for nomination. Yet, at the last, a kind of frenzy had fallen on them, a frenzy half of madness, half of exhaustion. And in a whirlwind of delirium, Wendell Willkie had received the nomination.

Suddenly, fantastically, Antoine saw again old Jay Regan's huge and saturnine face. "The imponderables of the people's conscience!" Absurd, insane. It had not been the donkey people who had thrown out the candidate-choice of the Bouchards. It had been some monstrous accident, some wild accidental joke, some hypnotism, something not to be explained in the reasonable words of reasonable men.

He said, with cold and venomous rage: "I tell you, we can't do anything with this Willkie! The best we can hope for is that he'll defeat Roosevelt. After that, God knows." He glared at his faction, and the others, his black eyes virulent. "I don't know! I don't know! But there's something very strange about all this!"

"If he defeats Roosevelt, there'll really be something very strange about it," said Nicholas Bouchard sourly. "Start your

435

worrying then. Any —— —— —— that gets to run for a third term in spite of hell and high water and the Daughters of the American Revolution can't be beaten by the Archangel Michael himself."

All the Bouchards were at this conference in the dark gloomy library of Armand's house. All but Armand, semi-conscious in his dusty room upstairs. Antoine looked slowly from one face to another, his dark face tightening, narrowing. He finally looked at Henri, bland of expression, harsh of feature. And Henri returned his regard with those pale implacable eyes of his that betrayed nothing at all.

Then it was that a cold and foreboding thrill of fear raced down Antoine's spine. There it is; there is the answer, he thought, against all reason, against all known logic.

"Willkie will win," said Henri, "unless you boys, and your friends, openly give him 'the kiss of death'; in other words, if you don't let labor catch on that you hope Willkie will be your heavy club to knock it down."

CHAPTER XLVIII

Christopher was leaving Endur for one of his frequent business trips to Detroit, when his nephew, Antoine, was announced.

It was a hot Sunday morning in July, and as Christopher selected the clothing he needed in order that it might be packed by his man, Edith kept him company, amusing him, as always, with her dry witticisms and slightly malicious sallies.

"When do you expect to be home, this time?" she asked, fanning herself with a magazine, and sluggishly glancing through the tall bare windows at the blaze of grass and sky beyond them.

"Oh, in a week or two. Eagle's getting under way fast, now. The British, as you know, are financing the building of the new plant. They're financing munitions and aircraft plants all over the country, which is an excellent thing. When the war breaks over us, if it does, we'll be in a sound position to manufacture armaments, tanks and aircraft of our own at a moment's notice."

"My God, this is a horrible thing to think about!" exclaimed Edith, bitterly. "It's a madness, a nightmare!" She paused. "By the way, I hear Peter's book is now in its third hundred thousand, and going better every day."

Christopher laughed shortly. "Your two remarks wouldn't have some occult connection, would they, pet?"

"They might," said Edith, grimly. She turned the nut-brown intensity of her eyes upon her husband. "You know, I think I don't like this family." She rose and put her arms about Christopher, and buried her face in his neck, tightening her arms convulsively. "I don't like you, either," she added, in a muffled voice.

He stood without motion for a moment, then hugged her strongly. "Frankly, I hate all the Bouchards," he said, kissing her smooth dark hair. He gently released himself, and hesitated. "You'll take care of Celeste?"

Her pale thin lips were suddenly compressed. "Can't I kiss you just once without your immediately mentioning your sister?" she demanded. Then she shrugged. "Oh, hell. It doesn't matter. Of course I'll take care of your precious lamb. She's doing very well, thank you, however. Quite calm and composed. Assembling a nice layette. You're all wrong about Celeste. She isn't porcelain. She's iron."

She smiled tightly. "I've got to be with her, not for her sake, but for Henri's. I expect him to appear any day soon, when least expected. And he must not see her alone."

It was then that Antoine was announced. Christopher was silent for an instant or two, his dry, pale face wrinkling. Then, with a gesture of his head, he dismissed Edith, who immediately slipped away into an adjoining room. Antoine, as urbane, darkly sparkling, and gay as always, appeared, saluting debonairly.

"Hah! On the way again, I see. Eagle, I suppose?"

"Yes. The new plant's under way, the one financed by British capital. We expect to be in production in about five weeks or so. Cigarette?"

Antoine accepted a cigarette, then seated himself gracefully on the broad window-sill. With his air of an *élégant*, he smoked slowly and easily, gazing out upon the broad and brilliant expanse of bare lawns below. Christopher continued to sort out clothing. The first locusts were shrilling violently in the hot still air. "What this place needs," said Antoine, "is a stockade at the end of the lawns."

"Can't you see it? There is one, down there," replied Christopher, with a slight smile.

Antoine smiled also, without turning his head. "One never knows where the hell he is with you, Chris," he said.

"Ah, you know me," said Christopher. "Always the well-bred reserve, the delicate reticence. What is it you want to do to me now? Or get out of me?"

Antoine turned to him slowly. A good position, thought Christopher. His face is in shadow, the window behind him, while I'm exposed. He began to laugh. "Tony, sit over here where I can watch the mobile features. You know, for an understudy you aren't very subtle. Besides, you shut off the light."

Antoine laughed with great enjoyment. He threw himself into a comfortable chair, where he sprawled in the most lazy of attitudes. "Can't we stop being fencing master-minds and really talk?" he asked.

"I'm asking you the same question," replied Christopher. He waited. But Antoine did not speak. He watched his uncle, smiling broadly and darkly the while as if deeply amused. "If you think you can put me on the defensive, child, I might remark that brighter men than you have tried it. So, go ahead," Christopher added.

"I really came on a friendly visit, only," began Antoine.

"Do tell!" said Christopher, softly. "Well, I'm listening. What scandal do you want to talk about now? You are the damnedest gossip, you know."

He lifted three ties and studied them critically. "Help yourself to a drink," he suggested.

Antoine went to the small portable bar at the end of the room and served himself a whiskey and soda. He returned to his chair, where he began to sip with enjoyment. "What do you think of Willkie's chances?" he asked.

"Excellent. If you follow Henri's advice, and don't bring up the heavy artillery in the shape of Big Business Boys and start shelling labor. I don't think Willkie would appreciate that, anyway. He isn't anti-labor. He never was. You'll kill him off if you bring up the phalanx of the heavy boys. And another thing: shut off some of the anti-Semitism your pet organizations are beginning to drivel. That's still an excellent way of doing Willkie in. Only last week, you remember, he said he didn't want the support of lunatics."

"Anti-Semitism," observed Antoine, "is always a good thing to feed the troops. They love it. Give the cattle something to hate."

"You'll find the hate coming back where you least want it," warned Christopher. He sat down and regarded his nephew coldly. "Have you observed, my precocious Machiavelli, that both candidates for the Presidency are conducting themselves like decent, civilized gentlemen, and it is only their supporters who are behaving like dogs and swine? Get some dignity and decency in our own campaign, and we'll win. By the way, I understand Wendell refused your invitation to dinner a few days ago. That ought to be hint enough for you."

Antoine shrugged. He began to frown. "All right. All right. Incidentally, I still haven't figured out how that Indiana clodhopper got the nomination."

"The ways of God are very mysterious," observed Christopher, with a bored air. "Another thing: that wasn't a bright move on the part of the Guardians of America, putting out the brilliant idea that Roosevelt's name is really Rosenfeld. Of all the damned——"

"Don't be vulgar," laughed Antoine. "I, for one, thought it clever. You overestimate the intelligence of the American mob."

But Christopher did not laugh. "I'll make you a prophecy: if Willkie loses, it'll be because of you bright young men. But you never learn." He glanced at his watch. "If you have anything to say, make it fast. I have only one hour and a half to catch my plane."

Antoine continued to sip leisurely. He swirled the yellow liquid in his glass. "It really isn't important. I only wanted to say that when you come back I'm calling a meeting again. My papa-in-law, Boland, will be there, too. Incidentally, I saw him two days ago, in New York. He was asking about my own papa. I told him he is expected to join the others in the family plot momentarily." He looked up now, at Christopher. "You still haven't an inkling about his will?"

"Not the least. Armand and I were never confidential, you know. What are you worrying about?"

"Nothing. Nothing. Just curiosity. I'd like to know, however, if my sister is properly protected."

Christopher shrugged, but made no comment.

Antoine watched him narrowly. "By the way, you've made

no decision about your tetra-ethyl lead patent for high octane gasoline?"

"No," said Christopher, smoothly. "At least, I haven't changed my mind. Henri's watching us too closely, you know. We can't let Germany use the patent, under present circumstances."

"But Eagle controls the Consolidated Tetra-Ethyl Corporation. You can make your own decisions, Henri or no Henri. What has he got to do with it? What's to prevent your letting our motor corporation in Germany use the patent?"

"Our motor corporation is manufacturing motors for Hitler, in case you've forgotten," said Christopher, casually. He lit a cigarette, with every suggestion of boredom.

"The Consolidated Tetra-Ethyl Corporation is in partnership with I. G. Farbenindustrie, in case *you've* forgotten," said Antoine. "What more natural than that they turn the patent over for Hitler's use? Damn it, he needs the high octane."

"There's another thing that's slipped your mind, Tony: Henri still has the controlling vote in Eagles. You know that; so why all this small talk?"

Antoine put down his glass, rose and began to walk softly up and down the room. "I told you: I saw Mary's father in New York, two days ago. He'd like to have that patent, or some hint of the process, anyway. Hitler's getting impatient with us. Papa Boland's got everything arranged for shipment of high octane gas through the Argentine; the tankers are lined up in the harbor. But it will help Hitler more if the oil can be cracked right there in Germany. I. G. Farbenindustrie is all ready to start the process. You are the one that's been holding it up, ever since Henri announced that the process was not to be given to Hitler under any circumstances."

"What can I do about it?" asked Christopher, in a neutral tone.

Antoine stopped abruptly before him. He said, softly: "You know the process. You developed it down there in Florida. It belongs to you. One of your chemists in Florida, still connected with Duval-Bonnet, can move over to Papa Boland. If you give the word."

Christopher was silent. He watched the cigarette smoke slowly curling through his fingers.

"We can get the Army O.K.," continued Antoine. "I saw Brigadier-General Henderson last week in Washington. The

Army won't stand in the way of the process being given to Germany."

Christopher gave no indication of the sudden sharp thrilling that ran along his nerves. He said, indifferently: "Isn't Henderson one of the brightest lights behind the America Only Committee?"

Antoine grinned. "Yes," he said. He added: "Incidentally, our motor company in Germany wouldn't lose by the transaction. And Henderson has a large amount of our motor company stock in Germany." He laughed.

"So," said Christopher, reflectively, "our noble general is quite willing that Hitler have this patent. We know one reason: the stock he has in our German company. But I think there is another, don't you?"

"What do you think?" replied Antoine, gently.

He stood before Christopher, and waited. There was a long silence. The shrilling of the locusts was more strident in the hot air. Antoine could not read Christopher's face.

Antoine almost whispered, his voice heavy with urgency: "Hitler needs that process. Immediately. For the bombing of Britain, which will break out on an unprecedented scale this fall. I hear he's going to try to bomb her out of the war. So, the matter is extremely urgent."

Christopher leaned back in his chair. "You know," he said, with increasing indifference, "I don't see how we can keep out of this war. We'll be in it, eventually, in spite of all your efforts, Tony."

"Yes, I know." Antoine was smiling. "That's why it's so important that Hitler get the patent at once. Boland can still ship oil to Hitler through the Argentine, even if we get into the war. He has cartels in South America, as you know, and Hitler will get the oil even if the supply is shut down right here in America. Roosevelt won't get anywhere in the Argentine with his Good-Neighbor policy, though he might be able to drag the other South American countries into an agreement with him. Remember, Franco's agents and priests have been doing good work in the Argentine; there are picked men in the Cabinet, there. The Argentine will do business with Hitler, for us and herself, whether we are pushed into this war or not. Our agents are working with Franco's agents right along. We've got the Church with us. Whatever happens, the Argentine won't declare war against Hitler, even if we do, and the other South American nations do. So, we'll have our listening posts there, and our outlets, and our propaganda stations, and our sanctuary for German agents."

Again, there was a deep silence. Christopher's cigarette burned itself away in his fleshless fingers. His face was a parchment mask. Then he said, thoughtfully: "All right. I'll let Boland have one of my men, the one best acquainted with the process."

He rose and went to the telephone, where he put through a long-distance call to Florida. Antoine waited, exultation dark and brilliant in his eyes. Christopher added: "A little change in the process, just a little, then there will be no grounds for a suit for infringement of patent."

After Antoine had gone, Christopher called Henri. "I'll be at the airport in fifteen minutes," he said. "This is deadly important. I've got to see you. Drive out as fast as hell."

CHAPTER XLIX

Francis Bouchard (the "frozen Frank," as his relatives called him) regarded his daughter Rosemarie in an ominous silence. Pale, blond, frigid, he seemed ageless, so brightly blue was his eye, so excellent and lean his figure. About his thin and angular mouth there were those attenuated folds of acid humor which always added a prepossessing expression to his whole gaunt face. He was an "Anglo-Saxon" Bouchard, and though he was much taller in stature, more athletic than Christopher Bouchard, and was conspicuous for his big narrow hands and long narrow feet, he had a curious resemblance to Christopher, and also to his own dead brother, Peter. He was noted in the family for his wit, his fastidiousness, and a peculiar kind of integrity which had nothing at all to do with his business affairs. He had always had a pitying contempt for Peter, but also an impersonal affection. He regretted Peter's death very much.

He was one of Henri's faction, for not only was he shrewd, but he also had a liking for the younger man. Determinedly detached and amiable, he kept his relationships with all the members of his family smooth and amicable, partly because he was too selfish to allow himself to be disturbed by feuds, and partly because he found his relatives entertaining. If one did not become too intimate with any of them, he would say. Besides, he believed in the possession of friends, and was very popular.

President of the Kinsolving Arms Company, subsidiary of Bouchard & Sons, he was enormously wealthy, and at least as avaricious as other members of his family. But he never allowed this avarice to become obvious. He appeared to be very generous, easy, with an astringent kindliness which deceived practically everyone, even his wife. He was beloved both by his two daughters, Rosemarie, and Phyllis Morse, and by his wife, and he loved them all. Rosemarie, however, was his favorite.

He sat with her alone in his own small sitting-room. Here he had always summoned his children when he had matters of importance to discuss with them, such as their delinquencies, their private troubles, and other problems. His house was grotesquely large, set in incredibly beautiful gardens. His library was famous, and he also had a fine gallery of original paintings which was the acute envy of Christopher, his particular friend.

His children had always regarded him with the utmost respect, and Rosemarie, enraged as she was, dark and suffused with violence, could not get over the habit of a lifetime. She surged with fury; she wanted to scream deliriously. But her father sat opposite her, his long lean legs crossed, his attitude negligent and quiet, and he looked at her with the blue sparkling eyes that were like sharp fragments of bitter glass.

"No!" she said at last, beating her knees with her clenched hands. "No! You'll all have to go somewhere else for your information."

"I've come to you, Rosy," said Francis. "Because you can give it to me. I want you to think about it. I've been candid with you; you can't repeat anything of what I've said to you without betraying me. And I don't think you'd ever do that, eh, Rosy?"

He smiled slightly. She flashed her black and vivid eyes at him, her scarlet thread of a mouth open viciously. And then she was silent, breathing roughly as if her heart was pounding too strongly in her smart breast. Her throat felt thick with turbulent passion. Then she said, hoarsely: "Dad, I can't tell you anything. It's not that I particularly mind, for ethical reasons. The women of the organizations I've helped to organize are foul and contemptible. Maniacs, perverts, imbeciles. Yes, they're all that. I hope that some day we'll have an adequate way of dealing with them, either by chloroform or sterilization." She smiled bleakly. "But it does happen that I rather agree with the principles of these organizations. We need women like these to advance the principles."

"It seems to me a fine commentary on the principles of your organizations that you require insane females and potential murderesses and perverts to advance them," said Francis. "Look, my dear, perhaps I haven't made things clear to you. I'm in with Henri. Kinsolving is a subsidiary of Bouchard & Sons. For that reason alone I would be in with Henri. But it also happens that I'm in with him for many other reasons, some of them personal."

"Not to mention the fact that your dead brother's wife is going to present Henri with a child?" Rosemarie smiled virulently. Her father's eye dwindled to a brilliant pinpoint. "Perhaps," he agreed, quietly. "God! You women. You can't get away from the bedroom, can you?"

To his surprise, his tumultuous daughter was suddenly very still. She said: "No. We can't."

Francis carefully lit a cigar with precise gestures. He tilted back his chair and regarded the ceiling thoughtfully. "It always seemed a humiliating thing to me to have anything to do with women—at least, in business. In earlier days, women weren't all mixed up with business. Now, they're everywhere, smelling and messing up the whole place, complicating things. Daughters were manipulated, it is true, to bring about better business connections through marriage. That was all right. But now you women have run riot all through business, like a pack of mares in heat. You're everywhere, stinking up politics, stirring up unholy messes in public life, shrilling at the top of your lungs even on Wall Street. I don't like having you sit there opposite me refusing to do something for me which is of the utmost importance to me as president of the Kinsolving Arms."

He went on, when Rosemarie did not answer, though she fixed her burning eyes furiously upon him.

"Christopher mixed his sister into his affairs, with the nice result we have now. Annette is tangled up with Henri. Antoine manipulates Burglar Boland through his little Mary. It goes on, all the time. And you, for instance, go on inventing the dirtiest organizations to revenge yourself on Henri, who's acquired another sweetheart. Pah. It smells. I could name dozens of other instances."

Rosemarie's thin dark face was scarlet. Her lips hardly moved when she said: "He always implied that when he could he would divorce Annette, and marry me. He lied. He was always a stony liar. I loved him, Dad," and now her hard voice shook.

"Yes," said Francis, thoughtfully, "I suppose you did. And I always hoped you'd get to marry him. But there was never anyone for him but Celeste. You've got to remember that. My dear," he added, with affection, "all this doesn't really matter. What does matter is that I'm part of Henri's faction, that if he goes down, I go down, too. That's why I've got to know, and completely, and accurately, the names of all the influential backers of your organizations, what their plans are, the complete lists of their memberships, and if and how they are allied with German organizations, and what German money helps support them."

Rosemarie's lips twisted in a sardonic smile. "You'd be surprised, Dad. By the way, did Henri ask you to get this information from me?"

"He did," acknowledged Francis, gravely. "In fact, when he told me you were the fine Italian hand behind these stinkers, I didn't believe it. But he finally convinced me. He told me, of course, that Antoine is one of the guiding angels of two of the more dangerous organizations. Is that true?"

Rosemarie's black brows drew together, but she said nothing. However, a look of surprise flashed across her face.

"Henri seems to be a little omniscient," she remarked, sneeringly, after a while.

"Henri," said her father, "knows a great deal." He paused. "Rosemarie, my dear, let's forget Henri. I'm asking you to do this for me. And for yourself. If you don't my darling, I'll cut you off with the proverbial nickel." And then, though he smiled at her with the deepest understanding and affection, she saw the remorseless sharpness of his acute eye.

"You wouldn't lose anything if I did cut you off," he went on. "For, if Henri goes down, and I go down, in the general debacle, what will you have left? Think of yourself, my darling."

She was deeply perturbed. The dryness and sparseness of her father's words had the greatest effect upon her. Her avarice, enormous as the avarice of all the Bouchards, came

445

strongly awake. Seeing her perturbation, her father took a box of cigarettes off his desk, and extended it to her. She took a cigarette with svelte, red-tipped fingers that quite visibly trembled. He lit it for her, then leaned back and waited for her to speak.

"You can't feel any loyalty towards that rabble," said Francis. "You can't really feel any sympathy for their aims. How could you? So, that is disposed of. The complete lists, Rosy. The names, backers, tie-ups with the German Embassy, German Intelligence, and the German Consulate. Nothing must be left out. And," he added, "I wouldn't mention any of this conversation to Antoine. It wouldn't be a good thing for you. We'd have to move prematurely, and, my darling, the fact that you're my daughter wouldn't cause me much more than the slightest passing regret."

"Dad," said Rosemarie, in a shaking voice, "you're a swine."

But he said, quietly and heavily: "I'm a man fighting for my life. Didn't it ever occur to you, Rosy, what your nasty intrigues would mean to me?"

"I didn't know you were in with—him!" cried Rosemarie. "You've got to believe that!"

"You never really gave the matter any thought at all," said her father, sternly. "You were so damned engrossed in your own filthy little hates and jealousies, and your natural viciousness. You've done me a lot of damage, Rosy. You've got to undo it. And before you leave this house."

He indicated his desk, and a thick sheaf of blank paper upon it.

"What good would all that do anyone, even if I gave you the information?" asked Rosemarie. "You couldn't stop the organizations, you know that. Even exposing them wouldn't do any good. They'd go underground." Her voice was shrill with desperation.

Francis stared at her emptily. "The Federal Bureau of Investigation would like the information," he said to her, relentlessly. "Don't jump, Rosy. Yes, we intend to turn over the complete lists when the time comes. And that time is soon coming."

Her desperation increased to sharp personal fear. "Dad, you couldn't keep my name out of it—at the end," and now her tone was pleading, distraught.

"No. Perhaps not. I know that, Rosy," said Francis. "But the fact that you gave us this information would mitigate in your favor. That's all we can promise you. Anyway, you're a Bouchard. I doubt you would be—inconvenienced. Come on, Rosy. We'll find out without you. It'll take a lot of time, however. And when we do find out, you'll not have a leg to stand on. This way you can save your skin. While you save mine, too."

She twisted her fingers together in her deep agitation and misery. Then she looked directly at her father, fear burning in her eyes. "Dad, Antoine's in it, you know. A lot of his money. He's been backing Jaeckle. And the America Only Committee. He, and Nicholas, and Jean, and Alexander. I don't care about the others. But I do care about Antoine."

A sensation of utter sickness struck at Francis' heart. What a foulness there was in women these days! The daughters and wives of the "best" people took lovers as casually as did the dirtiest strumpets and trollops of the streets. There was no decency in women, no honor, no respect for their miserable bodies. He stood up abruptly. It would not be expedient, just now, to strike his daughter violently across the face.

"There is the paper, and the pen, Rosy," he said, in a strained voice, and walked quickly out of the room.

CHAPTER L

Celeste, Edith reluctantly admitted to herself, possessed the iron of fortitude. With dignity, with lifted head, with calm and poise, she had faced her family, had looked them unswervingly in the eye, had silenced, at least in her vicinity, any malicious or ambiguous remark, had forced them in her presence to treat her with respect. Even if the venomous Christopher and the stalwart Edith and the sweet and faithful Annette had not stood behind her and beside her, her very indomitable manner and direct and steadfast look would have compelled strong admiration, and an assiduous outward show of acceptance. Despite her years of marriage, she had always been known as "little Celeste" to the family, and not with endearment but rather with mockery, because of Christopher. Too, she had lacked most of the traits of the Bouchard character, and had never been known for amusing conversation or ingratiating manners, two traits which most of the Bouchards fondly believed were attributes of their particular breed. In childhood, she had been fearful of her relatives, and shy, and silent, and not prepossessing in temperament. The family had early discerned that she was not truly a Bouchard, but a frightened stranger who instinctively loathed them.

As they had not admired or respected Peter, for similar reasons, Celeste and her husband had fallen far back in the consciousness of the family, who, during their European pilgrimages and residences, often totally forgot for years at a time that they existed. Their return, the curiosity and laughter about Peter's "opus," and then the sudden huge entrance of Henri into what the Bouchards considered the little and piddling picture of two unpopular and insignificant people, had brought the exiles into strong and brilliant focus in the vision of the family. They had forgotten almost entirely Christopher's devotion to his sister, and Christopher himself had been virtually exiled to Florida by the formidable Henri. Christopher's emergence from obscurity added to the vivid light now thrown on the small portrait in the corner.

The family, by a kind of grapevine, knew many, many things which Henri obtusely believed they either dared not know, or were too stupid to know. It was the immense shadow of this man looming behind Celeste which stilled tongues by nature malignant and cruel.

The Bouchards, then, had never admired Celeste in her own right until now. They had considered her brainless, dull and ridiculously ingenuous. Now, as she came among them, proud, silent, courageous and embittered, stricken with grief but valiant, they looked at her with new respect and even fondness. The sympathy they extended to her, as a young, rich and beautiful widow, was not entirely hypocritical. They, and especially the Bouchard women, began to speak of "poor Peter's child" with increasing firmness. Those who spoke thus, with cool and challenging eyes, were led by Agnes Bouchard, to almost everyone's surprise, for Agnes had been in the vanguard of those who in the past had amusingly derided Peter and Celeste. Then, of course, there was Annette, the frail but gallant, and in her sweet and gentle presence not even the most vulgar or brutal dared utter a malevolent word.

Also, family solidarity (the "rogue's loyalty," as Jules had called it) made them stand together in strong ranks against the possible whispers of snickering outsiders. They might laugh furtively among themselves, but never among their friends and associates.

Last, but not least, was their mortal fear of Henri Bouchard.

So it was that, after their first enjoying surprise and secret loud laughter, almost all the Bouchards, even among themselves, spoke only of "Peter's coming child." Antoine, to his fury, could do nothing. He was stared down, even by his immediate conspirators. Once the pompous Alexander, the pious and the ponderous, had said to the younger man: "I don't know what you are inferring, Antoine, but I can say this: It is in extremely bad taste, if not slanderous."

It had been no easy thing for Celeste, at the stern promptings of Edith and Agnes, and the gentle insistence of Annette, to face the family fully, to force herself to go among them, to accept, after the first sly smiles, their condolences and sympathy. Her eye had glazed, her face had flushed hotly. But she had not shrunk, she had not tried to hide, after the first few weeks when she had been almost beside herself with shame, sorrow, remorse and despair. She attended dinners given for her, very quiet and affectionate dinners. She had given small dinners, also, for her female relatives. Her new strong dignity, her new sureness, excited their admiration. It was only on the occasions when she saw Annette that her eyelids flickered a little, and her mouth trembled.

She had even gone to New York alone to see Mr. Hawkins, and to arrange with him for the allocation of the royalties from *The Fateful Lightning* to various refugee and foreign relief organizations in which Peter had been so desperately interested.

Her life, then, had taken on a heavy serenity and calm, without joy or anticipation, but very controlled and full of dignity. She regarded the coming child with somber indifference and weariness, as she would have regarded any other catastrophe in the long series of catastrophes in her life. When her relatives spoke of the child, she replied desultorily and with disinterest. It had no reality for her, no warmth. She made no plans for it, and, incredibly, never wondered as to its sex.

For she lived, now, in a complete suspension of emotion, in a sort of inertia and apathy. She had always been considered phlegmatic by the family, and this quality seemed enhanced in these days of waiting. It was not that she moved in a dazed stoicism, but rather that she gave an appearance of impassive and neutral control. And, this was not merely an outward manifestation. Her control extended to her disciplined thoughts, her movements, her words. She read much, watched the progress of the war with absorbed distress and intensity, walked, drove, wrote letters to distant friends in England and unoccupied France, and evidenced sincere interest in the coming Presidential elections. She slept calmly, never waking to tears and anguish, never suffering agitated dreams. She had forced herself beyond all this.

Edith had a word for all this: fortitude. She was only partially right, as Christopher suspected. For Christopher knew that Celeste had decided that she dare not think, nor allow herself to feel.

When Christopher was away, Edith spent the days of his absence with Celeste. She knew that Christopher's nervous concern for his sister was ridiculous. Celeste was not in the least disturbed at being alone. She was mildly pleased at the presence of Edith, for the two women had become moderately strong friends, but she did not express any wistful regret when Edith returned to Endur to be with Christopher. Edith had to struggle hard to repress her natural annoyance and jealousy, when, immediately after Christopher's return, he insisted on visiting his sister: "All alone up on those damned bleak hills, God knows what could happen to her."

It was a waste of time to point out to Christopher that Celeste had a houseful of servants, two nurses, and a doctor who called to see her at least once a day. He would only impatiently brush aside Edith's remark that not a day passed but that every female Bouchard called the big lonely house on Placid Heights to inquire about the health of the prospective mother, and that at least three times a week a delegation drove up on brief visits. As far as Christopher was concerned, his little sister lived in wild and precarious isolation on the top of some abandoned mountain, where only a strong eye in the valley below could catch any distress signal in the form of a tiny fluttered handkerchief from a high bastion. He had tried to induce Celeste to spend the days of her waiting at Endur, but when she had involuntarily shuddered, he had said, irritably, before she could speak: "All right, all right! I know you never liked the place."

On a hot Sunday morning in late August, Edith came up to Celeste's room, in the wake of the morning tray carried by the constantly beaming young nurse. "Well, my pet," she said, briskly, "Christopher's flying in from New York at noon, so I'll be trotting along. Is there anything I can do for you before I go?"

Celeste was sitting up in bed, propped up by pillows, and she looked movingly young and defenseless with her black bright hair on her shoulders. Her face had the polished patina of ivory, and her mouth was blooming with freshness. If it had an habitual tautness, if her dark-blue eyes were always a little too fixed, only a keen observer could detect it. She smiled at Edith, and glanced down indifferently at the tray being arranged before her. "No, darling," she said. "And thank you for staying with me. I hate imposing on you."

"No imposition at all," said Edith, pushing a rose back into a vase. She glanced through the windows at the warm soft slope of the hills. Even though it was still August, a mauve haze obscured the heated distance, and the hot quiet air was heavy with the fecund odors of approaching autumn. Trees rustled at the windows; the leaves glittered in the dazzling sunlight. All over the country the silence was blazing and too brilliant. Edith could see the far and blinding gleam of the river in the valley below. Everything was caught in a somniferous trance of sun and heat. Though it was still early morning, the locusts were already stridently shrilling, curiously emphasizing the silence.

When Edith had gone, Celeste ate her breakfast without hurry. Sometimes she stared through the windows, feeling in herself the heavy and motionless unreality and torpidity in which she now spent her life. Nothing had meaning for her. She looked at the morning newspaper, and, at its account of death and fury and destruction in Europe, she shivered slightly. She thrust the paper away from her. Something stirred in her heart at these stories, something agonized and piercing, which, had she allowed it, would have awakened her to shrieking and desperate life.

She allowed her nurse to bathe and dress her. The heat of the day rose strongly. Even the cool dusky rooms with their blue closed shadows were unbearable. Celeste, in her loose white dress, went out into the gardens, her large white

451

hat protecting her head. With gloved hands, she cut flowers, replied gently to the greetings of the gardeners. She did not encourage her nurse to follow her, and had been peremptory at the original suggestion. She walked slowly down the slope behind the house, and entered the cool green shadow of the tangled trees. White benches and chairs were scattered on the dark moist grass, and she sat down and removed her hat. Little sparkles of sunlight broke through the frondage overhead and danced over her dark hair and quiet expressionless face.

She sat without moving, her hands in her lap, looking emptily before her. Above her, in the hot still distance, she saw the glitter of the upper windows of the house which she and Peter had built less than a year ago, and the hot color of the red tiled roofs. No one was here in this small natural woods but herself. She heard the flutterings of birds in the dark boughs over her, and could catch little broken fragments of blazing blue sky between the petrified leaves. It was very still and peaceful here, and refreshing. A squirrel ran near her foot, and she watched its brisk scurryings idly. It turned its little head and regarded her with penetrating wild eyes, sitting up on its haunches, like a nervous and febrile child. She pursed her lips and whistled softly to the creature, and smiled. A bird suddenly flew through the warm green gloom, bearing a sudden flash of light on its eager wings.

There was a strong and vital stirring in her body, and Celeste put her hand over it, as if to quell it. The stirring grew more insistent, and now she was anxiously conscious of a dull but quick pain in her back. Apprehensive, she waited. The pain was gone as quickly as it had come. But her forehead was suddenly wet, and she was aware of an odd weakness.

Her term had almost passed, but the child was not expected for nearly three weeks, according to the doctor's calculations. Celeste sternly repressed her heart's new leaping, breathed deeply, sat back against the chair.

Yet she could not control the thoughts that now leapt insistently into her newly-disturbed mind. For the first time she thought intently of the child that had stirred so urgently in her body, calling her attention emphatically to its own importunate life. She saw it, for the first time, as an individual, a human creature endowed with potential consciousness and character and spirit, and not, as usual, as a lump of living flesh that had no connection with her at all.

She was enormously shaken. What would she do with this creature, how receive it, how regard it? It would be there, in that house, Peter's house, a presence, insistent, demanding, growing daily more aware. When her body was relieved of it, her mind and her soul would not be relieved. It would be with her always, until the day of her death.

She was suddenly terrified. In some vague way she had dimly fancied that once the child was separated from her it would disappear into the mists of the past and no longer be part of her. In her bemused state, she had thought that she could forget it when it had left her. But now its presence was close upon her, its life bound to her own.

She thought, for the first time: Will it be a boy or a girl? Her newly-awakened mind sharpened all her thoughts, made them too bright and clear. She said to herself: I hope it will be a girl. And at the thought of a daughter, a daughter who would live with her in that house, whose voice she would hear, who would soon run through these woods, her heart moved strangely and deeply, and her eyes filled with tears. And now the heavy apathy deserted her, and she felt faint and heady and too vivid with a kind of sweet and trembling joy.

She had not allowed herself to think of Henri during these past months. She did not think of him now. She thought only of her child, and the strong delirious sweetness that the thought of her child brought to her. It was all her child; it did not belong to anyone else. She had not seen Henri since Peter's funeral, nor, in her profound anguish, had she desired to see him. (Annette, in Celeste's presence, and in the presence of the family, had once remarked regretfully that "Henri is away so much these days, in New York, and Washington, that I hardly ever see him.") But Annette had brought friendly messages from him, that he hoped she was well, and she had repeated these messages firmly to Celeste in the presence of the other Bouchard women, and had looked at them all with her lovely light-blue eyes, so that they had not dared to glance aside.

Now, engrossed with thoughts of her child, Celeste did not think of Henri. She had built up an impassable wall between her consciousness and any awareness of him. Henri had nothing to do with this creature that now stirred so strongly and determinedly below Celeste's heart. She clasped her hands over her swelling body, and a bright deep smile stood on her lips.

All at once, she was impatient for the birth, for the sight of her daughter, for the external feel of her body. Her hands lifted a little, as if to take the baby, to touch its soft new skin, to caress its head and flesh. Her fright, her aversion, her terror and agony, had gone forever.

And now the sights about her, the dark moist earth, the trunks of the trees, the glittering fragments of sunlight that spilled upon her knees and hands, the glow of the red roofs far above her, seemed too poignant, too beautiful, to be borne. She had emerged from the colorless and formless world in which she had lived, and had stepped into sound and loveliness and pungent odors, her heart beating wildly and with a penetrating joy. She was like one emerging from the gray caves of death into vivid and burning life.

Tears ran down her cheeks; she tasted them at the corners of her smiling mouth. Their saltness was sharp and strong to her new consciousness. All her pulses were beating, as if a trance had been lifted from them. When another squirrel ran near her and peered at her inquisitively, she laughed aloud, and snapped her fingers at it, and laughed again.

And now her whole spirit was like a city that had been frozen and smothered under a black and freezing mist, and at last feels the sun of life and delight again. One by one, each forbidden tower in her mind rose from the mist. She ran into them all, throwing wide the doors and the windows, letting in the light, no longer in dread or fear or hopelessness or sorrow. She looked everywhere, fearlessly, sometimes with a little sadness, but always with courage.

She thought of Peter, and his quiet grave, and all the years she had had with him of love and understanding and pain and gentleness. These months, since he had died, she had thought of him only in confusion and anguish, shutting a door upon his remembered face when she remembered at all. It had seemed to her that he had not really died, but that he was waiting for her, dumb, lonely, in darkness, and that she had turned away from him in her remorse and grief. Now she opened the door and looked at him fully, smiling, her tears quickening. And it seemed to her that he smiled back, and held out his hand and laughed gently, indulgently and with love, as if she had been frightened by such little and insignificant things that had not touched him. Why, he must have known, always, she said to herself, with wonder and humility. She remembered how she had burst out to him on that last day, crying hysterically against herself, and how he had silenced her, and just touched the thin white streak in her hair. He had understood so much; he had wanted her to know some happiness, though he had not been able to give it to her himself. How can there be talk of forgiveness, between you and me? she heard him say, as she looked at him fully again. How can there be talk of forgiveness in such a huge universe, where there is so much pain and so much to do? When she left him to go elsewhere in the forbidden towers, she felt him looking after her, his face as radiant as the sun itself.

So much to do! There was all of life before her, perhaps not a life of delirious joy, but a life of serenity, strength and peace. There was a child to love and to know, and a place to be made in the world for that child. All at once she was filled with a sense of haste, of impatience, of desire to begin to live again. She had never really lived, except for those brief days and nights when she had been with Henri, and then they had been wretched days and nights, bound and not free.

She stood up, breathing quickly and lightly, as a liberated prisoner breathes. She pushed back her hair with swift hands, caught up her hat, and turned to the path that led back to the house.

It was then that she saw Henri in the arch of the trees, watching her.

CHAPTER LI

She saw him without shock, surprise or fear. She stood there in the green gloom of the trees, motionless, her hat dangling from her hand, her white loose dress faintly stirring, and he looked back at her quietly, the blaze of the sunlight throwing him into silhouette.

He began to walk slowly towards her, and she waited for him. He saw the brilliant blue light of her eyes, the stern delicacy of her face, so palely luminous in the shadow.

"Hello, Celeste," he said, softly. He held out his hands.

She did not move. But she felt her heart bursting in her breast; she felt the knotting of her throat, and the long trembling that ran along her body. She felt the moist earth slide under her feet, and the long upward swell of joy that rushed through her veins. She lifted her arms, and waited, and she uttered faint and smothered sounds.

He put his arms around her gently, and she pressed her hand into his shoulder, her fingers tightening in the warm light flannel of his coat. The peace and happiness she had experienced a few moments ago climbed to rapture, to ecstasy, and to a breaking sweet grief. She did not know she was crying, or that she was sobbing incoherent things. She only clung to him as a child clings, who has been lost.

"Such a little fool," he said, and loosened her arms, and wiped her eyes and wet cheeks. But her hands continued to grasp him unknowingly, and she began to laugh a little, breathlessly, murmurously.

"I didn't think you'd ever come back," she said.

He put his arm about her again, and sat down with her, on the white wooden bench she had left. He held her to him tightly.

"I didn't go away. You left me, you little imbecile," he said.

She could only look at him devouringly, and then, very slowly, the joy began to leave her eyes, and they became drained and dim. "I had to," she whispered. "You shouldn't have come back. You mustn't come again."

But he only smiled down at her. He said, at last: "I know. I know all about it."

She said, faintly, clasping her hands tightly together: "Then, you see why you mustn't come again."

"You were always a little fool, and a romantic," he replied. "As soon as I heard about the child, from Christopher, I knew that was why you'd gone away from me. But now—that circumstances have changed—it doesn't matter any longer, does it?"

With a sick shock, she saw that he still did not understand, that he was in graver danger than ever. She cried out: "You mustn't come again, not alone, not ever again! You've got to understand that, Henri!"

"Good God," he said impatiently. "Did you actually think that I intended to proclaim out loud that this is my child? Why can't you be sensible, Celeste——"

But she interrupted him, in a passion of fear: "They all know, all of them! If you came alone, if we tried to go on as we did before, there'd be no hiding it, in spite of what everyone would try to do!"

He frowned over this, baffled, trying to understand her.

"Well, then, if they all know, in the family, what does it matter? I've never taken the time to wonder whether they knew, or, if they knew, what the hell it mattered, anyway. As far as anyone else, outside of the family, is concerned, that doesn't trouble me in the least."

Her fear became frenzy. "Henri, you've got to realize that as long as you are married to Annette, you can't come here —alone! We can't see each other—alone!"

He stared at her, suddenly cold and inimical. "Look here, I've an idea that Annette understands all about it. So——"

She was silent, very white, and shivering. She felt his iron egotism, his formidable blindness and selfishness. At last she said, very faintly: "I can't tell you what I mean, Henri. Not yet. But you've got to trust me. As far as anyone else knows, outside the family, this is Peter's child." And she put her hand on her body. "But if others ever knew——"

"They won't," he said. "They never knew anything, before. Besides, I'm not sure whether I care a damn, anyway."

As in a flash of lightning, Celeste saw Antoine's face. She stood up, impelled by a sense of desperate hurry. He stood up, also, and put his arm firmly about her. She saw his face, changed now, as she had never seen it before, and very moved. He said, roughly: "What do you think I've gone through, all this time, knowing you were up here alone after poor Pete's death, knowing you were frightened and sick and wretched? I kept away; I knew you didn't want me to come. I knew it was all nonsense, but I had that much thought for you, at least, you addled little fool. I don't suppose you gave a single thought to what all this meant to me, did you?"

She pulled away from his arm. "I did! That is why I knew you mustn't come here! Can't you see? If you can't, I can't tell you, Henri."

She looked at him, in agony. He stood and glowered at her, his pale eyes flashing inexorably.

"I don't know what this is all about. I only know that I had to see you, in spite of your absurdity. I made Edith promise to be here with you, and I intended to stay away, for some time. But I had to come today. It had gotten to be too much."

She pleaded, with pathetic eagerness: "You can always come, with Annette, or with Edith, or with Christopher. But never alone, never again."

"And I suppose," he said, grimly, "that when my child is born I'm to keep my distance, and let you go through it by yourself? And then visit you nicely, with my wife, as an affectionate relative?" He added, with increasing roughness: "Have you thought what it means to me to have everyone speak to me of 'poor Peter's child'? And to know that it's always to be that way—'poor Peter's child'?"

He was about to say much more brutal things, violent and vicious things, but bit them back, in the face of her fear and white despair. He said, in a stifled voice: "Later, things will be different. How long, I can't say. I've always told you I couldn't marry you while Armand lives. You've known that. But when he dies, then Annette will give me a divorce, and we can be married. Not right away. That would be too obvious. But even then, for years, for always, my child must still be 'poor Peter's child'!"

My God! he thought. Even if I "adopt" the child, for the sake of appearances, he'll always think of that damned, miserable, poor weakling as his father! He'll be told that; I'll have to stand by and let it be done.

Something of what he was thinking communicated itself to Celeste. Her fear lessened in the rising of her compassion. She had never felt compassion for Henri before, and she was dimly amazed. His pale harsh face swam before her eyes. She held out her hands to him, and then when he didn't take them, she grasped his arms. Love gave her an unfamiliar cunning.

"Don't you see, Henri," she pleaded, "why you can't be here, now? Or ever alone with me, until—until you are ready to marry me? We've got to think of the baby. There —there mustn't be any sort of scandal about her——"

"Him," he corrected, automatically. Then he began to laugh a little. He drew her to him, gently. "All right, then. I see what's been in your mind all along, and I was a fool not to know it. It was all for the baby's sake, wasn't it?"

"Yes," she said, in a muffled voice, her lips pressed against his neck. His arms tightened strongly about her. "It's a hell of a thing," he said, softly. "There now, stop blubbering. It isn't good for you."

Then he held her face in his hands, and looked down at her with such moved passion as he had never shown her before. "My dear, tell me you are well, that you aren't too miserable?"

"Oh no, Henri, I'm not miserable! I'm happy. I was just sitting here before you came, thinking how happy I was!" She was laughing now, but crying too, and she turned her head and kissed his hand.

"We'll be happy again, my darling. It won't be long, perhaps. It won't be too bad, waiting?"

"I could wait forever, if you will just go on loving me," she answered, simply. "Nothing else really matters."

She smiled at him, her wet face shining with tenderness and new joy. And then, her face changed, and she cried out, sharply. He caught her arm. "What is it, Celeste?"

She struggled to speak, above the sudden awful plunging of pain in her body. She gasped for breath, while he held her. He saw the sweat start out over her lip and on her forehead. Her blue eyes dilated with fear and suffering.

Then he lifted her in his arms, quickly, and carried her out of the little woods, and up the uneven path towards the house.

Christopher and Edith, who had started out to the gardens behind the house to look for Celeste, were dumfounded to see Henri swiftly climbing the long slope towards them, carrying her in his arms. Christopher recovered first; he ran towards Henri and his sister. Henri, oblivious to everything but Celeste's extremity, looked up at Christopher, with alarm and ire. "Don't stand there!" he shouted. "Get someone!"

"Well," said Christopher, "I'll be damned."

CHAPTER LII

The child, premature by three weeks, was born two hours later. It was a boy, long and strong of body, but extremely thin, "like an eel," Christopher remarked, to Edith's indignation. The baby was not in the least red or wrinkled. It had considerable light hair, and square hands, and strongly

459

marked features, and did not resemble its mother at all.

"And if anyone thinks he is like Pete, then it'll be a triumph of imagination," said Christopher. (Edith later brought him a faded photograph of herself and Henri as children. She, a solemn little girl with a plain and frowning face, stood beside a high-chair, her dress, with the pointed lace at the hem, brushing the tops of her black tasselled boots. In the high-chair sat Henri, a pugnacious, square-faced child with a crest of light hair, pale staring eyes, and a heavy look. Christopher, seeing this photograph, burst out laughing. "Hide the damned thing; bury it!" he advised.)

Celeste was very ill. The months of fear and grief and despair, of forced courage and inner anguish, now exacted their fee of weakness and lassitude. It was not until six o'clock that night that Henri, her brother, and Edith were permitted to see her. She had slept all day, breathing uneasily, moaning a little. When she opened her eyes, she saw Henri's face bent over her in the lamplight. His expression was strained and grim, and when he tried to smile it was only a convulsive grimace. She tried to speak, but he put his hand gently near her lips. He felt their heat and dryness when she feebly kissed his hand, and at their touch he started a little and the nostrils in his broad nose expanded as if he had been overtaken by a sharp pang. She slept again, her hot and tremulous hand in his, and he sat beside her, not moving, only watching her, bent towards the bed. The doctors and nurses were there, but he did not see them. His eyes remained fixed on her, and each time that Edith and Christopher peeped into the room it seemed to them that he had not moved a muscle. Once or twice the doctors tried to persuade him to leave her, but he gave no indication that he had heard them.

Edith was uneasy. "I wonder what they'll think," she said to Christopher. She sat with her husband on the cool terrace, leaning back in her chair, exhausted. "Dr. Morton already has a funny look. They're scared to death of Henri. He always frightens people. Anyway, I saw them exchanging a look, and it was a very peculiar one."

Christopher shrugged. "You can count on their not repeating anything," he said. "The nurses are another matter."

"The family has been calling regularly for hours," said Edith, hopelessly. "I've told them no one can see the baby or Celeste for several days, but there's bound to be a delegation up here tomorrow morning, or even tonight. We've got to get Henri out of here."

"Call out the derricks, then," replied Christopher. His voice was so dull that Edith looked at him sharply. That pale wedge-shaped face, with its fine wrinkled skin like parchment, had aged, had become sunken and lifeless. It's no use, thought Edith, despondently, but with the old dark anger smoldering in her heart. "I think," said Christopher, "that I need a drink. Several drinks. Will you get me one, sweet?"

Edith went into the house. She returned with the frosty glass, and Christopher drank rapidly. He hated whiskey, but he exhibited a kind of hasty greed in downing it. The night was very dark and silent, except for the shrilling of crickets in the dry warm grass, and the occasional spasmodic fluttering of hidden trees. In the valley below, lights twinkled like distant stars, and once or twice an air-liner thundered overhead, its green and red navigation lights moving like colored planets through the moonless sky. All at once, there was a quickening of the wind, and from the sun-baked earth and grass there rose a strong and passionate odor.

"He hasn't seen the baby yet," said Edith. "I thought he'd be more interested."

"It's been hours," answered Christopher, almost in a murmur. "Why don't you try to get him out of there now. Tell him, if necessary, that something's wrong with the child."

Edith considered this for a moment. "I will," she said, listlessly. She sighed. "Of all the messes. I knew it was going to be bad, but not this bad. It's going to be very hard on Henri. It's always going to be hard. Even if and when he and Celeste are married, that youngster will always be known as Peter's child. That isn't going to be very nice for Henri. I know him too well."

It was fortunate that she didn't see the sudden malignant smile on Christopher's lips, nor his sudden expression of surprised pleasure. But she felt his malignancy, and she said, in a rising voice: "You've always hated him, Kit. You'll have a lot of fun watching him during the next few years."

"Nonsense," he murmured, languidly. "Anyway, you can't expect me to love him, can you? Who could? No one ever did, except a batch of women. I've always wondered what the secret of his charm was for the ladies."

"He's a man, not a polite cut-throat," she said, with considerable bitterness.

"Women are such atavists," Christopher remarked, with a loud yawn. "They prefer clubs to hand-kissing."

Edith went upstairs again. She peeped into Celeste's large pretty room, with the soft curtains blowing gently in the rising night-wind. In the background burned shaded lamps; around the white bed there was a large gentle circle of shadow. Henri still sat there beside Celeste, his relaxed hand near her cheek. Celeste slept, and it was evident that Henri, too, had fallen into a doze. The two nurses were whispering in the background, as they prepared various things at a table. Edith could see the black shining mass of Celeste's hair on the pillow, and her quiet white profile. She was breathing easily, now, and did not stir.

Edith hesitated. She glanced towards the fresh young nurses. They were smiling together. Nonsense, thought Edith, irritably, they probably are just having one of their obscure and obscene jokes; nurses are famous for them. They aren't thinking of us, at all. She tiptoed towards her brother. At the slight sound she made, the nurses turned quickly, their young faces respectful. They came towards her, and she smiled at them reservedly. Under their frank clear eyes she bent over Henri and shook him. He opened his eyes and stared blankly at her. She whispered: "Henri, we want you to see the baby. There might be something wrong——"

Now his eyes flashed suddenly. He moved stiffly in his chair, then glanced quickly at Celeste. He stood up, and bent over her. She slept peacefully. Edith, looking at the nurses out of the corner of her eye, saw them exchange a gleaming and significant glance, or, at least, she imagined that they did so. Her anxiety and anger quickened. She wanted to grasp Henri by the arm to hurry him, but he remained, bending over Celeste, for several moments longer, while she had to force her features into an expression of fond indifference.

Finally, Henri straightened up, and followed his sister into the quiet corridor outside. Edith closed the door behind them. Henri turned to her, and said in a rusty voice: "What is it?"

"It's the baby. There is a baby, you know," answered his sister, ironically.

Now Henri's face changed. "Yes? What is wrong?" he asked, harshly.

"Nothing." Edith sighed and shrugged. "But I had to get you out of there, Henri. I want you to do a little thinking, my pet. Do you know how long you've been here? Does

Annette know where you are? I haven't much time, my dear, but I want you to understand that you mustn't come here alone again. Come with Annette——"

The flesh about Henri's eyes tightened and wrinkled. Then he turned away from her. "I want to see the child," he said, with abruptness.

Edith, praying that one of the nurses would not follow them immediately, led the way down the hall to the bright airy room which had been prepared as a nursery. Henri saw nothing of the pictured walls or the white furniture. He saw only the crib, in a corner, far from the little night-light burning on a distant table. He went to that crib directly, and looked down in profound silence at his son.

Edith was not given to easy compassion, but as she watched her brother, his broad square hands tightening on the rail of the crib, his head and shoulders bent over the baby, she looked aside, a thick lump rising in her throat. She moved a step or two away, her eyes dim, dazzled in the faint light. Henri stood there a long time. The baby slept and moved his tiny lips restlessly. One small fist lifted spasmodically, then fell in a restless movement. The light curled softly over the big round head.

Edith heard Henri move. He had turned away from the crib, and he was smiling. "Ugly, isn't he?" he asked. "And isn't he very small, or something?"

His sister laughed softly and with a shaken sound. "No, he's beautiful, dear. And very big. Even though he's a little premature, he weighs nearly eight pounds. He's thin now, but you won't know him in a month."

The door opened and one of the nurses came in, her big brown eyes avid with curiosity. She rustled to the crib, and gazed down fondly at the baby. "He's darling, isn't he, Mrs. Bouchard?" she ventured, in a whisper. "Such a nice clean healthy baby, even if a little early. Doctor says he's doing fine."

Henri was about to speak, but he met Edith's firm and warning eye. He followed her out of the room. Alone with her, he sagged slightly, and passed his hand over his head.

"Go home, Henri," said Edith. "Everything's all right now." She hesitated. "Things will be better soon, I know."

But he turned away from her without a word, and went down the stairway.

CHAPTER LIII

Inspired by the same sadism that animated the Roman mobs fighting for front seats at circuses in order to watch every expression on the faces of the tormented in the arenas, the Bouchards flocked thickly to the big house on Placid Heights to visit Celeste. They were extremely disappointed if Henri did not happen to be there when they called. Almost to a man, they hated him, and feared him. They wanted to watch his face as they talked about the baby, or Celeste, or "poor Peter, who'll never see the little fellow."

But Henri had never possessed a "vivid" countenance. No one had ever been able to guess his thoughts. Even his rare violences had been gloomy, or dull, like a heavy November day. He had never displayed any conspicuous delight, enthusiasm or pleasure to the casual observer, and what little of these had ever broken through his stony reserve Celeste alone had seen. His native impassivity, therefore, protected him from the furtive malice of his family, as it had protected him in intrigues, plots and multitudinous machinations. It was this impassivity which had given him a kind of terribleness, a potential violence which no one ever desired to evoke.

He came with Annette, now a gallant as well as a pathetic figure to her relatives, who often stared at her with the unwinking speculativeness which passed as admiration with the Bouchards. He came as an interested relative, standing beside his wife as she laughed and murmured over the baby, touching the child gently with her little hand. But Edith saw, to her surprise, that he looked at his wife with a curious intensity, rather than at the baby, that he seemed strangely fascinated by her sweet and radiant face, and that when she turned to him, smiling, her eyes filled with bright tears, his features would take on an oddly moved expression. He was very kind to her, studying her openly, and when she would glance at him, with some remark about the baby, he

464

would reply with gentleness and slowness. Edith observed that he would sit beside her, as he had never done before when not compelled, and that often he would reach for her hand, to hold it. And Annette, not looking at him, would sit very straight, like a child in her chair, her eyes brilliant with joy and rapture. Her voice, always diffident and soft, would take on a more confident and merry note, and her relatives, staring, would be amazed at her gentle wit and volubility.

Edith, who had always felt some aversion for her sister-in-law, now was quite worn out with her pity and admiration. He's grateful to her, she thought. Now that gratitude seemed like an insult to the tender and valiant Annette, for her courage possessed a noble grandeur too lofty for compassion. Edith noticed that she never visited Celeste alone, and Edith, who had admired her before, now felt completely humbled in her understanding. But she was also overwhelmed with wonder. How could Annette endure this? How could she look at his misery, her betrayal, her loneliness and sorrow, with such an unflinching eye, and with such fortitude, and smile with such steadfastness as she did so? Of course, she loved both Henri and Celeste; Edith understood that. She intended to protect them, and their child. But, Edith thought sourly, there were heights to which love could mount which were hidden from more dull and selfish eyes.

Beside this gallantry, Celeste's courage seemed thick and obstinate, even sullen, as all defensive courage must be. She received the congratulations of her relatives with her slight stern smile, and listened to their praises of her child with pleased silence only. She appeared to be engrossed in her thoughts, and Edith, very wryly, wished her good luck with them. For Edith, these days, was blown about by a dozen different emotions, and was exhausted and made irascible by these conflicts. Sometimes she was enraged with her brother, and hated Celeste, because they were both a constant drain on her compassion. But always she regarded Annette with humility and tenderness.

Henri, who must have understood that he was a danger to his child, never came alone, though he had plenty of opportunities to be unobserved. However, he wrote to Celeste, constantly. Edith knew that. She saw how eagerly Celeste searched through her volume of mail, and how she would flush at the sight of a certain square envelope, and how eager she would be to be alone in order to open it. In the afternoons, she would sit up in bed, writing copiously, thanking her friends for their gifts and letters. Edith would come in, later, and unconcernedly carry off the mail, and stamp it. Celeste knew, of course, that Edith would see the thick envelope addressed to Henri at his office, but when the two women met again they did not speak of it.

Henri was often away from Windsor, making short and frequent trips to New York and Washington. He appeared very preoccupied after these journeys, and the thick seam between his eyebrows would be more pronounced, and the lines about his heavy mouth would be more gloomy than ever. Christopher told Edith that Henri had another gay love in Washington, a happy and vivacious young widow who was the owner of one of Washington's larger newspapers, but he apparently derived little permanent pleasure or relaxation from the lady. Upon his return, he would visit Placid Heights with Annette, and sit in abstracted silence while Annette chatted joyously with Celeste, or admired the baby.

There were many things to disturb him these days, and not all of them were connected with Placid Heights, Edith knew. The frightful "blitz" had broken out in the Battle of Britain, and the newspapers carried appalling stories of the devastation of English cities.

Edith did not love England. But, as England stood alone in an indifferent, hating or terrified world, her head high, bleeding from countless wounds, her eyes open and strong and full of desperate but unshaken courage, she inspired, in enemy and indifferent friend alike, the admiration that can be accorded only the heroic and gallant. "Will she stand?" asked the world. "I will stand," said England. "I will stand! Not by the help of God, not by the hands of fearful friends, not by the grace of heaven! But only by the help of my valorous heart, my intrepid blood, the grace of my unshaken people. I stand alone, but I stand undaunted, and neither fury of men nor the desertion of God can throw me down."

This was not the epic of kings, of captains or gentlefolk. It was the epic of the small people, the little shopkeepers, the starveling farmers, the factory and mill fellaheen, the street-walker and the shopgirl, the old flower-woman and the newsboy, the bedraggled mother in the tenements, the driver of drays, the shabby mechanic and the children in their ruined schools. It was even the epic of desperate thieves and gutter-rats, of miserable little scoundrels and drunkards, of chimney-sweeps and window-washers. It was the epic of the betrayed and bewildered and anonymous people. The Trojan heroes, the Wagnerian posturers, the captains with their swords and their braid: where were they now? The Greek chorus of the people, lifting their dim voices in one long swell of undaunted tragedy, shouted down the tinsel voices of the useless and the gilded. This was the agony of a whole people, and it possessed a grandeur and a loftiness beyond that of any king in torment, of any army in desperate retreat, of any Napoleon on St. Helena. It was the agony of a world, betrayed, abandoned and stricken by a hundred men who sat in every great capital of the world, and communed secretly together in growing consternation and wonder.

For it was slowly becoming evident that the people of England would not die, that England would not fall. Their king might possibly flee, their Parliament disperse in disorder, their ships steam away in the night with their freight of the treacherous, the frightened and the cowardly. But England would stand. The people would not die.

For a while even the foul enemies of the people of the world were silent. The treasonable broadcasts over the American radio were temporarily stilled. Only the voice of Winston Churchill was heard, a loud and strong and lonely voice, in the darkness and the fury, rising over the roofs and towers of a thousand cities, sounding clear and firm above the crackle of the flames and the scarlet of the hundred fires, above the shattering thunder of falling walls, and the weeping of a bleeding people. And the world listened to that voice of heroic resolution, of passionate faith and exultant if sorrowful pride.

"We stand alone," he said.

No, thought Edith, you do not stand alone. There is an unseen power in the passion of the hidden people, there is an unknown power in the prayers of lightless masses, streaming up from every dark boundary of every dark land.

Henri returned from Washington, and called Christopher to come to him from Detroit. Henri was fagged, but grimly content. "Well," he said, "we've put it through, with the help of our friends. The President will sign the Selective Service Act tomorrow. Our next job will be to put through greater and more effective aid to Britain, a kind of lending, or leasing, of matériel of war. She can't keep up the pace, and the resistance, without it. That's why we'll be up against a terrific fight in Congress, to prevent any such aid. The boys are certainly determined that the Fascists must win—especially in the State Department. But Hugo's working hard at it.

"By the way, there's a friend of his, Senator Anthrusters. Remember him? His broadcasts, his rallying of the Mothers against Conscription, his denunciations of 'the international bankers, and the Communists, the war-mongers, and Jews, and British imperialism,' and all the other shibboleths and slogans, will be something to remember, later. Hugo's thrown the fear of God into him. Hugo long suspected his tie-up with German Intelligence. At any rate, he's suddenly grown rich, and very vicious against any sort of American rearmament, conscription, support of Britain, and so on. Now, something's terrified him; I think Hugo helped. He's flying from his home State to Washington, today, for an interview with J. Edgar Hoover. Hugo's given him forty-eight hours, and then public exposure if he doesn't comply. Hoover's sent three men to guard him on the way, though I hardly think it necessary. Well, things are under way, though I can't see much light or hope, yet."

Two hours later, Henri, listening to the broadcasting of news, heard a bulletin that brought him upright in his chair with a loud exclamation. The air-liner in which the pusillanimous and subversive Senator Anthrusters had been flying to Washington had crashed mysteriously only two hours' flight from the Capital. With him had perished several other passengers, including three agents of the Federal Bureau of Investigation. No cause for the crash had as yet been discovered.

CHAPTER LIV

By the end of September, Peter's book had reached nearly four hundred thousand copies in sales, which were increasing rapidly. While all the critics had been unanimous that it was a "startling and sensational" piece of work, the majority were incredulous, and some were vulgar and full of ridicule in their comments.

A typical criticism of the latter sort was this: "In Part Three, the writer exceeds the bounds of public credulity. He calls this Part *The Plot Against America*. He ought to have called it *The Plot Against Common Sense*. Who are these Brouelles, these Maynards, these Uptons and these Crawfords, who are supposed to be involved in an international plot with others like them, in Paris, London, Rome, Berlin, Budapest, Warsaw, Vienna, and New York, to guarantee the success of Adolf Hitler in his alleged dream of world-conquest? Who are these fantastic financiers, these great industrialists, these bloated bankers, these gilt-and-scarlet clergy, these mad statesmen and politicians and liars and plotters, these hinted members of our own State Department and Congress? The author implies that all these names are fictitious, but that the facts are true and dreadful. One has only to observe the stalwart and passionate resistance of the British people, led by their so-called upper classes, to feel nothing but disbelief in the allegations in this book: that Britain is part of the huge international plot to make Hitler the supreme dictator of all the world. One has only to look at the furious resistance of the conquered but unconquerable French peasant and workingman and small shopkeeper and farmer, who will not accept the frightened dictates of Marshal Pétain, to know that France was never in a plot to become a vassal of Hitler's. Though Mussolini has stabbed fallen France in the back, one can be sure that the Italian people had no part in that act.

"Then the author's attack on the clergy is cowardly and unjust and scandalous. The Church has always opposed Mussolini and Hitler, in spite of the Concordat. Thousands of priests have already perished at the hands of Hitler's madmen, thousands of humble priests trying to protect and save their flocks, whether in Poland or Norway or Belgium or France. This vicious attack on an obscure but valorous body of dedicated men is one of the ugliest things this critic has encountered in twenty years.

"The author implies that the plot goes on in South America, where many Falangists are now living, and to which Franco did, admittedly, send many Spanish priests. Just at the very moment when our President is trying to consolidate South America in a Pan-American bloc, this book attacks the very people who are capable of achieving this bloc. The Argentine particularly is attacked. It is unfortunate that the author has made this glaring error. For last news reports state definitely that Argentina will lead all the other South American nations in an accord with the United States, and that, in the event of any unbelievable attack upon us, Argentina will be the first of our sister nations to declare war upon our attacker.

"The author goes on to say that Russia will soon be aligned with Britain and any other democratic allies against the Nazi murderers. It would be interesting at this point to know just how sheepish he would feel now in the face of the German-Russian Non-aggression Pact of August.

"The names of the great American industrialists, bankers, newspaper owners, manufacturers and politicians are admittedly fictitious, he says. But does he actually believe that any sane American might suspect that the famous Bouchard family, Mr. Hiram Mitchell of Mitchell Motors, Mr. Morse of the Morse National Bank, Mr. Jay Regan of Wall Street, and all our other famous and vigorous men who have advanced American progress, are actually in a plot to deliver us over to Hitler, for their own purposes? The Bouchards are now turning out huge quantities of armaments, chemicals, motors and other matériel of war for the use of Britain, and ourselves. Does this look as though they were plotting with Hitler for the conquest of America?

"I'd like to see the author's 'sources of facts,' which he mentions so passionately. I don't believe they exist. I don't believe any intelligent American will credit it, either."

It was rare that a critic answered or attacked a critic. But one courageous man wrote in rebuttal: "The famous critic of The ——— ——— Times has pointed out the heroic resistance of the British and French and Polish and Belgian and Dutch and Norwegian peoples as a definite denial of the facts in *The Fateful Lightning*. He eulogizes, and quite rightly, the dedicated, humble but fearless acts of the obscure clergy in the cities and villages and towns. But he overlooks the obvious and insistent fact that this epic of wild and grim resistance is being written by the obscure and helpless and anonymous people, not by their leaders, not by the powerful, the masters. The little peasant fighting to the death with his pitchfork, the starving saboteur striking down Nazi soldiers in the black streets of Paris or Brussels or Copenhagen or Warsaw, the little hungry priest standing so gallantly at his bare altar in his miserable little church and fearlessly denouncing the bloody invader: these are the inarticulate and voiceless people who have been so foully betrayed by the powerful of their own nations. When they shall have driven out the murderers, and destroyed them, it will be their epic. Their betrayers will have died, or fled into exile."

Another reviewer said: "It is disappointing to see an old and respected firm like Thomas Ingham's Sons publishing such incredible fantasies as *The Fateful Lightning*, and other murder mysteries. One has come to expect only the finest in contemporary literature from this House, and it is very disillusioning to your reviewer to find it descending to clap-trap and spectacular cheap lies for the mere sake of sensationalism. It can't have descended like this for the sake of money. I predict that *The Fateful Lightning* will be the year's worst flop."

Mr. Hawkins read these reviews with a wry smile. His consultations with the sales manager of the company were comforting. Reviewers or no, orders came in by letter, telephone and telegraph for *The Fateful Lightning*. He saw Peter's face, and quite involuntarily, he smiled his encouragement at this vision, as if he had heard a question.

"You can't sue a dead man for libel," said Antoine, indulgently.

But Robert Bouchard, his cousin (son of Emile and Agnes) replied hysterically: "But we can sue Ingham's! Good God, is the family going to stand by and let them publish this stuff about us?"

"If we sue, we identify ourselves with the 'Brouelles,' Bob."

"But everyone knows who the bastard meant!" cried Robert.

Antoine shrugged, lit a cigarette, and eyed it with interest. "Remember: 'If the cap fits, wear it'? Our only attitude should be one of ignoring the thing. Dignified silence, and all that. Being above the cat-calls of the monkey-men. The newspapers wouldn't dare identify us with the 'Brouelles.' They'd face a libel suit, and they know it. As for the people: who cares? Who reads books, anyway? A few hundred thousand impotent nincompoops with eye-glasses and dandruff on their shoulders. But the American people read nothing but the sports and financial news, the murder stories and the comic strips. The one way to focus the interest of this nation of morons on us would be for us to sue, so that the suit would be big news in the papers. If we keep our mouths shut, the nincompoops may read, and draw in deep breaths of awe and fear and indignation, but the mass of the people will remain brightly innocent and ignorant of everything."

He smiled. "I shudder to contemplate what would happen to all of us if the American people ever acquired the intelligence of a superior dog! But there's no fear of that, fortunately."

But Robert looked at him with his little, restive pig-eyes. "Well, it says here in the *Times* that the book has been bought by an English publisher, a Swedish publisher, and a publisher in Buenos Aires. And these people read, even if Americans don't."

Antoine shrugged again. "We won't need to worry about the English—soon. Nor, about the Swedes. As for the South Americans: the priests will take care that the book doesn't have very much of a circulation. What is wrong with you, Bob? You are always looking under beds and into closets for the bogyman."

"Oh, hell," said Robert, querulously. "And I don't think England's done. They're holding up damn well. And now we've got that cursed Lend-Lease to contend with. Why couldn't you fellows stop that?"

"We tried." Antoine's voice was still smooth, but there was a sharp and venomous glint in his eye. "We spent half a million dollars in propaganda fighting it. We had three hundred fat middle-aged sows parading around in front of the White House carrying placards against it. Mothers of America against Lend-Lease. Used to be Mothers of America against

Conscription, wanting to keep their baby-boys at home. We gave Jaeckle, alone, ten thousand dollars and stirred him up to a fine frenzy. We put out three hundred thousand dollars to various gentlemen in Washington, where it would do us the most good. We put full-page advertisements in every prominent newspaper in the country. We bribed newspaper columnists and radio commentators. We had hundreds of thousands of money-men and women writing their Congressmen. We had professional patriots bellowing at the top of their lungs. We had priests and ministers speak against it as an instrument to draw us into a 'foreign war.' Nothing," he added, with a dark and glittering smile, "was left undone in the way of coercion, bribery, hot-air and suborning politicians to defeat the measure. I'm damned if I know why it passed."

"There's something going on undercover that I don't understand!" ejaculated the dull and sluggish Robert with unaccustomed energy.

Now Antoine was not smiling. He rubbed his chin, thoughtfully. "Yes," he said, musingly, "there is something going on. I suspect it's coming right from the warm bosom of this very family. I think I smell a stench from Robin's Nest. Yes, yes indeed."

Robert stared at him affrightedly. "You mean Henri?" he said, and his voice was almost a whimper of fear. His big broad face, flushed with torpid blood and fear, turned on Antoine with acute apprehension. And then when he saw Antoine's fixed silent smile, so sinister, so full of detestation and hatred for his pusillanimity, his fear sharpened to terror. He lifted his pudgy little hands, overgrown with short black hairs, as if to defend himself from that lethal regard.

From early childhood Antoine had fascinated him, had led him, had subjugated him with refined and graceful brutality, had told him what to think and what to do, had even chosen, by suggestion, the wife for him. For Antoine he had always had a dull thick adoration, an open-mouthed and speechless passion, and that stolid and somewhat hysterical loyalty found only in the stupid man. No matter how Antoine maliciously betrayed him to the laughter of others when they had been children, no matter how Antoine had ridiculed, neglected, slighted or lightly insulted him, Robert had followed at his heels like a fat and lumpy puppy, regarding it as the height of joy if Antoine condescended to notice or to speak to

473

him. Antoine's grace, wit, brilliant smile, and air of assurance and savoir faire enchanted Robert, who had no grace, who had been cursed by a stature abnormally small and a breadth abnormally wide, and who had been born with natural fear already one of his major characteristics.

They were cousins: their fathers, Armand and Emile, were brothers. They had attended the same schools and universities, where Antoine had always been the gay leader and vicious contriver of escapades. He had remembered, at times, to include Robert in some of the escapades and less dubious events. Otherwise Robert, so stagnant, so stolid, so phlegmatic and obtuse, would have been the butt of the school if not completely overlooked. For he had not the slightest imagination, originality or color. He crept painfully through his classes, and only his own dogged and flat-minded persistence, his own obstinate drabness that could never imagine defeat, and Antoine's irritable coaching, kept him from total failure. He graduated with an average of C minus; even this surprised his parents: Emile, who loathed him, and Agnes, who felt for him only an indulgent and contemptuous pity.

His slow wit was reflected in his small red-veined brown eyes, sunken in rings of suffused flesh, in his pudgy oily nose squat against his face, and his sullen slack mouth. Emile sometimes declared that his son resembled Armand, his uncle, but Robert did not have Armand's look of wary shrewdness, and the occasional cunning and watchful flash of the eye, nor the swift crafty mind that had been part of his, Armand's, youth. Nor did he possess that frightened intuition, that aching perception and uneasy conscience that had so bedevilled the younger Armand. Besides, Armand had been auburn. Robert was muddy brown in coloring. It was true that he had Armand's short and trundling legs and little feet, but the body these supported was enormously wide and heavy, solid as stone rather than fat, with shoulders fantastically broad and beamlike. He swayed ponderously when he walked. Even in childhood, he had had no swiftness or any sinewy quality. His brownish hair was rough, coming forward like a shelf over his low brow, giving him a somewhat ape-like appearance, emphasized by two large and outstanding ears.

Robert's character, though trustful of Antoine, and slavish towards that sparkling cousin, was yet furtively virulent and secretly vengeful. He knew he possessed no prepossessing physical qualities. He knew that he was a vaguely ridiculous figure, with his big broad body and short trunklike legs, his lack of neck which set his big ball-like head squarely on his shoulders. For these physical traits, which he sometimes believed were actual deformities, he hated all the lovely and graceful and well-formed of the world, with the exception of Antoine. Finally, when he was in his thirties, the hatred had extended to everyone and everything, again with the exception of Antoine, and sometimes, of his little stupid wife. But the hatred was never violent or explosive, or even occasionally articulate. It lay in him like a thick, black and viscid pool, a pool of slow hot pitch.

Dimly, he must really have known he was a fool and a dolt, despised of everyone. In consequence, he became arrogant and vain, dogmatic, cruel and sluggishly resistive. His obstinacy became a byword in the family. Only Antoine, and he not always, could sway him from a preconceived notion or plan. All his attributes were brutish and obtuse. He delighted in brutality, especially those aspects of that quality which were gross and obvious. He had finally convinced himself that he was very clever, a deep fellow, with very profound thoughts, and extremely subtle and aware. "They'll not put anything over on me," was his constant thought. "I don't say much—but look out!" He saw himself as one of those silent men of history, misunderstood by contemporaries but revered by posterity. Besides these charming qualities, he also possessed the Bouchard avarice and voracity. He was sullenly violent, his expression was almost constantly glowering, and he had a craven and cowardly heart, fearfully fawning on those he suspected of the power to hurt him, overbearing to inferiors and those at his mercy.

He was pathetic. He had the capacity for a slavish adoration, an attribute common to the stupid and secretly hysterical. No one had ever discovered this but Antoine. Even though he had married Elsie Mitchell, granddaughter of the malignant and pious old motor magnate, Hiram Mitchell, he had never felt for her more than a vague and suspicious affection. Elsie had recently presented him with a small daughter with eyes like shoe-buttons but with the prettiest auburn curls, and Robert, very furtively, was beginning to show the child the first signs of uneasy adoration.

Robert was his father's secretary, and to Emile's surprise, he had displayed a certain dogged tenacity, a certain bull-dog devotion to details, a lack of imagination that secured him from doubt and hesitations, a certain bulky integrity and persistence, which made him quite invaluable to his father, who was vice-president of Bouchard & Sons. He would sit in his office like a fat and brooding toad, disposing of a mountainous daily mass of tedious details, dictating tirelessly to batteries of stenographers, attending to the endless routine of telephone calls and orders, never indicating any weariness or blunted exhaustion. He was like a mole, grimly digging. Emile was indeed happily surprised, and though he did not despise his son the less, he appreciated his peculiar talents. Moreover, he could be trusted, a most unusual characteristic among the Bouchards. But even Emile did not know that Robert could be trusted only when he did not adore. And he adored Antoine.

Robert hated practically everybody, but more than anyone else in the family he hated Henri Bouchard. Like all those who are the rejected of the earth, Robert had an almost insane egotism, a passionate belief that he was rejected because he was superior and misunderstood. He even welcomed overt dislike. But he could never endure complete neglect. Henri did not neglect him. He simply forgot the younger man's existence. He never saw Robert without staring at him momentarily and blankly, before recognizing him. He seemed to have difficulty in placing him. This was not all sincere. Part of it was deliberate contempt. Robert could have overlooked the latter, but he could never overlook the first sharp stare, the sudden drawing together of Henri's thick light brows before the recognition.

Robert feared Henri more than he had ever feared another human being. He had never had any encounters with Henri that were even slightly tinged with violence or disagreement, but Henri had only to enter his office, had only to glance at him, had only to pass him, to fill the younger man with a quite unreasoning terror. In Henri's presence he was completely dumb.

Antoine, then, found in Robert an eager and devoted servant in the work of ruining Henri. The very thought filled Robert with the wildest terror and the wildest joy and vengefulness.

Because of his many dangerous if sodden attributes, Robert was a great favorite with his wife's grandfather. His natural inclination to vicious hatred, his dull-wittedness, his stony vengefulness, his dogged tenacity and deep, innate brutality, endeared him to the psalm-singing, pious and deeply religious old motor magnate. The bent for sadistic cruelty and mercilessness and ugly malevolence which seems part of the character of the fanatically religious man were very strong in Mr. Mitchell, who compelled his many thousands of employees to sign a pledge to attend church at least once a week, to swear that they had never committed adultery or fornication, and to promise that they would never drink, smoke to excess, swear or practise birth-control. It followed, as a matter of course, that Mr. Mitchell hated mankind. He loved to have religious men, especially clergymen, about him. He had tried to secure the friendship of the Catholic bishop of his diocese, but that bishop, unfortunately for Mr. Mitchell, happened to be an honest and brilliant man. He rejected Mr. Mitchell's overtures with such firm and scornful incisiveness that Mr. Mitchell later imported two Ku Klux Klan clergymen from the deep South to head two of the more important and fanatical Methodist and Baptist churches in his city. Mr. Mitchell, in consequence, became a very violent anti-Catholic reactionary, and even the assistance of certain venal Catholic clergymen in Mr. Mitchell's own work of destroying American democracy did very little to alleviate his hatred for the Roman Church. He would use these virulent and misguided men, yes; but he plotted to destroy the organization to which they belonged when the convenient day arrived. When the bishop, suspecting Mr. Mitchell's machinations, removed one of the priests to a less vulnerable parish (and reprimanded him harshly in private), Mr. Mitchell's hatred for the Roman Church reached a new high pitch. He privately financed two of the most fantastic, the most sadistic and vicious anti-Catholic publications in America.

Mr. Mitchell was also one of the most lavish backers of the America Only Committee. Through Robert, he had met Antoine.

CHAPTER LV

There were moments when Antoine, amazed, found himself on the incredible edge of fantasy. In spite of the prodigious efforts of his faction, in spite of the enormous sums of money expended upon treacherous Senators and others in public life, including August Jaeckle, Bishop Halliday and many subversive organizations, in spite of venal newspapers and prominent magazines, in spite of prominent anti-British speakers who toured up and down America in increasing numbers, and radio and newspaper columnists who denounced the "war-mongers," the "imperialistic British," and "international Jewish bankers," in spite of many members of the State Department who adored Pétain and the Vatican and who crippled all efforts of the Administration to bring Pétain to a decent realization of what his cowardly perfidy to France might mean, the American people showed the most alarming symptoms of beginning to think for themselves.

A certain public poll disclosed the fact that seventy-five percent of the American people would assist Britain, "short of war," to defeat Hitler. A considerable portion of this percentage were Roman Catholics, a fact which disconcerted the plotters against America, who had fondly believed that at the final reckoning the Roman Church would be on the side of the destroyers of American democracy. In fact, many prominent Catholic churchmen denounced Hitler and Mussolini with passionate bitterness and hatred, and several well-known Catholic laymen published books and pamphlets urging America not only to assist beleaguered Britain to the fullest extent, but even to declare war upon Germany. The carefully planned disunity of America betrayed the most distressing signs of not coming to a head, of disintegrating. Even anti-Semitism, so meticulously organized, had done nothing but raise a bad smell in politics. It appeared that the American people would have none of it, and that small fanatical bands of agitators aroused nothing but disgust and distaste, even in those inclined to be anti-Semitic. Only the lunatics subscribed to the suicidal doctrine, and aroused laughter.

The "Negro Question," sedulously agitated in the South by the enemies of America, found few there to listen. It was in the Northern States that the evil problem was most mooted. Enemy agitators did succeed, in some measure, in creating resentment in the Southern States against the presence of Negro troops in certain sections.

But, all in all, to Antoine's complete amazement, the American people remained in odd mental health. Moreover, there was not that universal resentment and anger which had been expected against the Selective Service Act. Hundreds of thousands of young American men entered the Army and Navy with singular calm and interest, even willingness. The great war plants, partly financed by British money, drew the best of the mechanical workers.

All over America there was a strange but determined expectancy, a grimness and a sane preparedness for the worst.

"The imponderables of the people's conscience." The phrase came back to plague Antoine and his faction with increasing threat. There were warning signs that Catholic, Protestant and Jew no longer considered themselves as separate camps, but as Americans, faced with the final and desperate hour of choice between the things by which men die and the things by which they live.

The "donkey-people" were most unpredictably beginning to act like intelligent human beings, plagued by liars and thieves and rogues, by malefactors and mountebanks from all sides, only occasionally confused and annoyed, but always steadfast. It was infuriating. Certain venal priests, certain mad Protestant clergymen, might harangue their people with rising hysteria and hatred. Certain writers and newspapers might shriek aloud against Britain, against the "war-mongers," and weep copiously over the "mothers of America." But the people remained calm and expectant, and were daily growing more grim. More and more diatribes appeared in certain newspapers against "Communists who were endeavoring to force us into war, and foreign agents who wished to lead us into a conflict that could only bring ruin upon America." But their words reached only the eyes of the insane and the haters, and did little damage.

Like a terrifying dream, this began to permeate the consciousness of Antoine Bouchard. For the first time, he began to doubt.

"The imponderables of the people's conscience"! Was it really possible that there were such things, that there actually were tides of intense and passionate feeling among the peoples of the earth, which might urge them to rise as one man and destroy the universal enemy? Was this feeling instinctive, or were the forces of counter-propaganda stronger than the propaganda disseminated by Antoine and his kind?

Antoine preferred to think it was the latter. It was against all his aristocratic instincts to believe that the people actually had a heart and a soul, that they might be inspired by just anger and noble indignation against murderers. He had some evidence for his determined belief, though he could not see the faces of the shadowy foe that opposed him. The counter-propagandists were doing excellent work in Washington, and in the country at large. That was easily to be seen. But, could they have done such excellent work if the people had not been prepared, even eager, to listen and to follow them?

There was organization among the foes that opposed Antoine, and money, and power. He saw this. But, again, all this would have come to nothing but for the "imponderables of the people's conscience"!

The people, apparently, were dimly but strongly beginning to discern and feel the presence of those who would enslave and murder and exploit them. They might not, in their simplicity, be able to name names, or catch glimpses of the faces of their haters, but they felt their presence, heard the murmur of their secret voices, saw the fleeting shadows of them on the walls of the world.

Antoine began to doubt his very colleagues. He had never been entirely sure of Christopher Bouchard, his uncle. He had never been wholly certain of Hugo Bouchard. Of his family, he was sure only of Jean Bouchard, brother of Hugo, Alexander Bouchard, Robert, and Nicholas. Jay Regan, for all his affable promises, and deep friendly interest in the increasing momentum of the plans, had still done nothing very important. Only Hiram Mitchell, and Mr. Morse, Mr. Boland, and Joseph Stoessel of the Schmidt Steel Company, and certain potent others, could be relied upon. There was, of course, Joseph Bryan, Junior, Regan's strongest rival, and certain Senators and members of the State Department. But in Antoine's own family, only Jean, Alexander, Nicholas, and Robert were beyond question. Emile and Francis were definitely part of Henri's faction. Was it possible that Christopher had been playing a double game, and that Hugo had been working in sly secret among his colleagues in the State Department?

And, if so, in what horrible jeopardy had Antoine, himself, placed his faction!

These were the thoughts that so bedevilled him. He, himself, was impotent until his father died, and he knew the contents of his will. He had little fear that Armand would abandon him. Had it not been Armand, himself, who had forced his son into Bouchard & Sons, had literally compelled Henri to accept him? After all, Armand was his father. He had said nothing that might lead one to believe that he would betray his son.

Antoine had never been such a one as Henri, believing in his own personal star, his own personal potency. For Antoine was too subtle, too intellectual, not to know that there are certain imponderables that work with, or against, a man. Nor had he, in himself, that enormous lust for power which had operated so gigantically in the lives of Ernest Barbour, and his great-grandson, Henri Bouchard. There were times when Antoine simply wondered why he bothered at all. He had always been intrigued by the legend of his grandfather, Jules, and had, quite consciously, been a real "understudy." But there were many times when he was bored to complete ennui at the efforts he was making to become the power of the Bouchards.

He had only his light and humorous love for intrigue to keep him active in his plots. Intrigue was his genius. But even this sometimes bored him. He had the soul of a seventeenth-century gallant, and he found the ponderous and unprepossessing plotters of the twentieth century too ugly and colorless for endurance. They had no heart, no gaiety, no light and delicate touch. Above all, they were without humor and zest. They wanted only money.

Money, as such, had no peculiar charm for Antoine. It is true he had the Bouchard avarice, but it was an artificial one, at best. He wanted it because it was the visible sign of potency, because it apparently appeared valuable to others. His own personal fortune was so enormous that he needed no more.

Sometimes, he suspected he was a romanticist.

He enjoyed the spectacle of humanity for itself, alone. He

was the eternal dilettante. He was the sleepless manipulator. He knew that others, even the dull ones, suspected this, and distrusted him for it. Henri had called him a "play-actor," and though others had laughed at the remark, Antoine had not laughed. In fact, he had, with surprise, eyed Henri with more respect than at any other time. Who would have suspected that the Iron Man possessed such subtlety?

Antoine, in short, was a plotter for the sake of the plot, itself. He was beginning to lose enjoyment in a plot whose protagonists were so dull and drab. There was no one, anywhere, who had such vitality and power except Henri, and even he had no passion. He was a glacier, and glaciers were notoriously without brilliant color.

Antoine had always felt an alien in the world. He felt more alien than ever, in this year of 1941. He had only his endless interest in humanity, in its less desirable emotions, and his natural hatred for Henri, to keep him from becoming one vast yawn.

And then, quite suddenly, Armand died.

CHAPTER LVI

"When the Bouchards die, it takes them years to make up their minds," someone had once said.

In Armand's case, this had been particularly true. He had suffered from diabetes for over ten years. Insulin had saved his life, had preserved him from the swift death which otherwise would have overtaken him. Moreover, he had the strong tough peasant constitution, that can survive unbelievable assaults, and the peasant obstinacy which frequently balks death of an immediate prey. Terror of death, too, had kept him alive. In the midst of increasing comas (from which only huge doses of insulin could rescue him) that stubborn and resolute terror had withdrawn him from the dark gates, had lifted him again above the shadows and left him, gasping, on the thin reef of life. He clutched existence desperately.

In the confused recesses of his mind he had come to believe that the resolution not to die would defeat death indefinitely. In his case, strangely, he had demonstrated this over a period of years.

He had known that only the most careful of diets and constant hypodermics of insulin could keep him alive. But he had not had the courage to resist the table, and often, he forgot the insulin. When he did so, he was seized with terror. He never knew what made him forget. Dimly, he remembered that a man forgets those things he wishes to forget. Why did he wish to forget to employ the insulin, the elixir that enabled him to dodge man's final enemy. Finally, in his bewilderment and fear, he came to think of himself as his own foe, and, at last, to believe that he was two persons: one bent on death, one bent on life.

Sometimes the struggle exhausted him, filled his mind with vague nightmare shapes and forms. He found himself thinking the strangest and most terrible thoughts. Sometimes he felt himself a clear transparency, a mere consciousness, poised over dark pits, over whirling chaos. At these times he would struggle from his bed, stagger into his bathroom, and swallow a bromide with desperate haste.

Then he had come to the place where he dared think no longer. He suffered enormously, but he also suffered dimly. He forgot the insulin completely. He ate his huge meals, and then would go to his bed, gasping, his face purple, his heart laboring, and his mind would become nothing but amorphous confusion in which he was faintly aware of a suffering that was more than the suffering of a dying body.

And then, in the midst of his agony, he would open his suffused eyes and be amazed to discover that it was day, that the sunlight was streaming over his bed. Why, he had only just gone to bed, he had not slept for a single moment! Time, in a twinkling, had passed from midnight to noon. He would see the face of his stout nurse, and sometimes the face of his doctor, and he would be enormously surprised. He would try to speak, to express his incredulity. And then, suddenly, it would be Annette who sat beside him, white but smiling, her hand on his, or sometimes it would be his son, Antoine. He could only marvel.

He would muse for hours on all this strangeness. Was there really time? Was there really reality? The peasant's shrewd and exigent mind would retreat in awe before this puzzle. But he was not very frightened now. He felt very smug about this. Fear, he thought, came only with the consciousness that death was at hand. His fear having departed, he had defeated death again. If he was now too weak to leave his bed at all, if he was too weak to protest at the slight dabs of food fed to him by his nurse, he was not concerned. He was surely getting better.

He was quite sure of this. He would listen as his nurse read the headlines to him, the headlines which were daily growing more frightful. And he would try to nod gravely, vaguely delighted that the news no longer had the power to overwhelm him with mysterious terror. And then, as he contemplated this happy thought, he would look about him, and discover that it was dark, the lamps gone, the nurse vanished. That was very strange. Only a moment ago it had been four o'clock in the afternoon, and the nurse had been reading the paper to him. He could even hear her last accents. While, again frightened, he studied this phenomenon, he would feel a flash on his eyelids, and the nurse would be there again, in broad morning light, a basin and towel in her hands.

On this particular morning, his fear returned, and with it, his strength. He said to his nurse: "Miss Concord, where has the night gone?" He heard his voice, frail as glass, and as tenuous.

"You slept splendidly, Mr. Bouchard," she replied, in her genial voice, as she prepared to shave him. He was heartened. He smiled at her, closed his tired eyes. He felt her shave him. Then, opening his eyes to thank her, he saw that the room was dark, a single lamp blooming on a distant table.

Now, the hideous and oppressive memory of a dream recurred to him. He had not remembered this dream for many years. It came back to him in its full horror. Yet, it had not been an evil dream, only a strange one, and he knew, in a confused way, that it had carried comfort with it.

He had been very young when he had had this dream. There had been no disturbing event to encourage it, or explain it. He had just returned from Harvard for the Christmas holidays. He could smell the scent of the balsam tree in the great old-fashioned drawing-room, and between the folding-doors he could see the twinkling of the gold, silver, blue and crimson ornaments on it. It had been an unusually satisfactory Christmas. Jules, his father, had been in one of his rarer benevolent moods, not lightly jeering, as usual. Adelaide, his mother, with her gentle brown eyes, seemed happier. It was long before the first World War. It was still in those halcyon early years of the twentieth century when one felt the vast strong growing of America, and hope was in the air. He was happy to be home. He was never happy at school, for his plumpness, his peasant secretiveness and suspicion, his awkward wariness and hidden vulnerability, made him unpopular with his classmates. He was even happy to see fat and jovial and big Emile, home from Groton, and little silvery Christopher with his venomous "Egyptian" eyes. Celeste was hardly more than a baby, then, with bright-black curls and big blue eyes, always shy yet resolute. It had been a disagreeable term at Harvard, and home seemed very secure and pleasant. There were hints that the new automobile he had craved was to be his father's Christmas gift to him. At any rate, he had not been permitted to enter one of the big stables behind the house, only recently converted into a garage. He could see the automobile in his mind's eye: it would be very red and very shining, with crimson leather seats. He trembled with joy. He would be practically the only student at Harvard who would possess such magnificence.

It was on the first night, that he had that most appalling dream. He dreamt that he had been asleep, not for long, in fact, for only a very short time. But when he awoke, he was not in his bed. He was lying in a long dim white hall, very narrow, like a great corridor, whose farther reaches were lost in vague bluish mist. On both sides of this corridor there were wide marble shelves reaching from the marble floor to the marble ceiling, which was lost in floating gloom. And on every marble shelf there lay a sleeping form, wrapped in what appeared to be a white shroud. He could not see the faces of these forms, though he dimly guessed that some were men, some women, and some children. They slept as if dead. The light that pervaded the corridor was not constant. It was very faint, and sometimes Armand could not see about him. And then there would be a quickening of the light, like moonlight seen under water, and there would be a flow of nebulous illumination all down the length of the corridor, a crepuscular shine that would permit him to see the calm sleeping faces of his companions for a brief moment or two. It was the luminous pallor of a dream. Then he would guess that the sleepers were numberless, extending into infinity.

He was not frightened. He was only filled with wonder. And yet, there was a strange familiarity about the scene, as if he had been here many times before, had slept, had awakened. He remembered, very faintly, that sometime, somewhere, he had been very tired, so exhausted that he could not endure it, and that he had fallen alseep, to awaken a very short time later, rested, quite alert, and very calm, in this mysterious yet familiar place.

Then he felt, rather than heard, that someone was approaching him down the corridor. He saw the slight form of a young woman, in flowing white garments, her fair hair piled high on her small head. In her hand she held a golden flaming candle. All the floating mist about her became a round aura of golden light. She paused beside him. Her face had an aloof calm about it, motionless, yet not unkind. The candle trembled a little in her hand, which was as white and lifeless as marble. He heard her voice, echoless and indifferent. "You are awake? Then, it is time to rise and begin again. You have slept very long, this time."

"But I fell asleep only a moment ago," he murmured.

He saw her smile, inhuman, composed and withdrawn, and when he saw it he was filled with overwhelming terror. He felt the beating of renewed life all through his body, but that impersonal and stony smile repudiated him, despised his fear. He felt something inimical in her, yet it was not a personal enmity, but rather the enmity of a lifeless universe. She repeated: "You have slept very long, this time. Go, you are awaited."

He did not know where he was, who awaited him, or where he was going. But he did not want to go. Through all his consciousness he knew that pain and suffering waited somewhere for him in the outer confines of an enormous space, that heat and torment and death lurked there, and all weary confusion. He protested again. And the young woman only waited, a static and marble form now, unmoved as a statue, the golden candle in her hand. He could see her eyes, colorless and fixed, shining like white stone, implacable and inexorable, and her motionless frozen smile, and the endless shelves of the sleepers all about him.

He awoke from that dream, drenched with the sweat of complete terror. He literally fell from his bed, gasping. He saw the cold moonlight on the floor of his room, and the gleaming snow on the window-sills. He fumbled for a chair, fell into it, still gasping. He said to himself: What does that mean? But his trembling soul knew, and knew too well.

He did not soon forget that dream. He remembered it for years. It did not grow dimmer with time. Sometimes, in the very midst of his classes, or even when among friends, he saw the white fixed shining of that woman's eyes, illuminated by the golden candle. He began to hate her, wildly, desperately. He saw her as a horror, which had awakened him from peace and nothingness. She was his enemy.

Then, in time, the dream faded, quite suddenly, and was gone. He had not remembered it again until tonight.

And then, as he remembered it, it came back to him in full force. The quiet dark room with its blooming lamp retreated, yet was still about him. But closer than the room was the corridor with its endless shelves, and the waiting woman, and the prescience of waiting pain and torment and weariness.

This time, he thought, in his bottomless terror, I shall sleep, and I shall not awaken. I will close my eyes, and she will not know I am awake.

And then, the strangest of thoughts came to him, like a quiet voice: But, I have done nothing to deserve peace. I shall surely come back again, and again, and again, until I am no longer frightened and sick and covered with dirtiness.

He looked at his doom, and now a strange resolution and calm and resignation came to him. He felt humbled and full of sorrow. He sighed from the very pit of his heart.

When he opened his eyes again, the room was still dark, the lamp still burning. But Miss Concord stood beside him, her hand on his pulse, her eyes staring at him anxiously. He moved his stiff cold lips, and whispered:

"I want my son. Please call my son."

She was a blur of white as she drifted from the room. He watched her go. He was sure that he never took his eyes from the door, yet, oddly, he was next conscious of his physician at his side, and Antoine. "Very strange," he murmured, and smiled. His facial muscles were stiff and cold, also, and this puzzled him. He felt the slow congealed moving of them.

And then, the doctor completely vanished, or, at least, Armand saw him no longer. Antoine was sitting by his bedside, his dark inscrutable face glimmering in the lamplight. Armand saw nothing else in the room. He and his son were in one dim circle of half-light, and nothing else existed. The April rain murmured at the windows. There was a sudden breath of sweet, fresh air, damp and humid, sweeping through the dusky quietness.

Armand could only stare at his son. His last urge of life stood in his failing eyes. In his turn, Antoine saw the dying face of his father. Very few things ever disturbed him, or discomfited him, but for some reason Armand's expression, the long and steadfast regard, made him faintly uneasy. He had never seen Armand with such a look, somber, thoughtful, completely aware, and very sad. It was a mature look, cleansed of all shrinking, all fear, all diffused alarm.

Then Armand spoke, his voice labored and whistling, very meditative. He said: "It was a long time ago. My father sent for me. This was his bed. He was very proud of it. They said it was Robespierre's bed, once. Robespierre. He died in this bed." He moved his hand feebly over the mattress beside him.

Antoine inclined his head gently. Armand could see the black and thoughtful glitter of his tilted eyes. The young man waited.

"Now, I'm going to die in it," Armand went on, his voice so low that Antoine had to lean forward to hear it. "Robespierre's bed. I never thought how appropriate, my father dying in it. He was guillotined, too, like Robespierre. He knew that, at the last."

And now his regard was grave and mournful. What is he trying to tell me? thought Antoine. Had his father been maudlin or frightened in this supreme hour of his dying, Antoine would have felt far more at ease, and very cynical. He knew that venal men frequently experienced pangs of cowardly terror in the face of death. He had believed that his father would reveal these, and that it would be very interesting to observe him, and would have a macabre and amusing quality. But the face that lay on the pillows, though formless and slack with approaching dissolution, possessed eyes that were more alive, more potent, more poignant and urgent, than they had ever been in the height of life. Moreover, there was no fear in them, only a profound understanding and heavy sorrow. There was no sign in them of that craven repentance, that shrinking remorse, which so often assailed the dying. Too, in this hour, Armand possessed a strange dignity, a coherence of personality, which he had never revealed before.

Now a pale gleam passed over his features. He moved his head a little. He had not taken his steadfast regard from Antoine, and now it quickened.

"My father sent for me, just before he died. It was like this. He lay in his bed, and I sat beside him, as you are sitting, Antoine. He said some things to me. I don't think he meant to say them. They were unimportant. What he didn't say was the important thing." He paused. "He was a very strange man, my father. He was a bad man. But he was very amusing. And superior. None of his sons could come up to him. He was the most grown-up man I ever knew." And now Armand's voice took on a stronger and firmer quality, and there was a look about him of renewed vitality.

"He wasn't afraid to die. He was never really afraid of anything. That is why he was so fascinating. He never trusted anyone, except, perhaps, my mother. He never trusted his sons. He had reason not to. I think he hated us. Yes, I am sure he did. Just before he died, he sent for me, and I sat near him. He told me about his will, and he enjoyed himself. That was because he knew we hated him. Or, he thought so. Perhaps he was right. I think he was thinking what we would do with what he had left us, and that amused him."

And now Armand lapsed into the French patois of his early youth, the language his father had used with so much elegance, so much grace, that the idioms had been pure music. On Armand's lips, the peasant's lips, however, they were rough and graceless, but, oddly, much more sincere.

Antoine, whose French was fluent, rich and aristocratic, felt an obscure distaste for these uncouth accents, but acknowledged that they had a certain rough dignity, even grandeur, on those heavy peasant lips, and a native appropriateness. And there was even a subtle change on Armand's face. It had never been delicate of outline, or refined of expression. But now it took on strength and earthiness, a coarse resolution and simple nobility.

"And even as my father talked to me, amusing himself as he hinted at his will, there was the strangest emotion in me. I had always feared him, for he had the most penetrating wit, and a cruel inventiveness of epigram. I had always been a young and lumbering boar, and I must have amused him very frequently, though, doubtless, he despised me. Nevertheless, who but I remained to him? His other sons he distrusted. I, at least, did not have the wit—he believed—to be vicious or plotting."

And now Armand smiled mournfully. His short fat hands, overgrown with gray and auburn hair, lifted a trifle, then dropped back on the bed.

"Yes," he said, reflectively, "there was the strangest emotion in me as he told me of his will. I stared at him. I

489

forgot what he was saying. Suddenly, it seemed very dreadful to me that he was dying. I did not know why. I had never loved him. I had always feared him, and avoided him. And yet, it was very dreadful that he was dying. I never understood. All at once I cried out to him: 'But I do not want you to die!' "

Antoine was silent. Again, Armand turned his head toward him, and fixed those queerly steadfast and quiet eyes upon him.

"My father was very surprised. I shall never forget the look that flashed over his face, as if he was enormously perplexed and amazed. He even lifted himself on his pillows, quite high, to stare more closely at me. I think he died, still amazed. It had never occurred to him that anyone might want him to live. Love, he did not expect. Trust, he was too intelligent to believe might exist. And yet, he knew I was sincere. He knew I was very sorry. That was what so perplexed him."

Armand paused. His regard was more penetrating, and quite humble. "I should like you, my son, to be sorry. I do not know why you should be, just as I am not sure why I was sorry when my father died. But, nevertheless, I should like it to be so."

Antoine smiled inwardly. He thought, with sharp cynicism: But you knew your father's will! However, despite himself, his voice had a peculiar gentleness in it when he said: "I *am* sorry. Believe it, I am sorry."

Armand smiled. It was a dark and very sad smile. He said: "I do not know why, but I believe you. At this moment, you are sorry. You do not know why; I do not know why. Is it because you are sorry that I must go through death, or is it sorrow that I am not to live? It is very confusing. I think, perhaps, that you are sorry that I have suffered, and still suffer. I should like to believe that, in preference to believing you feel the same sorrow you would experience should a dog die, of whom you were indifferently fond. Yes, I should like to believe that. I think I do. For only if I have that belief can I tell you what I must."

Suddenly, he was suffocating. He gasped: "Lift me up!"

Invisible hands lifted him and put him higher on his pillows. He did not wonder at the hands, though Antoine had not moved in his chair. All Armand's last energy, his desperate urgency, was concentrated on his son. Antoine, in his turn, was sincerely glad that his father was speaking in his French patois, for he wished no one to understand what the dying man was saying.

Now Armand reached out, and his clammy hand, of a claylike texture and dampness, and as cold as clay, grasped Antoine's hand. The young man felt its urgent strength. From his higher position, Armand was closer to his son, also.

"What has there been between us?" he asked. "Less, perhaps, than there was between my father and me. And, yet, perhaps, it was the same, in a fashion. Then, I was the son of a man similar to you; one such as you was my father. Nevertheless, though I often see my father in your face, and hear his voice in yours, and watch his very gestures in your own, and his step, there is something lacking in you, my son, that was in my father, Jules Bouchard. You have thought I was very dull and undiscerning. But I always knew what it was you lacked, though I had no words for it then. Perhaps I have no words now, though I am struggling for them."

Antoine was startled. He frowned a little, delicately. Some obscure conceit in him was annoyed. However, he listened more attentively to his father when he resumed:

"What I must say to you now could never have been said to my father, never, in all his life. For it would have been untrue to him. You have his wit and grace, his genius for intrigue, his inexhaustible plotting. But there the resemblance ends." He paused, then added in a stronger, surprised voice: "I knew this with my instinct, but not with my mind, until now!" His face flashed with an oddly brilliant smile, as if he had been told some joyful news. "It gives me much happiness, my son, to know all this with my heart and my mind!"

What is the poor wretch trying to tell me? thought Antoine. But he made his expression attentive. Again, despite himself, there was the strangest weight in his chest. Armand's amazing strength, too, his resolve to speak, his determination to resist death, filled Antoine with a faintly superstitious astonishment.

"All my father's attributes were bent towards one sole object: power," continued Armand, and now his voice was quite normal, no longer gasping, but filled with energy. "He must have power. He must take that power from Paul Barbour, the son-in-law of Ernest Barbour, who was my own great-uncle. It is very strange of me to remember that: that, indirectly, the blood of Ernest Barbour flows in me, and in you. It was bad blood, that, the blood of Ernest Barbour.

It was strong in my father. I thought it was strong in me. I was glad to know, at last, that it was not. I am even happier to know that that blood is not strong in you, my son, though once I believed it was. There was the lust for power in that blood, a very evil lust.

"My father had that lust. You do not possess it. You have acted as if you possessed it; you have pretended. It was, perhaps, a family tradition to desire power: that is what you have believed. It was intolerable of you, you thought, not to have the lust. You have always admired your grandfather; it flattered you that you resembled him, and I have seen you contemplating his portrait when you thought yourself unseen. It frightened me, the resemblance. But I was not so frightened when I realized that there was the final ultimate in him which you did not possess."

He turned his eyes to the portrait above the distant lamp, and instinctively Antoine looked also. All of the portrait was in diffused shadow except for the gay and satanic black eyes that stared so vitally from the frame. Armand nodded, and smiled. "It is lacking in you, what he possessed," he said. "That is why, now, I am so glad. That is why I am speaking to you like this."

Antoine frowned slightly. He regarded his father with a certain uneasy surprise.

Armand continued to speak. His voice was much fainter now, but it had a disembodied clarity and penetration.

"In spite of all my father's attributes and graces and wit and intellect, he was a plebeian. He had the plebeian's brutal lust for possessions. He seized and grasped. That was his nature. He must triumph, in the variety and richness of his possessions, over those he hated. And he hated all men. That is the mark of the plebeian: his avarice and his hatred. At the last, perhaps they are the same.

"It gives me much joy, my son, to know that you were never avaricious. You have pretended you were. You have pretended, even to yourself, that the lust for power—the plebeian's attribute—and the desire for possessions, lived in you. But these marks of the dull and the brutal man are not in you. You are an aristocrat. You might even be a great man, could you but rid yourself of your pretenses, and the ugliness and death and weariness that must inevitably follow them. As they have followed me."

Antoine did not speak. He moved his chair backwards, only a trifle. But the gesture was significant. It was an instinctive desire to remove himself from the faint circle of light that enclosed his father and himself; it was an instinctive desire to recoil from his father's most mysterious and subtle eyes, which, in this hour of his death, saw everything. The young man felt stripped, and an embarrassed anger filled him.

"You have hated so many in the family!" cried Armand, and he clasped his hands together very tightly, and shook them with a last vehemence. "You did not really know why you hated! But I have known. You hated them because they were parvenus and plebeians. You will deny this, even to yourself. But, some day you will acknowledge it. I want you to acknowledge it very soon, for otherwise, you might be destroyed. As I have been destroyed."

He pressed his clenched hands, covered now with a cold dew, to his breast, and his burning eyes implored his son desperately. Antoine rested his elbow on his knee; he lifted his narrow dark hand and covered his mouth with it. Over that hand, his eyes, brooding, dark and hooded, regarded his father intently.

Armand spoke again, and his voice was full of bitter pleading and humility: "I am praying that it is not too late. Had I known earlier, when you were a child, and a youth, that you did not possess those attributes of my father, I might have done much. But your face, your voice, your gestures, deceived me that you were another one such as he. It was not very long ago that I began to guess. I did not believe. There was so much evidence to the contrary. Now I know that what I had guessed at was true.

"I might have saved you so much had I been able to speak out of clear knowledge. I might have been able to tell you of my disgust for myself and others, my exhaustion, my weariness, my loathing of what I am and what I have done. You have all thought that I was a coward. It is true. But you did not know of the thing which made me afraid. You thought I was weak, but you did not know why I was weak. You have thought that it was perhaps some frail and uneasy stump of conscience in me that tormented me in the midst of all that I was doing. Perhaps, in a fashion, that is slightly true. But, my son, you see, it was because I knew what was right and what was wrong, and yet did not have the courage to resist the wrong. Because I, too, was a plebeian, and had the lust for possessions, and avarice, and the desire for power. And when, as I grew old and sick, these lusts faded, I discovered that I was impotent. Others had taken the power from me, the power to undo the evil I had done, and which they were now doing. It was this that really killed me," he added, with profound and moving simplicity.

Antoine did not speak. The hooded eyes above the shelter of his quiet hand became a little more brilliant, a little more narrow. Armand stared at them with hopeful despair, searching, eager. He could not read them.

"Do not want the things that will kill you, my son," he whispered, hoarsely. "They are nothing. They are stones, covered with dust. You have enough. Go away."

And now the two men regarded each other in a profound and most portentous silence. Antoine did not move, except that one finger of his hand rose a little as if to conceal his eyes. Armand could see his son so clearly in the lamplight, which shone like a bright pale outline over the shape of his sleek and narrow small head. He could see the set of his elegant thin shoulders, the lines of his compact and graceful body. He could see his fixed and unreadable eyes.

And then the dying man cried out loudly, as if in a frenzy: "You must tell me that what I have believed of you is true! You must tell me! I cannot die in peace unless you tell me it is true!"

His slack mouth fell open as he gasped stridently. A gray shadow ran like water over his wet face. His eyes dilated, flamed and started. He lifted his hands in an abrupt gesture, the gesture of a man who is drowning and sinking beneath smothering waves.

Antoine stirred. He looked aside. He said: "It is true."

He stood up. The nurse and the doctor, who had been there all this while, uncomprehending, bent over Armand. He did not feel their ministrations. He still stared at his son, all the last urge of his life in his eyes, imploring, desperate.

"It is true," repeated Antoine. He turned away. He walked slowly from the bed. He stood beneath his grandfather's portrait. The eyes gazed down at him, his own eyes, cynical, bright, full of dark laughter and bottomless gay contempt. For a long time Antoine stood there, looking at Jules, and it was as if he looked into a mirror.

When he turned around again, the nurse, sighing heavily, was drawing the sheet over Armand's closed eyes, his strange and aloof smile, which had in it an unreadable sorrow and resignation, a mournful and bitter wisdom.

CHAPTER LVII

No one wept at Armand's funeral, except little Mary, Antoine's wife, who, in her childish way, had been very fond of him. She was covered with grief and remorse. She cried in Antoine's arms: "If only I had made him keep to his List! But I didn't! I let him eat what he wanted, and now I really killed him!"

"No, dear," said Antoine, with unusual gentleness. "He killed himself."

She stared at him with wet eyes, while the others in the family regarded them silently. "You mean," faltered little Mary, "that he killed himself because he wanted to eat the things he shouldn't have wanted?"

Antoine hesitated. Then he said: "Yes. Yes, that is true."

Annette did not weep. She was unusually quiet, and her little face had a dwindled and profoundly meditative look. She, alone, had loved her father. She looked at him as he slept in his bronze coffin, and was glad that he was dead. Though Henri made a gesture as if to restrain her, she bent over Armand and gently kissed his stony cheek. She whispered to him, her breath warm on his lifeless lips: "Good-bye, darling. Don't forget me."

Celeste looked at her brother as he lay there, majestic in death, and she thought: But I never knew him at all. Emile, big, stout, misshapen and black of eye, stared at Armand; he did not know that Armand, dead, resembled him very closely. Christopher looked at his brother, also. He thought: He never could stomach us.

Henri said nothing at all. He stood at the foot of the casket, and thought: Not for the reasons you wished it, but for my own, it is better that you died. I will do as you wanted me to do, but not for your reasons. Only for mine. In the end, it will be the same.

The other relatives were profoundly curious about Armand's will. They had always despised him, felt only amused contempt for him. They remembered his cowardice. They were sorry for him, of course. But they, too, believed it was better that he had died. They regarded Annette and Antoine curiously. The greatest of the Bouchard fortunes had now passed into their hands.

Armand was buried with his family in the private cemetery originally purchased by Ernest Barbour. He lay near his father and his mother. All about them, Bouchards and Barbours slept under great bowed willows and evergreens. The cemetery was like an immense and well-tended park, with flower-beds and winding gravelled paths. The family had never liked mausoleums. They preferred the earth, the strong earth, from which their peasant bodies had come, and which they instinctively loved. Here, in a quiet and lovely corner slept Gertrude Barbour, Ernest's beloved daughter, grandmother of Henri and Edith, who had died in her pathetic youth. Beside her lay her husband, Paul, and at her left hand slept her daughter, Alice Bouchard. Not far away her brothers slept. Godfrey Sessions Barbour, brought from his beloved France—(Godfrey, the great American composer, and his wife, Renée Bouchard), and Reginald, snatched from the grasp of the Mennonites in his death, and Guy, murdered in the Pennsylvania hills, and Charles, the dull and obscure, who had died of typhoid fever so very long ago. Near them, on a low but strangely lofty eminence, dominating the whole cemetery as a king dominates his kingdom even in death, lay Ernest Barbour, and on each side of him lay his wives, May Sessions and Amy Drumhill, their bodies long one with the earth. Amy's children lay below her, to the left of the beautiful lonely eminence: Elsa Barbour and Lucy Van Eyck, and John Charles. (It was her son, Paul, who lay near Gertrude, his wife.)

Scattered far and wide, in that cemetery, lay numerous others, part of that empire of family and power which Ernest had founded. Their names were carved on simple marble and granite stones. Jules Bouchard, in a circle of gravelled paths and flowers and trees, lay beside his wife, Adelaide, in her grave which had not yet sunken, and poor Peter. His brothers were there, too, François and Leon, and Leon's wife. And many, many others.

Few ever visited those quiet and more humble graves near the high stone walls, the graves of Armand Bouchard, and his wife, Antoinette (grandparents of Jules), and their beloved son, Jacques, the cripple, who had killed himself. (Jacques had been removed from the outer side of the walls of the Catholic cemetery, and Armand and Antoinette had been taken from within those walls, and all had been buried here at the order of Ernest Barbour.) Here, in this distant spot, lay also Ernest's parents, Joseph and Hilda, who had never returned to their beloved England, and their daughters, Dorcas and Florabelle. There were shafts, too, in memory of Martin Barbour, who had died in the Civil War, and of Honoré Barbour, much loved cousin of Jules. But Martin lay buried in some lost grave in the South, and Honoré had fallen far into the gray sea.

Husbands lay beside wives and parents, and children lay there, too. On the bronze gates of the cemetery was welded the plaque: Barbour-Bouchard. Gardeners were here, constantly tending, weeding, trimming, planting. Above the tops of the walls stood the heads of great trees, in which birds sang in the sunny silence of the summer. Not far away was the small but exquisite chapel which Ernest Barbour had built.

The new raw earth near Jules and Adelaide was disturbed again for Armand. They laid him there, and the red clods fell on his coffin. His many relatives and innumerable acquaintances left him to his sleep, and the bronze doors closed after them. April rain fell on his grave. A bird or two picked at evicted worms on the oozing clods, above the spot where his silent heart lay. His head was near the roots of a mighty evergreen, which one day would penetrate his body and his skull, and claim them.

The relatives returned to the house which he had built to hear his will. But they were shocked into complete amazement and bewilderment. For the lawyers told them gravely that there was a stipulation with regard to the will:

It was not to be opened for a year, or until America had declared war on Germany, or until Henri Bouchard gave the signal. If America had not been embroiled in the war, or Henri had not given the signal, then, at the expiration of a year after Armand's death, the will was to be opened.

CHAPTER LVIII

Celeste had named her child Land Burgeon Bouchard. Land Burgeon had been her mother's father, a harsh and ribald old man of great integrity, and possessing a very dirty tongue. But he had been tough, and he had been disillusioned, and like most men of his kidney, he had been kind, just and compassionate. He had died long before Celeste had been born, but she possessed, as a legacy from her mother, a dark portrait of him.

It was an ugly portrait, but full of life and vitality. The short and wiry old man was painted sitting in a huge carved chair, his large and knobby bald head bent forward over his chest, as if he were deformed, his gnarled hands clenched on the head of his cane, his big bristling chin belligerently thrust outwards. He had a wrinkled and irascible face, very ugly, with a huge Roman nose, a thin wide mouth all tightness and grimness and cynicism, and little beetling eyes, choleric and contemptuous. But his great bald brow had a cold nobility about it, and his expression, though bitter and disingenuous, had no craft, no cruelty. The wide white points of his collar came up about his sallow jowls; the cravat was knotted below them like a hangman's knot. It was the portrait of a great gentleman, bawdy, ferocious, but all honor.

I should like to have known him, thought Celeste, standing beneath that portrait with her child in her arms. He wasn't a liar, her mother had told her. He also never liked the Bouchards, Adelaide had added, with a sad and twisted smile. He had called Jules "that French jackanapes with the priest's face." He never called the Bouchards by that name; he used the English translation: Butcher! Celeste smiled, remembering her mother's stories of her father, how he used his cane lavishly when enraged, how his tongue had been famous for its ribaldry, caustic epigrams and abusiveness. But, he had been a man of integrity—and he could never endure the Bouchards. None of his grandchildren had inherited any of his facial characteristics, though Adelaide had often declared that Celeste's eyes, direct and steadfast, had something of her grandfather's expression. Yes, thought Celeste, I should like to have known him.

She lived very quietly with her little boy on Placid Heights. He was eight months old now, and, to his mother at least, very precocious. He had a mass of light and virile hair, light grey eyes with a bold look, a short strong nose and a strong chin. But his mouth was tender, if firm, and when he smiled several dimples sprang out in his cheeks. And when he smiled so, his amazing resemblance to his father disappeared in an expression of great sweetness. He was a good, quiet and self-contained baby, much attached to his mother. He rarely cried, and played for hours by himself with his multitude of toys. When Celeste held him close to her breast, he wound his little hands strongly in her hair, but very gently, and his grey eyes were luminous. Celeste would feel the weight of tears behind her eyelids, and the knot of grief and love in her throat.

She guarded him jealously, with a kind of fierceness. He had several teeth now, and could pull himself up in his crib. She was certain that he could say a few words, though his nurses disagreed. Celeste would carry him into the gardens and let him roll on the warm May grass, laughing and shrieking with joy. She would expose him to the sun, and rejoice in the stocky strength of his little body. Bouchard: Butcher! No, he would be no butcher, this little one. His mother would see to that, to the end of her life. She would take him away, some day, so that he would not be corrupted.

All her life, now, was in this child. She talked to him, sang to him, played with him. And as she did so, the rigidity of her features began to relax, the stiff sternness of her mouth softened, the white still grief of her expression lifted.

When her relatives called upon her, she was reluctant to let them see the child. They thought, slyly, that this was because his resemblance to Henri was so startling. But that was not the reason. She was afraid of their contagion. She made the excuse that he was asleep, or being fed, or out with one of his nurses. When the war was over, she said, she believed she would take the child to England, or perhaps to France, after the hoofprints of the boar had been washed away in its own blood.

Sometimes the relatives would whisper to each other: "She seems to have forgotten Henri entirely. A nice thing for him!"

They could never tell what Henri was thinking. He, apparently, had not seen the child since the day it had been born. Annette came often to Placid Heights, alone. She, alone, saw the child very often. Celeste would let her play with him on the grass; she would laugh merrily as he pulled her soft bright ringlets. She would kiss him passionately, laughing and half-crying together, clasping him to her small shrunken breasts. Then she would look up at Celeste, who would be watching her broodingly, and her large light-blue eyes would be full of radiant tears.

It had been exquisite agony for Celeste the first few times that Annette had come to her and had seen little Land. But even that had gone now. She seemed grateful for Annette's gentle company, but when Annette would kiss and fondle the baby something hard and tight and dark would grip Celeste's heart. She could hardly prevent herself from snatching him from Annette's arms in a kind of blind jealousy which was inexplicable even to her. Later, she would feel the most excruciating compassion for Annette, and an immense sadness. She would not let herself consider whether Annette knew the truth, and in time, she came to believe that Annette had no suspicion at all.

In fact, as her fierce protectiveness grew, she persuaded herself that the family had no suspicion, or that, if they had, they were beginning to forget.

On April 10, 1941, Mr. Hull declared that an agreement with the Danish Minister for the use of Greenland as an American base had been signed.

On May 27, 1941, the President, in a radio address, declared an unlimited national emergency. He announced that the Battle of the Atlantic now extended from the icy waters of the North Pole to the frozen continent of the Antarctic.

The subversive organizations of America went into a frenzy, into feverish and renewed activity. The "war-monger" President was hastening America into "this terrible foreign war." Subversive newspapers, speakers, Senators, Congressmen, politicians, labor leaders, prominent and public figures, and many others, shrieked that "American boys would soon be dying on foreign soil."

But the people were calm, expectant and grim. It was the

people who were silent amid the huge and frenzied uproar. The "imponderables of the people's conscience" were felt throughout all America, watchful, disillusioned, undeceived and intent. The soul of America was felt, growing stronger every hour, the simple and still uncorrupted soul of an enlightened people.

When Germany invaded Russia on June 22, there was a rising murmur throughout America like a deep but resolute sigh of relief, and a sound as if a gigantic army rose to its feet and tightened its belt.

"We haven't lost, yet," said Antoine to his faction.

That faction, through its newspapers, more than hinted that the President should be impeached. It, too, felt great relief at the German invasion of Russia. Its suborned newspapers drew a deep breath, then exultantly cried that Hitler would now destroy "bolshevism" in Europe, as he had long promised. The newspapers, also, made quite merry over the consternation and confusion of the American Communists, now that Hitler had broken the Pact between Germany and Russia. Not only the newspapers were merry: the American people, even in this terrible hour, could lean back and laugh heartily at this dilemma of the timid and pallid American Communists, who had declaimed so earnestly on "British imperialism," and "foreign wars in which we have no stake," and "war-mongers who would rush us into a conflict that is no concern of ours." The America Only Committee had had its share of members from among the American Communist Party, and their withdrawal in confusion and complete funk heightened American mirth hugely. It was not until later that the mirth became just anger. It was apparent, said the American people, that the Communists knew no loyalty to America, but only to the party line in Russia. They were no better than the fascists, after all. During the past two years, the American Communists had attacked the President as viciously as the native fascists had attacked him, and there had been a suspicious similarity between their propaganda and the Nazi venom. With the stupidity of their kind, and the obtuseness, the Communists soon boldly demanded American intervention in the war, ignoring the anger and the outraged laughter of the people.

"In the end, it is probably a good thing that Germany attacked Russia," said Antoine. "I was afraid that it would consolidate American opinion against Hitler. But the antics of the American Communists have enraged the country, and

I am delighted to see that public opinion has recoiled to its original caution of 1939."

But he spoke without his original liveliness and gaiety. He spoke with somberness and heaviness, strange manifestations for the elegant and insouciant Antoine.

"It's Armand's damned mysterious will that's annoying him," said the family, delightedly seeing his dark face, pale, now, to sallowness, and the brooding and hooded expression of his eyes.

The Russian time-table, Hitler had announced, was six weeks. The world, fantastically, believed him. The Germans rushed through the Ukraine, a bloody gray horde. Cities smoked in the wheat-fields. The rivers vomited bodies on the torn shores. Villages crumbled and dissolved under the thunder and lightning of steel and explosives. From the great flat stretches of the bleeding Ukraine came one long groan of agony and death.

But the six weeks passed, and though the Germans were at the gates of Moscow and Stalingrad and Leningrad, and Russian blood fell upon the thirsty earth, Russia did not collapse, did not surrender. The world watched, amazed and incredulous. The Russians retreated, died. The Russian sky turned red with the fire of countless villages and towns. But Russia did not fall.

CHAPTER LIX

"We can soon strike," said Henri, to Christopher, in August, 1941.

"When?" asked Christopher. "Are you waiting for war?"

He was very curious about Henri. Did the swine know the contents of Armand's will? If he did, he said nothing that could give the slightest hint. One never knew about him, his thoughts or his plans. Yet, Christopher began to believe that Henri knew what the will contained.

As if he guessed Christopher's thoughts, a livid flash passed over Henri's pale eyes. He smiled a little. "If you mean: Am I waiting until Armand's will can be opened? the answer is no. Suppose you leave the rest to me."

Christopher inclined his head humorously. But he did not feel humorous. His vanity was stung again with humiliation. If Henri knew the contents of the will, why, then, did he not move with regard to Celeste? Unless, and now Christopher felt a sickened pang, the will expressly prohibited Henri from any marriage with Celeste, or any divorce from Annette. If it was this, then, what was to become of Celeste, and her child? Was it possible that the dull and stupid Armand knew of the affair, and had provided against it? Was it possible that Antoine had told his father? If so, then everything was lost.

He looked up again to see Henri watching him with cold cynicism. And then all the hatred of years flared up viciously in Christopher. He clenched his hands. Henri rose and walked to the windows of his office. He did not want Christopher to see his smile now. Let him stew, he thought.

"We can soon strike," he said, his back to Christopher.

They never spoke of Celeste these days, though her name hung between them threateningly.

That August night, when Land Burgeon Bouchard was just one year old, Henri returned home for dinner, and was greeted sweetly and gently, as always, by his wife, Annette. He was too engrossed in his own thoughts to see that she was even paler than usual, and her eyes had a strange and steadfast shine. They ate their meal in silence, broken only by an occasional comment by Annette on the humid heat of the day, and her suggestions that a storm was imminent.

Henri glanced idly through the open french windows. The west was a sultry blaze of crimson. High in this fuming light the thunder-heads were piled in purple masses. It was very hot and still. Even the locusts were silent. The trees hung heavily, their tops tinged with scarlet. In the brilliantly clear yet spectral air of sunset the grass had a peculiar vivid greenness. As Henri watched, thin lances of pale fire pierced the thunder-heads, and were followed by a far rumbling. All at once the motionless trees stirred uneasily, and a cool and sulphurous breath passed into the quiet room. The atmosphere was ominous with the coming storm.

"Yes," said Henri, "we're in for a bad one. Well, we need it."

After the meal was concluded, and Henri was about to rise, Annette spoke. There had been a silence for some time. She spoke very quietly, her regard fixed upon Henri, her little hands clasped together on the table.

"Henri, I'd like to talk to you, if you don't mind."

There was something in her sweet voice that prevented his impatience. He looked at her sharply. She was so still. She was even smiling, though he could see, in the peculiar vivid air, that her upper lip was beaded with moisture. But her blue eyes were unfaltering and very bright. He drew his chair back to the table, and waited. "Yes?" he said, in his dull and monotonous voice.

The instinct in him which was always aroused at the hint of danger awakened now. Even his skin was aware, prickling strangely. But he showed no sign of this. He sat there, stolid and immovable, waiting.

He saw the movement in her thin white throat, as she swallowed thickly. He saw that she was trembling slightly. She still looked at him directly, and she still smiled. But the smile was painful.

"Please don't be angry with me, darling," she said. (How clear and firm her voice was, but how strained!) "But I've thought about this for a long time."

"What?" he said, heavily.

He saw her little pale fingers tighten together. She lifted her chin a little higher and gazed at him valiantly.

"First, I've got to ask you a question, Henri. Please be honest with me. Please answer me, if you know. Do you know about Papa's will—what it contains?"

He was silent. He stared at her somberly. Then, all at once, he pressed his hands upon the table, pushed back his chair, and got up. He went to the windows, and stood before them, looking out unseeingly at the rising thunder-heads against the crimson west. He heard a soft movement beside him. Annette stood there, facing him. She put her hand on his arm. But he would not look at her, though his muscles flinched at her touch.

"Henri," she whispered, urgently, "I must know."

"Why?" he muttered, not looking at her. But she saw his grim stark profile in the dark and stormy light.

She sighed deeply. "Please believe me. I must know. It is so very important to me. Henri, if you know at all, you must tell me." Now her voice broke. "Henri, I've got to know. Don't ask me why. I can only tell you this: I can't bear not knowing."

He did not speak for a moment or two. Now his harsh profile was dogged and stern. "Yes, I know," he said.

She dropped her hand. She stood beside him, still and waiting, all her passionate pleading in her eyes. Slowly, he looked down at her, and then suddenly turned away again.

"Please tell me," she said.

He was silent once more. But he could feel her waiting, gently obstinate, strongly determined. Then he spoke: "You know the provision. War, or a year, or when I give the word. That was your father's express condition."

She said, breathlessly, pleading: "Tell me, Henri."

He turned to her again, his mouth opening on impatient words. Then he saw her face. He felt his rare compassion for her. His face became quite gentle.

"Even though your father wouldn't want it, Annette?"

But she said, looking into his eyes: "Tell me, Henri."

He hesitated. Then he told her. He watched her closely as he did so. She did not move. But her eyes became vivid and brilliant blue light. When he had ended, she smiled a little, and sighed, over and over.

"Dear Papa," she murmured. She moved a step or two away. Then her face saddened. "But, poor Antoine. It will be terrible for him. I can only hope that Papa knew best."

All at once, she seemed exhausted, broken. She moved away, blindly, fumbled for the chair, and fell into it. Her head dropped on her breast. Her hands hung at her sides, slackly. The stormy light, falling in a shaft through the windows, lay on her fair hair, so that it was like a halo. Henri could not see her face. He had turned to watch her go, but he did not move from his position.

"Believe me, your father knew best," he said, with unusual gentleness.

But she did not speak.

"You won't, of course, tell this to anyone?" he added.

But she did not seem to have heard. He frowned a little. He began to move towards her when she spoke, and the sound of her voice, oddly strong and without emotion, stopped him abruptly. It was all the more odd to hear that voice, for she had not stirred in her chair, had not lifted her head. It was as if her voice came from near her, and not from her lips, themselves. Henri's heart began to beat heavily, with a dull pounding, at her words:

"I am glad you've told me. It's solved so many things. You see, Henri, I want a divorce. I couldn't ask you until I knew."

And now there was only silence in the room, broken by the gathering mutter of thunder and the stirring of the restless trees. Henri stood at the window. His hands had knotted into fists. His face was in darkness.

"Why?" he asked, at last.

Her figure was only a blur now, in the spectral gloom, her hair a diffused gleam. Her head had fallen a little more, but that was all.

"I couldn't ask you before," she said, and her voice was a sibilant and piercing whisper. "But now I can. I've wanted a divorce for a long time. I—I've wanted to be alone. I've never been happy."

And then she felt her husband beside her. He had placed his hand on her shoulder. At his touch she sighed, over and over, and shivered a little. He felt her long trembling.

"No," he said, gently, "you've never been happy. I know that. I've never made you happy; I never tried. I'm sorry, my dear. Very sorry. But, there it was. I don't believe I could ever have made anyone happy."

She did not lift her head. But her hand rose, and fell upon his fingers, which still lay on her shoulder. He felt their cool trembling touch, and something contracted painfully in his chest.

"It wasn't your fault," she said, faintly. "We shouldn't have married, in the beginning. It was my fault, really. I—I couldn't be anything to you, dearest. I couldn't give you children. When—I knew—that was when I should have let you go. But I was selfish."

He said, in a strange loud voice, foreign even to his own ears: "You were never selfish, Annette! It wasn't in you to be selfish." He added, and now his voice faltered, roughly: "I was never fit for you, my dear. No one was. You've always been everything that was good and kind and sweet and loyal. I'll never forget you, Annette. Never."

She drew a deep breath. Then, very gently, she put aside his hand. She stood up and faced him, frail and small, but very gallant. She was even smiling, though her color, in the thickening gloom, was so ghastly that it was the face of a ghost that confronted him.

"But I want you to forget, darling," she said, softly. "You see, I'm going away. Perhaps I'll never come back. I wouldn't

506

want you to remember me, not in the least. Except, perhaps, if you were ever fond of me, just a little."

He said, his voice shaking: "I have been fond of you, Annette. I think only I really knew what you are."

She lifted her hands involuntarily, and he took them quickly, holding them with strength. They were so cold and thin, and lifeless. He said, without thinking: "Annette, won't you change your mind?"

He felt her fingers stiffen. She drew back her head, and her clear blue eyes fixed themselves on his, steadfastly.

"No, Henri. I've thought of this for a long time. I really want a divorce. It would make me—more content. But," and her lips shook, "I'm so glad you asked me! I can't tell you how glad! I can't tell you how happy it makes me!"

He dropped her hands. She continued, quite firmly: "I wanted to know, before everyone knew, about Papa's will. It was best, wasn't it?"

And then, with shocked compassion, with profound gratitude and humility, he understood. He was so stunned that his vision whirled before him with sparks and flashes of light.

"It was best for you," she whispered.

He took her into his arms and pressed her head against his shoulder. He could not speak. He could only hold her, his fingers in her soft hair. She could feel the pounding of his heart, his deep sighs. She clung to him, not strongly, but gently. When he turned her face up, and kissed her lips, her breath stopped, and her eyes closed.

CHAPTER LX

One evening Annette called her brother, Antoine, and asked him to come to Robin's Nest, alone. Henri was in Washington again, she said, and there was something which she wished to say to Antoine.

Her tone and words, though quiet, even indifferent, caused

507

some inner excitement in the subtle Antoine. He came at once. His sister, in her mourning black, seemed frailer to him than ever, though she was quite composed. He saw that she regarded him somewhat intently and sadly, and that there was something personal in her regard. He kissed her with real affection, and sat near her, holding her hand.

"Well, my pet, what's bothering you now?" he asked, lightly. He reached up to tuck a soft bright curl behind her ears. His touch, his voice, his affectionate manner, almost broke her heart. For the first time she felt an unreasoning bitterness against her father. She bit her lip to keep it from a treacherous trembling. Perhaps Papa and Henri had been wrong all the time. She looked at her brother's dark narrow face and shining black eyes, and again her bitterness rose until it was a taste of gall in her mouth.

She withdrew her hand from his, but her expression was all love. She hesitated, looked away from him. "I want to tell you, first of all," she murmured. "You're my brother, and so, I thought it best. It's all so confusing, you see. But I know you'll understand, Tony dear."

"Well, Nita," he said, as she hesitated, using his old pet name for her. "What is it? Is it really so important?" But he knew it was important, and leaned alertly towards her.

She drew a deep breath, then said, steadily: "I am going to Reno in a week or so, dear. I'm getting a divorce from Henri."

He stared at her blankly. He had drawn back from her a little. His hands tightened on the arms of his chair. He began to smile; there was a dancing glitter in his eyes. "Yes?" he said. "Yes? Why?"

When she did not answer, he said: "At this late date? You remember, I advised you to do that over a year ago. Why now? Why the sudden change of mind?"

She gazed at him unwaveringly. "I think it best," she answered, with calm.

He stood up, unable to remain sitting. He walked quickly up and down the room, his hands in his pockets. His face was inscrutable, but darkly elated. Then he swung back to her.

"Reno? Why Reno? Why not here, in Pennsylvania? And, on what grounds?"

Before she could answer, he continued, swiftly: "Adultery?"

"Adultery?" she murmured, drawing her fine light brows together and regarding her brother with mingled reproach and affront. "That's absurd, Tony. You know it. I am going to sue for a divorce on the grounds of incompatibility, of course."

Now his expression darkened. He stood beside her, scrutinizing her almost savagely. His eyes narrowed, became malignant. "So," he said, softly, "he's throwing you out at last, eh? So he can marry that bitch?"

She rose quickly to her feet, shaking violently, her eyes blazing. "Tony! How dreadful of you!"

But, engrossed with his own tumultuous thoughts, he exclaimed: "He couldn't do it while our father was alive, no! How can he do it now? What does he know about our father's will? Does he know? God, I'd like to know about that!"

He began to walk up and down again, with increasing swiftness. He passed and repassed his sister, who stood in desperate silence, watching him. He stopped before her, glaring down at her. But she knew he did not see her.

"He must know about the will, or he wouldn't dare demand a divorce! He must know it is safe! My God, why is it safe? What is in that accursed will?"

She reached out and caught him by his arms. She shook him a little. "Tony, you don't understand! He didn't ask me for a divorce. It was I who asked." She paused. Her voice quivered, and she swallowed. "Please believe me. I am telling you the truth. I've never lied to you, have I, Tony? When I asked him for a divorce, he asked me if I wouldn't change my mind."

Antoine stopped, rigidly, in the very moment when he was about to wrench himself from her. Now he was smiling again, evilly. "So," he said, softly, "he asked you to change your mind, did he? Now, I wonder why? I really wonder why."

He threw back his head and laughed, silently. Then he pushed his sister back into her chair, and sat beside her. "Tell me some more," he said.

She could not endure the sight of his gloating, his dark smile and laughter. She dropped her eyelids convulsively. When he tried to take her hand again, she withdrew it with a shudder. Papa was right, she thought. But her love for her brother was like a terrible ache in her heart.

Her words were so low that he could hardly catch them when she spoke. He bent his head towards her. "You are wrong, Tony. He asked me to change my mind because he

509

was sorry for me." Now he saw the slow silvery tears dropping from beneath her lashes. "He was so sorry for me. But, he was glad, too. He was glad to be rid of me. I can't blame him. I should never have married him. He never wanted me."

His elation faded. He scowled at her closed white face. Then he took her hand again, and rubbed its coldness between his own hands. Now he was all heaviness, all presentiment.

"You are telling the truth, Nita?" he asked, insistently. "You did ask for a divorce? Would you mind telling me why?"

She did not open her eyes. She said, feebly: "Because I can see at last how wrong it was of me to have married him. It's been nearly sixteen years now. All this time—I've held him. It was wicked. Yes, I can see it now. I only hope it isn't too late for him."

Her low and faltering words struck like stones against him. He was no longer gloating, no longer exultant. Henri would not have acceded to the divorce had it not been safe, had he not some assurance that it was safe. Then, there was nothing in the will that could ruin Henri should he divorce Annette. Antoine moistened his cold dry lips.

But still, he could not resist asking: "I don't quite understand. Has he agreed to the divorce?"

"Yes," she whispered. "It is all arranged. His lawyers are drawing up settlements. But I am going to refuse—anything. I have more than enough. I—I don't know what is in Papa's will, but I know that he wouldn't have forgotten me. Besides, I have part of Mama's money, too."

He saw that she was terribly ill and broken despite her valor. He looked at her intently, and for the first time he thought of his sister's suffering. A black and evil shadow settled on his features.

"Annette," he said, harshly, "you are a fool. You are releasing him so he can marry that—that trollop. Don't you know that?"

She turned to him swiftly, and he saw the bright blue fire of her eyes. But her tone was very quiet and unmoved: "I don't know what you're talking about, Tony. I don't think Henri intends to marry again. I hope he may. I hope there is still enough time to—to right things. For him. I don't care whom he marries, so long as he is happy. That is all that matters."

He stared at her gloomily. "Annette, you know you can

ruin him, even now, don't you? Don't you think you owe something to yourself? Don't you think there should be justice for you? You know that all these years he's been unfaithful to you, that the things he has done with other women have been a scandal. Haven't you any pride? Is there nothing I can say to make you change your mind, and drop this divorce?"

He thought: If he marries Celeste, then he'll have Christopher, and others.

She said, clearly: "I don't believe Henri has been unfaithful. If he has, then it is still my fault. What had I to give him? I was nothing to him. He could have divorced me many times, but he didn't. He has been—kind—to me."

"Kind!" He burst into ribald laughter. "Only because of our father! Didn't you know even that?"

But she answered with grave steadiness: "Yes."

He was about to speak, then was silent. He studied her with piercing scrutiny, and she did not turn away from him. Then, shrugging slightly, he went to the windows, and stood, with his back to her. He played with a tassel on the draperies. She saw his thin dark hand moving restlessly, and with little abstracted tuggings. All at once, she was vaguely startled. She discerned that there was something quite strange about her brother. She looked at him earnestly, at his lean and elegant figure, and the outline of his small-boned sleek head. What was there that was so changed about Antoine? She could not tell. But involuntarily she took a step towards him, and said, softly: "Tony?"

He did not turn for several moments, and then he did so, reluctantly. Now, she could not see his face, for it was averted, bent aside. However, she caught the impression of brooding and somberness.

She made a small and fluttering motion with her hands. "Tony? Is there something wrong? You don't seem quite yourself, dear."

He lifted his head and gazed at her. He is tired, exhausted, she thought, all her love for him opening wide in her heart. There is something wrong! "Tony," she said, impulsively, "is it anything I can help?"

"No," he answered, with indifference. Then he came back to her and stood before her, and again she had the impression of strangeness, of tired immobility. But when he spoke again, it was with gentleness: "Nita, what are you going to do?"

She pressed her hands quickly together, palm to palm, and though the evening air was hot and close, he saw that she shivered just a little. But she was smiling. "You mean, after I get my divorce? I don't know, dear. What can I do? I can't stay here. I only know that."

"So?" he said, tentatively, as she hesitated.

She walked back into the room, and now it was she who turned her back to him. She stood, holding onto a chair. She began to speak, as if to herself:

"What is there I can do? All my life, I've lived uselessly, devouring the provender that could have been used to better advantage by others. I've eaten food I never earned, and worn clothes that were bought with others' money. It has just begun to occur to me that I'm a parasite, that I have no reason to live. If I had had children, there might have been some excuse for my existence."

Her voice was very soft and firm. But, somehow, Antoine felt a sharp sad contraction in his chest.

"Yes, there was a reason," he said. "Our father loved you. You gave him what little happiness he ever had. What would he have done without you, Nita? And, I think I've loved you, too."

But she went on as if he had not spoken: "A useless, foolish life. Worst of all, it isn't ended, yet. There ought to be something I could do," she continued, with soft vehemence, and he saw that she had clenched her little white hands and was pounding them soundlessly on the back of the chair. "Once, I thought I might do something with my music. But, there seemed no reason. Perhaps I didn't have ambition enough, or talent enough. If we had been poor, something, perhaps, could have been done. I never had sufficient energy of body, and no one ever told me this did not matter. I was pampered and coddled all my life, until I came to believe that I was really something quite precious!" And now she laughed, so softly and drearily. She shook her bent head, again and again, as if overcome with her sorrowful mirth.

"No one is precious," she went on, while he watched her, full of pain. "No one deserves anything he does not earn. I've never earned anything. I've never given anything. I am just beginning to see— Now, I am stranded. And it is all my fault."

"No, darling, it wasn't your fault." He went to her but did not touch her. "You had ill health all your life. And then, you married—him—and he did nothing to make you happy."

"Happy!" She turned to him with such swiftness, such impassioned wildness, that he was startled. "Why should anyone make another 'happy'? As if happiness were something to be given, like a piece of jewelry or a Christmas present! No one can give another man happiness. It is something he acquires himself, something he buys himself with his own energy and his own desire. How dare we say to anyone: 'Please, please, make me happy! I'm weak and stupid, and have no resources in myself, no valor or kindness or selflessness, which can make me happy!' How presumptuous! How disgusting! How greedy!"

She was ablaze with her passion and anger, and trembling violently. He watched her, amazed.

She continued, almost incoherently: "We blame others for our misery, and despair and impotence. If we are wretched, we never admit to ourselves that we were weak, or cruel, or comtemptible. If we fail, it is never our fault, no. Perhaps we couldn't endure to look at our own mediocrity and sterility, or ask ourselves if we ever, at any time, had anything to give. It is much easier, and much, much more comfortable, to blame it on parents, or husbands, or wives, or circumstance, or lack of opportunity. Then our ego isn't hurt. We can think of ourselves as abused martyrs, whom no one ever loved, or helped, but only neglected."

He said, irascibly: "Do you think you deserved the treatment you've received from him?"

"Yes!" she cried. "I had no right to marry him! I knew he was marrying me because Papa had bribed him, and that, in a way, he was weak, too, putting power above peace. I knew I was indulging his weakness. I knew he was being bought by Papa, for me. Yet, I was indecent enough to accept the bargain. But I didn't have the courage, or the pride, to accept all the conditions of the bargain, and be contented that at least I had married him. No, I must want him to love me, too! I must begin to hope that he might find me endurable, might even come to want me for myself!" And again, she burst into dreary and bitter laughter. "I wasn't cheated by Henri. I cheated myself."

She walked away from him, distractedly. "Never speak to me of what he 'owed' me, or how he 'betrayed' me! He owed me nothing. He never betrayed me, because he never wanted me, had never promised me anything. He never pretended. At least, he was honest."

She stood by the dark windows now. She put her hands over her face, and stood like that, in sudden stark silence, not weeping.

Slowly, Antoine sat down. He rested his elbow on the arm of the chair and put his hand over his mouth. He stared heavily at his sister. Her words repeated themselves over and over, in his mind, like sick echoes. He felt an awful barrenness and disintegration in himself, which had nothing to do with her, and nothing at all to do with pity. All at once, he was enormously tired, and there was a choking dryness in his mouth.

He said, mechanically: "Still, I don't think you should divorce him. I think his share in this should be made public."

She turned to him, electrified, passionate. "Made public? What do you mean, Tony?"

When he did not answer, she came to him rapidly, and stood before him, her little hands clenched, her blue eyes fiery. "Tony, what do you mean? Tony, I've thought you cared a little for me! But, you'd do this to me? To your sister?"

"Don't talk like a fool, Annette. What have you to do with it?"

But she said, in an even wilder tone: "I want peace, I tell you! I want to forget everything! Yet, if you ever tried to hurt him, to malign him, Tony, I'd have to defend him, to deny everything you said! You think I wouldn't? I would, Tony. I swear to it. Wherever I was, I would return to help him. Don't you think I owe him that much?"

Now his deep and volatile rage rose to the surface. " 'Owe him'? What do you owe him? Do you know about our father's will? Don't you ever wonder how he might have influenced our father? Don't you ever suspect that he might be robbing us?"

"Robbing us?" She stopped, and smiled whitely. "Are we destitute? Only a week ago, Henri told me that in my own right I am one of the richest women in America. And I know that Mama left you two-thirds of her own estate, to come into your hands after Papa's death. What more do we want, Tony? What more do you want? You are married to a rich woman, Tony. What more?"

He was silent. But very slowly, the black and fiery embers of rage died in his eyes. He said, dully: "It's useless to explain to you, Annette. You'd never understand."

He stood up. They regarded each other speechlessly.

Then, with a faint sound, she came to him, and laid her head on his chest. "Tony," she whispered. "Be good to me. Love me a little. I've always loved you so. Don't forget I'm your sister. Help me, Tony. You are all I have."

Instinctively, he put his arms about her, and held her to him tightly, his compassion like a hot knife in his heart.

CHAPTER LXI

Jay Regan said to Henri Bouchard one early September day: "Not more than three months, I would say. And not directly from Hitler. I'm looking towards Japan."

Henri nodded gloomily. "Yes. But who, besides ourselves, knows this, or will see it?"

The old man smiled delicately. "My dear Henri, you mean: Who would believe us?"

Henri laughed shortly. "Well, put it that way, if you must. 'Who would believe us?' "

"Frankly," said Mr. Regan, "I don't blame them. If I should go to Washington, to the White House, and say: 'Mr. President, stop staring eastward. The danger is there, yes, waiting. But the first blow will come from the west,' what would be the result? Mr. Roosevelt would look at me long and steadily, in a certain disconcerting way he has, and then he would smile a little. That would be all. He would redouble his attention eastward, more firmly convinced than ever that the danger lies there. No, my dear Henri, a reformed thief is always under suspicion that he has not really reformed, or that he has an ulterior motive at all times."

"We have," remarked Henri, grimly. "But it also happens that our own ulterior motive is coincidentally connected with the safety, and survival, of America. Couldn't you convince the President of that?"

Mr. Regan shook his head, and now his smile was caustic. "When he saw me, quite accidentally, in Washington about a year ago, he said: 'Well, Jay, how's tricks?' I would say that his expression wasn't exactly amiable, though the remark was ambiguous enough. Mr. Roosevelt is a very subtle man, Henri. He also asked about you."

They laughed together for a moment. Then Mr. Regan said: "The only ones, besides ourselves, who know, are our enemies. And you can be sure that they are not talking too much. We can do very little except make our own plans for the inevitable day when America will be caught napping. You know, Henri, I've never consulted military men very much. I've left that to our lobby. Now I wish I knew a few admirals. I might persuade them to watch the Philippines, and Hawaii."

Henri brooded on the matter, while Mr. Regan watched him closely. Then the old man said: "My boy, you've done well. You have the explosives ready, and the arsenal filled. When are you going to move?"

"Not until war has been declared. Or a year has passed since Armand died. I don't know why he added that. I didn't know. Unless," and his smile was grim, "he didn't trust me all the way. Though he did say I could give the signal."

He betrayed an uneasy thought by the twitching of his broad and heavy lips. So, thought Regan, you are wondering what sly and nasty little afterthoughts are also included in the body of the will, about which you hadn't been informed, either.

Dead men, he observed to himself, frequently take the most treacherous and cruel revenges, which they had been impotent to take in life.

"I don't know why he didn't trust you, in everything, as you seem to imply," said Regan. He waited, but Henri made no comment. His square strong hand tapped with only the slightest restlessness on the other's desk.

Then Regan said: "I've heard a rumor, Henri. That Mrs. Henri is going to divorce you."

Henri looked up, alertly, frowning. "Where did you hear that?"

Regan shrugged. "Frankly, I don't remember. It was the slightest rumor. Is there any truth to it?"

Henri hesitated. Then he replied, his pale and relentless eyes expressing nothing: "Yes. I see it's no secret. No one has been told; it has been entirely between myself and my wife. And I'm certain she has told no one, yet." He added: "If it's around, now, what is the general reaction?"

Regan shrugged again. "A little uncertainty, among the

large stockholders. You know how temperamental the Market is. Of course, if Armand's will were known it might have a lot of influence, particularly, I might add, if the contents were favorable to you."

When Henri did not speak, and only stared penetratingly at his old friend, Mr. Regan continued: "If, for instance, the presidency of Bouchard & Sons passed to Antoine, with Armand's fifty-one percent of stock, and your wife were to receive several large blocks of stock in the subsidiaries, adding her weight to her brother's, that would have, at least, a disturbing effect on the Market, and particularly, on our friends, who know Antoine's—sympathies."

Henri did not speak, though his eyes flashed with an ugly look. Regan said: "You are certain that what you have told me about the will is correct?"

"Yes," said Henri, with a quick impatience which betrayed his uneasiness. "I was there, when it was drawn up. I know all about the trust funds. I know the witnesses. The attorneys are my friends. They have assured me that nothing of the original draft was changed. But," he said, after a moment's somber reflection, "they did not tell me whether anything else was added, later."

"Well, then, in the main, everything is as you have said. I will pass the rumor around, judiciously. Anything that might have been added is of no importance, of course?"

"I don't know," said Henri, with annoyance. "It could only be of personal importance."

"Well, good God, man! Why don't you order it opened, then? And see?"

Henri bit his lip. He said: "I don't know. I think, for our own sakes, that opening it just now would be premature. I'm waiting for war. Armand was of the opinion that if a year passed after his death, and we were not in the damn mess, then the chances were that we never would be. That is why there is that other condition. So," he added wryly, "I'm torn between wanting to see what the infernal will has had added to it, if anything, and the necessity for waiting."

Mr. Regan rubbed his chin. "Suppose there is some codicil about a divorce, eh? What then, if your wife has already divorced you?"

Henri turned to him directly. "I have persuaded her to wait, until the will is opened. I persuaded her that she owed that to her father's memory." And he smiled now, a smile that was excessively nasty.

After a little, Mr. Regan said, idly: "There might be some provision about your not remarrying, in the event of a divorce, or of your wife's death."

"Then," said Henri, very quietly, "there shall be no divorce, and no remarrying."

Mr. Regan stared at him a long time. "You know," he said, finally, "you are really marvellous. Really marvellous, Henri."

He thought of Jules Bouchard's daughter, waiting in loneliness and obscurity and shame on Placid Heights, and he smiled inwardly. Jules' beloved daughter, who must await the will of a dead man, who must await the word of a living man who loved her much less than he loved power.

I hope, thought Mr. Regan, that Jules is enjoying this. He had always hated Jules very much.

CHAPTER LXII

It had been in August when Agnes Bouchard had informed Celeste that Annette intended to divorce Henri. Celeste had made no remark. She had merely regarded Agnes in silence, then, after a few moments, she said: "I can hardly believe it. Why? There seems no reason."

But when Agnes would have cynically elaborated, Celeste changed the subject. She asked Agnes if she would care to see little Land, who was now walking a few steps by himself. Agnes followed her up to the nursery, where the serious strong baby was standing in his crib, and calling his mother impatiently. He stared at Agnes with his pale bright eyes, and smiled a little. Agnes did not particularly care for children; however, she liked Land as a person, not a child. Her own grandchildren, she would say, were mere "blobs. Protoplasm." But this child, with his gravity, the determined tilt of his chin, and his strong straight stare, filled her with respect. She said: "Hello," as she would have said it to a contemporary, and he smiled quickly in answer.

Celeste looked at him tenderly. She lifted him in her arms

and kissed him with sudden passion. She buried her face in his warm neck, so that Agnes would not see the tears she could not prevent from rising to her eyes. But Agnes, who was both astute and subtle, was quite aware of them.

Celeste had suffered in her life, but nothing had been much worse than the long dead period of waiting which now ensued for her. She would not allow herself to acknowledge why she waited, or why she watched every road that led up Placid Heights. When her heart bounded at the sound of a car winding over the gravelled driveways, when a door opened and she heard a masculine voice, she would try to control herself with desperate sternness. When her relatives called upon her, she tried to pierce behind the veil of friendliness that masked their faces. No one spoke of any pending divorce. She dared not ask, or hint. She could only wait and watch. If it were true, she thought, he would have come. He would have been the first to tell me. And then, with sudden coldness, she would think: If it is true, why doesn't he come? Can it be that he will never come again?

She had not seen Annette since Agnes had told her of the rumor. Annette had called her on the telephone frequently, but Celeste, however she tried, could tell nothing from her voice. Annette, as usual, had been only loving and serene, asking about the baby, repeating her endless invitations, which Celeste never accepted, and promising to drive up shortly to see her. But for some reason, when Celeste replaced the receiver, she found that her hand was cold and damp, and trembling.

Within a very short time, her new color, her new vitality, her new plumpness, began to disappear. A strained and haggard expression deepened about her eyes; her lips whitened. She had been fond of driving through the early autumn countryside with little Land. Now, she sent him with one of his nurses and remained behind, sitting under the trees near the house so that she could watch the hot and shimmering roads that climbed the hills. When she would see the dust of an approaching car, her heart would swell to the point of suffocation. But when she could identify it, her mouth would go dry, and burn with the bitter acid of disappointment.

Slowly, as time passed, a dull yet fiery core of pain settled in her chest, a core that was also the wildest and deepest anger, and shame. She tried to reason with herself that the rumor was most probably false, that no divorce was intended, at least not until Armand's will was opened. But Agnes, she

519

remembered, was not given to scandal-mongering. She never repeated anything that was entirely without foundation. Now Celeste bitterly reproached herself for her "damnable" reserve. Why had she not allowed Agnes to elaborate on the subject? Why had she risen so precipitately and urged Agnes up the stairs to the nursery? She remembered the sudden roaring and swimming of her senses after she had heard the rumor. She had felt the tightening of all her veins, the trembling of her body. Her rising had been flight, in truth. But why? She hated herself for the instinct which had made her run from the room, with Agnes following closely behind.

I was always a coward, really, she thought to herself, with self-hatred and self-contempt. Yes, Agnes was right, that day. She said I was a coward. I am. I always was. If I had had any courage, at any time, much of what has happened would never have been, and so much suffering would have been saved, for myself and others.

Again, like a vivid nightmare, she remembered that day, so very long ago, when she had watched Henri leave her for the last time, before her marriage to Peter. She could see herself again, at her window, and the way his shadow followed him under the poplars. And then, feeling her mournful child eyes upon him, he had turned, and lifted his hand in a final salute, smiling back at her. Then it was that the wildest passion had come to her. She had wanted, with every beat of her heart, every instinct, to throw open the long french window, to run to him across the grass, crying to him to wait, and not to leave her. She had remained, rooted there stiffly and coldly, like stone, while her spirit had pursued him, calling to him in despair.

But, she thought, I did not have the courage to declare openly that I had made a mistake. I was afraid of the laughter. I was afraid of the newspapers, which had made such a disgusting scandal of my breaking my engagement to Henri, and becoming engaged to Peter. I was afraid of such inconsequential mean things, such unimportant things. So, I let my life be ruined, and the lives of others, too, because I was afraid of transient laughter, and transient humiliation.

When she remembered this, she would think to herself: Perhaps he is right not to come. How could he trust me again? He knows I am a coward, that I run when I want to stay, and stay when I want to run. If he never comes again, I shall deserve it.

But there were other occasions when her shame seemed too much for her to bear, when she had the maddest dreams of approaching him publicly and crying out against him. She was terrified, on these occasions, and would run to her room and lock the door behind her, appalled.

She felt completely friendless. Her brother was increasingly absent from Windsor. She had at first thought of asking him, in her growing despair and suspense, but on the few occasions that she saw him, her tongue would become thick and numb.

However, one night she could endure her agony no longer. She called Christopher, at Endur. Edith had told her that he was expected at eight that night. It was now nine. Christopher was alarmed at her voice, so hoarse and low, and demanded, over and over, her assurance that she was perfectly well. He had hardly entered his own home, when Celeste's call had come to him, and Edith expressed her opinion of his departure in a tone that was corroded with acerbity.

Christopher found his sister waiting for him. He had expected to find her hysterical, broken, over some as yet unexplained calamity. The child, perhaps. But he was extremely angered to see that she was quite calm, if somewhat pale and strained, and that when she greeted him she asked him some ridiculous question about his recent trip.

"Look here, my dear," he said abruptly, "what is all this? I've just flown in from Los Angeles, and before that I was on the go constantly. I'm not as young as I used to be. I'm damned tired. Yet, you call me as if your house were afire, or your baby kidnapped, or the place full of thieves. Couldn't it have waited until tomorrow?"

She looked at him without speaking. And then he saw that there was a glazed blind look in her eyes, as if she had suffered long and shocking pain, and that she was calm only because she dared not be otherwise. He took her hand, and held it strongly. "All right, darling," he said, quietly, "what is it?"

He put her in a chair, and sat near her. She pressed her hands rigidly on the arms of her chair, and turned to him. "Christopher," she said, "I've got to know. Is Henri really getting a divorce from Annette?"

"Divorce?" he exclaimed, astounded. "What gave you that idea? Who told you?"

"Agnes," she said, simply. "Over a month ago. And Agnes never repeats silly rumors without foundation."

She looked pleadingly at her brother. She was startled to

see how ghastly he became, and how immobile. His light silvery eyes flashed evilly. He said, as if to himself: "And he never told me."

He turned to his sister, but she knew he did not see her. He was really seeing the man he hated more than he had ever hated anyone.

"Why didn't he tell me?" he asked.

"I don't know," whispered Celeste. "I don't know!" And then, in a stronger tone: "But it might not be true, you know. Armand's will hasn't been opened. Perhaps there can be nothing definite until——"

Christopher's face changed. "Yes. Of course. But, why didn't he tell me? Or you?" He felt his mortification in him, like a disease. "He hasn't been here?"

"No. He never comes. I asked him not to. But, he should have come, in spite of that."

Christopher began to laugh. He got up. "Damned inconsistent. Well, he's showing discretion, at last." He added, scrutinizing his sister: "You might, of course, ask him to come."

"No. Never! If he never came, I'd never send for him, Kit."

Her voice was passionate, vehement. He turned away. "Then, we can only wait. Until Armand's will is opened. Though, frankly, it would be more decent, and less open to gossip, if he allowed Annette to divorce him before we knew the contents of the will."

He had a thought which made him wrinkle his parchment-like forehead, but he did not communicate it to his sister.

"I can't stand the waiting," she said, suddenly. "Kit, I must go away!"

"You'll do nothing of the kind! The talk has died down. Your going away would only stimulate it."

"Then, I must wait, just wait? I can't stand it!"

He regarded her gloomily. "You must. There is nothing else to do. Shall I send Edith up here to stay with you for a while?"

"No."

He felt that she was distraught, when he left her. Once or twice he even thought of going to Henri, but the memory of that harsh and relentless man made him quail.

It was the next night, a night of warm rain and gray skies, that Annette came to see Celeste and her baby. Annette, as usual, was warm and tender, but Celeste, who was never at ease now with her niece, was very silent. In her extremity, she had lost all sense of any possible wrong to Annette. There were even times when she regarded her with dark and bitter coldness and resentment. She knew this was cruel, but the feeling returned with greater strength each time.

Annette played with the baby in his nursery. It was not for quite a while that Celeste observed some change in Annette. It was not that she appeared more frail, or more tired, or more gently sad. Rather, there was a sense of delicate strength in her, and contentment, and serene quiet. Celeste forgot her frozen resentment, in her uneasy curiosity.

They went to Celeste's sitting-room for tea. It was then, while stirring her tea, and helping herself to a small cake, that Annette said, in the most casual and thoughtful of tones: "Celeste, would it shock you terribly if I told you I am divorcing Henri? Divorces, I know, aren't common in our family. Perhaps it is the Catholic heritage."

She continued to stir her tea. She did not look at Celeste for some moments. When she did so, slowly lifting her eyes, she saw that Celeste's head was bent. But otherwise, there was no sign from her.

Annette's eyes filled with compassionate tears. She sipped a little tea. The cup tinkled in its saucer. "You don't think it dreadful of me, do you, dear?" she asked.

Celeste lifted her head. Even in the warm dusk of the room, Annette could see that she was pale and rigid.

"Annette," she said, and her voice was strained and thick, "what will you do?"

Annette shrugged her shoulders, and sighed and smiled. "It has just recently come to me that I'm a very useless woman, Celeste. I've just had a physical examination. It's true that I'm not exactly a tennis-playing athlete, and that I have no muscles." She laughed softly. "But my doctors assure me, as they always have, that I have a fine constitution. A few scars on the lungs—but that is all past. Not much of a body, but an excellent nervous system. I need an interest in life, they tell me. So, I think I shall engage in some sort of relief work. You remember Lucille Wanamaker? She is organizing a British relief agency, to operate in England. She has already collected an enormous sum, to be spent for clothing and food, and in cooperation with the Red Cross, she intends to distribute these things to the bombed-out evacuées. She needs volunteers. I can drive an ambulance, and help with the distribution."

Celeste, forgetting herself in her sudden concern for Annette, exclaimed feebly: "But you can't! You've never been strong! It will kill you."

Annette carefully laid down her cup and saucer, before answering. And then she clasped her hands on her thin little knee and looked at them for quite a while. She began to speak, in a very low tone:

"I think that most of the ailments of American women, and their everlasting neuroses, come from not having anything worthwhile or significant to do. You can't ail, you can't imagine dreadful and incoherent things, if someone needs you. I, myself, have done nothing all my life but accept affection and care, and think of my own pursuits and my own desires."

She paused. Celeste looked at her, her eyes dazzled with tears. Forgetting everything, she leaned towards the other woman and laid her hand on her knee.

"No, dear, you are wrong. You've never thought of yourself. You've always helped others, and understood so much. None of us ever deserved you, Annette."

Annette smiled. She put her little hand over Celeste's. "How good of you, darling, to say that. But, it isn't true. What have I ever done? I've given money to charities. But I never saw those who benefited. Frankly, I don't think I even cared to see them. They were something nebulous, and unreal. I'd like to see those I can help. I'd like to talk to them, and help them with their problems. Somewhere, I know there is misery and suffering that can be alleviated, not only by money, but by sympathy and kindness. I feel I must do this. For the sake of my soul, perhaps," and she laughed, a little tremulously. "A whole world in agony, Celeste, and millions of foolish women sipping tea and playing cards, and whimpering with fear that we may be involved in the war. And, of course, we shall be. It is inevitable. I don't want to remain one of the whimperers, Celeste."

Celeste pushed back her hair with her old bewildered and uncertain gesture. She stared at Annette with a moved and sorrowful look. She said: "At one time, when Peter was alive, I was really living, Annette. Now, I am not. Nothing seems to matter to me, very much. I have become narrow and selfish. Everything is unreal, beyond me." She stopped abruptly, for her voice broke with tears.

"You have a child, Celeste," said Annette, softly, and with pain. "You have accomplished something."

But Celeste stood up, in acute restlessness. She started to speak, then stopped. After several poignant moments, she said: "Annette, why are you divorcing Henri?"

Annette rose, also. She forced herself to look at Celeste directly, and yet with detachment. She felt the rapid and painful throb of her own heart, though she concealed it with a smile. "Because, it's gone on long enough, Celeste. He never cared about me, though sometimes I think he's had some affection. It's been awfully long. And very wrong of me. It isn't very soothing to know that one's husband married one—for an advantage. But I've deceived myself all these years. Now I know it's no use. It gets worse, as time goes on. It isn't fair—to either of us. I'm not a child, Celeste, though I've continued to think I was, for too long. I see now that I have a life of my own to live, and that I can live it, if I have the courage. It is now or never."

Celeste stared at her in a silence in which there was a sort of white grimness. She moved away a little, and began to rearrange a bowl of garden flowers on the tea-table. She said, almost inaudibly: "It was he who was wrong. He had no right to treat you as he did, Annette. He is a cruel man."

"No!" cried Annette. She came to Celeste, and took her by the arm. "It was I who was cruel. Believe me. I married him, knowing he didn't want me except for a personal advantage. I ought to have had more pride."

"He was cruel," repeated Celeste, and now she was breathless with sudden passion. "If he hadn't been cruel, and vicious, he wouldn't have married you, knowing that he could give you nothing. He never tried to make you happy, Annette! It was the least thing he could have done. It was only honorable. But he never tried; he never treated you with anything but indifference. Worst of all, he constantly humiliated you!"

Her dark blue eyes glittered in the dusk. She stepped back from her niece. She was breathing with great distress.

Annette was alarmed. Her fragile color disappeared. "You are wrong, Celeste! He was often very kind to me. You don't know! How could you? When I asked him for a divorce, he asked me to change my mind."

"He—" began Celeste, then her mouth went dry, and she stood, petrified.

"Yes, dear. He did ask me to change my mind. Finally, he

525

persuaded me to wait until things were settled, and Papa's will was opened."

She wondered, in her huge distress and fright, why Celeste suddenly appeared so gaunt, so haggard, and why her eyes blazed wildly. What have I said to upset her so? she thought, in confusion.

"Why should he ask you to wait?" said Celeste, and she spoke as if her tongue had swelled enormously, and was choking her.

Annette began to tremble. Something had gone horribly wrong. She fumbled for words in her aching throat. "I—I don't know, Celeste. I, myself, thought it better not to wait. I've been sure that Papa has made everything right for Henri, in his will, and that a divorce wouldn't matter."

Celeste had begun to smile, darkly, and with increasing wildness. "Don't you understand, Annette? He is afraid there is something else in the will. He is afraid that if there is a codicil, forbidding him to divorce you, he will lose everything he has perjured himself for. Can't you see?"

"No!" said Annette. She withdrew her hand from Celeste's, and now, for the first time, Celeste saw Annette's anger and indignation directed at her. But she was too distracted to care.

"And, Annette," she continued, very loudly, "if there is such a codicil, what will you do? Will you divorce him, then?"

Annette was silent. She walked away from Celeste with stumbling steps, so sick and dizzy that she feared she would collapse.

Celeste's loud wild voice pursued her: "Why doesn't he open the will now, Annette, and know for sure? He can give the word."

Annette swung back to her, quickly, her small white face afire. "Does it ever occur to you, Celeste, that it is too early to open it, that Henri has work he must do, before it is opened? That to open it prematurely might spoil all his plans? Don't you know at all that he has something more important to think about just now than women?" She lost control of herself in her extremity, and selfless indignation: "Don't you know that even you are not as important to him as the work he must do?"

And now the words she had spoken unthinkingly, in her vehement passion, lay between them like a sword that could never again be sheathed. They stared at each other over it, hardly breathing, their eyes locked. A sudden icy coldness wrapped all Annette's body; her throat closed in despair and anguish. She spoke again, while Celeste, pallid and frozen, waited: "Celeste, I should not have spoken. I hoped I might never need to speak. I won't say I am sorry. It is too late. But I can tell you this: if there is such a codicil in the will, I won't divorce Henri. He is still more important to me than anyone else on earth, including myself."

Celeste had never seen her niece like this. Even though the dark room heaved and spun about her, even though her heart was flaming with shame and agony, even though she experienced the most awful desolation and sickness and horror of her life, she was still conscious of Annette's wide, light-blue eyes, steadfast, undaunted and clear as bright water.

For speechless and terrible moments they confronted each other. Then, Annette began to sigh. She dropped her head and turned away. She left the room. Celeste watched her go. Unable to move, she listened acutely. She heard the sound of Annette's car turning down the driveway. She ran to the window, and flung it open. The car had reached the first turn.

Then Celeste cried out, though she knew Annette could not hear: "Good-bye, Annette! Good-bye, darling, dear! Good-bye, good-bye!"

She dropped on her knees before the window. She pressed her cheek distractedly against its cool darkness. Her hands fell to her sides. She began to weep, but without tears.

CHAPTER LXIII

Though Henri had seen Celeste some dozen times in the past year, their encounters had been casual and distant, in the homes of relatives. However, he had been greatly pleased at the improvement in her appearance, at her look of serenity and health, and her color. She had always greeted him with pleasant indifference, and then had directed all her attention to Annette or others.

Henri's first impression, as he walked into Celeste's drawing-room this early October night and she rose from before the fire to face him in stern and iron silence, was that she had lost all the freshness and color she had acquired in the past year, and that it was an embittered and hardened woman who faced him. She made no such banal remark as: "Why have you come?" She only said, at last: "Please sit down, won't you?"

He did. She sat down at some distance from him, and waited, all coldness and withdrawal. He said, after a hard silence: "You look ill, Celeste. What is wrong with you?" His voice was impatient.

"Do I?" she asked, dully, and moved a little, so that she was slightly averted from him. "It is the weather, I suppose. I hate the winter. That is why I am going to California for a while."

"Yes. I heard that. That's why I came tonight."

She turned to him quickly, and smiled unpleasantly. "That is why you risked being indiscreet, I suppose? But, why should it concern you, anyway?"

The sound he made was even more impatient, and very rough. "The longer I live," he observed, "the more I wonder why we ever treat women as though they mattered. The Orientals are much more sensible than uxorious Occidentals, or rather, Americans. I don't like women. I never did. They are a damn, necessary nuisance." And then he began to smile. "Very necessary, sometimes."

She flushed angrily, but said nothing.

"I happen to find you necessary, Celeste," he continued. "For some reason, you were always necessary to me. I've never liked you much, as a person. I thought that as I grew older, my necessity for you would lessen. It didn't, much to my surprise." He waited for her comment, but she had lifted up her head, and was now regarding him with flashing scorn, mixed with humiliation.

"There were times," he went on, "when I thought you possessed more than the birdlike brain of most women. You returned from Europe a woman. I had had considerable feeling for you as a girl; I had much more for you, as a woman. Not that I'd ever expect that any woman could be a 'companion' to me, by God!"

He laughed contemptuously. "However, I could always talk to you with some stimulation, between your bouts of pouting and righteous indignation, and your attitudes. Yet, each time that I come back to you, you are there with blazing eyes and nasty remarks. Agnes once said you were a Victorian. I'm beginning to believe it."

Celeste said nothing. He saw that her throat was throbbing with considerable violence, and that her lips had parted as if she was finding it difficult to breathe. A look of extreme fury glazed her eyes.

Henri stood up, leaned against the mantelpiece, and regarded the fire pleasantly. "Of course, you aren't going to California," he said.

Celeste's repressed rage was so great that she felt a voluptuous impotence. As she stared at him, she was convinced that she hated him as she had never hated any creature before.

"You are wrong," she said, thickly. "I am going."

He turned his large head to her, and asked casually: "Why?"

But her anger had become too swollen for speech.

He went on, still standing at ease, and still speaking casually: "I never made you any promises. That was understood, from the beginning." He paused, to watch curiously the flood of scarlet rush over her cheeks and forehead. "I did say, that when certain circumstances would permit, we would consider marriage. Or, rather, that I would consider it. You were quite agreeable, I think I remember."

She sprang to her feet, suffocating with shame, something tearing agonizingly in her chest. "Go away!" she cried.

He suddenly changed, becoming implacable and ruthless. He stared at her, and she saw the relentless disks of his pale eyes.

"I don't like dramatics," he said, coolly, eyeing her as if she were some offensive creature. "They're always false, or hysterical, or whipped up for effect. Behave yourself, Celeste."

She cried out, incoherently, lost to everything but her shameful suffering: "You said that when Armand—died—!"

His impassiveness increased as she lost control of herself. He watched her drop her head on her arms, which she had leaned on the mantelpiece. He heard her weeping. The two deep furrows between his eyes became deeper.

"Yes, I remember," he said. He took a step towards her, then stopped. "That's quite true. But something else has come up. I can't open Armand's will—I can't divorce Annette—until events make it safe to do so. It won't be long. Perhaps a month, two months."

She lifted her head, and turned on him wildly. "You are

such a liar, Henri! Did you know that Annette has been here, that she told me that she intends to divorce you?"

He was startled. His expression was at first lowering, then it changed, and became thoughtful. "Yes?" he said. "And then?"

Celeste pressed both her hands fiercely to her breasts, as if to control the leaping pain of her heart. She looked into his eyes. "She said, however, that if the will specifies that you—are to lose if there is a divorce, then nothing will make her let you go."

Henri's light thick brows drew together so that his eyes were only pale bright pinpoints under their overhanging ridge. He watched Celeste curiously, as she waited, and he heard the hoarse panting of her voice.

He spoke quietly: "I told you, one time, that I couldn't marry you until Armand died, that I dared not risk a divorce. I thought you understood that the things which I was trying to accomplish were more important than ourselves. After Armand died, I said, and the danger to my work was over, then we could consider the matter. You remember that?"

"Yes, yes!" she exclaimed, with fervid and uncontrolled impatience. "I remember all that! But, you could open the will now, if you wished!"

He shook his head with granite stolidity and slowness. "No. It is too early. I told you: in a month, two months——"

She suddenly regained control of herself, but her face remained white. She could actually say, with quietness: "And after the will is opened, and you have accomplished what is necessary—which I know is necessary—and there is still some codicil there which will cause you personal loss if you divorce Annette—" She swallowed convulsively: "A loss that has nothing to do with the work you will have concluded, but is personal——"

He dropped his hand from the mantelpiece, and faced her fully. He said, with great slowness and emphasis: "Then, I shall not divorce Annette."

Her shock was so great that she appeared to dwindle, to shrink, to disintegrate. She stared at him with eyes suddenly grown enormous and dim. "I thought," she murmured, faintly, "that everything was delayed only because of the things you are doing, for the sake of America, and of yourself, and that when these were safe, you—you——" Her voice failed her.

"I would throw up everything, eh?" he finished, with a smile so dark and ugly that she felt a hideous fainting sickness in herself. "I would throw up a lifetime of effort, and scheming, and planning, and struggle, and ambition—for you? For a woman?" He began to shake his head, and his smile widened, became even more ugly. "Why do you think I returned to America? What do you know about me? Do you actually think, even after all these years, that I am the kind of man who would throw up his whole life for a woman? Do you think I am one of your movie heroes?" And now he seemed obsessed by a cold and violent rage of his own. "Can't you American women understand that to men who are not mere masculine copies of yourselves a woman is always only secondary? And that the sort of men you would have, fawning on your footsteps, abandoning all ambition and pride and accomplishment just so they might sleep with you, are caricatures, disgusting and contemptible and loathsome? Yet, how you damn women love 'em!"

Far off in the dim and whirling recesses of her awful suffering and shame, Celeste could only murmur: "O God. O God." She could see Henri no longer; he was only a whitish shape in a blowing mist. Somewhere, she was conscious of a core of fire burning, searing her.

Her lips, feeling gigantic and swollen, moved, and she said, hoarsely:

"And the baby? What of the baby?"

She could hear his voice, which came to her from some immense distance, but very clear and cold: "From the beginning, you understood that things were to be on my own terms and not on yours. I made you no promises, but I thought you understood that we'd always be together, married or not married. Armand is dead. The work I have to do will soon be done. If it is possible to divorce Annette, without injury to myself, I shall divorce her. We can be married, then. If I cannot divorce her without hurt to myself, then we cannot be married. However, in two months, perhaps less, it will be safe for you and me to be together again. It will be safe for me to visit you whenever I wish, and to see my child at any time."

Her senses came back in a vivid rush at his words, and to her they seemed so infamous, so terrible, that she was shocked into full consciousness. She reached for her chair; she fell into it. She could hardly believe what she had heard. She began to shiver, drawing her body together as if it had been

531

touched by ice. She could not speak; her throat had closed.

He watched her with that detached and cruel curiosity which was one of his strongest characteristics. "You are thinking," he observed, "about the boy. Don't you know that we are all rich enough so that nothing else will matter? Besides, who would dare say anything to him? Who would dare blaspheme all this money?" And he laughed a little.

She looked at him from the pit of her indescribable suffering, and said, simply: "I don't understand you. I never did. You are a liar. I—I thought you cared what happened to—to the baby, if not to me. But, you don't. You care only for yourself." She caught her breath deeply, then exhaled it, a long and broken sigh of extreme and exhausted pain. "You haven't seen him since the day he was born. You never wanted to see him."

He smiled, oddly. "You are wrong again, my darling. I see him very often. I've made it a point. Not in this house, of course. And now, I suppose," he added, with contemptuous impatience, "you will be very enraged with poor Edith, with whom you have left the baby frequently, at her request? You will scream in her face, I suppose? That would be like you, Celeste. And, no doubt, you will stop it?"

But, to his great surprise, she was not enraged. Instead, her face changed. Tears suddenly rose to her eyes, and spilled over her cheeks. She turned her head away. "No," she said, very softly, "I won't stop it. That surprises you, doesn't it, Henri?" After a little, she added: "I can accept it that I am not the most important thing to you, but I can't accept it that the baby isn't."

He came near her then, and said, looking down at her indulgently: "Perhaps, in a way, he is. It won't do him the least harm if another Bouchard name isn't added to the one he already has, but it will do him considerable good if I can leave him one of the biggest fortunes in the world, and a powerful position."

She stood up, and now her emotionalism was gone, and she could look at him directly, with dark calm. "I think I understand everything now, Henri. I won't take the baby away. You can see him even more often, if you wish. I shall arrange it with Edith, who loves him quite a lot, herself. But, I don't want to see you again. You'll think I am a female egotist, and perhaps I am. But I do know this: No matter what happens, no matter if there is nothing in Armand's will to prevent a divorce and a marriage to me, I don't want you to come back. I don't want you on any terms, yours or mine. Somehow, there is nothing left in me now."

He began to speak, impatiently, then stopped. He had never seen Celeste like this, so strong, contained and resolute. The thin white lock in her dark hair was no whiter than her face. Her eyes were intensely blue, and very still. He saw that she looked at him with no passion, no anger, no outrage or pain.

"You mean," he said quietly, "that you couldn't bear the truth?"

She shrugged; she was very tired. "Perhaps. I can even admit that. But no: I think it is because you are cruel. I always knew you were both brutal and cruel. But I knew it with my mind. I didn't know it with my heart. Now I know it with everything, and I can't bear to have you near me again."

While he watched her with narrow intensity, she continued, with immense simplicity: "When I was young, I was always afraid of cruel people. I've been trying to find out, lately, why it is I ran away from you, and married Peter, when I did love you all the time. But I know now. It was because I instinctively sensed you were cruel, and not just cruel in a relentless and impersonal way, an ambitious way, but in a personal way, also. That is something I can't forgive. I've believed, all these years, that your cruelty was an essential thing, a necessary thing, for dominance in a thieving and predatory world. But I didn't think it could extend to those you might think you loved, that you could strike down, in sheer viciousness, those who had no defense against you. It is a cowardly thing, Henri. It is not cowardly to strike down enemies who will destroy you. But it is terrible to strike down those who love you, or are weaker than you, and for no other reason than a deep sadism. You are a sadist, Henri."

He was silent. He leaned his elbow on the mantelpiece, and gently bit his index finger as he watched her with blank thoughtfulness.

She sighed, lifted her hands, and dropped them. "So, that's all, Henri," she said.

She turned and walked away from him. He saw her straight proud back, the fine and delicate lines of her slight figure. She did not hesitate or stumble. In a moment, she had passed through the archway, and he could hear her soft unhurried steps mounting the stairway.

Once up in her room, she sat on the edge of the bed in

the darkness, staring blindly before her, her lips and eyes as dry as dust. She felt no pain, only a profound and sinking desolation of spirit beyond anything she had experienced before in all her life, and it was like death to her.

CHAPTER LXIV

Annette wrote to Celeste: "Can you ever forgive my rudeness and boorishness and bad temper, darling? I know that I said things to you which are really unforgiveable, but I am hoping that you will overlook them, and remember how much we have always loved each other, and what friends we were. Can you bring yourself to forget that wretched afternoon, and go on as if nothing had ever been said?"

Celeste wrote back, immediately: "I have already forgotten. Nothing was said, really. Even if there was, how can I weigh it against our whole lives? There are bound to be disagreements and misunderstandings in every human relationship, but these aren't of any importance, dear."

But she knew that nothing would ever be the same again between herself and Annette, and, in its way, this was as terrible a circumstance to her as her final break with Henri. In actual fact, as Celeste implied in her letter, nothing had been changed. Fundamentally, this was true. But Annette had broken the brittle pretense between them that Celeste's affair with Henri was unknown to her. Deep in her heart, Celeste had believed that Annette had always known, but she had refused to think about it. Henri, from the beginning, had been aware that his wife was not really deceived. But Annette's silence had been like a concealing garment over a nakedness of which all were aware. She had torn aside that garment and revealed the nakedness. Neither she nor Celeste would ever forget that appalling moment of revelation.

In her own way, Annette was as friendless as Celeste. But Annette's friendlessness was even more painful to her, for there was a deep and vulnerable necessity in her for love. Her life had not cured her of this. Her attachment to Celeste was much stronger than Celeste's attachment to her, for Celeste had a core of hardness which withstood the final shock. Soon to be deprived even of Henri's casual presence, Annette felt herself bankrupt, now that she had smashed the painfully poised relationship between herself and Celeste. She had no one but her brother, and him she had never trusted.

In the long days and nights of her increasing suffering, she told herself the agonizing truth, over and over, that no one is safe from the assaults of living so long as he is not a fortress in himself, so long as he must rely upon another creature for love, understanding, or even for companionship. If his own company is not the most desirable, if another's hurt must also be his hurt, then he has opened some of the gates of his fortress, and made himself vulnerable to attack. He has deprived himself of that impregnability which is necessary for peace.

Why, all my gates are open! she said to herself, with wry sadness. But, in revolt, she also thought: Yet if one withdraws completely, he is like a snail, a bi-sexual snail, procreating in the narrow confines of a shell and producing only its own image, retreating always, blind always, and never admitting that anything exists beyond itself.

As always her sad reflections came to only one conclusion: she must make herself needed, somewhere, somehow; she must make herself useful. The habits of a whole lifetime shrank from this. But, she thought, with unusual grimness, I have a soul to save—my own.

She refused to listen to the complaints of her fragile body when she began to take an active part in the local Relief Organization. She learned to knit; she learned to roll bandages. She was the organizer of the local blood bank in connection with the Red Cross. She mended clothing and learned to make simple garments. She contributed huge sums of money to the American Freedom Association, and to relief societies who sent vast amounts of clothing and medical supplies to Britain and to Russia. Later, after her divorce, she intended to take part in the relief efforts in England. If she was exhausted at night, she also experienced the anodyne of weariness. I am actually working, she would say to herself, with ironic surprise, as her maid undressed her and prepared her for bed.

The family watched her with amazement, and with a reluctant compassion. Her brother protested. But she would only smile and declare that she felt first-rate. And, strange to say, her frail health did not decline. In fact, her fragility became that keen wiriness so often found in small and active people. If it had not been for that cancerous ache in her heart, she would have been happier than at any other time in her life.

Thanksgiving Day, 1941, was approaching. Annette and Celeste had not met for several weeks. But the whole family in Windsor, and some of the Chandlers in New York, were invited to dinner at the Emile Bouchards'. Celeste's impulse was to refuse. Then she saw the ridiculousness of the situation. She, alone, would be absent. There would be many sly comments. Worse, Annette would believe that Celeste had not "forgiven" her.

It had been hard enough in the past two years for Celeste to meet Henri and Annette in public with casualness and poise, aware always of inimical and curious eyes. Now, it would be much more terrible. The family, informed, naturally, by its own peculiar grapevine, must surely know of her break with Henri, and her quarrel with Annette. Unreasoningly, she believed this. She would stand alone, open to contempt and laughter, now. Nevertheless, she must go to that dinner. Each member of the family took his turn in the holiday entertaining of the rest, and it had become a tradition despite the fact that it had never yet occurred that every member was on speaking terms with all the other members, at the same time. This lady and that had been avoiding each other for several weeks; this gentleman and that hated each other malignantly, and had not met since last Thanksgiving Day. Enmity, intrigue and plotting might be going on among factions and sub-factions. Yet, on Thanksgiving Day, or Christmas, they met with open geniality, shook hands, drank together, joked, gossiped, and laughed heartily.

Peter and Armand were dead. They would be more present, in their absence, than they had actually been in life. Peter had almost always sat beside Annette. Jean ("deadly little Jean") would be there now. Armand, gormandizing next to his sister-in-law, Agnes, would have his place taken by Henri. In a way, thought Agnes, laying the place-cards, there was a great deal of irony in this situation.

Agnes, who was a subtle woman, felt a kind of vast fatality in the air at this Thanksgiving. She, like almost everyone, believed that America would soon be involved in the roaring conflagration that sent its long flames across the Atlantic. How long would it be before laden Thanksgiving tables would be lighter, and certain chairs would be empty? As she filled flower-vases all over the rich and profuse mansion which she and Emile had built together (robbing Europe of many of its treasures) she felt a deep and spiritual malaise. She felt also that she was not alone in this. Millions of American women were looking at their tables, and wondering, with sadness, as she was wondering. The fruit or flower center-pieces were trembling continually in the cold gales that swept across the oceans, and no tight walls, no locked doors, could keep out their deadly breath. The windows, so heavily covered with rich draperies, shivered with the unheard rever-berations that reached America from the great vomiting guns in Russia.

For the first time, Agnes felt some mournful sadness for the Bouchards. Some sympathy for their plight as members of humanity. Some affection even for the worst of them. She scrutinized her lavish table with more anxiety and sternness than usual.

But she knew also that terrible things would not end when the war ended. Evil had been too deeply plowed into the living earth of the whole world. Cruelties and abominations had become too much of a habit to countless millions of men. Mania and sadness had invaded too many brains, had scarred and crippled too many souls. What had begun in only one decade would continue for many decades, perhaps for cen-turies. One could not say, when war ended: "It is over, and done. Let us forget. It happened yesterday. There is tomor-row before us."

It would not be over, would not be done. It could not be forgotten. It would happen today, and tomorrow, and the day after tomorrow, so long as man recorded his history. The evil had been plowed too deep. Blood had flowed too abun-dantly for the earth to absorb it quickly. Hatred had known too strong a blossoming for its seeds to die. This most hor-rible thing would be contemporary when the peace-tables had gathered dust, and the diplomats who had signed the peace had long been dissolved in the earth. It would remain, like a pestilential and stricken mountain, among the events of men, time out of mind.

Celeste had put her child to bed, and had just turned out

537

the light, when she was summoned to the telephone. It was a call from New York.

"Hello!" said a lively, masculine voice. "Celeste, this is Godfrey."

"Godfrey?" repeated Celeste, her mind frantically searching.

"Godfrey Barbour. Remember me? In Paris, and Cannes, and half a dozen other places?"

"Why, certainly, Godfrey!" exclaimed Celeste, somewhat dazed. "Where on earth are you? I thought you were in London, last? What are you doing here?"

The young man chuckled. He had a very agreeable voice, faintly British. "Complications! Complications!" he said. "But I'll tell you later." His voice changed. "Dreadfully sorry about Peter, Celeste. Didn't hear about it until yesterday, in New York. What am I doing here? Why, my child, I'm living, at the present time, with a friend, Alfred Milch, the movieman. Ever heard of him? We're old friends. He used to run over from England to produce pictures in Paris and Germany, but no go since Hitler. Nice Hebraic chap. We're discussing my going to Hollywood, where he is to produce three thrillers, and he's trying to induce me to go along. My 'art' might get some appreciation there."

Celeste was still dazed, but also amused and excited. Godfrey Barbour, she was enlightened by the gentleman himself, had arrived in New York less than a week ago, by Clipper. Yes, he said, he could be persuaded, with not too much effort, to come to Windsor this very night, by plane, and join the family relatives tomorrow. "You're the only one of the family I've ever met, really," he said. "Are they really as frightful as they say?"

"Not really," laughed Celeste. She was becoming delighted, remembering Godfrey. "I'll call Agnes immediately, after we've done. Agnes? She is my brother Emile's wife. You'll be quite dizzy making out the relationships. I'll have a car waiting at the airport for you. You'll stay with me, of course. I've the most enormous house. And," now she hesitated a little, "I also have a baby. Over a year old. Fifteen months, in fact."

She felt refreshed and anticipatory when she had concluded her conversation. She sat near the telephone, smiling to herself. How was Godfrey related to the family? She tried to disentangle the relationships. Godfrey was the grandson of Godfrey Sessions Barbour, oldest son of Ernest Barbour. He, too, could claim the legendary Ernest as his great-grand-father, as could Henri. Henri's grandmother had been Gertrude Barbour, sister of Godfrey. This Godfrey, in his hatred for his father, Ernest, had assumed his mother's maiden name, Sessions, but upon the birth of his son, Aristide, he had reverted to his real name. It was this son, Aristide (whose mother had been Renée Bouchard), who was the father of the present Godfrey, a young man about Celeste's own age. Godfrey's mother had been an English girl. Both of his parents were now dead.

The Bouchards had shown no interest whatsoever in the dead Aristide, or in his son, Godfrey. In truth, they had not at all forgotten that Ernest Barbour had been the father of the great American composer, Godfrey Sessions. But Godfrey's son, Aristide, had aroused no curiosity or family interest in them. Some of the older Bouchards had remembered him as a dull fat little man, "black and greasy," as Armand had expressed it, resembling the spare blond Godfrey not in the slightest. His appearance, and his temperament, came from the early Bouchards. (He was a grandson of the original Armand Bouchard.) They had heard a rumor that he had lived a great deal of his time in England, and there had married that obscure English girl, whom no one had ever met. Young Godfrey had been born in England, but had lived the greater part of his life in Paris.

Upon his death, it was discovered that Ernest Barbour had provided generously for his son, the first Godfrey, but in a cautious manner. Not trusting the artistic nature, he had created a French trust fund for Godfrey. Eugene Bouchard, great friend and brother-in-law of Ernest (he had married Dorcas, Ernest's sister), had been the father of Renée, Godfrey's wife, and he, too, upon Ernest's promptings, had established a French trust fund for his daughter. These funds had, for many years, provided a very comfortable subsistence for the first Godfrey and his wife, but through subsequent decades changing conditions had reduced the income considerably. Upon the death of the first Godfrey's mother, May Sessions Barbour, wife of Ernest, it was discovered that she had left her favorite son over seven hundred thousand dollars. Godfrey, displaying a shrewdness quite inconsistent with his general character, had founded a British trust fund for his son, Aristide, out of his legacy, a trust fund of respectable proportions. He used the balance to augment his own shrinking income.

The first Godfrey had been the composer of four excellent symphonies, but one only was now played with any degree of regularity. He had also composed innumerable sonatas, concertos and serenades. Only a few of these were well-known. His son, Aristide, upon the death of Godfrey (whom he had adored in his dull, taciturn way), had attempted to revive his father's compositions in every European capital. He had financed several orchestras. As a result, his income, already shrinking through vicisscitudes of the years, was almost completely devoured. Upon his death, it was found that he had been able to leave his son, young Godfrey, less than twenty thousand dollars.

Young Godfrey, in somewhat the manner of Antoine Bouchard, had been a dilettante. He had shown an easy aptitude for the piano, he had an excellent baritone voice, could paint quite well, and had written two thin volumes of poetry. But none of his talents was remarkable. Having a great deal of intelligence and shrewdness, he early saw that he must earn his living. He had invested half his legacy in a French moving-picture concern, which he later had to take over, himself. He was able to obtain the services of third-rate French actresses, only, and their male counterparts, but as he wrote the scripts himself, and showed much genius in directing and producing, he had just begun to acquire considerable fame as a producer of small but fine pictures, when the war broke out.

Peter and Celeste had come across him quite accidentally. When they had first gone to live at Cannes, they had attended a party given by a neighbor, a handsome elderly woman who was a retired and famous actress. At that time, Peter had responded wonderfully to the clear warm air of Cannes, and often accepted invitations before his illness again became enervating. There were many guests there, and Peter and Celeste had moved smilingly from one group to another, when they had been accosted by a very pleasant and personable young man.

"I say," he had said, with a smile, "I think we are relatives. Are you connected with the famous, or the infamous, Bouchards, of America, the big gunmen?"

Peter had laughed. He had liked Godfrey at first sight. He admitted that he was indeed one of the "big gunmen." Godfrey had then gone on to explain the relationship. He had the most witty way of talking, and free expressive gestures inherited from his French grandmother, and he was so affable, so gay, so gently clever, that both Peter and

Celeste had been charmed. They saw there was no malice in him, but only brilliant humor, and that his jokes were on himself, and never on others. He talked volubly, but so fascinatingly, that the hearer was never impatient. It was evident that he had an enormous zest in life, and that he found almost everything amusing, delightful and full of interest. One could not imagine him ever being bored, or cruel, or sullen or vengeful. He was, at that time, living with the actress' granddaughter. Both the old and the young woman adored him. He and his mistress were permanent guests at the villa.

He had talked to Celeste and Peter almost exclusively that night, while his pretty little mistress scowled in a corner. He confessed his impecunious condition, but with such gaiety that he made it seem one of the most delightful conditions in the world, and one to be envied. But when Peter had inevitably spoken of Hitler and Naziism, the young man's face had changed, had become strangely dark, strong and brooding. Moreover, he had appeared oddly distressed. Later, Peter learned that the elder and wealthy actress was one of Hitler's great admirers, and that she, and her friends, were serving him as a sort of aristocratic espionage service among the decadent and depraved members of the Salons Internationals. When Peter learned that, he was no longer surprised at the sudden disappearance of Godfrey some six weeks before. He heard that Godfrey had gone to England, and had vanished there, leaving his mistress and her grandmother bewildered and desolate. Peter and Celeste had not seen him again.

As Celeste recalled all these things, she remembered Godfrey very clearly. Before his disappearance, he had often come to their own villa, and Peter had enjoyed his company with simple pleasure. As if he stood before her now, Celeste could see Godfrey's slight and active figure, full of wiry strength and vivid health. She remembered his extraordinary flaxen hair, so pale that it was almost white, and his very dark brown eyes that were always glinting and mirthful. His complexion, too, was dark, and so threw his hair into startling contrast. He was indeed all contradiction. He had the Barbour short broad nose, strong and harsh in contour, with wide nostrils, and the square Barbour chin with its deep dimple. But his mouth, though firm and sharp of outline, was also kind, and very often, gentle. Five years had not

541

blurred Celeste's memory of him. She saw him in her mind's eye, with all his features undimmed.

She called Agnes, and explained the situation. Agnes was quite diverted, and pleased. "A real Barbour!" she said. "We've forgotten, it seems, that the Great Paterfamilias was a Barbour. Any resemblance to the rest of the family?"

Celeste hesitated. "Well, no. He is both dark and light. And very witty, and very charming. Peter and I were very fond of him."

"And he is to stay with you, my dear?"

"Yes," said Celeste. "I'm becoming an elderly widow now. Do you think there might be scandal?"

"I think not," said Agnes, wryly.

She asked, a little later: "Is he rich? His grandfather was Godfrey Barbour, old Ernest's son. There ought to be money there."

Celeste replied, with considerable dryness: "If his fortunes haven't improved during the past five years, and I have a feeling they haven't, then he is practically penniless. He did say something about going to Hollywood with a producer friend of his. Godfrey is interested in moving pictures, you know."

"O my God," said Agnes. "So, he's that sort, eh?"

For some reason, Celeste was annoyed. But she knew that anything she might say in Godfrey's defense would only further distort the picture of him.

She awaited his arrival with pleasure and excitement. Godfrey had been her friend. She realized how bankrupt in friendship she was, that she must await the coming of a single human creature with such anticipation.

CHAPTER LXV

A light fine snow had begun to fall in the evening, so that the dark earth sparkled as if sprinkled with sequins. It was cold and sharp and fresh, and for the first time in many years Celeste felt suddenly festive. The fixed and burning pain in her heart seemed less unbearable tonight. She dressed herself carefully in a gown of black and white, and then, hesitating and smiling, she tucked a white flower in her hair. The face she confronted in the mirror might be stern and pale, with a red mouth whose outlines might be sharply cut and stiff, but it was also a beautiful face.

When she heard the sound of the returning car, she ran quickly downstairs, and was waiting in the hall at the foot of the stairs when Godfrey Barbour entered. She saw the door open, and out from the dark the snow swirled in, a scattered and disintegrating cloud of whiteness, and she heard the voice of the chauffeur, speaking encouragingly: "There now, easy, sir, another step here. Right it is."

Celeste's hand reached out fumblingly and clutched the banister, as she stood there, waiting, a straight and slender figure, all lovely outlines in its black, white-touched gown. But her new color had suddenly gone, and there was a strange, dreadful beating in her breast. For she heard uncertain and hesitant steps, a hard tapping, and then Godfrey's well-remembered and gay voice: "Can't get used to these damned things!"

Now the cloud of snow-particles were sucked back into the night, and Godfrey was entering, the supporting chauffeur compassionately at his side. Celeste stared. Her hand lifted and pressed itself fiercely against her heart. For the young man she saw now was in the uniform of a Royal Air Force captain, and he swung himself forward awkwardly on crutches. His right leg had been amputated above the knee.

But none of the gaiety, none of the life and the zest and the bright humor had gone from that dark face, now so emaciated and parched with suffering. The dark brown eyes sparkled upon Celeste; the jaunty cap was perched at a debonair and precarious angle on the extraordinary flaxen hair. Weaving dangerously on his crutches, he lifted his hand and saluted Celeste and laughed with pleasure at seeing her. He totally ignored the chauffeur, who had literally caught him in his strong arms, and was holding him balanced while he completed the salute.

"Celeste!" cried the young man, joyously. "It's the old girl, herself!"

But Celeste's vision had dimmed, so that she saw nothing but swirling rainbows. She flung out her arms. She ran to Godfrey, and put those arms tightly about him, hugging him

543

in a kind of frantic despair and sorrow. She pressed her head against his shoulder, and then kissed his cheek, sobbing over and over beneath her breath.

"Hey, what is this?" cried the young man, at last, gently taking her chin in his hand and searching her face. "Is this a proper greeting, I ask you? Why the tears, my pet? Here, let me look at you."

But Celeste clung to him, weeping. "O Godfrey, how terrible, how terrible! You never told me!"

And Godfrey said: "What's wrong, dear?" His kind brown eyes, ordinarily so merry, were now full of subtle pity and concern. "You've changed, Celeste."

She was outraged that he thought of her. She held one of his arms with both hands. She shuddered at the sight of the crutches. "Come into the room!" she cried. "Where you can sit down, and rest."

But he gently resisted. Now he no longer smiled, though his expression was still kind. "Celeste, my love, I'm not a cripple, really. I can get about on these damn things first-rate. It's a matter of learning new balance. And in a few months I'll have a fine wooden leg, and only a little limp. You'll never know the difference. And now, be a good girl, and watch me manipulate with my customary dexterity."

She dropped her hands. She watched him swing away from her awkwardly, swaying. She saw his fine strong back twisting his uniform into pathetic ridges, and the painful tilting of his shoulders. The back of his flaxen head looked so valiant, so undaunted and determined, tipping backwards as he thrust his body forward with the crutches. His neck reddened, and so did his ears, with the unusual effort, and strain. Celeste suddenly closed her eyes on a spasm of pity and grief. She followed him. She did not assist him, though she ached to do so. She sat down quietly, watching him as he fumbled and swayed and manœuvered himself into a chair. Then, with a sigh and a little laugh, he placed his crutches carefully side by side against a near-by table, and turned his attention upon Celeste. His face was damp and glistening, his smile a little fixed.

"Well, now," he said, "tell me everything." He helped himself to a cigarette from the table, and lit it. She saw that his hands were trembling.

She said, in a low voice: "Godfrey. Why?"

The light he held flared up, and she saw his face a moment, stark and dangerous and full of cold hatred. Then that expression had gone, and he appeared thoughtfully indifferent. "Why? It just happens, sweet, that I hate Germans. Not just Nazis; not Hitlerites; not Junkers or soldiers or duelling students. Just Germans. The lovely, kind little German burghers gouging each other in the shops and the offices and the small businesses; the sweet German mädchen who is treacherous, mean and greedy; the handsome youth with the fresh cheeks who is not even a barbarian, but just a cowardly murderer; the German man in the street, the German woman at the markets, the German farmer and the German hausfrau. I hate them all, Celeste. I want to see them die."

He spoke with such detachment, even indifference, that his words were enhanced in their ferocity, rather than diminished. He had put his cigarette to his lips; she saw the sudden strong burning of its tip as if he had drawn a quick savage breath. He was staring before him.

"It wasn't love for England, my sweet, that sent me into the Air Force. It wasn't tenderness for dear old filthy, lying, crafty and greedy France. It was only hatred. You see, I know so much about Germans. I lived in Germany quite a few years."

She had never seen Godfrey like this, and even when he shrugged his shoulders, smiled again, his eyes dancing as of old, she was still horror-stricken at the cold and deadly look he had worn for an instant or two, and the iron and ringing sound of his quiet voice. She thought: What a terrible thing it is for the Germans to have this on their conscience: that they have made men hate them so that these men could forget all civilized instincts of gentleness and compassion, and hate with even greater ferocity.

"It is not Hitler. It never was Hitler," said Godfrey. "It was, and is, always the German people. Hitler just catered to their instincts, and was able to get his brothers-under-the-skin to help him in Europe. And in America, probably."

"A drink?" asked Celeste, after a moment's silence.

"Yes," he answered, smiling at her fondly. He watched her. "Come. A little more of that whiskey, pet. A lot more. And very little of the soda."

They sat before the fire, glasses and ice sparkling on a small table near them. Celeste gave a glass to Godfrey. She watched him as he gulped its contents quickly, as if he was enormously thirsty. "More?" she said, when he removed the glass from his lips. She was not surprised, and only sad, when he nodded. He watched her pour the golden whiskey into the glass again, and add the soda, which hissed loud in the warm, firelit silence. This time he did not gulp. He sipped, his elbow on his left knee. She tried not to look at the stump, which was so neatly folded into its blue trouser. She fixed her attention on Godfrey, and it seemed to her that as the moments passed the squeezing pain about her heart was becoming unbearable.

The mask of Godfrey Barbour was there, smiling and attentive as always, even gay and light and zestful. But there were moments, she discerned, when the old mask would slip aside, and show his new and dreadfully real face.

"Do you want to tell me about it, Frey?" she asked.

He still smiled, yet he gave the impression of frowning, also. He shook his head. "No, I don't, Celeste. I will tell you this, though." He tapped his stump. "This happened over Berlin. We were given industrial targets before we set out. Always industrial targets! They're probably most necessary, I admit. But, I wanted something else. I wanted to kill Germans more than I wanted to blow up an airplane factory or a tank plant. Just wanted to kill Germans, male or female, big or small. You see, I would prevent them from breeding more Germans to harass the world some twenty-five years from now. I turned off the scheduled flight. I got the plane over the residential districts for a few split seconds." He paused. He sipped again, took the glass from his lips, and looked at the fire. There was a red reflected glow in the sockets of his eyes, and it gave him a terrible look. "All the bombs went there, from my Thunderbolt. All of them. Right on the houses, the streets, the shelters. I was killing Germans. You can't know what joy that brings to a realistic man, Celeste."

He looked down at his stump, long and fixedly. "That's when this happened. But it was more than a fair exchange. I had probably killed scores of Germans. I paid for it with half a leg. It was little enough."

He held out his glass to her automatically, and again she filled it.

"And now," he said, in his old tone, light and warm with affection, "what have you been doing, Celeste? You know, I heard about Peter. He suffered so, poor old chap. And the baby? I suppose I may see him?"

Celeste glanced aside, and he wondered, fleetingly, at the closed and uneasy expression of her mouth. She said: "Oh, of course. But tomorrow, Frey. We'll have dinner soon, when you are ready. Your room is ready." She paused, then said in a quicker, livelier voice: "You don't know how good it is to see you again! Peter and I were so fond of you, Frey. He often spoke of you after we had come home."

"Good old Peter," he murmured, and there was genuine sadness in his voice. "I suppose I should have written, after I went to England. But I couldn't think of anyone there, at Cannes, along the Riviera, without feeling sick. You and Peter were different. Yet, you were there. I wanted to cut myself away, clean."

"Yes, I understand," said Celeste, softly. She looked at him with tenderness. Some old painful rigidity in her was relaxing, some old painful wariness and distress.

They talked now, of the war, of the probability of America's embroilment, of the family he had never seen. He was particularly interested in the last. But he laughed in protest as Celeste tried to unravel the complexities of relationship. "That's enough!" he cried. "You make it sound like incest."

Celeste was suddenly pale and rigid again. She looked aside. "It is," she murmured. "Spiritual incest. You don't know the Bouchards, Godfrey."

"I bet I'll find them interesting!" he said.

Celeste asked him if he had married, and he shook his head, laughing. "No. I was never in love. Not really. Except once, perhaps."

"And you couldn't marry her, Frey?"

He leaned forward to place his empty glass very carefully on the table. All his movements were slow and precise. She saw his profile, and it was no longer open and careless, as she remembered it, but secret and restrained. Yet, his mouth was smiling.

"No," he said, indifferently. "She was already married. Very unfortunate. There was nothing I could do. Her husband was my friend."

He turned to her now, and there was a bland smoothness, opaque and unreadable, about his eyes, which reminded her, painfully, of Henri. She stared at him, and to her dazed senses it seemed that there was something about him that was powerfully suggestive of the absent man. She pushed her chair back a little.

He saw this, and frowned to himself. Had he frightened her, or aroused her suspicions? My darling, he thought, why the hell do you think I came here, anyway?

They went in to dinner. The dining-room was now no longer chill and empty for Celeste, nor full of dreary cold shadows. The candles burned warmly, throwing soft flickering lights upon her face. Godfrey was delighted and exuberant about the dinner. "You don't know what all this means after rationing!" he cried. "All the roast beef I want, by God! And butter! And sugar. It's a miracle!"

He ate with appetite. He was so gay and pleasant and simply happy. His shrewd remarks and epigrams kept Celeste helpless with laughter. It had been so long since this room had heard her laughter, or her voice, eager and alive as now. She forgot his mutilation. Her face glowed; her eyes were blue dancing lights. He did not remark on the streak of whiteness in her hair, nor did he appear to glance at it. But he knew it was there; he was completely aware of it. Sometimes, in the intervals of her laughter, he saw the marks of pain about her mouth, and the mauve shadows under her eyes.

They sat for hours at the table. When they finally returned to the fire for coffee, Celeste felt young and free again, light and dizzy. And they sat by the fire until the last coals had turned to ash, and midnight had long gone.

For the first time in many weeks, Celeste fell asleep as soon as her head touched the pillow, and she smiled a little, as she slept. The house, formerly so deserted and desolate to her, so barren of human life and joy, closed about her warmly like the friendly walls of home.

CHAPTER LXVI

It had always seemed to Celeste that pain had been her familiar from her earliest consciousness. She had become so accustomed to it that on the few and scattered occasions when she had known happiness there had been a kind of hysteria in her joy, a disorientation, as if she had become drunk. Sometimes she had thought: I think I can bear anything with ease, except happiness. For happiness had always created a wild tension in her, a thrilling spasm which caused her heart to beat too rapidly for comfort.

But the pain her final separation from Henri had produced had been too much even for one so inured to suffering. She had abandoned, in her grief, all pretenses of living normally, of revealing to the outside world even the show of tranquil existence. Even her child had not been able to lift from her mind the crushing blackness and desolation, the long cold misery of hopelessness and sorrow. She had begun to wander, as Armand had wandered, through the empty rooms of her house, looking blindly through windows at the autumn landscape, feeling in herself no response to any stimulus, no care and no desire. A thousand times she said to herself: But I always knew what he was.

But her reason was impotent against this ball of cold and iron weight in her throat and breast. She never cried out in despair, for despair is the sister of hope. She had no hope. There were times when she asked herself: What is to become of me? But even the silence that answered her question had no power to agitate and torture her. A thick dullness had begun to settle on her face, to echo in her voice, to make all her gestures languid and heavy. She did not care whether others knew. When Christopher visited her and talked to her, when her other relatives literally forced her to come to their houses, she answered them, and looked at them, with an endless weariness and emptiness. She heard them as from a far distance, and they had begun to lose dimension for her, so that they appeared like wearisome and annoying shadows from which she must soon deliver herself.

Her mornings had been the worst of all, for during sleep she often forgot her desolate state. For a few seconds she would lie peacefully on her pillows, vaguely staring at her windows and thinking of her child. Then the initial pain, for only a few instants, would return like a mortal agony, and she would turn her face down as if to drive memory from her in one convulsive act of suffocation.

She did not think of Henri acutely. He was only a symbol of her pain. She did not long for him, nor even desire that he should come to her. Her suffering was like a disease, which she could only endure numbly. There had been one time when she discovered that she could no longer breathe with comfort, and that the slightest exertion provoked breathlessness and sharp pain. Then, she had been frightened. If she died, what would become of her child? She had visited her physician, who, after a few shrewd questions, and quiet scrutiny, had shrugged and prescribed sedatives for her. The sedatives had dulled the violence of her anguish, had left it throbbing far off from her. It had also dulled her thoughts. One day, she was amazed to discover it was the middle of November. Time had stood still for her.

It was no wonder then, that when she awoke the morning after Godfrey Barbour's arrival and did not feel that old hideous plunge into agony, she was utterly amazed. She sat up in bed, and waited. But she felt nothing but a curious sense of consolation and tranquillity. Everything, too, had taken on clarity, and was no longer outlined with the dim haze of drug-induced lethargy. She saw the rim of bright snow on the window-sills, the crystal branches of the tree that tapped the shining glass. She saw the pale and sparkling blue of the November sky, streaked here and there with white veils. She sprang out of bed and looked out over the brown hills, glittering with frost, and the dark vitality of the evergreens that surrounded the house. The room was full of fresh cold air, but she stood in her nightdress, her hands and face pressed against the window, and the clear and brilliant light lay on her pale face and in her staring eyes.

Her maid, entering discreetly, was surprised to see her mistress standing there, and was even more surprised when Celeste turned, smiling. Was Mr. Barbour up? she asked, and when she heard that he was, she hurried through her bathing, and then studied the dress she would wear. She finally chose a crimson wool. She discovered that her hands were trembling, that a thin and excited pulse was beating in her throat. On the way from her room she passed a bowl of red roses. Smiling, she took a flower and thrust its stem through her black hair.

She ran down the stairs to the breakfast room, whose south wall of windows was filled with flowering plants. Godfrey was standing there on his crutches, looking out over the hills and the white plain of shining snow that lay between them and the house. He turned when she entered, and stretched out his hand, laughing. "Hello! This is a fine place you have here, my pet! And how well you are looking this morning!"

She caught his hand impulsively between her own, and cried: "O Frey, you don't know how glad I am that you are here!"

He looked down at her, and was silent, though his smile

550

was wide. But his eyes narrowed a trifle, searchingly. And then he said: "Are you sure, Celeste? You are really glad?"

"O yes. So very glad. I've been so lonely, Frey." Her words, her voice, her look, were simple and moving, like a child's, and because he was both subtle and intuitive, he guessed that she had been suffering for a long time for some reason unknown to him. Was it poor old Pete? Certainly: that was it. He remembered her devotion to Peter, and a pang of something sharply like jealousy passed through him. How lonely she must have been, indeed, in her grief. Her family, then, was no comfort to her, no joy. Not even the child, evidently. His heart suddenly rose giddily as he saw how fresh she appeared this morning, and how the deep blue of her eyes was alive and sparkling. She had such a pure simplicity, this poor darling little creature, such candor and openness. He looked down at the hands that held him, and impulsively he lifted one and kissed it.

He wondered how she would take this. But when he looked up, she was smiling, and her cheeks were glowing. He drew out a chair for her, and she let him do it, to his gratitude, and did not appear to notice how he swayed on his crutches. He sat near her, and surveyed the pleasant table with its crystal and silver with open admiration. "I'd forgotten, really, how nice peace is," he said. "And how nice snow is, and the country, and lighted houses. I think I'm going to like America. When you come down to it, I'm an American, after all. Or am I?" he added, pausing with his glass of orange juice near his lips.

She pretended to regard the question seriously. The air about her was all lightness and childlike gaiety. Then she shook her head. "I'm afraid not. You were born in England, weren't you? Your father was born in France. What does your passport say?"

"I've a British passport. But really, I'm an American. By the way, in Manchester, I discovered a family of Barbours who I believe belong to us. Shopkeepers. There was a chap who was one of our mechanics. A fresh and sturdy brute of a young fellow, with pale grey eyes like stone. Remarkable damn resemblance to a photograph of a mutual relative, Henri Bouchard." He paused, with some surprise, for all at once Celeste's color had gone, and her lips had changed. She had dropped her eyes; her hand lay quietly on the table silver. "Did I say something wrong?" he asked.

She looked up quickly. Her expression was quite dead.

"No, not at all. But it's very interesting about those Barbours. Do tell me more, Frey."

"There isn't very much to tell," he said, watching her with furtive keenness. "I met the family. Working-class, but good and healthy. Yes, they were our Barbours. This young chap's great-grandfather had been a George Barbour, who had got a start in America, and then had been robbed by his brother's son, our good old Ernest Barbour. Georgie had gone back to England, and opened a draper's shop. This young chap, Edward, however, was a fine mechanic. He said he was going to patent an invention of his. Something about a radio detector, or something equally mysterious. Said he had some fellows very interested. Hope something comes of it. There's a drive in him. When I told him I was done, and was going to America, he wanted to know if I could interest some people here. I have the blueprint in my luggage, and perhaps, if I have the time, I'll haul it out and give it an airing among the boys, for their opinion."

Celeste was listening with interest. Her color was returning, but very slowly. When she spoke, it was with an effort. "That would be nice for—what did you say his name was?"

"Edward. Edward Barbour."

After breakfast, Celeste ordered the baby to be brought down for inspection. Godfrey insisted upon holding him upon his knee, and dandled him. The child played with his buttons, and fingered the bit of ribbon and the medal on his chest. He looked up at Godfrey without shyness, and an odd contained smile. "Handsome little devil," said Godfrey. "And believe it or not, he's got Ed Barbour's eyes. That curious bright pale grey. It must run in the family. Crops out here and there in the generations."

Celeste called for a car, and they drove out into the brilliant November light. Celeste's spirits had returned in good measure. She laughingly indulged Godfrey when he insisted upon getting out of the car and standing in the thin layer of snow. "I'm going to like America!" he exclaimed. The car had stopped near a thick woods, and Godfrey surveyed the tall bare trees with pleasure. A pheasant whirred near them. In the distance a farmhouse chimney fumed against the pale pure blue of the cold sky. A dog barked, and the echo of his barking fell back from the woods with sharp clarity. Shafts of radiant sunshine and shadows of scudding clouds raced over the white and undulating valley. Godfrey took off his blue RAF cap, and the cold fresh wind blew through his flaxen hair. A stain of color appeared on his thin and sunken cheeks. When they were back in the car, and turned homeward, he began to sing. He held Celeste's hand, and the warmth of his own penetrated through her glove. Soon, she was laughing with him, and singing foolish popular songs. Her face was pink, framed beautifully in the rim of fur that lined her woolen hood. She had forgotten Godfrey's lost leg, and when his crutches clattered down at their feet, she joined in his merriment and pretended to be shocked at his profanity. Their bodies were warm and close under the fur robe.

She did not even try to analyze the light delirium of her senses when she dressed to go to the family dinner. It was not exactly joy or delight, she knew. It was, rather, a release from unbearable black tension and cold close misery. She put on a white-and-silver gown, and put silver flowers in her hair. She had never worn this gown. She surveyed herself in her mirror with pleasure, her dark full mouth smiling and soft.

It was Godfrey who put her cape of white fur over her bare shoulders. She was too bemused to notice how his hands lingered a moment or two, or how his fingers brushed her soft flesh. But when she turned her head and glanced up at him, her heart stopped strangely for a moment. For he was very pale, his mouth set, and his eyes were full of a peculiar light.

She knew that Henri and Annette would be at Agnes' dinner. But not once during the drive to Emile's home did she think of Henri. It was as if her consciousness had enclosed the thought of him in a hard thick capsule that could not be penetrated. However, by the time her car turned in up the long avenue that led to the house she was conscious of a vague chilliness, and a dimness in her mind.

CHAPTER LXVII

Even the family's cruel anticipation of watching the meeting between Henri and Celeste had taken second place to their curiosity with regard to Godfrey Barbour. It had been so long since there had been an active Barbour in the family. They speculated upon his penniless state, his reasons for coming to America, and his appearance. Was he a musician like his grandfather, the first Godfrey? Perhaps he even wrote books, God forbid! Was he looking for charity from the family? If so, he had come to the wrong place. They were annoyed that Celeste had given so little information to Agnes, and Agnes was exasperated when they asked her the same questions repeatedly. "I tell you, I don't know," she would say. "He arrived last night. That's the full extent of my enlightenment. But Celeste did sound excited and pleased. She and Peter were great friends of Godfrey's, in France."

"Oh, he's probably one of those damned refugees, then," said the vitriolic Rosemarie, to her dark and simpering sister, Phyllis. "Or looking for cash for a lot of vermin-stricken Free French or Poles, or God knows what."

"The country is overrun with the creatures," said Phyllis. "We'll live to regret it. That's the Communist influence, of course. They're all Communists."

Celeste and Godfrey arrived somewhat late. When they were announced, a rustling murmur ran over the family, congregated around the fire in one of Emile's great ornate drawing-rooms. They hardly saw Celeste in her radiant silver gown. For, when they saw Godfrey in his uniform, swinging along on his crutches, an amused and watchful smile on his mouth, the whole family drew one long breath, and held it. A strange and heavy silence fell over them, and they stood in awkward fixed attitudes of uneasy shock. The blazing firelight glimmered on the jewels and sequinned gowns of the women, but it was as if those gowns had been draped upon motionless dummies and the faces turned to Celeste and Godfrey were tinted plastic masks.

Celeste had never possessed much social poise, but this sudden discomfiture of her relatives gave her the advantage. With high serenity, and smiling a little, she introduced her guest. She brought him, on his crutches, to one group after another, and he looked at them all with a fresh and intent interest, his eye flashing over each face shrewdly. As he progressed, those already introduced stared after him expressionlessly.

He met the little, dark and dimpled Jean, ageless in his small plumpness and eager affability, and his great blond and stupid wife, Alexa. He gathered that Jean was the brother of Peter, Celeste's dead husband, and president of the Sessions Steel Company, subsidiary of Bouchard & Sons. He saw the real charm of this vivacious little man, which to him, for he was not naïve, compensated a great deal for the natural villainy which sparkled in his dancing bits of eyes. His children eyed Godfrey with that blank curiosity which displayed the modern fashion of lack of manners.

Then there was the bachelor, Nicholas Bouchard, fifty-three years old, son of Leon Bouchard, brother to Jules, president of the Windsor National Bank, and director of both the Manhattan Merchants Trust Company and the internationally potent Morse National Bank, controlled by Jay Regan. Godfrey was not prepossessed by Nicholas, "that dirty man," for Nicholas was short and uncouth, obstinate and avaricious even to the most casual glance, tenacious and truculent of expression, and cunningly astute. His complexion was greenish, and his rough short hair, once of a greenish cast also, was now composed of untidy patches of uncombed gray. He had successfully resisted the attempts of his sisters-in-law to marry him off, and now that they had failed, they contemplated him and said, openly, "Well, it was a blessing for some woman that he never married." He was not only ungroomed, but gave the impression of soiled linen and unpressed clothing. He grunted when Godfrey was introduced to him, did not extend his hand, and stared after the young man with narrowed green eyes both cruel and mean.

Alexander, "the Deacon," magenta of complexion, enormous of swollen belly, with big legs, big smooth-skinned face, and gray curling hair, inspired Godfrey with distaste, as did his smirking, mean little wife with her simper. He was vice-president of Sessions. He greeted Godfrey in a booming voice, and interjected a platitude about blood being thicker than water, after all, and Godfrey had the feeling that little was needed to provoke him into giving a sonorous short sermon. It was evident that he believed himself to be the virtuous pillar of the family.

There was tawny Hugo, and his amiable and handsome Christine, and one of his daughters. Hugo, the politician, never forgot that every man was a potential voter, and though he knew that Godfrey was a British subject, he could not refrain from the politician's beaming address. He shook hands with heartiness.

There was Christopher, suave and parched, with his silvery "Egyptian" eyes, who acknowledged the introduction with polished cordiality. "Danger," thought Godfrey. He liked the plain, smart dark Edith, who looked at him with such direct and appraising nut-brown eyes, and he wondered how she could endure her husband. Francis was there, with his comely and horsy Estelle, and though Godfrey recognized the rascal, he also admitted to himself that in many ways Francis might be considered a "good" man. He passed over the short, dark, fat Robert with indifference, repelled by his surly and stupid face, and smiled engagingly at his pretty little wife.

Emile, his host, big, dark, bloated and very affable, had disgusted him instantly, and he had been conscious of a shrinking repulsion for him, but a great understanding. Agnes, he admired, as a "shrewd baggage," but an honest woman.

He looked at Rosemarie, Francis' daughter, and admired her smart and ugly perfection, and instantly thought to himself that here was a natural wanton and a deadly woman. He was not annoyed at her satirical survey of him and the quirk of her painted lips. He was only interested by the evidences of her heartlessness and greed and opportunism. Phyllis Morse, her sister, he considered a fool, with her fussy manners and her mean narrowed dark eyes. She was a vulgarian, he decided. Her husband, son of the powerful Richard Morse of the Morse National Bank, he dismissed as a robot, fearful, intolerant and dull. The eldest of her little girls was there, Bernadette, and he was startled at the clear blonde beauty of this sixteen-year-old girl with her radiant blue eyes. His sensibilities were not readily touched by anyone, but he lingered with the child, conscious of a feeling of strange sadness in himself. Later, when he learned that Phyllis destined her for a nunnery, he was as incredulously outraged as if he had been informed that she was to be sacrificed to Moloch on a smoking altar. Someway, he decided, this child must be saved from her monstrous mother's plannings, and he wondered if her very beauty had not inspired the unattractive Phyllis in her determination to immure her.

By this time, Godfrey was a little dizzy with the number of his relatives, and their relationship to each other and to himself. Celeste, gayly amused, tried to enlighten him upon each introduction, but after a while he began to shake his head muzzily, and greeted each new stranger with a laugh.

Some of the big, blond and silent Norwoods were there, whom he vaguely understood to be a collateral branch of the family by reason of the marriage of Jules' mother, Florabelle, to one Major Norwood far back in ante-bellum days. He did not try to memorize their names. He saw that, despite their wealth and position, they were nonentities. He gathered that a certain beefy young man was named Ernest Barbour Norwood, and when he looked at the large florid face and the empty blue eyes, he could hardly restrain some ribald laughter. This young man was a little less silent than his immediate relatives, and inquired at once if Godfrey was deeply interested in the coming game between Notre Dame and Yale.

While these introductions were taking place, Antoine and his little wife, Mary, arrived. (Henri and Annette were still absent.) Immediately upon seeing Antoine, Godfrey's flagging interest was revived and stimulated. He recognized a fellow dilettante, a European of taste and polish and intellect, a man of wit and grace and accomplishment. "Decadent as hell, like all of us," thought Godfrey, shaking hands with Antoine with real warmth and pleasure. And Antoine, looking keenly at the other, felt the same instantaneous magnetism of recognition, and though he had planned on being amused he was, rather, inspired by liking and fellowship. "I saw you once, in Paris!" exclaimed Godfrey, with enthusiasm, "though we never met. It was at the Marquise de Durand's salon. You were going it strong with her little protégée, Eloise, and though I suspected we were relatives in a way, I didn't think it delicate to interrupt."

"Ah, the Marquise!" said Antoine, in French, with his dark sparkling smile, and adding something highly improper, but very witty.

"Ah, Eloise!" said Godfrey, also adding a remark in the same language. They laughed together. If Antoine had been

557

curious at the sight of this young man with his stump and his uniform, and prepared to be humorous about him, he forgot it instantly. "Let us find an opportunity to get into a corner later, and converse," he said.

Little Mary stared emptily from one to the other, her pretty brows drawn together as she ruminated over these mutual remarks and tried to understand them with her limited French. She thought their sprightliness very odd, indeed. It had been a long time since she had seen Antoine so gay.

It was just then that Henri and Annette were announced, and though Godfrey was delightedly absorbed in his pleasure with Antoine, he could not but be aware, with his acuteness, that an odd silence had ensued, as at the coming of some feared and hated high personage. He thought: Why, it's as if a warning fanfare had been sounded, and the ranks had separated to admit his passage!

Celeste was standing near him, fluid and beautiful in her silver gown, and again that acute sensibility of Godfrey's became aware of a sudden rigidity in her, a paleness and coldness. He faced towards the archway, with the most intense curiosity.

When Henri entered, with Annette, he understood immediately. This was the image of Ernest Barbour, to the last pale short eyelash and curve of thick light brow. This was Ernest Barbour of the pale disklike eye, and heavy stony lips. Godfrey looked at his relative, and knew him for the antithesis of everything which he and Antoine represented, everything which was gay and warm and vital and suave, and everything which was decadent. Antoine was murmuring in his ear: "Here is the Power of the Bouchards. Old Stone Face. The Iron Man. And, it isn't a pose. He really is as repulsive as he appears. The lady with him is my sister." And Antoine's voice became softer. Godfrey glanced at him in surprise. Antoine was staring at Annette with brooding gentleness, and the most peculiar sadness.

Celeste, for some reason, did not appear to be able to move. Godfrey gave her a surprised glance, and then allowed himself to be piloted by Antoine to the new arrivals. Antoine did not attempt to assist Godfrey, swinging awkwardly on his crutches, but he slowed his step, and once, as he looked swiftly at the other man, his dry brown face tightened and drew together as if in discomfort and sympathy.

Godfrey was touched by Annette, and felt an immediate affection for this fair little creature with the large and beautiful blue eyes. He saw only goodness and sweetness in her, and understanding. He saw, also, as she watched him approach, that those eyes filled with quick and painful tears. Somehow, this did not annoy him, as it had annoyed him in Celeste. With his subtlety, he discerned that it was not pity that inspired her, so much as sorrow and regret. He took her little hand, and kissed it.

And, as he did so, he felt in all his flesh the stolid strength and power of the man who waited beside her. He shook hands with Henri. Henri's hand was dry and hard and broad, and without the slightest pressure in the palm. Godfrey's natural sprightliness and swift gaiety were momentarily quelled. But he looked at Henri, and their eyes locked in instant and devastating dislike and repulsion.

"I believe," said Godfrey, with reserve, "that we have the same great-grandfather. My grandfather and your grandmother were brother and sister. What does that make us?"

"Some sort of intangible cousins, I believe," said Henri, with complete indifference. He added: "It's odd that I never heard of you."

"Oh, I heard of you," replied Godfrey. Now the twinkle returned to his brown eyes. He shifted a little on his crutches.

Henri's broad shoulders moved in a parody of a shrug. He looked with brutal frankness at Godfrey's stump and his uniform. "Where," he said, "did you get that?"

Godfrey looked down at his stump, and carefully and slowly let his eye travel over his uniform. He assumed an expression of great surprise. Seeing this, Antoine smiled delightedly, stood back on his heels at ease, and waited.

"Oh, these!" exclaimed Godfrey, in a fresh, naïve voice. "I never really noticed them before. Funny, isn't it? Things can happen to one, and one never notices. Haven't you found that out yourself, Henri?"

Henri's pale harsh face changed; a stain of rough color appeared on his broad cheekbones. He stared inimically at the other. Some of the relatives close by, sensing something interesting, moved slowly towards them. Annette, uncertain and confused, looked humbly from one man to the other.

Godfrey settled himself on his crutches. His dark and mobile face was glowing with boyish enthusiasm. "Well, you see, I got myself a commission in the Royal Air Force. Quite accidental, you know. In fact, I was surprised, myself, when I found myself in uniform. A quite Alice-in-Wonderland reaction. Dreamlike, and all that. And then it was that a funny thing happened: it didn't seem grotesque at all, but quite natural."

"Natural?" repeated Henri. His voice was dull, but Antoine knew he was enraged at this baiting. Smiles appeared on the faces of the gathering relatives.

"Well, yes," said Godfrey, lowering his voice confidentially. "Not at first. Sort of as if I'd gone down the rabbit hole, like Alice, and come upon all sorts of queer places. I'm a British subject, you know, but like quite a few of my class, I didn't particularly care for England. You'd be really surprised to discover how many like me really didn't care for old England. Boring, y'know. Stolid, and plum-puddingish. All that sort of thing. And then, there I was in uniform. Must have been the working of my subconscious mind. 'Subconscious mind,' said I, when I discovered myself in this predicament, 'what the hell have you been up to?' And then it came to me, very neat. I just hated Germans. All Germans. Every last man jack of 'em. Every boar, and sow, and piglet. So, says I, it's very simple. I'd gotten into this pantomime suit so that I'd have a chance to kill human pork. Lots of pork. Very simple."

Henri was silent. Godfrey regarded him with his laughing eyes. And then, with an inclination of his head, he turned to Antoine, who moved away. Godfrey moved with him. Antoine tucked his hand in Godfrey's arm, not for assistance, but in fellowship.

"You know," said Antoine, "I love you. I really love you."

Godfrey saw Celeste at a distance, isolated. In her shining silver gown she was like a slender pillar of ice.

Godfrey, his eyes meditatively upon Celeste, said absently to Antoine: "You all hate each other thoroughly, don't you? Why?"

"It's a family tradition," said Antoine, grinning. "We've built it up carefully, through the ages. If we started to love each other, it would knock hell out of the legend. And where would we be?"

CHAPTER LXVIII

They went into the immense dining-hall. Gallery of horrors, thought Godfrey. He had long been accustomed to the gloom and decay of European dining-rooms, but there had been no pretense about them, no artificiality. But here was pretense, affectation self-conscious and determined to be natural.

Emile's pretentious château, high on its groomed terraces, had a false and disoriented air at the best of times. The dining-hall emphasized this air. It was filled with an uncertain and shifting light, that drifted down from the gigantic candelabra which, though blazing with a multitude of tall thin tapers, were unable to lighten the spectral and clammy atmosphere. The walls were far and dim and cold, shrouded in tapestries and banners ragged and subdued with time. Everywhere, Godfrey was conscious of the stony dusk, and of distant draped lances and scarred armor. The family took their places about the huge refectory table, dripping with lace, and burdened with crystal and silver glimmering faintly under the pale taper-light. This medieval room was grotesque, in robust and blazing America, and Godfrey glanced about him with cynicism politely concealed. His covert glance absorbed the grave dim portraits among the banners, and he wondered where Emile had got them. He smiled at the smug suggestion that these far and remote painted faces were those of illustrious ancestors. It was an insult to these faces, and their old tradition. He came to a rather cruel conclusion about his relatives. "Vulgar bastards with delusions of grandeur," he thought to himself. One could never entirely erase the mark of the peasant—the mark of the beast, Godfrey called it, happily remarking to himself that he, also, probably bore this mark.

Amusing himself with his secret thoughts, he looked about the table. Antoine there, so dark and so elegantly sophisticated, had no visible mark of the beast. Godfrey's eye travelled over each face, plump or thin, predatory or vapid, savage or sullen, watchful or stupid, and his delight grew. At last his glance touched Celeste, and stopped, abruptly. She sat opposite him, silent and motionless, her beautiful hand just touching a wine-glass. In that uncertain and moving crepuscular light, he drank in to the full the stern and delicate modelling of her white face, its high-bred strength. The thin snowy streak in her hair was smoothed back from the fine planes of her forehead. Her mouth, for all its dark bright color, was carved rigidly as from tinted stone, and her blue eyes, seldom lifted, had a bemused dull abstraction which assured Godfrey that her mind had fled away from her body. She looked at no one directly. Beside her on her right sat the magenta Alexander and on her left was her brother-in-law, little effervescent Jean. She spoke to neither. And they, in turn, ignored her as if she were not there. Why was this? mused Godfrey, angrily. Had she fallen into disfavor with the Family? If so, she appeared not to care.

At his own right sat Annette, and each time that he turned to her she looked at him with a swift and shining smile, shy and warm. Such a frail lovely little thing! He had an impulse to kiss her tenderly. On his left was big stupid Alexa, who, though she was fifty now, was as blonde and smooth as butter.

Nice people! thought Godfrey. He no longer felt related to any of them except Antoine, sitting at a little distance. When he met Antoine's merry significant look, he knew that his thoughts had been read. He smiled back in return. Antoine was too far away for chuckling conversation. Later, perhaps.

He studied them all, wondering at them cynically. They were not even decadent, with the exception of Antoine. There was a perfume to decadence, even if it was the perfume of death. There was a grace to decadence, a mature glaze, an adult awareness. It had the beauty of something exquisite which had died. Even in its death, it was far more poignant, far more noble and lofty, than the life which was here: predatory and mean and avaricious and brutal. The barbarians, he remarked to himself, have taken over. *Vive le barbare!*

Emile, he noted gratefully, had a French chef. He had not expected this. He ate with enjoyment. The wines were perfection. The Bouchards, he noted, apparently did not care for wine. They had swilled themselves full of horrible cocktails and acrid whiskey, in great quantities, before dinner. They knew it was expected of them that they be judges of wine, and it amused him enormously to see them sip, their eyes narrowed, their lips pursed, as if they were sternly passing judgment. But the glasses, after that first ostentatious sip, remained almost full.

Godfrey felt buoyant. He, too, had "swilled" before dinner. One needs an anaesthetic, he would say, to be able to endure a universe in which there was not the slightest evidence of relevancy. Aristotle was wrong. Nothing led anywhere.

Jean politely inquired as to Godfrey's plans. When he informed them frankly of his coming mission to Hollywood, he saw the amused and superior quirks of their mouths. But Alexander scowled. "Rotten stuff," he remarked, his color becoming more magenta than ever. "Depraved stuff. Immoral. We've got the Hays Office, and the Legion of Decency, but the filth creeps in. Besides, motion-picture stock hasn't paid any dividends lately."

"Al Milch," said Godfrey, "is going to make shorts for the United States Government. Perhaps you'd call it propaganda."

But the big blond Norwood interrupted: "You'll need money, you know, for that sort of thing."

Godfrey saw the sudden intent curiosity on the faces about him. He chuckled to himself. He knew they were dying to know if he had money. He waved his hand airily. "Money!" he said, with sublime contempt. The faces became dissatisfied. And uncertain. He had not enlightened them.

He continued: "We expect to do some war pictures, too. Try to show the German swine in perspective. I'll love to do that."

"Propaganda!" exploded Alexander, shifting weightily in his chair as if his buttocks had been stung. "So that's what Hollywood is up to! Pack of Jews determined to get us into the war! But we won't. By God, we won't!" And he struck the table so heavily and meatily that his silver danced. "They won't get us into this war."

Godfrey's smile remained. But now it was dangerous, and fixed. He looked at Alexander attentively, as if he was studying him. "No?" he said, softly. "I'm afraid you're mistaken. America will be in this war soon. A couple of years too late, as usual. You can't do a thing about it. It will be done for you."

He had expected amused shrugs and indifference, and was surprised to see how suddenly intent and wary every face appeared, except Celeste's, which remained stony and white as an image. Henri even leaned forward a little, his pale eyes unblinking. Nicholas grunted uncouthly. Francis lifted his hand and concealed his mouth with his long bony fingers. Emile's black brows knitted. Christopher turned in his chair to face Godfrey. Every other man and woman stared at Godfrey as at a strange and outlandish creature.

He looked at them all, and a huge repulsion and disgust for them filled him.

"You can't do a thing about it," he repeated, in that same soft voice. "You'll be attacked. And soon. Oh, I know all about your six thousand miles of water on the west, and three thousand miles of water on the east. We've heard all about it, in Europe. But I hardly thought it possible that Americans could be so stupid. I had a higher opinion of you. I'm sorry it isn't justified."

Nicholas leaned back in his chair, and thrust his thumbs in his vest. He glowered at Godfrey. "So we'll be in the war, eh? Damned nonsense. They wouldn't dare attack us. Lot of propaganda. Can't scare us. Who the hell would jump us? Eh? Eh?"

"Japan," said Godfrey.

A stupefied silence filled the great dining-hall. Even the many servants stopped in the very act of lifting silver dishes. The candelabra glimmered down on so many statues. But Henri had begun to smile inscrutably. He rubbed his lip with his index finger.

Then Hugo cried, throwing back his snowy mass of hair: "Japan! What rot! Why, we have the Japanese Mission right now in Washington, and as a member of the State Department, I can assure you, young man, that any slight differences with Japan that we have had in the past are now being resolved amicably and satisfactorily."

"Nevertheless," said Godfrey, amiably, "it will be Japan. Tomorrow? Next week? Next month? I don't know. But it will be Japan. You'll see. Is it really possible that you, especially, are so bloody stupid? Or is it to your interest to pretend to be?"

Then Phyllis said, in her high acid voice: "Oh, you're just an Englishman! You'd love to get us into this Communistic war! It's all just British imperialism, and Russian propaganda. Our priest, Father O'Connell, told us so, and he is quite an authority on international affairs."

Her banal remark brought sudden scowls down upon

564

her from the rest of the family, which had never become reconciled to her Catholicism. "Keep that Roman trash to yourself," said her amiable sister, Rosemarie, under her breath.

But the family, though they had scowled automatically at Phyllis, had heard only too clearly Godfrey's last remarks.

"Our interest?" repeated Jean, with raised eyebrows. He smiled, all his dimples appearing. "According to legend, we, the Bouchards, the Dynasty of Death, ought to offer up sacrifices to the Four Horsemen, or something, at the prospect of war. We'd make profits out of war: *ergo*, war, by all means. Yet, we don't want war; we won't have it."

Godfrey leaned his elbows on the table and bent towards Jean. He studied him meditatively. He frowned with thoughtfulness. "Yes. I see. I know. That's what's bothering me. Why?"

Jean smiled radiantly. But his dancing black eyes were minatory. He did not reply.

Godfrey shook his head reflectively. "There's something here," he remarked, "that definitely smells on ice. Yes, definitely."

Nicholas and Alexander exchanged swift looks. Nicholas coughed, with loud boorish noises. He said: "Nonsense. Don't go looking for bogie men. Ridiculous. Are you a halfwit? You've lived in Europe too long. We've got a cleaner and clearer point of view here. Japan! Hell! Why should Japan attack us? Why? I ask you."

"And I," said Godfrey, "am asking you. You know the answer. Don't you?"

When Nicholas, glowering, did not answer, Godfrey turned with a wide and relaxing smile to the others. He inclined his head towards Agnes, who had been listening with tense interest. "Am I ruining your dinner party, dear?" he asked.

"My darling, no," she replied, with a laugh. "You are making it interesting. You have no idea how stupid and stolid these Bouchards are at dinner parties. They eat, leave the table, and go promptly to sleep with their eyes open. Do go on."

"Then," said Godfrey, expansively, "I will proceed at once to make myself even more disagreeable, in the interest of stimulation. You know, my dear family, I don't like you. Even when I didn't know you, I didn't like you. I'd heard all about you. I followed your careers with the most flattering interest."

Robert, the dull, interrupted rudely, with a glare from his fishy eyes: "Let's talk about you, shall we? Maybe you're more interesting."

"Oh, I am, I am!" cried Godfrey. "You've no idea how absorbing I am! You could read about me for weeks with unflagging passion. I've lived all over Europe. I've seen the marionettes and I've seen those who manipulated them. Very amusing. To some people. In a way, it wasn't amusing to me. Perhaps I am, by nature, more sanitary."

Now he looked at Celeste again. He was gratified to see that her stoniness had softened. Her dark blue eyes were turned on him steadfastly. There was a tremulous line all about the carving of her lips. My dear darling, he thought, there is something or someone here that is tormenting you. I don't know who he is, but I'll strangle him. Just continue to look at me like that, and you'd be surprised at the dragons I can beard.

"Didn't all that traveling about cost money, lots of money?" continued the dull Robert. The family seemed content to let this ox of a young man bait the newcomer, for they were smiling faintly. But Henri was not smiling. He had folded his arms solidly on the table, and his big bull-like head was bent towards Godfrey with an interest that the young man preferred to consider flattering.

"Money!" cried Godfrey. "I had money, my child. Not a great deal. Papa was unfortunate in his investments. He was involved in the pawnbroking scandal, and I believe he lost a lot of money with the Match Man. The names of both rascals escape me just now. But no matter. I, myself, am more careful. I managed to scrape along. With the assistance of friends."

Now he encountered the eye of Antoine, who was delightedly listening. Antoine saluted as Godfrey's glance touched him. The young man, stimulated, prepared for wilder flings, at this salutation from a friend.

"You've probably got a pension from the British Government," suggested Robert.

"To return vulgarly in kind, yes," admitted Godfrey. "But very little. I really didn't want to take a pension at all, just for losing a leg in the joy of killing Germans."

Phyllis interrupted, with a faint squeak. "How can you be so bloodthirsty! I never heard anything like this! I think the Germans are much libelled. Father O'Connell——"

"Damn Father O'Connell, who probably harbors Nazi

literature under his black robes," said Godfrey, genially. The table burst into a roar of laughter. Godfrey was flattered. Apparently it took little wit to arouse the stable mirth of his relatives. Phyllis glared at him with hatred. He turned away from her with a momentary stiffening of his mouth.

Francis spoke, seriously: "But really, now. I'm interested in this moving-picture business of yours. I take it that one needs a great deal of money to produce pictures. How are you going about it?"

"Well, you have a good story, and then you go to the bank, or to other backers, and you say: 'Look here, old chap, I've got something rich here. You'll like it. I have the stars picked. What do you say?' Then they chew about, and frown, and scratch their chins, and go to the barber, and take an hour or two off to visit a particular lady friend, and come back all refreshed and full of ginger. Then, they get down to facts and try to rob you. If you're clever, you rob them. Or, at least, you compromise. I'm not much on all this. I'm leaving it to Al Milch, who has been struggling with the vermin for years. I'm more on the fragile side, myself. When the money is guaranteed, I go to work. I think we'll succeed in Hollywood. Al already has a fine reputation, and I am modestly swinging on his coat-tails."

Then Henri spoke: "You said something about war pictures and Government propaganda films. I'd like to know more."

Godfrey looked into his stony eyes doubtfully. Then he began to explain. The family, not overly interested, began to yawn, to look heavily at their plates. But Celeste, who had come to life like a statue turned to flesh, listened with strained attention.

It was right in the very midst of his exposition that Godfrey became aware of something. While Henri appeared to look only at him, he very often looked at Celeste, without the least change of expression, however. It was a hard male look. Godfrey's mouth went on moving, but his quick mind had retreated into itself. He did not like that look, directed so often, so piercingly, at Celeste. It indicated contemptuous and arrogant possession. He found opportunity to glance at Celeste. But she was looking only at him, and when their eyes met, she smiled swiftly and brightly.

Is there something up, there? thought Godfrey, with angry uneasiness, and something that was very much like alarm and dread. But when he saw Celeste again, she was still gazing only at him.

Henri stirred, moved his folded arms a trifle, after Godfrey had concluded, and said in an abstracted voice: "Very interesting. I am going to think about it."

Alexander, upon seeing Henri's interest, became interested, himself. "I've a lot of Cordon-Imson-Blaine stock," he said. "Know anything about it? Hasn't paid a decent dividend since the Crash."

Godfrey answered with the utmost gravity: "Al Milch has a tentative agreement with them for a release. I'll take your matter up personally with Mr. Cordon when I arrive there."

"Um," muttered Alexander. "Nice of you."

The family again became hilarious. Alexander, bewildered and indignant, removed the cigar from his mouth and glared at them. Even Celeste laughed. To one man, at least, the sound of that laugh was startling. It was the one sound he heard above the general hilarity, and it was clear and ringing and fresh, like a brook released from winter ice. He turned his slow implacable eyes upon her, and studied her new color, and the gentle mirth of her flushed face. And then when he had seen her face, he turned again to Godfrey and regarded him in moveless silence.

"I, too, have a block of Cordon-Imson-Blaine stock," said Christopher. "War pictures, you say? I understand the people are sick of them, and want something more appropriate to their mass donkey-minds. Such as a bleached-blonde trollop's legs in provoking attitudes, and a well-rounded pair of buttocks."

Godfrey gave Christopher his attention, and scrutinized him with the greatest candor. "You think that's what they all want, do you?" he said, thoughtfully. "You think that's our modern substitute for bread and circuses? Well, I disagree with you. Of course, there is a goodly sprinkle of imbeciles among the mass of people, I admit. But I really think there is a goodly sprinkle, too, in proportion, among our class. Or, pardon me," and he bowed his head with brief irony, "I should say: your class. I haven't yet reached your level. Anyway, perhaps none of you need look far to find dim-wits among your acquaintances. Or even among your family. I understand I haven't met them all."

Christopher grinned. He took his cigarette from his mouth and surveyed Godfrey with bright interest. "For which you ought to thank God," he admitted.

But now Godfrey was genuinely grave and serious. Slowly, he let his eye travel from one face to another, and at each face he paused, as if in abstracted scrutiny. Then he began to speak, with much quietness: "You know, I wondered about all of you. I wondered if you were what I had heard. I listened in Paris, in Moscow, in Berlin, in Rome, and in London. Sometimes, from a distance, I caught glimpses of some of you. When I pieced everything together, it was pretty terrible."

"Really?" said Rosemarie, with a coquettish tilt of her head, and an exaggerated simper. "You flatter us."

But Godfrey said, with such indifference for her on his suddenly pale face that she was infuriated: "When I say terrible, I imply a connotation different from the usual one. I mean it was frightful that any such powerful group and family of men, with such international influence, could be so stupid, so obtuse, so coarse and greedy and brutish, and so totally unaware of the world of men about them. If you had been elegant gentlemen, for instance, like our dear Antoine," and his sternness relaxed a moment while he and Antoine bowed ceremoniously to each other, "it would not have been so reprehensible. Aristocrats are really very innocent; they are so completely unaware of anything. But you are peasants; you are really very gross brutes, you know. You are as plain as dirt. You are as plain as the common people. That is what surprises me—that you can be so totally unaware of your own kind, and what they are thinking. And that you do not feel with them."

Phyllis clapped her hands together with a sharp little sound. "I knew he was a Communist all the time, or at least a radical!" she shrilled.

But they all ignored her. They, to the last man, stared at Godfrey fixedly, and only from Antoine's face was that predatory and hating expression absent. Some of them had flushed at his honest insults. Others merely drew their brows together over ambushed eyes, and waited for him to have done. Agnes, however, formed a silent "bravo!" with her crimson lips, and sat back to enjoy herself.

"Perhaps," said little Jean, gently, "you could enlighten us as to what our—kind—is thinking? And where you got all this very intriguing information?"

But Godfrey said, as if the other had not spoken: "I have found this strange new thinking, not in the capitals of Europe, but in the scattered and straggling villages of Russia, in the working-class districts of British laborers and mechanics and draymen, in the subdued and desperate towns of France. It seemed to me at one time that I no longer drew a breath in a little village or town than the Germans exploded into it, and there I was galloping away, remembering I was an Englishman. That's beside the point, however. I talked to the people for years. I am, by nature, not a lover of the rabble. But you'll find rabble everywhere, not only in the workman's cot, but in the middle class, in the salons internationals, and among the great of all Europe. So, when I say 'the people,' I mean those human beings who still have uncorrupted minds, and hearts that can feel and understand."

He paused. The silence in the dining-hall was intense. And Godfrey looked at Celeste on an inexplicable impulse. There was a blind and dazzled blaze on her face, a kind of brilliance that was touching and arresting. And another man looked at her and felt a vice of fury tightening in his breast. He remembered a day very long ago, when Celeste had sat at this very table, opposite Peter Bouchard, just returned from Europe, and that she had listened like this, with the same full and radiant look upon her face, and the same parted lips. Though his arms were still folded on the table, his fists clenched.

Godfrey said, with penetrating quietness that came back in thin echoes from the stony walls: "If I had found this thinking in only a few instances, I would have admired it, regretted that it was not more common, and have forgotten it. But it was universal! Universally, among the most divergent sorts of people, there is a growing and really earnest preoccupation with human welfare and human advancement, not only in material things, but in the ethical field, also. And strange to say, this deep and fumbling preoccupation is sometimes inarticulate, but always passionate and dynamic. If I were a mystic," and he smiled briefly, "I would say that the people had been permeated by some vast and unknowable Cosmic force. It has nothing to do with religion. In fact, the clergy, as a class almost, were totally unconscious of it, and I have no doubt that when they discover it they'll invoke hell-fire on it. It is something deeper. It is part of the universal flow and tide of an awakening human spirit."

No one moved or spoke. His voice had been so penetrating, so quiet and yet so sincerely emphatic, that it had thrown a kind of enchantment over them, over even the grossest and most cynical and depraved. They were hypnotized by the pale set sternness of his features, by the flash of his dark eyes. Antoine's hooded gaze did not move from him, and a cigarette burned unnoticed in his hand.

Godfrey drew a deep quiet breath. "Herbert Spencer believed, not only in physical evolution, but in the evolution of the human spirit. If he were alive today, he would feel justified in his belief. Evolution is at work in the minds of men, so long sunken in the morass of greed and irresponsibility and hatred and lust."

He paused. Now all could see the strain and exhaustion which had temporarily been hidden under his exuberance and light gaiety. He was a sick man, remembering suffering. But in his way, he was as indomitable as Henri. His forehead glistened with dampness, and very simply, he took out his handkerchief and wiped it away.

Celeste was still gazing at him, with that brilliant light brightening steadily on her face. Her lips were trembling. It was as if she was listening to words of life after long entombment.

"Beautiful, beautiful!" said the vicious Rosemarie, in a lyrical voice. "But it still sounds like the old stuff put out by the fellow-travellers."

Godfrey looked at her with a bitter glow of his eye. "I think you are flattering Communism too much. It seems that every hint that the people are awakening to the conscience of their moral responsibility to one another is called Communism." He shook his head. "I happen to know Communism, my dear."

"I confess all this is beyond me," said the tawny Hugo, with benign condescension. "But then, I'm only a member of the State Department. The Department hasn't heard anything about this 'new spirit' yet. It hasn't arrived in any diplomatic pouch."

"Yes, I know," said Godfrey, slowly. "And it never will." He directed his attention to Agnes. "My dear, you must forgive me. I've been monopolizing the conversation at your table, and that isn't very polite, is it?"

Agnes said satirically: "I beg of you not to stop. This is the first intelligent conversation I've heard at this table in lo! these many years."

Godfrey reached for a cigarette from a silver box. A servant, listening in the background, hurried to light it for him. Godfrey glanced up idly. The man, in livery, had a most peculiar expression on his heavy face. It was shining. For a moment or two their eyes held in profound acknowledgment.

Godfrey spoke again, as if thinking aloud: "I understand the Bible speaks of certain men as being the 'scourge of God.' Perhaps Hitler is that scourge, today. For if it had not been for Hitler and his bloody violence, I doubt that we would have awakened at this time to a realization of our moral apathy and indifference. It took Hitler to make us understand what man can endure with dignity and fortitude and compassion and selflessness in the face of death and destruction. And I believe, I know, that the people see now to what appalling levels we can descend when moral responsibility is lost, and when every man is concerned only with his own belly. The German people will remain, I hope, an eternal reminder to all the rest of us of man's potential degradation; they have given us a full view of the other face of all of us: the face we usually keep turned toward darkness. If the Germans only remain as a symbol of man's complete disgrace and infamy, they will have served their frightful purpose."

He waited for someone to speak. But no one did. Antoine played with his cigarette-holder, Christopher smiled slightly behind the thin fingers spread across his mouth; Henri leaned solidly on the table and stared at a point near Godfrey's head; Annette looked at Godfrey with a gentle and radiant humility in her eyes; Celeste seemed tremulous with life and eagerness; Agnes smiled with wry approval at her strange guest; Francis was grave and thoughtful, Edith was thoughtful. But the others merely regarded their plates glumly, or smoked, their eyes averted.

Godfrey sighed. He was quite exhausted. He put his lean hands on the table as if to push himself away. "You've got to learn, all of you, that there is one thing you must hereafter take into consideration at all times: the people's conscience. If you don't—" and he spread out his hands significantly— "you are done. Completely."

Antoine walked beside him as they all left the dining-hall. "By the way, do you know Jay Regan—you know, the Wall Street financier?"

"No," said Godfrey, laughing. "I'm afraid not. Why?"

"I just wondered," mused Antoine.

"I wouldn't mind knowing him," said Godfrey, with a grin.

Antoine gave him a curious glance. But he said nothing.

CHAPTER LXIX

The fire was roaring merrily in the vaulted living-room when they returned there. Agnes came to Godfrey, and said, with an affectionate smile: "You know, you really are a member of the family. You are as rude as the rest of them. I was brought up to have manners. The Bouchards never acquired them. They aren't gentlemen. Neither, darling, are you."

"But I'm an honest man!" protested Godfrey, laughing. "At least, comparatively honest. Can you say that for the rest of them?"

"Some are, in their own mysterious fashion." Agnes looked at Henri, who stood at a distance talking to Francis. "And one or two are gentlemen. Antoine, for instance, is quite authentic. I'm not sure I like gentlemen, either. They remind me of Inquisitors."

Godfrey was suddenly very restless, as well as exhausted. He looked about for Celeste. She was sitting at a distance from the fire, and her brother was sitting beside her. She was talking listlessly. Christopher had his arm across the back of her chair, his head bent towards her. Her attitude expressed weariness, and again she was pale, her small gestures without life. The room was now full of noisy talk and loud laughter. Antoine was standing beside Godfrey, but they did not speak to each other.

Finally, Godfrey, still not taking his eyes from Celeste, said to Antoine: "I've known Celeste a long time, Tony. She seems to have taken Peter's death very hard. They were devoted, you know. Are there any signs that she is recovering?"

He felt Antoine make a slight movement beside him. And then Antoine's derisive voice said lightly: "Celeste consoled herself a long time ago."

Godfrey turned to him so quickly that he swayed on his crutches. He looked disturbed and shaken. "Yes? Is she expecting to marry again, soon? She didn't tell me."

573

Antoine studied him with cynical keenness. Ho, ho! he thought to himself. But he said, with that same derisive lightness: "Marry? I don't think so. Perhaps it isn't possible. Sometimes there are previous commitments, you know."

Godfrey looked at him in silence, and the fluid lines of his face hardened. And Antoine looked back, darkly smiling. Then Godfrey, without a word, swung himself away.

He directed his way through clumps of Bouchards, who parted automatically to let him pass. He felt their amused and contemptuous or inimical eyes following him. He didn't care. They weren't really his family, he felt. Though he shared, in some measure, their blood, he was an alien. They knew it. He would never be part of them. He was suddenly sorry that he had come.

He was moving towards Celeste, when suddenly he stopped. Henri, apparently without locomotion, had appeared before Celeste and Christopher. He was looking down at both of them, and smiling. Godfrey heard his voice through the noisy clatter:

"Chris, something's come up. Come in to see me tomorrow. It's very important."

"Of course," replied Christopher.

There was a pause. But Godfrey saw Celeste's face, as cold and as expressionless as plaster. She had dropped her eyes. Her hands lay in her lap. And Godfrey saw Henri's face, also, tight and harsh and brutal, as he looked at her.

"Are you feeling better, Celeste?" Henri asked, goadingly. "We haven't seen much of you, lately."

Celeste lifted her head and looked at him with slow directness. "I was not ill," she said. Her voice was clear, if without inflection. She stood up, and her brother rose with her. Her manner was quiet and composed, but when she glanced about, Godfrey saw the swift blue flash of her eyes. He lifted his hand and signalled to her that he was coming. She smiled, now, and again the immobility of her expression broke into delicate planes of light. He swung towards her rapidly.

"I'm really very tired, Godfrey," she said. She put her hand on his arm. "And the baby has a feverish cold. Will you take me home?"

He put his hand over her own, and pressed it. "Of course, my dear. At once. I'm tired, too."

He turned to Christopher and Henri. The latter was regarding him with that hard and stony ruthlessness of his, now enormously increased. Christopher was smiling, but with a speculative air, not at all pleasant. "You will excuse us?" said Godfrey, courteously.

Henri said nothing; Christopher inclined his head.

"You gave us a very interesting evening," Christopher said. "Thanks." He saw his sister's eyes, fixed on Godfrey. They were radiant and soft, and her parted lips were smiling, as if preparing to break into eager laughter. Christopher's brows drew together, uneasily.

"Good-night. I hope we'll see each other again, soon," said Godfrey. Henri did not reply. Christopher replied cordially. The two men stood side by side, watching Godfrey and Celeste, as they moved towards Agnes to say good-night. Finally, they had gone.

There is really something very satisfying in this, thought Christopher. But something very damn familiar, too. Henri was speaking, without the least emphasis: "He's staying up there with Celeste, eh?"

"Yes," said Christopher, wryly. "I think it's perfectly proper. She's not a young girl, you know. She's a widow." He added, innocently: "And I think the baby's quite a chaperon." He turned to Henri and offered his platinum case. "Cigarette?"

Henri looked down at the case with distaste, then his broad strong fingers fumbled for a cigarette, and took one. Christopher lit it for him. Henri held it, like all amateurs, between the tips of his thumb and index finger. Also, he held it at quite a distance, as if it was obnoxious.

He turned a little and regarded the fire. Again he spoke, indifferently, and with a monotonous inflection: "Get him out of that house. As soon as possible."

Christopher said nothing. He looked at the back of that big head, and suddenly he tasted salt in his mouth, and felt a furious expanding of his heart. All the years of humiliation, of subservience, of fear and appeasement, of hope and self-disgust and hatred, overwhelmed him. All these years, he had been so cautious, considering whether each little or great matter would hurt him. All these years, he had considered only himself. What had it brought him? He had betrayed his sister; he had watched her later betrayal. He had become a panderer, a lackey. And in the end, he had watched her heart break, and had seen the hopeless anguish in her eyes. If she now had a chance of happiness, she must have it, come hell or destruction.

He said, almost whisperingly: "No. No."

He walked away from Henri. He felt a wild exhilaration.

His head whirled. He stepped as if moving on clouds. He came to Edith, and took her arm, and she was startled at his look, excited, as mobile as quicksilver. "My dear," he said, "I think I'm drunk!"

"Drunk?" repeated Edith. She scrutinized him. "Nonsense. You aren't drunk. Something's happened."

"Oh, it has, it has!" he exclaimed, and he pinched her arm gently. "It's a wonderful thing to be free. I ought to have tried it before. Don't look so confused, pet. It's just that I'm having the most excellent time."

CHAPTER LXX

Whatever painful suspicions Godfrey now had, they were slowly dispersed and half forgotten during the next days. For Celeste, with a sincerity and pathetic eagerness he could not doubt, urged him to extend his stay. "You don't know how lonely I've been," she pleaded, with simplicity. So he called his friend, Alfred Milch, and persuaded him that "matters of family importance" made it impossible for him to return to New York now, but that they would meet in Hollywood about two weeks hence.

Pleasant happy days, bright with sun and blazing winter snow, followed one after the other. Godfrey was invited to the homes of his relatives, with Celeste. Celeste invariably refused. When she explained to Godfrey, he was conscious that she was not being frank with him; her words were evasive and inconclusive. But she urged him to go. "It'll do no harm," she would say, wistfully. In politeness, he had to accept. When he returned, no matter how late, he found Celeste waiting for him, reading by the fire, and upon his entrance, she would rise, smiling, her hand out-stretched.

"You know, they really hate me," he told her. "They are suspicious of me. I'm an alien. They want to study me more closely, to see whether I have any menace in me. I've pretty well convinced them by now that I'm a very harmless, and very penniless, person, so their interest is subsiding. How have you endured them all these years, my dear?"

"I haven't really," she assured him, laughing.

He would sit down near her, and light a cigarette, and would puff at it thoughtfully. "The women are much better, some of them. Edith, especially, and that darling little Annette." He turned for agreement to Celeste, but once again, that baffling mask of thick coldness had slipped over her features, and again, he felt that warning uneasiness in him that was so threatening to himself.

He would talk to her of his ambitions, with such pristine enthusiasm that he fired her, also. When she said: "Godfrey, I'm so enormously rich. Do let me back a picture or two," he was too realistic, too honest and without hypocrisy, to protest, or pretend to refuse. Instead, he expressed his gratitude, joyfully, and immediately called his friend, Al Milch. Coming back from the telephone, he balanced himself on one crutch and hilariously waved the other. Celeste ran to him, exclaiming with fear that he might fall, and they hugged each other in mirthful delight, disposing kisses with the most immense enthusiasm.

There was an eternally youthful quality about Godfrey which Celeste had met in no one else. It awakened her own buried youth. They drove about the country. They went to the village and bought immense quantities of foodstuffs. Godfrey boasted of his culinary achievement, and invaded the kitchen, and was so charming, so gay, that the cook could not help but be enchanted. They played with the baby, who rolled in the snow, and staggered on his short strong legs like a wool-wrapped cocoon. Sometimes friends of Celeste's came, and sometimes a few of the family, and everything was informal and high-spirited and careless.

For the first time, Celeste was playing. The fund of subjects to be discussed between herself and Godfrey was inexhaustible. They talked for hours over dinner; at times they talked almost till dawn. No matter how worn the subject, Godfrey gave it a special uniqueness and freshness and vitality. He was seldom grave, now. Celeste had been sad too long, he had observed, acutely. He loved to see the laughing sparkle of her eyes, the redness of her laughing lips, and her mirth was the sweetest and most intoxicating sound in the world to him. She followed some of his more subtle arguments with flattering intensity. He had taught her to drink a cocktail or two before dinner, and the bright fillip this gave her loosened the bands in her mind, so that an unsuspected merry and childlike gaiety was released, witty and quite clever.

Christopher, visiting them, noticed this. So did Edith. She said one night, very casually: "Do you know, I think Celeste might fall in love with our gallant adventurer."

And Christopher said: "She might. She might, indeed. I hope so."

Edith had turned then, and stared at him, but he had taken up a book and had begun to read. Edith frowned.

There was a sweet delirium in the days, for Celeste. Health and vitality came back to her. The house, no longer empty and sad and full of suppressed gloom, became gay, also. Flowers were everywhere. Fires roared. Celeste's happy voice, and Godfrey's laughter, and the shouts of little Land, came back from every room, every hall. There was a gentle recklessness about them, like a holiday. In the meantime, November had gone, and December had come, a calm and snowy December full of shining blue light.

Godfrey had begun to hope. By now, he had persuaded himself that what he had seen so obscurely and fleetingly at that Thanksgiving dinner had been his own imagination. Though he had visited Antoine at his home, Antoine had said nothing, only remarking very sympathetically that it was an excellent thing that Godfrey had come, for Celeste had been "distrait" for a long time. "She should marry again," he said, casually. "Someone who could teach her to play and to enjoy life. She's had a grim time of it."

Godfrey was too intelligent and too realistic to reflect that he was poor and that Celeste was an heiress. He had a moment or two of doubt about his lost leg, but again, his realism made him shrug. "I'm still a man, with most of my members," he would say to himself, with a smile.

He loved Celeste. He had loved her almost from the first hour when he had met her. (He had also liked Peter, to the point of great affection.) Moreover, he understood women thoroughly. He knew what pleased them, in general, and what displeased them. They interested him very much, as human beings, apart from their femaleness. He liked them. He enjoyed their company, even when they were fools. If they were beautiful, they delighted him; if they were intelligent, they intrigued him. He pitied their weaknesses, and admired their great and unsuspected strengths. He believed that the ages had much maligned them. It was a favorite saying of his that if men would only learn to understand women better, and to acquire the art of pleasing them, they, themselves, would derive immense benefit and pleasure from the effort. Godfrey firmly believed that though many things were valuable in life, human relationships, and the delight and sweetness which these could bring, were the most valuable.

Did Celeste love him now? he would ask himself. He had never had any such doubts about any other woman. He had always known, and availed himself of the knowledge. But, with Celeste, he could not know completely. He knew that she was very fond of him, that she had only to see him to become radiant, that her voice took on a sweet high breathlessness when she spoke to him. But how much of this was due to a pathetic loneliness he had alleviated? How much was gratitude that she had found a friend and a companion, full of sympathy and affection? How much was mere congeniality, and similar tastes, and mutual laughter and understanding? And then he would think to himself, buoyantly: But what else is there to love, anyway? Passion there was, of course, and vehemence, but both of them had seen enough of these exhausting aspects, and would prefer them now in gentler and more mellow guise. Even if, as far as Celeste was concerned, they might always be absent, no matter. The other things were much more durable.

He became preoccupied with his thoughts, and more grave and pensive. Noting this, Celeste was frightened and perplexed. Had she begun to bore him? Was he tired of being here on Placid Heights, with herself and her child? Perhaps her conversation was too light and inconsequential. But, O God, she would think, I've had so many years of being serious and taking the world on my shoulders! I'd like a little surcease, now. I should like to laugh, even for a little while, and pretend, just a little, that nothing is of tragic importance.

She was thirty-five, now, no longer young, but she still had the pure and easily bewildered naïveté of a child. She would lie awake at night, thinking of Godfrey, her thoughts so busy with him, so humble over her inadequacies, that the old monstrous pain, huge and black, became like an ominous mountain far in the distance of her consciousness. When she would meet him in the morning, she would peep at him wistfully. When he would look at her, and smile, and suggest a ride, or a romp in the snow with the baby, her face would light up and her eyes would dance with pleasure. While the final arrangements were being made with her lawyers and Godfrey, in her pleasant living-room, she would listen with eagerness to technical discussions of motion-picture making, and there would be a shining quality about her. When she declared, quickly, that she wanted no profits, she did not notice the acrid hidden smile of her lawyers, and looked only at Godfrey, who laughed and patted her hand, and assured her she was no business woman.

He had many things, therefore, to make him hope. And on the morning that Mr. Milch irritably called him from Hollywood and suggested that he had had holiday enough, Godfrey decided to discover just how much foundation there was for this hope.

There had been an ice storm during the night. The morning sun, blazing and whitely incandescent, shone on a crystal world, in which every twig, every tree trunk, every evergreen frond, every eave and fence-post and telephone line was encased in brilliant glass. Godfrey and Celeste went out alone to look at it. They saw the distant hills, now purple as hyacinths in that clarified and too poignant light, and a sky that was also crystal and pure as ice. When they spoke, their voices rang from them in crystalline echoes. All was so silent, so still, so luminous, so very sharp, that finally they did not speak, but stood side by side, their hands locked tightly. The houses in the valley below were like doll-houses; pillars of blue smoke stood upright over their chimneys. The light on the snow reflected back the sun until they were blinded.

They went back into the house, and sat by the fire. Celeste's cheeks were crimson. She held out her hands to the fire, and smiled shyly at Godfrey, who was smoking in silence. She discovered that he had been watching her keenly, and she could not explain to herself the sudden springing of her heart, her sudden awareness.

He threw his cigarette in the fire, and spoke with gentle abruptness: "Celeste, my child, I must leave for Hollywood not later than the day after tomorrow. I don't want to go, but I must. I have a living to earn."

All the brightness was wiped from her face. It became pale and dull. She turned to the fire again, and after a moment, in a difficult voice, she said: "Yes. Of course. I understand." She sighed. "I'll be awfully sorry. You have no idea how sorry."

He leaned towards her now, and took her hand. "Darling, look at me."

She did so. Her mouth quivered. She tried to smile. He kissed her hand.

"I want to ask you something, my dear," he said, softly. "Perhaps it's a little soon. But I've got to know. Have I any chance at all?"

He had known she was naïve, that perhaps she would retain this pure virtue to a great age, to the end of her life. But he could hardly believe it when he saw her astonishment, and when she pulled her hand quickly from his, and then stared at him in white silence, he, himself, was astounded. Had she really been so blind? And now there was a sick and peculiar aching in his chest.

"I love you, Celeste, my darling," he said, the words pushing themselves out painfully from a throat suddenly dry and thick. "I thought you knew."

She did not speak. Her eyes filled with slow tears. She lifted her hand, rested it on the arm of her chair, and concealed her profile from him.

And now there was silence in the room. The sun streamed in through the windows in one long wash of profound radiance. The fire crackled on the hearth. Trees snapped outside. There was no other sound. Godfrey was leaning towards Celeste, waiting, his hands dropped and clasped before him.

"I think we've been happy here, together," he murmured. "Perhaps I banked too much on that." He regarded the fire reflectively. "And perhaps it was too soon."

She dropped her hand now, and he saw her touchingly wet cheeks, and her quivering mouth. She tried to speak, but she had to make several efforts before she succeeded:

"Yes, dear, a little too soon." Her voice was shaking.

He became quick and sympathetic, the ache in his chest abating somewhat.

"Yes, of course! I understand. Poor Peter——"

But he saw, now, that she had become rigidly grave, and bleakly stern.

"Godfrey, it isn't Peter," she said, steadfastly.

He gazed at her speechlessly, his head bent. And waited.

She pressed her hands together, palms and fingers stiff. She began to shiver.

"I can't be a hypocrite to you, Godfrey," she said, still looking at him with strong valor. "I loved Peter. I honestly did. From the first time I met him. I loved him until he died.

I shall always love him. But not the way you think. It—It was never like that."

He fixed his brown eyes on her steadily, and was silent, while he missed nothing of her speechless anguish and misery. Then he said, with the greatest gentleness: "Then, it is someone else?"

She did not reply. But her head bent a little.

He looked down at his crutches, as if he would take them and begin to walk up and down the room. And then he just sat there, and looked at them, as if there was nothing else on his mind.

"It would be impudent of me, of course, to ask—" he said.

He was startled at the sharp and bitter clarity of her voice, and its loudness, as if she spoke in self-loathing and uncontrollable self-contempt: "You might as well know, Frey. Everyone else does. I thought perhaps one of the family had been kind enough to enlighten you! I thought you knew, and still didn't care! I was grateful for that. You see, it's Henri."

He still looked down at the crutches. His merry mouth was now sharp and thin with shock. But I think I always knew, he thought. He said, not lifting his eyes to her: "He's married, though. To little Annette. So——"

But her words poured out at him, swiftly, like flung pellets of ice, and he did not recognize this voice, so brittle, so stinging, so embittered and full of breaking agony, as if all her control had broken down and she must speak for very inability to do otherwise. She told him of her old engagement to Henri, which she had broken, and of her marriage to Peter. She told him, in hard, loud, unemotional tones, of the fourteen years of almost complete exile. She told him how she had never forgotten Henri, that she had wished never to return, because she felt she dared not, for Peter's sake. She did not hesitate or fumble as she told him everything, her return, her meeting with Henri, their subsequent affair.

And Godfrey listened, numbly, never taking his brown eyes from her. Once or twice, he heard the tense anguish of her short laugh, dreary and choked.

"I had made a mess of everything. I didn't seem to care. Nothing mattered at all. I had no pride, no shame. He came and went as he pleased. I did whatever he said." She suddenly put her hands to her throat, as if an unendurable pain had stabbed her there. "He told me over and over, that he made no promises. He only said that if and when it was safe, and feasible, for him to divorce Annette, he would do so, and we could be married. It seemed that nothing could be done until Armand died, and his will was known."

She told him of the will, and the conditions. And he listened, not moving a muscle, only watching her distraught wildness, her aimless and jerking gestures. If he was shocked and horrified, there was no sign of it.

"Then," she continued, still in that hard, loud, hurried voice, "Peter became very ill. I never thought of anything else. I take some comfort, remembering that. And then, he died." She stopped for a moment, and he saw the rigidity of her white throat, and her difficulty swallowing. "I discovered, too, that I was going to have a child, that it was too late to do anything about it."

Then Godfrey made an uncontrollable movement. His pale lips parted. His hands, shaking a little, fumbled for a cigarette. He lit it, stared blindly at the still burning match that he held (as if he did not know what it was) and then flung it into the fire. He said, very quietly: "Henri's child, of course?"

"Oh, yes, yes!" Her smile was even wilder, more mocking. "The family knew. But I owe them some gratitude. They never spoke of it. They always speak of 'Peter's little boy.' Family pride, I suppose. Yes, I am grateful."

Godfrey smoked slowly. He said, in a casual voice: "And Henri has made no move?"

"I tell you, it's the will! He must wait until he decides that the proper moment has arrived to open the will! I've tried to understand. I really did understand," and her voice now broke quickly, with a heart-shaking pathos. "I understood. There were things to be considered besides myself. I wasn't unreasonable. I was willing to wait. I didn't want him to open the will prematurely, just to satisfy me. It wasn't that which made me break with him."

Her voice was hoarse and breathless, and she waited a little, breathing heavily, before she could continue:

"I broke with him. Because he is cruel, and brutal. Because he is a sadist. Because, even though I knew he loved me, he could not resist tormenting me. He is a bad man, Frey. A very bad man. I had always known it. I had tried to overlook it. But there came a day when I couldn't, any longer."

Godfrey threw his cigarette into the fire. He watched its engulfment in the flames. He said: "Then you have broken with him?"

"Yes." She whispered this, as if she had no more strength left for loud speech. Her head fell on her breast.

They sat like this for a long time, with only the crackling of the fire and the snapping of the trees outside to break the silence. It seemed to Godfrey that the sunlit room had become very cold. He gazed at Celeste's fallen head and hands, and his heart was wrung with the most profound compassion and love that he had ever known in all his life.

And then he said, with the deepest gentleness: "You haven't forgotten him, though, have you, darling?"

She put her hands to her face. Her voice came to him, muffled, broken. "No. No. I've tried. But it's no use. It'll never be any use. There isn't any hope. He's finished with me, no matter what the will contains. He'll never come again. He's forgotten. He doesn't care."

Godfrey sighed. He rubbed his cold hands together. There was no heat for him in the roaring and leaping fire.

"You are wrong, my dear, poor child. He hasn't forgotten. I saw it at once, that Thanksgiving day. I saw him look at you."

She pressed her fingers deeper over her face. A murmured laugh, harsh and broken, came through them. "Not if the will forbids it! Not if he loses anything by coming! He told me so. Quite frankly." She dropped her hands and turned to him. He saw her white and ravaged face, her dry eyes full of bitter and sardonic light. Then her expression changed, and she said, almost incoherently: "What do you mean, Godfrey? About his still remembering? About his not having forgotten?"

And he sighed again, knowing finally there was not the least hope for him. He saw that, in her eyes, suddenly poignant, suddenly desperate and fixed. He averted his head. "It's quite true. He hasn't forgotten. He will come back. Perhaps very soon."

"I won't see him! I won't speak to him!" she cried, in a wild and distraught way. She clenched her hand and struck her knee with it. "I won't see him!"

But he only looked at her and smiled drearily. He fumbled for his crutches. He said nothing.

She saw his gesture. All at once, she burst into tears. She rose and fell on her knees before him and put her arms about his neck, and dropped her head on his shoulder. She clung to him, distractedly. After a little hesitating, he put his arms about her, and held her to him, as if she were a heart-broken child, and he gently kissed her cheek and the top of her head. He comforted her in silence.

After a long time she was quiet. She lifted her head, and showed him her wet face, relaxed and exhausted, now. "Godfrey, dear," she said, humbly. "Ask me again. Six months from now. A year from now."

He smoothed her disordered hair, and sighed. "No, dear," he said, tenderly. "I won't ask you again. You see, there would never be any use."

CHAPTER LXXI

Christopher had just returned from a flying trip to Detroit this burningly-cold December Sunday morning, when he was called to the telephone. It was Henri.

"I am alone here," said Henri, in a low and monotonous voice. "Annette's in New York. I want to talk to you. It's very important." He paused. "I've just returned from New York, myself. I've opened the will."

Christopher's pulses jumped. But he answered indifferently: "I'll be over in an hour."

The wire hummed with silence. Christopher knew the line was still open. After a long moment or two, he heard the click of the receiver as Henri hung it up. Christopher smiled evilly to himself. He returned to Edith, who was waiting impatiently for him in the breakfast room. He told her of the conversation.

"He wanted me to ask, all breathless and tremulous and eager, what the will contained," he said, with satisfaction. "But I didn't."

"How could you restrain yourself?" she asked, mockingly. But he saw that she was alert and concerned.

Christopher began to laugh. "I've an idea. He wouldn't have called like that, if it hadn't contained everything he wanted. There was something he wanted to know, too. I've an idea that Godfrey's nesting up at Placid Heights has caused him some bad minutes. He's human, after all, by God! I hope," added Christopher, with pleasure, "that he's been squirming."

"Did you tell him that Godfrey had left for Hollywood yesterday, my amiable pet?" A certain look of strain had left Edith's face since yesterday.

"Indeed I did not! If I had been a really vulgar person, I might have hinted that we could all expect some exciting news from Placid Heights soon. Somehow, I wish that were true." Christopher's expression had become musing now, and a little sad. "I really wish it were true. I didn't care for our gay adventurer, personally, but he seemed just the thing for little Celeste."

Edith looked at him wryly. But she made no comment. She saw that, in spite of his nastiness, he was enormously excited and anticipatory.

Don't bank too much on influence over Henri, after the wedding-bells have rung, she thought. No one will ever have much influence over my darling brother. But you'll never learn.

When Christopher arrived at Robin's Nest, he saw that Henri had just completed a considerable breakfast before the fire in the living-room. Henri had never cared much for food, except as sustenance. But Christopher noticed that this had been quite a breakfast. He was further diverted when Henri offered him an excellent cigar, and took one, himself. A servant carried the wreckage of plates and covered silver dishes away. Henri's broad pale face was really amiable, and relaxed. When he smiled at his brother-in-law, the smile actually reached his eyes for the first time in Christopher's memory.

"There was nothing in the will that prevents me from divorcing Annette," said Henri, calmly. "We had a talk in New York. She won't even return here. She is going directly to Reno. Her maid is packing her trunks now."

Christopher was surprised. It was not like Henri to speak out like this, without preliminary remarks that had nothing to do with the case. He was even more amused when Henri said, with the most genial frankness: "I hope that pipsqueak has left Placid Heights?"

Christopher meditated. Should he hint that perhaps some agreement had been reached between Celeste and Godfrey? But his own inner excitement and exultation were too much, even for him.

"He has," he said. "Yesterday. I wasn't taken into anyone's confidence, but I think Celeste had something to do with it."

Henri smiled again, with satisfaction. When he looked at his smoking cigar, it was without distaste. He actually appeared quite warm and human, even faintly boyish. Christopher eyed him cynically.

"He wasn't a bad chap," said Henri. "I've made some arrangements of my own, directly with his friend, Milch. After thorough investigation, of course. They ought to produce something good down there. I understand Godfrey has considerable talent. I'm interested in Milch's plans."

So, he doesn't bear me any malice, thought Christopher. And was amazed at his own sense of relief.

And then he was again surprised, for Henri appeared genuinely reflective and grave. "At that dinner," said Henri, regarding his cigar intently, "I thought he appeared quite at an advantage. I thought, at first, that he was something of an idealist—like Peter. Then I saw that he was a realist. There was something bold about him, too, and no nonsense." He smiled a little. "In spite of his general coloring, I thought he resembled the Old Man a lot," and he glanced up at the portrait of Ernest Barbour above him. He did not look away for several moments, and became even graver. "Yes, there was considerable resemblance. I could see that eventually I might like him. Later, I intend to see a lot of him, here and there. I suspect that on occasion he might be a liar, and a rascal, and unscrupulous. But when has all that been a vice with us?"

Christopher laughed, without comment. But he watched Henri narrowly.

"But he had other things, too," Henri went on, reflectively. "He had given a leg, not because he was an idealist, but because he wanted to kill something he thought was detestable. To him, it was a fair exchange. I like men who pay the price, and no heroics, afterwards. Yes, I like him. I talked to Milch, myself, last week."

So, thought Christopher, that is what precipitated matters, and was back of Milch's hurry call to Godfrey. He smiled inwardly. Henri, then, had squirmed, indeed. How much did he offer Milch to get Godfrey out of here? he asked himself. Of course, it wasn't handled as crudely as that. It was all business, naturally. Christopher was delighted.

"Did you inform Milch what sort of pictures you'd prefer?" he asked.

Henri smiled, and again his smile reached his eyes. "I never interfere with another man's business, especially if I know nothing about it. But, on a tentative offer of unlimited backing, I had a few suggestions."

He added: "And, by the way, I don't think we'll be bothered any longer by our little friend with the candid eyes: August Jaeckle. The investigation has been completed. Two investigations, in fact. The most important showed that he received over fifty thousand dollars during the past six months direct from Berlin. The other, that he has what the French call a *petite amie* in Pittsburgh. Of course, Mrs. Jaeckle doesn't know about it, but a small hint to August persuaded him he'd better stop his propaganda."

"Excellent!" said Christopher. "And—other matters?"

Henri leaned back in his chair. "I'm going to call a meeting for Tuesday, right here. All the boys. Ours,—and Antoine's. And, by the way, Antoine will receive a copy of Armand's will this morning—by special messenger." He looked into the distance, gently musing. "I'm not naturally a curious man. But I'd like to be there when he receives it."

Christopher did not speak at once. Then he said, oddly: "I've always considered myself an intuitive person. I don't know what's behind it, but I've seen a change in our sprightly dancer lately. A kind of thoughtfulness. Somehow, I'm not so sure the will is going to be an overwhelming shock to him."

Henri frowned, sourly. "I hope you're wrong."

He went on: "There was something else I wanted to tell you. Bishop Halliday won't be broadcasting again. For the duration. We discovered, quite accidentally, of course, that he has a nice block of stock in Marshal Goering's little iron works, in Germany. Someone explained to him that the United States Government might do a little impertinent investigating if the facts were presented to it."

And then, abruptly, he stood up, his back to the fire. He said, with sudden quietness: "New York is afraid. Washington is afraid. It's Japan."

"Japan," repeated Christopher, without emphasis.

"The Japanese Mission is in consultation with the State Department just now. A satisfactory agreement is expected. By the optimistic. But not by others with whom I talked."

"You think the attack will come from Japan?"

"I have no doubt of it. When, I can't say. I don't know. But Hitler has given his command to the Japanese Government, and they have no choice. The command came through two weeks ago. I don't think the Mission knows it. Yet."

"It may blow over."

Henri shrugged. "Perhaps. I don't think so."

He said: "Everything is ready. That's why I'm calling a meeting for Tuesday. Among other things, I'm going to talk about Japan."

He stood before the fire, immovable, rocklike. "I've just discovered, too, that in spite of my orders, a large cargo of platinum, grain, oil and machinery left the Argentine two days ago. For Franco, of course! But destined for Germany. I informed the British Government. It will never reach Spain."

He continued: "Whoever is responsible for that isn't going to like the result." Without a change in tone, he said: "Hugo will be here on Tuesday. I expect him to be in a state of shock."

Christopher leaned back in his chair, and said, pleasantly: "I seem to smell a lot of heavy blackmail in the air. I hope you are keeping a supply of restoratives on hand for the boys."

Henri smiled briefly, but said nothing. However, he looked at Christopher with long attentiveness.

He then sat down and outlined curtly what his plans were, and what he intended to do. Christopher listened closely. At the end, Henri said: "I'm leaving for South America in about eight weeks, with a certain Commission."

A servant came to the door and said that Mr. Bouchard was wanted for a long distance call from Washington. "Today?" said Henri, frowning. He excused himself and went to his private, soundproof booth on the second floor.

Christopher felt very content. His thoughts afforded him pleasure. Occasionally, as he sat before the fire, waiting, he smiled. He smoked constantly. Eventually, however, he became aware that Henri had been gone a long time. For some reason, this caused him disquiet. He stood up and began to pace up and down the room, silently. Sometimes he paused to look out at the winter landscape. There was no sound in the house. Everything was still and shining.

He turned from the window to see Henri standing in the archway, and he was very white. "Pearl Harbor has just been attacked," he said, and his voice was quiet and controlled.

CHAPTER LXXII

Celeste was out in the new bright fall of snow with little Land. She watched him stagger about, shrieking, gathering up handfuls of the shining stuff in his mittened hands, and throwing it up in the air so that it sparkled like a small cloud of diamonds. She put him on his sled, and pulled him about, and they both shouted with laughter in the clean air when he deliberately fell off. Celeste's furs were powdered with white. The wind stung some color into her pale tired face. She caught the little boy in her arms and kissed him passionately. He struggled for a moment, then suddenly became preternaturally grave, staring at her cheeks, which were suddenly touched here and there by a quicksilver drop. Thoughtfully, he pushed one away with his mitten.

"Mama cry," he said. "Tummy-ache?"

"Tummy-ache, darling," she agreed. "A very bad tummy-ache. But not in the usual place. We're at war, honey. And you don't know what that is yet, thank God!"

She set him down again, and again he waddled off on his strong legs. He found a black twig, forked and glittering with ice. He put it tentatively into his mouth. Celeste protested. He regarded her with his light-gray eyes, which had become expressionless. "Don't!" cried Celeste, with passion. The child, startled, dropped the twig, and frowned at her. "Don't look at me like that!" cried Celeste, with even more passion. Then, at his genuine bewilderment, she ran to him, knelt in the snow, and hugged him, kissing his warm neck. "Don't mind me, darling," she whispered, incoherently. "But please don't look at me like that, ever! I can't stand it."

She let him go once more, and he went off. She still knelt in the snow, watching him with sad urgency. She did not hear the purring of a car as it turned up the long driveway from the valley. But the child heard and saw. He shrieked with delight. "Papa!" he called.

He ran down the driveway. He fell once or twice, picking himself up with a howl, and then continuing. Dazed and numb, Celeste slowly got to her feet. It was Henri's black car standing there before the house, and it was Henri, in his rough gray coat and gray hat, who was serenely stepping out of it. Celeste turned cold and still. She could not move, or even think.

Henri ignored her, standing on the snowy rise, silhouetted in her furs against the burning blue sky. He saw the child, and began to laugh, strongly. He struck his gloved hands together with a loud sound. He bent down, extending his arms. Little Land increased his staggering speed. He flung himself into Henri's arms. Henri lifted him and kissed him heartily, and the child hugged him with ecstasy. "Well, well, old fellow!" cried Henri. "You're damn wet, you know. Take that paw out of my face."

The scene splintered into a thousand dazzling and dizzy fragments before Celeste. Her breath was smothered in her throat. She began to gasp, loudly, with dry and tearing sobs. But she still could not move, for all the bursting pain in her heart, and the whirling of her head.

As in some incredible and too bright dream she saw Henri climbing up towards her, still carrying the rosy and happy little boy. Henri kept fighting off the wet mittens that wanted to pat his face. He was laughing as Celeste had never heard him laugh before. Now he looked up at her, and his eyes were actually dancing. "Hello!" he called. "Can't you keep this brat dry?"

But Celeste heard Land's voice, shrieking over and over: "Papa! Papa!" She heard it numbly, stunned.

Henri stood before her now, the boy on his shoulder. "Edith and I had a hard time getting him to say that clearly," he remarked, in a confidential and warm tone. "He could only say it last week. Damn!" he added, thrusting aside the mitten which again caressed him. "Look here, stop pawing me or down you go."

"Candy," demanded Land, bending down to thrust his round rosy face into Henri's. And then, as an afterthought, he kissed his father wetly, and with enthusiasm.

The snow about her was no more white and motionless than Celeste. Her dark-blue eyes were fixed and glazed with shock. Henri ignored this.

"I hope," he said, casually, looking fully at her, "that his nurses are reliable. We'll be leaving him in about eight weeks, and we won't be back for at least two months. Can you trust them?"

"Trust them?" she whispered, dully.

Henri put the child down. Land promptly hugged his legs, almost upsetting him. Henri disengaged himself, and Celeste saw his harsh laughing profile under the brim of his hat. He managed to pull a cluster of little lollypops out of his pocket and pushed them into the baby's eager hands. "Go off somewhere and eat them quietly," he said.

Celeste murmured, faintly: "He mustn't. It's almost his dinner time."

"Never mind dinner time," said Henri, airily. "You don't know anything about boys. They can stuff themselves every half hour." He paused, and smiled at her. "It'll be summer, in South America, when we get there."

She did not speak. Her lips began to shake. And now he took her by the arms, firmly, and looked down at her. She looked up at him, dumbly, her eyes slowly filling.

"Hello, Celeste," he said, softly.

She could not make a sound. He pulled her to him, and kissed her lips, over and over. They were cold and stiff as ice. Then, very slowly, they warmed and softened. She uttered a choking cry, and clung to him. She began to weep, and he held her to him gently, and let her have her way.

She was conscious only that the huge and monstrous pain in her breast had left her, that something was melting and warming all through her flesh. She heard his voice, sometimes close, sometimes as from a distance, and it was grave now, and steady.

"You haven't heard the news, Celeste? We're at war. Japan has attacked us. War, Celeste. And I've work to do. I want you with me. In seven weeks, we can be married. Annette has already left for Reno."

But she only cared that his arms were about her, strong and steadfast, and that her pain was gone.

Little Land had seated himself on his sled. He had pulled the cellophane from all the lollypops, and, in ecstasy, he was tasting them all, in careful order.

CHAPTER LXXIII

There they were, sitting in a great circle before him in the wide warm drawing-room at Robin's Nest. A thick December snow was falling, ominous and silent, a fitting background for the atmosphere of this room, also ominous and silent, minatory and watchful, full of gigantic suspicion and enmity. A large fire burned on the enormous hearth, filling the duskiness of this inner air with lances and flares of rosy, restless light. It was still afternoon, but the skies outside were all long gray folds, swelling with storm and sullen anger, and a strong wind beat against the windows with a groaning sound. Smoke curled languidly from cigar and cigarette. At every elbow was a table on which stood tall crystal glasses filled with amber liquid. Here and there the firelight picked out a polished black shoe, the glint of eyeglasses, the glare of a bald head, the glimmer of a seal ring, the sudden deadly and inimical flash of the eye of a foe.

Henri stood beneath the portrait of Ernest Barbour. Had he been another man, those gathered there would have suspected him of theatricalism, of striving for a melodramatic effect. But even his enemies could not suspect this. Some of them, with a ridiculously superstitious uneasiness, felt that two identical faces looked down at them, and that these faces curiously contributed power to each other. It was two men, then, that they confronted, waiting, two implacable and dangerous cold men, with pale basilisk eyes and wide heavy mouths formed of gray stone.

Henri looked at the circle of faces about him—his Family. Here was the power of the Bouchards, part of the power of America. And he thought: There is not one among them that I can trust. Dogs, weasels, snakes and wolves! A huge contempt rose up in him, a wild but icy surge of strength such as might imbue a man who secretly knew he could blast them at his will. He felt no regret that he could not trust them.

He was only loathingly exhilarated that he had power over them, that he could destroy them, that, in the end, they must obey him. He moved his broad heavy shoulders under his coat; he felt the flexing of his muscles. They did not know what he thought, but they saw the sudden arctic blaze of his colorless eyes, the sudden flare of the nostrils in his short broad nose. Even though he stood at ease, his hands in his pockets, they felt all that he was, and all felt a prickle of foreboding like a cold wind over their flesh.

He had called them, and they had come. Not one had dared not to come. He had waited until they had comfortably settled themselves with cigars and cigarettes, and whiskey. He looked at one especially: Antoine, white as plaster, with eyes that were like hot holes in his face—Antoine, who had been so undone by his father's will. He had received a copy of that will the day before; it had been sent him, without comment, by Henri's lawyers. For a moment, as he stood there, Henri glanced a few times with secret curiosity at his brother-in-law, and with secret dour amusement. Give the devil his due: the volatile and gracefully avaricious Antoine betrayed no signs of discomposure or fury. He did not even appear to be stricken. Henri had expected much more than this white fixed calm, this elegant and silent composure. Henri allowed himself a moment or two of curious speculation and faint surprise. He was also annoyed. He liked to think that he understood all men completely, that he could foretell their reactions. It was irritating that Antoine could sit there, so silent, so unmoved, that his hand did not shake, and that his attitude was one of courteous attention and interest. Antoine might have felt the world shake beneath his polished shoes; he might have seen the walls of his private city collapse with a great thunder. But he surveyed the ruin with calm, and with a kind of civilized grandeur of detachment, a Petronius-like cynicism and a faint shrug. Even, perhaps, with acrid amusement.

Henri thought, with hatred and rising bitterness: He is a gentleman, that damned dancer and posturer. And with sudden clarity, he thought: I've hated him before, but I hate him more now. I've never pretended to be a gentleman. This is no world for courtiers, for *élégants*, for the civilized man. It is still a world of dinosaurs and tyrannosaurians.

He became aware of the immense silence with which they watched him. He smiled a little. His consciousness of the power within him made him stand a little straighter. He began to speak in his penetrating if monotonous voice:

"I'm not going to beat about the bush. I've been to Washington, as you all know. And I've come back to explain matters as simply as I can."

Antoine spoke, in a gentle musing voice: "Do be very simple. Our intellects aren't subtle enough to grasp innuendoes."

A stir went through the others, and surly or sly smiles appeared momentarily. Henri looked hard at Antoine. "I'm not dealing in subtleties, though I suspect you, yourself, would prefer them."

Antoine shrugged, but very faintly and indifferently. For one instant Henri felt rage, as the precarious advantage passed fleetingly to Antoine. He had hopefully suspected that Antoine's composure might be only a pose. But that shrug, exquisitely tired, but exquisitely contained, convinced him to the contrary. There was, apparently, some profound weariness in Antoine, the weariness of the civilized man confronted with brute force that not only annoyed his fastidiousness, but bored him. Henri turned from him. If he was to state his case, calmly and with brutal incisiveness, he must not look too much upon Antoine. But though he did not look at the other, he felt his quiet and cynical regard, his delicate scrutiny, his curious interest.

Henri's voice, in consequence, was harder and harsher than before, when he resumed:

"I am not going to tell you the name of the man with whom I have been in conference for two days in Washington. Perhaps you will soon guess.

"This is what he said to me: That since the beginning of the depression of 1929, capital and industry have shown themselves to be bankrupt as far as national leadership is concerned. You may, or may not, agree with this, however. He further said that we have had a chance to perpetuate our leadership in the United States, but that when we became so indifferent, so sunken in ourselves and our greeds, that we permitted veterans of American wars to sell apples on the streets, and other nasty little events of the early nineteen-thirties, and that when we did nothing to alleviate starvation, and the distress of the people, and insisted that the President then in office use dictatorship methods to subdue the panic that was rising from one end of the country to the other, to a point of complete chaos, we morally bankrupted ourselves in the eyes of the nation. We lost the trust of the people, and aroused nothing in them but hatred and suspicion."

He paused. Christopher lifted his cigarette to his lips and puffed languidly. "It seems," he murmured, "that I've heard all that before, somewhere. I believe the Communist press went into that extensively."

Again, to his cold rage, Henri felt the light balance of power pass momentarily from him, at this baiting. But he did not reply. He surveyed Christopher grimly. So, he thought, savagely, you feel safe enough now, do you, you white snake?

He waited until the malevolent murmur of amusement at Christopher's baiting subsided again into a properly attentive silence. Now he knew that he really did not have a faction at all. That every man in that room hated him.

He resumed, without the slightest inflection in his voice:

"We must admit certain basic facts. It is not sentimentality on my part when I say that in the past we've never assumed any responsibility for the welfare of the American people. We, and our associates, and brothers-in-arms, have formed a selfish protective organization for our own advantage. We became a self-contained and greedy hierarchy with a total disregard for the people, upon whom, in the final analysis, we live. We have depended, and must depend, upon the goodwill and well-being of the people, for our very existence, though we seem to have forgotten that fundamental fact in the general scramble for profits. We have forgotten that we cannot exist, in America, as a prosperous and well-ordered capitalistic-industrial-democracy without that goodwill, without the well-being and trust of the people."

He paused again. He looked at Antoine's faction: the "deadly little Jean" with his amiable dimples and sweet attentiveness, and the green and dirty Nicholas, at the sullen and bewildered Robert Bouchard, at Alexander of the magenta face and great belly. They had begun to smile maliciously, putting up their hands to hide their smiles, and their eyes surveyed him with dangerous interest.

Jean spoke, softly and with an air of surprise: "For the great-grandson of Ernest Barbour, and on the evidence of your own remarkable record, your defense of 'democracy' is somewhat startling. But do go on. I didn't really mean to interrupt."

Involuntarily, Henri glanced at his own faction. Christopher, "the silvery snake" seemed involved in pleasant and infuriating thoughts of his own. Emile, "the bloated black rat," regarded Henri with opaque amiability. Hugo, tawny and huge, appeared cautiously uneasy. Only Francis, of the icy blue eyes, studied Henri with careful sympathy and thoughtfulness.

Henri's heavy gray mouth took on a vicious but indomitable expression. He repeated, with emphasis: "Only in a democratic society, with its religion of free enterprise and open competition, can we, the Bouchards, and our class, survive. I don't need to call to your somewhat obtuse memories what has happened to the great industrialists and capitalists under Hitler and Mussolini, and what bloody payment they received from their masters when they had served their purpose. I must make emphatic to you the stark truth that our welfare and existence are bound up inextricably with the welfare of the American people. When that welfare is jeopardized by our own blindness, then we are ready for destruction. There are some of you here, apparently, who are too blind, too stupid, and too greedy, to grasp this fact."

"There is no doubt," said Antoine, with a gracious gesture and an elegant inclination of the head, "that we are blind, stupid, and greedy. So, we agree with you all the way."

Again, a faint amused murmur arose, but Henri, who was aroused now, quelled it instantly by one pale and minatory flash of his eye. Each man felt that flash literally in his own flesh, and now a rigid alertness was apparent among them, a kind of wary fear. Henri sensed that fear. He smiled grimly.

He said: "It may be a thought new to all of you that Mr. Roosevelt saved us from destruction when he took office in 1933. Is your memory so short? The very NRA which we all fought so strenuously, actually raised prices and saved our capitalistic-industrial system. Have you really forgotten the temper of the country at that time? If I remember rightly, there was not one of you who didn't shake in his shoes, and begin to think of shipping gold out of the country to Canada or Europe. We were the most panicky class in America." He glanced at Nicholas. "I have a faint memory that you were treated for an embarrassing ailment by a whole battery of physicians until Mr. Roosevelt declared a bank holiday."

As if relieved from a really unbearable tension, the whole room burst into wild and discordant laughter at Nicholas' expense. He sat on the edge of his chair, huddled together, and looked from one to the other of the convulsed men with greenish hatred and fury. Henri listened to the laughter,

597

smiling darkly. He let it have its way. He lifted his hand and gently bit his index finger.

Francis exclaimed: "We've done Henri an injustice. He really does have a sense of humor!"

Now they looked at him, if not with sympathy, at least with more cordiality.

He went on: "Yes, I remember our panic. We were doomed. We wrung our hands. We ran around like blind ants, whimpering. Mr. Roosevelt saved us. We owed him gratitude, at least. But instead of that, we accused him, in our press, of being a Communist, a visionary. We apparently didn't realize that if it hadn't been for the slow and painful amelioration of the lot of the American people, after 1933, we might have had a revolution, or complete anarchy."

"We might," said Antoine, musingly, staring before him as if this were the most casual of conversations, "have called out the police and the military. You never thought of that."

Henri uttered a short loud laugh. "You've lived too long in Europe, Antoine. Do you actually believe that the American people could have been subdued by policemen's clubs and the guns of our army, which was then a very puny organization? And do you actually believe that those same policemen and soldiers would have fired on their fellow-Americans? Remember, even the most stupid man had absorbed in our public schools the fundamental principles of democracy. Do you think Americans are docile and hoglike Germans, or tired and degraded Frenchmen, or hungry Italians? Forget our foreign Northern cities. Try to remember our Western States, and our South, where lived the descendants of Britons who had an inherited memory of freedom and decency. Some of you will deny that the common people are possessed even of the dim brain of an amoeba. I was guilty of that stupidity, at one time. I've received a little enlightenment since then."

No one answered. He continued: "You've lived too long in your own gigantic Vatican, among your own cardinals and bishops of industry. You've lived in a kind of mystical belief in your own omnipotence, forgetting that you have no Fuehrer to protect your interests, and no robot army to enforce your decrees with machine-guns. You are vulnerable. You're covered with dozens of soft spots. And don't believe that the American people didn't know it, either."

And then he said: "We have never convinced the American people of the divine right of capitalists. We never shall."

He allowed the silence to become deep. He allowed them

all to think. And he watched them closely. He saw the guarded hating faces of Antoine's faction. He saw the interested but wary faces of his own.

Then Antoine said, very softly, almost caressingly: "God damn the people. God damn them always."

Henri smiled. His sense of power swelled in him. But he could feel a little surprise at the hint of impotence in Antoine's words. It was strange that this most dangerous and elegant man should feel impotence. It suggested a most curious and inexplicable exhaustion, even surrender.

"Do you expect me to defend the people? What I have been telling you have been facts, only. I am a realist. I predicate my affairs on facts. What I personally feel about the 'people' has nothing to do with the fact that I must deal with them. I only know that I must adjust myself to what exists, and proceed from there."

He paused again. Now his voice became stronger, quicker: "We are now at war. I don't think any of you will contradict me when I say that we've done everything we could, by bribery, by lies, by subornation, by corruption of public officials, by the buying of certain radio henchmen, by the maligning of labor, by our subsidy of certain clergymen, by our newspapers, by powerful subversive propaganda, by secret agreements with certain Middle European associates, by the forming of subversive and powerful Committees, by intrigues in South America, by the smearing of Russia, by avalanches of pamphlets and little leaflets, and God knows what else, to keep America out of this war. We've had our cartels which supplied Hitler with what he needed to conquer the world. We've even made him promises."

He stopped. Now every man sat up straight in his chair. The faces of Antoine's faction were rigid and expressionless. They looked at him with eyes so lethal and piercing that he could only look back at them as if momentarily hypnotized.

He said: "Some of us have even tried anti-Semitism to divert the attention of the American people from our real purpose. We have jeered at Britain, and besmeared her. We have tried to arouse the indignation of the people against Lend-Lease. Some of us have worked in every way, with unsleeping energy, to ensure the victory of Hitler over all the world, and the eventual enslavement of our own American people. I can only say now, and with personal satisfaction that, so far, you who have done all this have failed. It is now my purpose, and the purpose of many other powerful

599

men who are with me, to see to it that you shall continue to fail. You can't win. Not now."

His voice rose, became irresistible with power, with triumph and exultation:

"Perhaps some of you believe you can still destroy America, can still insure Hitler's conquest. But, I call to your mind certain facts: you could not, in spite of your efforts, prevent national conscription, prevent Lend-Lease, nor corrupt the sentiment of the people against Hitler. You could not destroy the decent indignation of seventy-five percent of the American people against Hitler, and their hatred for him. For all your newspapers and your hired liars and your suborned Congressmen, you could not crush the admiration of the American people for Britain's valor, nor could you arouse their overwhelming suspicion against Russia. You tried. You tried very hard. But, you failed. You had forgotten one thing: the imponderables of the people's conscience."

And now Antoine lifted his head, and straightened in his chair. Regan had said that. He had said that to Henri, most probably. We are lost, then, thought Antoine. And felt nothing in himself at all.

In the huge pent silence of the room, Henri continued: "You had your isolationists in Congress. You had their sworn promises. But you could not prevent them, in the end, from voting unanimously for war against Japan and Germany. That ought to have meant something to you."

He waited. But no one spoke. He looked from one face to another, slowly. They hated him. They feared him. But, they believed him. A dark shadow of infuriated uncertainty and frustration appeared in the eyes of Antoine's faction.

And then Henri said: "Some of you are making mental reservations, even now. You think you can still see a way to insure Hitler's conquest. Or, at the worst, you think you can force a negotiated peace which will be to Hitler's advantage. Don't. You can't win. I am not speaking for myself alone. I have others like me with me. I have the American people."

He walked back and forth a few paces. They felt his exultation, his enormous and contemptuous disgust and hatred for them. Then he turned swiftly, and said:

"There are a few more facts I want to bring to your attention. The American Legion and other powerful organizations have been advocating, for the past two decades, that in the event of a national emergency, such as war, when it becomes necessary to conscript human beings for the service of the nation, capital and industry be conscripted by the Government, and that industry be operated by the Government, not for profits, but for the welfare of the nation as a whole.

"This idea has penetrated into the consciousness of the American people. And so, in this present dire need of the nation, either you coöperate, with all loyalty, and produce material of war to the maximum, without mental reservations, without personal and international ambitions, forgetting your plots and your lies and your commitments to Hitler, or the President will go before Congress, which is now in a proper mood, and this Congress will pass a law to conscript industry for the duration."

A wave of shocked terror, of incredulity, swept over them. Factional differences were forgotten now. All of them looked at each other in profound alarm, seeking reassurance from other faces. But the reassurance was not there.

Henri watched them. He waited a little. Then he said, slowly, softly: "I am not speculating. I tell you this can happen, will happen. Unless you coöperate. But that is not the end. If we permit the Government to conscript industry, now, and eliminate profits entirely, the Government, and the people, might then get the idea that this is not a bad thing at all, and this control would most probably continue permanently, even after the peace is signed. Thus, we shall have Socialism.—And we, ourselves, will be responsible for this catastrophe."

Nicholas said, hoarsely, after a burst of obscene profanity: "God damn it, the Government wouldn't dare!"

Henri replied calmly, with a nod of his head: "I assure you it would. A plan has already been drawn. The eminent gentleman who told me of the plan informed me that it will go into effect at the very moment you show signs of continuing as you have been doing. I had a most interesting discussion with that gentleman. In the shadow of the White House. He convinced me, most thoroughly, that what we've considered to be the amorphous jelly-fish condition of the American people is really a very solid and jagged avalanche, which can roll over us and destroy us, and leave not even a smell behind."

Now a complete and sudden disorder blew into the room. Nicholas, Jean, Alexander and Robert Bouchard jumped to their feet, began to walk quickly about. Even

Hugo and Emile were infected. They, too, got up, began to pace up and down in utter distraction. Of Antoine's faction, only he remained seated. And he watched his friends with that elegant and composed detachment which was so curious to Henri, turning quietly in his chair to follow their frantic movements. He was like a civilized gentleman languidly observing the distraught antics of lower animals.

And then, he turned his sleek and narrow head toward Henri, and upon his dark dry face there appeared the oddest and most radiant smile of malignant enjoyment. He rested his elbow on the arm of his chair, and cupped his sharp chin in the palm of his small hand. He sat like this, not moving, his smile deepening.

Christopher and Francis in their turn, exchanged long significant looks, inscrutable but contented.

Then little Jean, all his gracious amiability gone, all his dimples vanished in vicious furrows on his round smooth face, swung virulently upon Henri:

"You are lying. We know what you've been up to. Do you think you can bamboozle us with words?"

Henri leaned back against the wall. He fastened his pale immovable eyes upon his relative, and said quietly: "I'd be sorry to see you try anything. For I'd be messed up, along with all of you. I hope, for my own sake, that you'll see the light."

Jean was about to say something contemptuous. His little hand had even risen in a disgusted and dismissing gesture. But as he looked at Henri, his face changed. His hand dropped. And then he was silent.

Then it was that Antoine turned gracefully in his chair, and said, right in the midst of the noisy disorder in the room, looking directly at Christopher: "You were in this from the beginning, weren't you?"

Christopher smiled, and inclined his head. "Yes. Always. But you knew, didn't you?"

Antoine actually laughed softly. He seemed delighted. "Yes. I believe I did. Congratulations."

Then Antoine rose, without hurry, all his movements elegant and languid. He looked at his faction, his tilted black eyes sparkling, his smile brilliant. He commanded their attention, though he said no word, nor made any gesture. They stopped in the very act of their disordered pacing, and stared at him.

"Boys," he said, gently, "I think we're done. Yes, I really think we're done."

Complete demoralization took hold of them now. They stared at him, pale, haggard, blinking and swallowing visibly. Then slowly, one by one, they returned to their chairs and fell into them. They dropped their heads. They stared before them, dully.

Antoine turned graciously to Henri, standing there like stone, smiling grimly. "I may ask you a question?" he said, with a light bow that infuriated the other man. But Henri only inclined his head.

"It is true that I am not very bright," said Antoine. "And my mind seems a little confused. In all humility, I want to know this: If we cooperate, as you have so tactfully suggested, producing material of war at a reasonable profit, what guarantee have we that the Government will relax its control after the war, and permit us to build up our resources to withstand a readjustment afterwards?"

Henri said, watching him closely: "This will depend upon your cooperation now, and above all, upon the confidence and respect we inspire in the people. If we assume our rightful position and show loyalty and comparative disinterestedness, we may even win a place at the peace table. And this will be very valuable in the allotment of spheres of industrial reconstruction in the devastated countries of Europe. I am sure you are imaginative enough to know this holds practically unlimited possibilities."

He looked at Antoine doggedly. His face became congested and thick. It cost him a profound effort, but he said, sullenly: "I hope also that you will continue with Bouchard & Sons. I have something very interesting in mind."

Antoine gazed at him with the utmost thoughtful gentleness. He appeared to muse, as if some sweet thought had come to him. His eyes glittered, but whether it was with intense amusement, Henri could not know. Then Antoine bowed deeply from the waist, like a dancer. "You interest me very strangely," he said. "Shall we have a talk, tomorrow, alone?"

Henri was nonplussed for a few moments. He stared somberly at the younger man. He even moved a little on his strong spread feet. He could not understand this civilized and graceful surrender, this admiration for a successful foe that sparkled so amusedly in Antoine's eyes. So, he merely nodded, and when Antoine turned away from him, he rubbed his ear in uncertain speculation. Somehow, his triumph was a little dimmed. In his defeat, Antoine was still unruffled, still completely contained.

Henri waited until all were seated again in their chairs, Antoine's faction still staring dully before them, Henri's faction sharing with quite vulgar satisfaction in his own triumph. And then he spoke again, louder, clearer, and with really ringing emphasis:

"Unless, finally, we come to the point where we all realize, not only the Bouchards, but all the powerful of America, that we are no longer a dynasty ruling from the top, but must depend upon the goodwill, not only of our own people but of all the other peoples with whom we must eventually come into contact in a constantly widening sphere of activity, we shall perish. And other men, wiser than we, will take our places. This is inevitable. This is the stark reality we must face.

"This is our final hour."

And now, as if impelled by an irresistible compulsion, he turned his head and looked up at the face of Ernest Barbour. The portrait looked down at him intently, as immovable, as inexorable as himself.

And then Henri turned to his silent kinsmen, each of whom was sunk in profound and private thoughts of his own. He said, with deceptive lightness:

"There is just one other little thing, and it embarrasses me to bring it up. I'm going to be right on the job, all the time. I'm going to know everything. You are going to tell me everything. Because, if any of you should prove refractory at any time, and continue with some of your—shall we say extra-curricular activities, such as you have been engaged in, and of which I am very completely aware, with records and so on, then I shall turn these exhaustive records over to certain Government investigative agencies, who can make things very uncomfortable for you. I have given that certain gentleman in Washington some hint of what I have garnered, here and there. It would hurt me very much to give him these records. But he made me promise to do it. In that event, I can guarantee that you will rue the day you didn't take my advice.

"I've told you I shouldn't like to do it. After all, it would involve the family. But, I'd have no other choice. For, you see, that would be the only way I could save myself from positive

Government vengeance, punitive measures, and complete annihilation."

He added, after he had let Antoine's faction brood upon this with impotent and silent fear and fury:

"I know that you will also inform your associates of this. It might save them a lot of unpleasant things, in the long run. And, as for some of you in the family: if the worst comes to the worst, I have ways of smashing all of you. I have been planning these ways for months."

Little Annette, solitary and silent, looked through the small windows of the transcontinental plane, and her pale triangular face was quite calm. She did not feel abandoned, or lost, or even heart-broken. Her sorrow was a quiet thing, part of her life, and now at last she realized that it always had been a part, and probably always would be.

But there was no weakness in her, no hopelessness. She looked at the huge masses of white and rolling cloud, so like an ocean, with dark and jagged towers of mist thrusting through them, like enormous ruins. And then, as she watched, the sun suddenly struck them, and every tower, every rampart, was awash with gold.

She smiled. She said aloud, softly: "Yes, there is a place for me. Somewhere, surely there is a place."

EPILOGUE

Mr. Cornell Hawkins stood by his dusty window and gazed down unseeingly at Fifth Avenue, swirling darkly in a wet thick snow.

Perhaps it was his imagination, but it seemed to him that there was a quicker and more hurried tempo in those who swarmed the street below, that a dusky urgency was upon them, a certain universal grimness. The dark and lowering sky hung threateningly overhead, a sky that looked down now on a world completely at war, completely engulfed in tragedy, completely face to face with its final hour.

He had often wondered how America would react to its inevitable destiny of long agony and suffering and death and sorrow. He remembered the last war, when there had been a certain jubilation, a sense of adventure, among the people. There had been bands, and songs, and marching, and the gay flutter of flags. There had been the joyful release from monotony, a burgeoning belief in mighty and glorious things to come after this war which was only a turbulent and crashing threshold that opened on the shining land of the future.

He did not believe that the American people were now so naïve, so childlike. He believed there was no joy or exhilaration among them. He believed there was only sadness and anger, and full knowledge of what was to come. America had come of age; in blood and bitterness and righteous hatred she raised her sword in the red light of war.

He had lived too long, he was too wise, to believe that any great and dazzling hope and rapture awaited the world after its anguished struggle with the forces of evil that lived in itself, and its conquest of those forces. Pain and loss, exhaustion and despair, would most probably come to it. It would feel that it could not go on. It would rest, panting, among its ruins, and would look about it with dull eyes in which there was not even a frantic horror. It would not even be hopeless. It would only be very tired, and very cold, and it would shudder.

How long would it be before it could rise again, and with bleeding hands begin to build once more? How much of its bitterness and hatred and memory could it obliterate from itself? How much of its deep death, and its darkness?

The shock of remembered conflict would be in all its flesh. For many years it would see again the ruined cities, and the multitudes of dead or weeping faces. The graves would not sink soon; the saturated and surfeited earth would not soon be pleasant and tranquil again. Where the plow struck, it would strike bones.

Long after the white walls of the world were again intact, and commerce again streamed across unthreatened oceans, the winds would still carry the cries of those who had so innocently died, of those who had been betrayed, of those who had been tormented. For this had not been a war of governments. It had been a war of peoples. It had been a war of the spirits of men. Every blade of grass would remember that it had been dyed red; every root of every tree would feel the dead entwined with it.

Evil had come, and man had risen to face it—afraid, yes, desperate most certainly. He would conquer it, as he had conquered it before. One must believe that, thought Mr. Hawkins. One must not dare not to believe it.

He sighed. He saw Peter's face. He heard Peter's voice once more, stronger and clearer now, and triumphant:

"No matter what comes, no matter what men die and suffer, the earth will remain. The earth will abide, forever. And with it, will abide men's hope, now and always, living again in their children, reaffirming their faith that there is a destiny for them among themselves, and with God."